PRAISE FOR

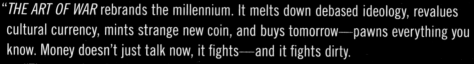

"*THE ART OF WAR* rebrands the millennium. It melts down debased ideology, revalues cultural currency, mints strange new coin, and buys tomorrow—pawns everything you know. Money doesn't just talk now, it fights—and it fights dirty.

"The story is relentless—its violence harsh, its sex brutal, its art graphic and unflinching. Ideas pop like cluster bomblets: some provoke thought, some sick hilarity— others are just weird and twisted. And yet, against the odds, stretched taut through the cynical mayhem, a thread of humanity persists, tenuous but unbreakable. What else could a reader ask for?"

—Jamie Delano, author of *Hellblazer*

"An astounding adaptation of Sun Tzu's ancient text that made me think about its application in an entirely new way."

—Brigadier General (Ret.) Stephen N. Xenakis, U.S. Army

"Imaginative, provocative, powerful, and disturbing, Kelly Roman's *THE ART OF WAR* should be required reading for those concerned with the future of America and its place in the world."

—Minxin Pei, professor of government, Claremont McKenna College

"*THE ART OF WAR* is a dark, powerful, incredibly well-written story that illustrates the good, the bad, and the ugly realities of living by strategic codes—and what happens if you violate them. I found it very hard to put down."

—Adisa Banjoko, founder, Hip Hop Chess Federation

"Filled with demon drones, nano scouts, and genetically engineered soldiers—once I'd started it I couldn't put it down."

—Peter Rojas, cofounder, gdgt, Engadget, Gizmodo, Joystiq

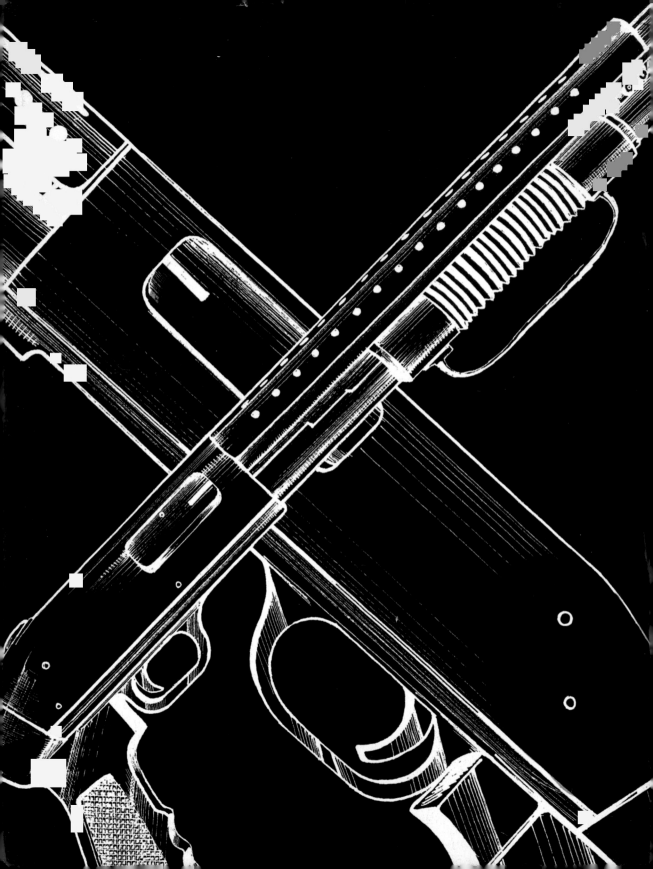

THE ART OF WAR

A GRAPHIC NOVEL BY
KELLY ROMAN

ILLUSTRATED BY
MICHAEL DeWEESE

HARPER  PERENNIAL

NEW YORK • LONDON • TORONTO • SYDNEY • NEW DELHI • AUCKLAND

HARPER ⬭ PERENNIAL

FIRST EDITION

Designed by William Ruoto

Library of Congress Cataloging-in-Publication Data is available upon request.

ISBN 978-0-06-210394-9

12   13   14   15   16   SCPC   10   9   8   7   6   5   4   3   2   1

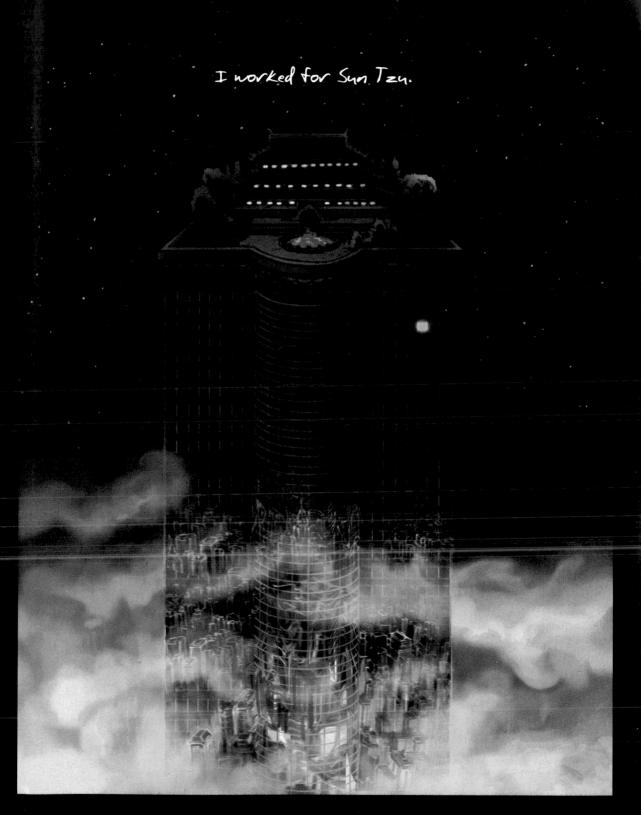

I worked for Sun Tzu.

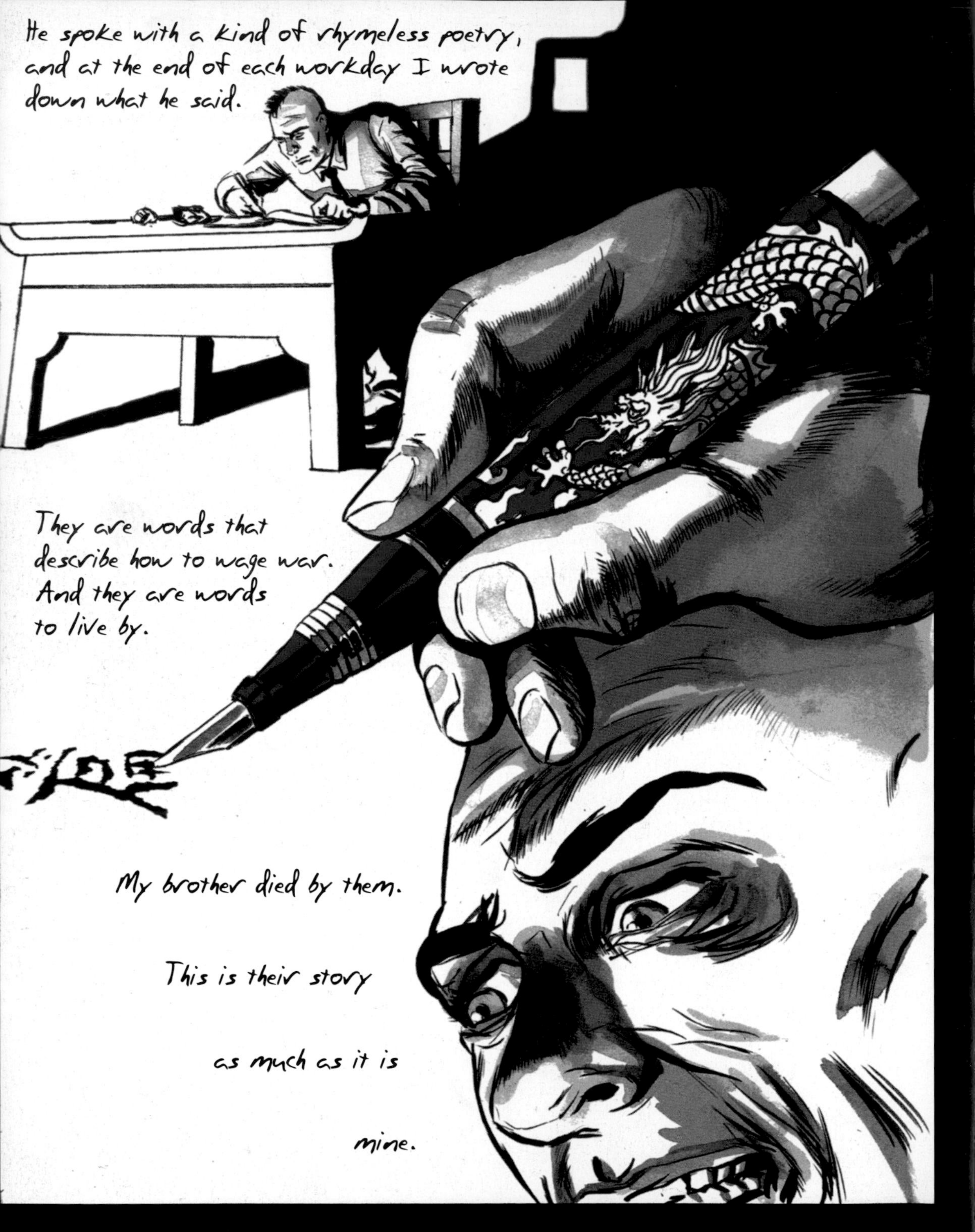
He spoke with a kind of rhymeless poetry, and at the end of each workday I wrote down what he said.
They are words that describe how to wage war. And they are words to live by.
My brother died by them.
This is their story
as much as it is
mine.

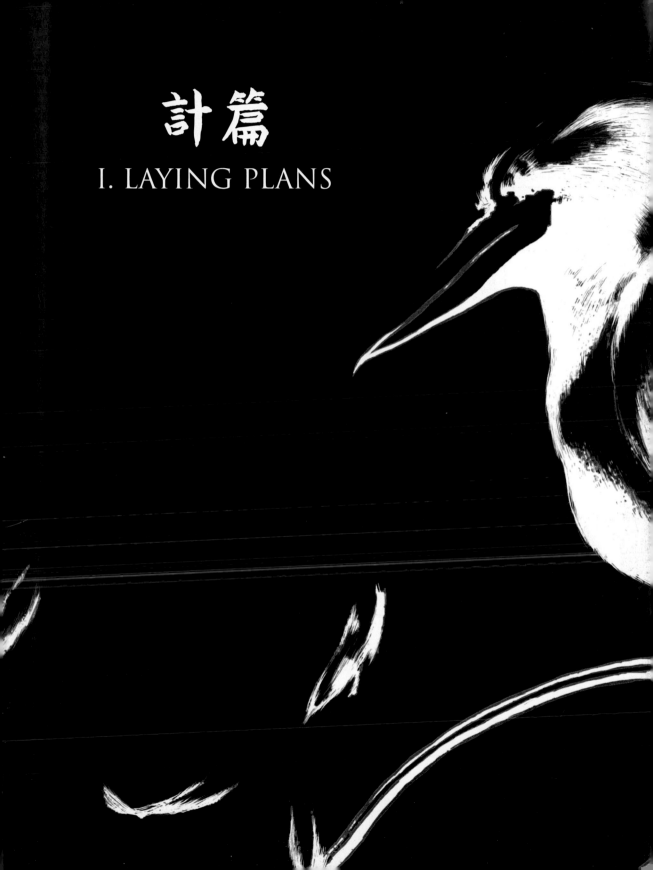

計篇

I. LAYING PLANS

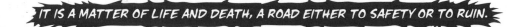

SUN TZU SAID: THE ART OF WAR IS OF VITAL IMPORTANCE TO THE STATE.

IT IS A MATTER OF LIFE AND DEATH, A ROAD EITHER TO SAFETY OR TO RUIN.

HENCE IT IS A SUBJECT OF INQUIRY WHICH CAN ON NO ACCOUNT BE NEGLECTED.

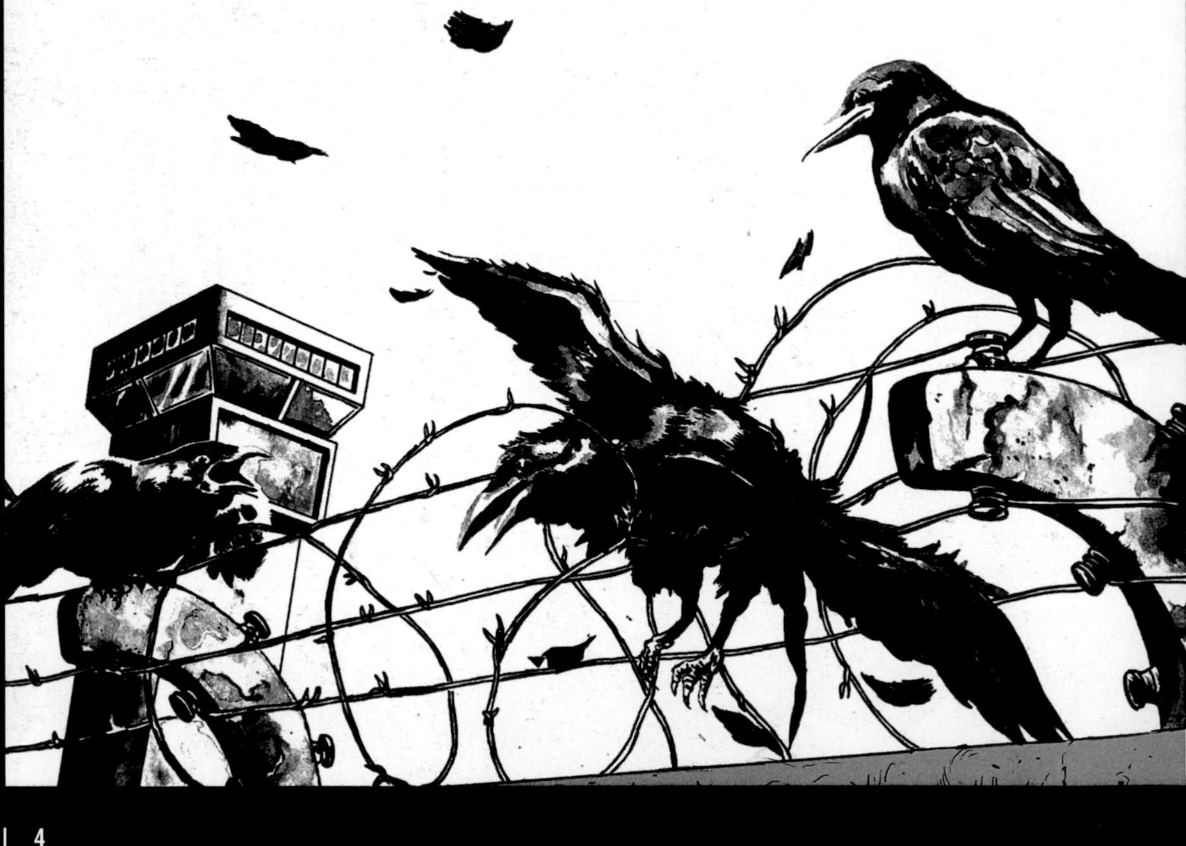

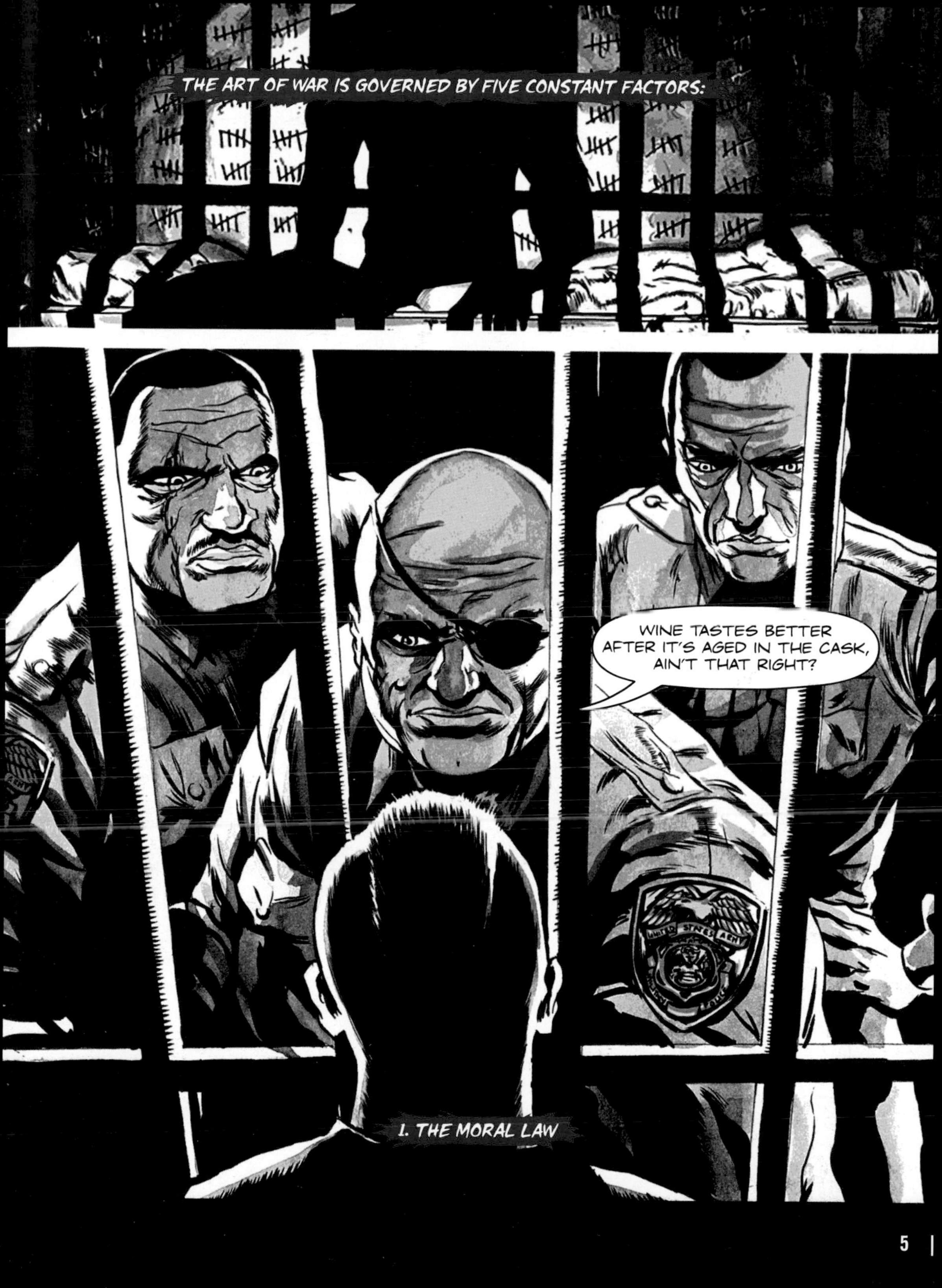
THE ART OF WAR IS GOVERNED BY FIVE CONSTANT FACTORS:
WINE TASTES BETTER AFTER IT'S AGED IN THE CASK, AIN'T THAT RIGHT?
1. THE MORAL LAW

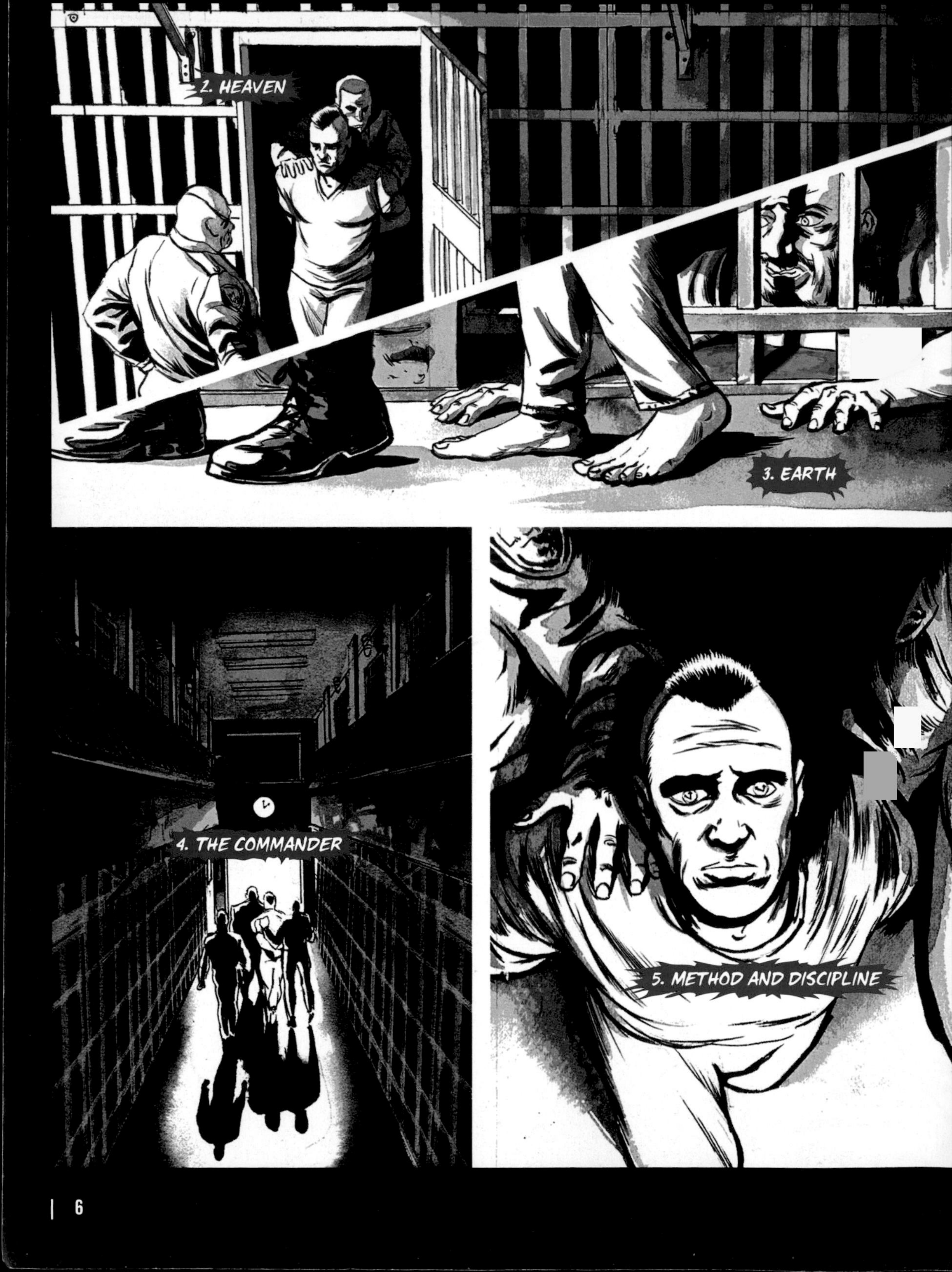
2. HEAVEN
3. EARTH
4. THE COMMANDER
5. METHOD AND DISCIPLINE

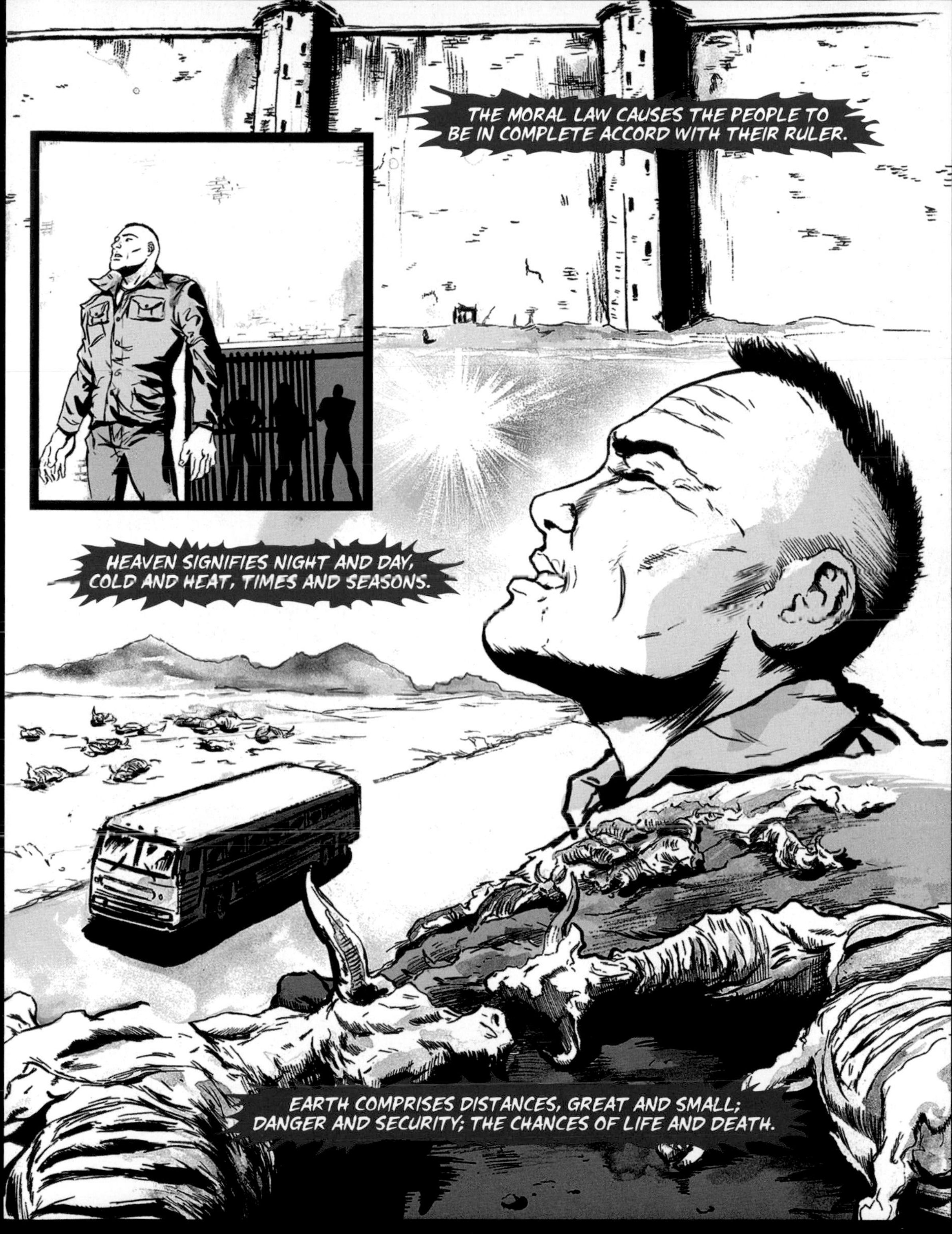
THE MORAL LAW CAUSES THE PEOPLE TO BE IN COMPLETE ACCORD WITH THEIR RULER.
HEAVEN SIGNIFIES NIGHT AND DAY, COLD AND HEAT, TIMES AND SEASONS.
EARTH COMPRISES DISTANCES, GREAT AND SMALL; DANGER AND SECURITY; THE CHANCES OF LIFE AND DEATH.

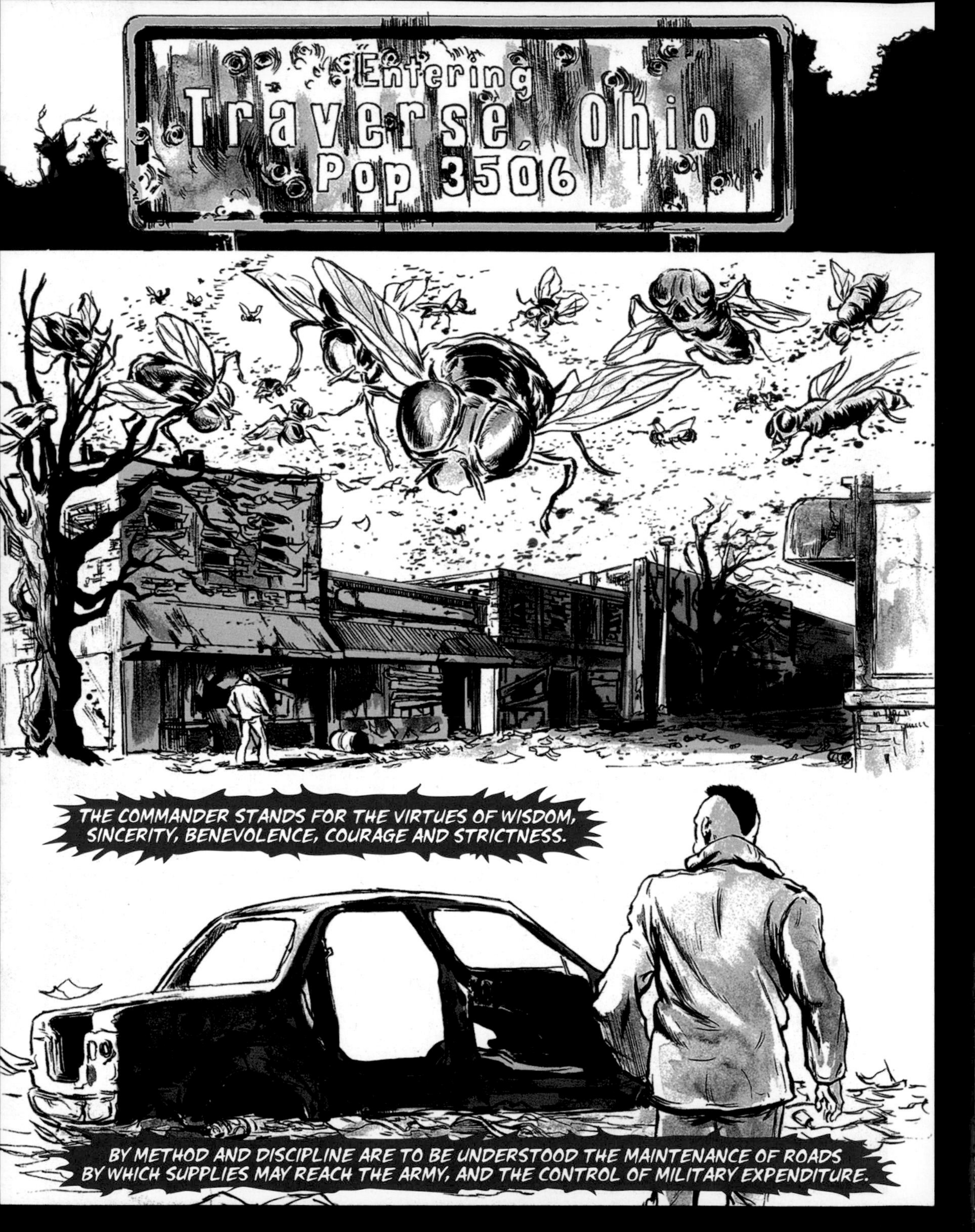
Entering
Traversé, Ohio
Pop 3506
THE COMMANDER STANDS FOR THE VIRTUES OF WISDOM, SINCERITY, BENEVOLENCE, COURAGE AND STRICTNESS.
BY METHOD AND DISCIPLINE ARE TO BE UNDERSTOOD THE MAINTENANCE OF ROADS BY WHICH SUPPLIES MAY REACH THE ARMY, AND THE CONTROL OF MILITARY EXPENDITURE.

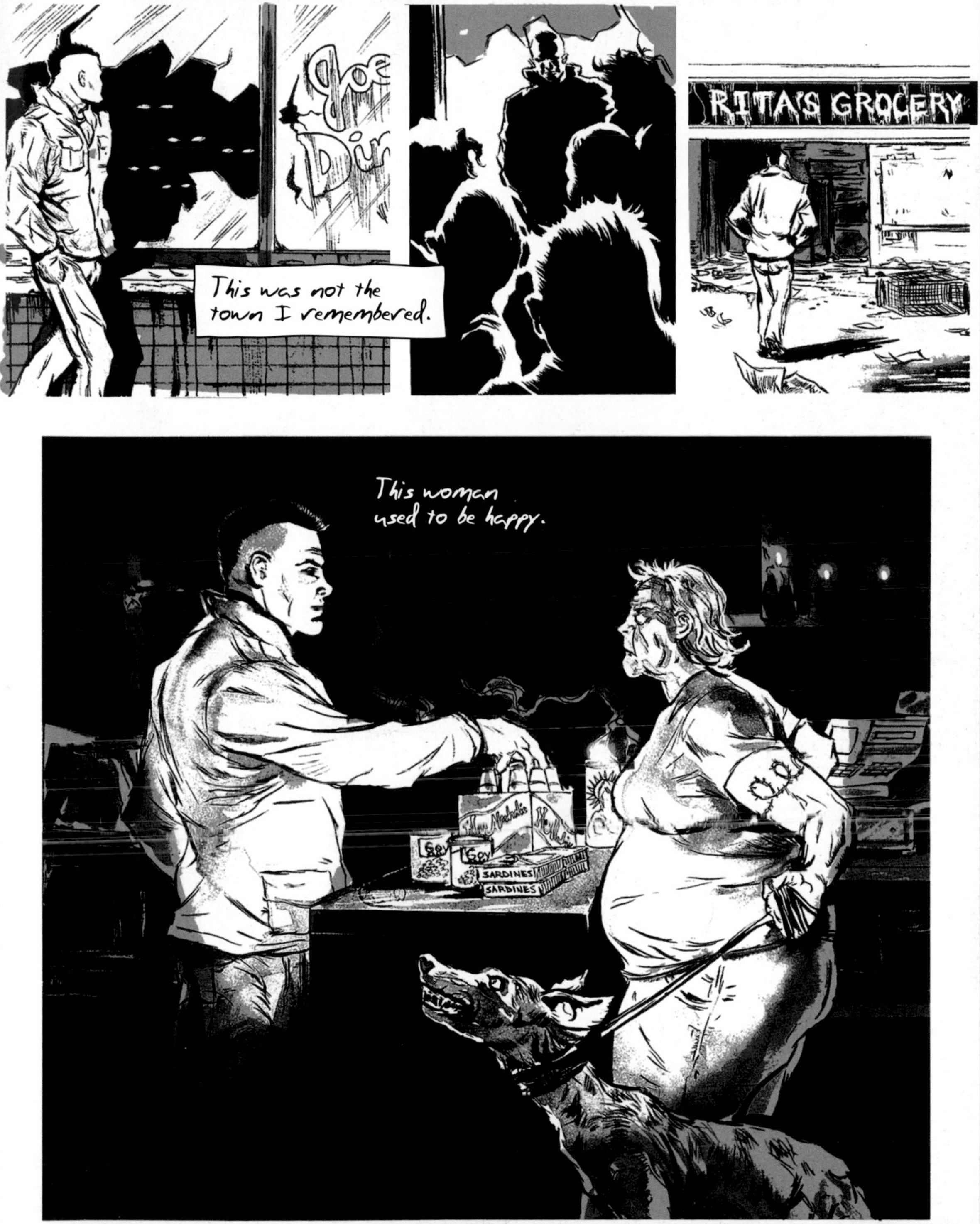
This was not the town I remembered.
RITA'S GROCERY
This woman used to be happy.
SARDINES
SARDINES

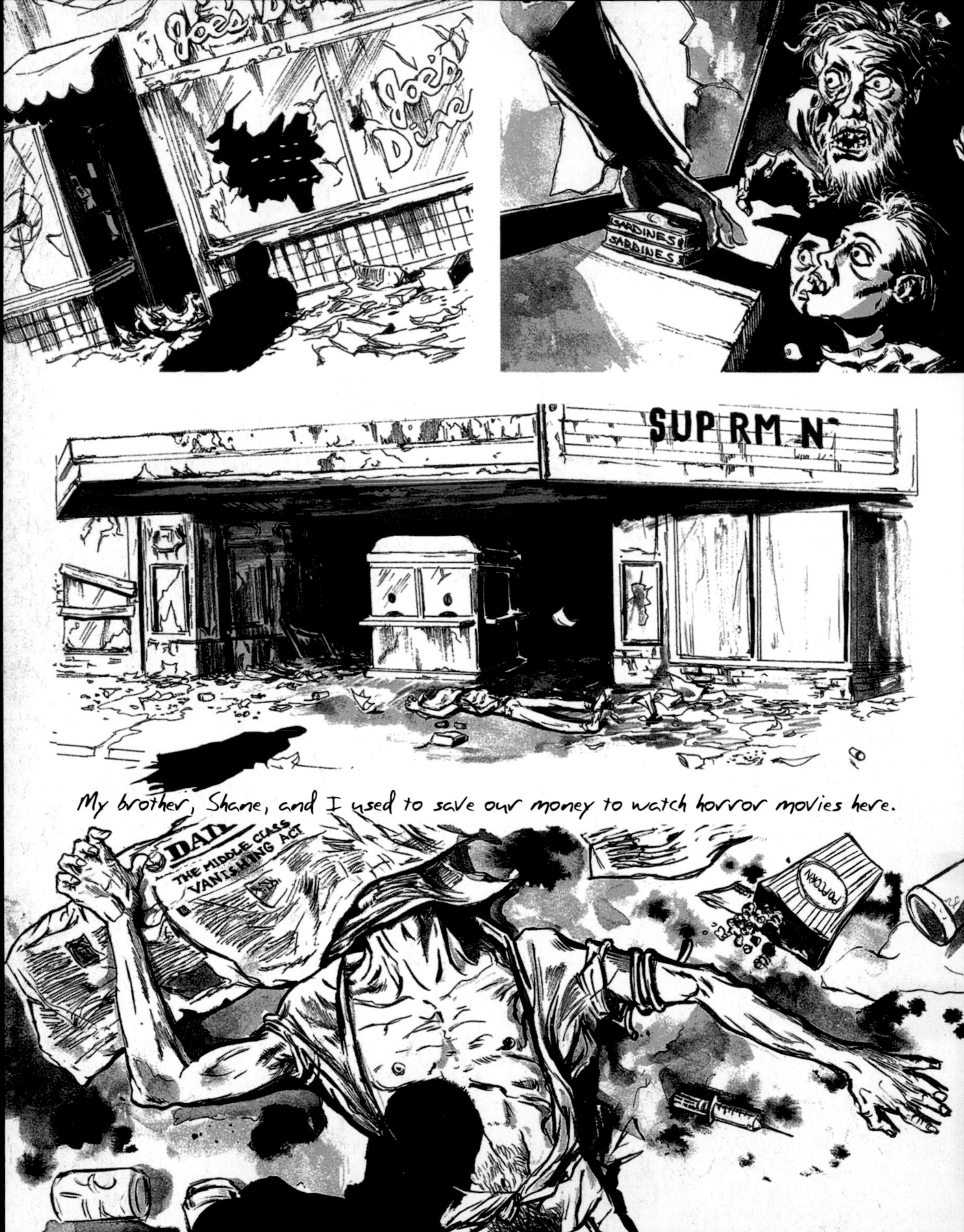
Joe's
Joe's
SARDINES
SARDINES
SUP RM N
My brother, Shane, and I used to save our money to watch horror movies here.
THE MIDDLE CLASS VANISHING ACT
POPCORN

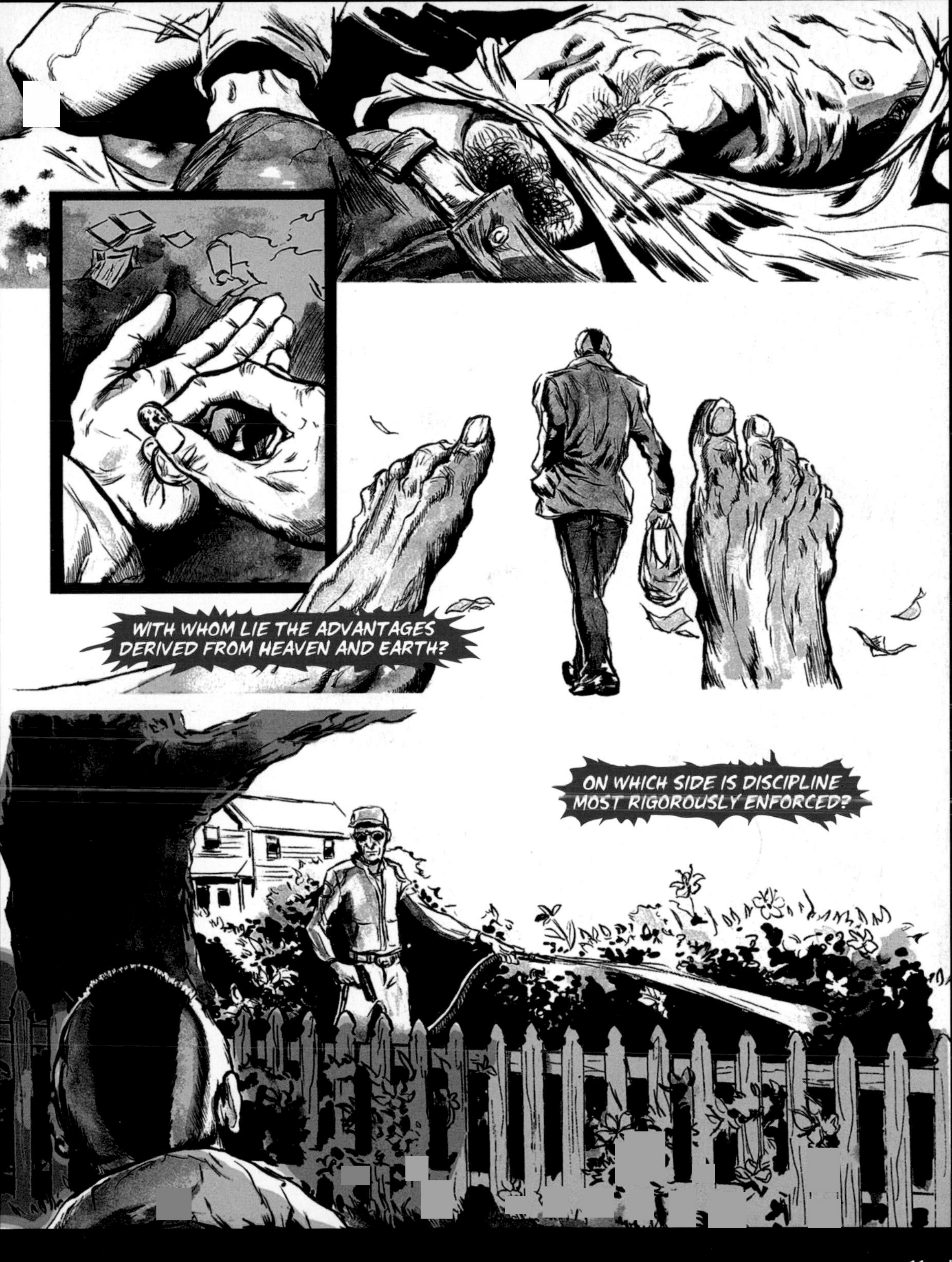
WITH WHOM LIE THE ADVANTAGES DERIVED FROM HEAVEN AND EARTH?
ON WHICH SIDE IS DISCIPLINE MOST RIGOROUSLY ENFORCED?

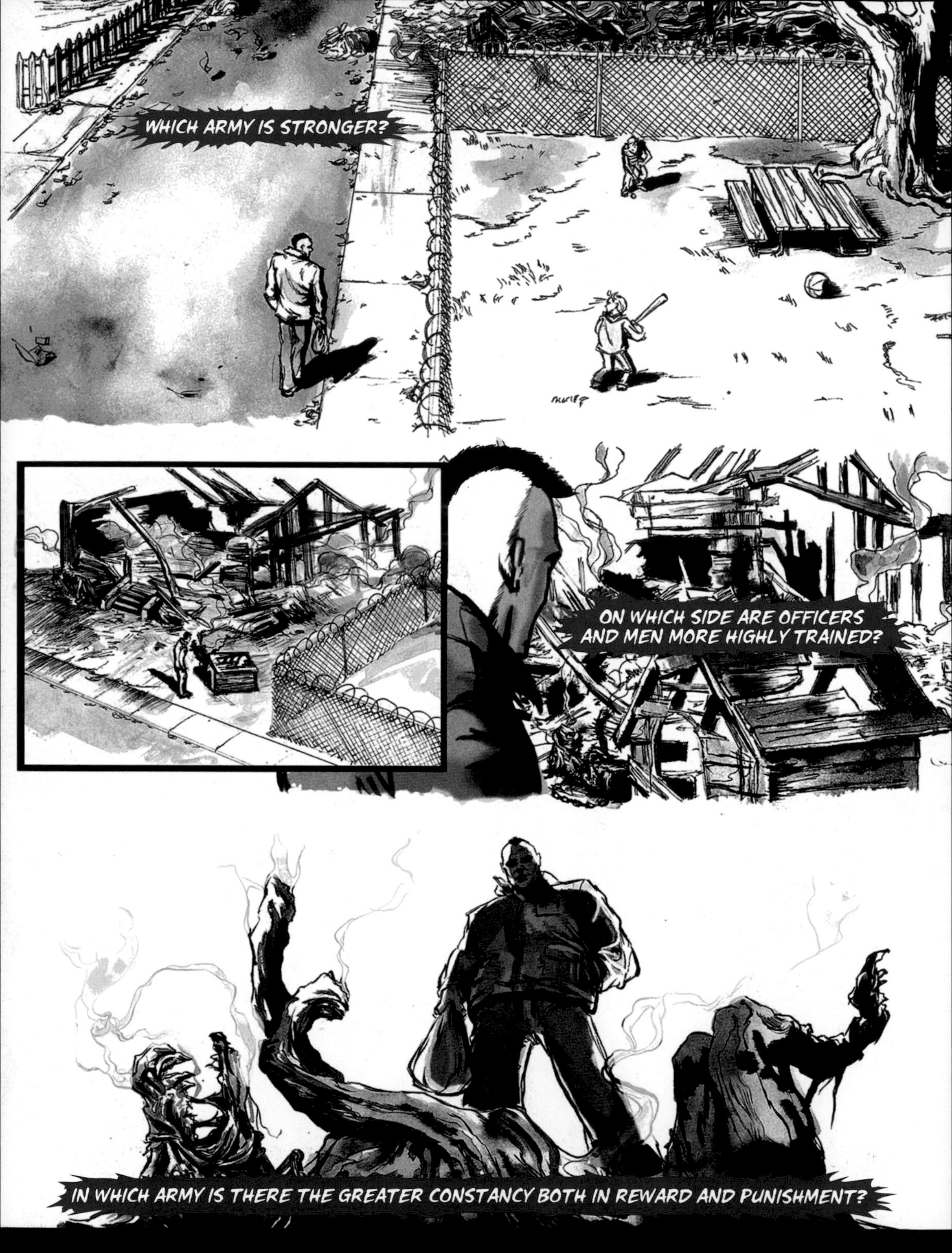
WHICH ARMY IS STRONGER?
ON WHICH SIDE ARE OFFICERS AND MEN MORE HIGHLY TRAINED?
IN WHICH ARMY IS THERE THE GREATER CONSTANCY BOTH IN REWARD AND PUNISHMENT?

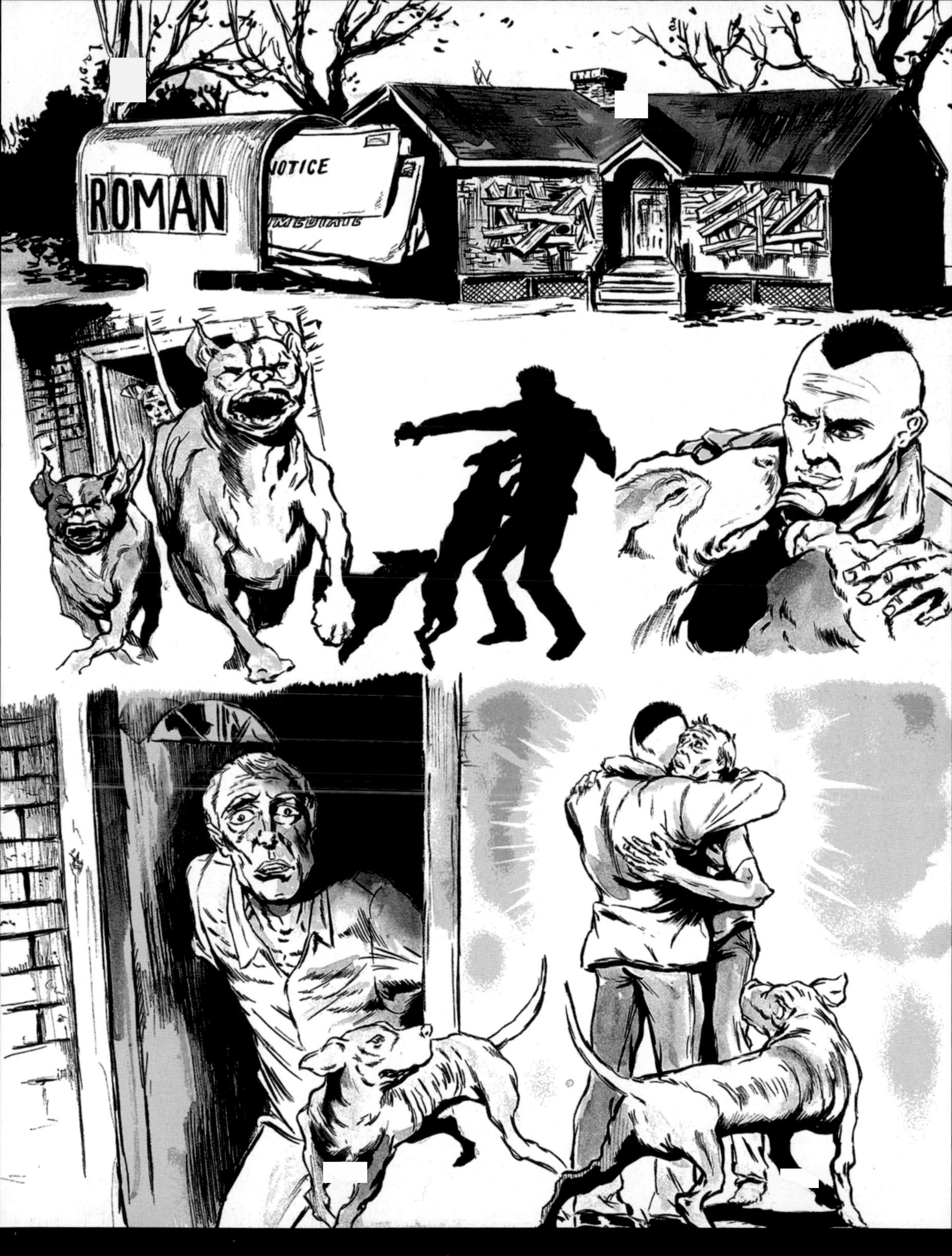
ROMAN

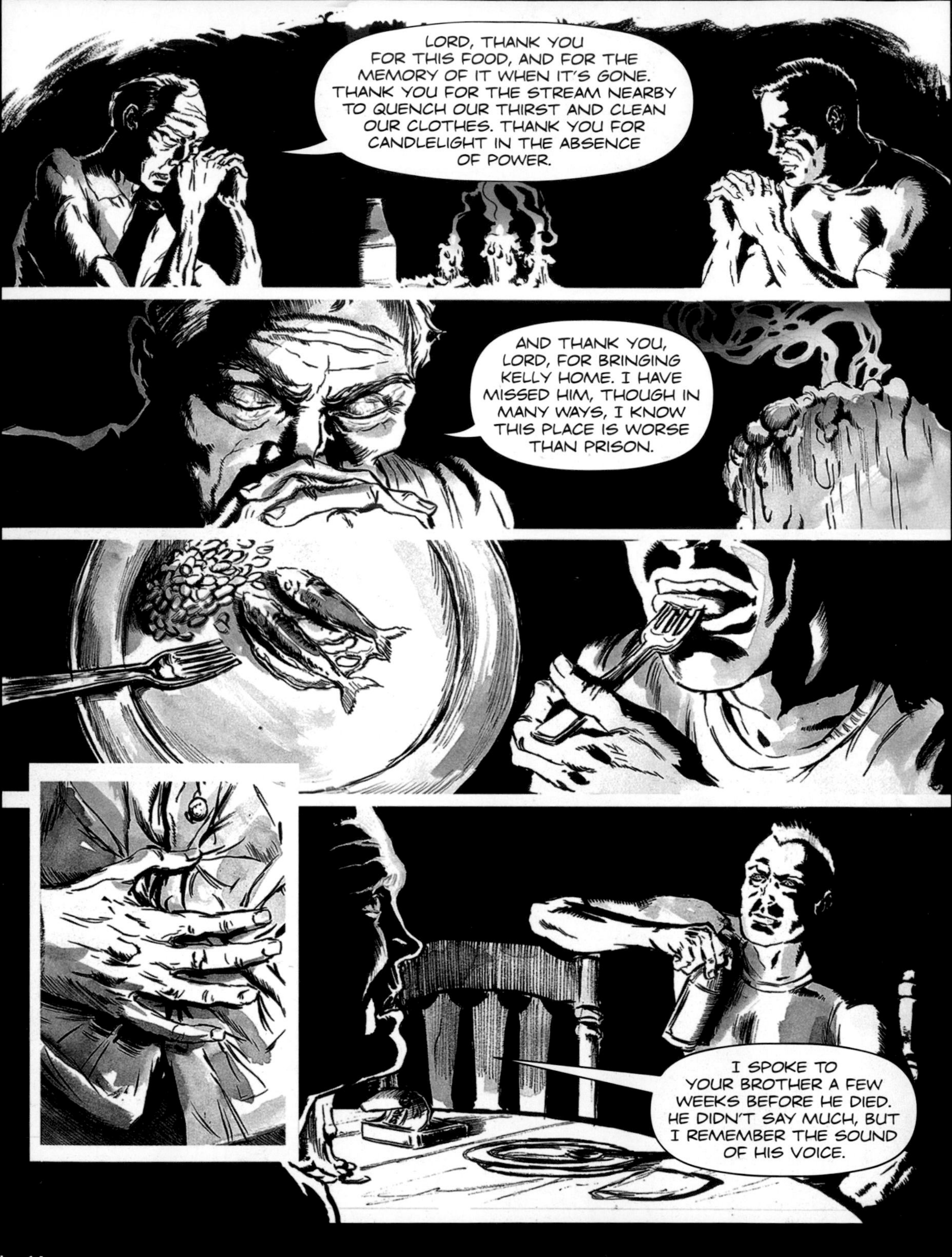
LORD, THANK YOU FOR THIS FOOD, AND FOR THE MEMORY OF IT WHEN IT'S GONE. THANK YOU FOR THE STREAM NEARBY TO QUENCH OUR THIRST AND CLEAN OUR CLOTHES. THANK YOU FOR CANDLELIGHT IN THE ABSENCE OF POWER.
AND THANK YOU, LORD, FOR BRINGING KELLY HOME. I HAVE MISSED HIM, THOUGH IN MANY WAYS, I KNOW THIS PLACE IS WORSE THAN PRISON.
I SPOKE TO YOUR BROTHER A FEW WEEKS BEFORE HE DIED. HE DIDN'T SAY MUCH, BUT I REMEMBER THE SOUND OF HIS VOICE.

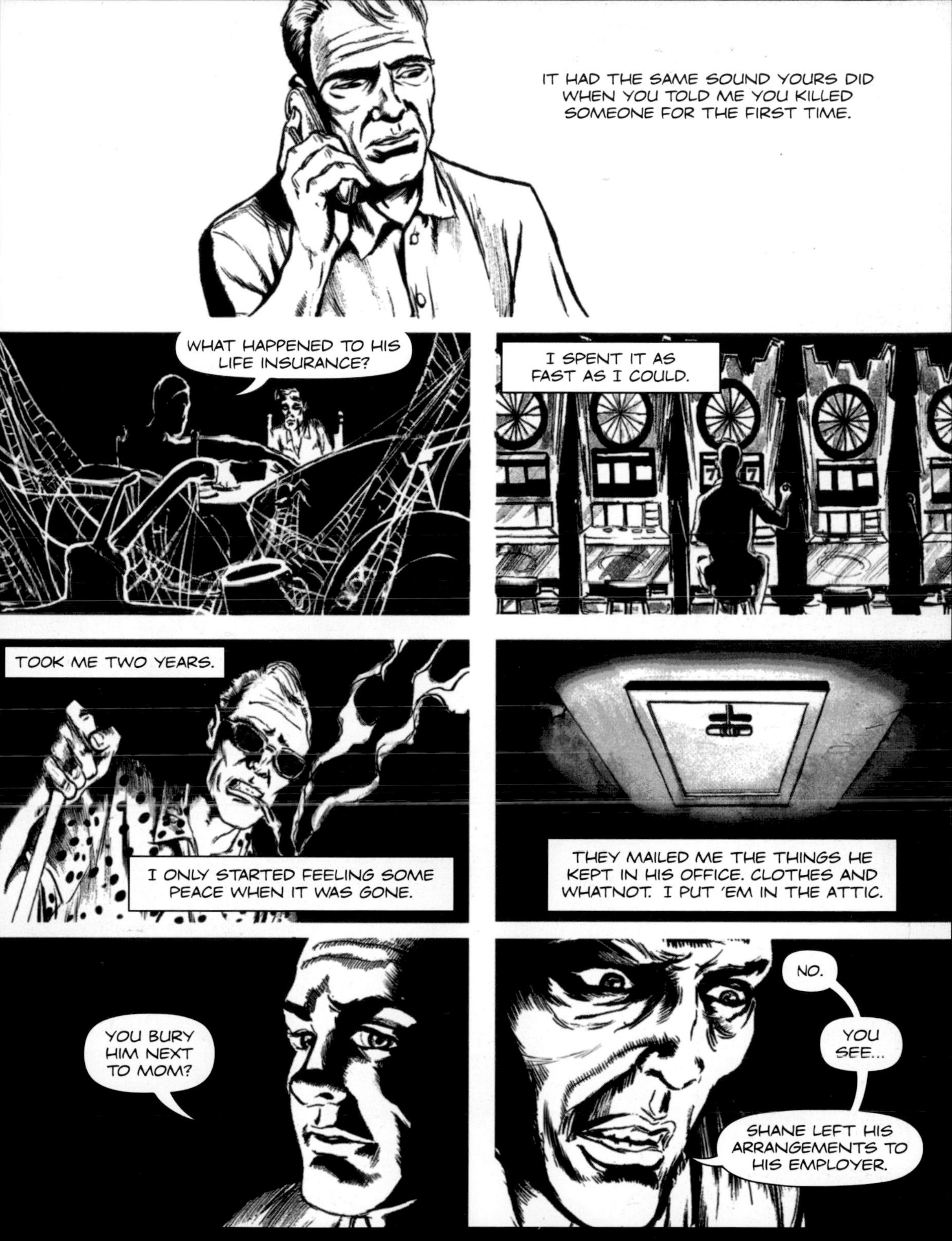
IT HAD THE SAME SOUND YOURS DID WHEN YOU TOLD ME YOU KILLED SOMEONE FOR THE FIRST TIME.
WHAT HAPPENED TO HIS LIFE INSURANCE?
I SPENT IT AS FAST AS I COULD.
TOOK ME TWO YEARS.
I ONLY STARTED FEELING SOME PEACE WHEN IT WAS GONE.
THEY MAILED ME THE THINGS HE KEPT IN HIS OFFICE. CLOTHES AND WHATNOT. I PUT 'EM IN THE ATTIC.
YOU BURY HIM NEXT TO MOM?
NO.
YOU SEE...
SHANE LEFT HIS ARRANGEMENTS TO HIS EMPLOYER.

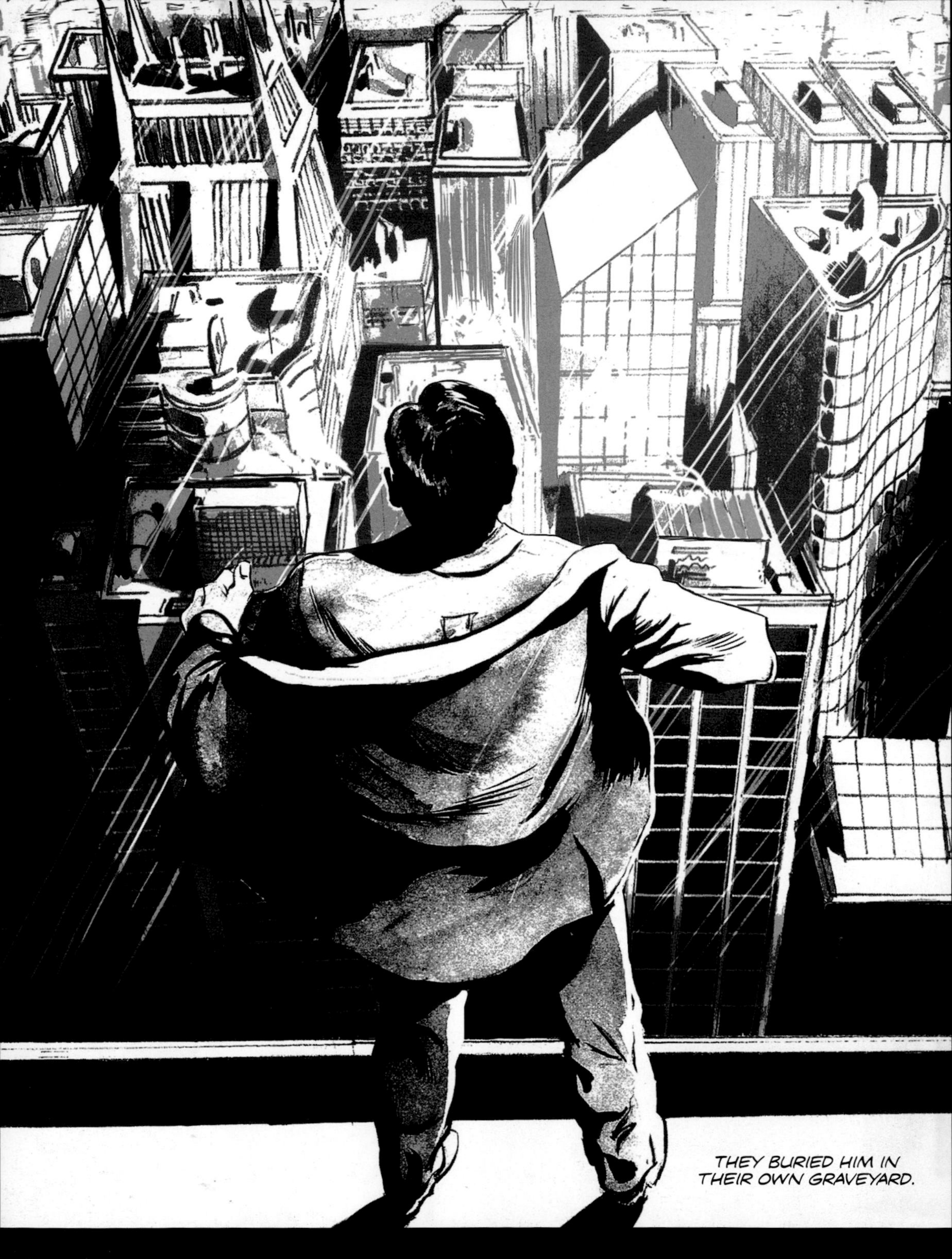
THEY BURIED HIM IN
THEIR OWN GRAVEYARD.

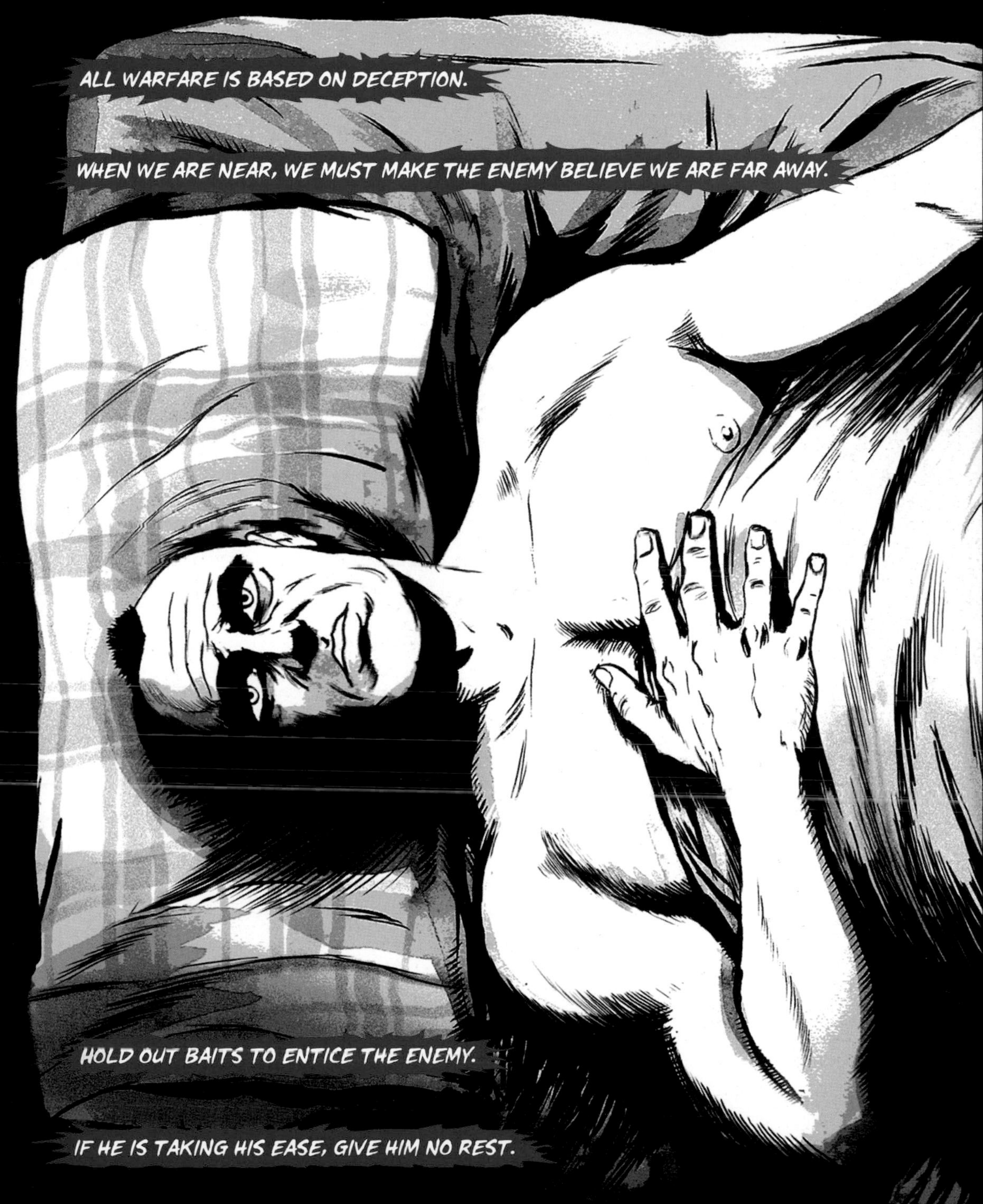
ALL WARFARE IS BASED ON DECEPTION.
WHEN WE ARE NEAR, WE MUST MAKE THE ENEMY BELIEVE WE ARE FAR AWAY.
HOLD OUT BAITS TO ENTICE THE ENEMY.
IF HE IS TAKING HIS EASE, GIVE HIM NO REST.

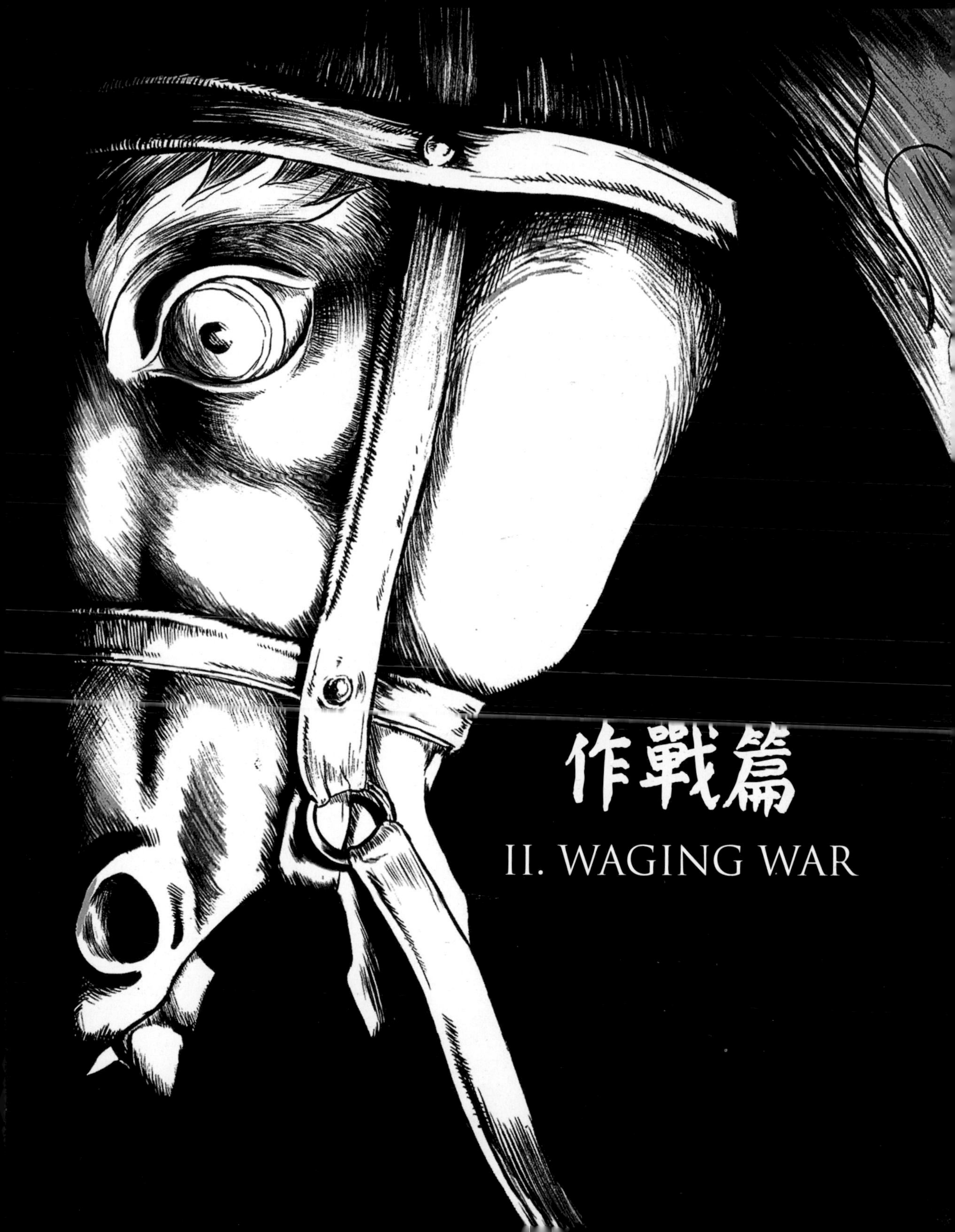

作戰篇

II. WAGING WAR

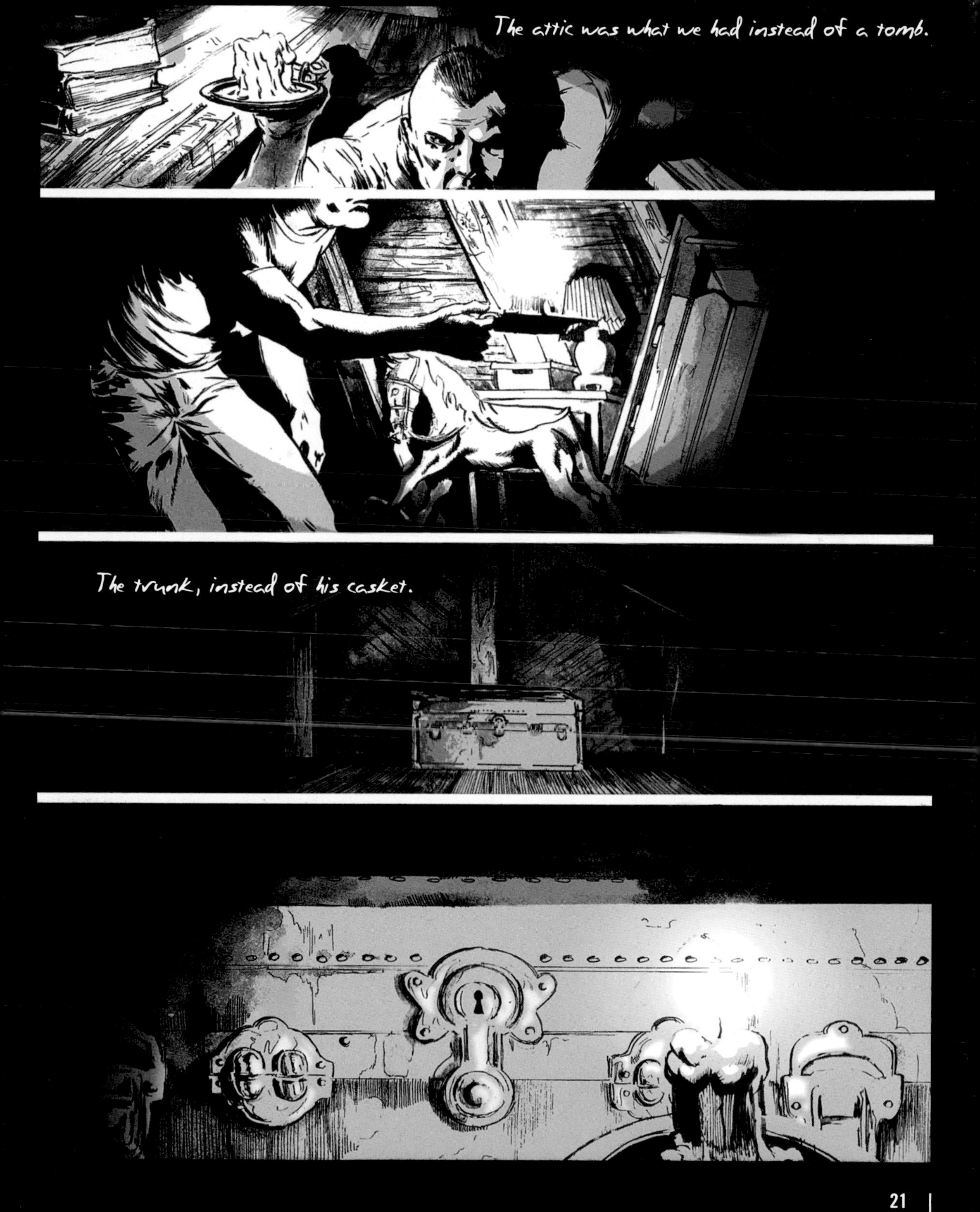

The attic was what we had instead of a tomb.
The trunk, instead of his casket.

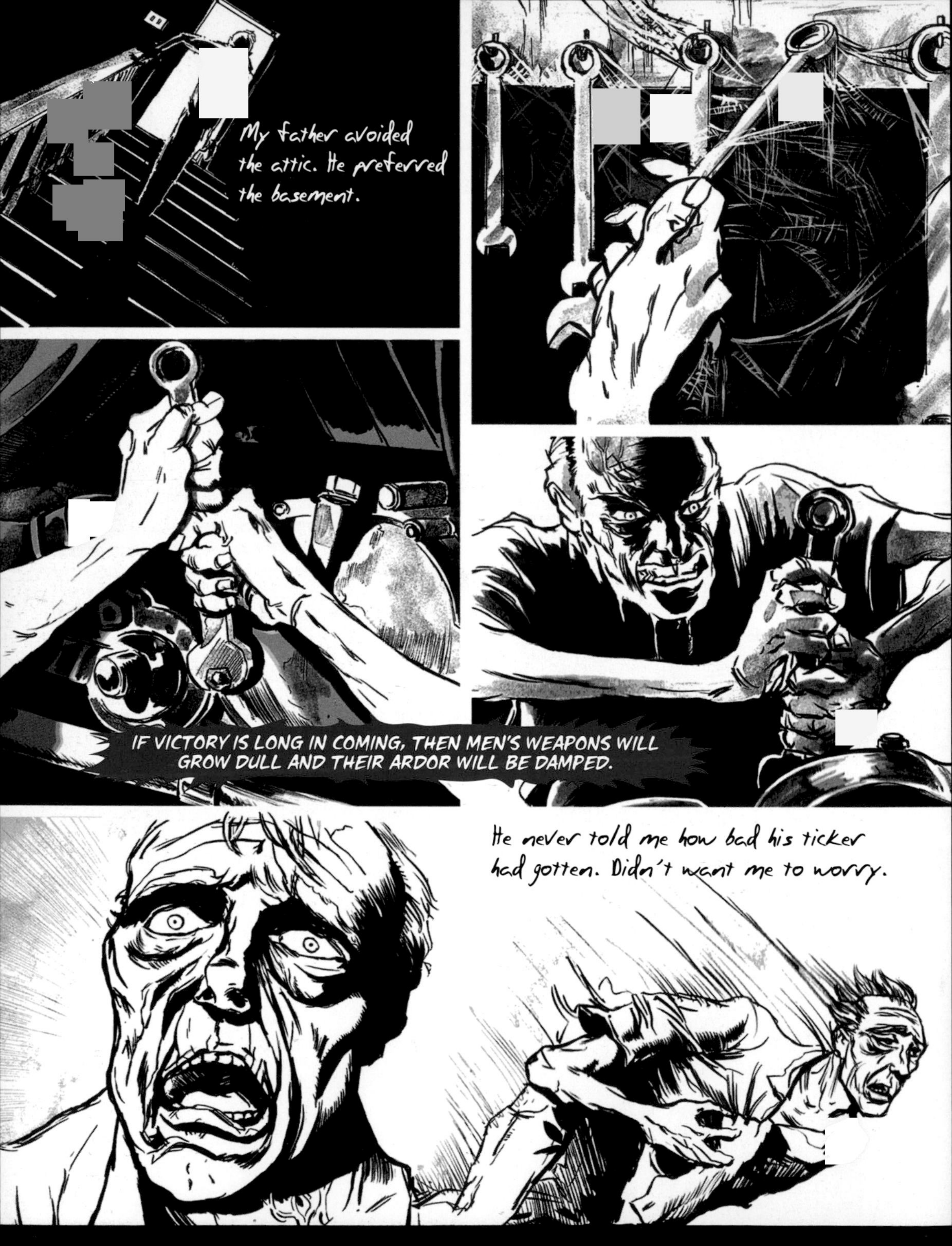
My father avoided the attic. He preferred the basement.
IF VICTORY IS LONG IN COMING, THEN MEN'S WEAPONS WILL GROW DULL AND THEIR ARDOR WILL BE DAMPED.
He never told me how bad his ticker had gotten. Didn't want me to worry.

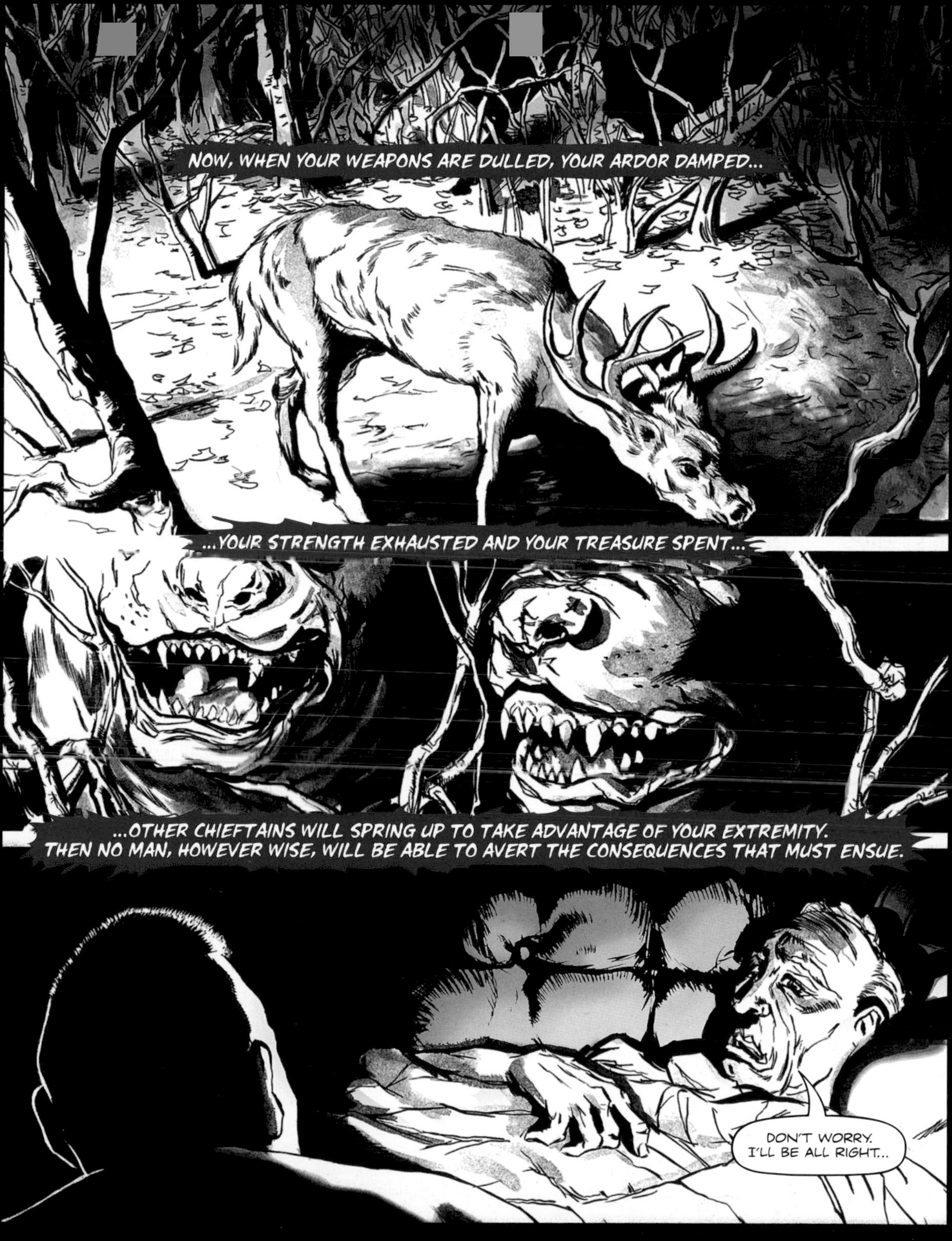
NOW, WHEN YOUR WEAPONS ARE DULLED, YOUR ARDOR DAMPED...
...YOUR STRENGTH EXHAUSTED AND YOUR TREASURE SPENT...
...OTHER CHIEFTAINS WILL SPRING UP TO TAKE ADVANTAGE OF YOUR EXTREMITY.
THEN NO MAN, HOWEVER WISE, WILL BE ABLE TO AVERT THE CONSEQUENCES THAT MUST ENSUE.
DON'T WORRY. I'LL BE ALL RIGHT...

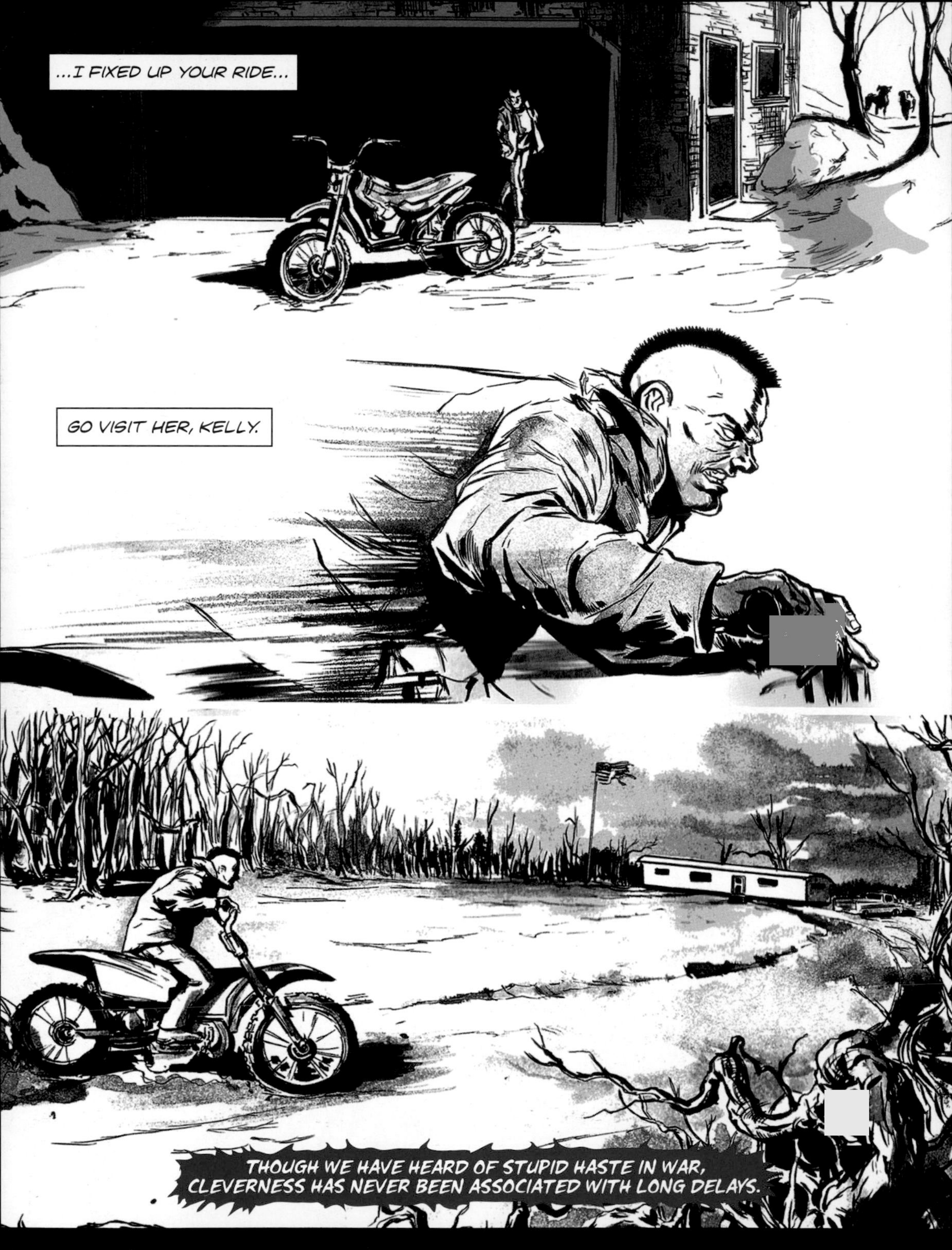
...I FIXED UP YOUR RIDE...
GO VISIT HER, KELLY.
THOUGH WE HAVE HEARD OF STUPID HASTE IN WAR,
CLEVERNESS HAS NEVER BEEN ASSOCIATED WITH LONG DELAYS.

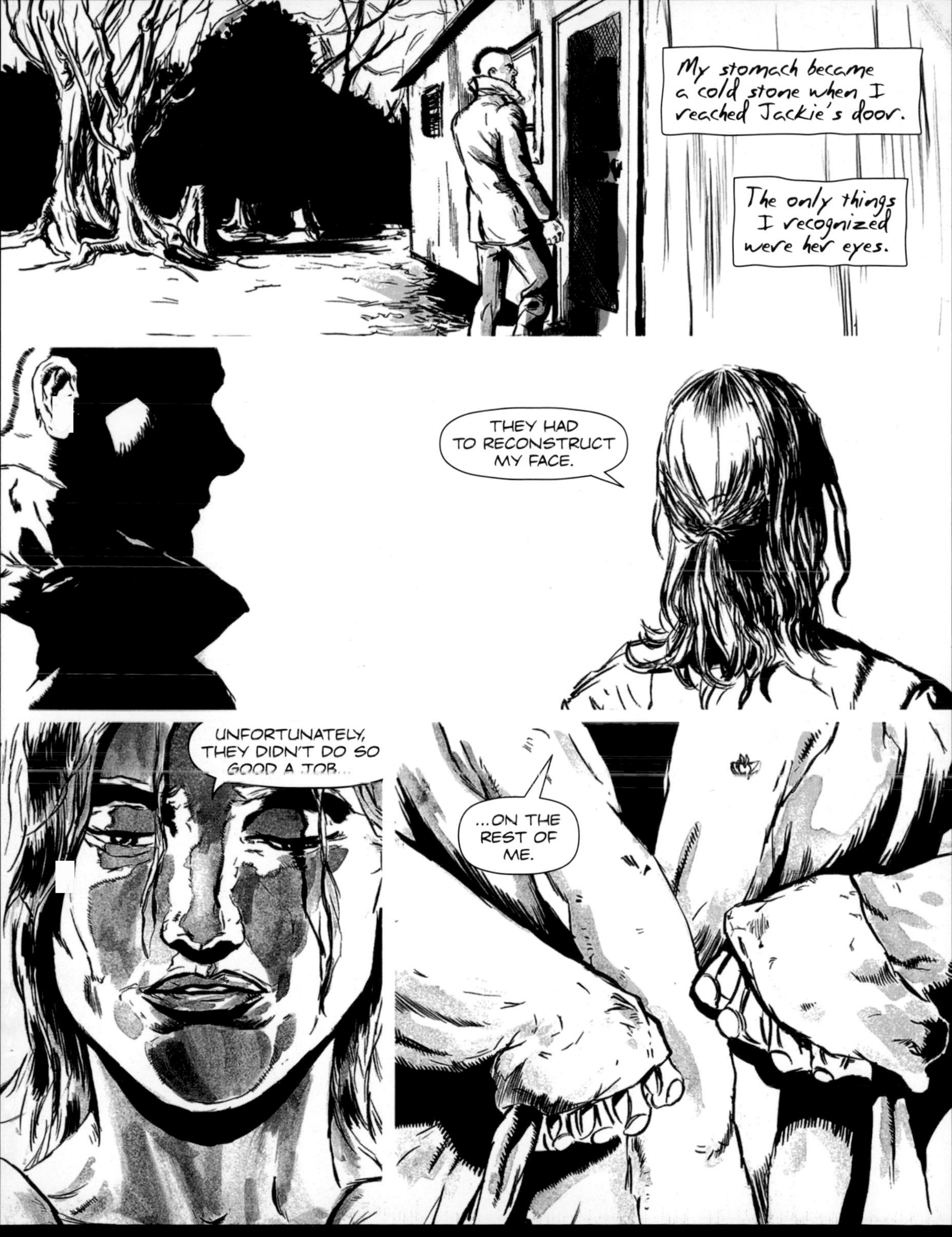
My stomach became a cold stone when I reached Jackie's door.
The only things I recognized were her eyes.
THEY HAD TO RECONSTRUCT MY FACE.
UNFORTUNATELY, THEY DIDN'T DO SO GOOD A JOB...
...ON THE REST OF ME.

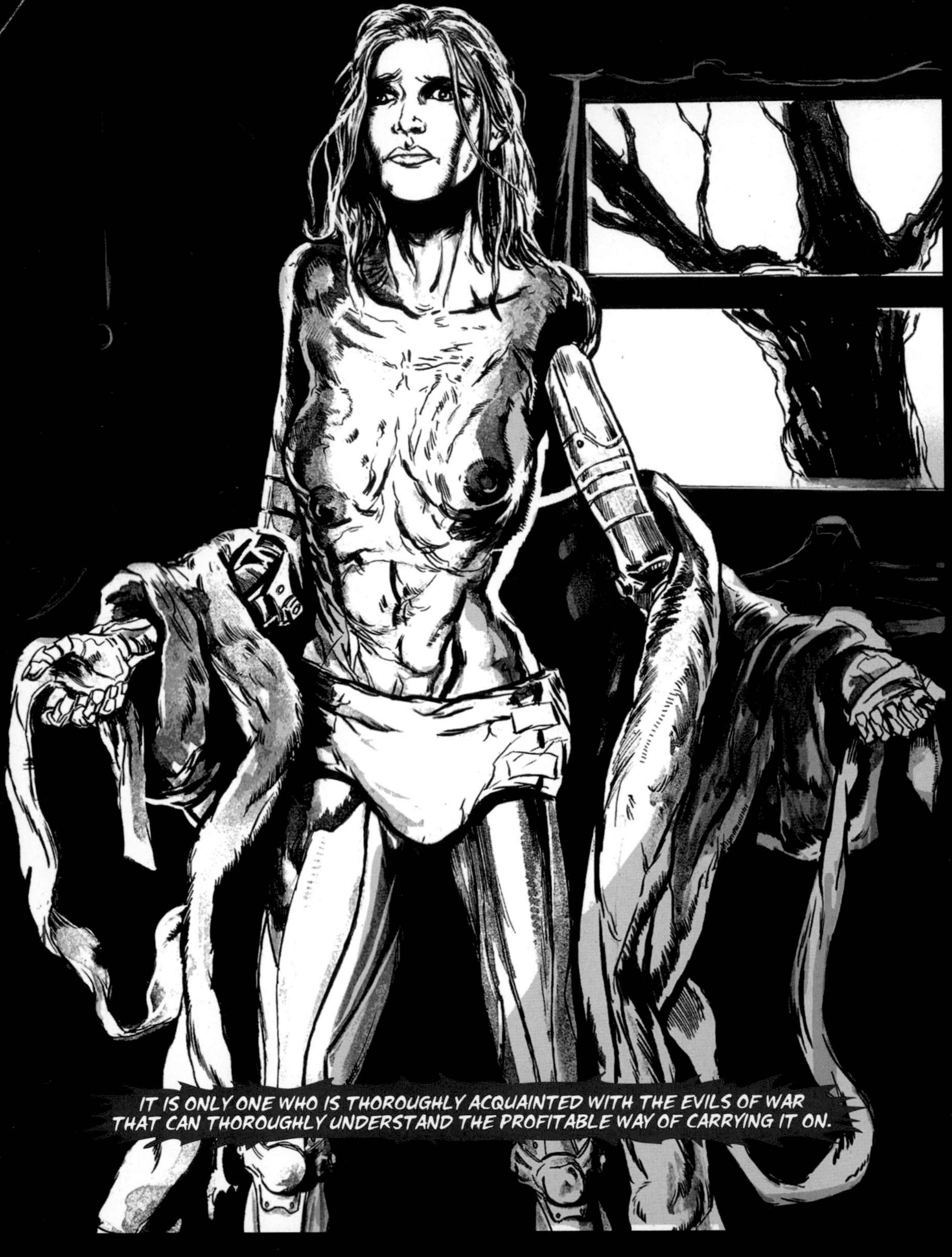
IT IS ONLY ONE WHO IS THOROUGHLY ACQUAINTED WITH THE EVILS OF WAR THAT CAN THOROUGHLY UNDERSTAND THE PROFITABLE WAY OF CARRYING IT ON.

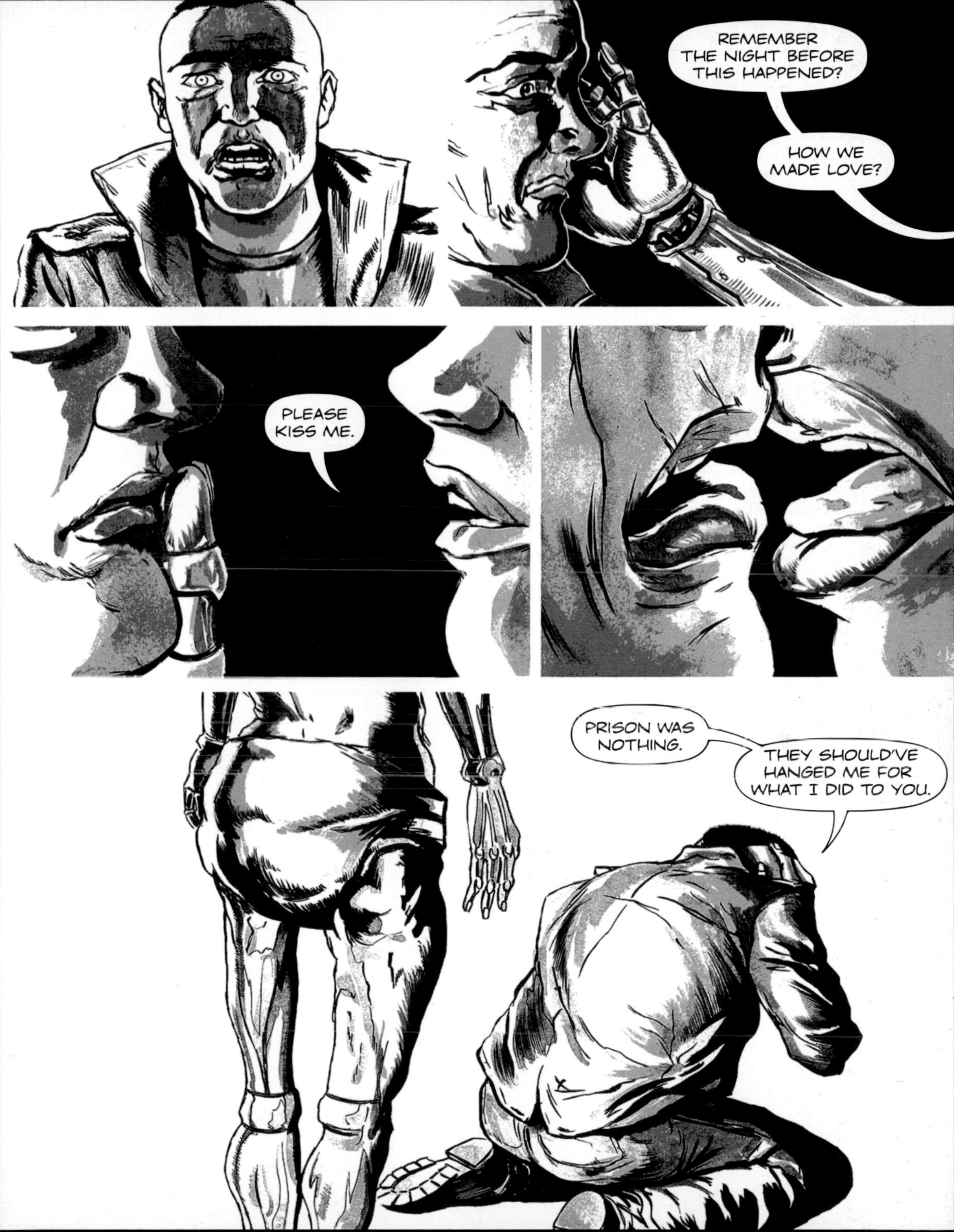
REMEMBER THE NIGHT BEFORE THIS HAPPENED?
HOW WE MADE LOVE?
PLEASE KISS ME.
PRISON WAS NOTHING.
THEY SHOULD'VE HANGED ME FOR WHAT I DID TO YOU.

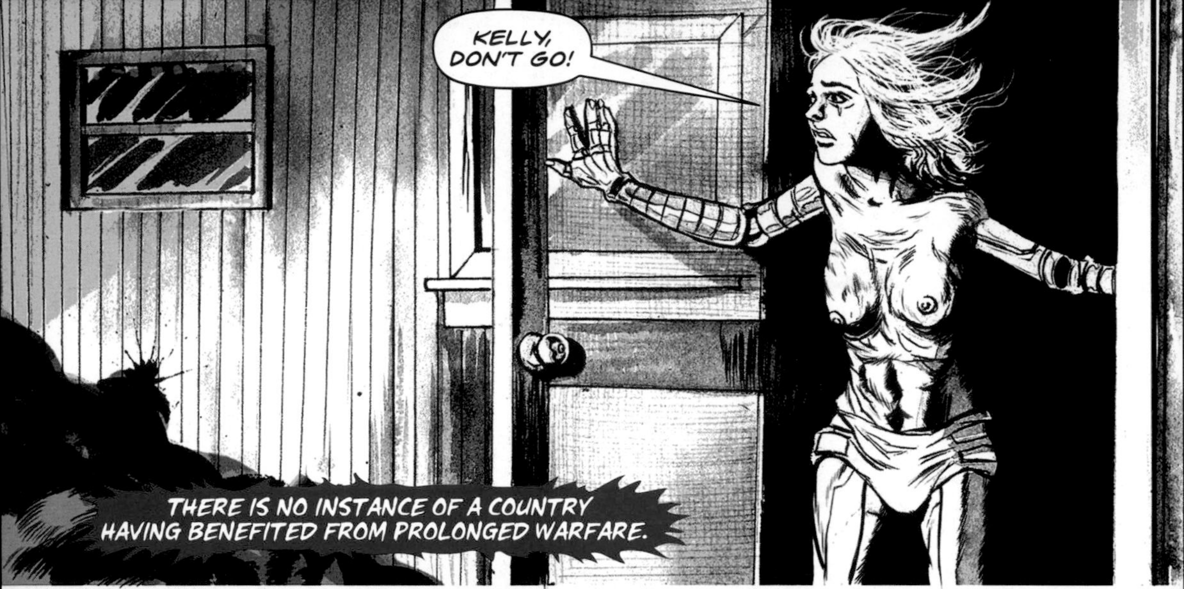
KELLY, DON'T GO!
THERE IS NO INSTANCE OF A COUNTRY HAVING BENEFITED FROM PROLONGED WARFARE.

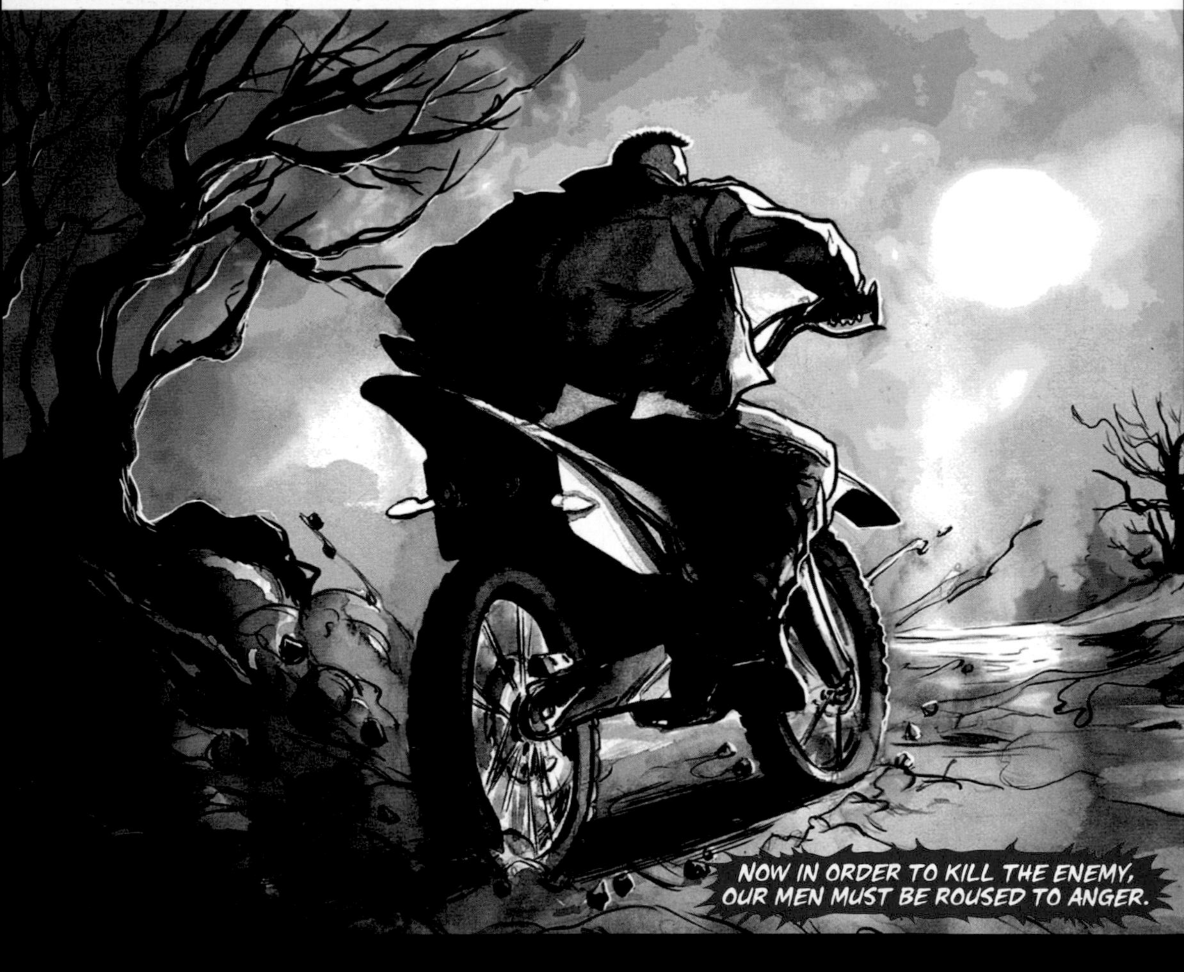
NOW IN ORDER TO KILL THE ENEMY, OUR MEN MUST BE ROUSED TO ANGER.

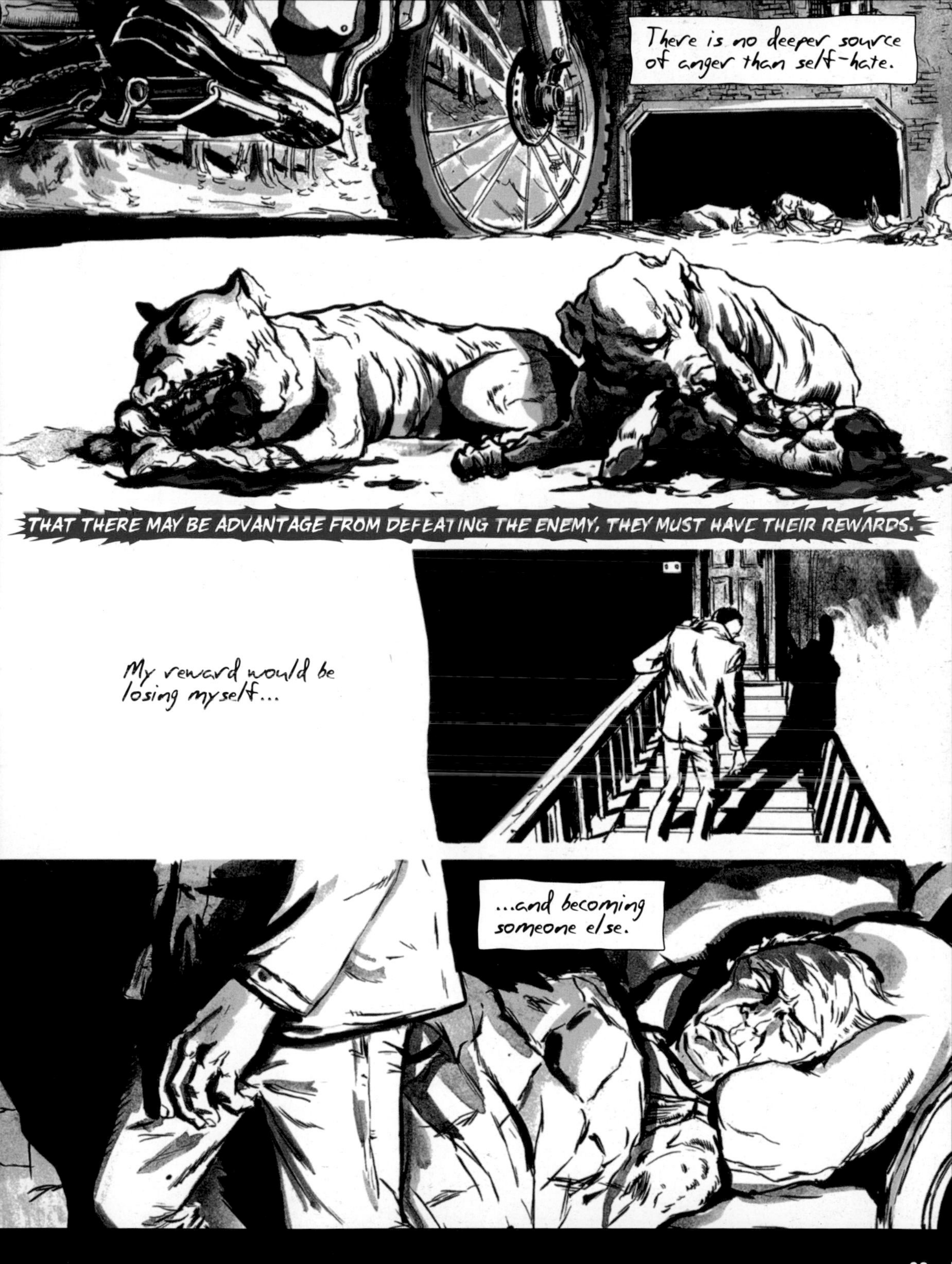
There is no deeper source of anger than self-hate.
THAT THERE MAY BE ADVANTAGE FROM DEFEATING THE ENEMY, THEY MUST HAVE THEIR REWARDS.
My reward would be losing myself...
...and becoming someone else.

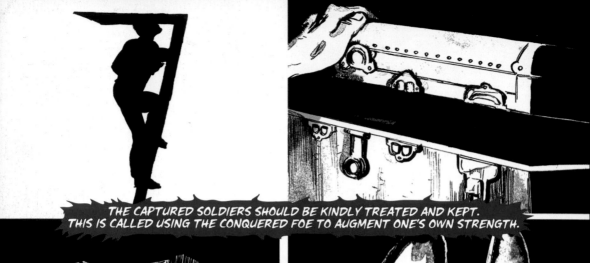

THE CAPTURED SOLDIERS SHOULD BE KINDLY TREATED AND KEPT.
THIS IS CALLED USING THE CONQUERED FOE TO AUGMENT ONE'S OWN STRENGTH.

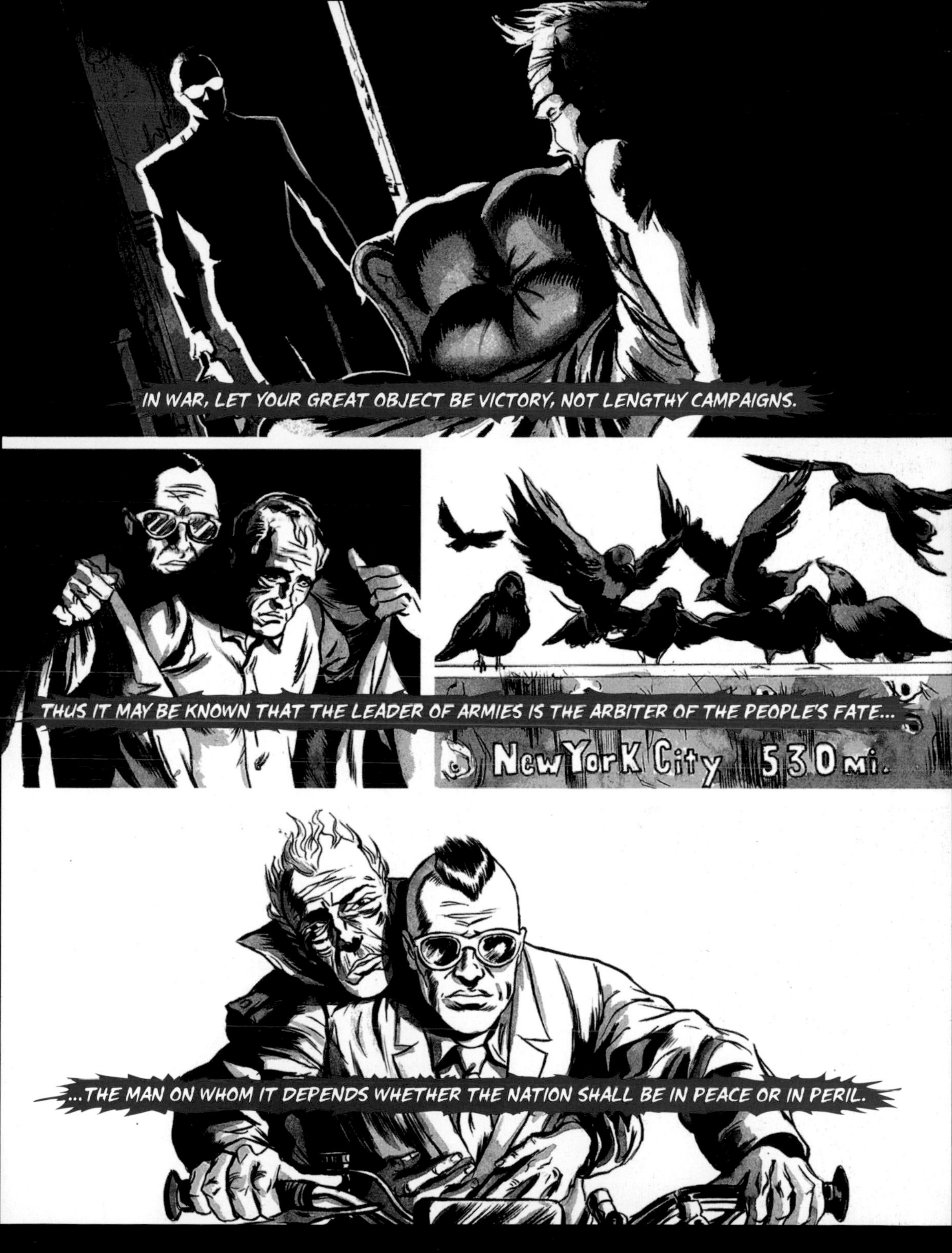
IN WAR, LET YOUR GREAT OBJECT BE VICTORY, NOT LENGTHY CAMPAIGNS.
THUS IT MAY BE KNOWN THAT THE LEADER OF ARMIES IS THE ARBITER OF THE PEOPLE'S FATE...
New York City 530 mi.
...THE MAN ON WHOM IT DEPENDS WHETHER THE NATION SHALL BE IN PEACE OR IN PERIL.

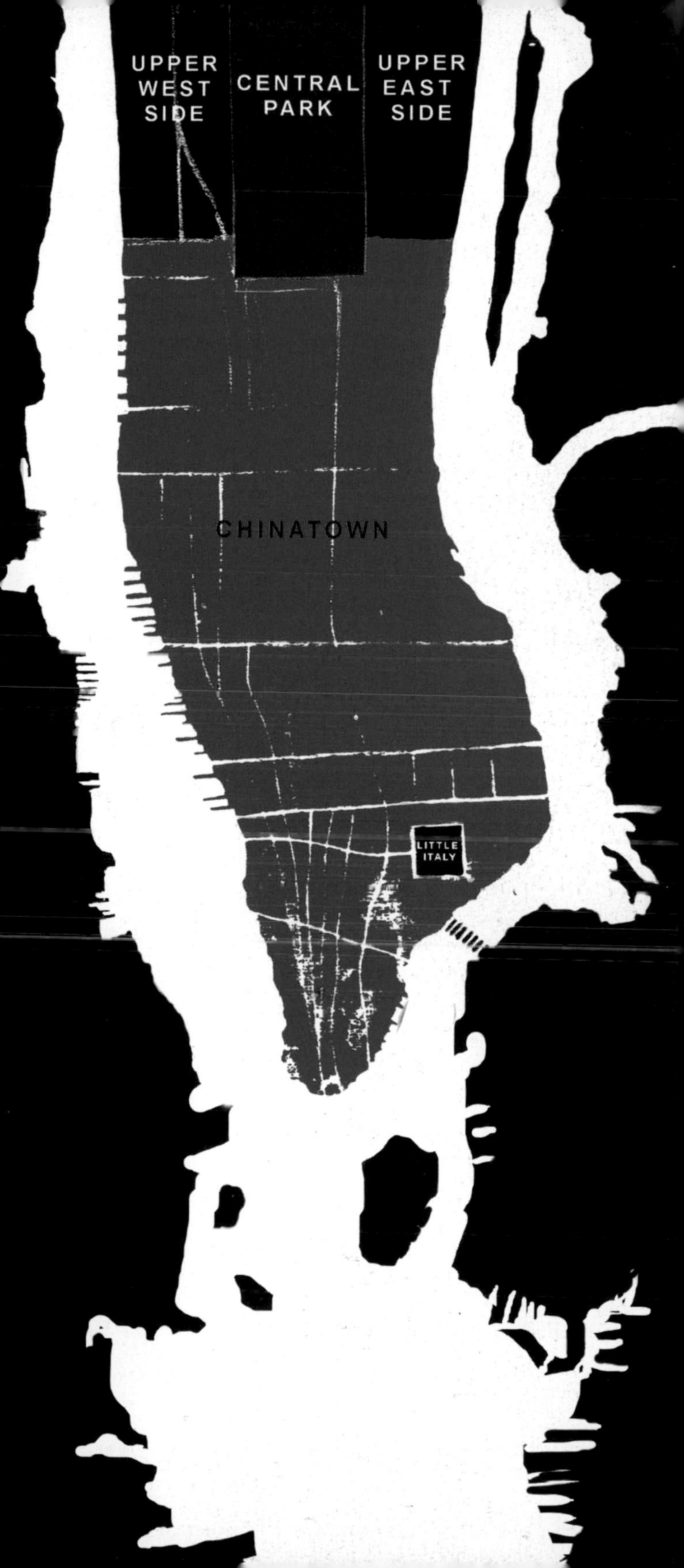
UPPER WEST SIDE
CENTRAL PARK
UPPER EAST SIDE
CHINATOWN
LITTLE ITALY

謀攻篇

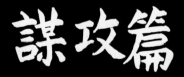

III. ATTACK BY STRATAGEM

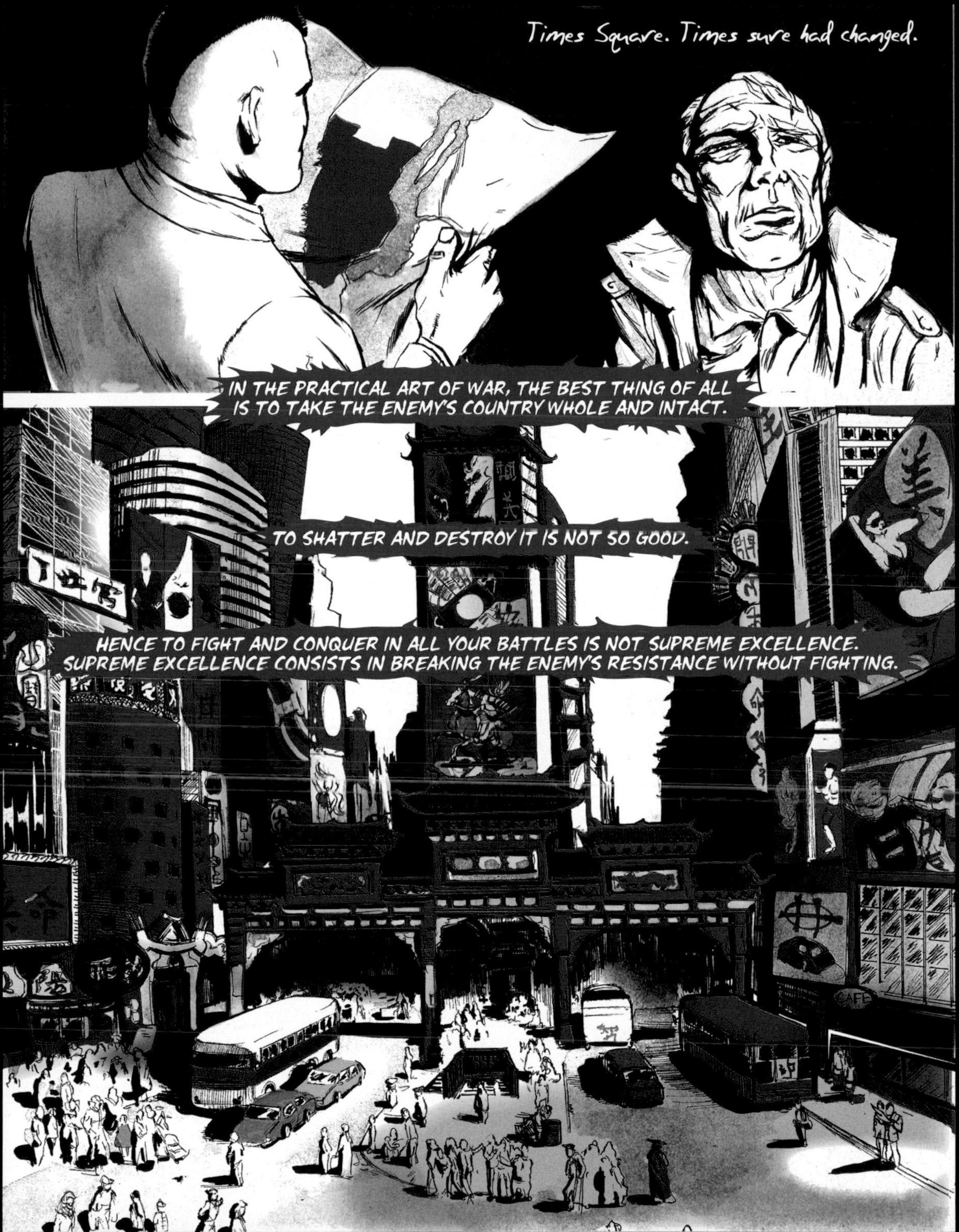
Times Square. Times sure had changed.
IN THE PRACTICAL ART OF WAR, THE BEST THING OF ALL IS TO TAKE THE ENEMY'S COUNTRY WHOLE AND INTACT.
TO SHATTER AND DESTROY IT IS NOT SO GOOD.
HENCE TO FIGHT AND CONQUER IN ALL YOUR BATTLES IS NOT SUPREME EXCELLENCE. SUPREME EXCELLENCE CONSISTS IN BREAKING THE ENEMY'S RESISTANCE WITHOUT FIGHTING.
CAFE

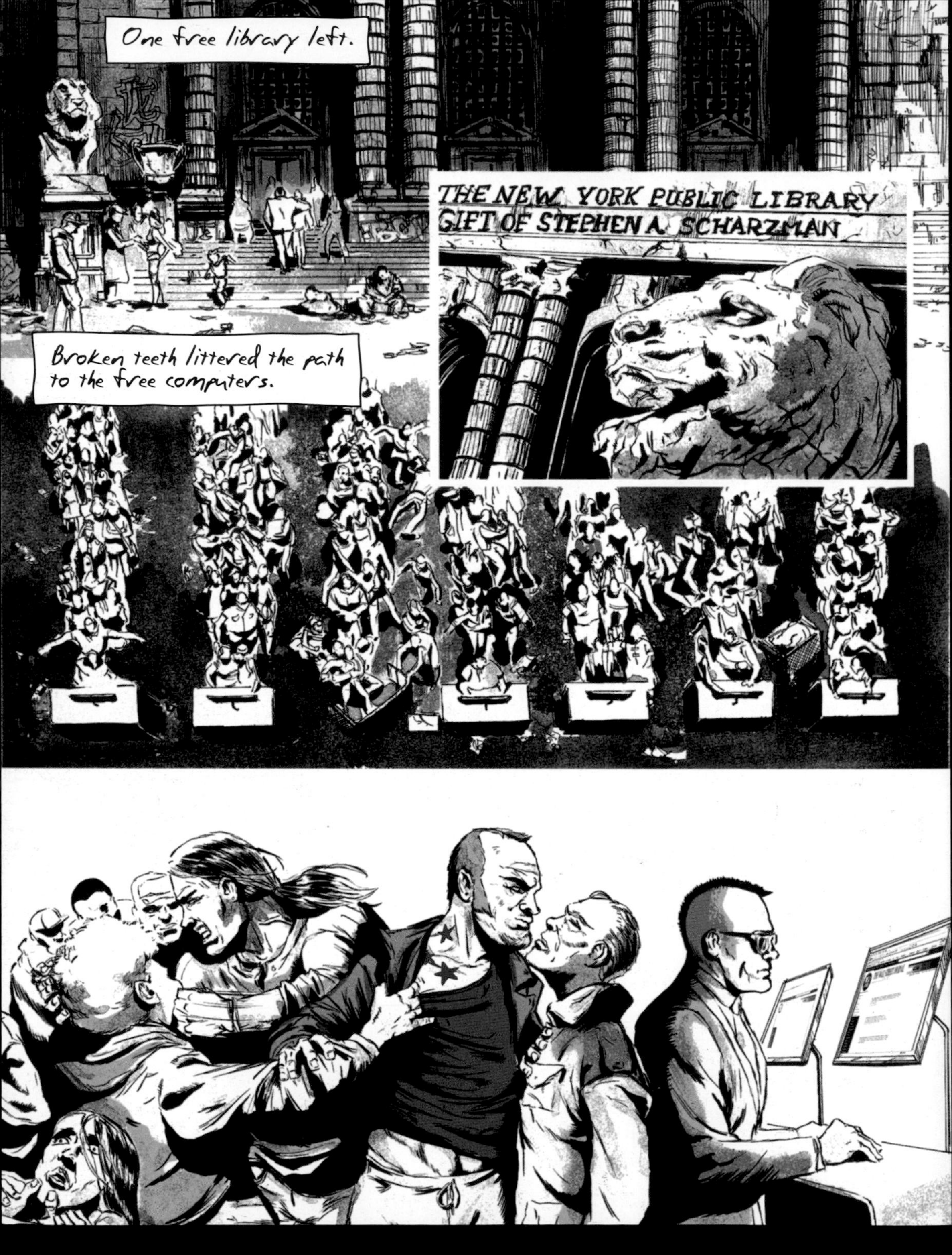
One free library left.
THE NEW YORK PUBLIC LIBRARY
GIFT OF STEPHEN A. SCHARZMAN
Broken teeth littered the path to the free computers.

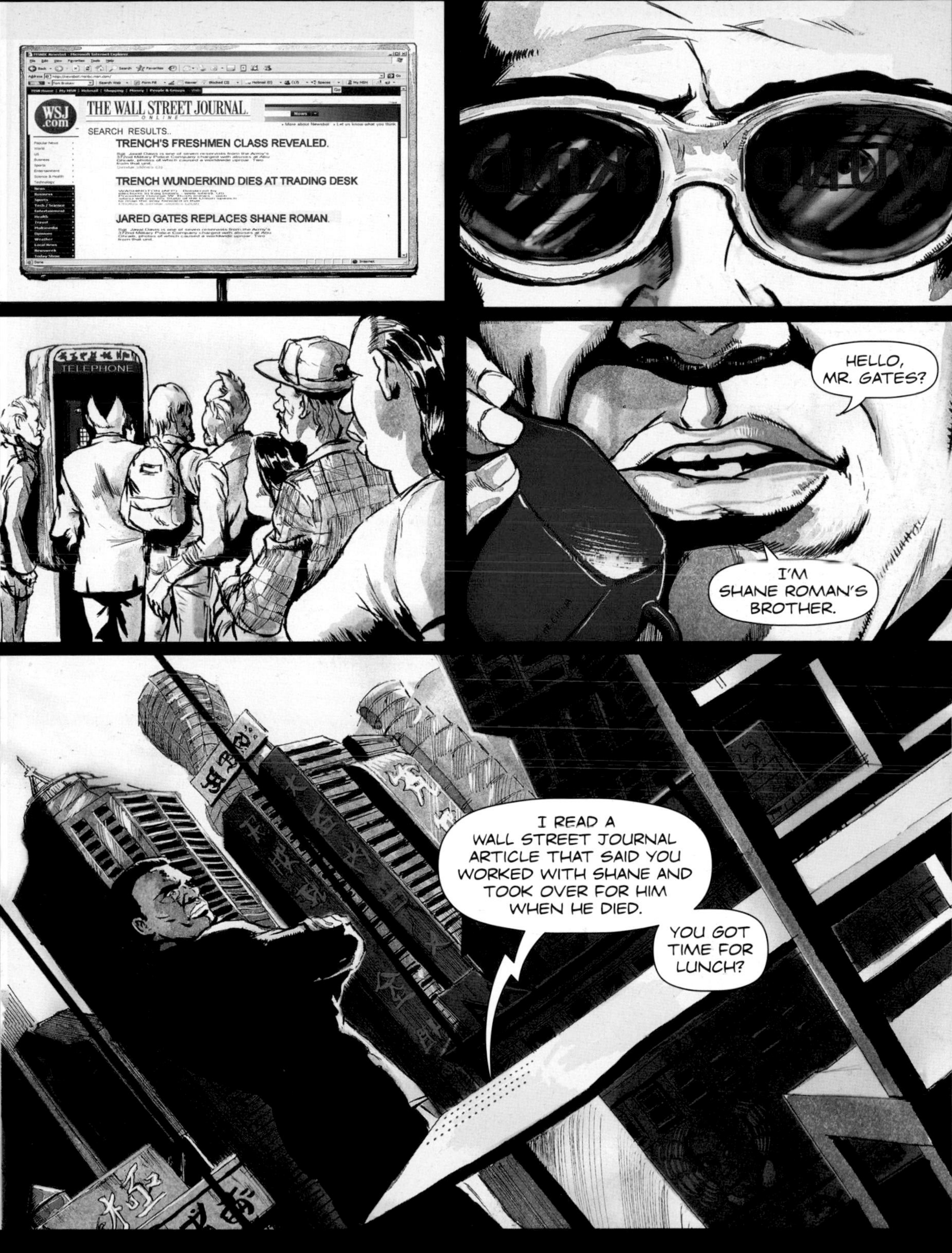
WSJ .com
THE WALL STREET JOURNAL. ONLINE
SEARCH RESULTS..
TRENCH'S FRESHMEN CLASS REVEALED.
TRENCH WUNDERKIND DIES AT TRADING DESK
JARED GATES REPLACES SHANE ROMAN.
TELEPHONE
HELLO, MR. GATES?
I'M SHANE ROMAN'S BROTHER.
I READ A WALL STREET JOURNAL ARTICLE THAT SAID YOU WORKED WITH SHANE AND TOOK OVER FOR HIM WHEN HE DIED.
YOU GOT TIME FOR LUNCH?

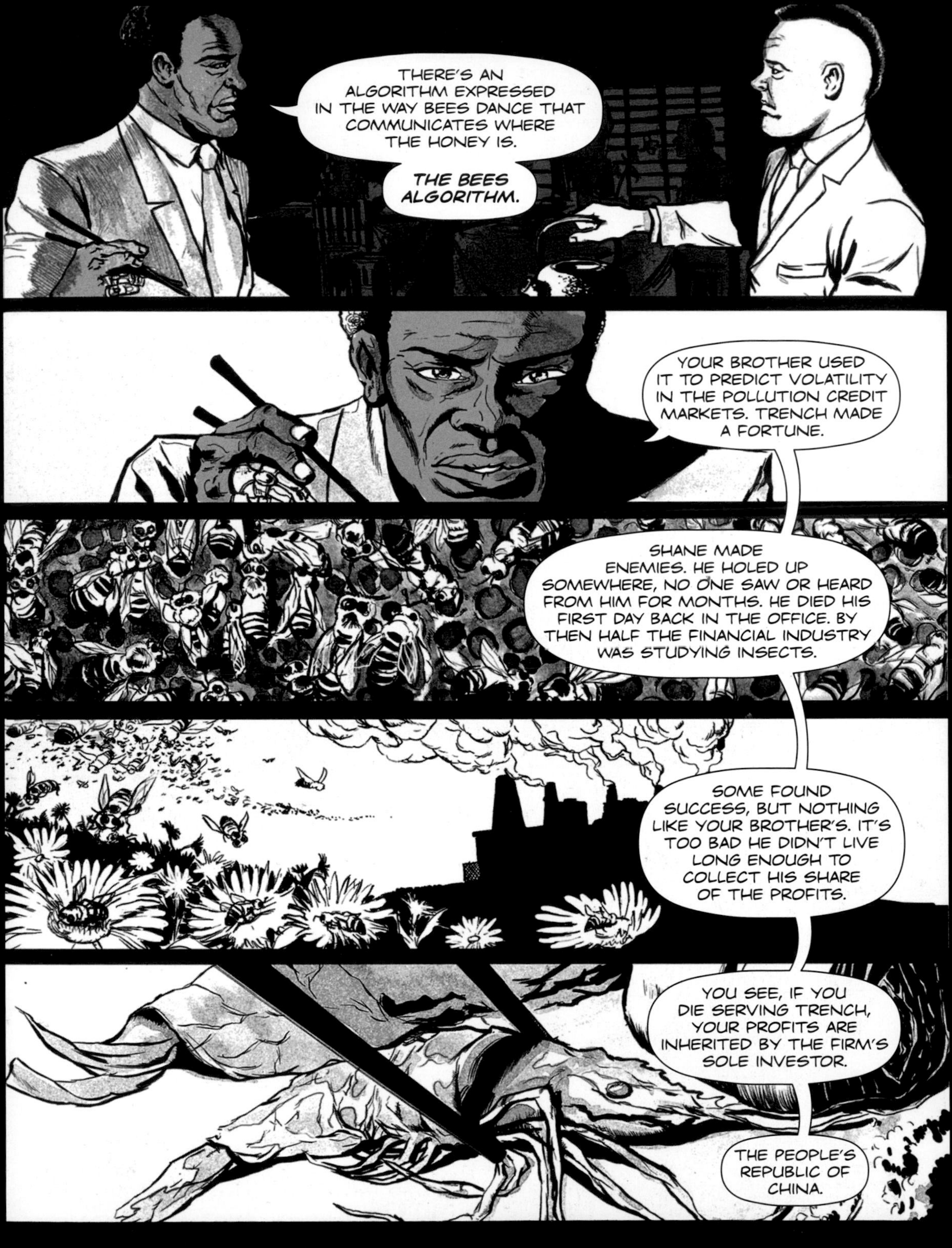
THERE'S AN ALGORITHM EXPRESSED IN THE WAY BEES DANCE THAT COMMUNICATES WHERE THE HONEY IS.
THE BEES ALGORITHM.
YOUR BROTHER USED IT TO PREDICT VOLATILITY IN THE POLLUTION CREDIT MARKETS. TRENCH MADE A FORTUNE.
SHANE MADE ENEMIES. HE HOLED UP SOMEWHERE, NO ONE SAW OR HEARD FROM HIM FOR MONTHS. HE DIED HIS FIRST DAY BACK IN THE OFFICE. BY THEN HALF THE FINANCIAL INDUSTRY WAS STUDYING INSECTS.
SOME FOUND SUCCESS, BUT NOTHING LIKE YOUR BROTHER'S. IT'S TOO BAD HE DIDN'T LIVE LONG ENOUGH TO COLLECT HIS SHARE OF THE PROFITS.
YOU SEE, IF YOU DIE SERVING TRENCH, YOUR PROFITS ARE INHERITED BY THE FIRM'S SOLE INVESTOR.
THE PEOPLE'S REPUBLIC OF CHINA.

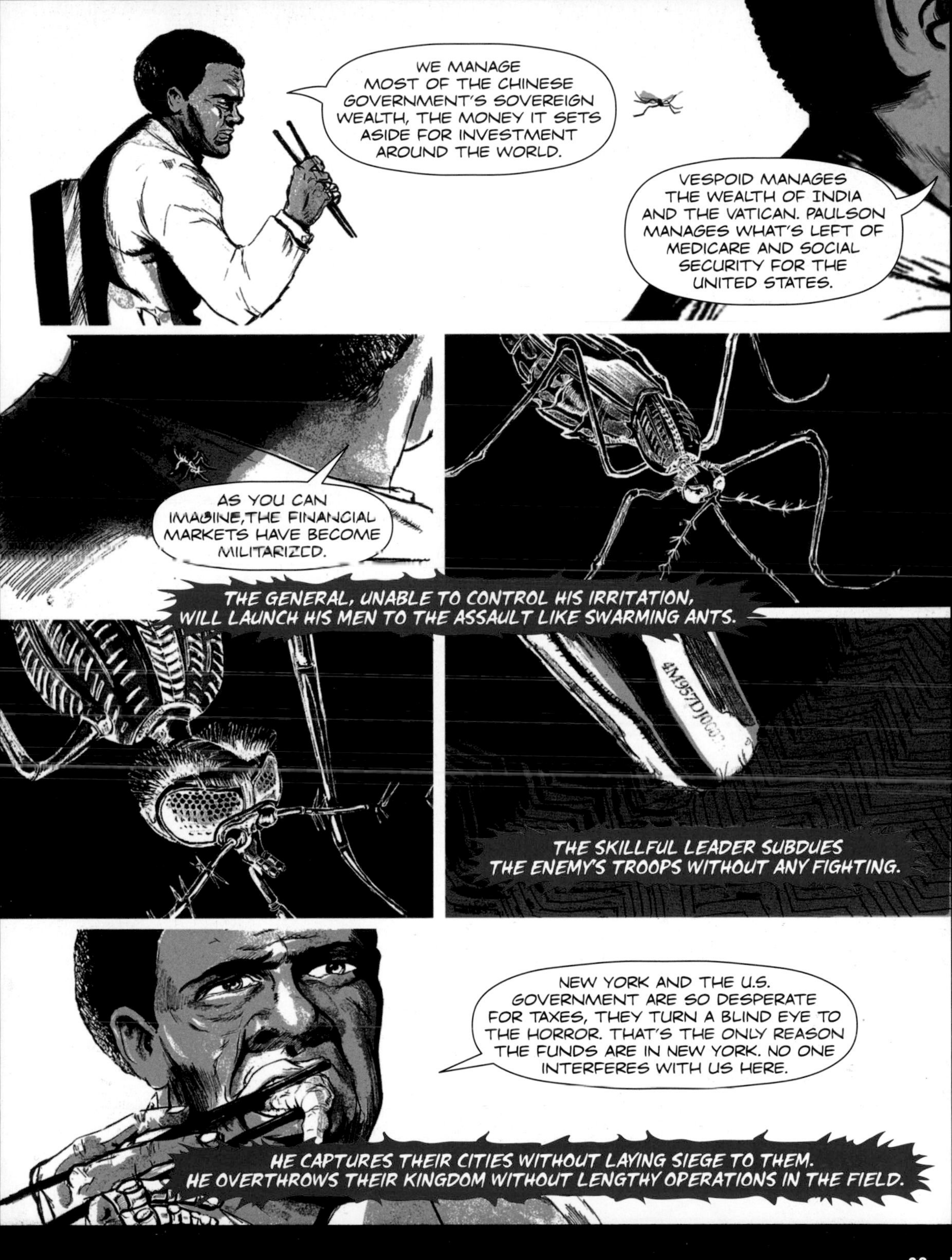
WE MANAGE MOST OF THE CHINESE GOVERNMENT'S SOVEREIGN WEALTH, THE MONEY IT SETS ASIDE FOR INVESTMENT AROUND THE WORLD.
VESPOID MANAGES THE WEALTH OF INDIA AND THE VATICAN. PAULSON MANAGES WHAT'S LEFT OF MEDICARE AND SOCIAL SECURITY FOR THE UNITED STATES.
AS YOU CAN IMAGINE, THE FINANCIAL MARKETS HAVE BECOME MILITARIZED.
THE GENERAL, UNABLE TO CONTROL HIS IRRITATION, WILL LAUNCH HIS MEN TO THE ASSAULT LIKE SWARMING ANTS.
THE SKILLFUL LEADER SUBDUES THE ENEMY'S TROOPS WITHOUT ANY FIGHTING.
NEW YORK AND THE U.S. GOVERNMENT ARE SO DESPERATE FOR TAXES, THEY TURN A BLIND EYE TO THE HORROR. THAT'S THE ONLY REASON THE FUNDS ARE IN NEW YORK. NO ONE INTERFERES WITH US HERE.
HE CAPTURES THEIR CITIES WITHOUT LAYING SIEGE TO THEM. HE OVERTHROWS THEIR KINGDOM WITHOUT LENGTHY OPERATIONS IN THE FIELD.

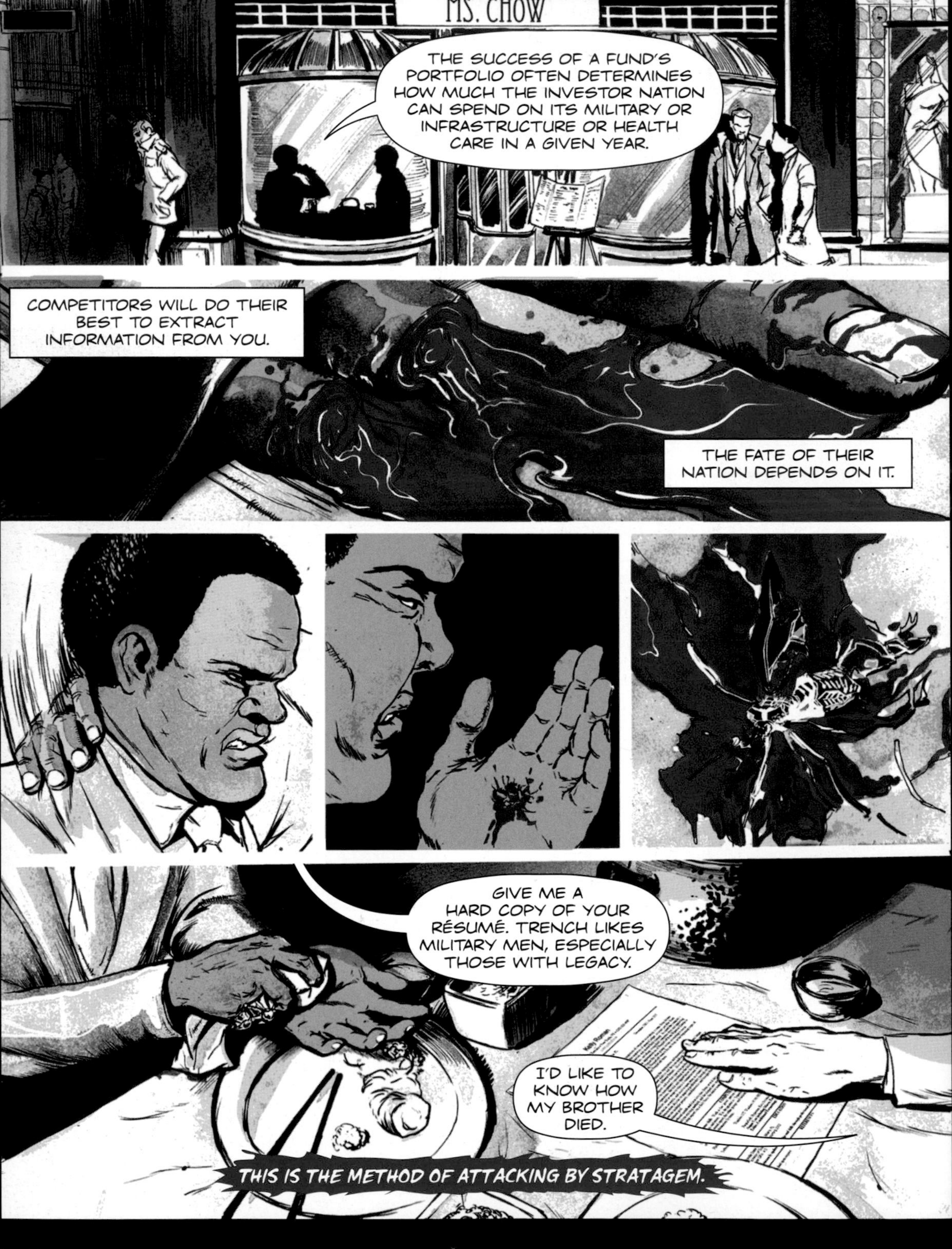
MS. CHOW
THE SUCCESS OF A FUND'S PORTFOLIO OFTEN DETERMINES HOW MUCH THE INVESTOR NATION CAN SPEND ON ITS MILITARY OR INFRASTRUCTURE OR HEALTH CARE IN A GIVEN YEAR.
COMPETITORS WILL DO THEIR BEST TO EXTRACT INFORMATION FROM YOU.
THE FATE OF THEIR NATION DEPENDS ON IT.
GIVE ME A HARD COPY OF YOUR RÉSUMÉ. TRENCH LIKES MILITARY MEN, ESPECIALLY THOSE WITH LEGACY.
I'D LIKE TO KNOW HOW MY BROTHER DIED.
THIS IS THE METHOD OF ATTACKING BY STRATAGEM.

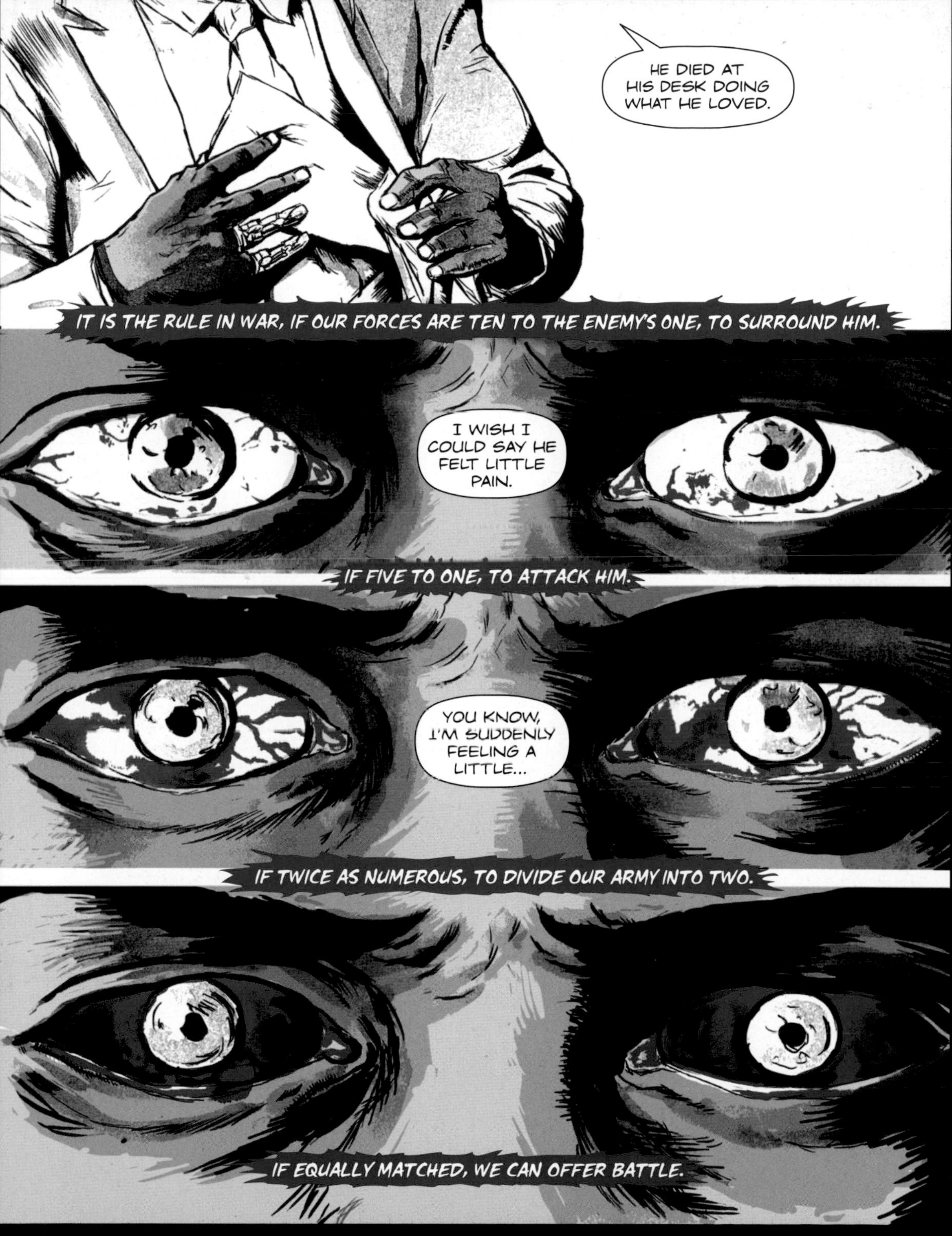
HE DIED AT HIS DESK DOING WHAT HE LOVED.
IT IS THE RULE IN WAR, IF OUR FORCES ARE TEN TO THE ENEMY'S ONE, TO SURROUND HIM.
I WISH I COULD SAY HE FELT LITTLE PAIN.
IF FIVE TO ONE, TO ATTACK HIM.
YOU KNOW, I'M SUDDENLY FEELING A LITTLE...
IF TWICE AS NUMEROUS, TO DIVIDE OUR ARMY INTO TWO.
IF EQUALLY MATCHED, WE CAN OFFER BATTLE.

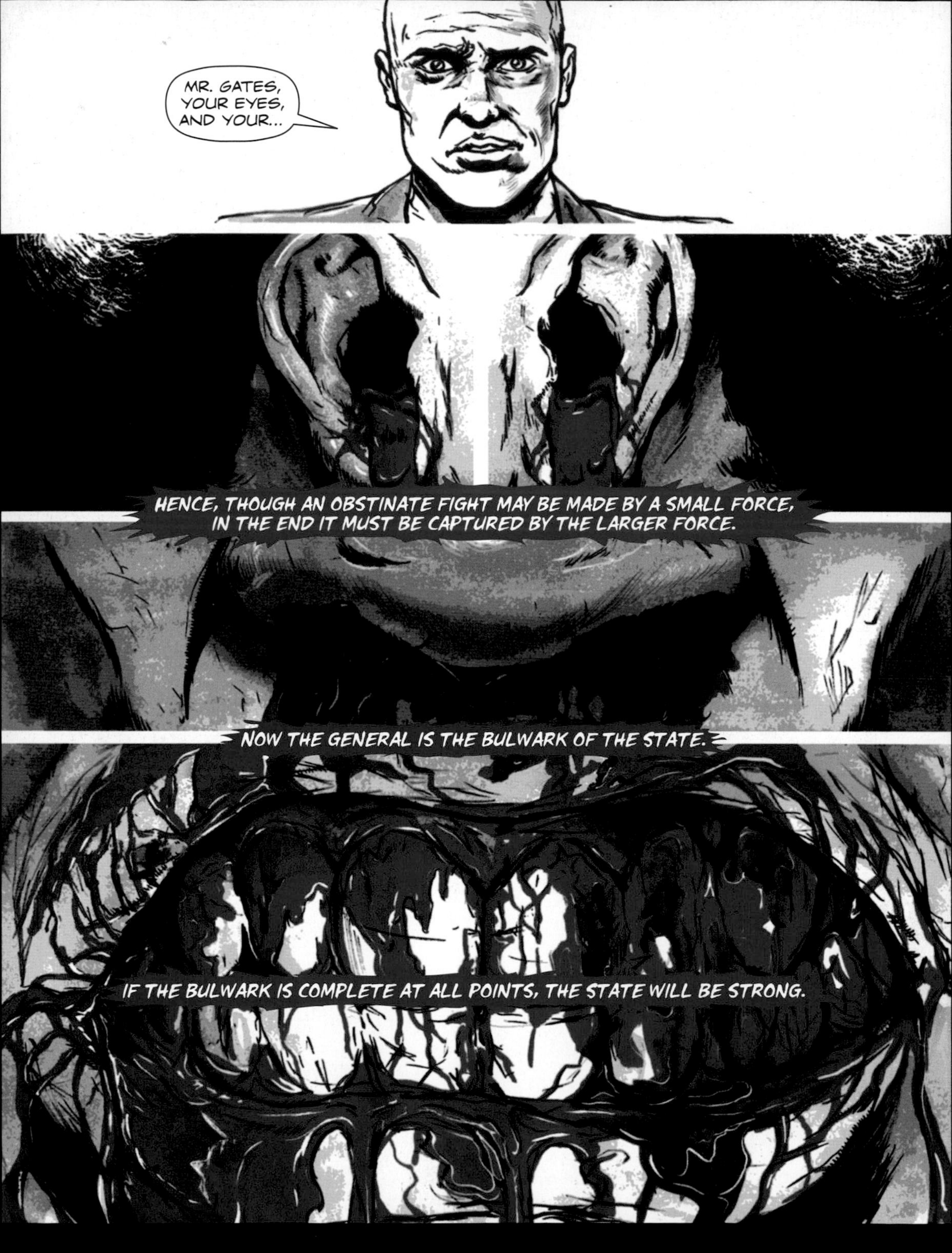

MR. GATES, YOUR EYES, AND YOUR...
HENCE, THOUGH AN OBSTINATE FIGHT MAY BE MADE BY A SMALL FORCE, IN THE END IT MUST BE CAPTURED BY THE LARGER FORCE.
NOW THE GENERAL IS THE BULWARK OF THE STATE.
IF THE BULWARK IS COMPLETE AT ALL POINTS, THE STATE WILL BE STRONG.

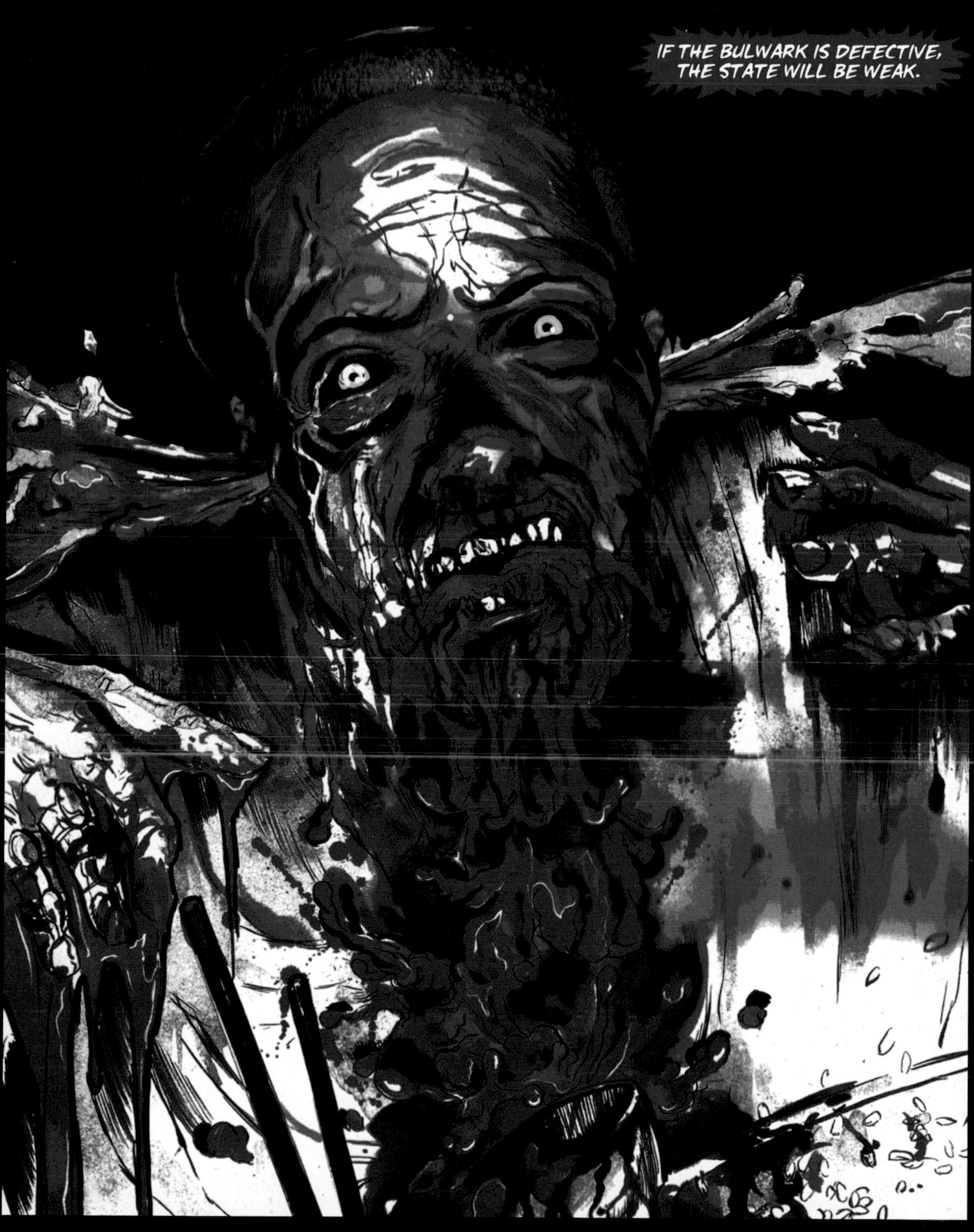
IF THE BULWARK IS DEFECTIVE, THE STATE WILL BE WEAK.

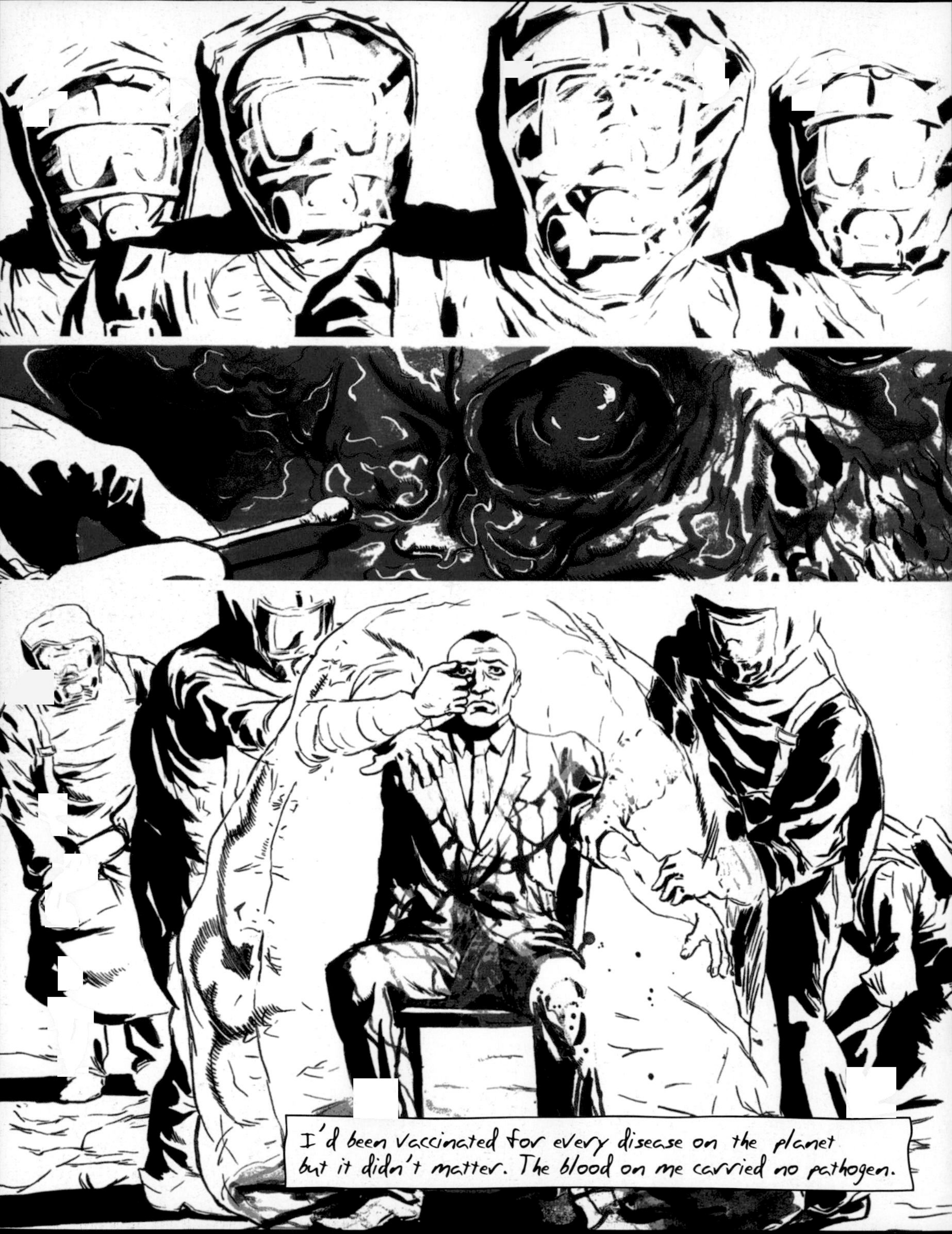
I'd been vaccinated for every disease on the planet but it didn't matter. The blood on me carried no pathogen.

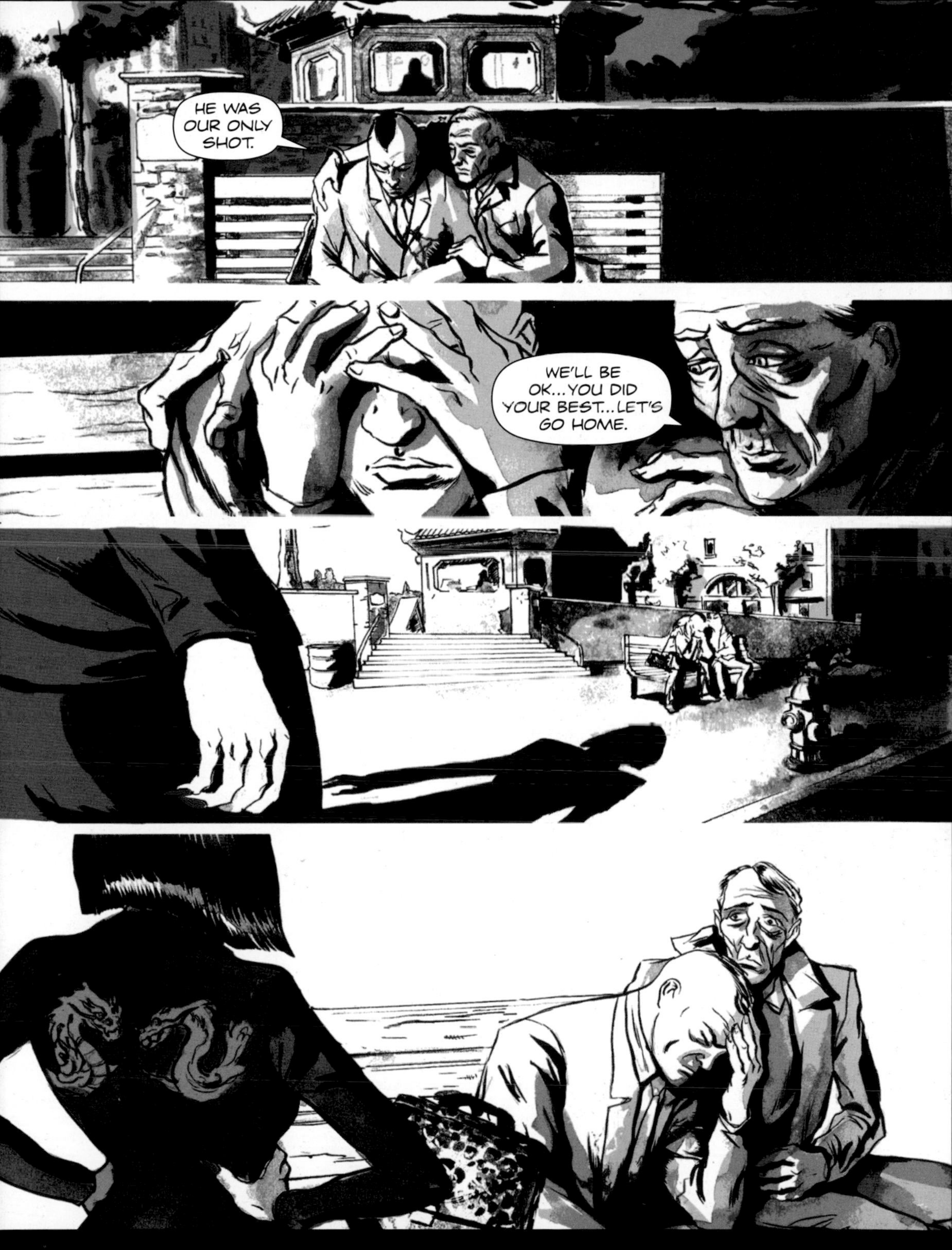
HE WAS OUR ONLY SHOT.
WE'LL BE OK...YOU DID YOUR BEST...LET'S GO HOME.

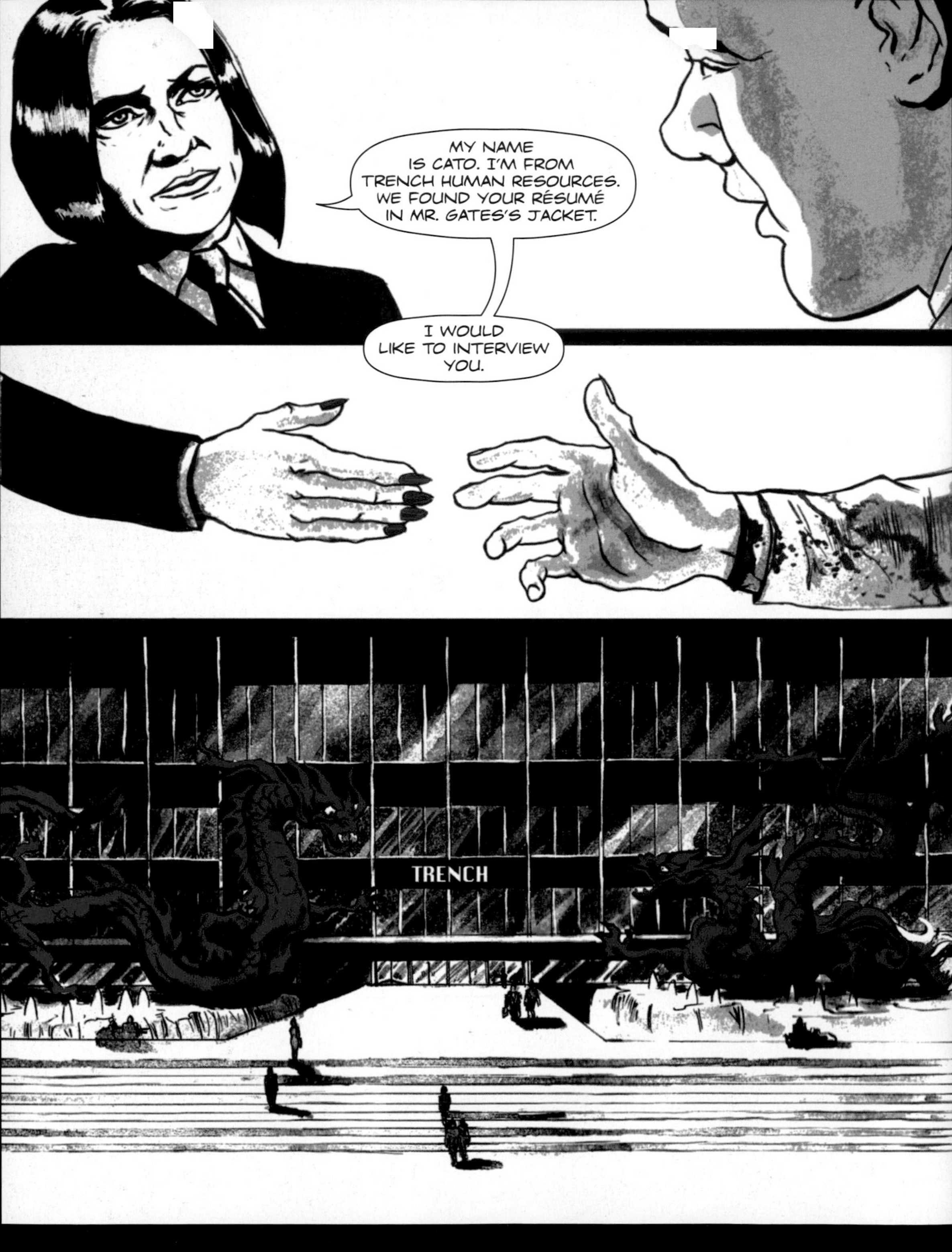
MY NAME IS CATO. I'M FROM TRENCH HUMAN RESOURCES. WE FOUND YOUR RÉSUMÉ IN MR. GATES'S JACKET.
I WOULD LIKE TO INTERVIEW YOU.
TRENCH

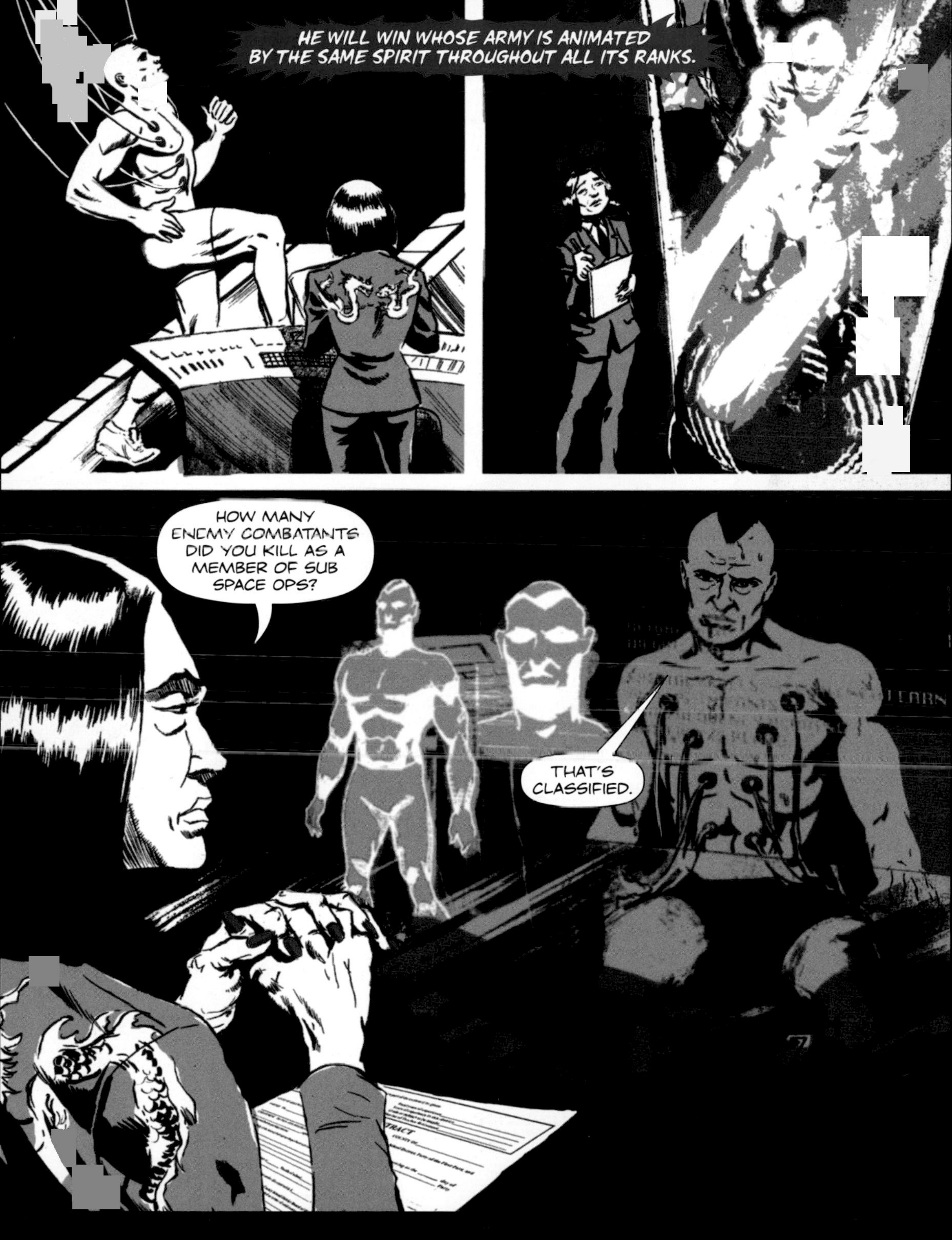
HE WILL WIN WHOSE ARMY IS ANIMATED BY THE SAME SPIRIT THROUGHOUT ALL ITS RANKS.
HOW MANY ENEMY COMBATANTS DID YOU KILL AS A MEMBER OF SUB SPACE OPS?
THAT'S CLASSIFIED.

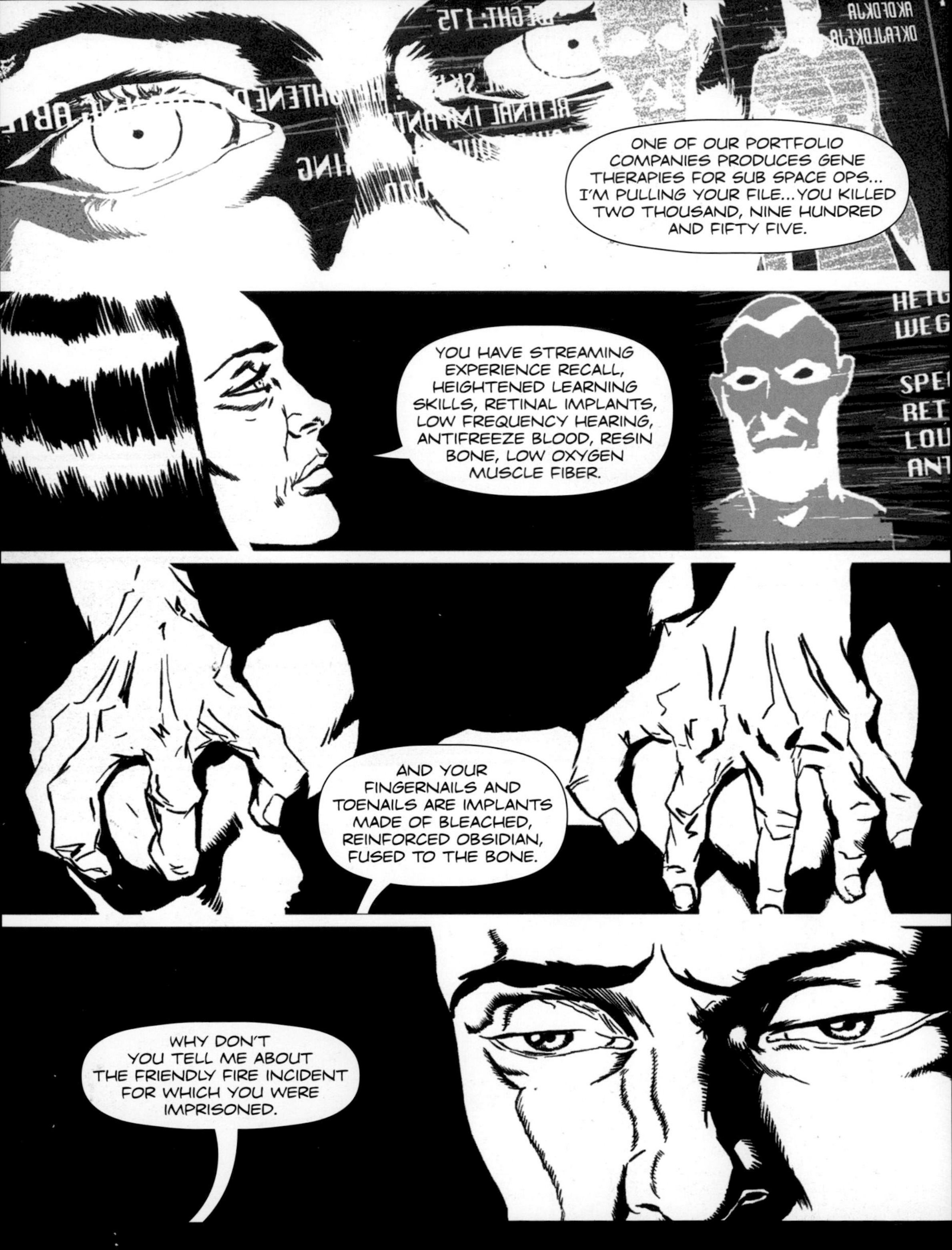
ONE OF OUR PORTFOLIO COMPANIES PRODUCES GENE THERAPIES FOR SUB SPACE OPS... I'M PULLING YOUR FILE...YOU KILLED TWO THOUSAND, NINE HUNDRED AND FIFTY FIVE.
YOU HAVE STREAMING EXPERIENCE RECALL, HEIGHTENED LEARNING SKILLS, RETINAL IMPLANTS, LOW FREQUENCY HEARING, ANTIFREEZE BLOOD, RESIN BONE, LOW OXYGEN MUSCLE FIBER.
AND YOUR FINGERNAILS AND TOENAILS ARE IMPLANTS MADE OF BLEACHED, REINFORCED OBSIDIAN, FUSED TO THE BONE.
WHY DON'T YOU TELL ME ABOUT THE FRIENDLY FIRE INCIDENT FOR WHICH YOU WERE IMPRISONED.

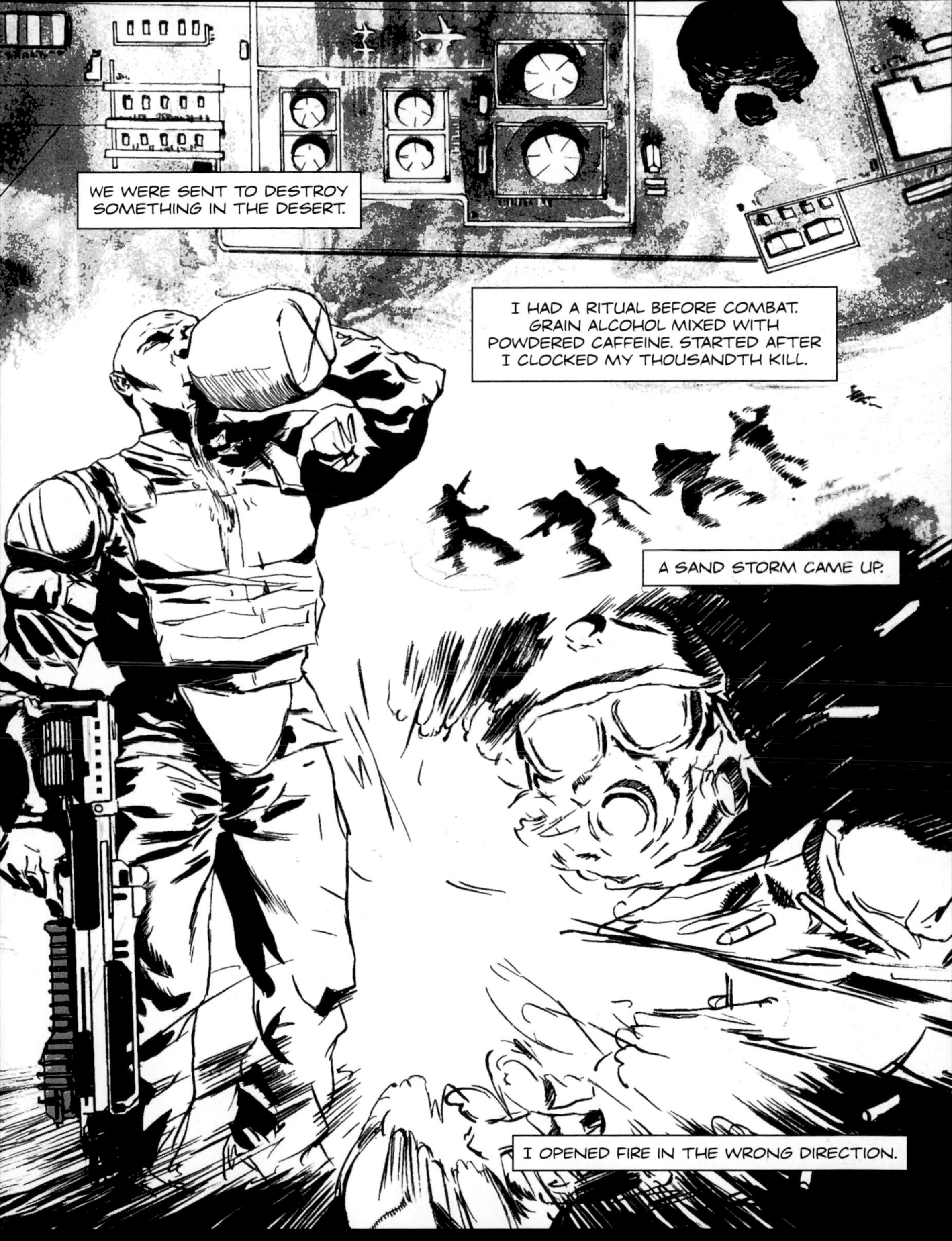
WE WERE SENT TO DESTROY SOMETHING IN THE DESERT.
I HAD A RITUAL BEFORE COMBAT. GRAIN ALCOHOL MIXED WITH POWDERED CAFFEINE. STARTED AFTER I CLOCKED MY THOUSANDTH KILL.
A SAND STORM CAME UP.
I OPENED FIRE IN THE WRONG DIRECTION.

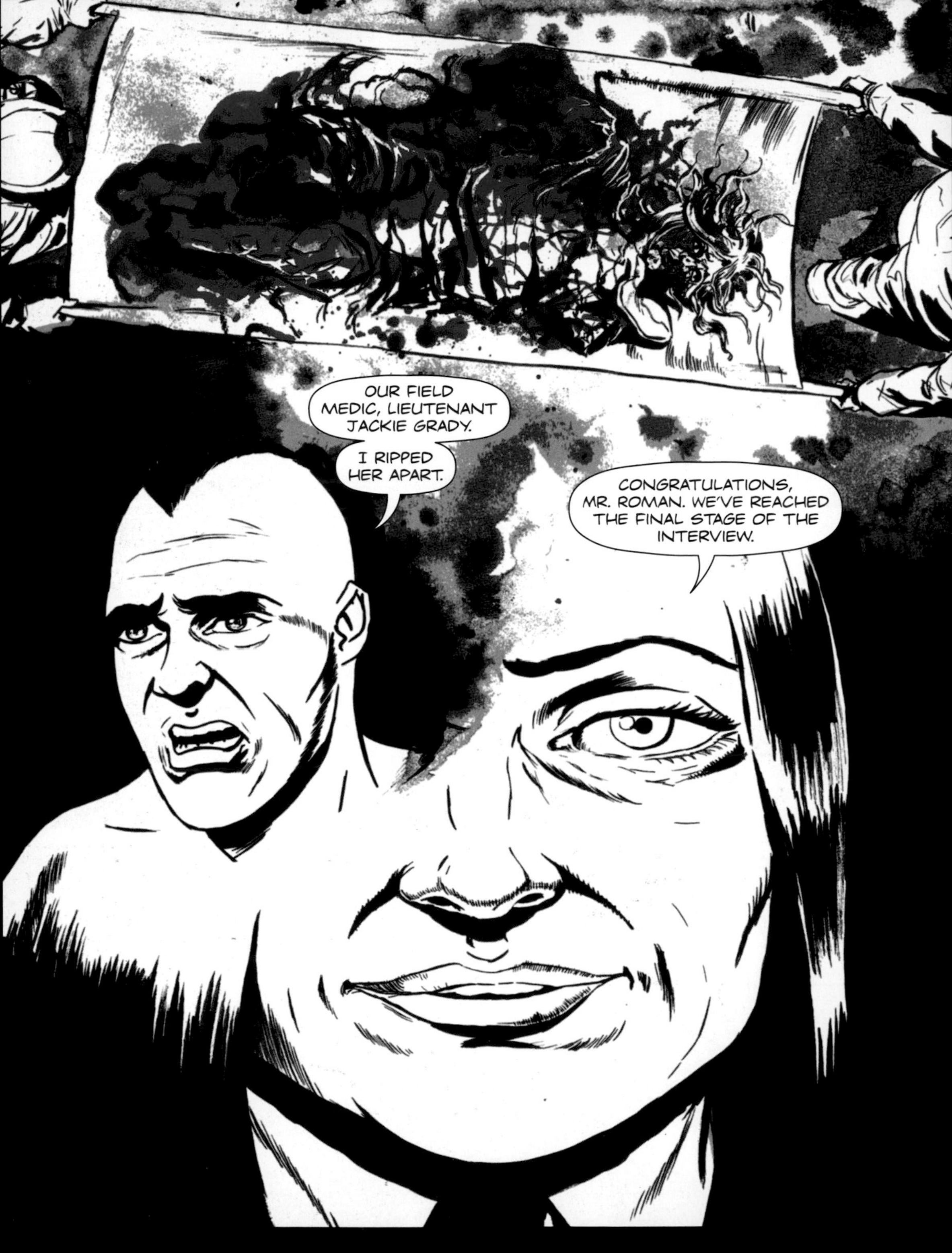
OUR FIELD MEDIC, LIEUTENANT JACKIE GRADY.
I RIPPED HER APART.
CONGRATULATIONS, MR. ROMAN. WE'VE REACHED THE FINAL STAGE OF THE INTERVIEW.

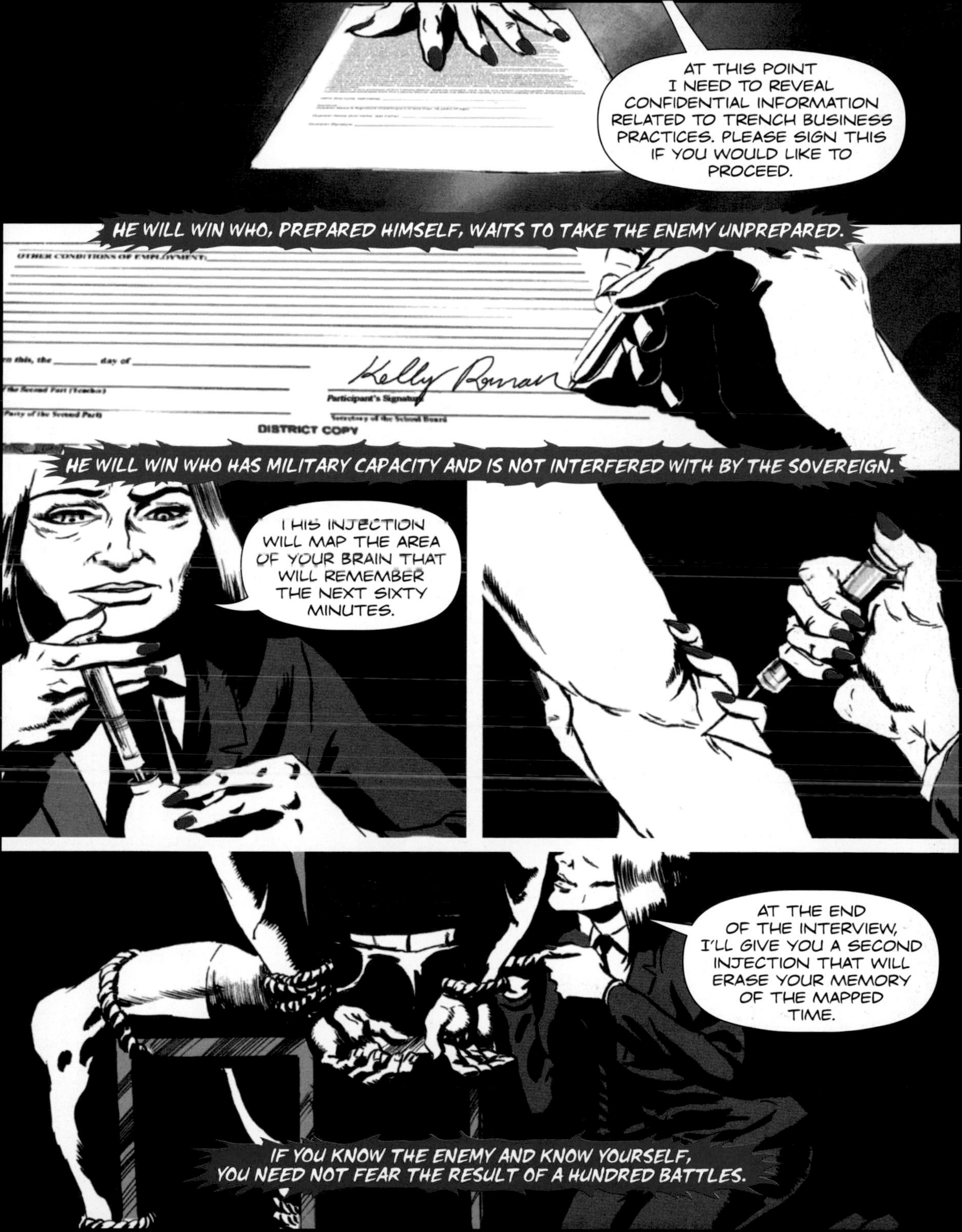
AT THIS POINT I NEED TO REVEAL CONFIDENTIAL INFORMATION RELATED TO TRENCH BUSINESS PRACTICES. PLEASE SIGN THIS IF YOU WOULD LIKE TO PROCEED.
HE WILL WIN WHO, PREPARED HIMSELF, WAITS TO TAKE THE ENEMY UNPREPARED.
OTHER CONDITIONS OF EMPLOYMENT:
Kelly Roman
DISTRICT COPY
HE WILL WIN WHO HAS MILITARY CAPACITY AND IS NOT INTERFERED WITH BY THE SOVEREIGN.
THIS INJECTION WILL MAP THE AREA OF YOUR BRAIN THAT WILL REMEMBER THE NEXT SIXTY MINUTES.
AT THE END OF THE INTERVIEW, I'LL GIVE YOU A SECOND INJECTION THAT WILL ERASE YOUR MEMORY OF THE MAPPED TIME.
IF YOU KNOW THE ENEMY AND KNOW YOURSELF, YOU NEED NOT FEAR THE RESULT OF A HUNDRED BATTLES.

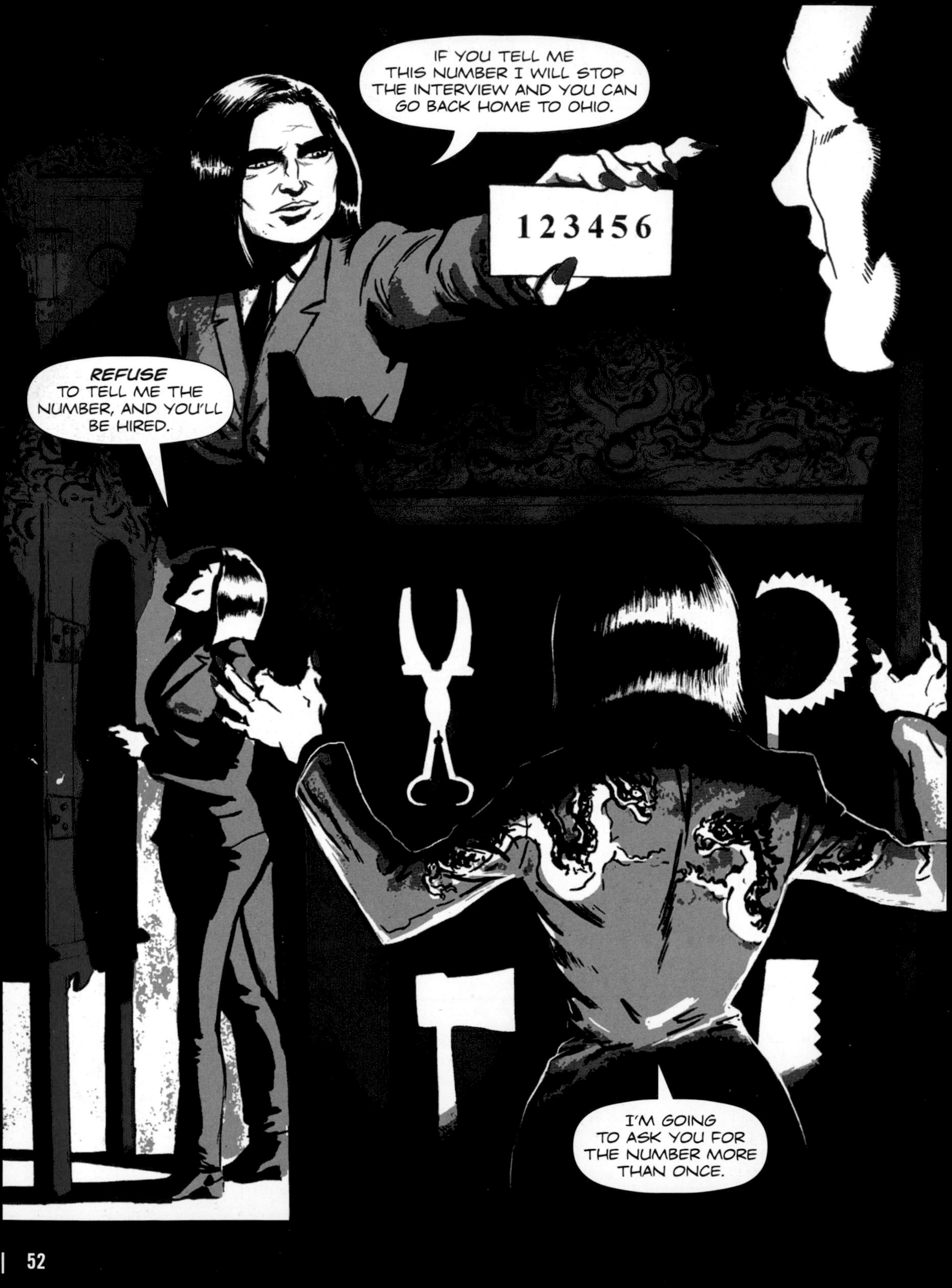
IF YOU TELL ME THIS NUMBER I WILL STOP THE INTERVIEW AND YOU CAN GO BACK HOME TO OHIO.
123456
REFUSE TO TELL ME THE NUMBER, AND YOU'LL BE HIRED.
I'M GOING TO ASK YOU FOR THE NUMBER MORE THAN ONCE.

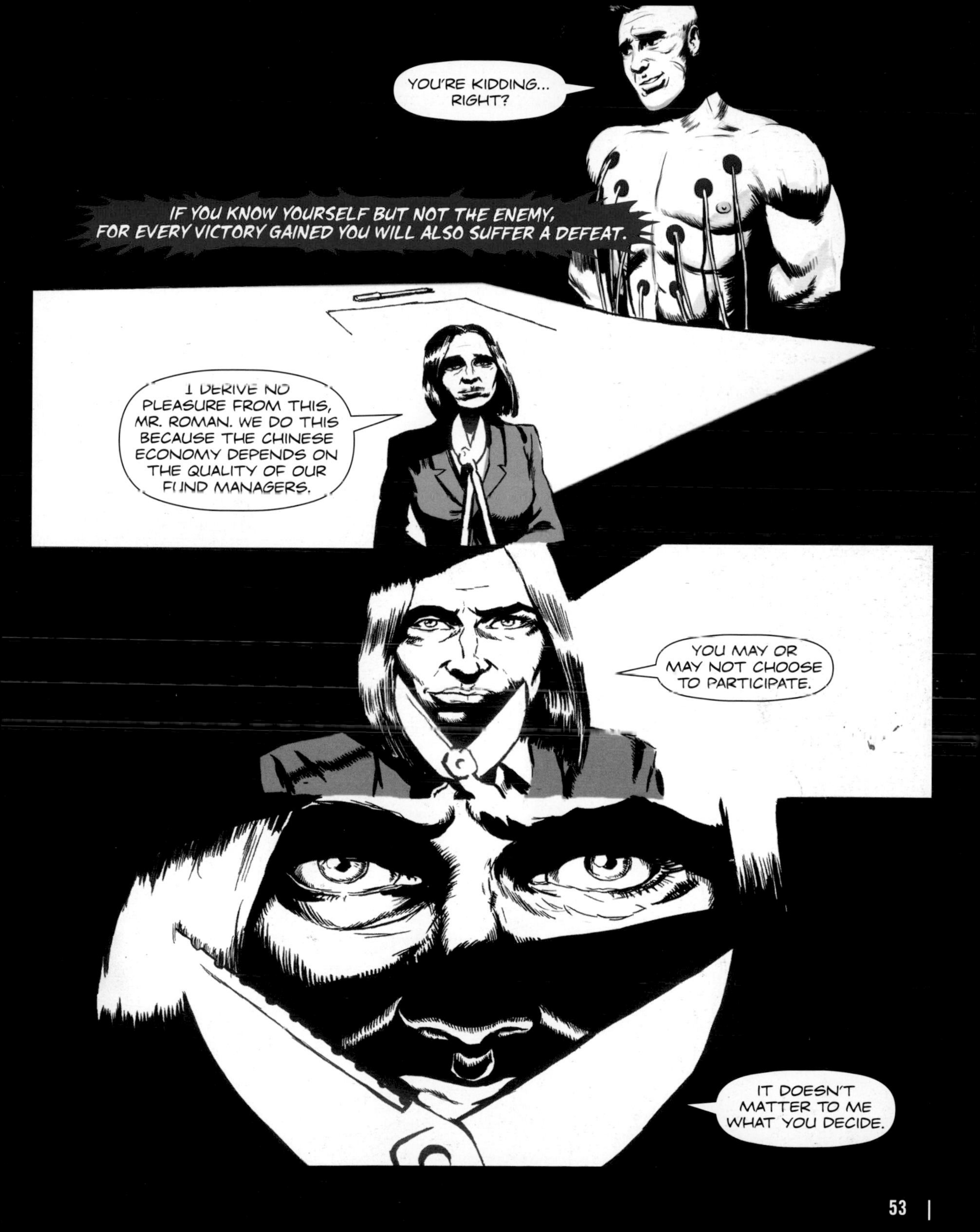
YOU'RE KIDDING... RIGHT?
IF YOU KNOW YOURSELF BUT NOT THE ENEMY, FOR EVERY VICTORY GAINED YOU WILL ALSO SUFFER A DEFEAT.
I DERIVE NO PLEASURE FROM THIS, MR. ROMAN. WE DO THIS BECAUSE THE CHINESE ECONOMY DEPENDS ON THE QUALITY OF OUR FUND MANAGERS.
YOU MAY OR MAY NOT CHOOSE TO PARTICIPATE.
IT DOESN'T MATTER TO ME WHAT YOU DECIDE.

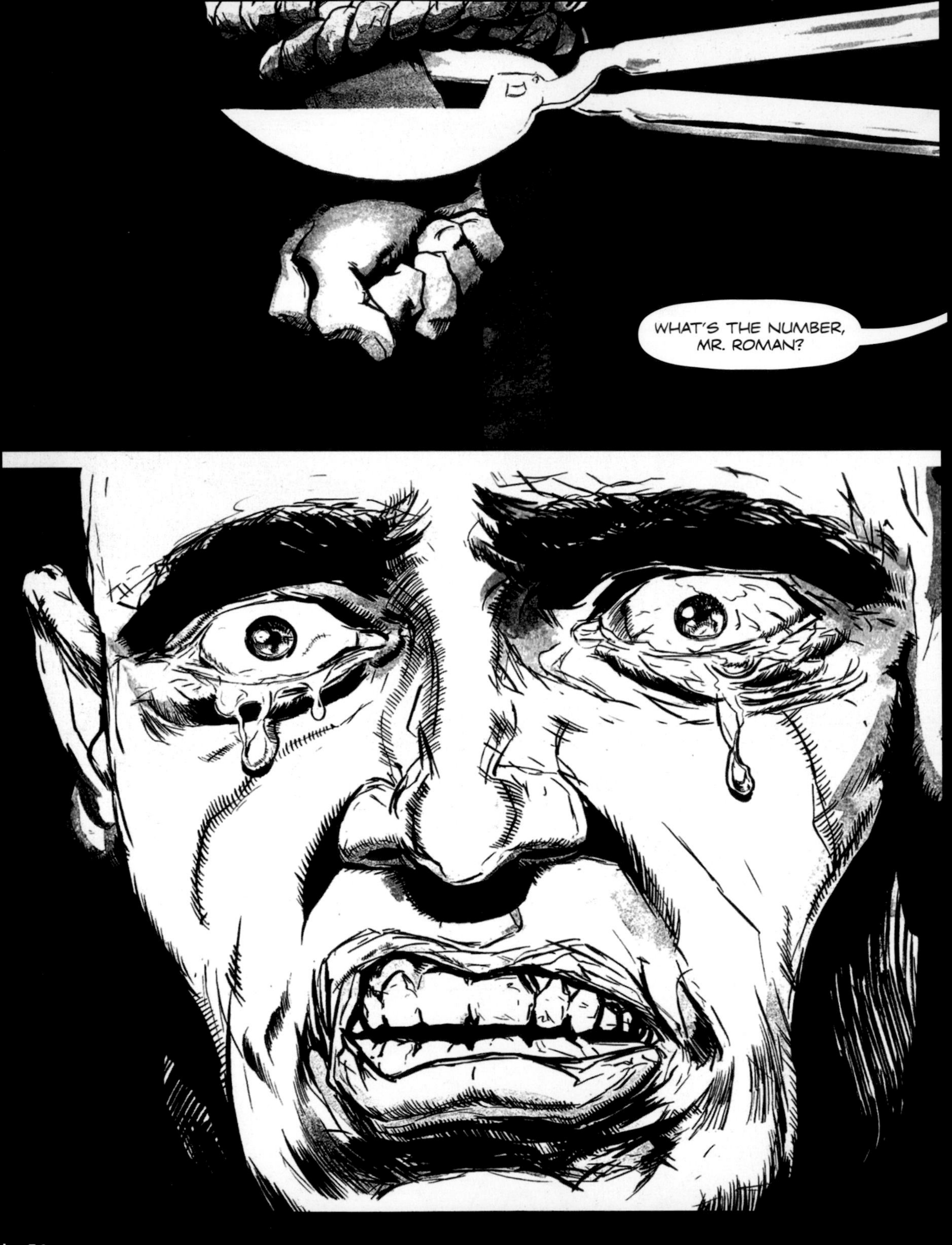
WHAT'S THE NUMBER, MR. ROMAN?

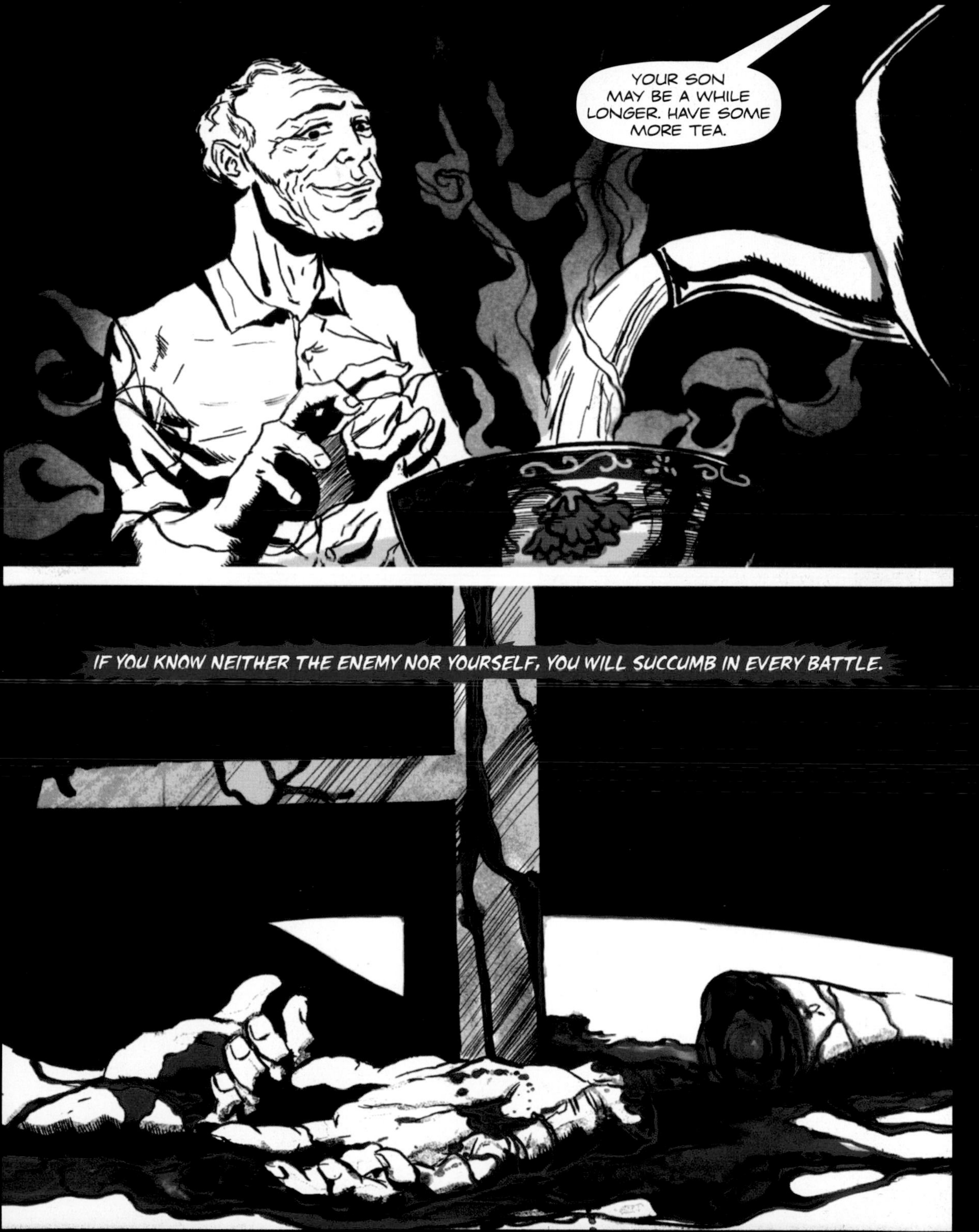
YOUR SON MAY BE A WHILE LONGER. HAVE SOME MORE TEA.
IF YOU KNOW NEITHER THE ENEMY NOR YOURSELF, YOU WILL SUCCUMB IN EVERY BATTLE.

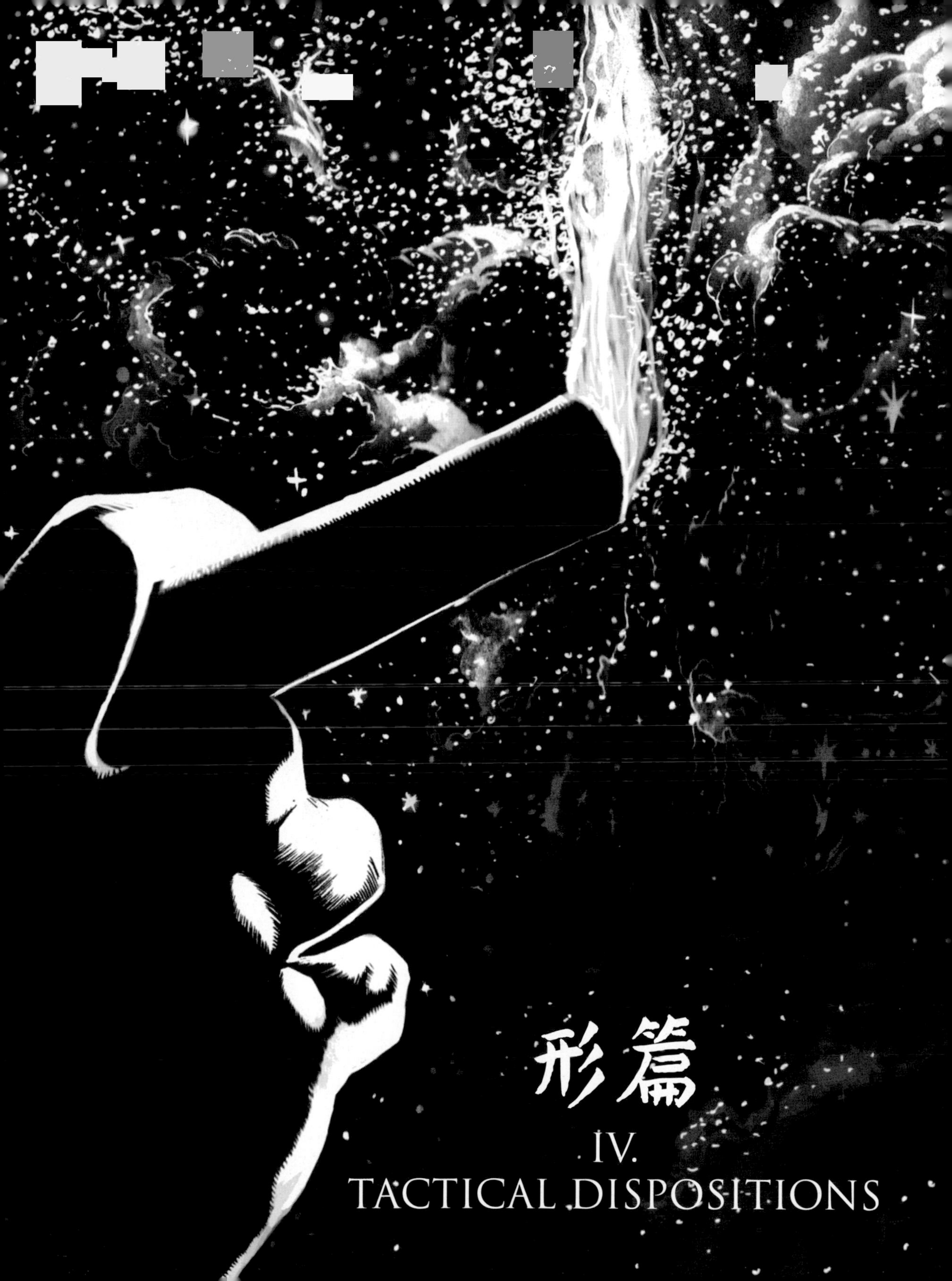

形篇

IV. TACTICAL DISPOSITIONS

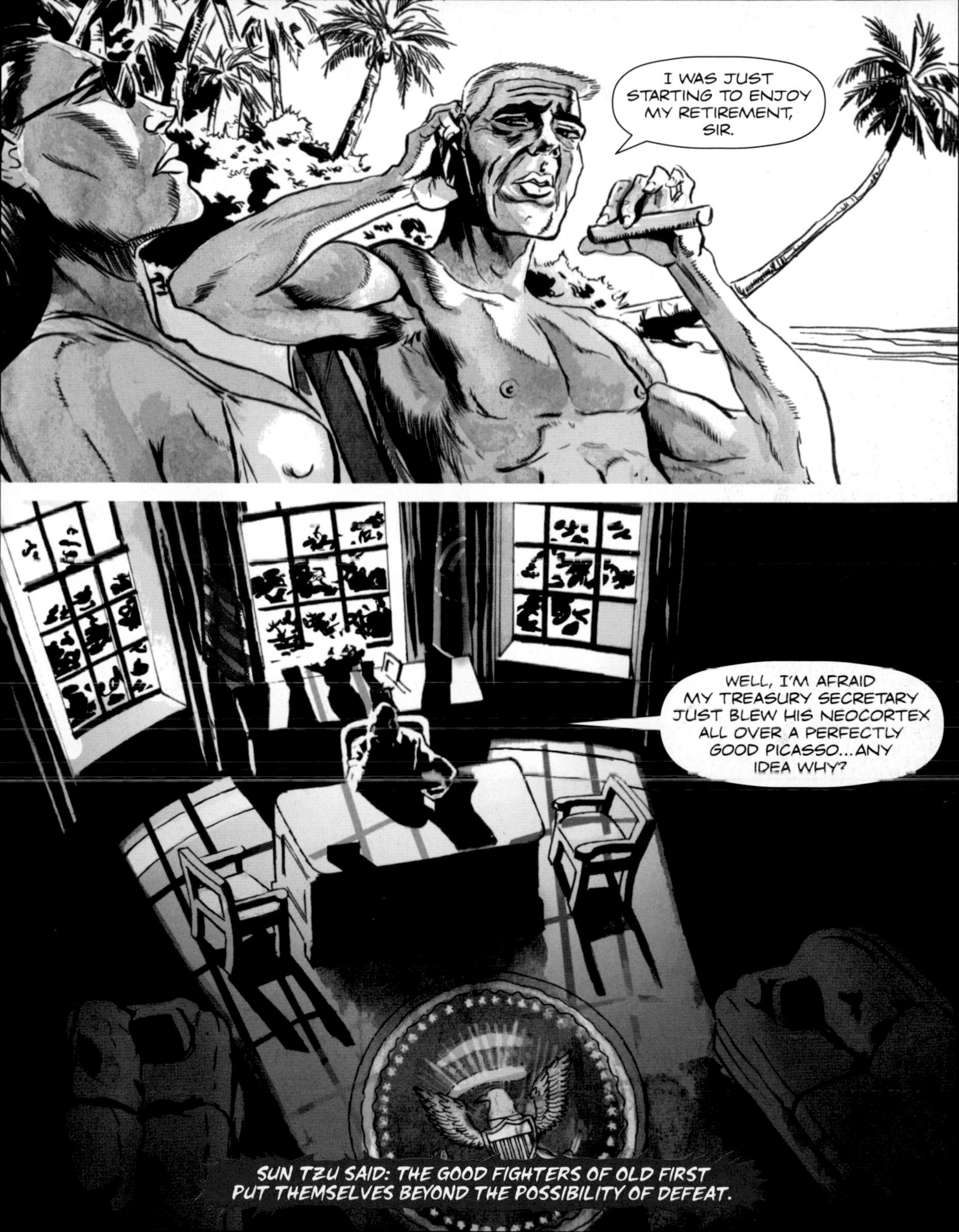
I WAS JUST STARTING TO ENJOY MY RETIREMENT, SIR.
WELL, I'M AFRAID MY TREASURY SECRETARY JUST BLEW HIS NEOCORTEX ALL OVER A PERFECTLY GOOD PICASSO...ANY IDEA WHY?
SUN TZU SAID: THE GOOD FIGHTERS OF OLD FIRST PUT THEMSELVES BEYOND THE POSSIBILITY OF DEFEAT.

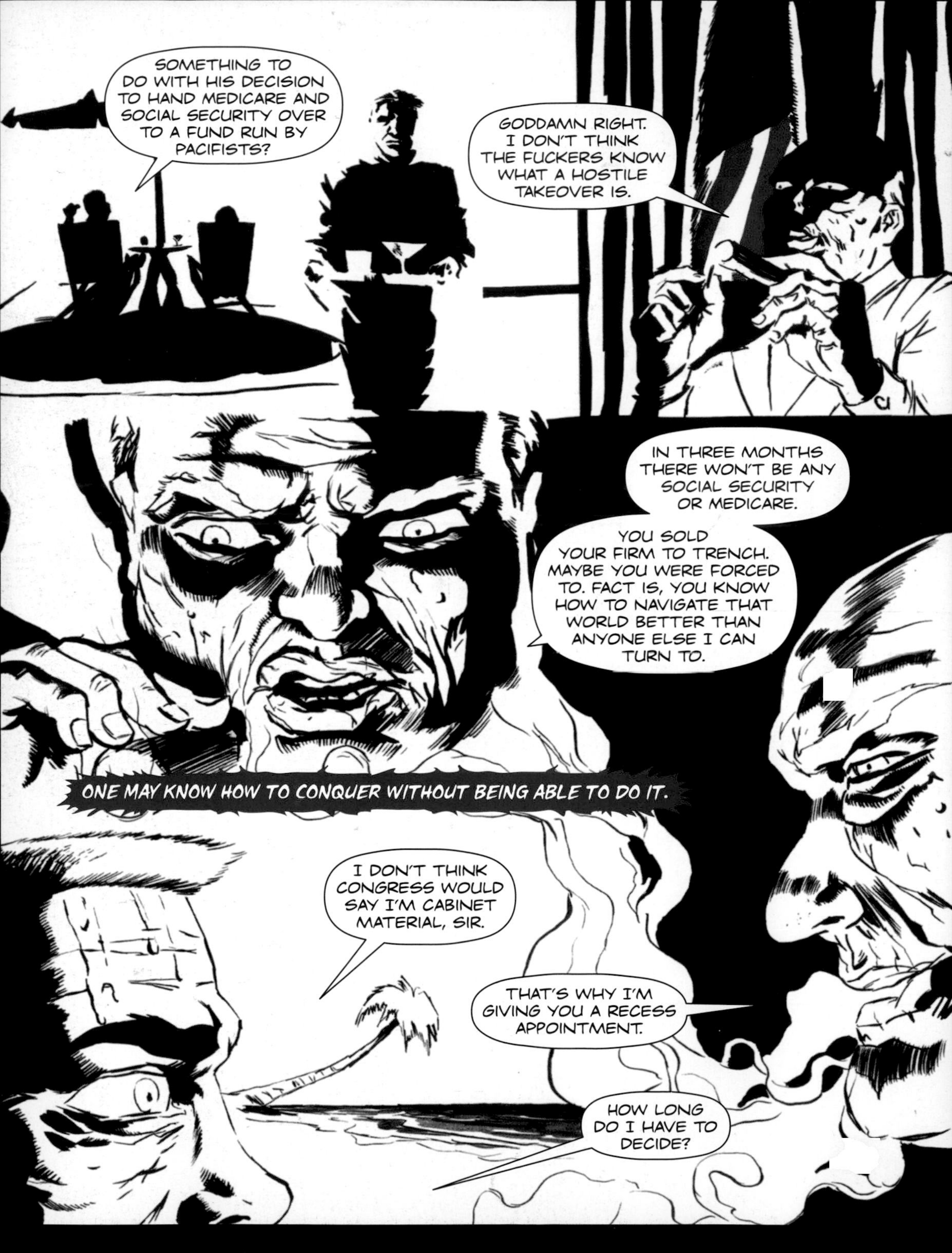
SOMETHING TO DO WITH HIS DECISION TO HAND MEDICARE AND SOCIAL SECURITY OVER TO A FUND RUN BY PACIFISTS?
GODDAMN RIGHT. I DON'T THINK THE FUCKERS KNOW WHAT A HOSTILE TAKEOVER IS.
IN THREE MONTHS THERE WON'T BE ANY SOCIAL SECURITY OR MEDICARE.
YOU SOLD YOUR FIRM TO TRENCH. MAYBE YOU WERE FORCED TO. FACT IS, YOU KNOW HOW TO NAVIGATE THAT WORLD BETTER THAN ANYONE ELSE I CAN TURN TO.
ONE MAY KNOW HOW TO CONQUER WITHOUT BEING ABLE TO DO IT.
I DON'T THINK CONGRESS WOULD SAY I'M CABINET MATERIAL, SIR.
THAT'S WHY I'M GIVING YOU A RECESS APPOINTMENT.
HOW LONG DO I HAVE TO DECIDE?

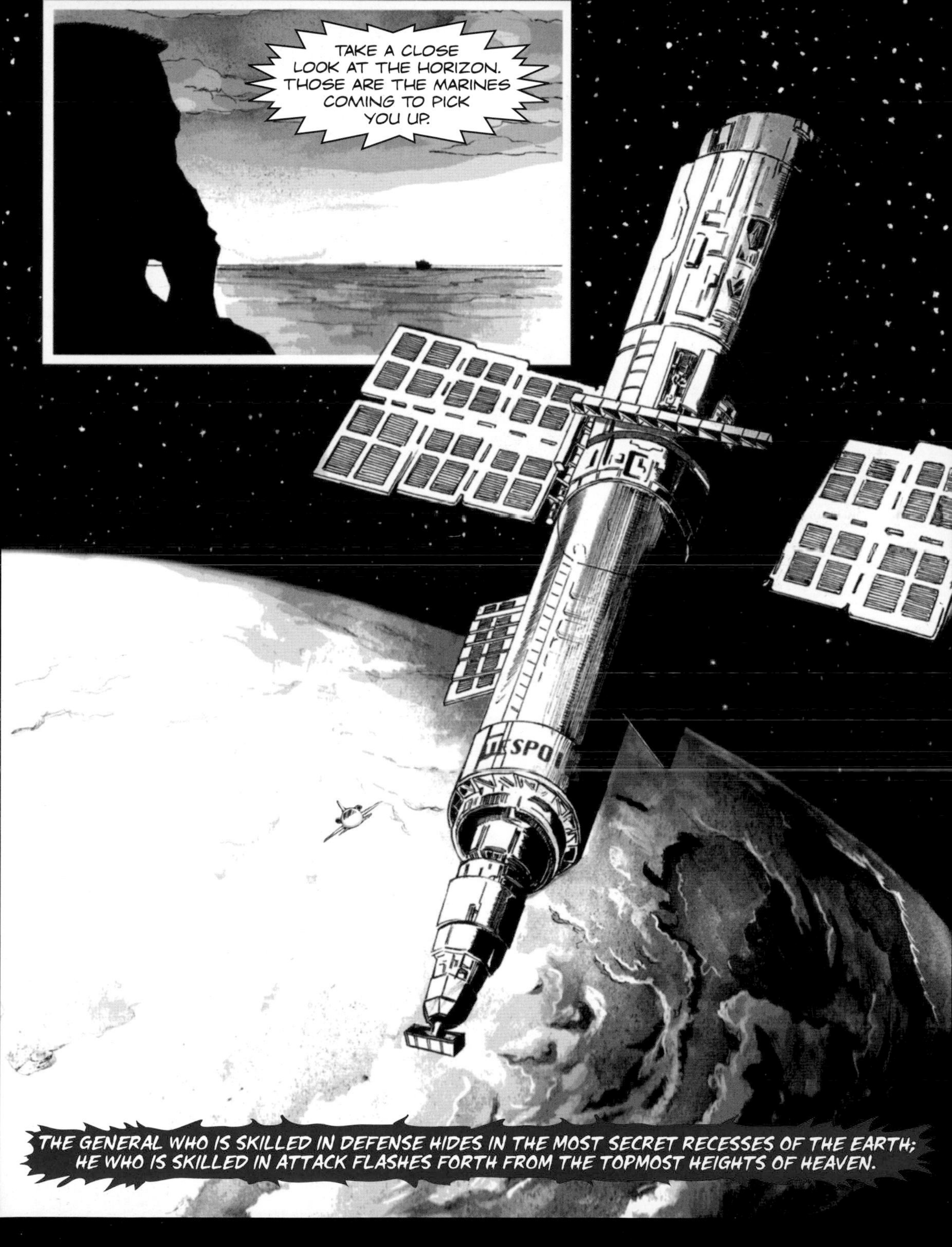
TAKE A CLOSE LOOK AT THE HORIZON. THOSE ARE THE MARINES COMING TO PICK YOU UP.
THE GENERAL WHO IS SKILLED IN DEFENSE HIDES IN THE MOST SECRET RECESSES OF THE EARTH; HE WHO IS SKILLED IN ATTACK FLASHES FORTH FROM THE TOPMOST HEIGHTS OF HEAVEN.

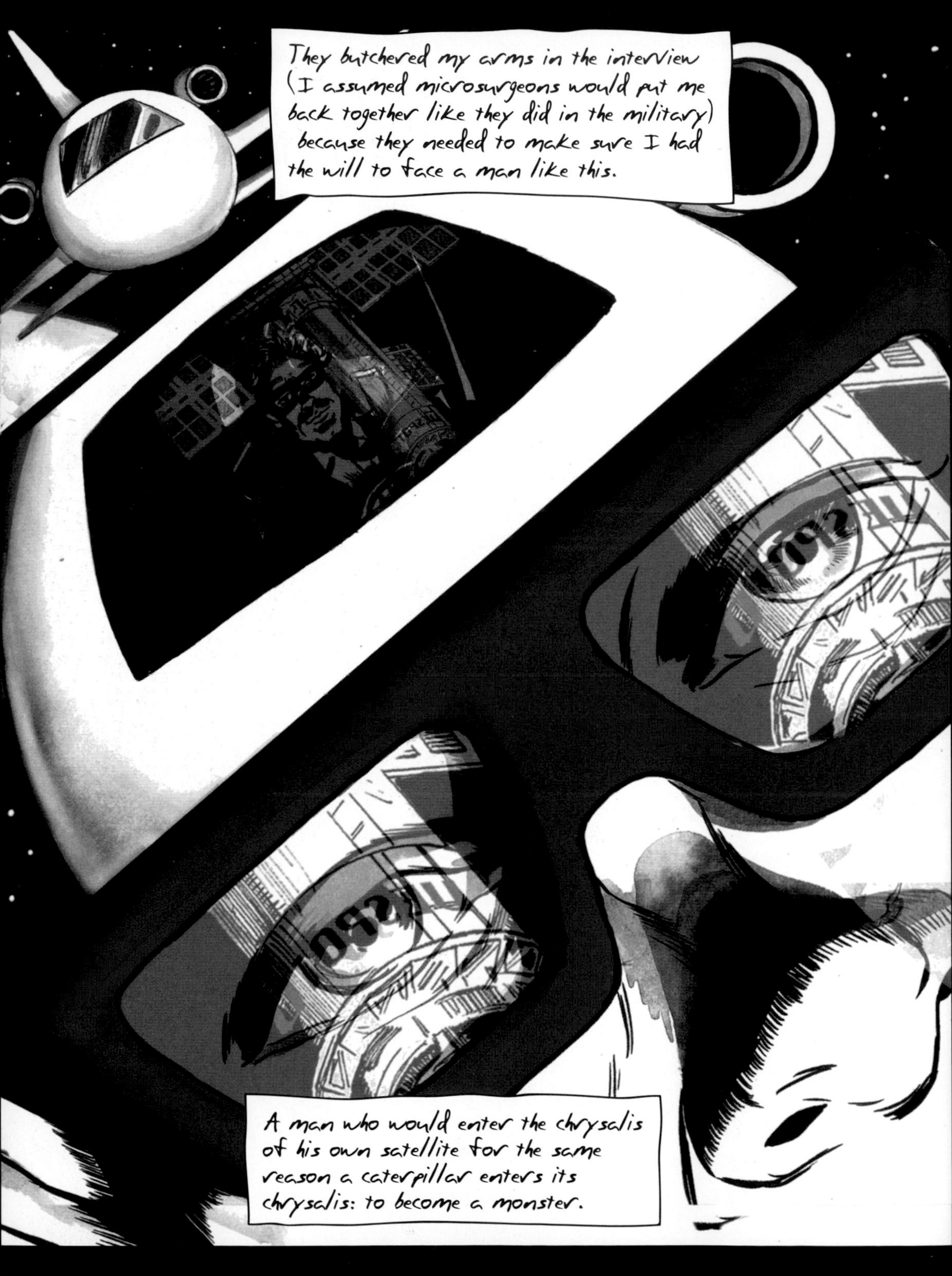
They butchered my arms in the interview (I assumed microsurgeons would put me back together like they did in the military) because they needed to make sure I had the will to face a man like this.
A man who would enter the chrysalis of his own satellite for the same reason a caterpillar enters its chrysalis: to become a monster.

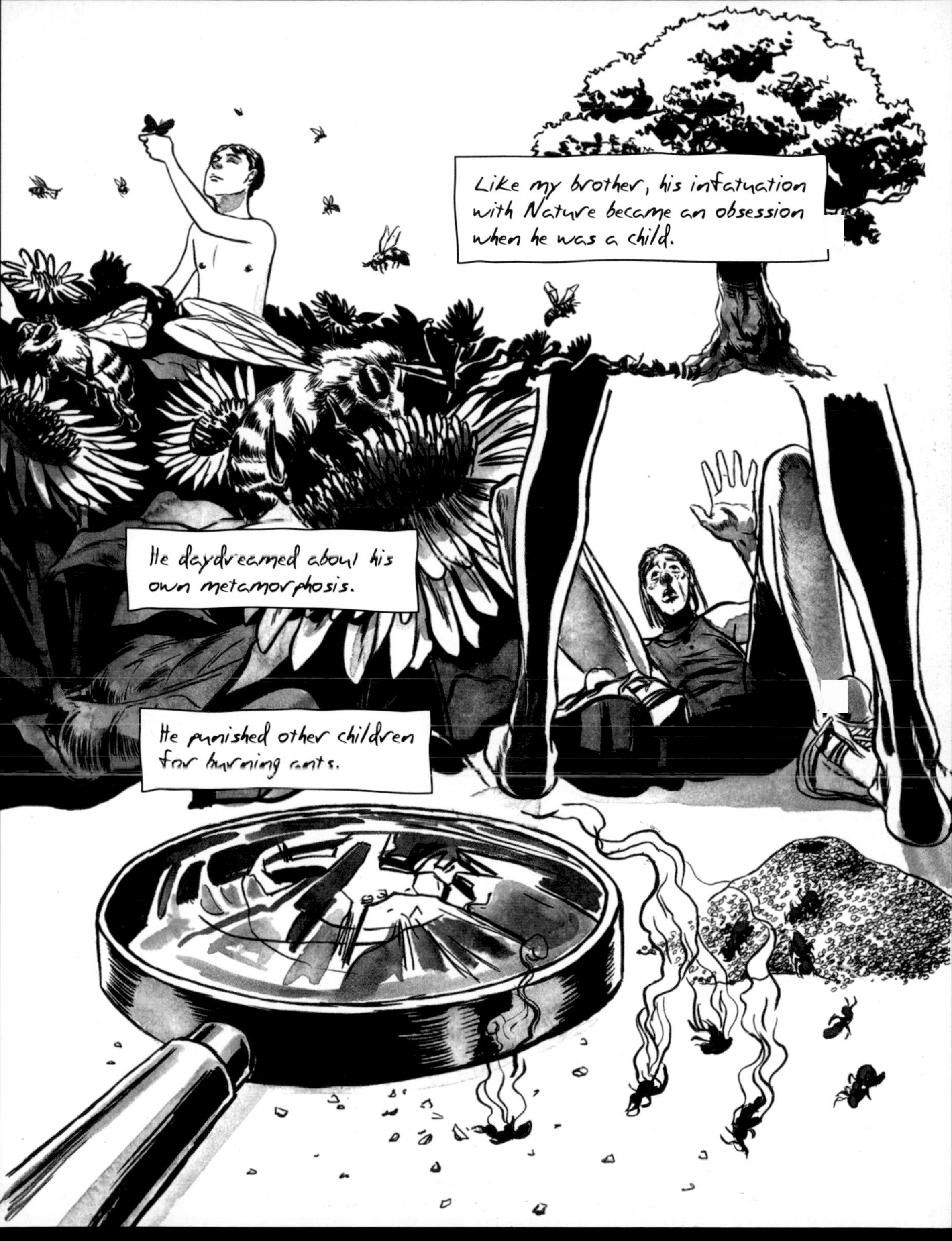
Like my brother, his infatuation with Nature became an obsession when he was a child.
He daydreamed about his own metamorphosis.
He punished other children for burning ants.

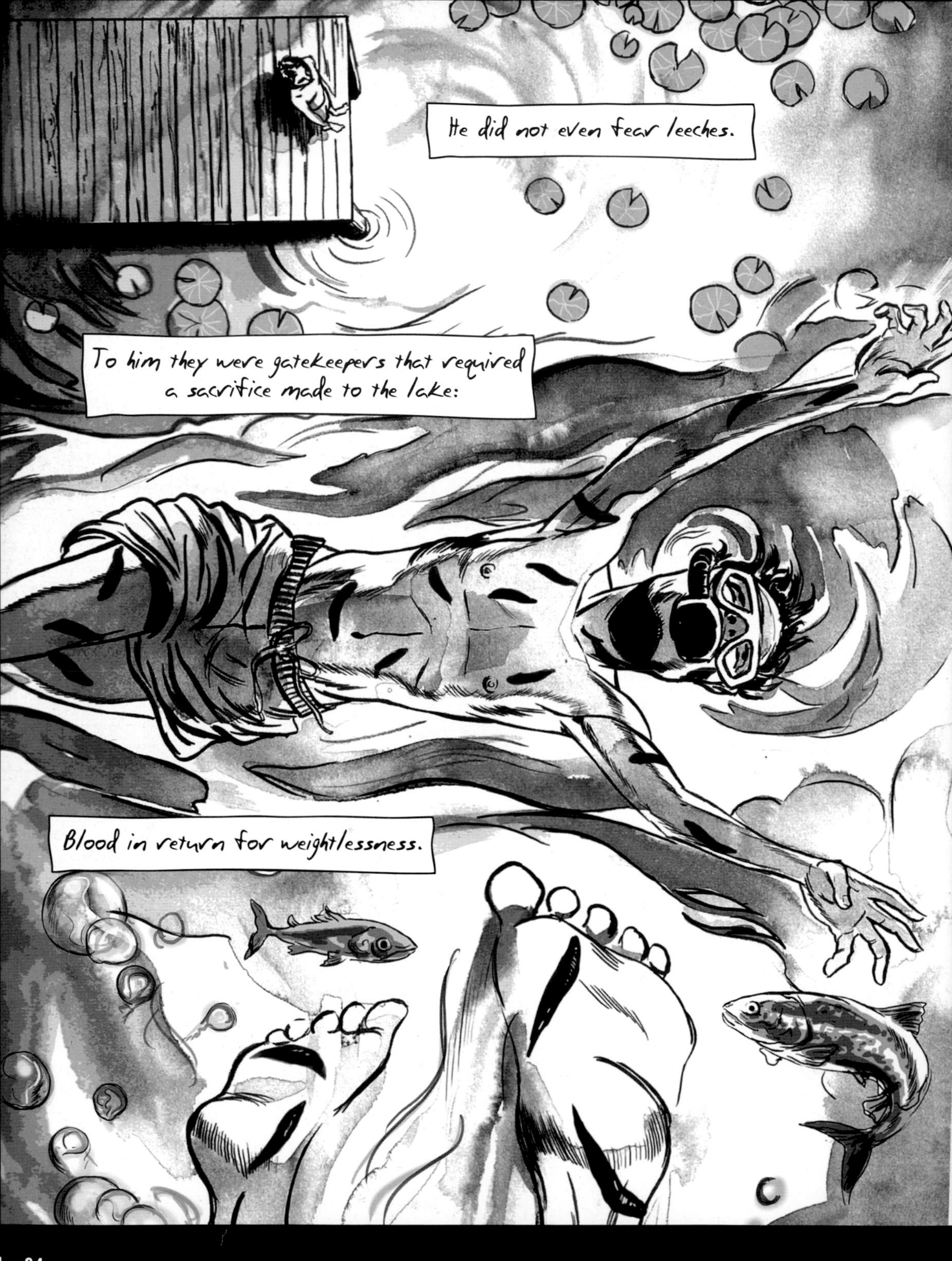
He did not even fear leeches.
To him they were gatekeepers that required a sacrifice made to the lake:
Blood in return for weightlessness.

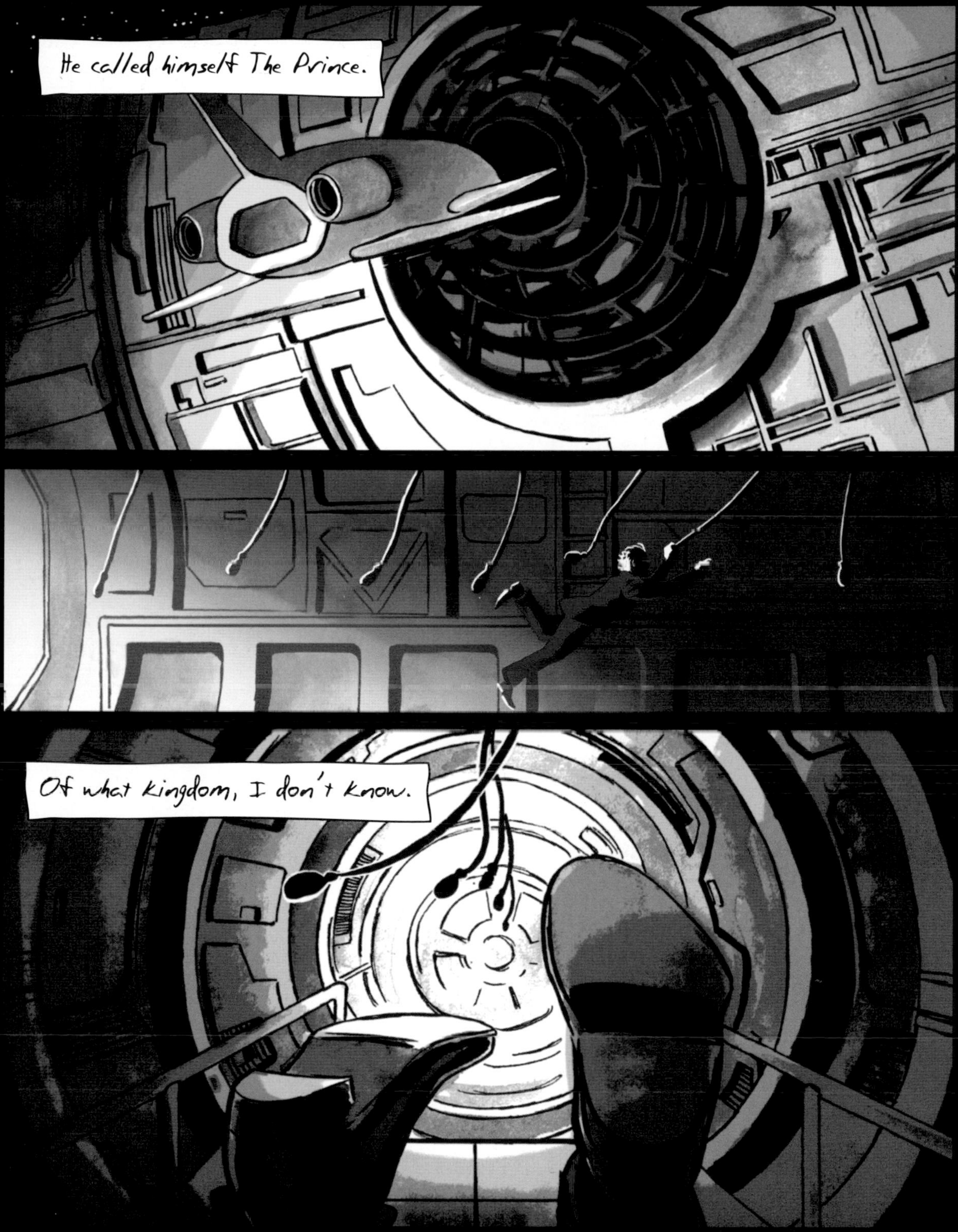
He called himself The Prince.
Of what kingdom, I don't know.

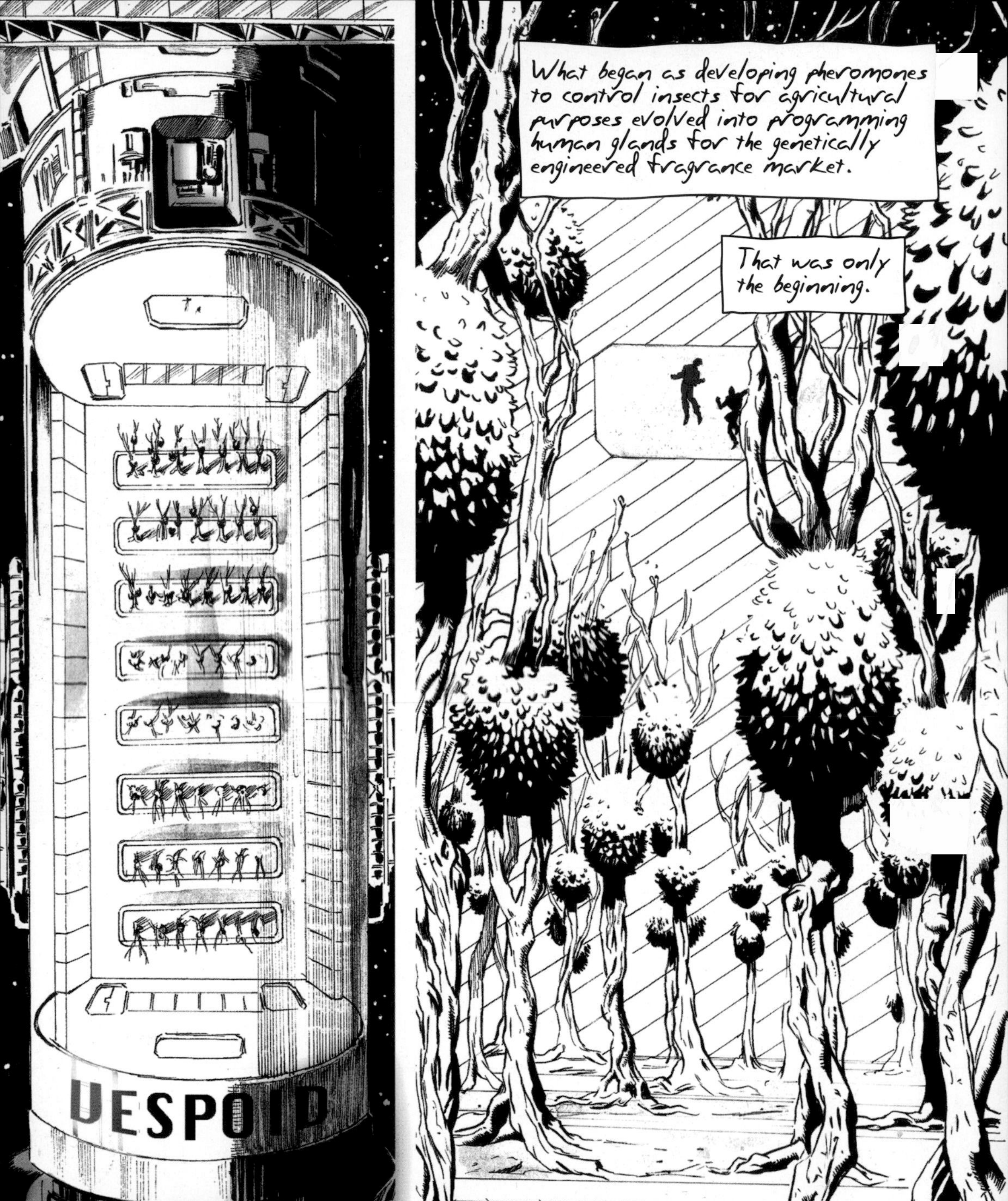
UESPOID
What began as developing pheromones to control insects for agricultural purposes evolved into programming human glands for the genetically engineered fragrance market.
That was only the beginning.

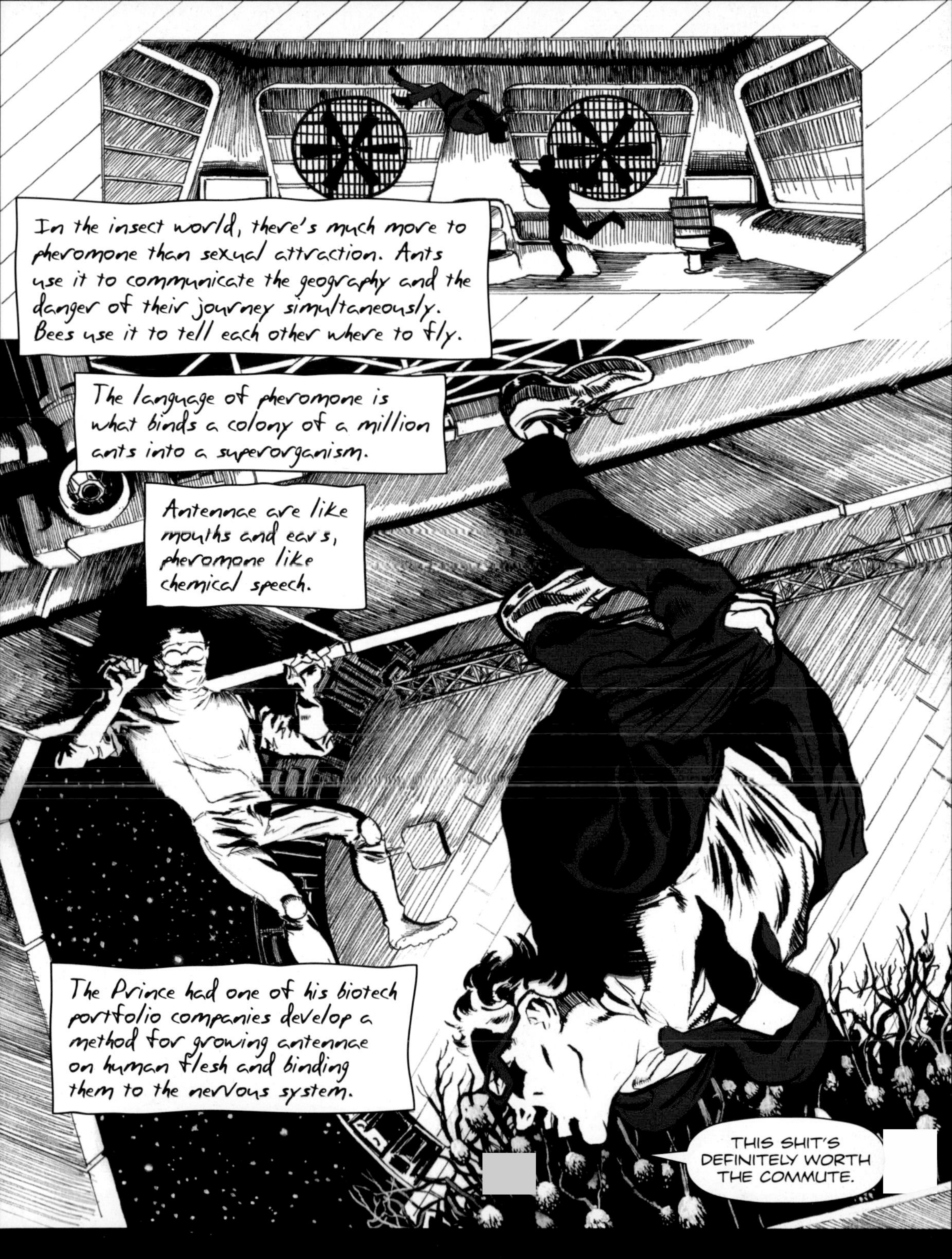
In the insect world, there's much more to pheromone than sexual attraction. Ants use it to communicate the geography and the danger of their journey simultaneously. Bees use it to tell each other where to fly.
The language of pheromone is what binds a colony of a million ants into a superorganism.
Antennae are like mouths and ears, pheromone like chemical speech.
The Prince had one of his biotech portfolio companies develop a method for growing antennae on human flesh and binding them to the nervous system.
THIS SHIT'S DEFINITELY WORTH THE COMMUTE.

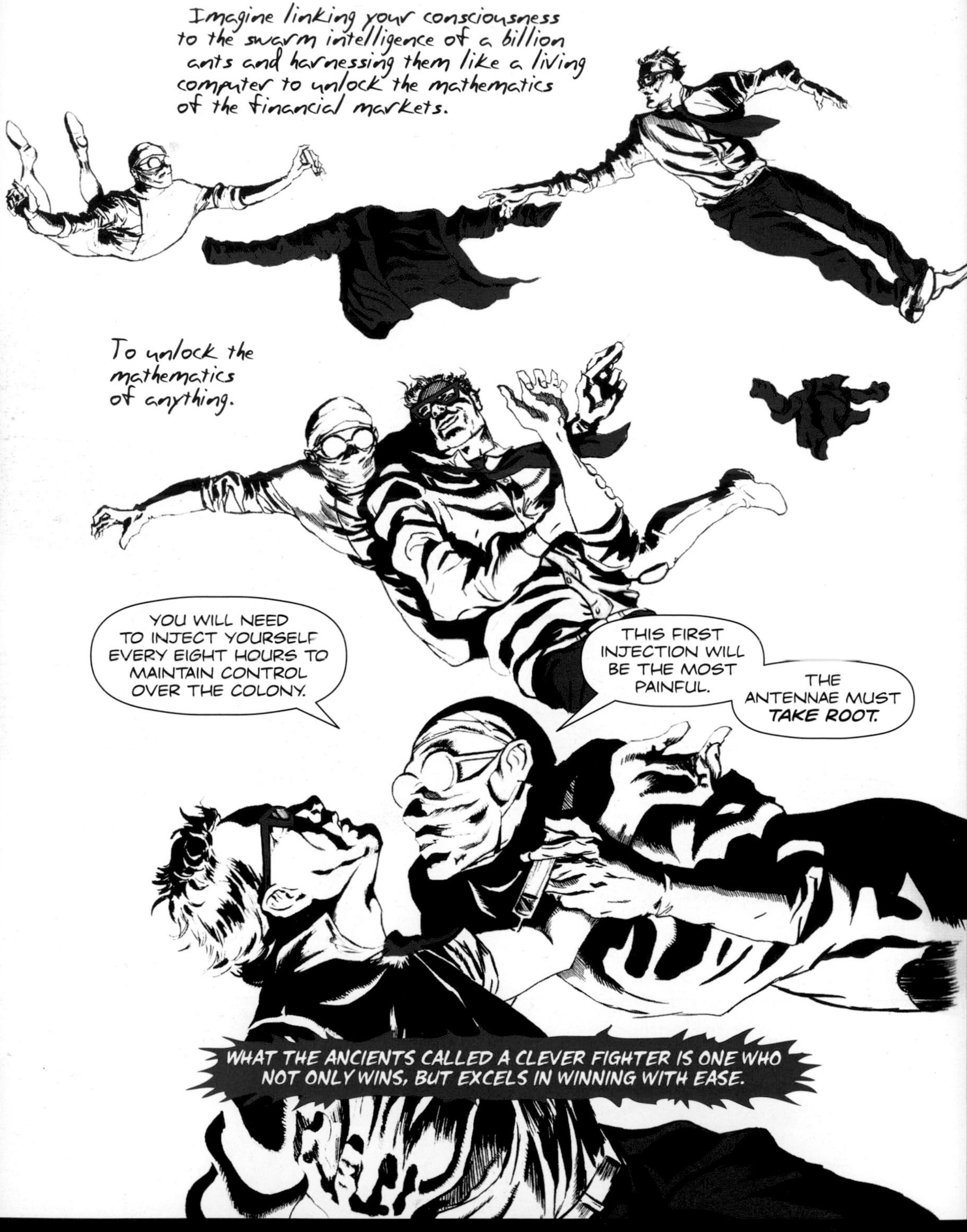
Imagine linking your consciousness to the swarm intelligence of a billion ants and harnessing them like a living computer to unlock the mathematics of the financial markets.
To unlock the mathematics of anything.
YOU WILL NEED TO INJECT YOURSELF EVERY EIGHT HOURS TO MAINTAIN CONTROL OVER THE COLONY.
THIS FIRST INJECTION WILL BE THE MOST PAINFUL.
THE ANTENNAE MUST *TAKE ROOT.*
WHAT THE ANCIENTS CALLED A CLEVER FIGHTER IS ONE WHO NOT ONLY WINS, BUT EXCELS IN WINNING WITH EASE.

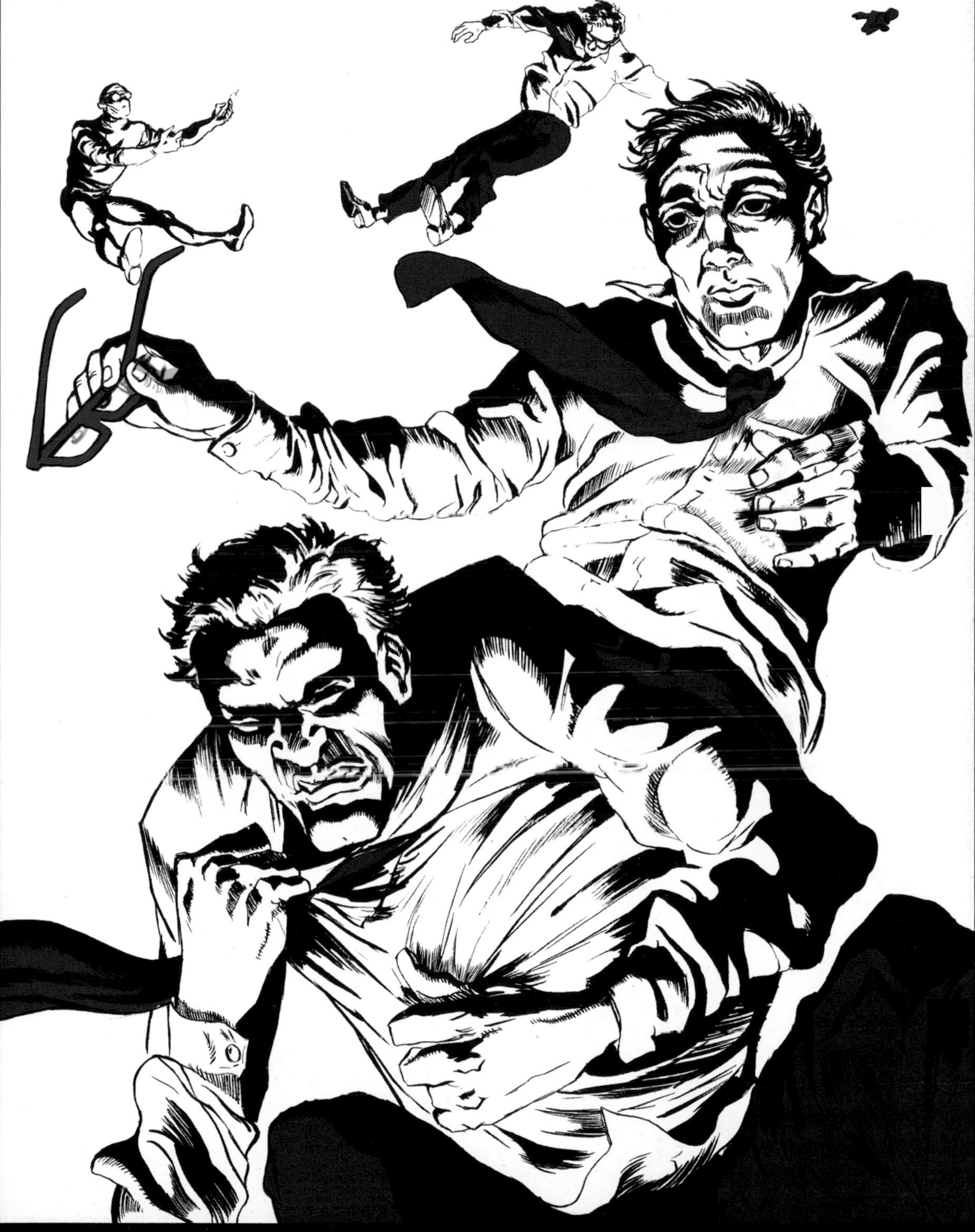

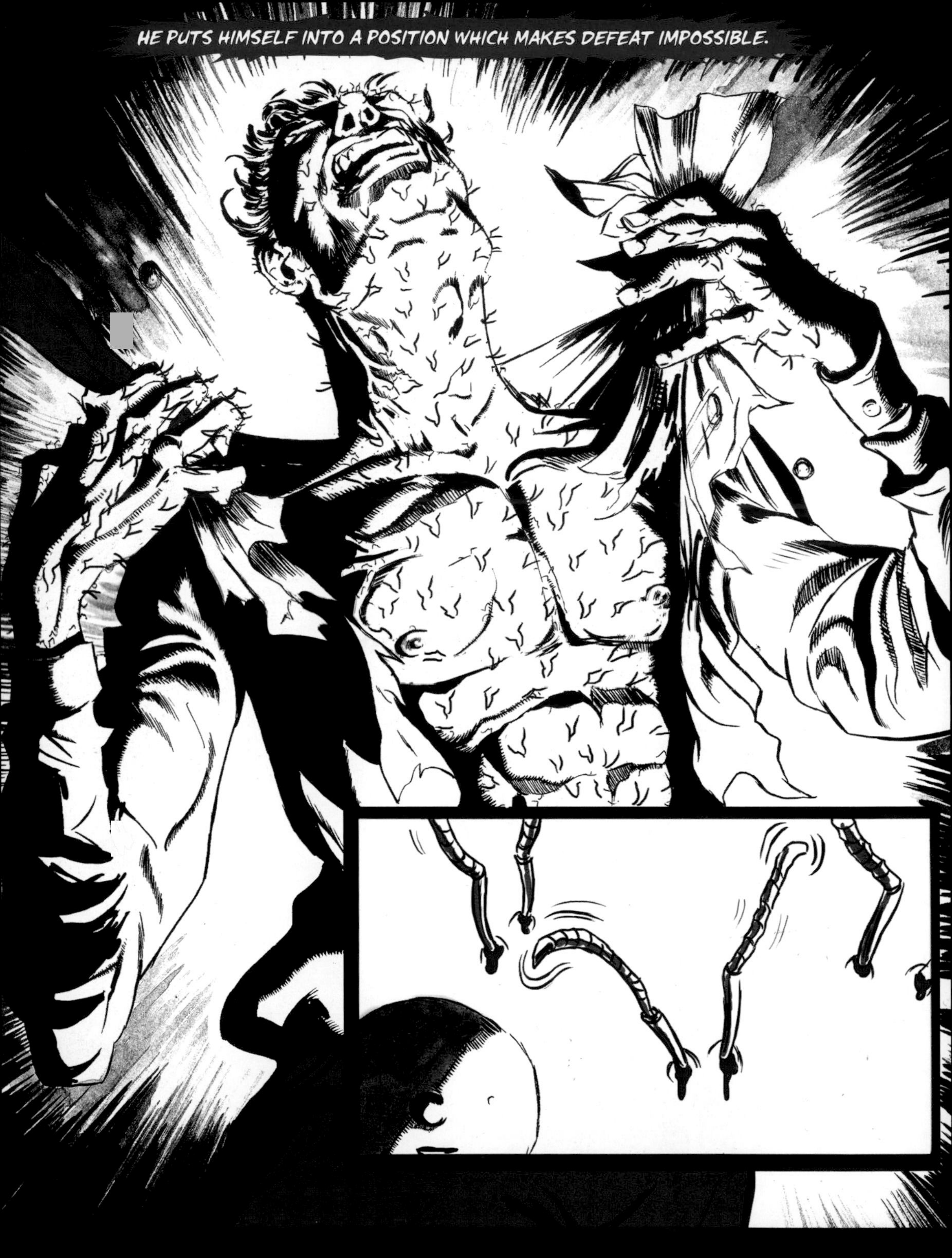
HE PUTS HIMSELF INTO A POSITION WHICH MAKES DEFEAT IMPOSSIBLE.

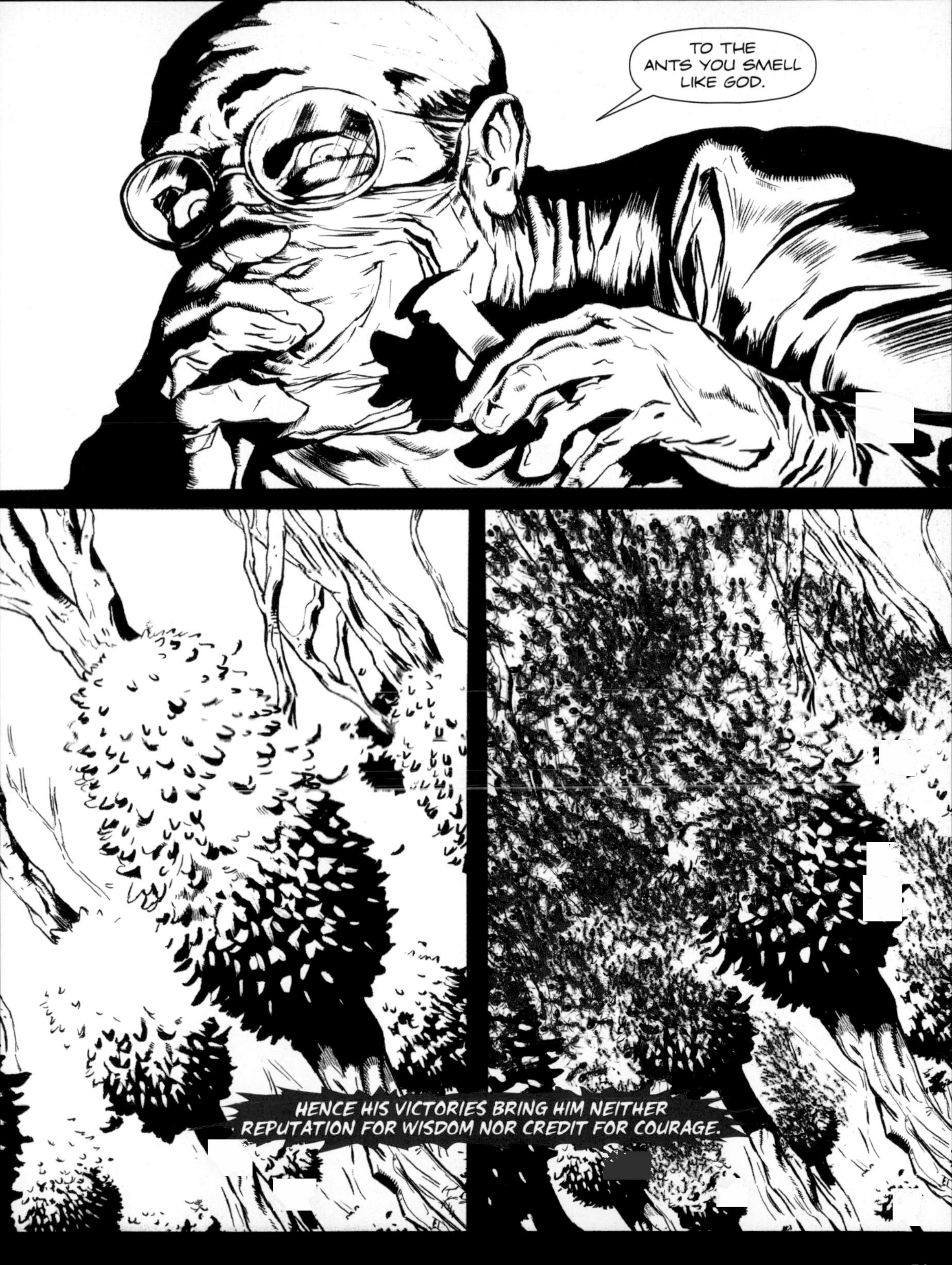
TO THE ANTS YOU SMELL LIKE GOD.
HENCE HIS VICTORIES BRING HIM NEITHER REPUTATION FOR WISDOM NOR CREDIT FOR COURAGE.

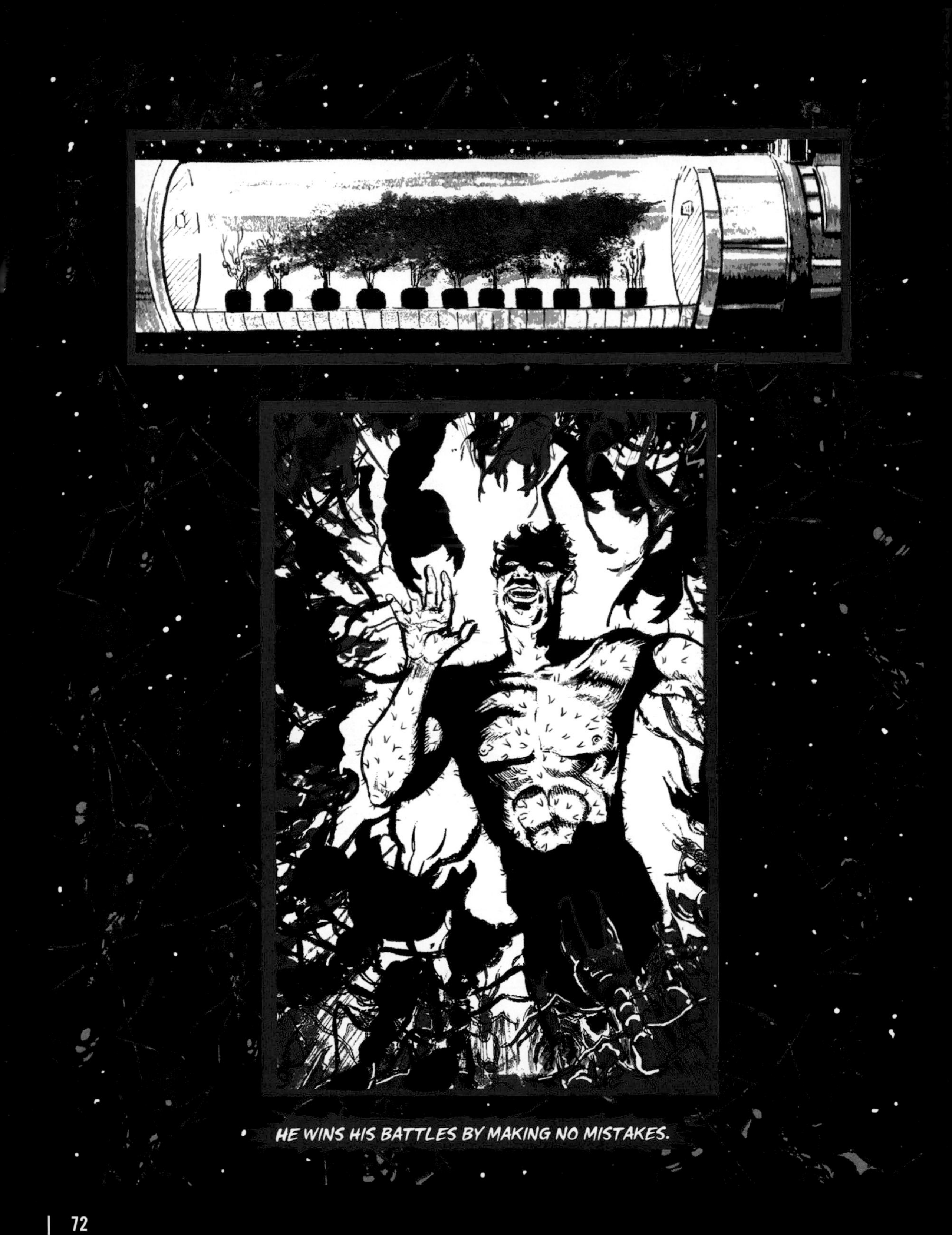
HE WINS HIS BATTLES BY MAKING NO MISTAKES.

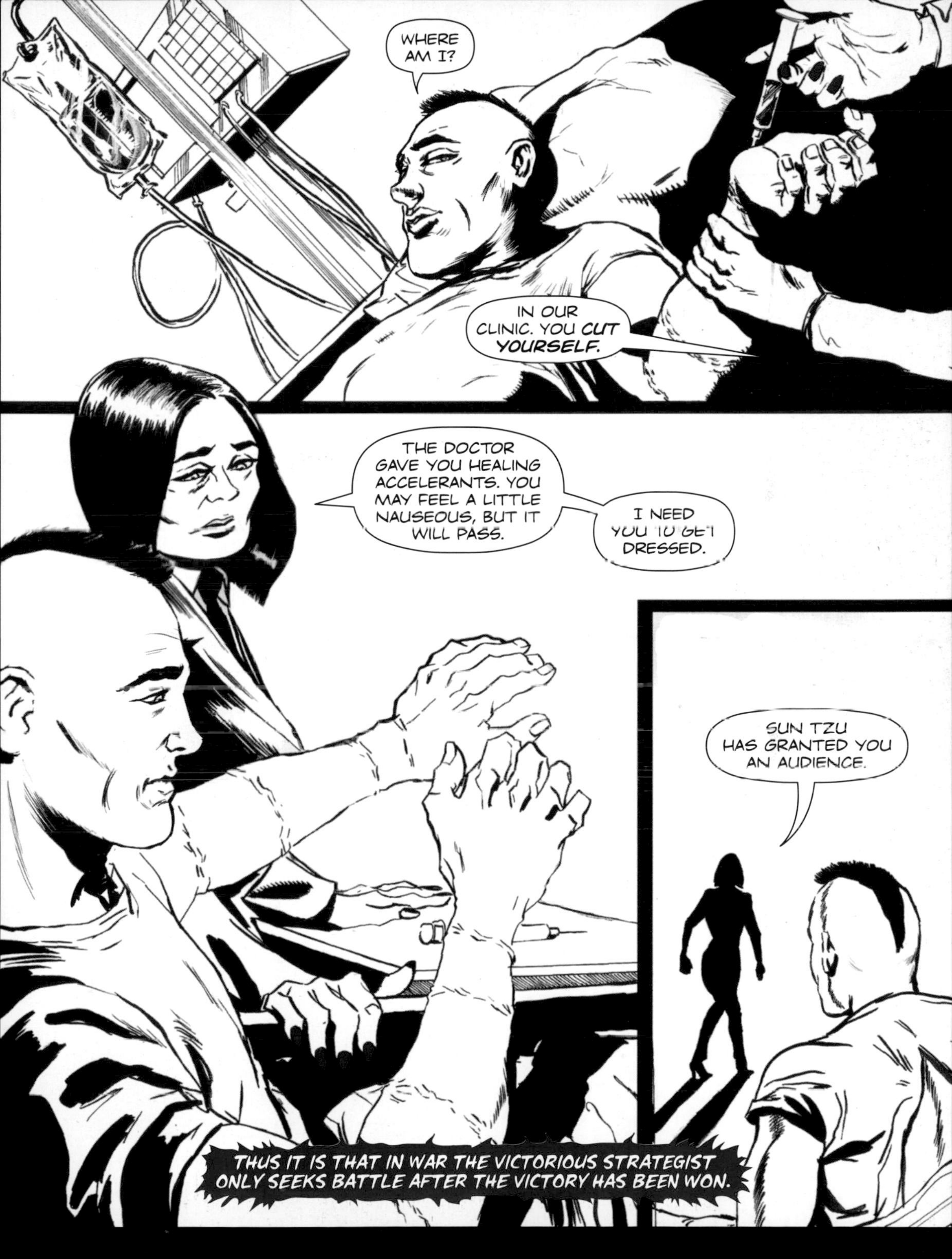
WHERE AM I?
IN OUR CLINIC. YOU CUT YOURSELF.
THE DOCTOR GAVE YOU HEALING ACCELERANTS. YOU MAY FEEL A LITTLE NAUSEOUS, BUT IT WILL PASS.
I NEED YOU TO GET DRESSED.
SUN TZU HAS GRANTED YOU AN AUDIENCE.
THUS IT IS THAT IN WAR THE VICTORIOUS STRATEGIST ONLY SEEKS BATTLE AFTER THE VICTORY HAS BEEN WON.

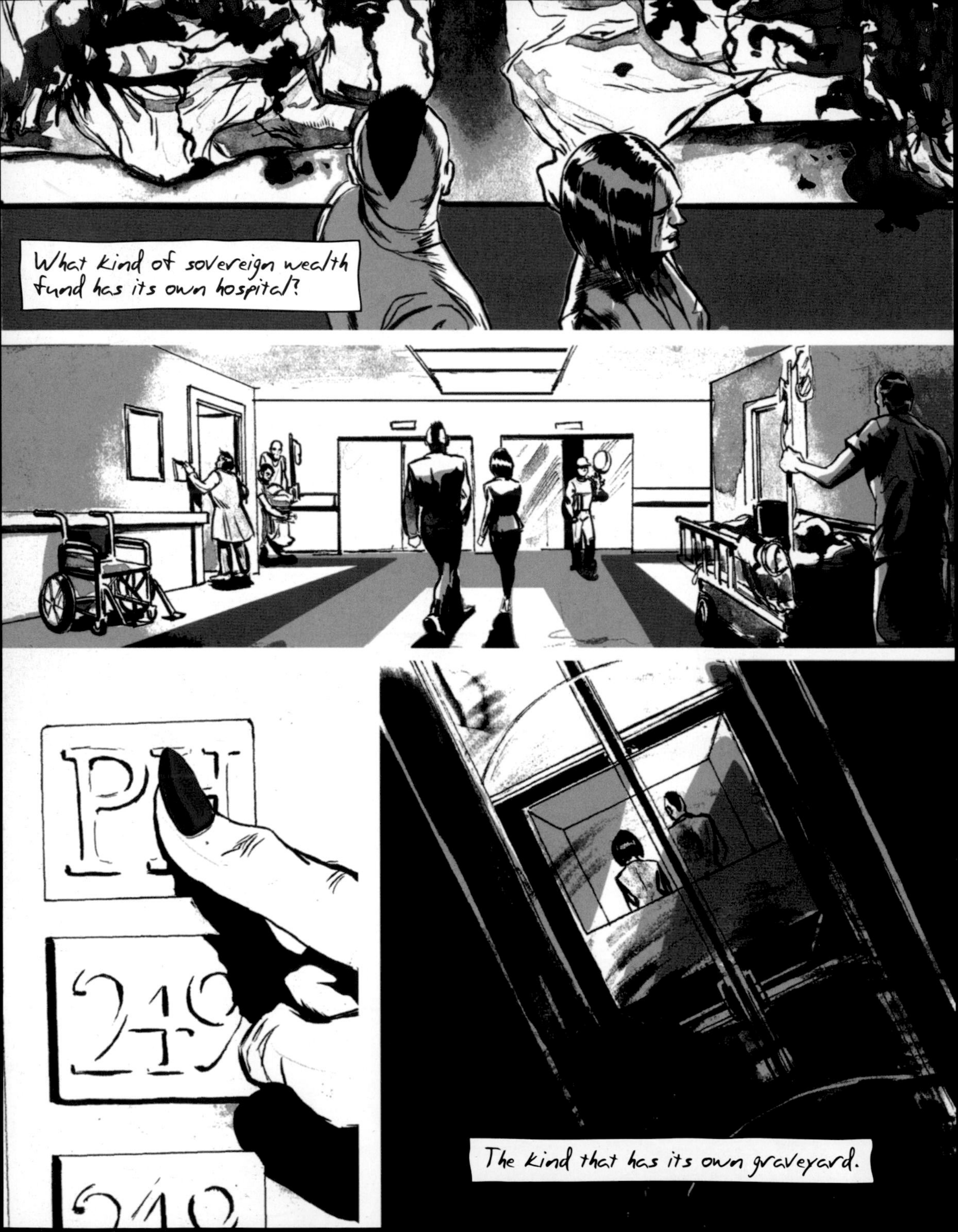
What kind of sovereign wealth fund has its own hospital?
The kind that has its own graveyard.

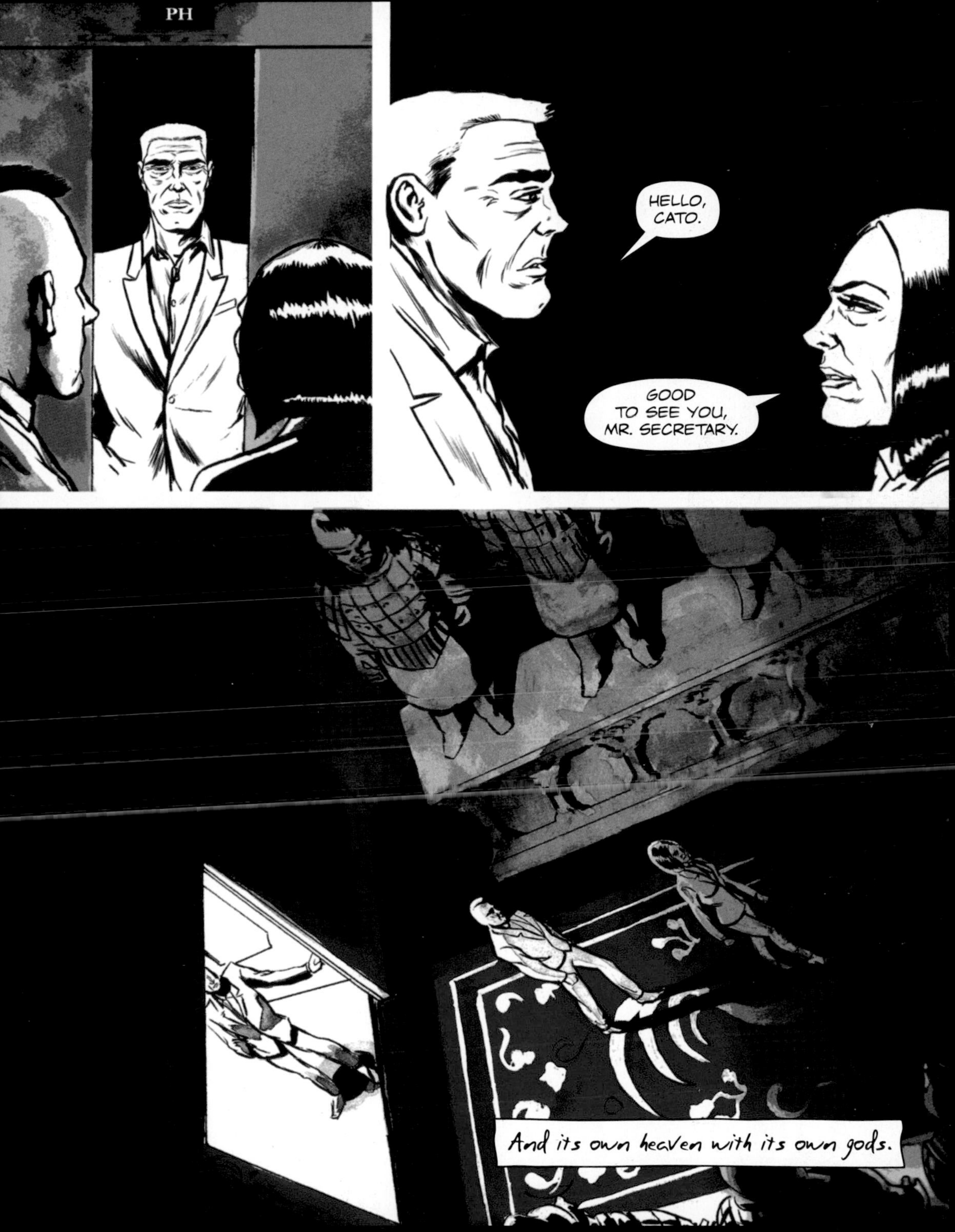
PH
HELLO, CATO.
GOOD TO SEE YOU, MR. SECRETARY.
And its own heaven with its own gods.

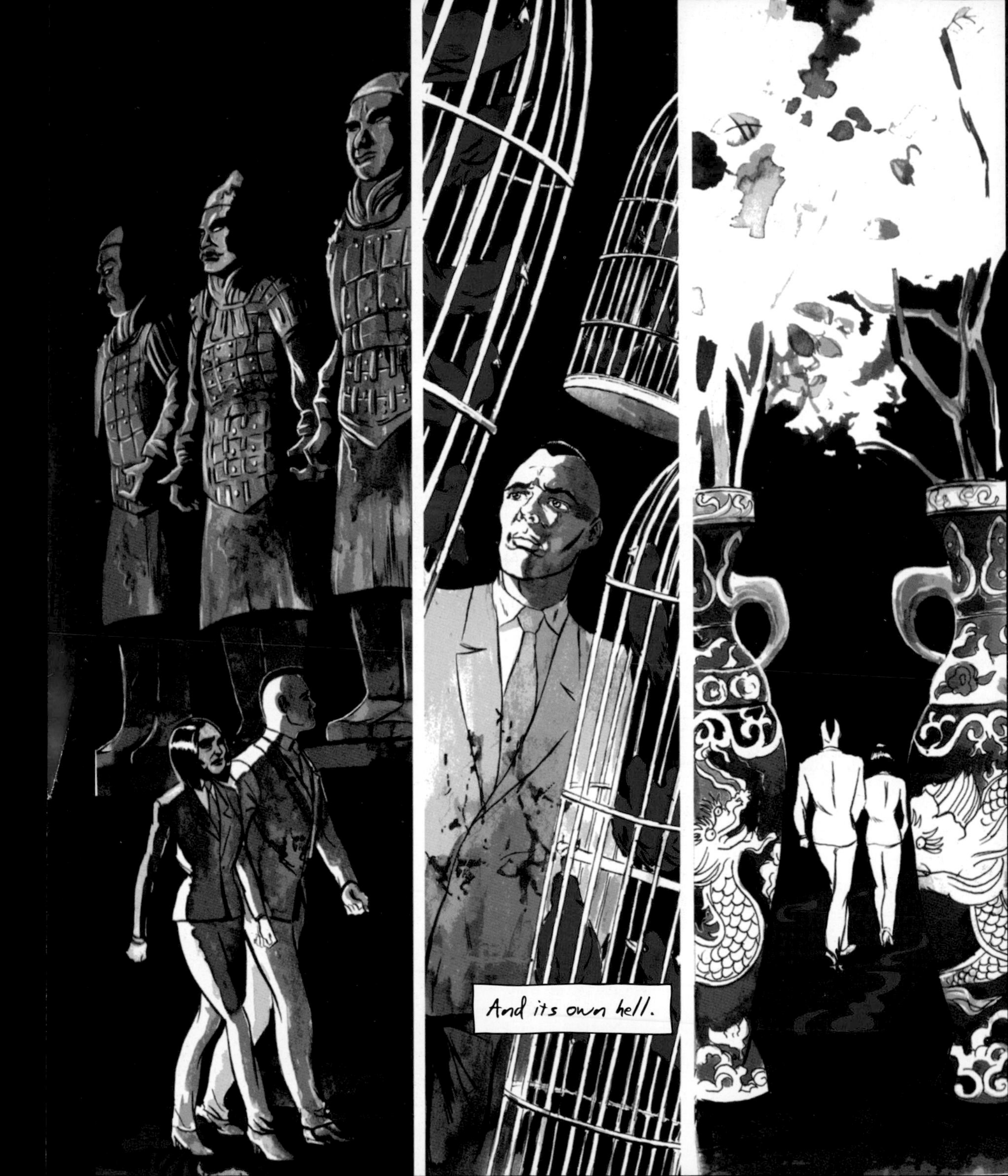
And its own hell.

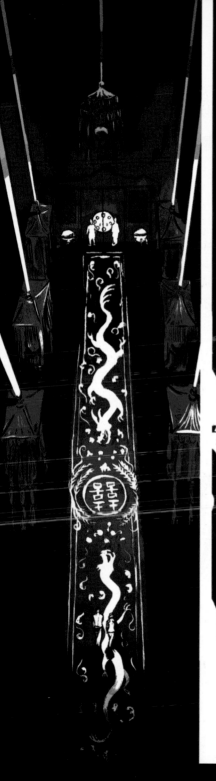

I'LL WAIT HERE FOR YOU.

The air outside was cold.

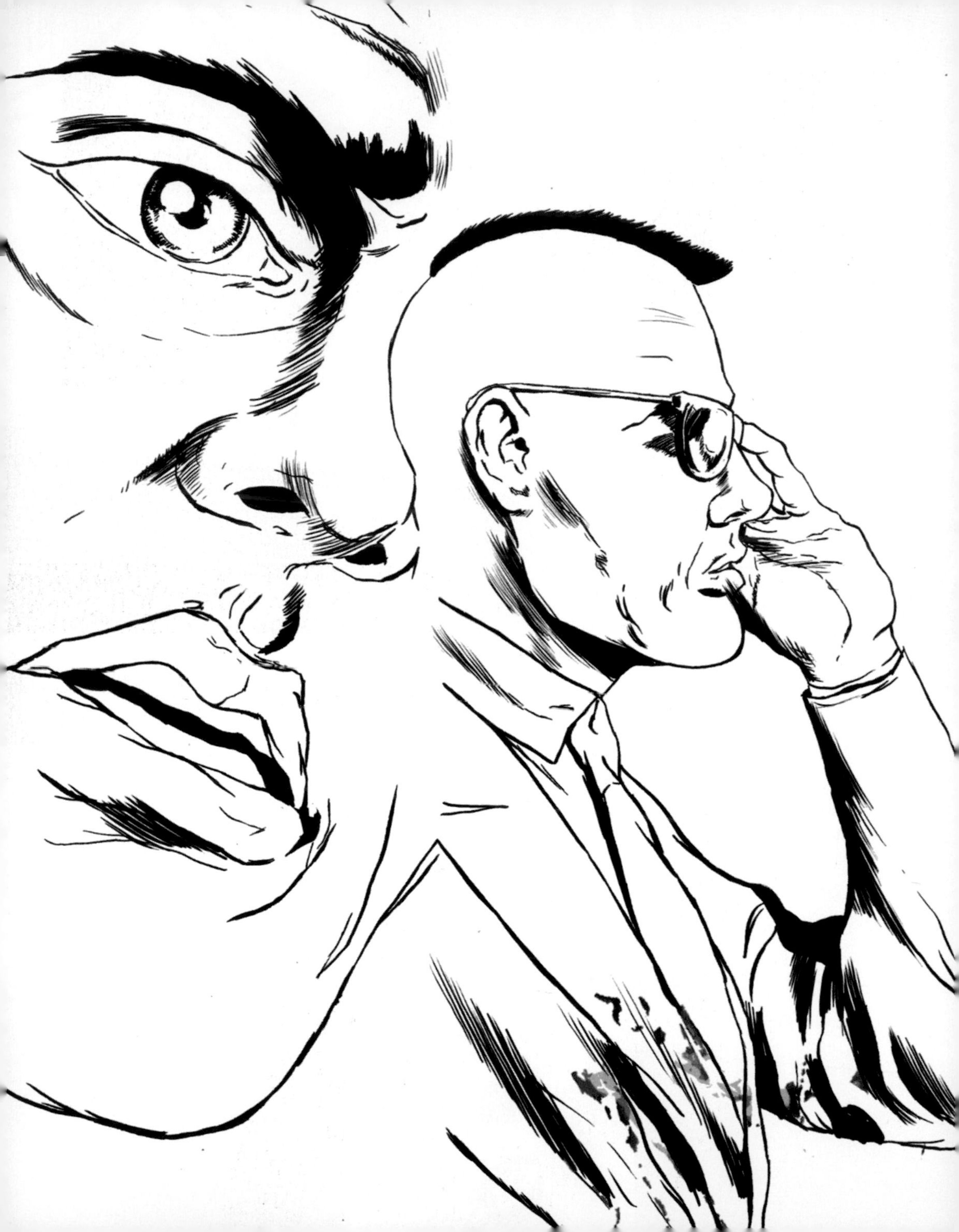

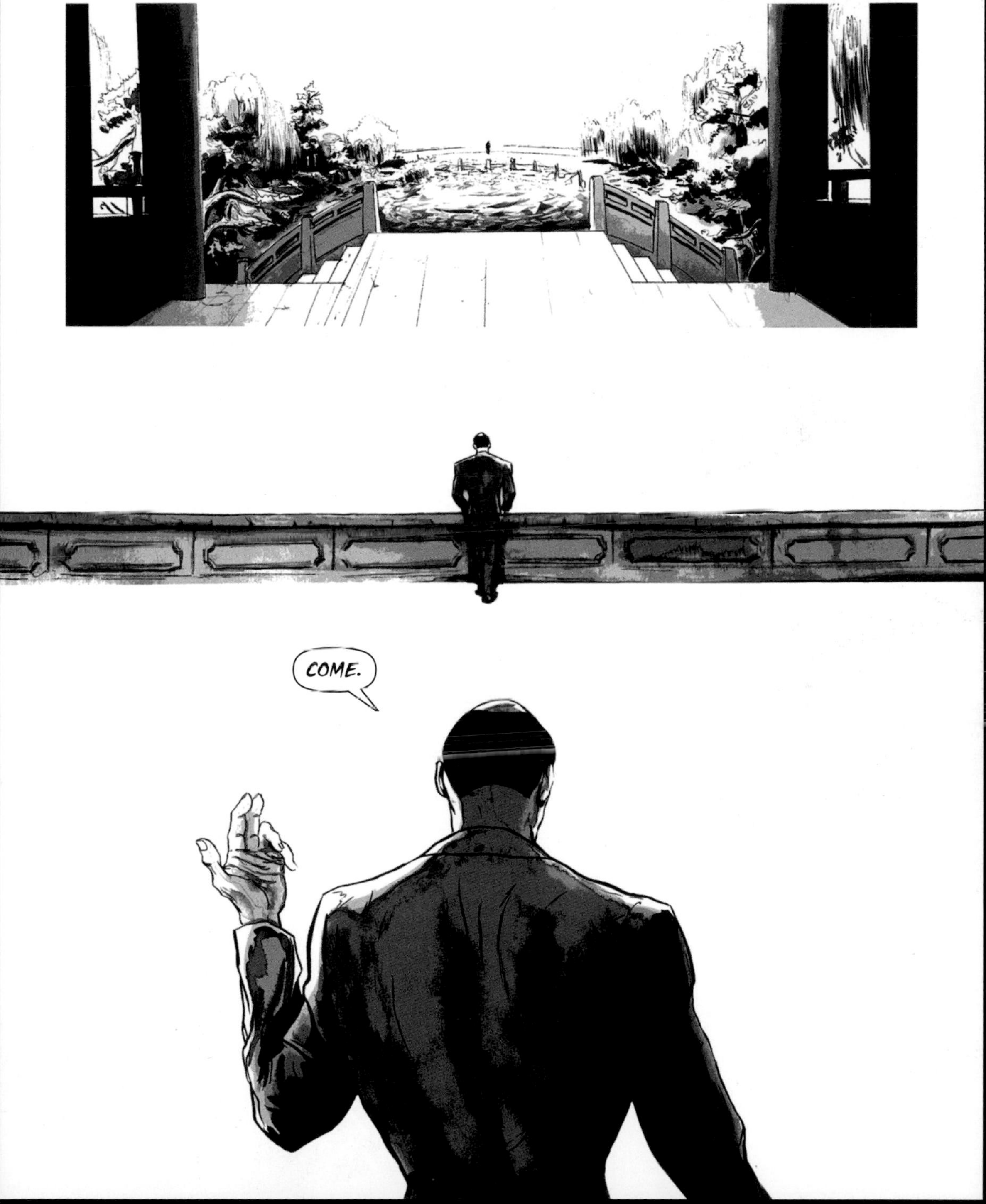
COME.

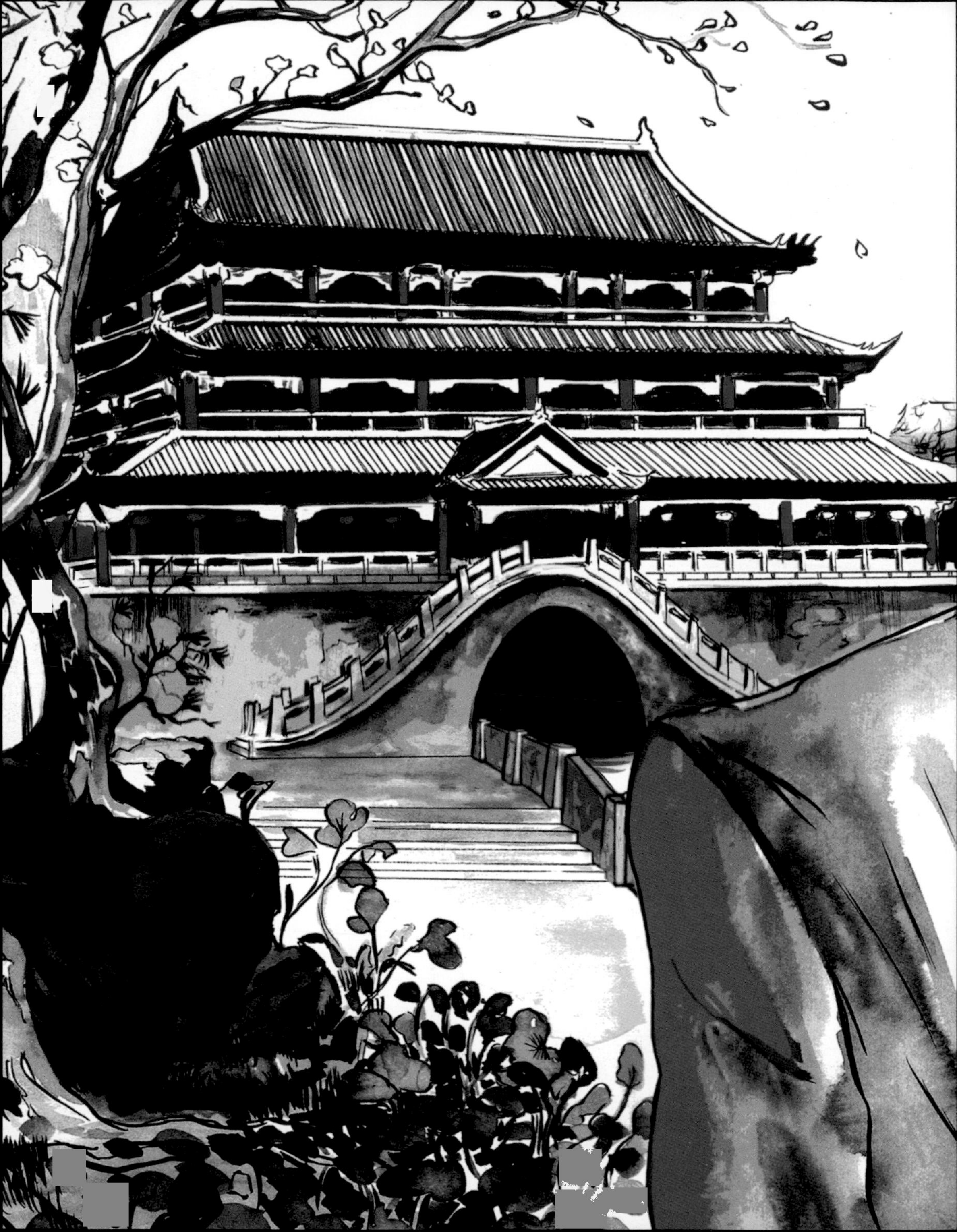

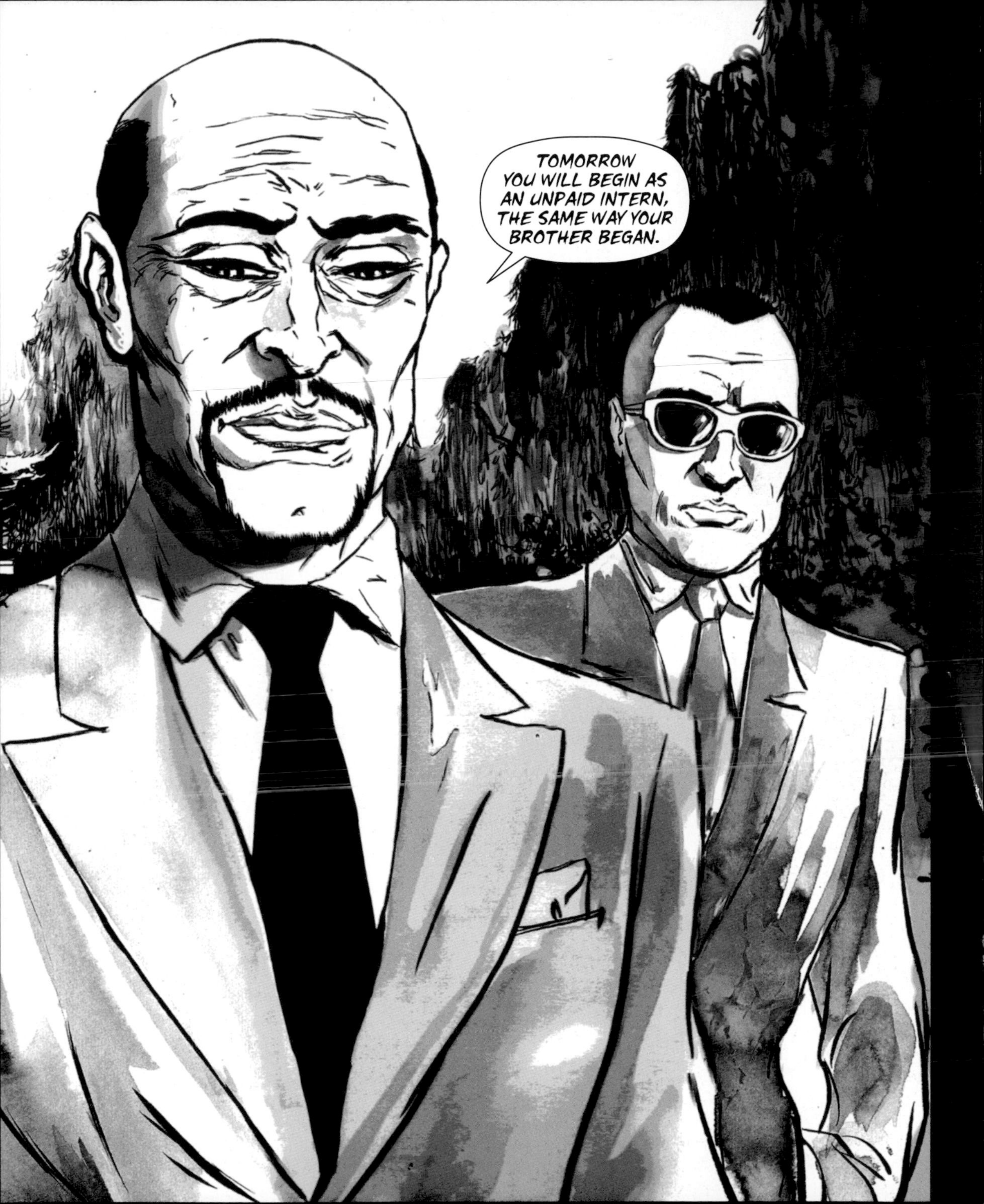
TOMORROW YOU WILL BEGIN AS AN UNPAID INTERN, THE SAME WAY YOUR BROTHER BEGAN.

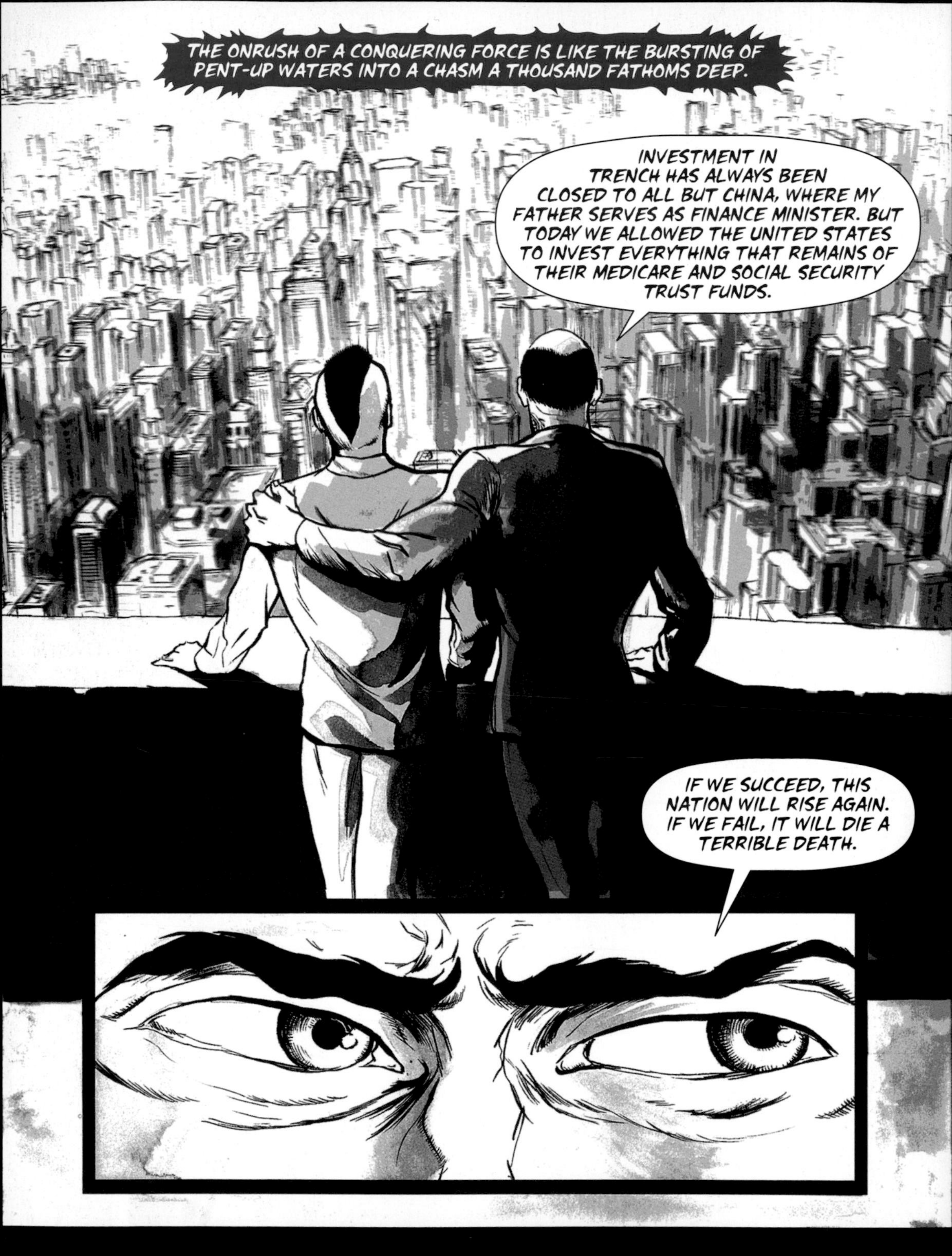
THE ONRUSH OF A CONQUERING FORCE IS LIKE THE BURSTING OF PENT-UP WATERS INTO A CHASM A THOUSAND FATHOMS DEEP.
INVESTMENT IN TRENCH HAS ALWAYS BEEN CLOSED TO ALL BUT CHINA, WHERE MY FATHER SERVES AS FINANCE MINISTER. BUT TODAY WE ALLOWED THE UNITED STATES TO INVEST EVERYTHING THAT REMAINS OF THEIR MEDICARE AND SOCIAL SECURITY TRUST FUNDS.
IF WE SUCCEED, THIS NATION WILL RISE AGAIN. IF WE FAIL, IT WILL DIE A TERRIBLE DEATH.

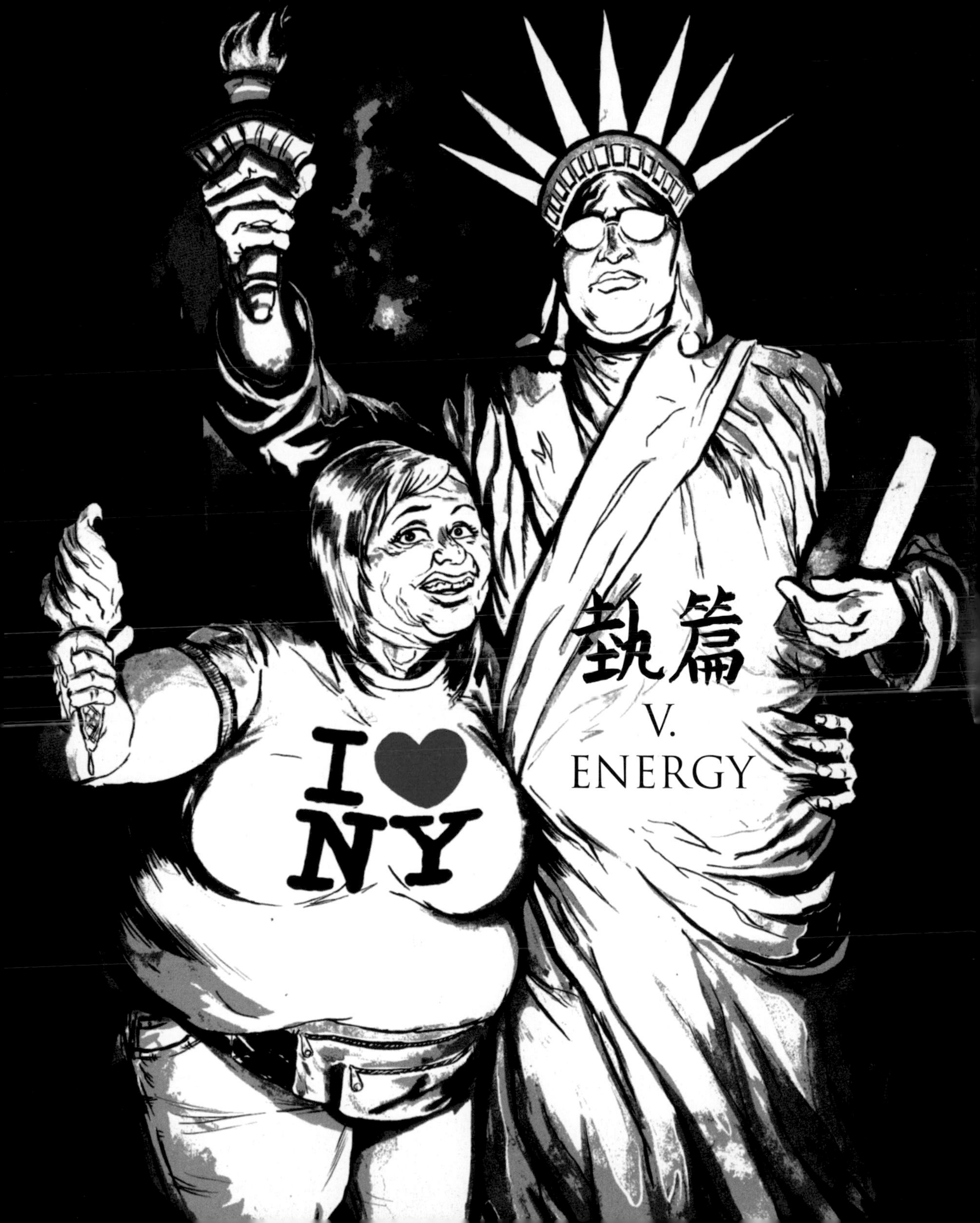

I ♥ NY

埶篇

V. ENERGY

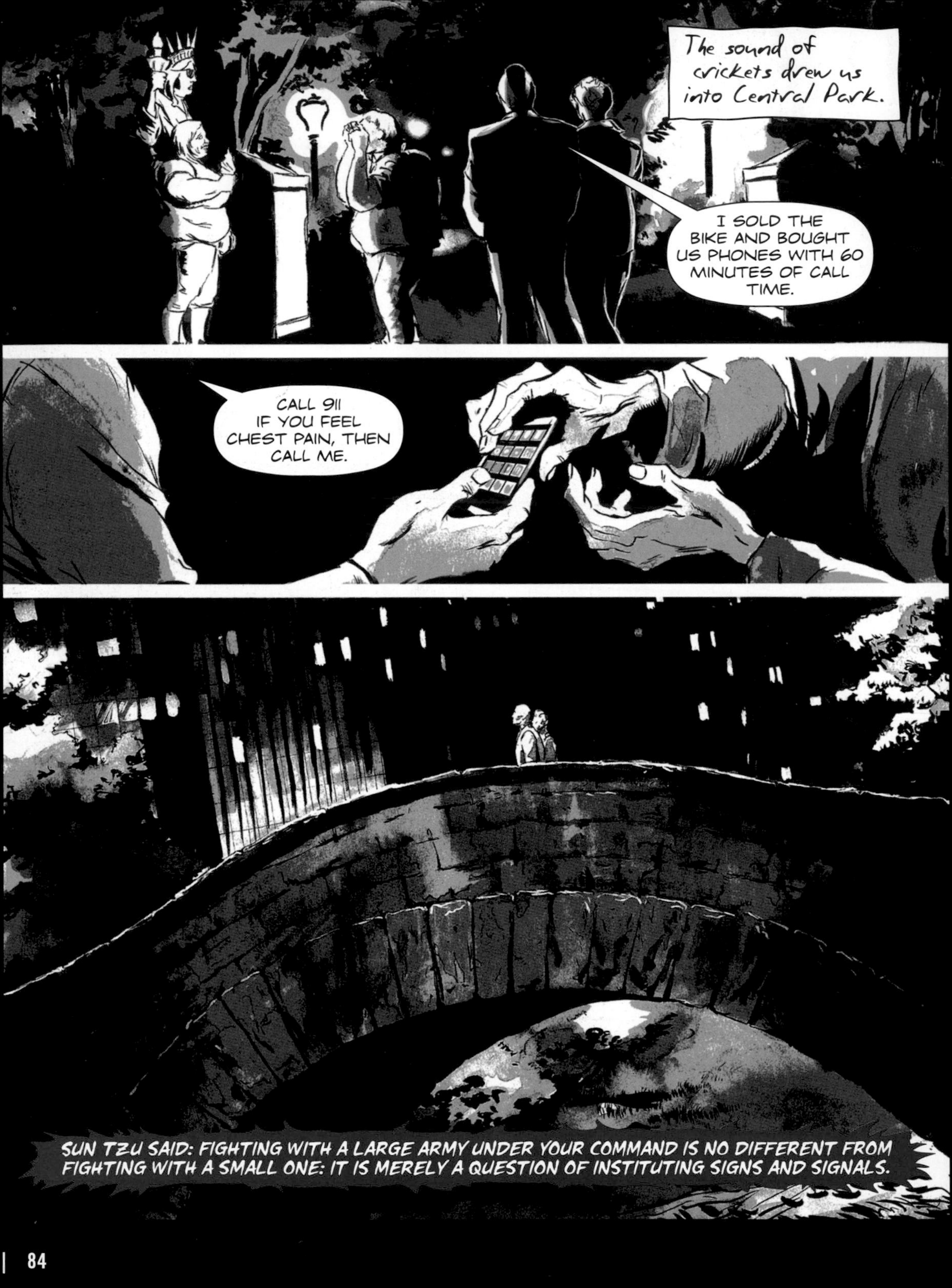
The sound of crickets drew us into Central Park.
I SOLD THE BIKE AND BOUGHT US PHONES WITH 60 MINUTES OF CALL TIME.
CALL 911 IF YOU FEEL CHEST PAIN, THEN CALL ME.
SUN TZU SAID: FIGHTING WITH A LARGE ARMY UNDER YOUR COMMAND IS NO DIFFERENT FROM FIGHTING WITH A SMALL ONE: IT IS MERELY A QUESTION OF INSTITUTING SIGNS AND SIGNALS.

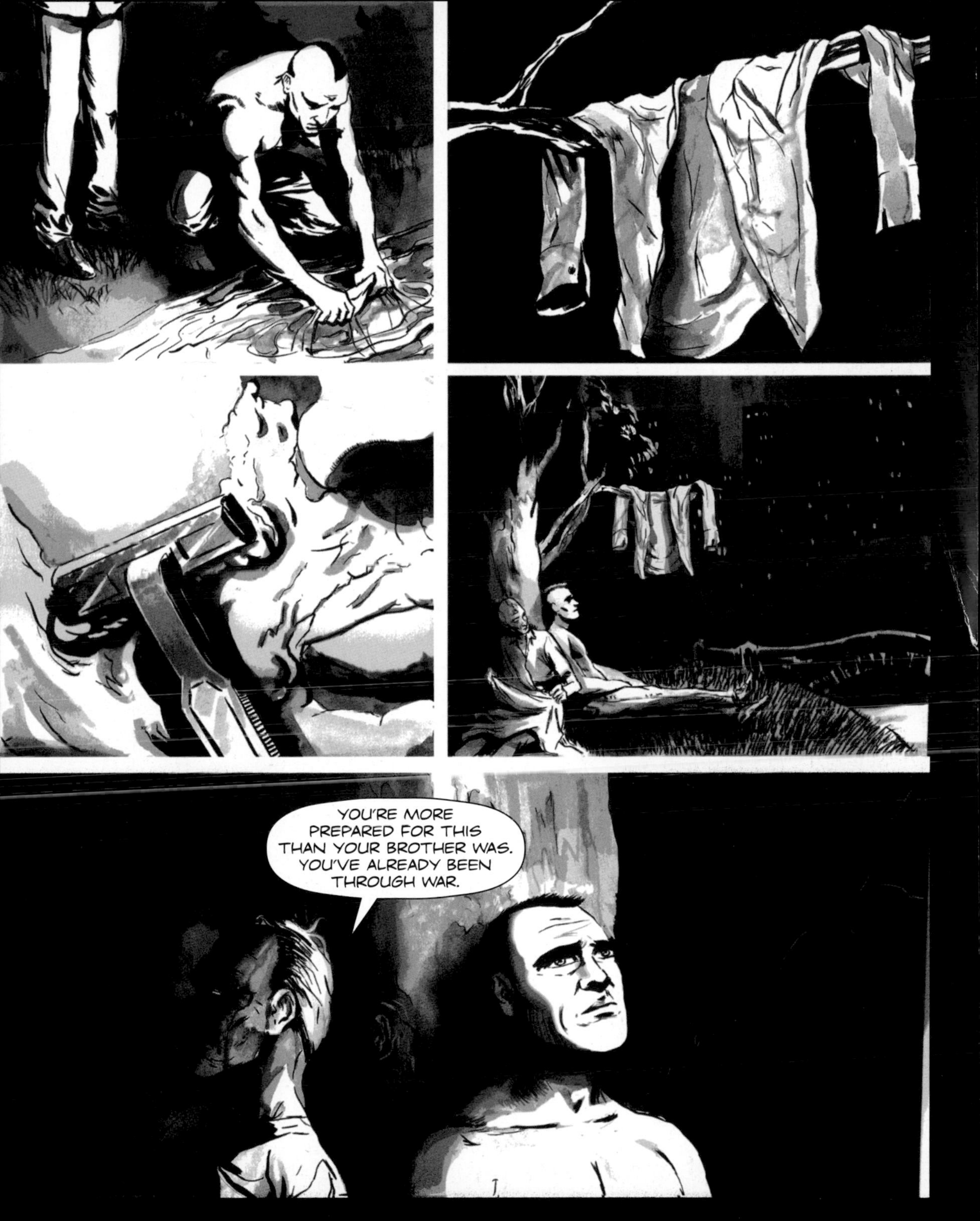
YOU'RE MORE PREPARED FOR THIS THAN YOUR BROTHER WAS. YOU'VE ALREADY BEEN THROUGH WAR.

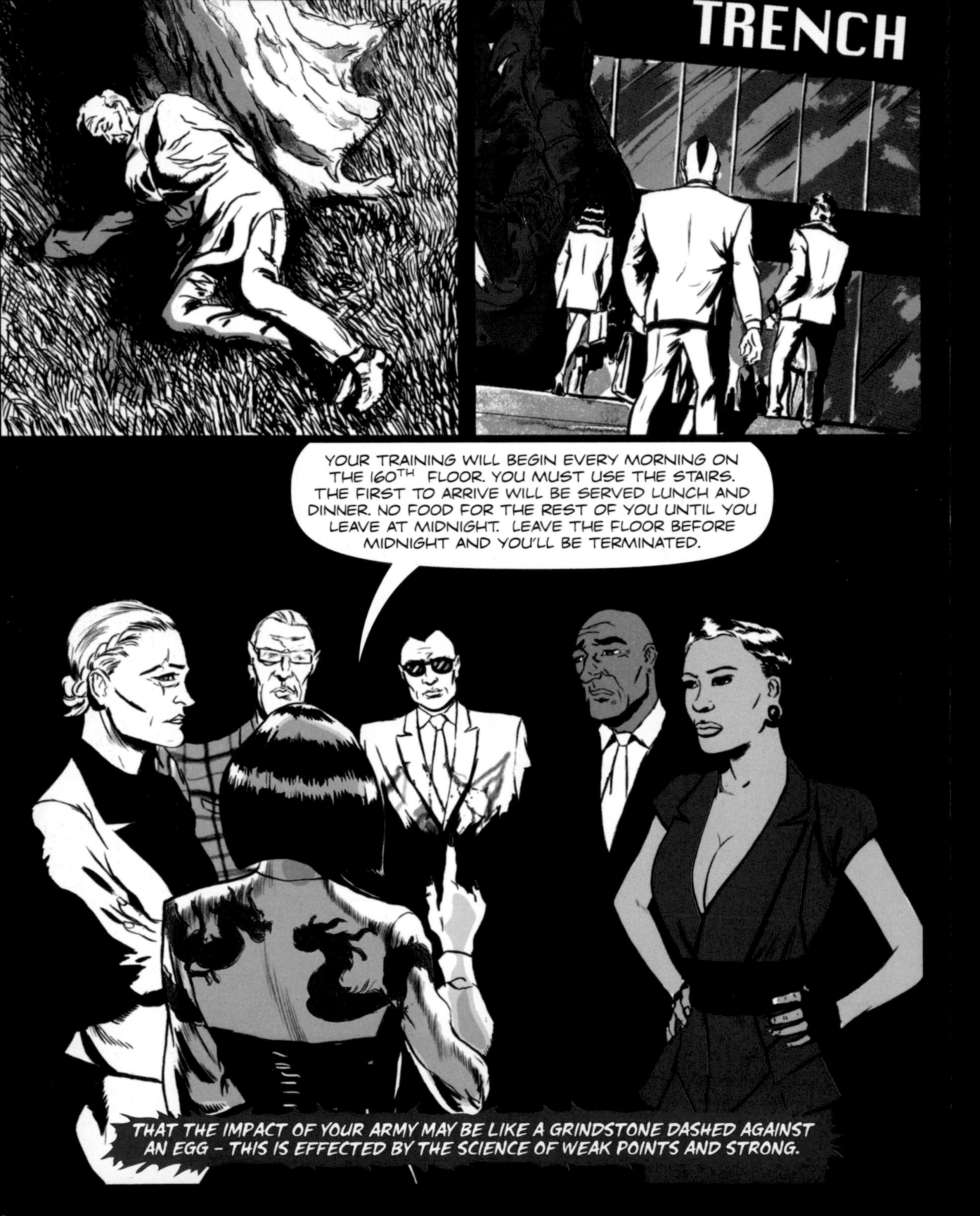
TRENCH
YOUR TRAINING WILL BEGIN EVERY MORNING ON THE 160TH FLOOR. YOU MUST USE THE STAIRS. THE FIRST TO ARRIVE WILL BE SERVED LUNCH AND DINNER. NO FOOD FOR THE REST OF YOU UNTIL YOU LEAVE AT MIDNIGHT. LEAVE THE FLOOR BEFORE MIDNIGHT AND YOU'LL BE TERMINATED.
THAT THE IMPACT OF YOUR ARMY MAY BE LIKE A GRINDSTONE DASHED AGAINST AN EGG – THIS IS EFFECTED BY THE SCIENCE OF WEAK POINTS AND STRONG.

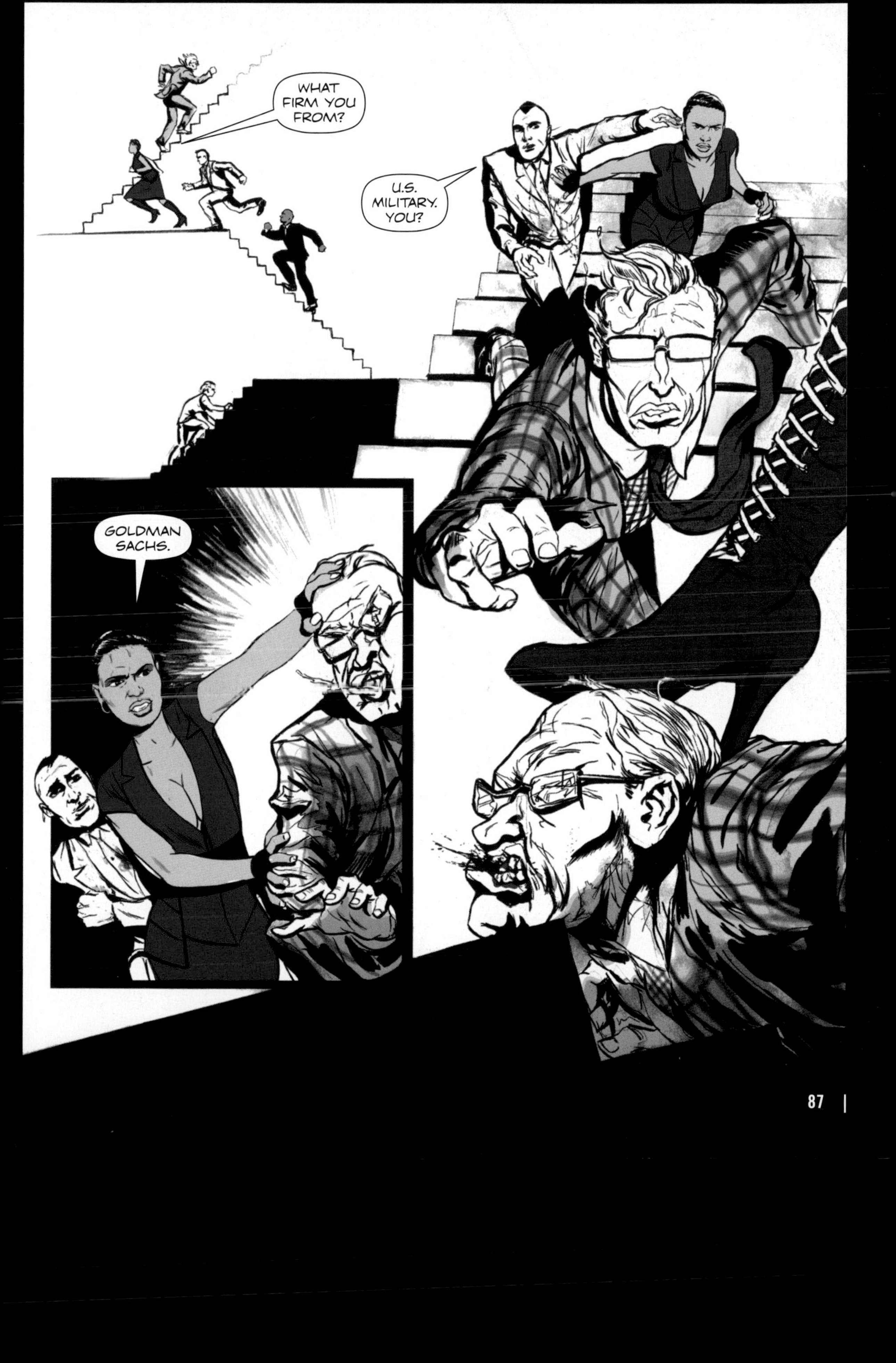
WHAT FIRM YOU FROM?
U.S. MILITARY. YOU?
GOLDMAN SACHS.

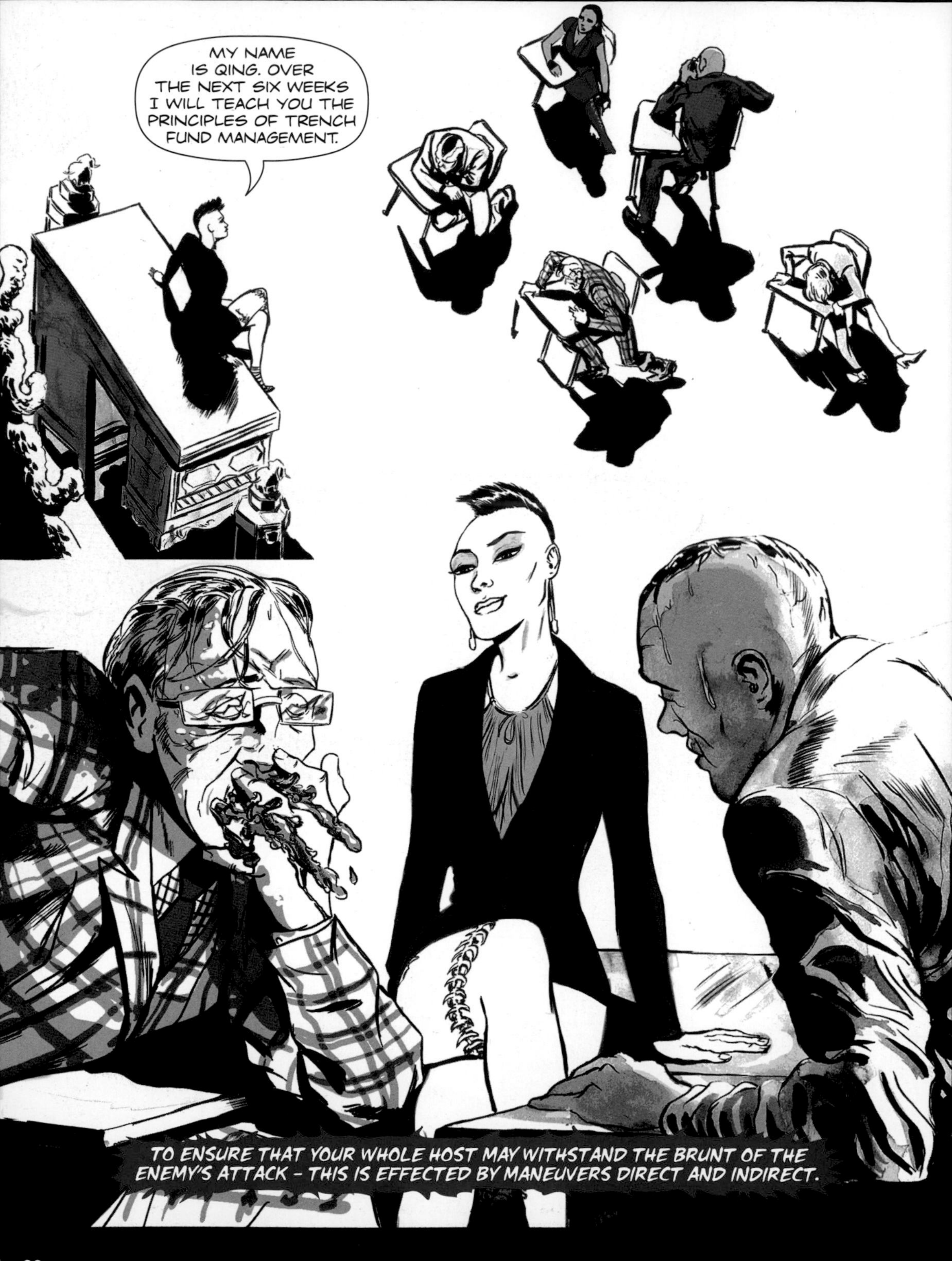
MY NAME IS QING. OVER THE NEXT SIX WEEKS I WILL TEACH YOU THE PRINCIPLES OF TRENCH FUND MANAGEMENT.
TO ENSURE THAT YOUR WHOLE HOST MAY WITHSTAND THE BRUNT OF THE ENEMY'S ATTACK - THIS IS EFFECTED BY MANEUVERS DIRECT AND INDIRECT.

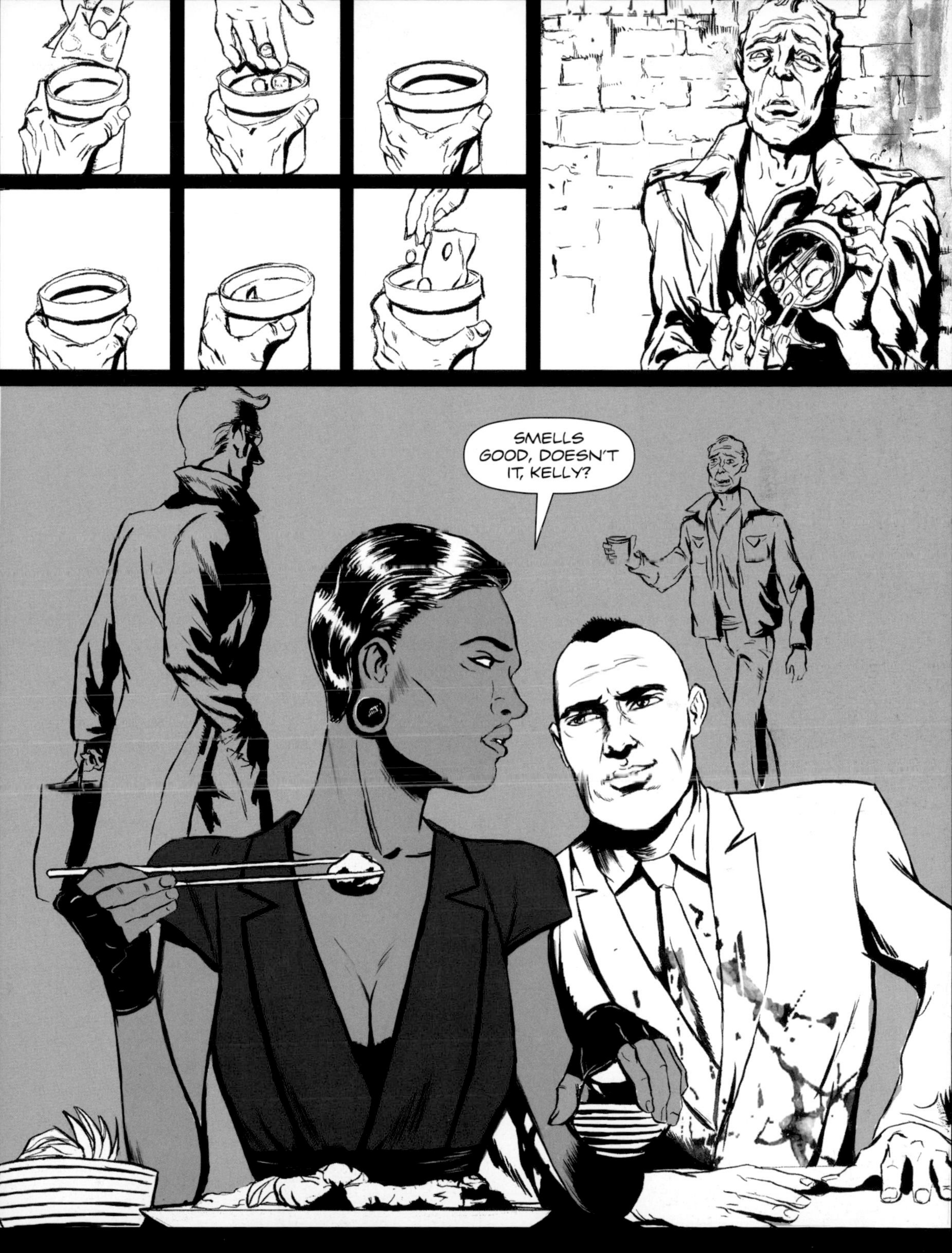
SMELLS GOOD, DOESN'T IT, KELLY?

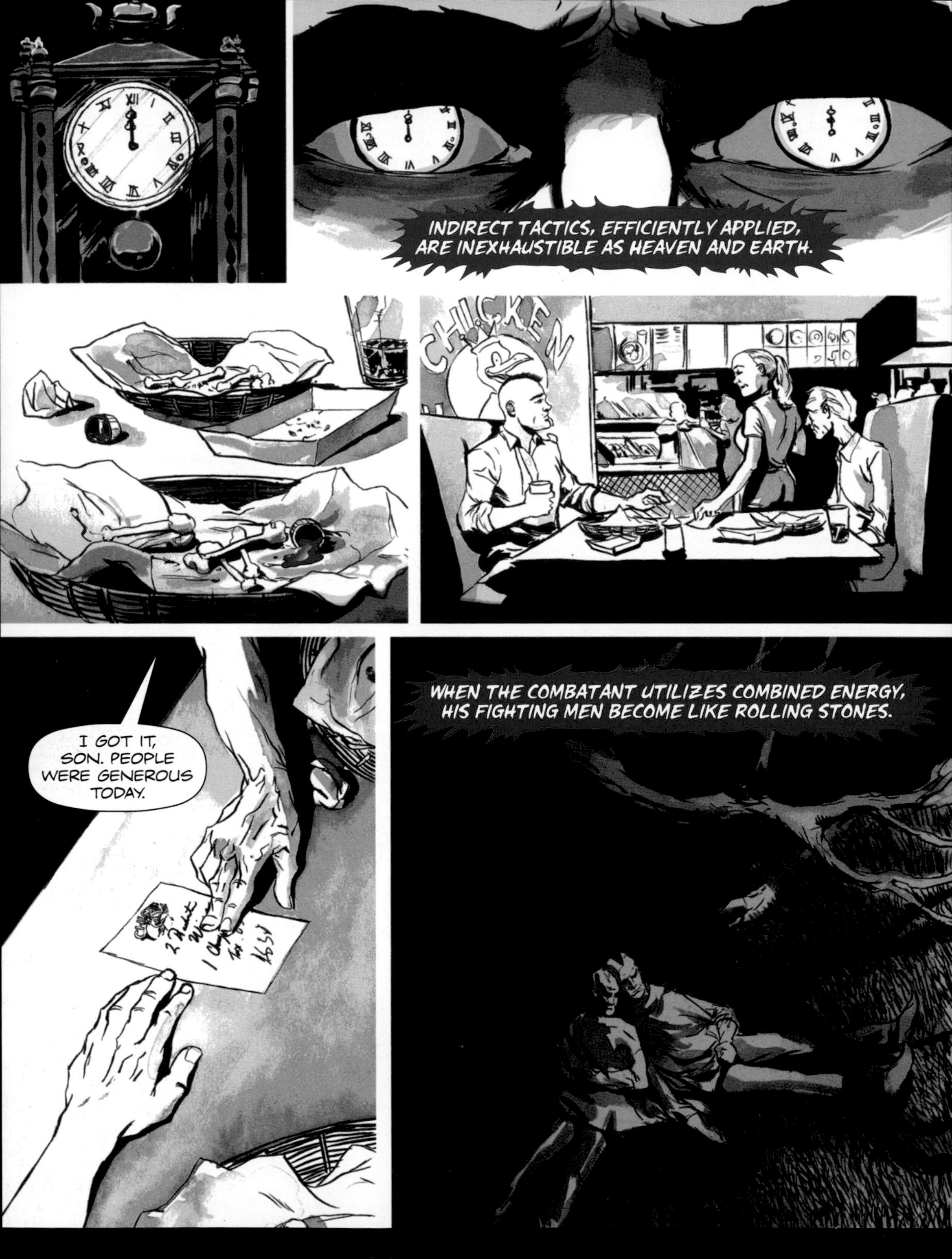
INDIRECT TACTICS, EFFICIENTLY APPLIED, ARE INEXHAUSTIBLE AS HEAVEN AND EARTH.
CHICKEN
I GOT IT, SON. PEOPLE WERE GENEROUS TODAY.
WHEN THE COMBATANT UTILIZES COMBINED ENERGY, HIS FIGHTING MEN BECOME LIKE ROLLING STONES.

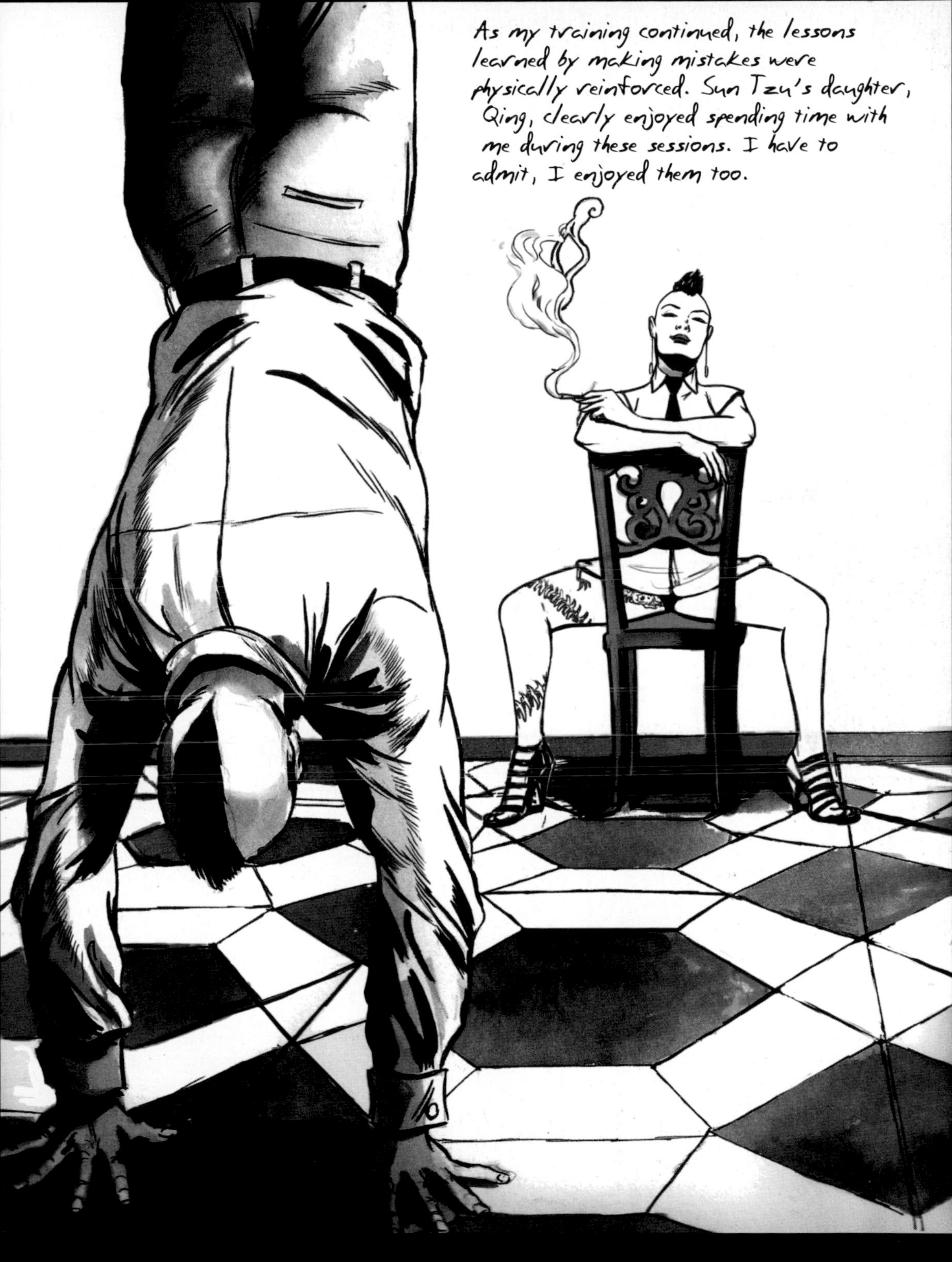
As my training continued, the lessons learned by making mistakes were physically reinforced. Sun Tzu's daughter, Qing, clearly enjoyed spending time with me during these sessions. I have to admit, I enjoyed them too.

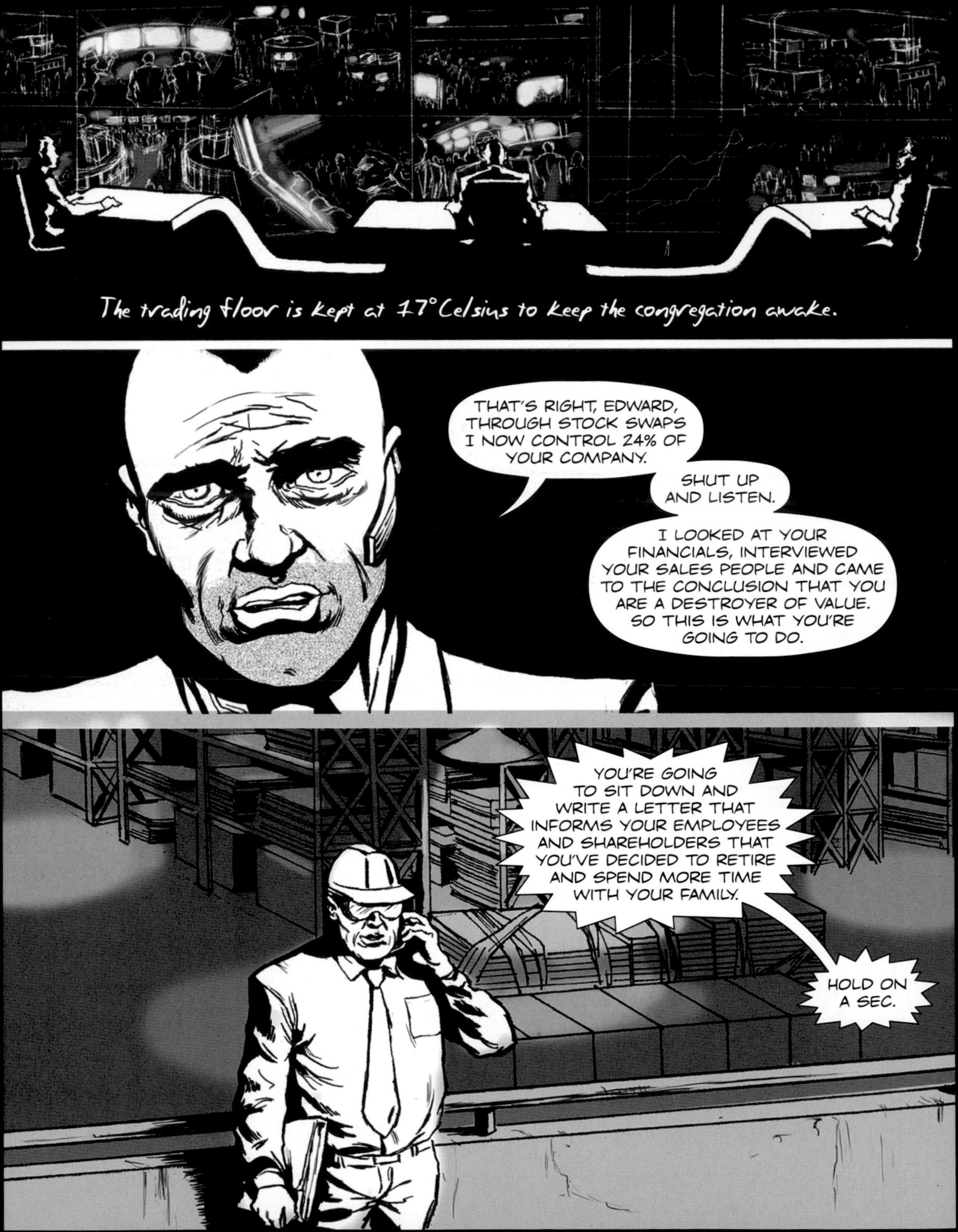
The trading floor is kept at 17°Celsius to keep the congregation awake.
THAT'S RIGHT, EDWARD, THROUGH STOCK SWAPS I NOW CONTROL 24% OF YOUR COMPANY.
SHUT UP AND LISTEN.
I LOOKED AT YOUR FINANCIALS, INTERVIEWED YOUR SALES PEOPLE AND CAME TO THE CONCLUSION THAT YOU ARE A DESTROYER OF VALUE. SO THIS IS WHAT YOU'RE GOING TO DO.
YOU'RE GOING TO SIT DOWN AND WRITE A LETTER THAT INFORMS YOUR EMPLOYEES AND SHAREHOLDERS THAT YOU'VE DECIDED TO RETIRE AND SPEND MORE TIME WITH YOUR FAMILY.
HOLD ON A SEC.

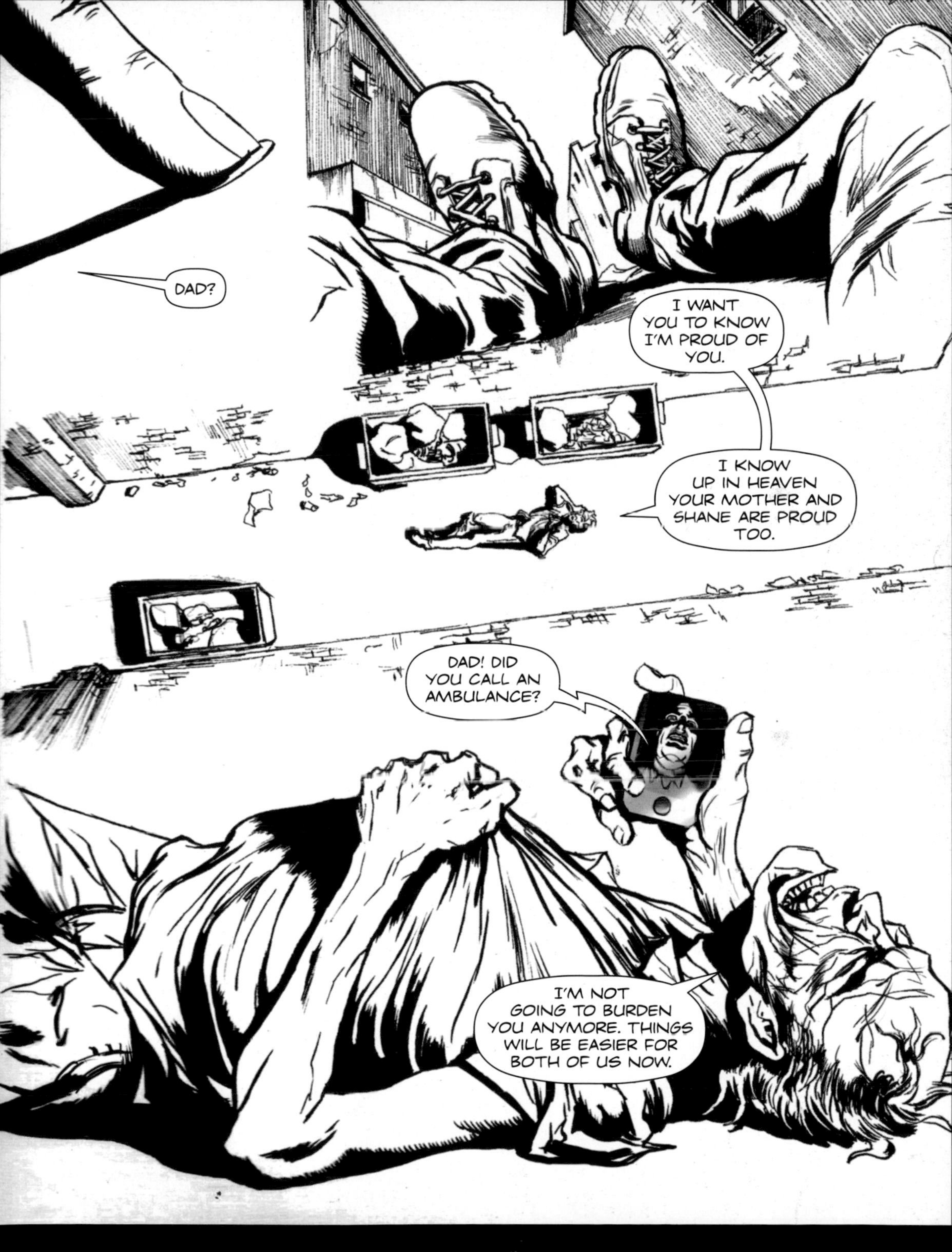
DAD?
I WANT YOU TO KNOW I'M PROUD OF YOU.
I KNOW UP IN HEAVEN YOUR MOTHER AND SHANE ARE PROUD TOO.
DAD! DID YOU CALL AN AMBULANCE?
I'M NOT GOING TO BURDEN YOU ANYMORE. THINGS WILL BE EASIER FOR BOTH OF US NOW.

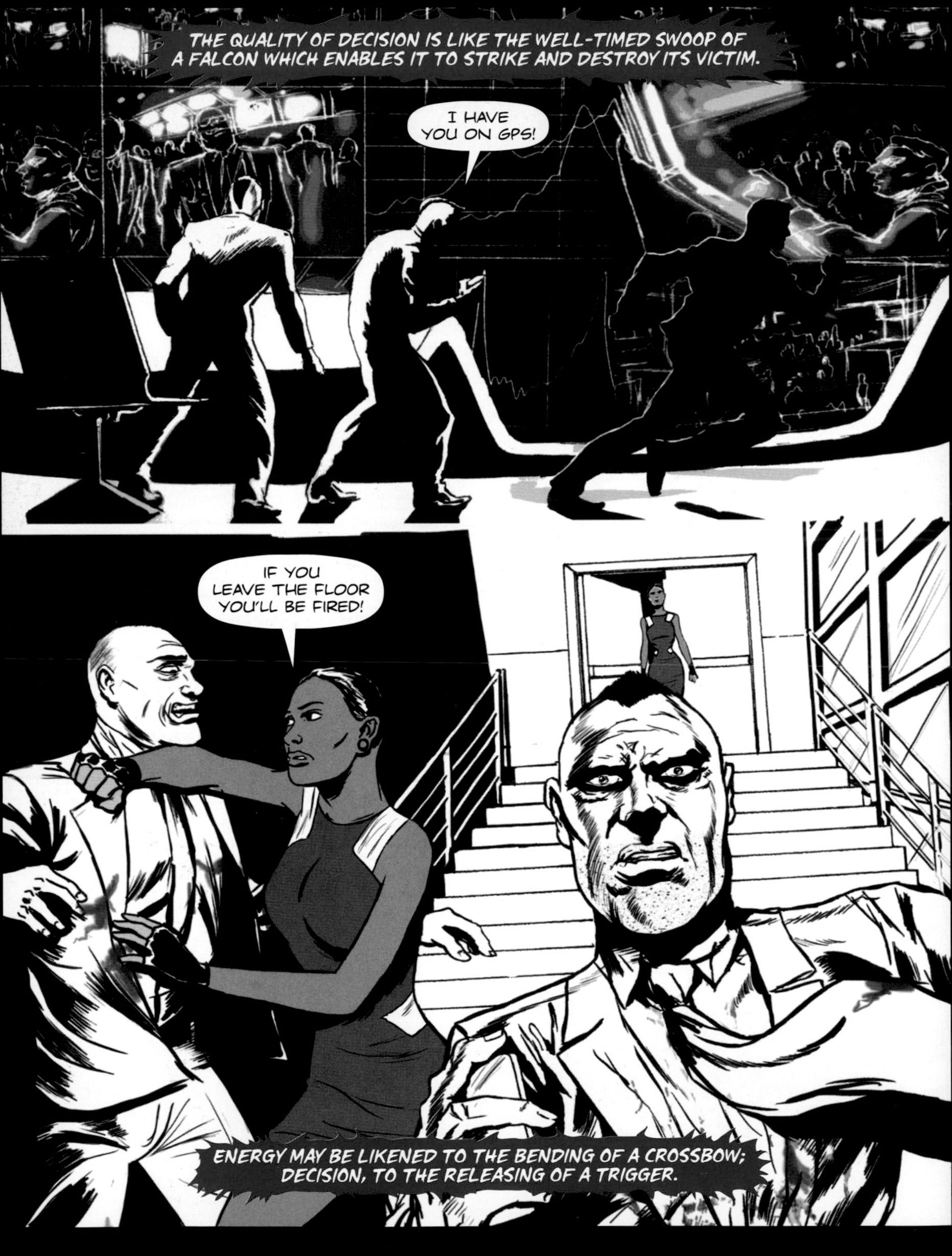
THE QUALITY OF DECISION IS LIKE THE WELL-TIMED SWOOP OF A FALCON WHICH ENABLES IT TO STRIKE AND DESTROY ITS VICTIM.
I HAVE YOU ON GPS!
IF YOU LEAVE THE FLOOR YOU'LL BE FIRED!
ENERGY MAY BE LIKENED TO THE BENDING OF A CROSSBOW; DECISION, TO THE RELEASING OF A TRIGGER.

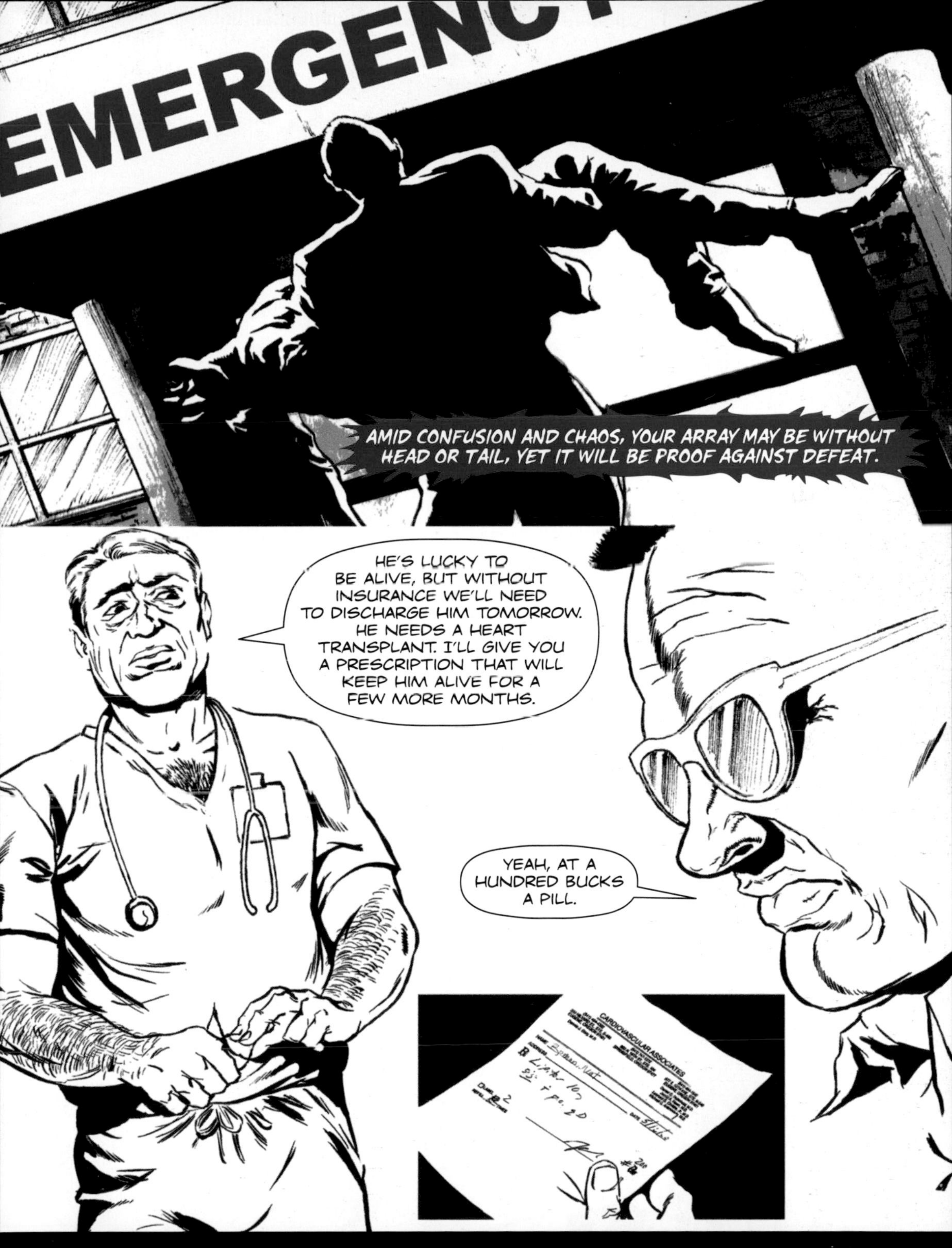
EMERGENCY
AMID CONFUSION AND CHAOS, YOUR ARRAY MAY BE WITHOUT HEAD OR TAIL, YET IT WILL BE PROOF AGAINST DEFEAT.
HE'S LUCKY TO BE ALIVE, BUT WITHOUT INSURANCE WE'LL NEED TO DISCHARGE HIM TOMORROW. HE NEEDS A HEART TRANSPLANT. I'LL GIVE YOU A PRESCRIPTION THAT WILL KEEP HIM ALIVE FOR A FEW MORE MONTHS.
YEAH, AT A HUNDRED BUCKS A PILL.
CARDIOVASCULAR ASSOCIATES

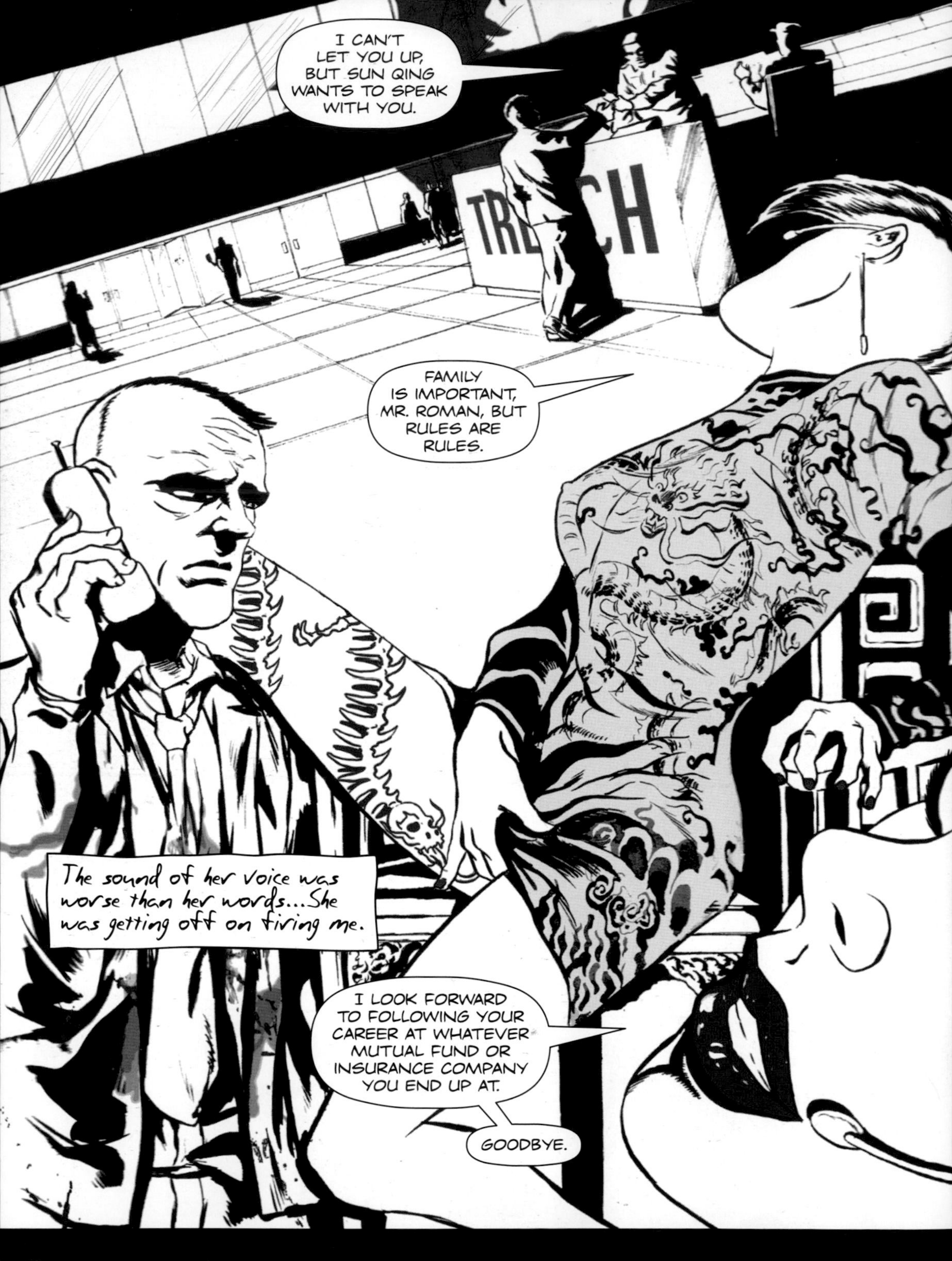
I CAN'T LET YOU UP, BUT SUN QING WANTS TO SPEAK WITH YOU.
TRE CH
FAMILY IS IMPORTANT, MR. ROMAN, BUT RULES ARE RULES.
The sound of her voice was worse than her words...She was getting off on firing me.
I LOOK FORWARD TO FOLLOWING YOUR CAREER AT WHATEVER MUTUAL FUND OR INSURANCE COMPANY YOU END UP AT.
GOODBYE.

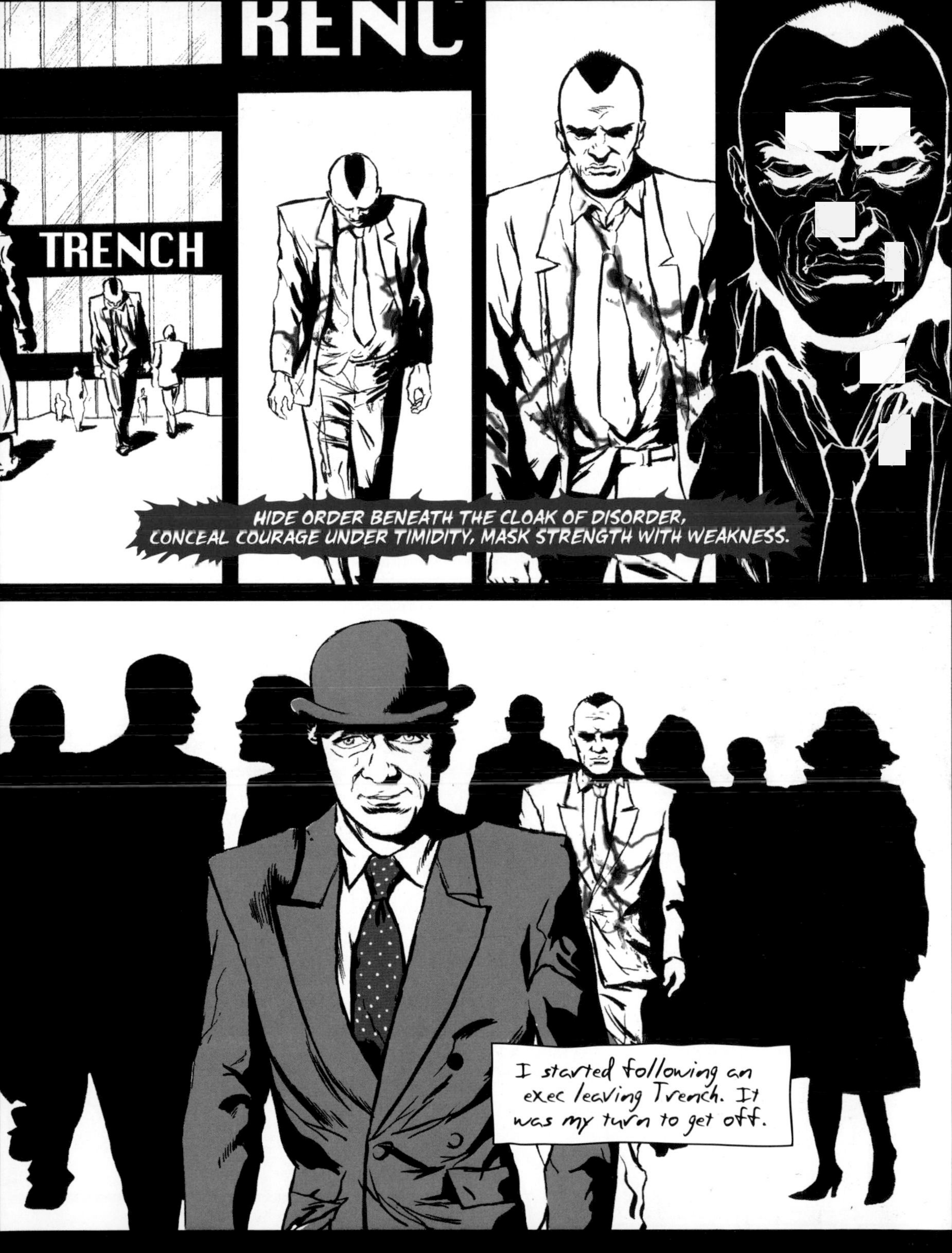
TRENCH
HIDE ORDER BENEATH THE CLOAK OF DISORDER, CONCEAL COURAGE UNDER TIMIDITY, MASK STRENGTH WITH WEAKNESS.
I started following an exec leaving Trench. It was my turn to get off.

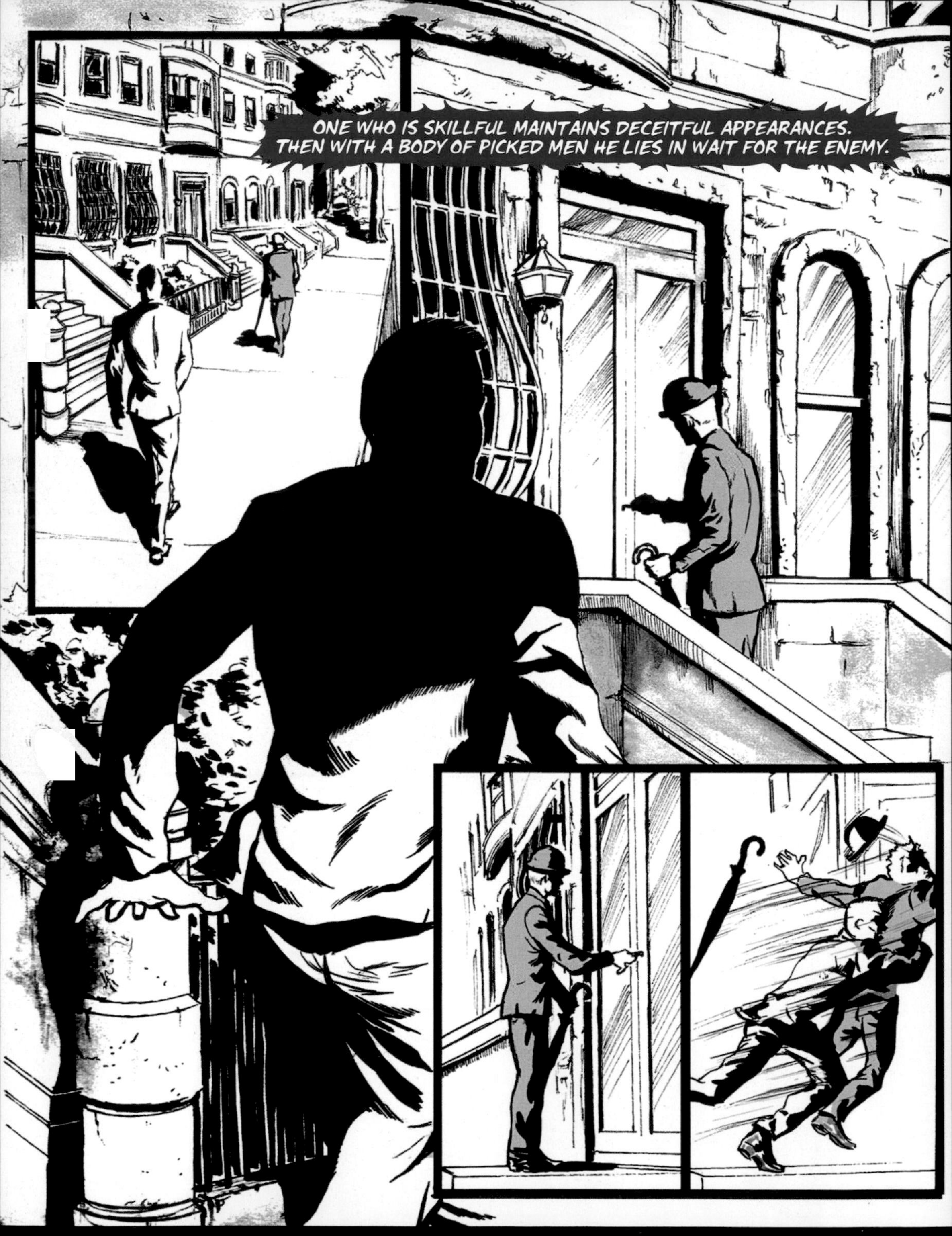
ONE WHO IS SKILLFUL MAINTAINS DECEITFUL APPEARANCES.
THEN WITH A BODY OF PICKED MEN HE LIES IN WAIT FOR THE ENEMY.

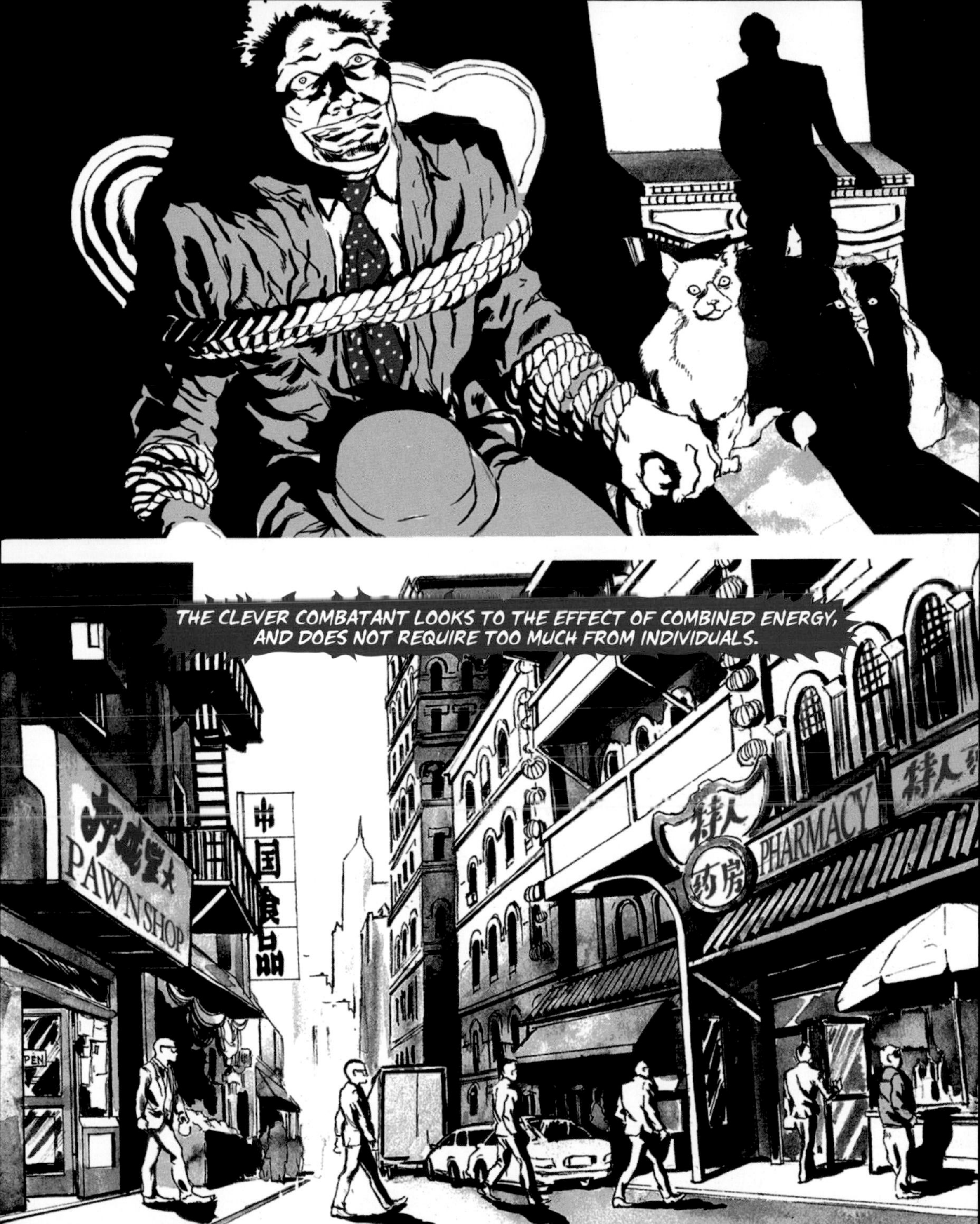
THE CLEVER COMBATANT LOOKS TO THE EFFECT OF COMBINED ENERGY, AND DOES NOT REQUIRE TOO MUCH FROM INDIVIDUALS.
PAWN SHOP
中国食品
药房
PHARMACY

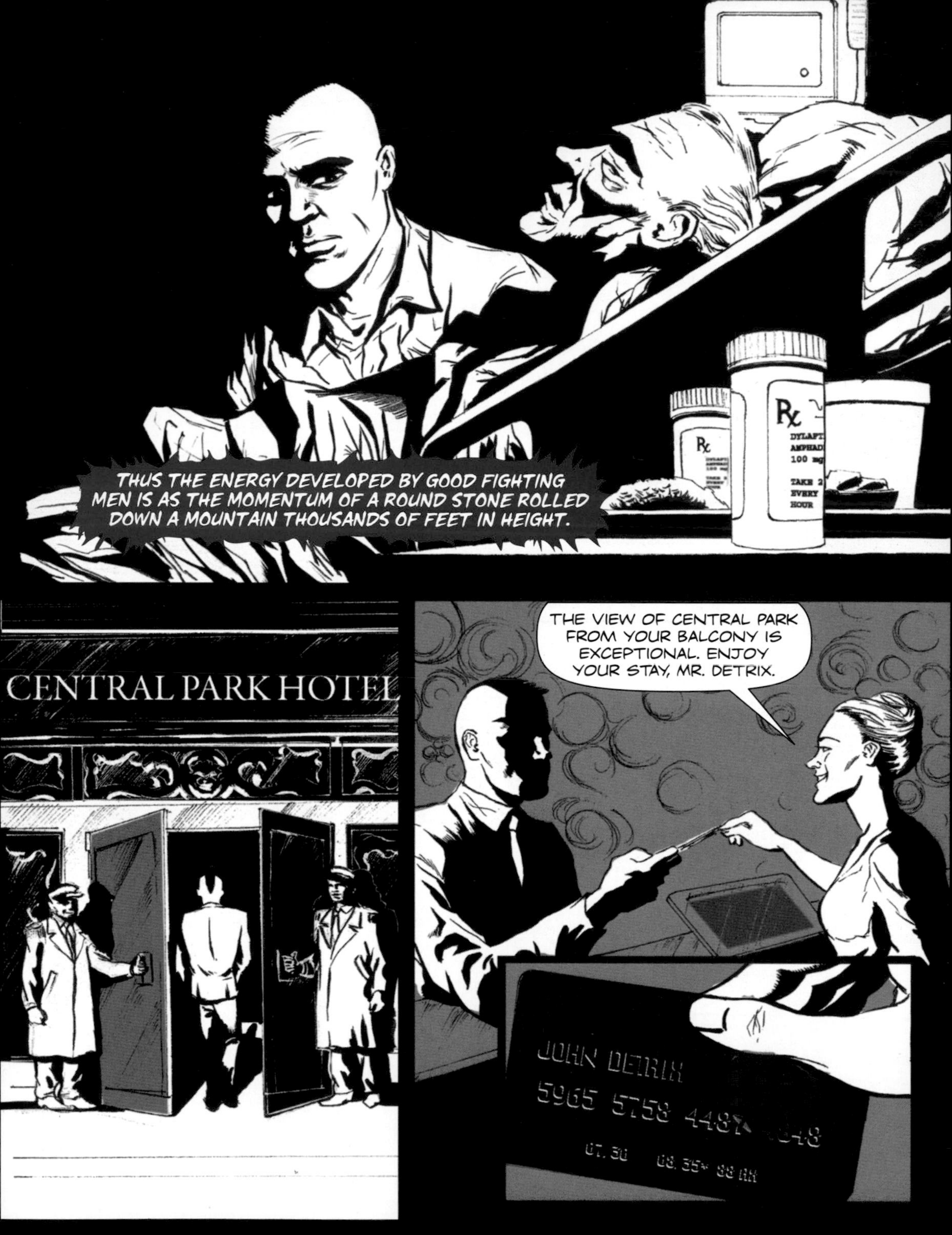
THUS THE ENERGY DEVELOPED BY GOOD FIGHTING MEN IS AS THE MOMENTUM OF A ROUND STONE ROLLED DOWN A MOUNTAIN THOUSANDS OF FEET IN HEIGHT.
CENTRAL PARK HOTEL
THE VIEW OF CENTRAL PARK FROM YOUR BALCONY IS EXCEPTIONAL. ENJOY YOUR STAY, MR. DETRIX.
JOHN DETRIX

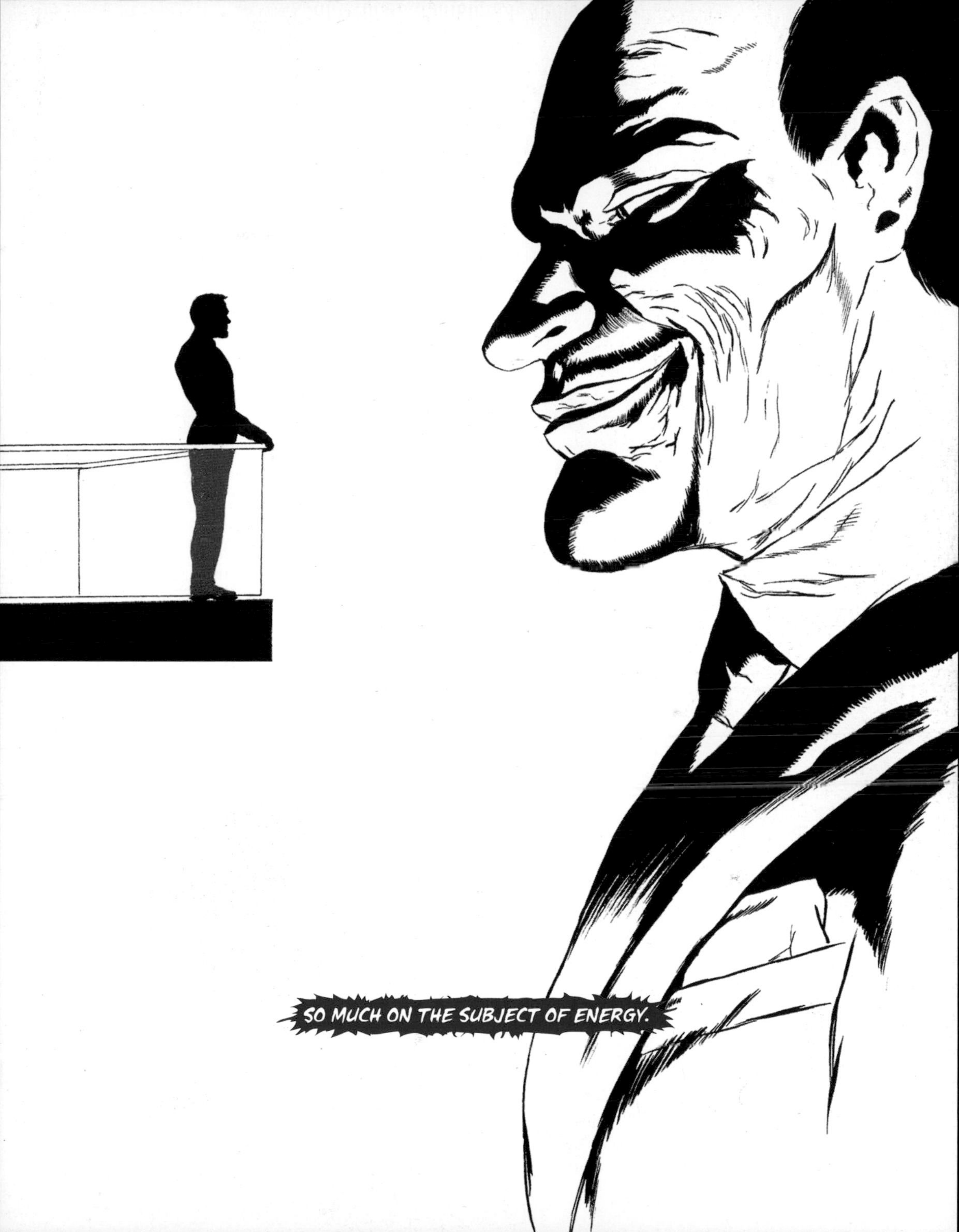
SO MUCH ON THE SUBJECT OF ENERGY.

虛實篇
VI.
WEAK POINTS AND STRONG

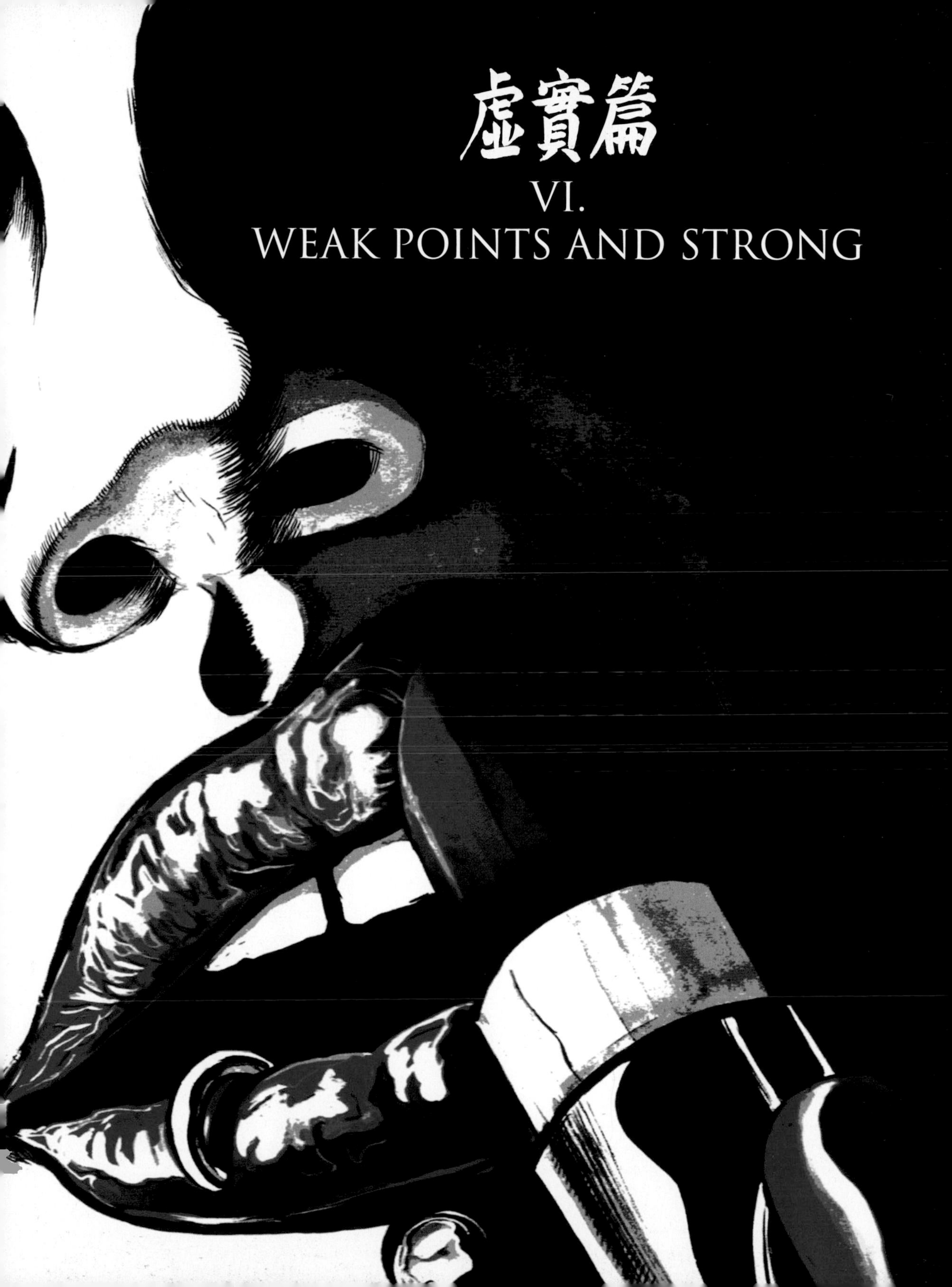

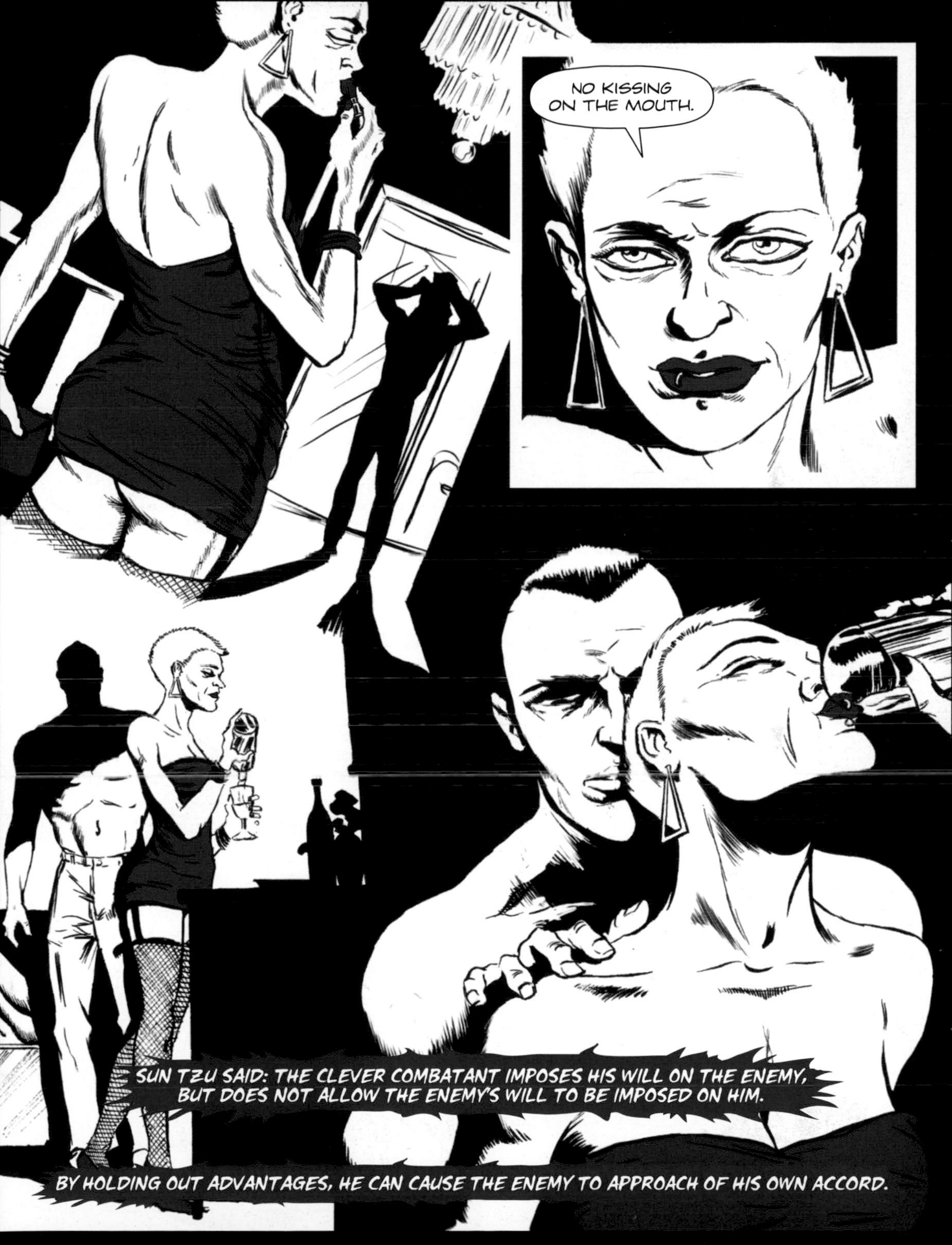
NO KISSING ON THE MOUTH.
SUN TZU SAID: THE CLEVER COMBATANT IMPOSES HIS WILL ON THE ENEMY, BUT DOES NOT ALLOW THE ENEMY'S WILL TO BE IMPOSED ON HIM.
BY HOLDING OUT ADVANTAGES, HE CAN CAUSE THE ENEMY TO APPROACH OF HIS OWN ACCORD.

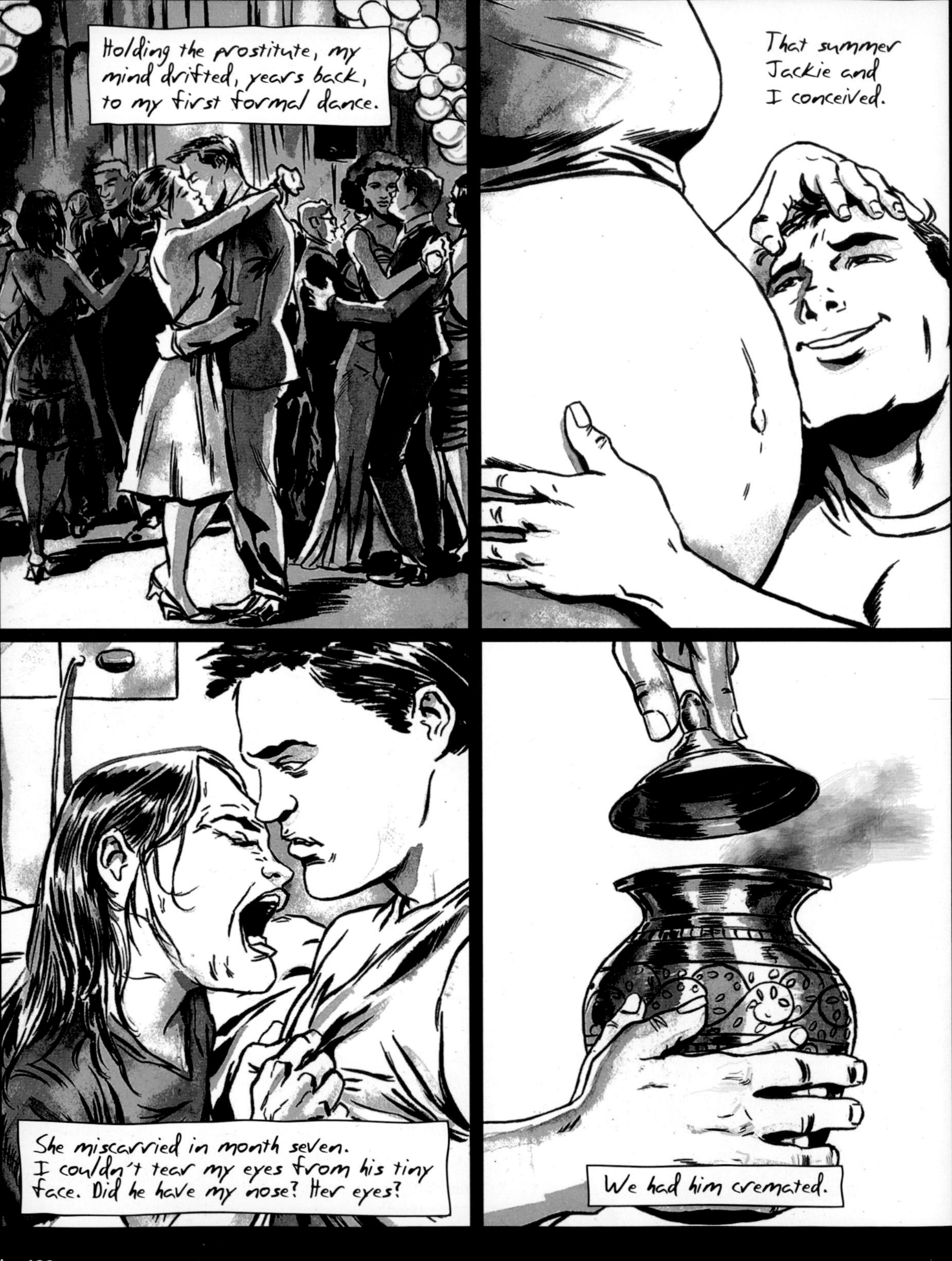
Holding the prostitute, my mind drifted, years back, to my first formal dance.
That summer Jackie and I conceived.
She miscarried in month seven. I couldn't tear my eyes from his tiny face. Did he have my nose? Her eyes?
We had him cremated.

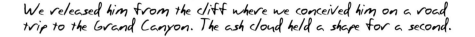

We released him from the cliff where we conceived him on a road trip to the Grand Canyon. The ash cloud held a shape for a second.

That was our boy up there.

We both needed to replace the pain with a mission. That night we decided to join the army.

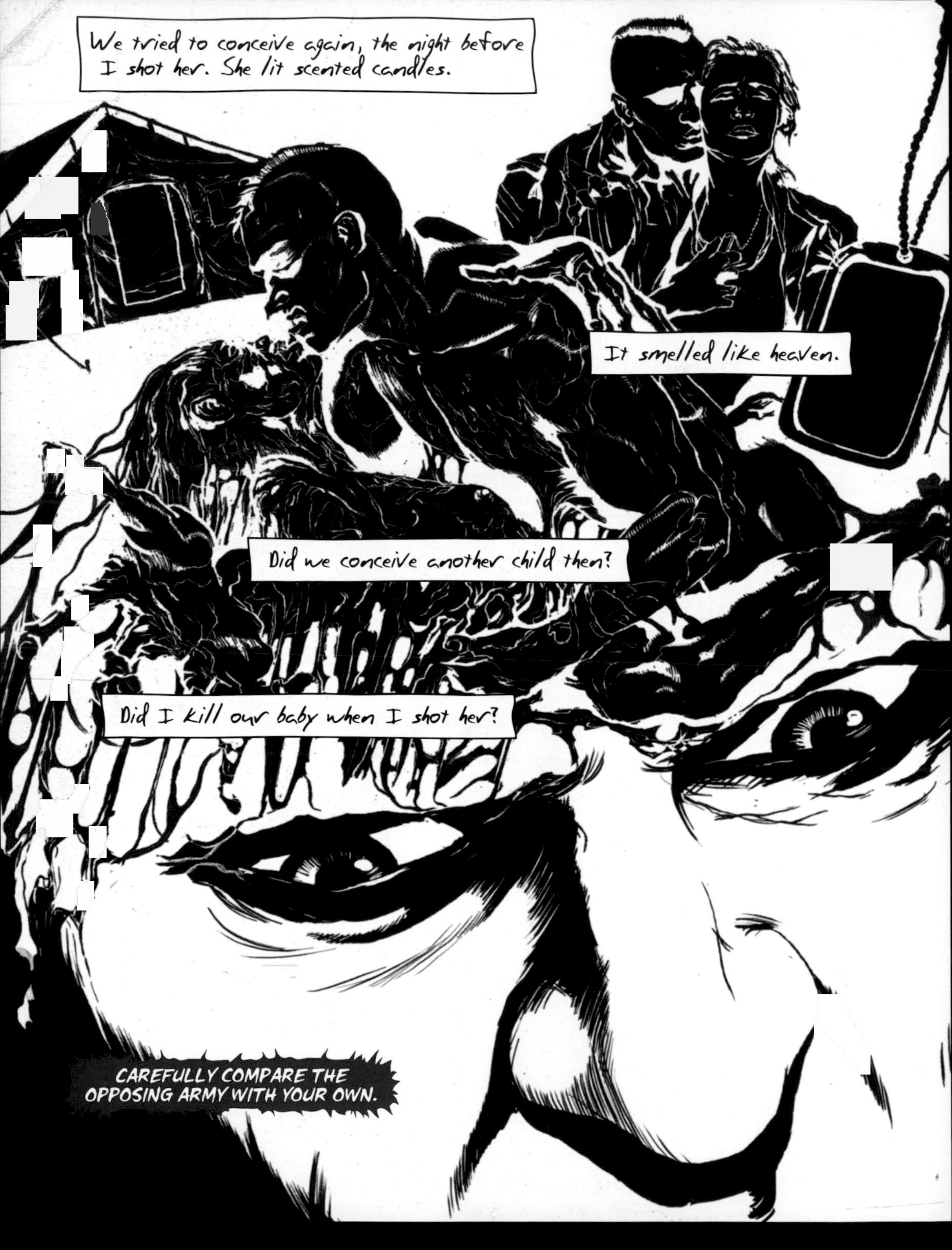

We tried to conceive again, the night before I shot her. She lit scented candles.
It smelled like heaven.
Did we conceive another child then?
Did I kill our baby when I shot her?
CAREFULLY COMPARE THE OPPOSING ARMY WITH YOUR OWN.

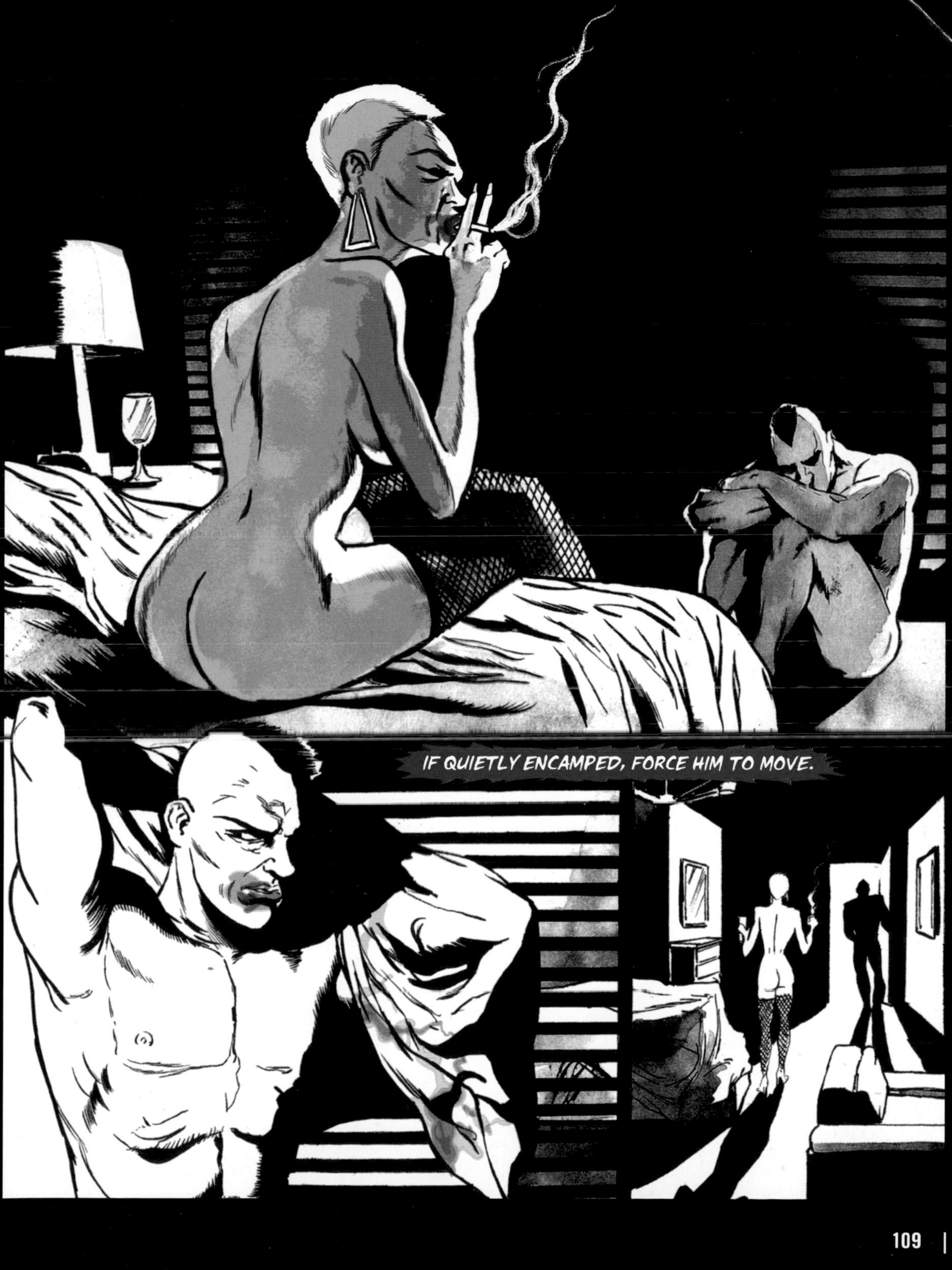
IF QUIETLY ENCAMPED, FORCE HIM TO MOVE.

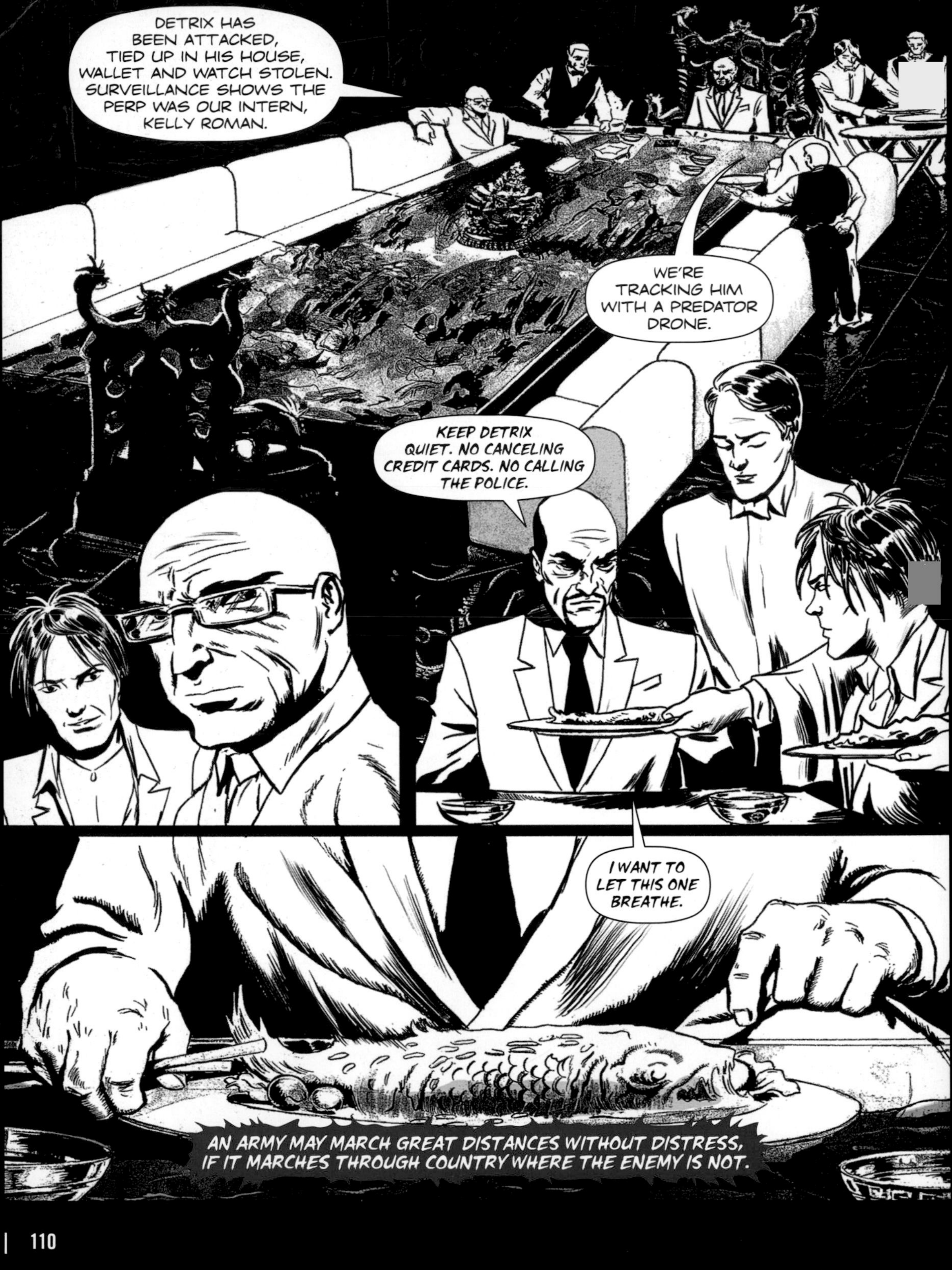
DETRIX HAS BEEN ATTACKED, TIED UP IN HIS HOUSE, WALLET AND WATCH STOLEN. SURVEILLANCE SHOWS THE PERP WAS OUR INTERN, KELLY ROMAN.
WE'RE TRACKING HIM WITH A PREDATOR DRONE.
KEEP DETRIX QUIET. NO CANCELING CREDIT CARDS. NO CALLING THE POLICE.
I WANT TO LET THIS ONE BREATHE.
AN ARMY MAY MARCH GREAT DISTANCES WITHOUT DISTRESS, IF IT MARCHES THROUGH COUNTRY WHERE THE ENEMY IS NOT.

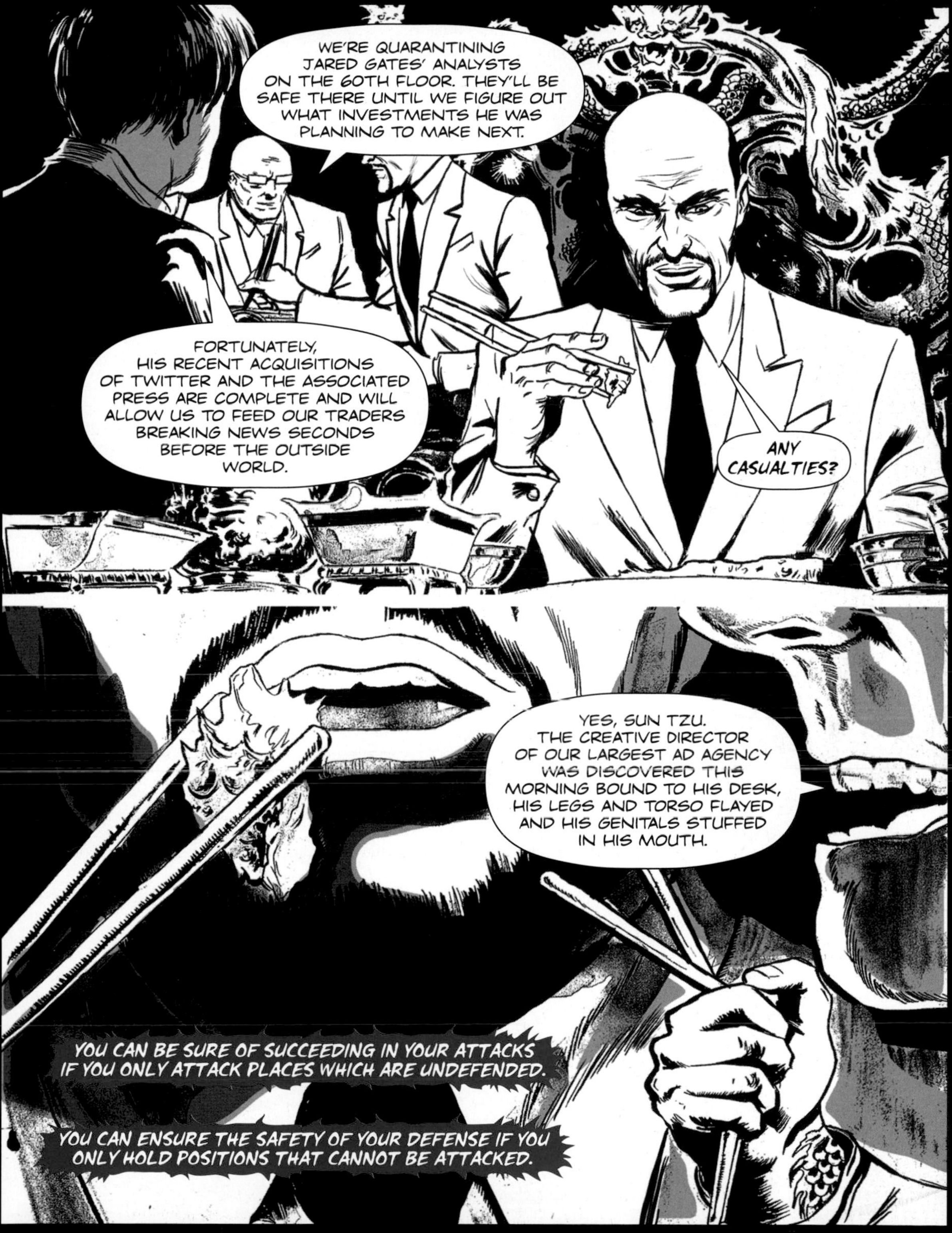
WE'RE QUARANTINING JARED GATES' ANALYSTS ON THE 60TH FLOOR. THEY'LL BE SAFE THERE UNTIL WE FIGURE OUT WHAT INVESTMENTS HE WAS PLANNING TO MAKE NEXT.
FORTUNATELY, HIS RECENT ACQUISITIONS OF TWITTER AND THE ASSOCIATED PRESS ARE COMPLETE AND WILL ALLOW US TO FEED OUR TRADERS BREAKING NEWS SECONDS BEFORE THE OUTSIDE WORLD.
ANY CASUALTIES?
YES, SUN TZU. THE CREATIVE DIRECTOR OF OUR LARGEST AD AGENCY WAS DISCOVERED THIS MORNING BOUND TO HIS DESK, HIS LEGS AND TORSO FLAYED AND HIS GENITALS STUFFED IN HIS MOUTH.
YOU CAN BE SURE OF SUCCEEDING IN YOUR ATTACKS IF YOU ONLY ATTACK PLACES WHICH ARE UNDEFENDED.
YOU CAN ENSURE THE SAFETY OF YOUR DEFENSE IF YOU ONLY HOLD POSITIONS THAT CANNOT BE ATTACKED.

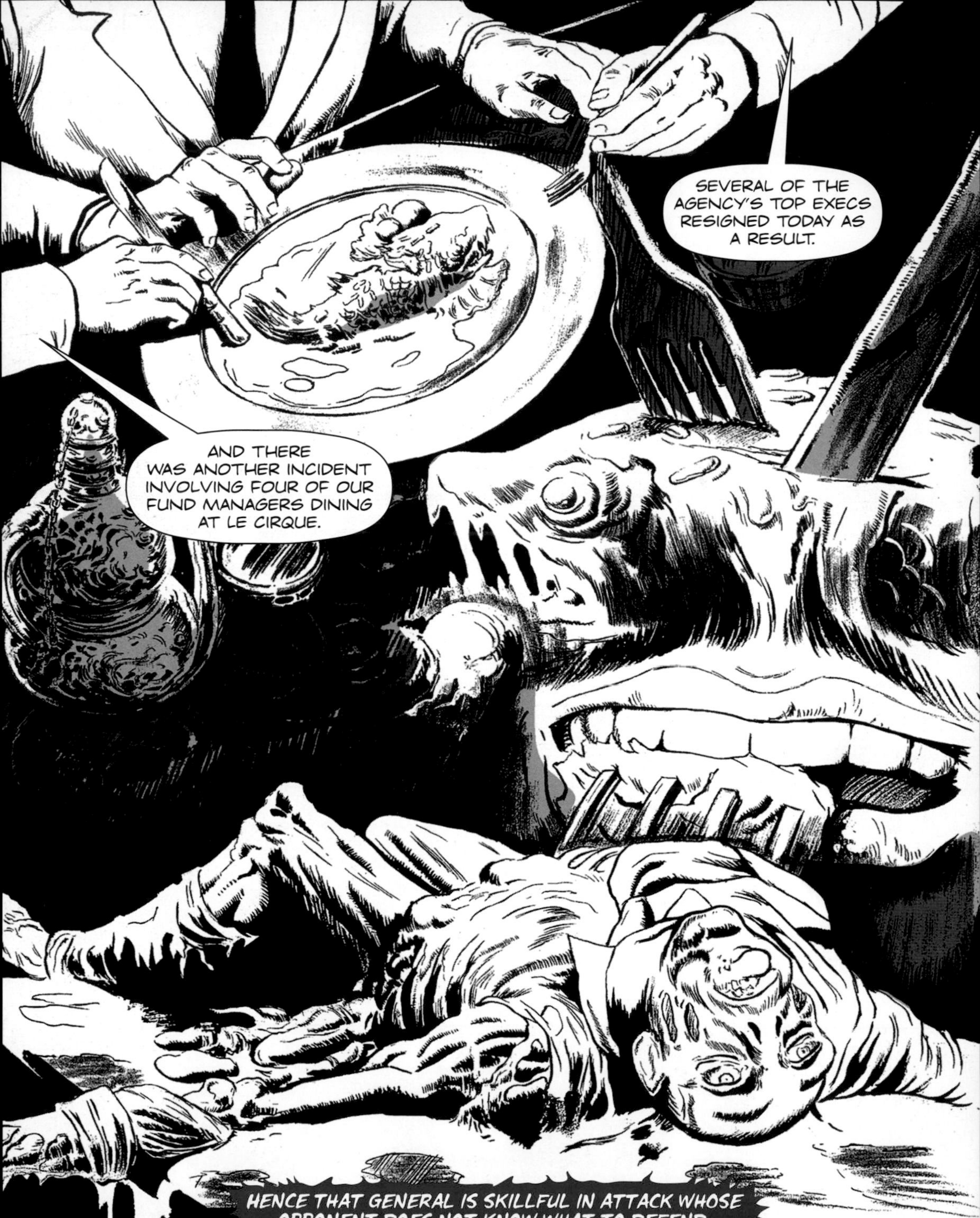
SEVERAL OF THE AGENCY'S TOP EXECS RESIGNED TODAY AS A RESULT.
AND THERE WAS ANOTHER INCIDENT INVOLVING FOUR OF OUR FUND MANAGERS DINING AT LE CIRQUE.
HENCE THAT GENERAL IS SKILLFUL IN ATTACK WHOSE OPPONENT DOES NOT KNOW WHAT TO DEFEND.

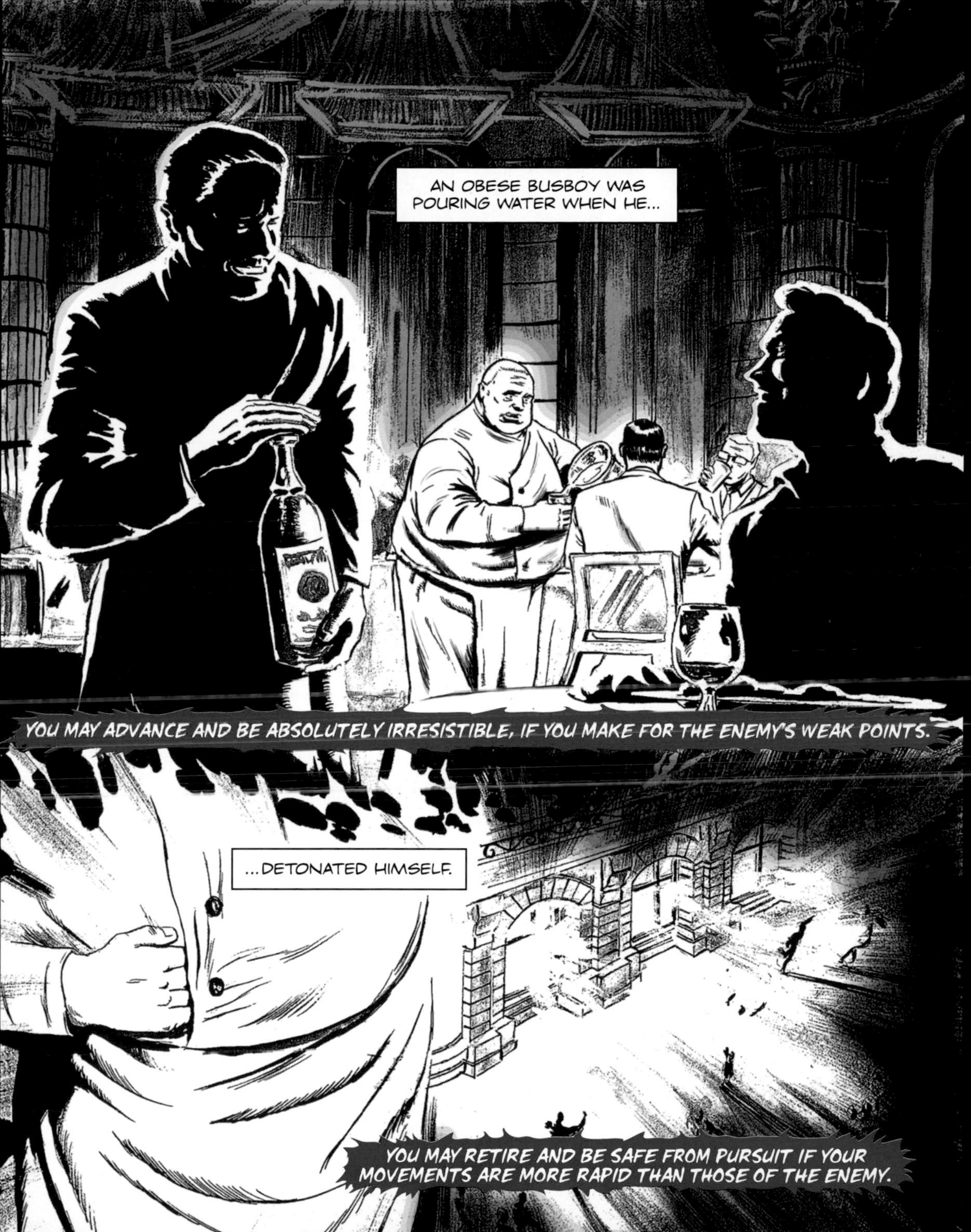
AN OBESE BUSBOY WAS POURING WATER WHEN HE...
YOU MAY ADVANCE AND BE ABSOLUTELY IRRESISTIBLE, IF YOU MAKE FOR THE ENEMY'S WEAK POINTS.
...DETONATED HIMSELF.
YOU MAY RETIRE AND BE SAFE FROM PURSUIT IF YOUR MOVEMENTS ARE MORE RAPID THAN THOSE OF THE ENEMY.

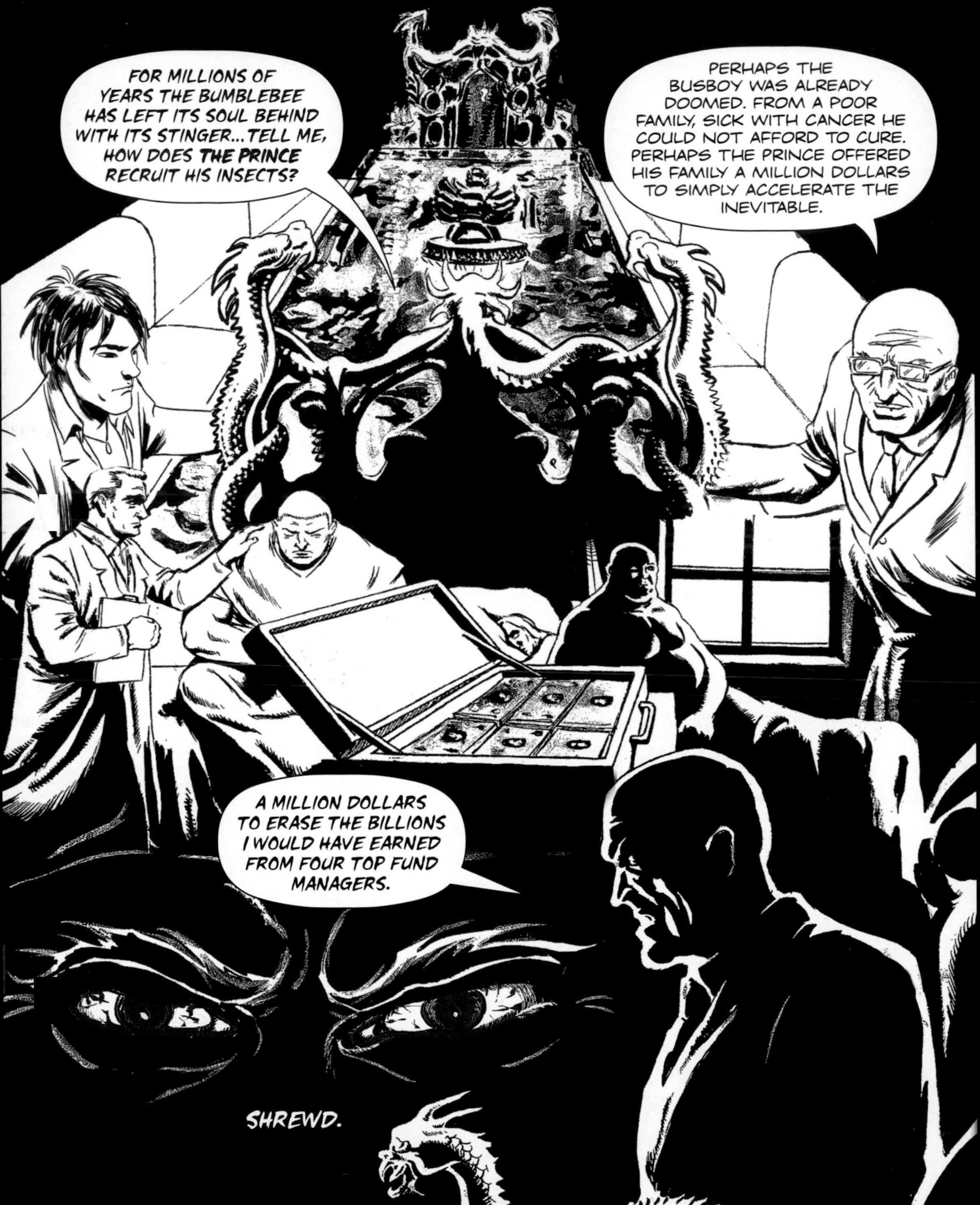
FOR MILLIONS OF YEARS THE BUMBLEBEE HAS LEFT ITS SOUL BEHIND WITH ITS STINGER...TELL ME, HOW DOES **THE PRINCE** RECRUIT HIS INSECTS?
PERHAPS THE BUSBOY WAS ALREADY DOOMED. FROM A POOR FAMILY, SICK WITH CANCER HE COULD NOT AFFORD TO CURE. PERHAPS THE PRINCE OFFERED HIS FAMILY A MILLION DOLLARS TO SIMPLY ACCELERATE THE INEVITABLE.
A MILLION DOLLARS TO ERASE THE BILLIONS I WOULD HAVE EARNED FROM FOUR TOP FUND MANAGERS.
SHREWD.

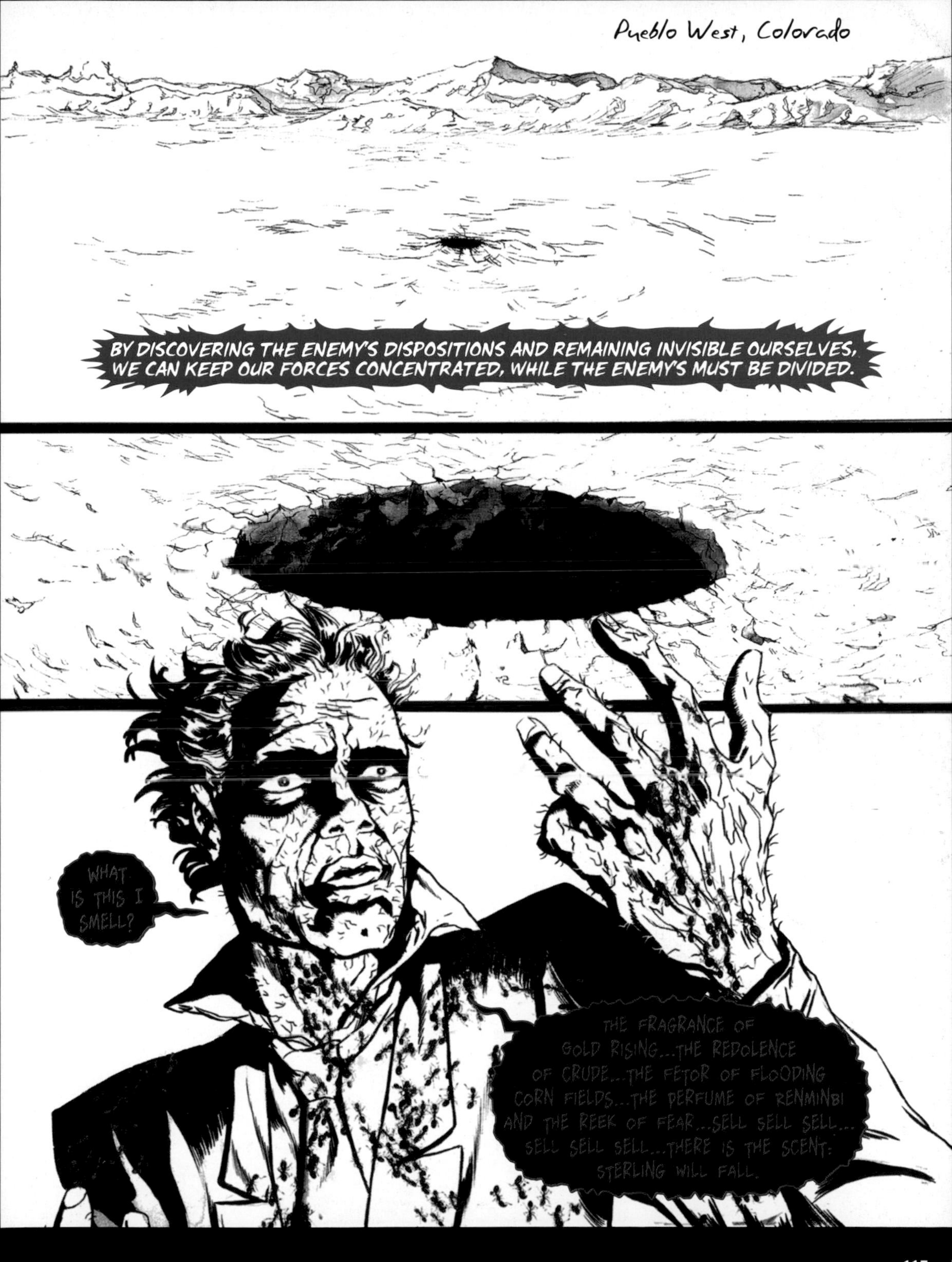
Pueblo West, Colorado
BY DISCOVERING THE ENEMY'S DISPOSITIONS AND REMAINING INVISIBLE OURSELVES, WE CAN KEEP OUR FORCES CONCENTRATED, WHILE THE ENEMY'S MUST BE DIVIDED.
WHAT IS THIS I SMELL?
THE FRAGRANCE OF GOLD RISING...THE REDOLENCE OF CRUDE...THE FETOR OF FLOODING CORN FIELDS...THE PERFUME OF RENMINBI AND THE REEK OF FEAR...SELL SELL SELL...SELL SELL SELL...THERE IS THE SCENT: STERLING WILL FALL.

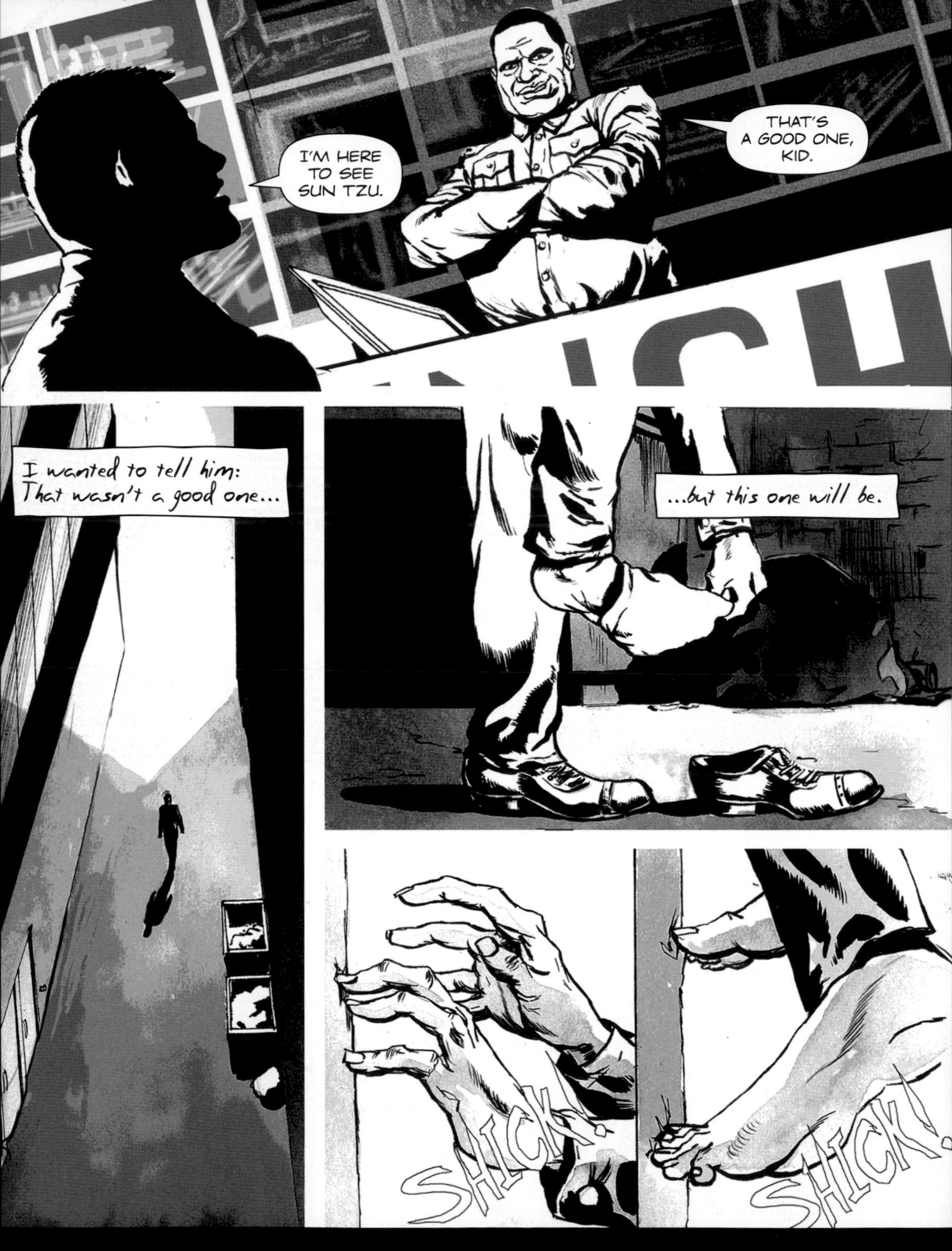
I'M HERE TO SEE SUN TZU.
THAT'S A GOOD ONE, KID.
I wanted to tell him: That wasn't a good one...
...but this one will be.
SHICK
SHICK!

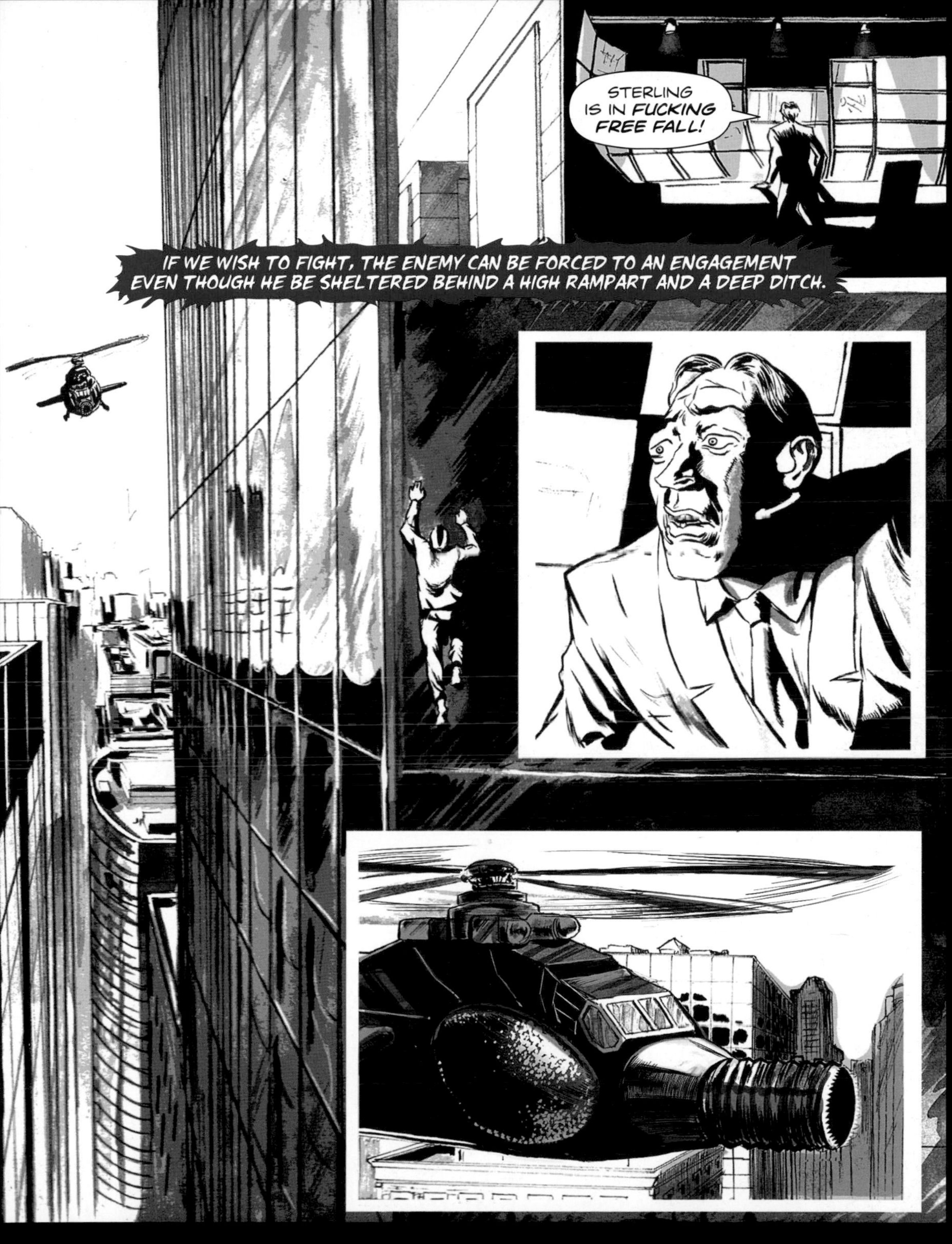
STERLING IS IN FUCKING FREE FALL!
IF WE WISH TO FIGHT, THE ENEMY CAN BE FORCED TO AN ENGAGEMENT EVEN THOUGH HE BE SHELTERED BEHIND A HIGH RAMPART AND A DEEP DITCH.

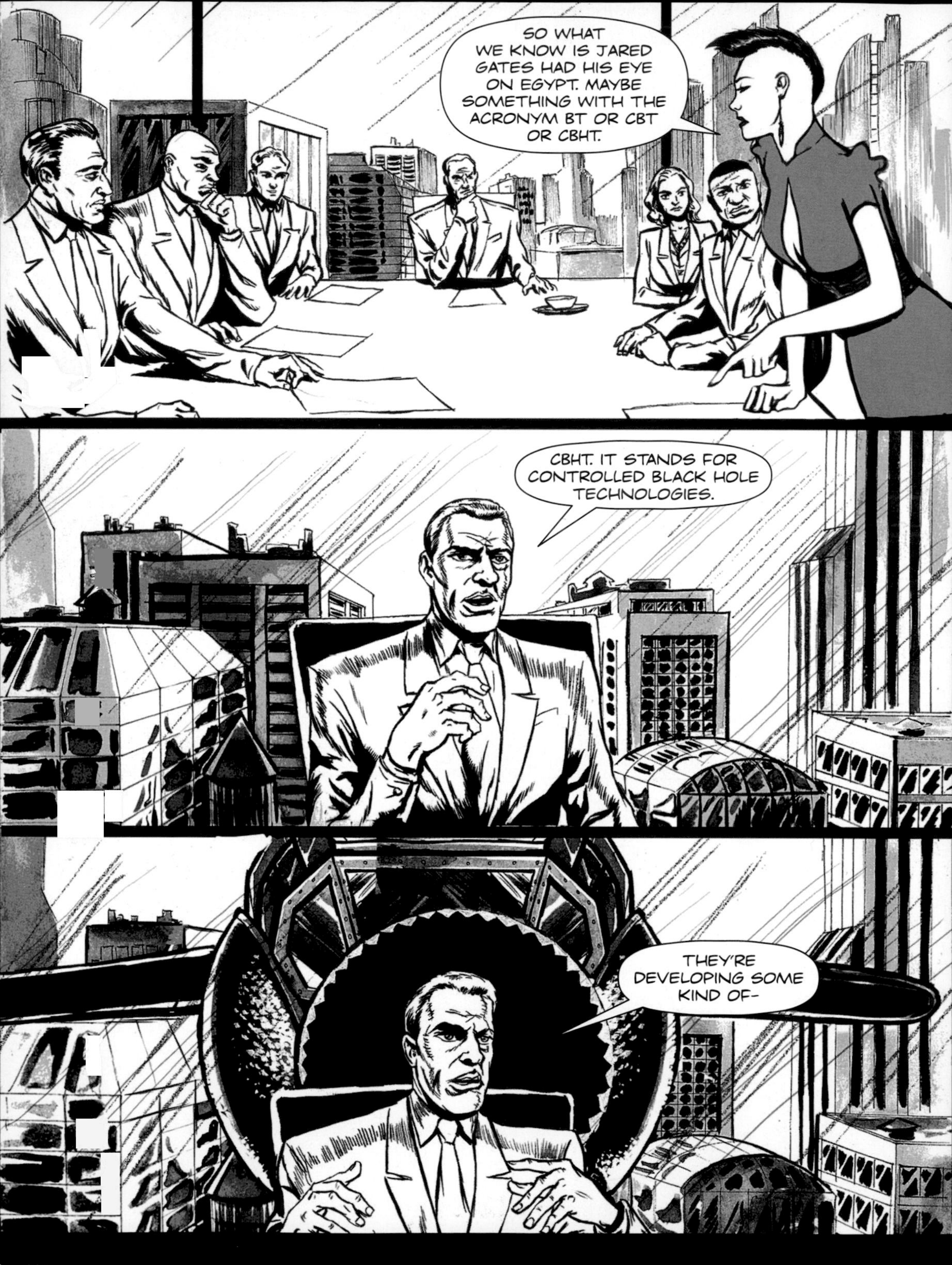
SO WHAT WE KNOW IS JARED GATES HAD HIS EYE ON EGYPT. MAYBE SOMETHING WITH THE ACRONYM BT OR CBT OR CBHT.
CBHT. IT STANDS FOR CONTROLLED BLACK HOLE TECHNOLOGIES.
THEY'RE DEVELOPING SOME KIND OF-

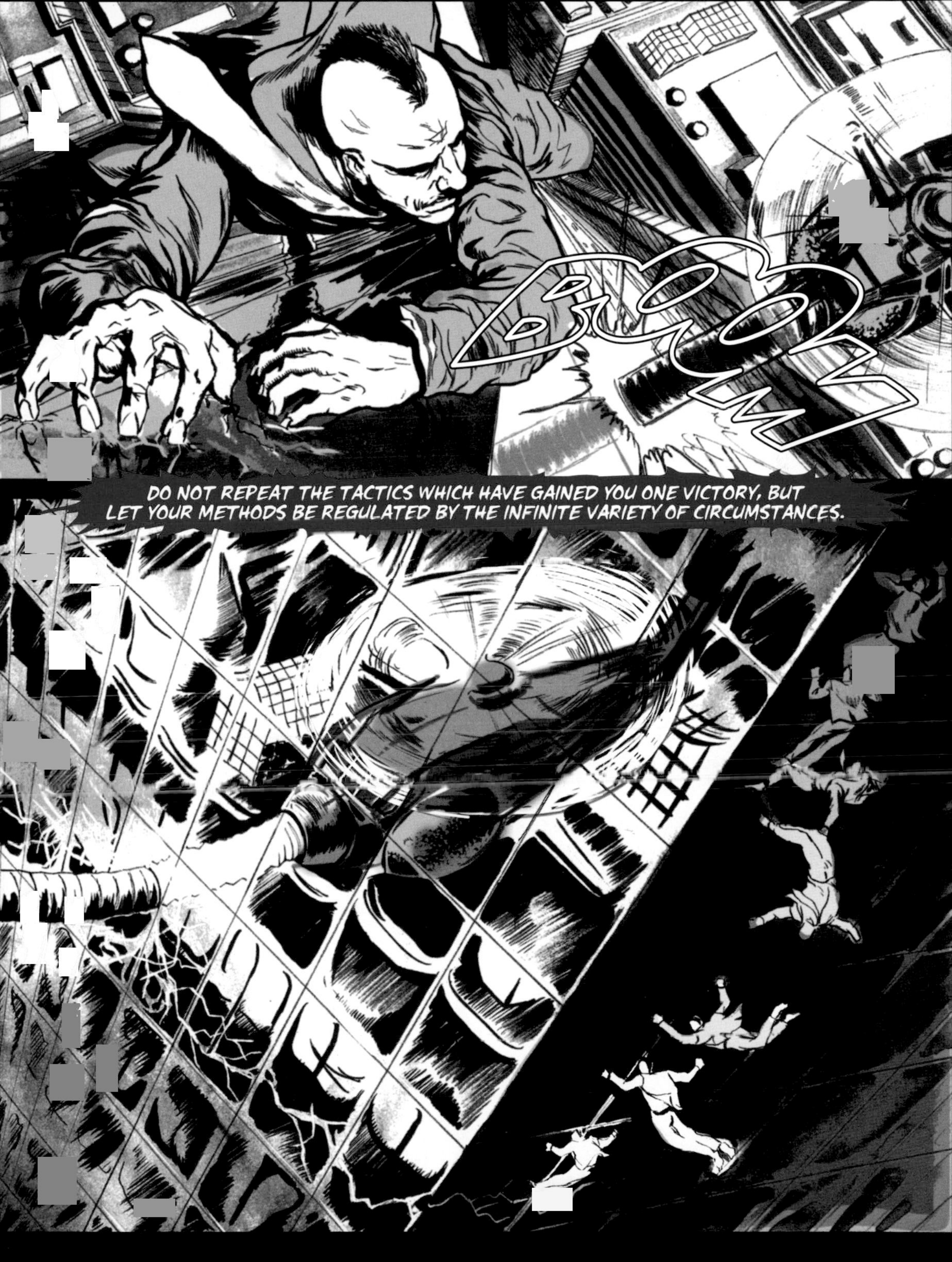
DO NOT REPEAT THE TACTICS WHICH HAVE GAINED YOU ONE VICTORY, BUT LET YOUR METHODS BE REGULATED BY THE INFINITE VARIETY OF CIRCUMSTANCES.

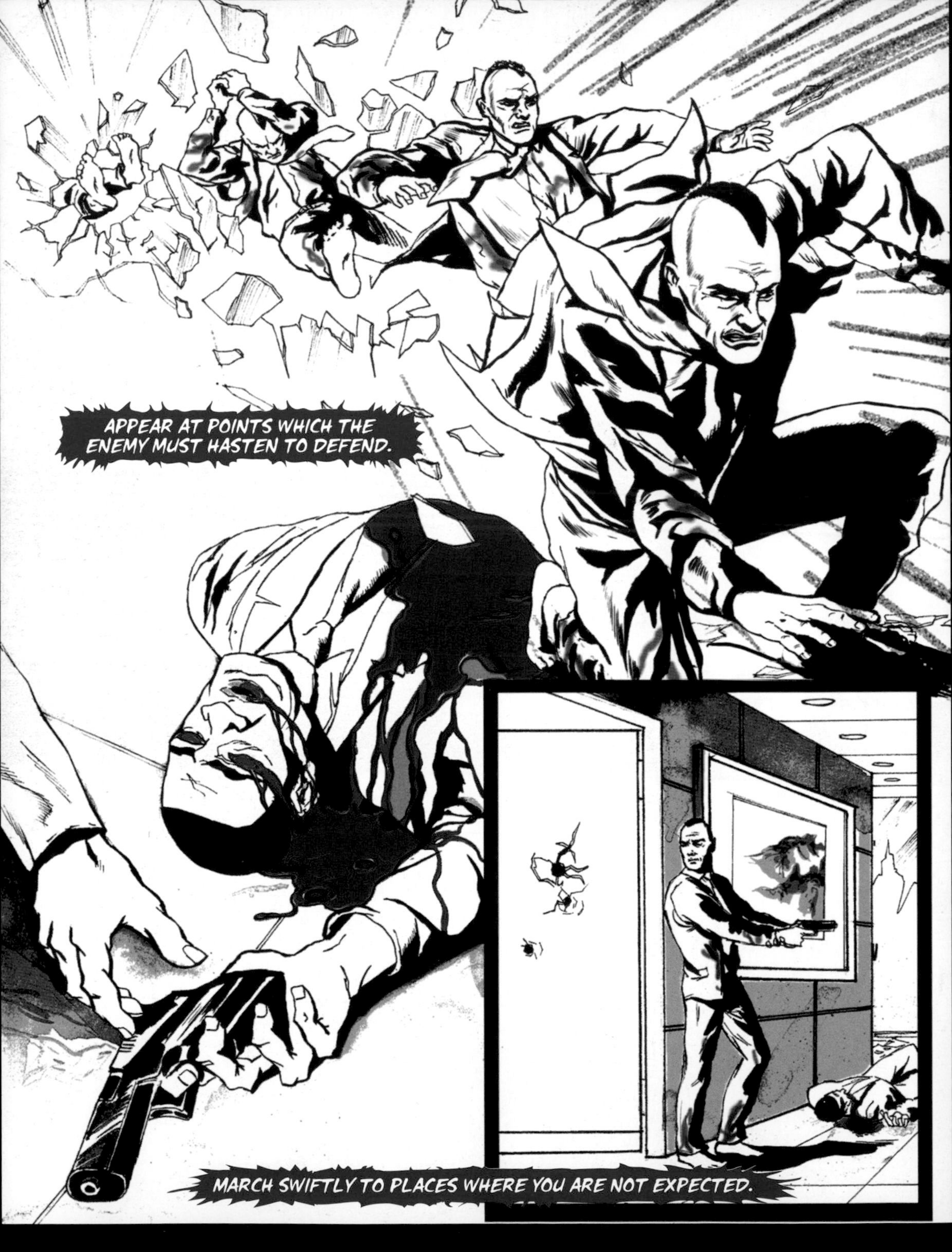
APPEAR AT POINTS WHICH THE ENEMY MUST HASTEN TO DEFEND.
MARCH SWIFTLY TO PLACES WHERE YOU ARE NOT EXPECTED.

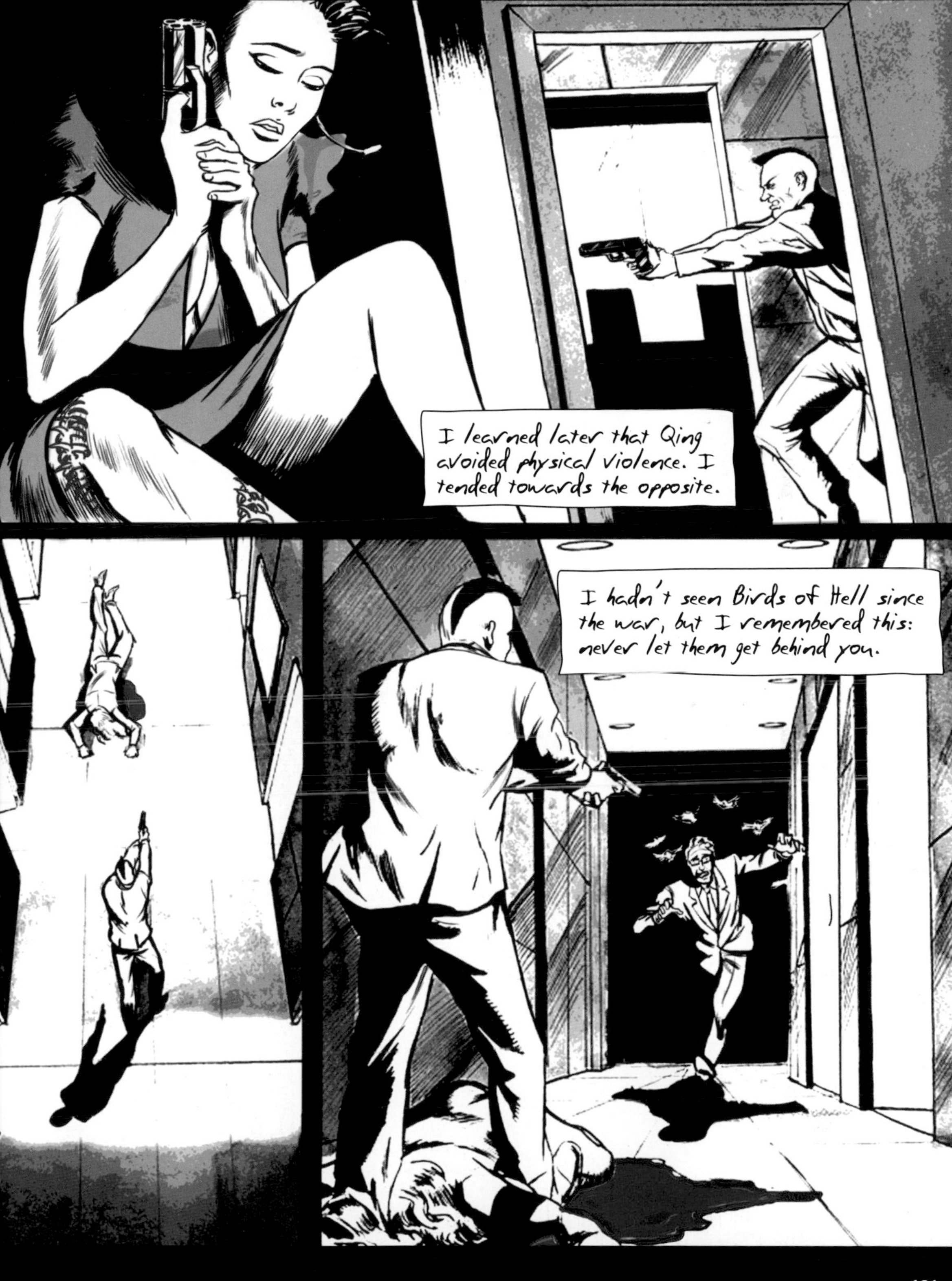
I learned later that Qing avoided physical violence. I tended towards the opposite.
I hadn't seen Birds of Hell since the war, but I remembered this: never let them get behind you.

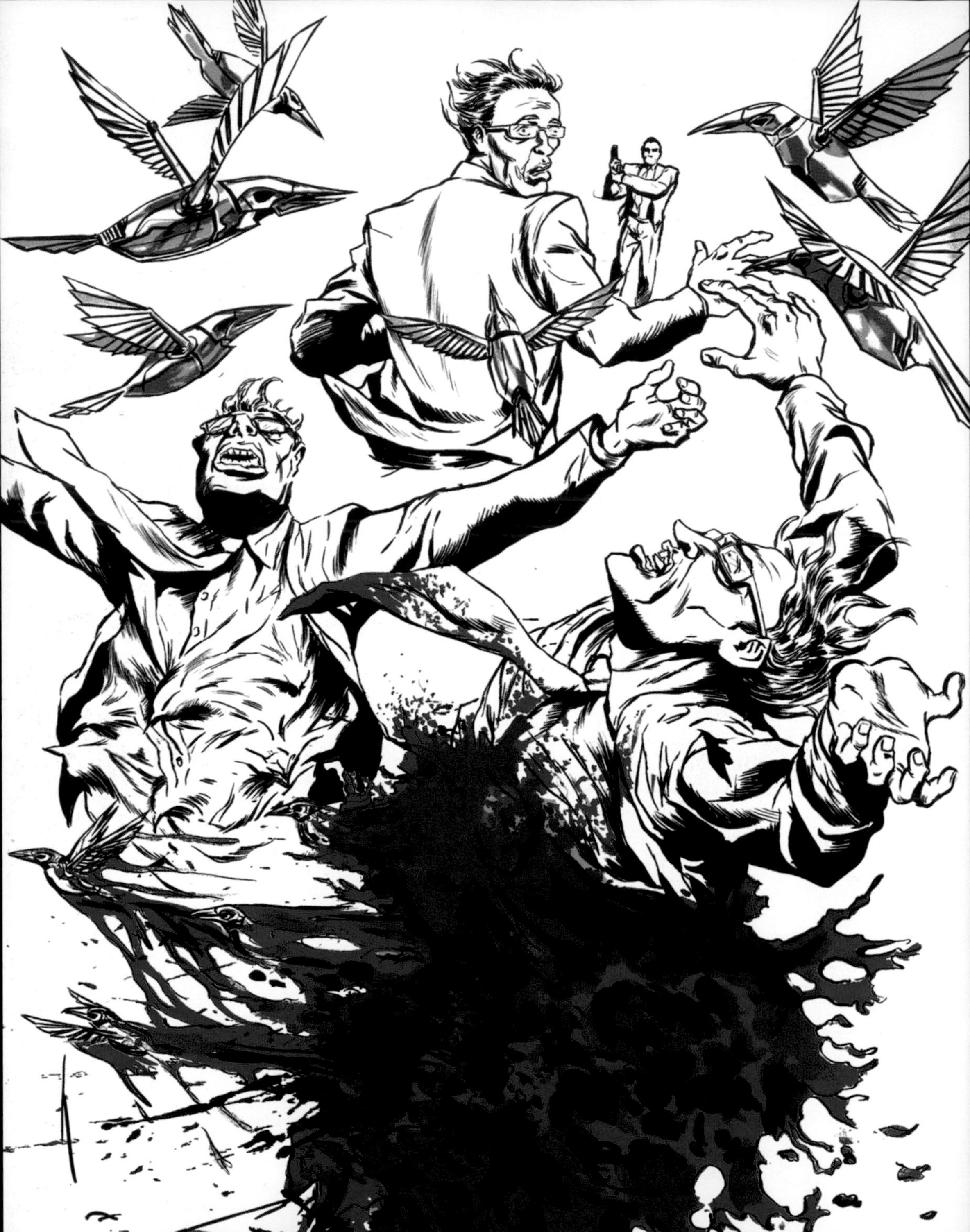

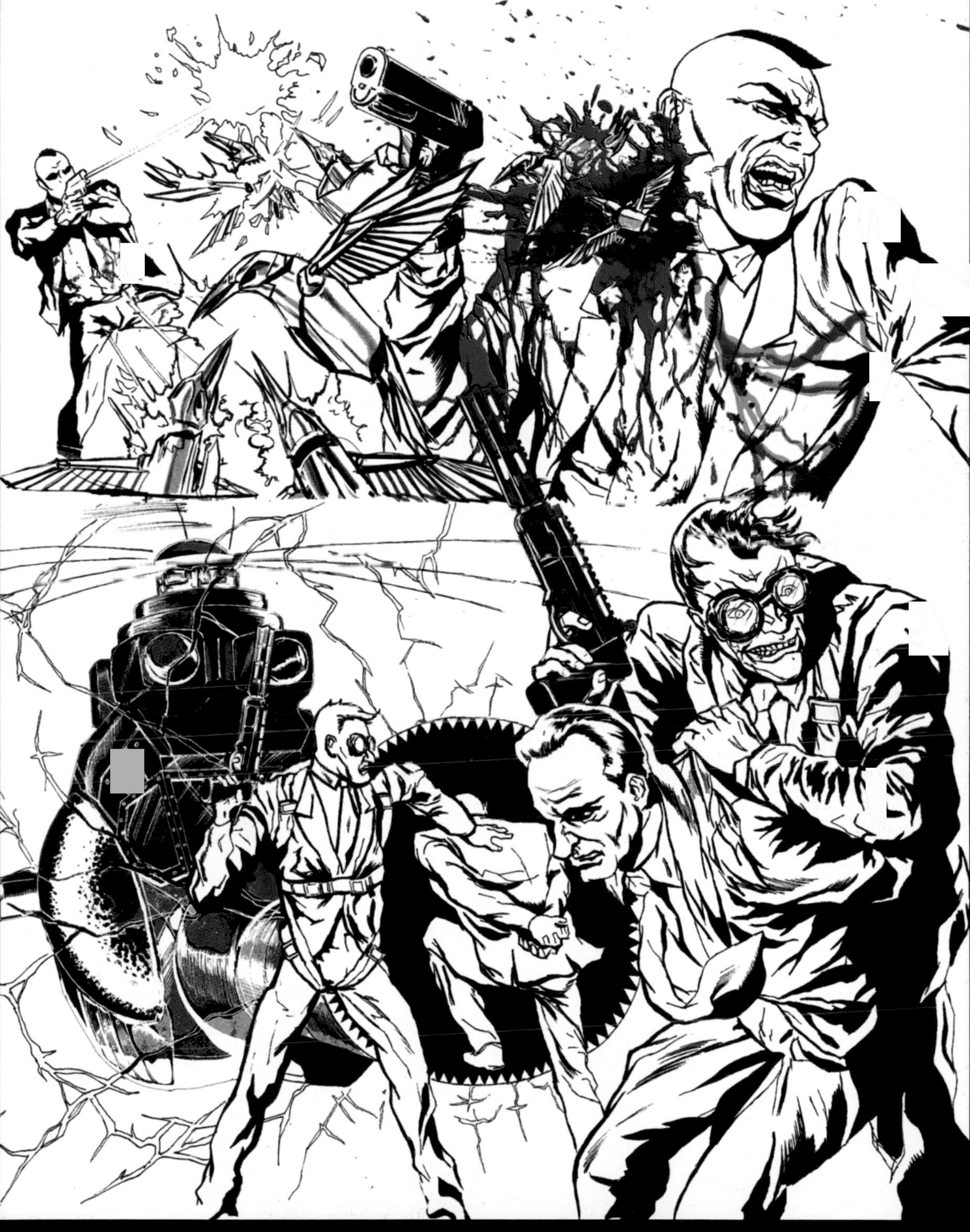

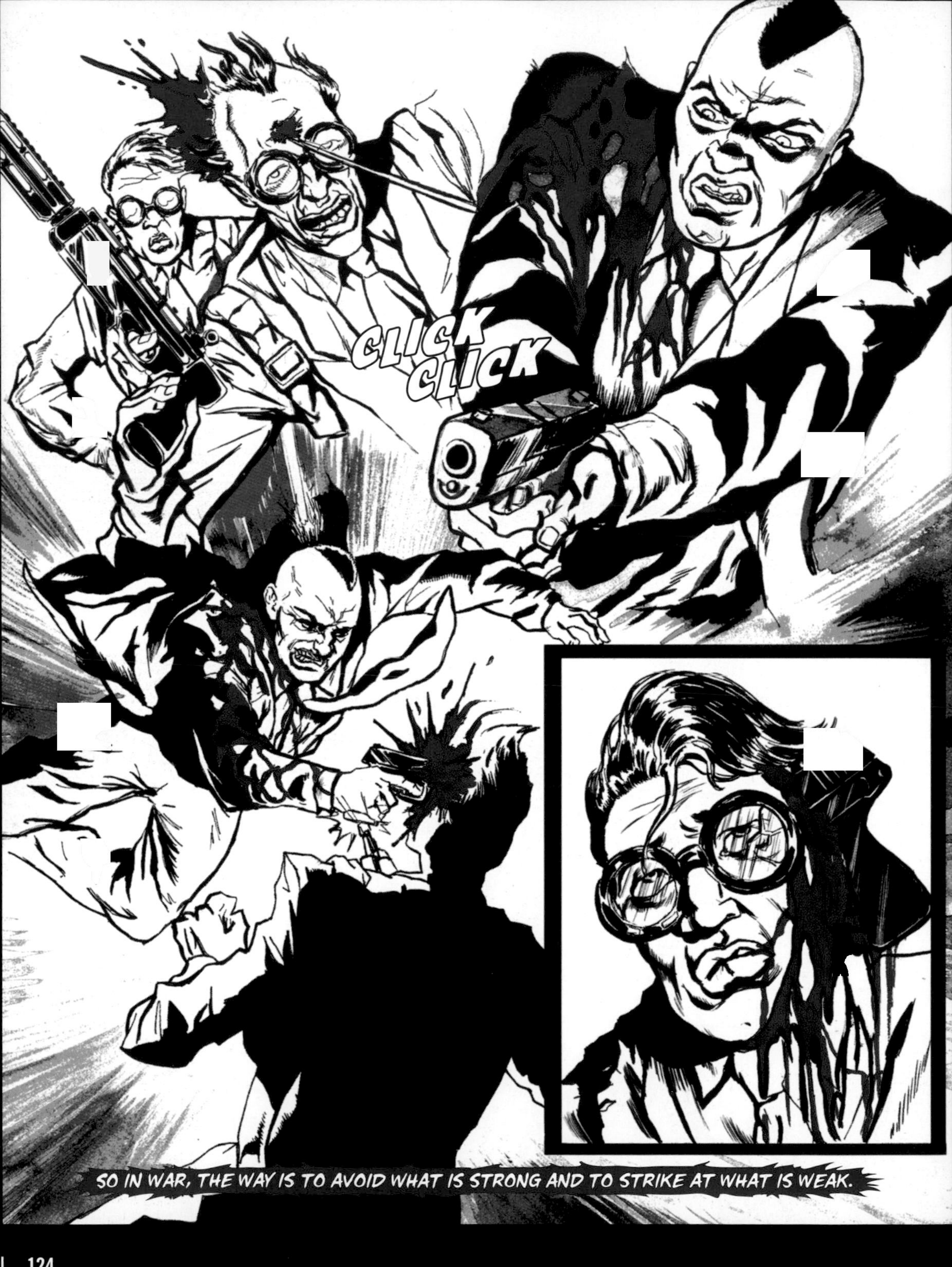
CLICK
CLICK
SO IN WAR, THE WAY IS TO AVOID WHAT IS STRONG AND TO STRIKE AT WHAT IS WEAK.

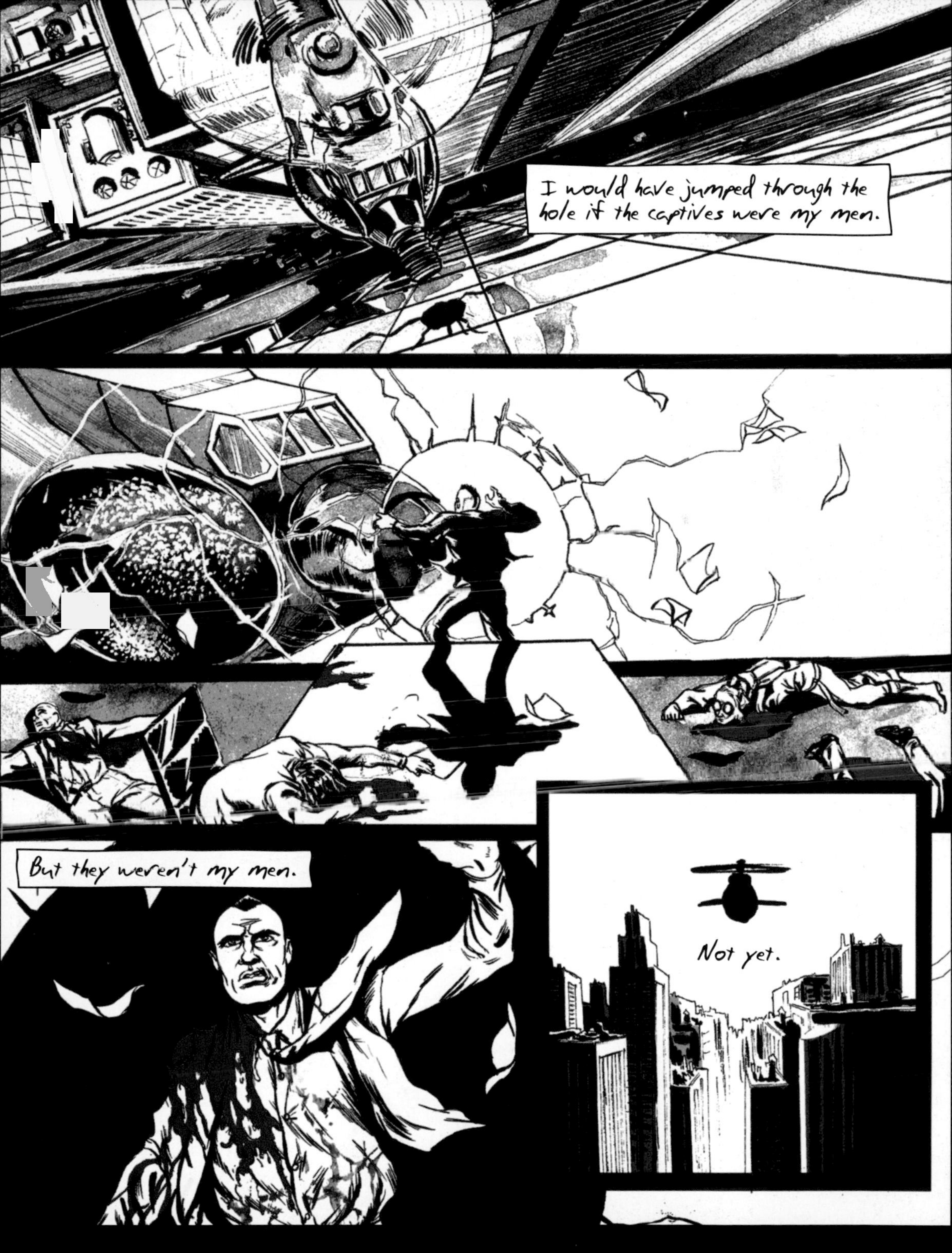
I would have jumped through the hole if the captives were my men.
But they weren't my men.
Not yet.

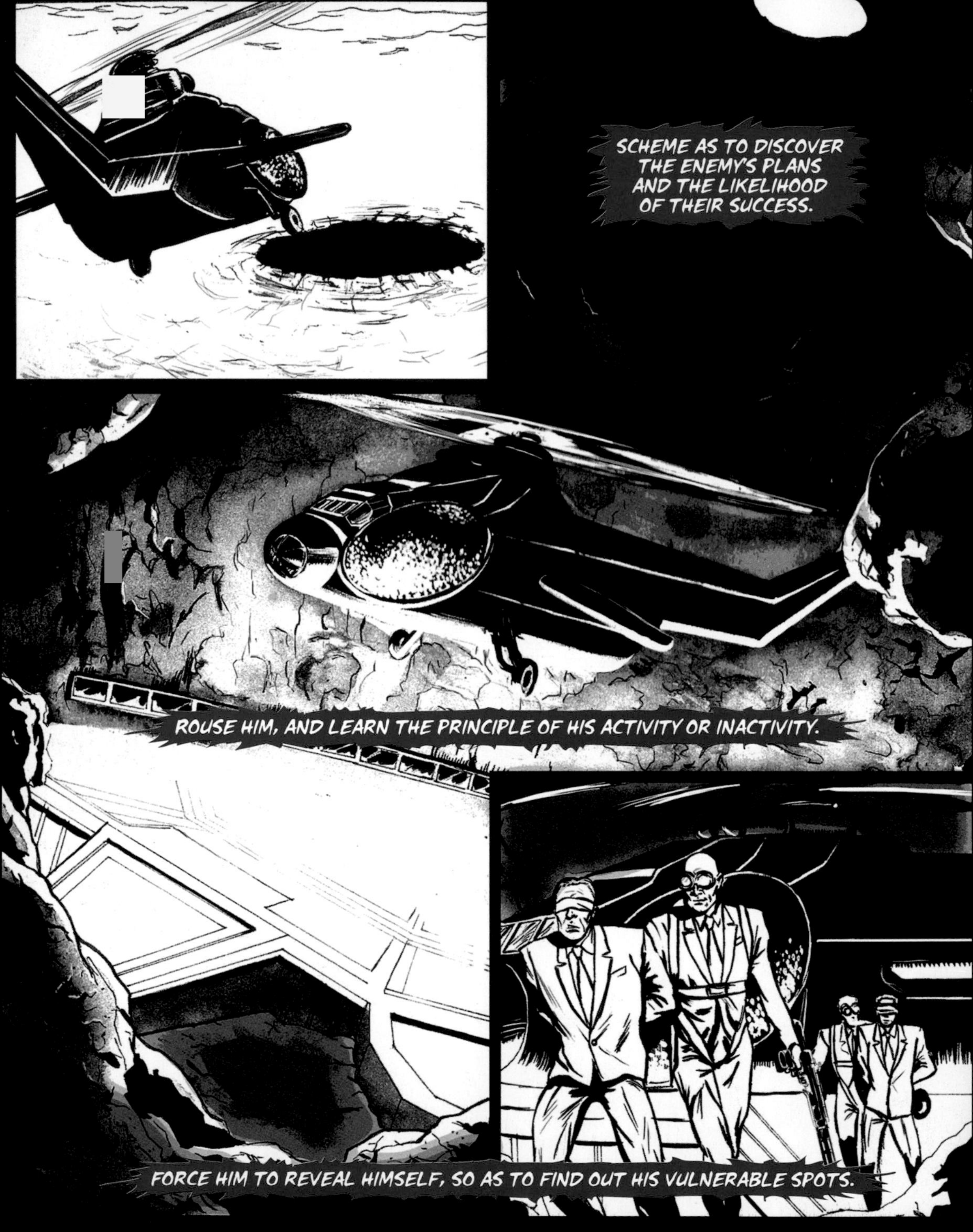
SCHEME AS TO DISCOVER THE ENEMY'S PLANS AND THE LIKELIHOOD OF THEIR SUCCESS.
ROUSE HIM, AND LEARN THE PRINCIPLE OF HIS ACTIVITY OR INACTIVITY.
FORCE HIM TO REVEAL HIMSELF, SO AS TO FIND OUT HIS VULNERABLE SPOTS.

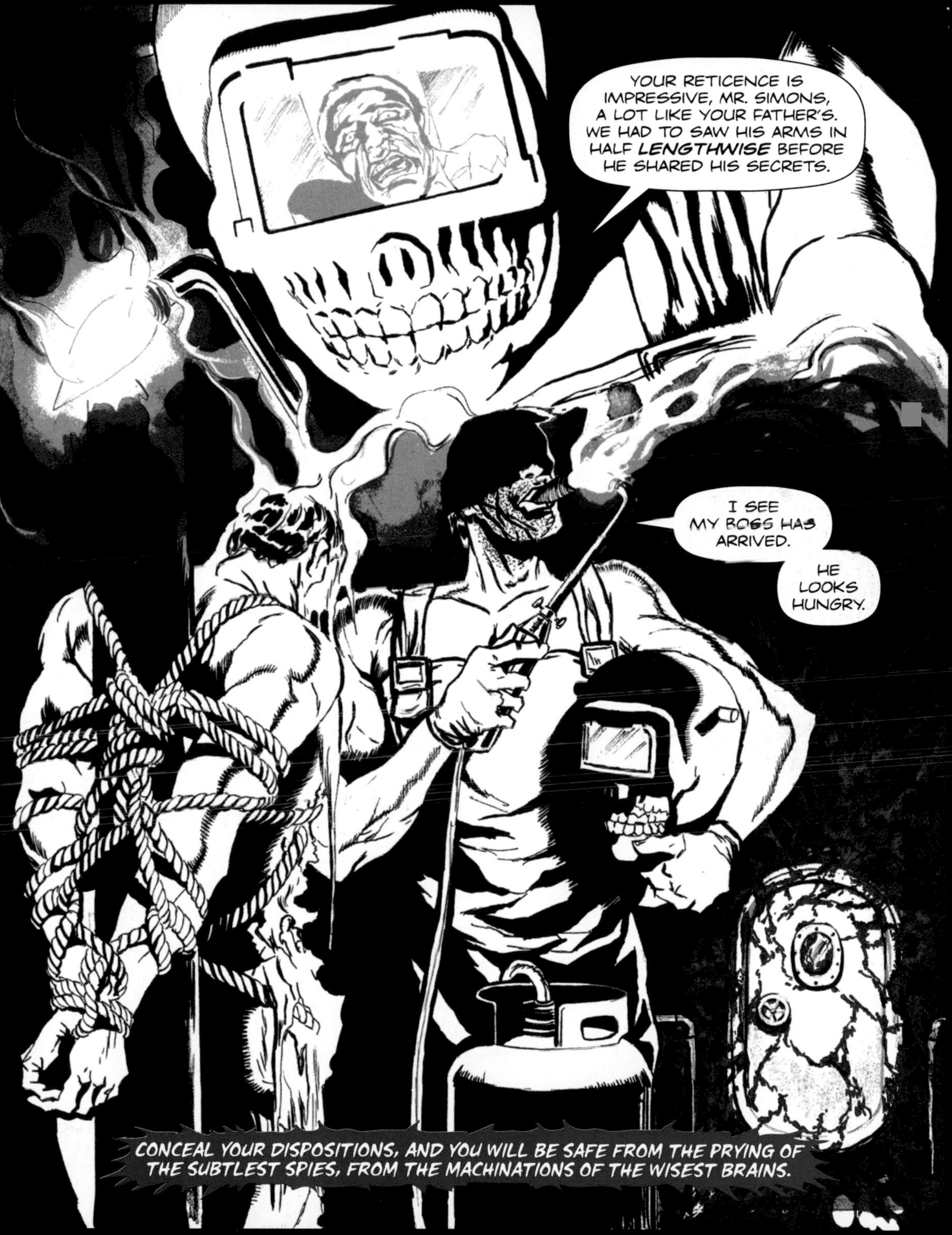
YOUR RETICENCE IS IMPRESSIVE, MR. SIMONS, A LOT LIKE YOUR FATHER'S. WE HAD TO SAW HIS ARMS IN HALF *LENGTHWISE* BEFORE HE SHARED HIS SECRETS.
I SEE MY BOSS HAS ARRIVED.
HE LOOKS HUNGRY.
CONCEAL YOUR DISPOSITIONS, AND YOU WILL BE SAFE FROM THE PRYING OF THE SUBTLEST SPIES, FROM THE MACHINATIONS OF THE WISEST BRAINS.

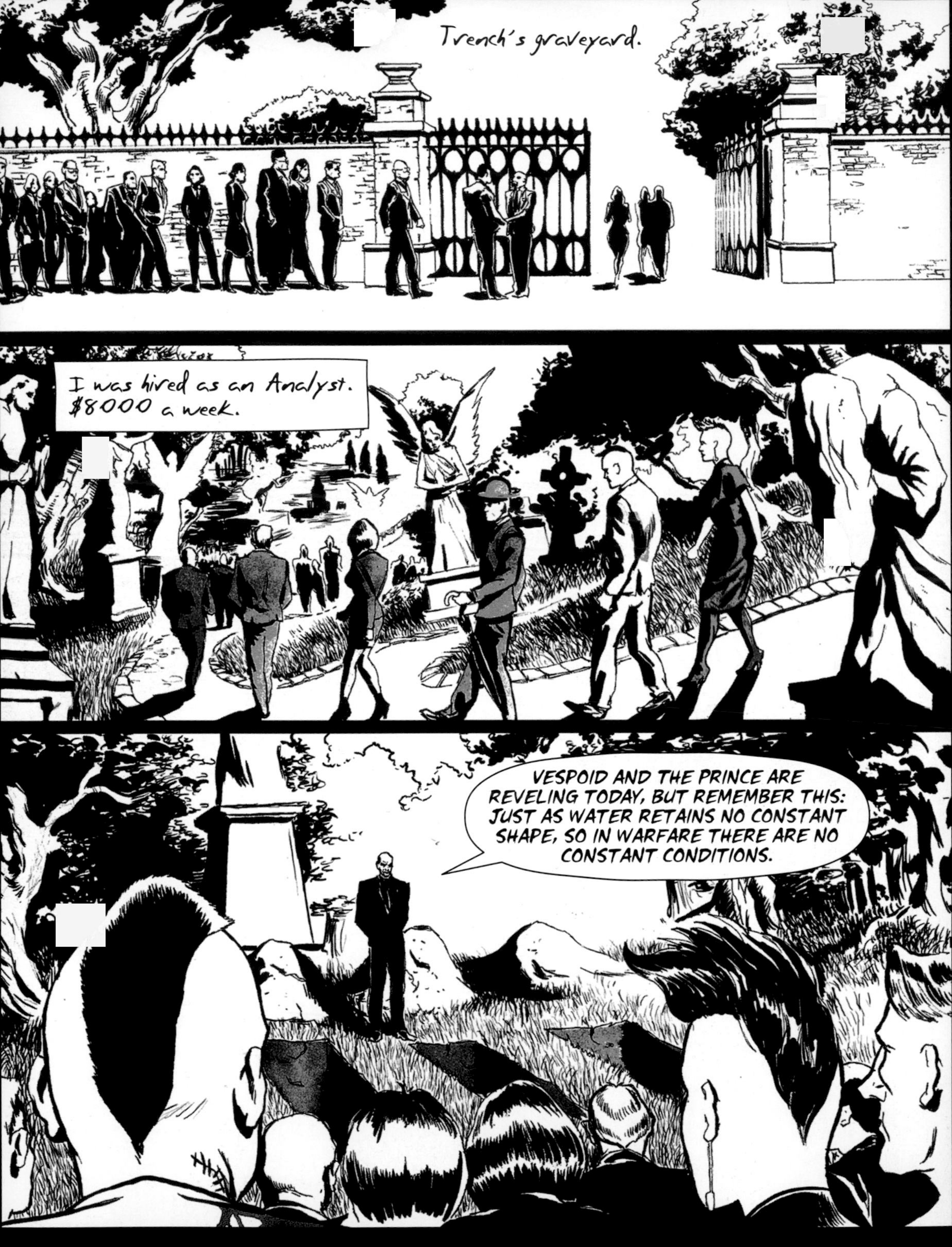
Trench's graveyard.
I was hired as an Analyst. $8000 a week.
VESPOID AND THE PRINCE ARE REVELING TODAY, BUT REMEMBER THIS: JUST AS WATER RETAINS NO CONSTANT SHAPE, SO IN WARFARE THERE ARE NO CONSTANT CONDITIONS.

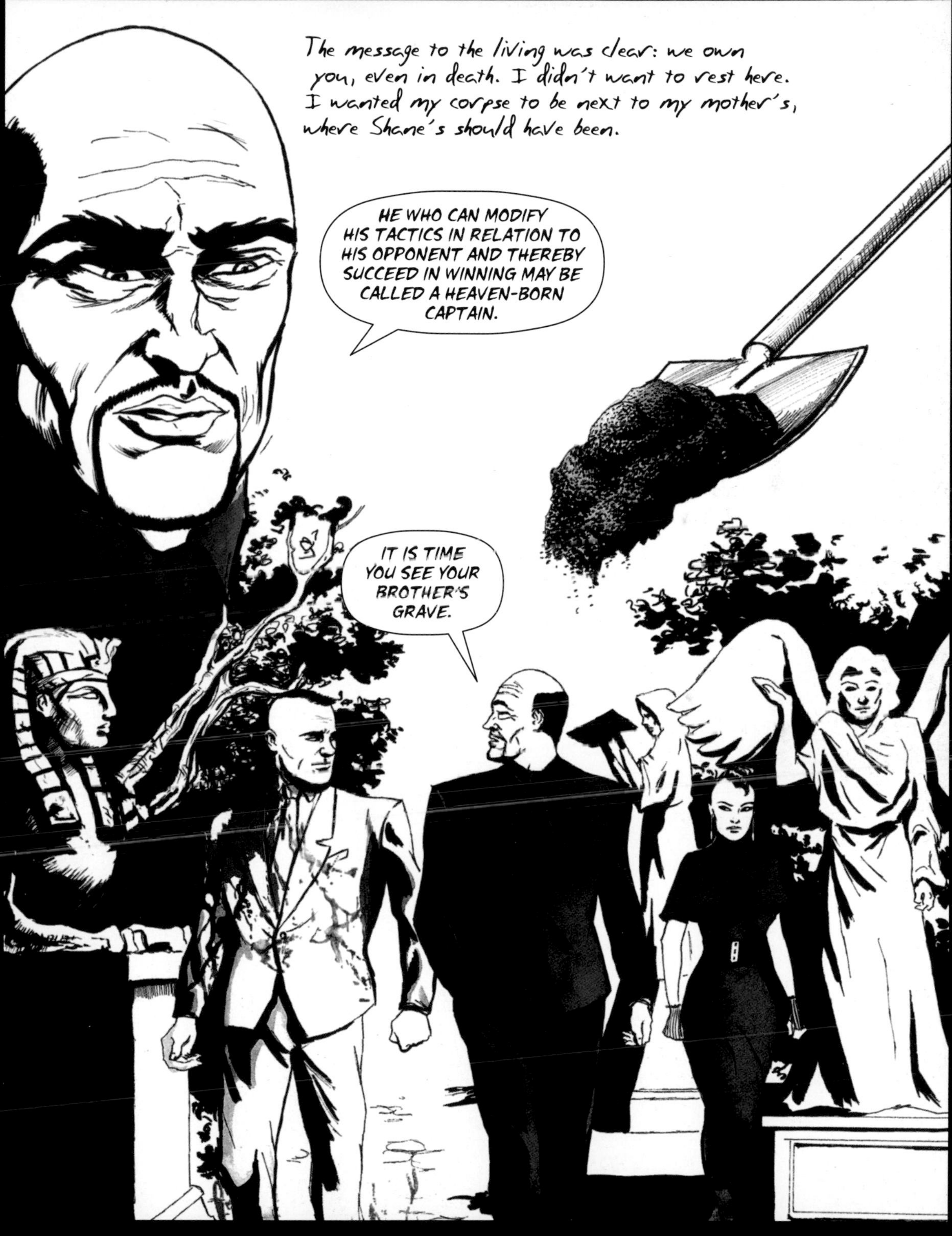
The message to the living was clear: we own you, even in death. I didn't want to rest here. I wanted my corpse to be next to my mother's, where Shane's should have been.
HE WHO CAN MODIFY HIS TACTICS IN RELATION TO HIS OPPONENT AND THEREBY SUCCEED IN WINNING MAY BE CALLED A HEAVEN-BORN CAPTAIN.
IT IS TIME YOU SEE YOUR BROTHER'S GRAVE.

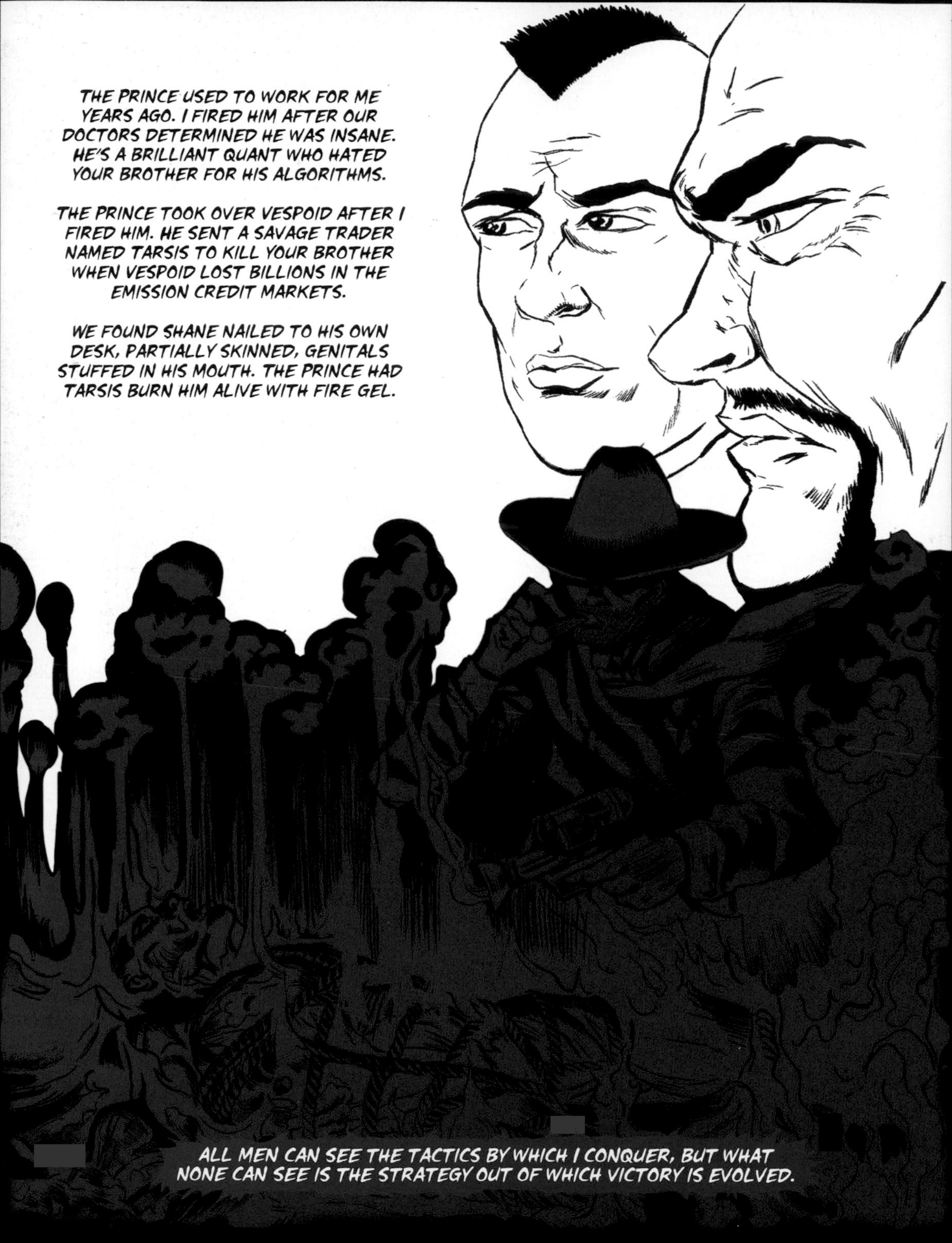
THE PRINCE USED TO WORK FOR ME YEARS AGO. I FIRED HIM AFTER OUR DOCTORS DETERMINED HE WAS INSANE. HE'S A BRILLIANT QUANT WHO HATED YOUR BROTHER FOR HIS ALGORITHMS.
THE PRINCE TOOK OVER VESPOID AFTER I FIRED HIM. HE SENT A SAVAGE TRADER NAMED TARSIS TO KILL YOUR BROTHER WHEN VESPOID LOST BILLIONS IN THE EMISSION CREDIT MARKETS.
WE FOUND SHANE NAILED TO HIS OWN DESK, PARTIALLY SKINNED, GENITALS STUFFED IN HIS MOUTH. THE PRINCE HAD TARSIS BURN HIM ALIVE WITH FIRE GEL.
ALL MEN CAN SEE THE TACTICS BY WHICH I CONQUER, BUT WHAT NONE CAN SEE IS THE STRATEGY OUT OF WHICH VICTORY IS EVOLVED.

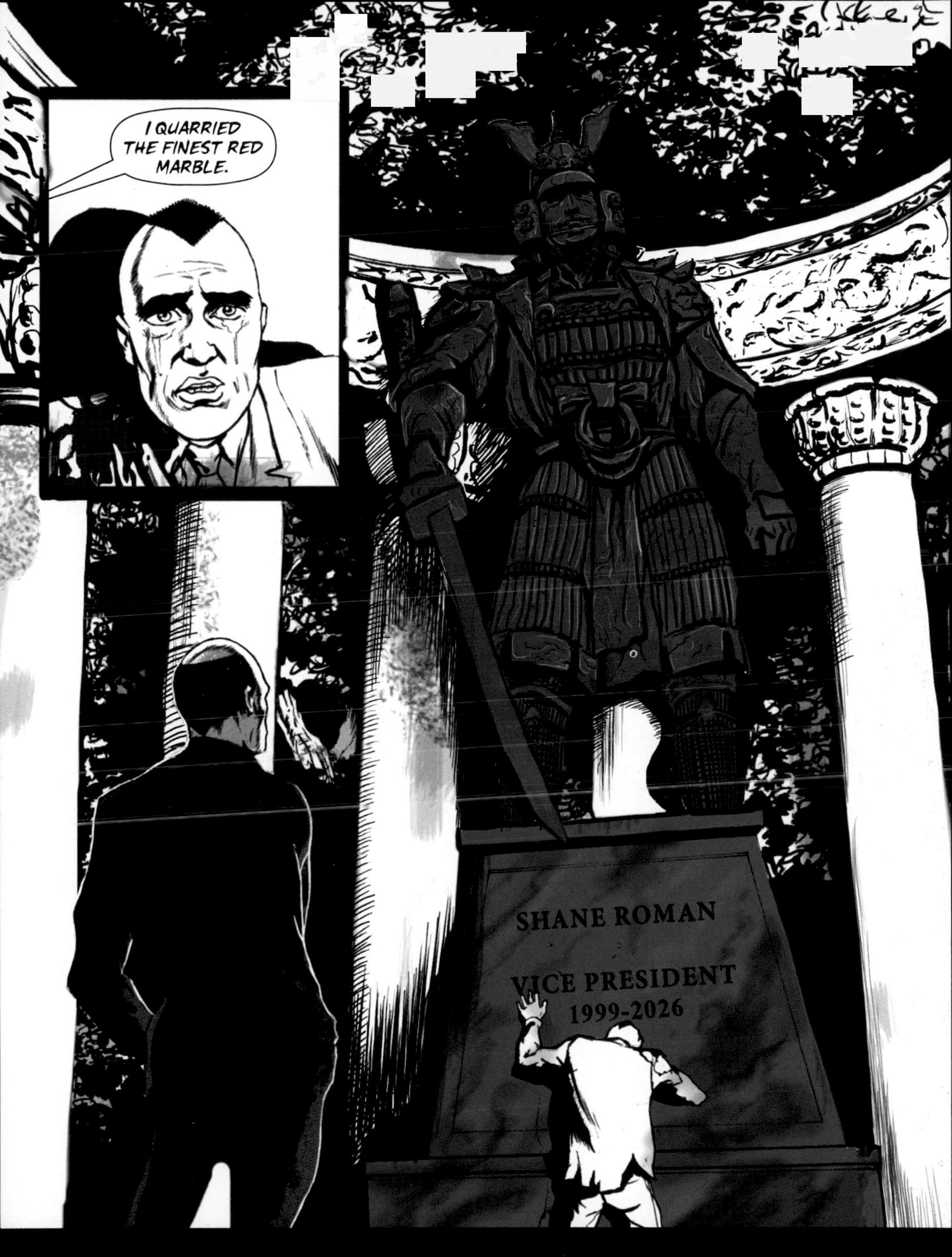
I QUARRIED THE FINEST RED MARBLE.
SHANE ROMAN
VICE PRESIDENT
1999-2026

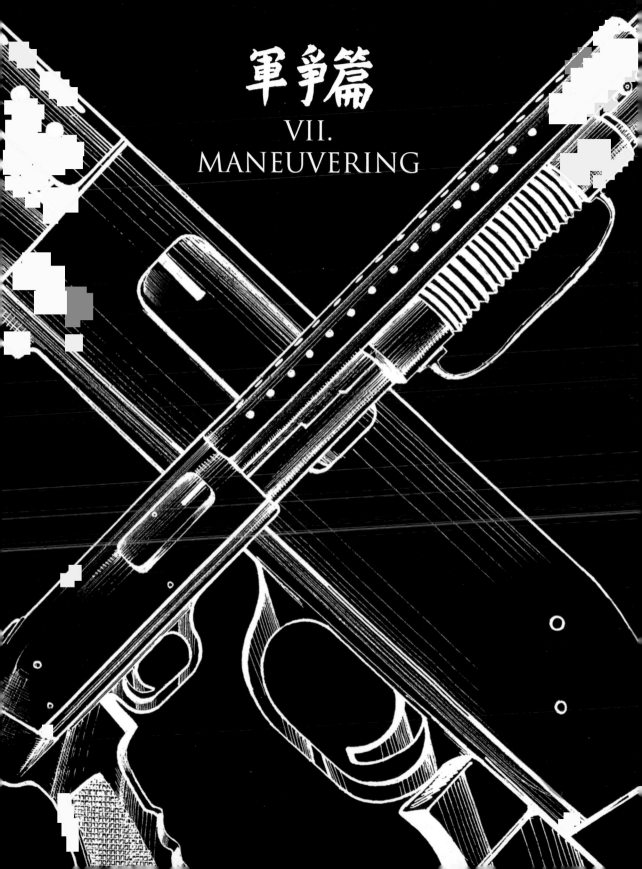

軍爭篇
VII.
MANEUVERING

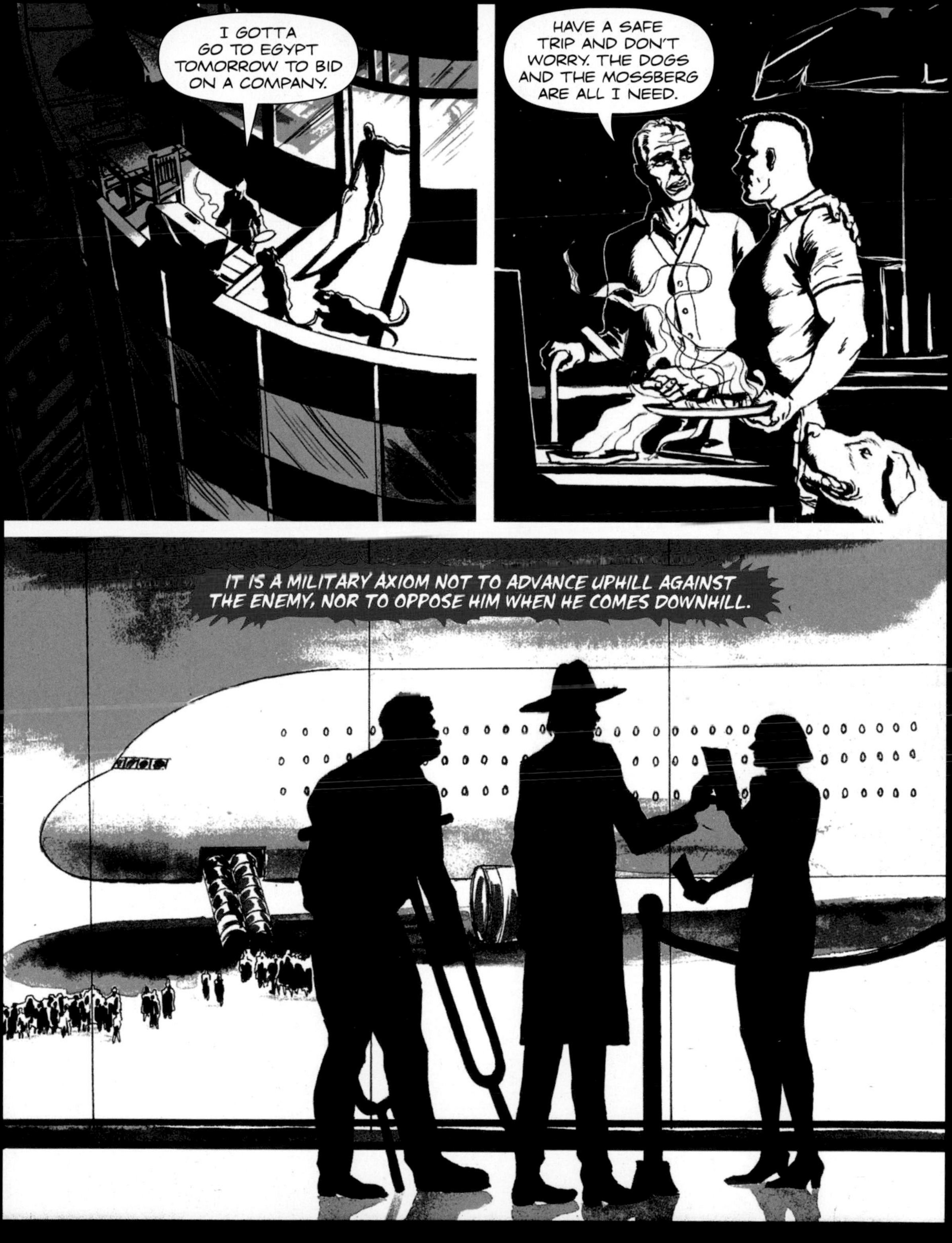
I GOTTA GO TO EGYPT TOMORROW TO BID ON A COMPANY.
HAVE A SAFE TRIP AND DON'T WORRY. THE DOGS AND THE MOSSBERG ARE ALL I NEED.
IT IS A MILITARY AXIOM NOT TO ADVANCE UPHILL AGAINST THE ENEMY, NOR TO OPPOSE HIM WHEN HE COMES DOWNHILL.

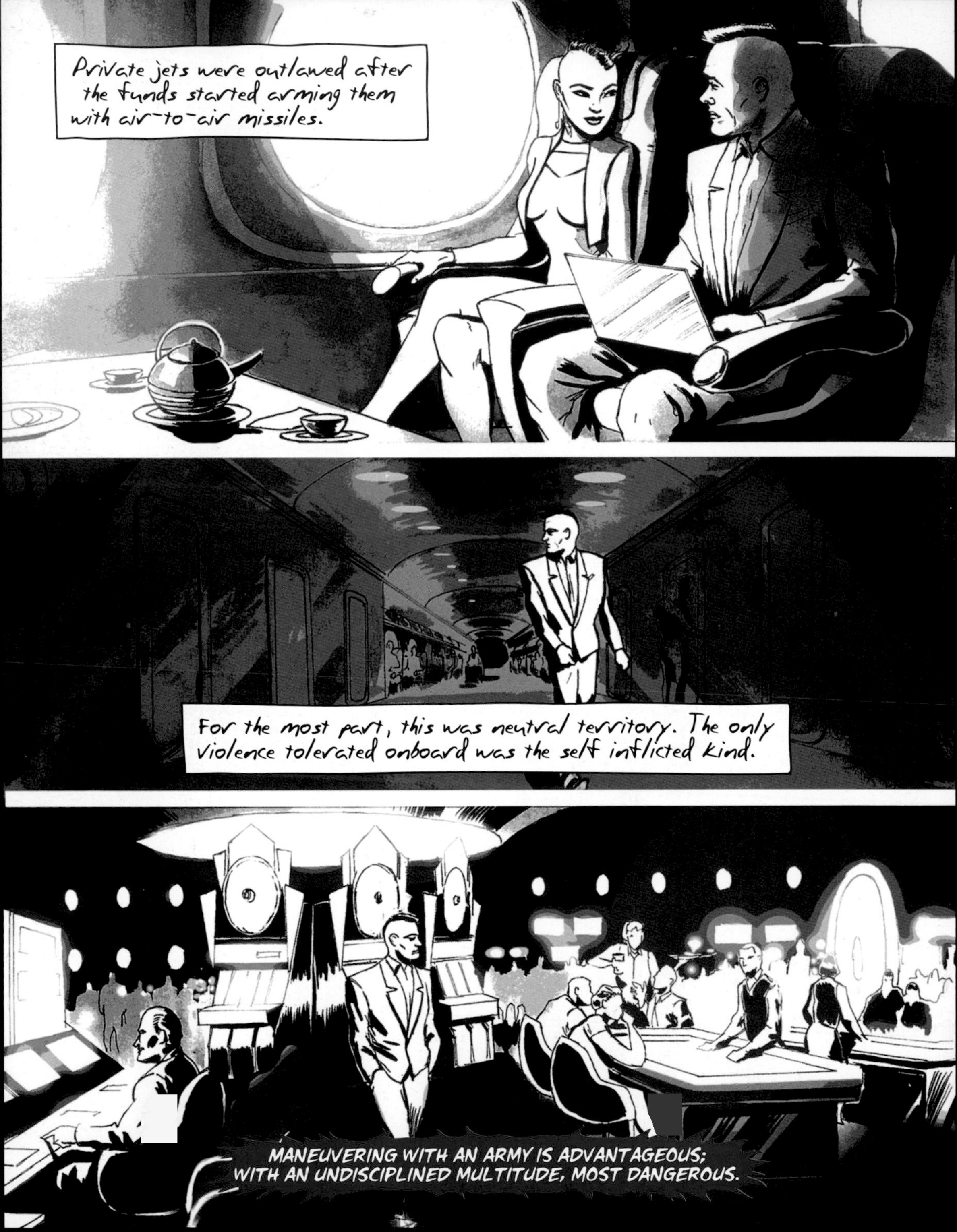
Private jets were outlawed after the funds started arming them with air-to-air missiles.
For the most part, this was neutral territory. The only violence tolerated onboard was the self inflicted kind.
MANEUVERING WITH AN ARMY IS ADVANTAGEOUS; WITH AN UNDISCIPLINED MULTITUDE, MOST DANGEROUS.

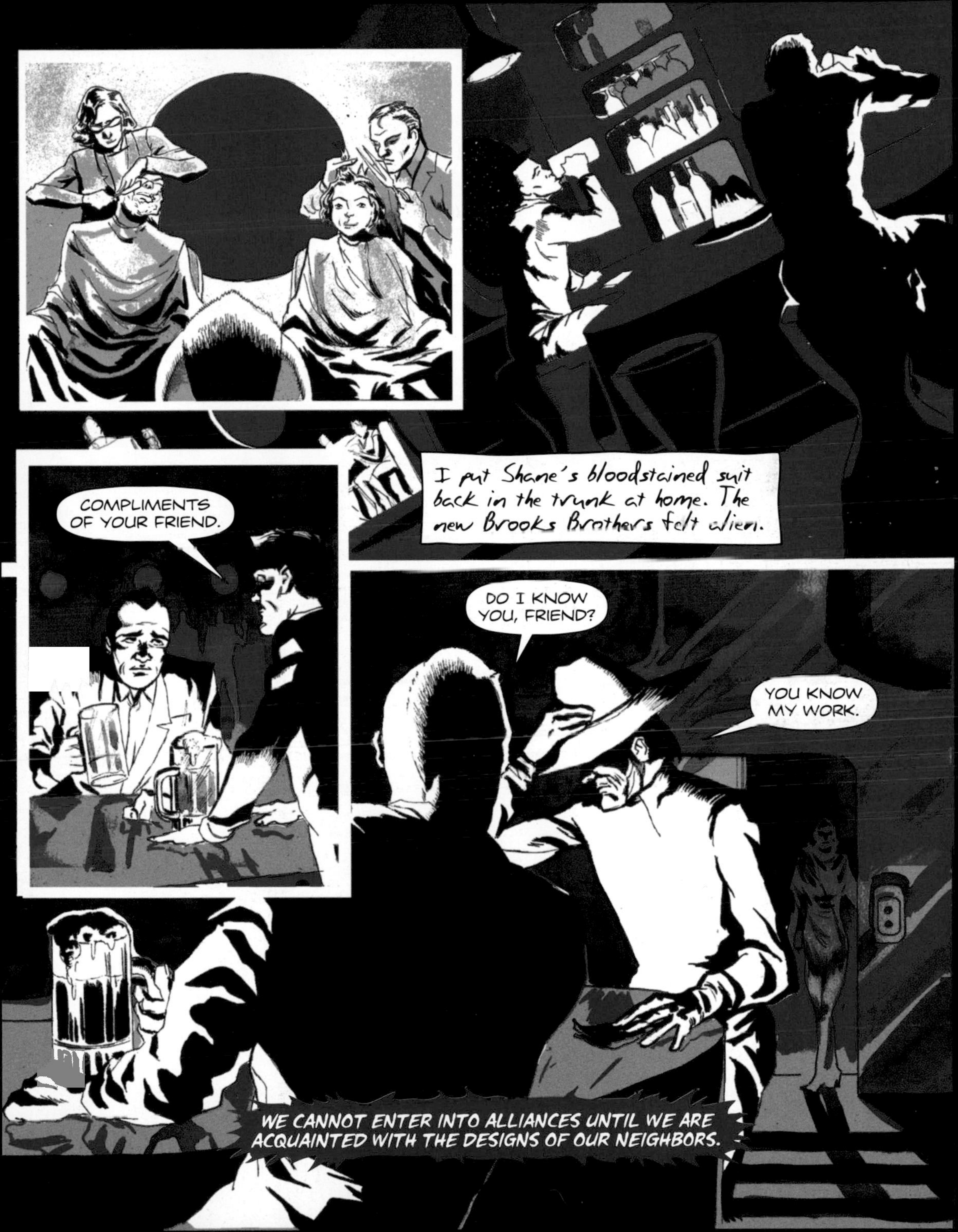
I put Shane's bloodstained suit back in the trunk at home. The new Brooks Brothers felt alien.
COMPLIMENTS OF YOUR FRIEND.
DO I KNOW YOU, FRIEND?
YOU KNOW MY WORK.
WE CANNOT ENTER INTO ALLIANCES UNTIL WE ARE ACQUAINTED WITH THE DESIGNS OF OUR NEIGHBORS.

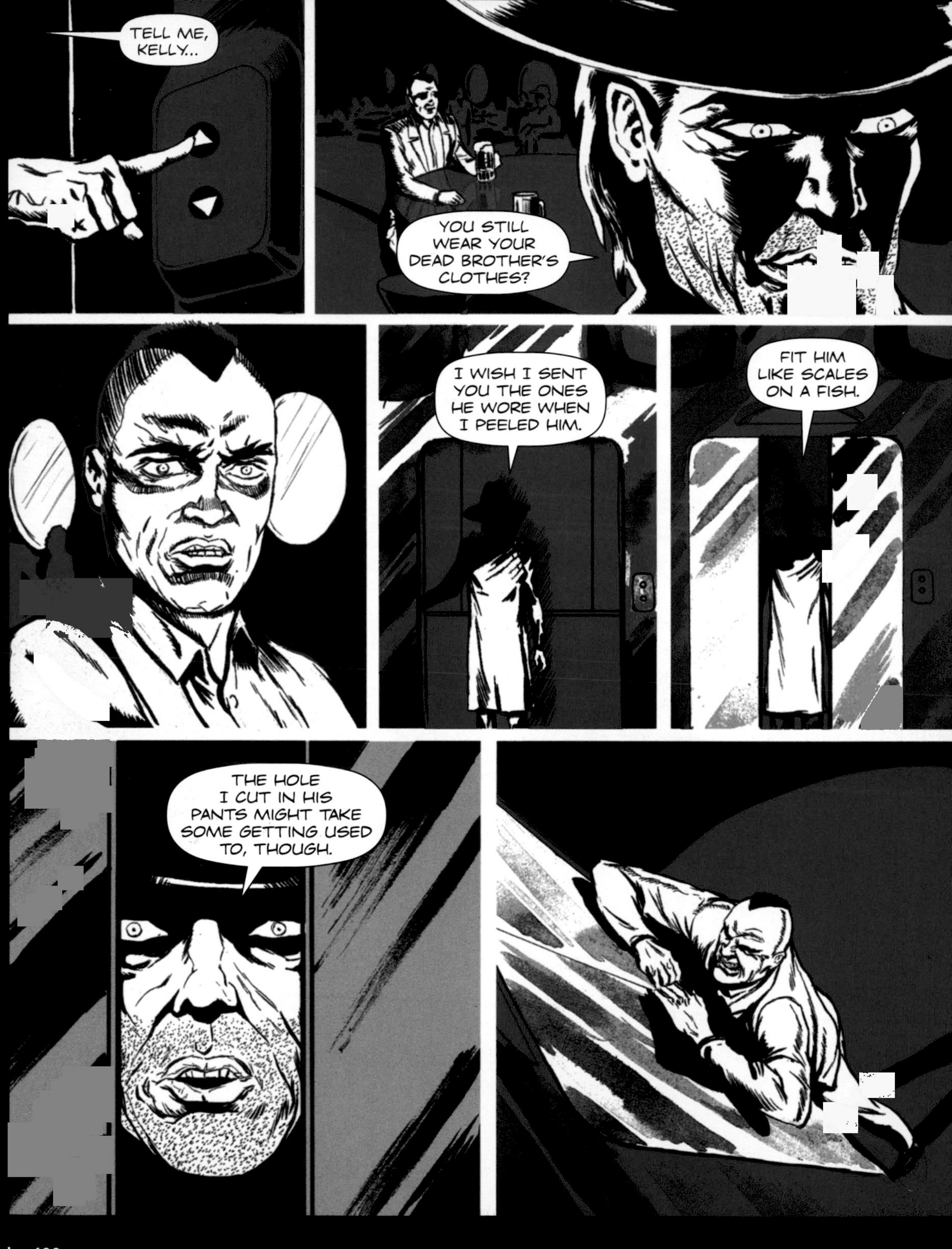
TELL ME, KELLY...
YOU STILL WEAR YOUR DEAD BROTHER'S CLOTHES?
I WISH I SENT YOU THE ONES HE WORE WHEN I PEELED HIM.
FIT HIM LIKE SCALES ON A FISH.
THE HOLE I CUT IN HIS PANTS MIGHT TAKE SOME GETTING USED TO, THOUGH.

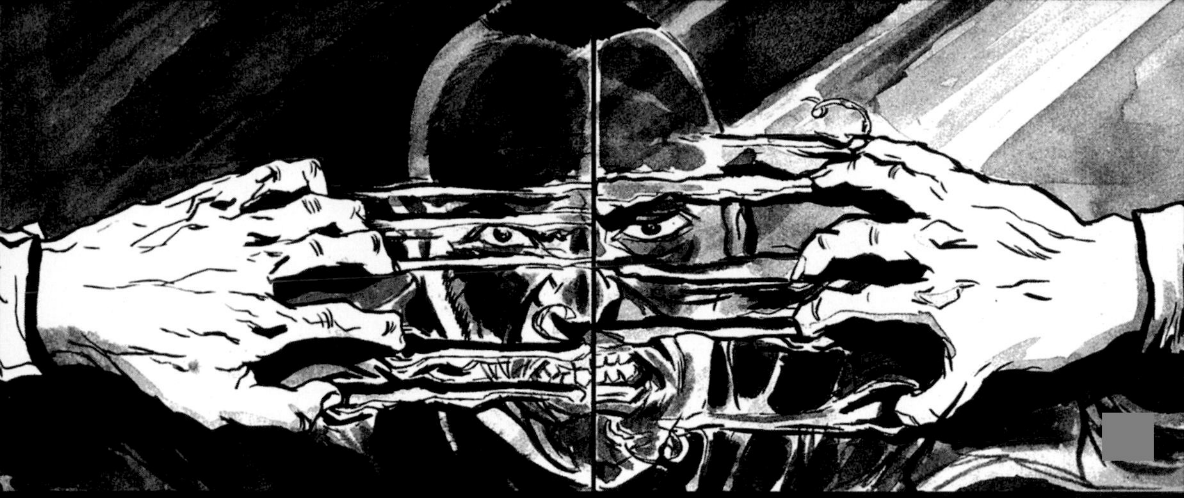

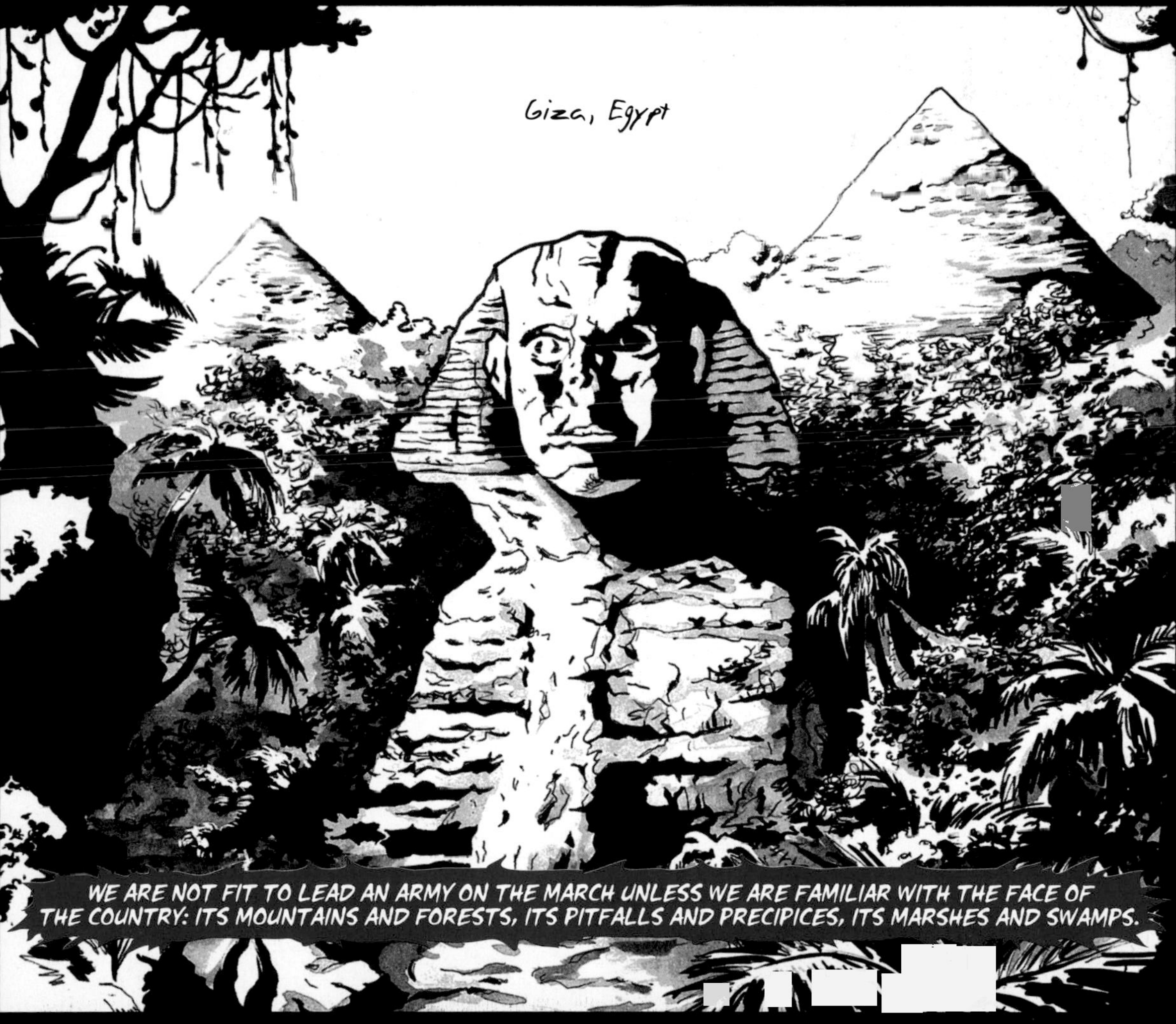
Giza, Egypt
WE ARE NOT FIT TO LEAD AN ARMY ON THE MARCH UNLESS WE ARE FAMILIAR WITH THE FACE OF THE COUNTRY: ITS MOUNTAINS AND FORESTS, ITS PITFALLS AND PRECIPICES, ITS MARSHES AND SWAMPS.

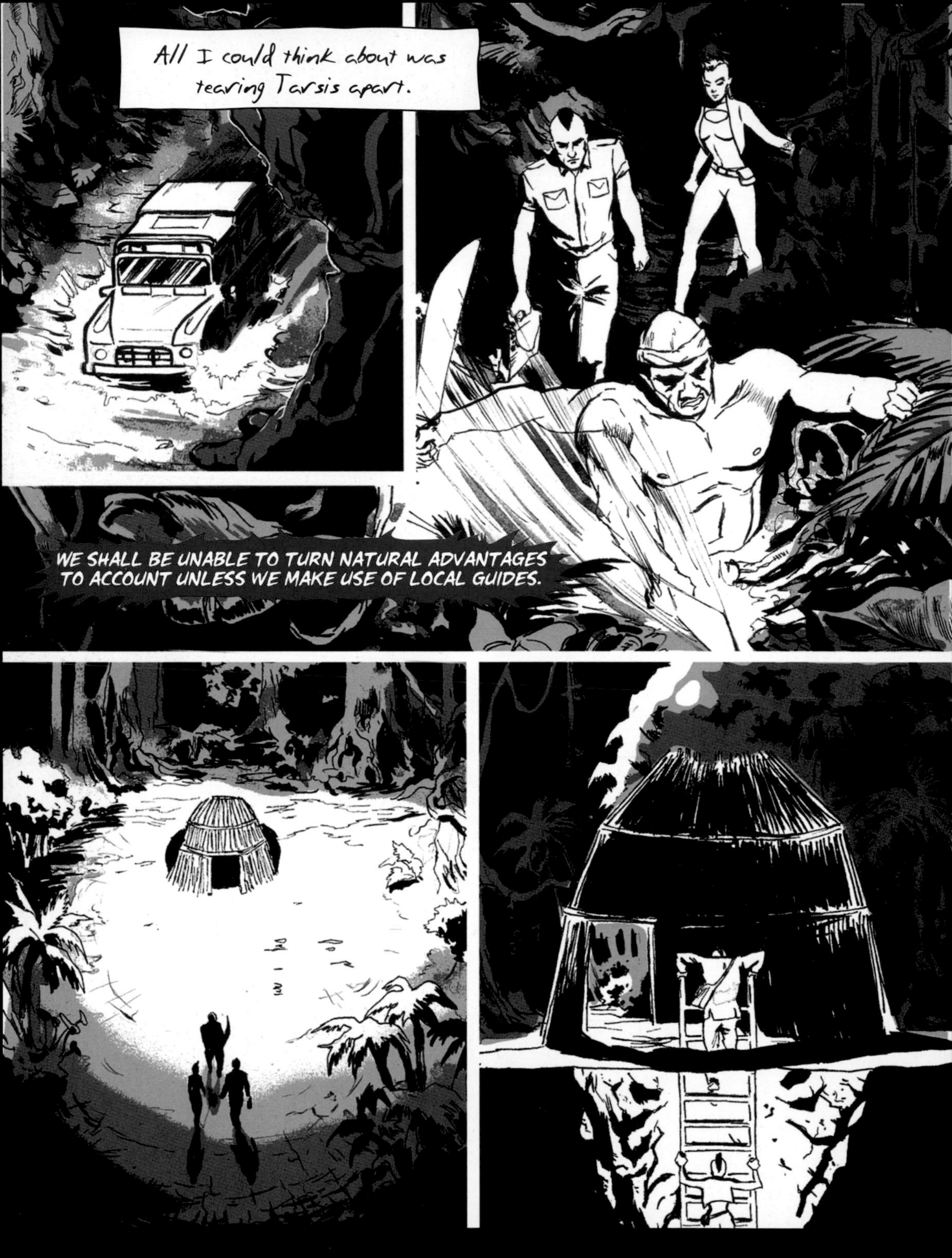
All I could think about was tearing Tarsis apart.
WE SHALL BE UNABLE TO TURN NATURAL ADVANTAGES TO ACCOUNT UNLESS WE MAKE USE OF LOCAL GUIDES.

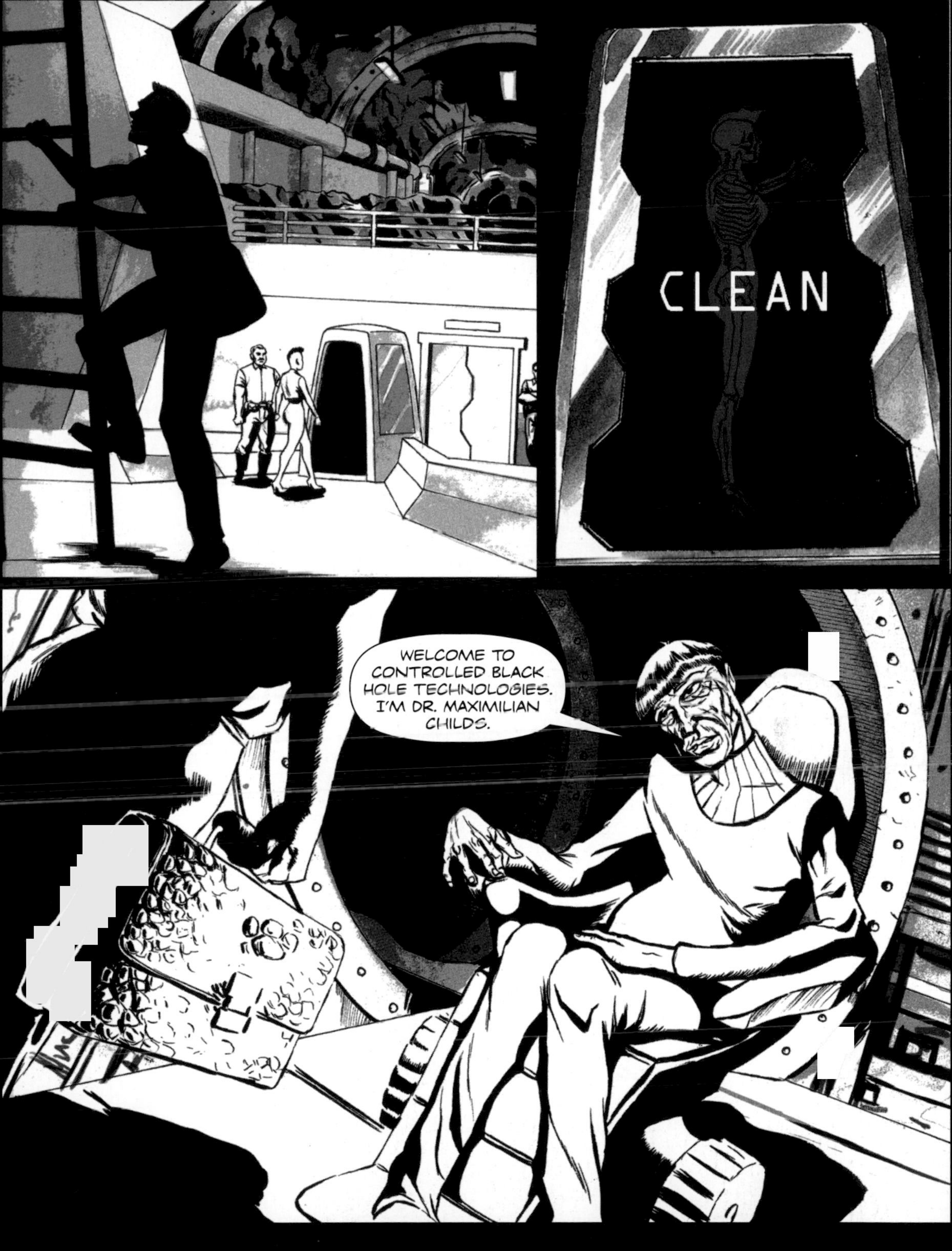
CLEAN
WELCOME TO CONTROLLED BLACK HOLE TECHNOLOGIES. I'M DR. MAXIMILIAN CHILDS.

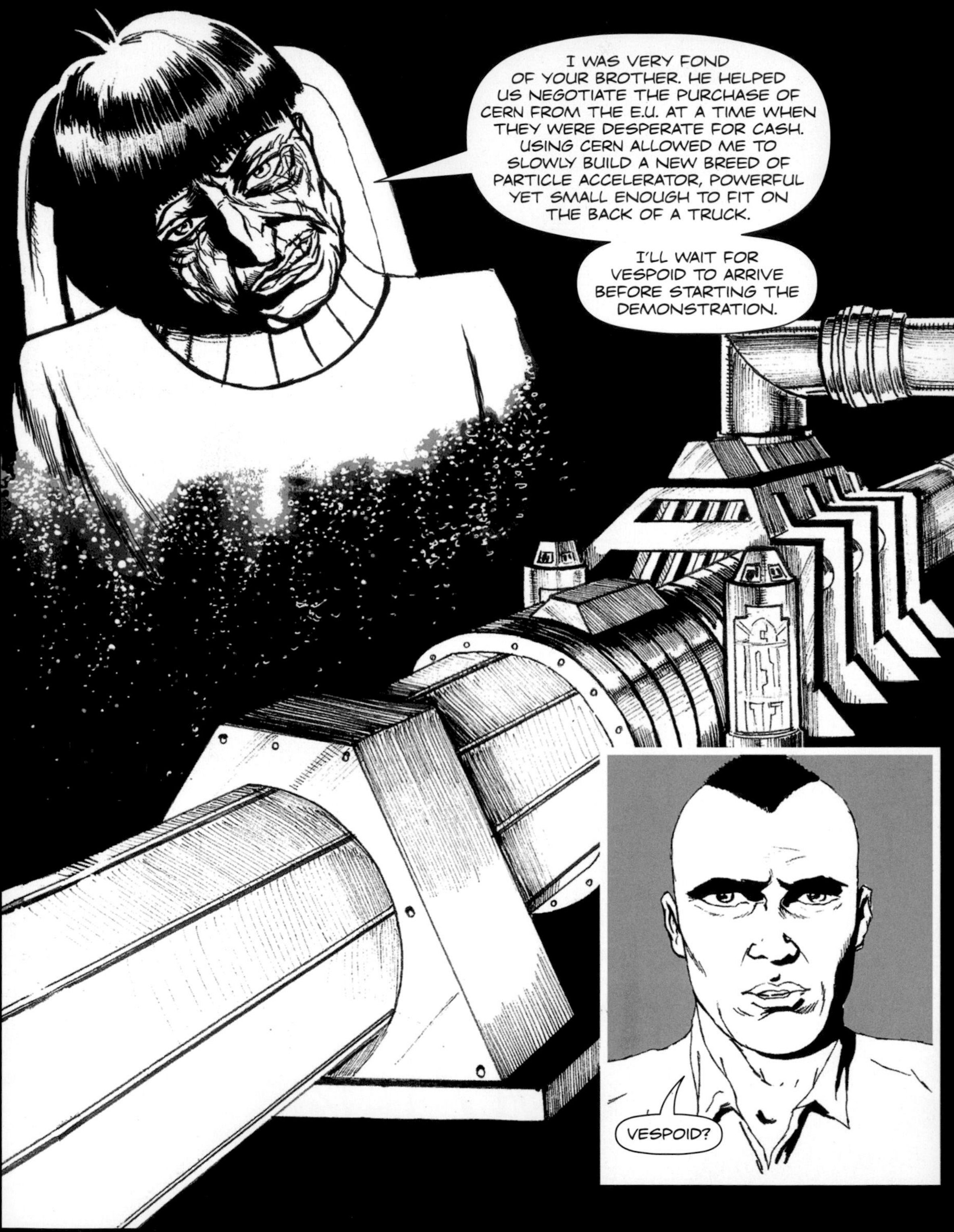
I WAS VERY FOND OF YOUR BROTHER. HE HELPED US NEGOTIATE THE PURCHASE OF CERN FROM THE E.U. AT A TIME WHEN THEY WERE DESPERATE FOR CASH. USING CERN ALLOWED ME TO SLOWLY BUILD A NEW BREED OF PARTICLE ACCELERATOR, POWERFUL YET SMALL ENOUGH TO FIT ON THE BACK OF A TRUCK.
I'LL WAIT FOR VESPOID TO ARRIVE BEFORE STARTING THE DEMONSTRATION.
VESPOID?

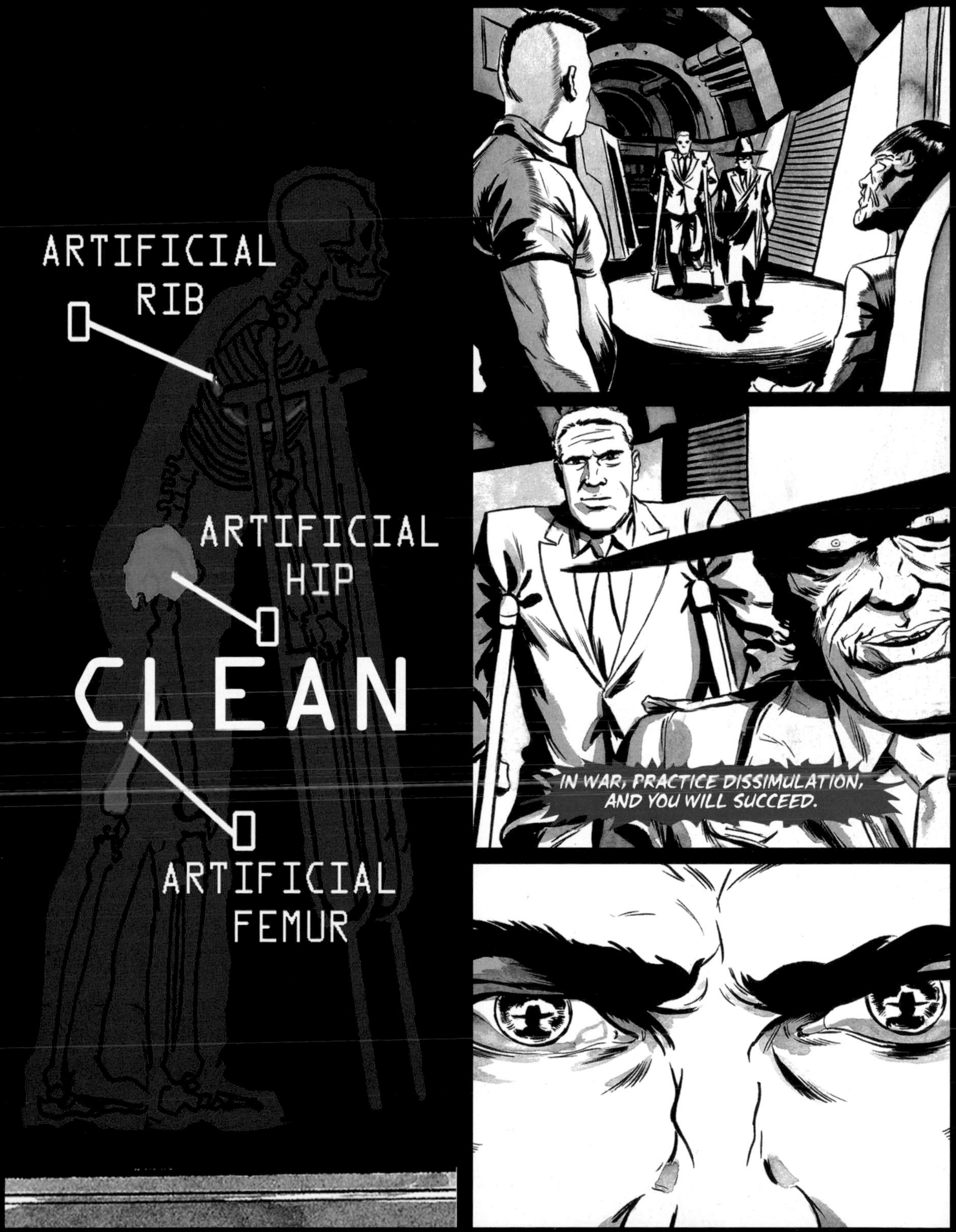
ARTIFICIAL RIB
ARTIFICIAL HIP
CLEAN
ARTIFICIAL FEMUR
IN WAR, PRACTICE DISSIMULATION, AND YOU WILL SUCCEED.

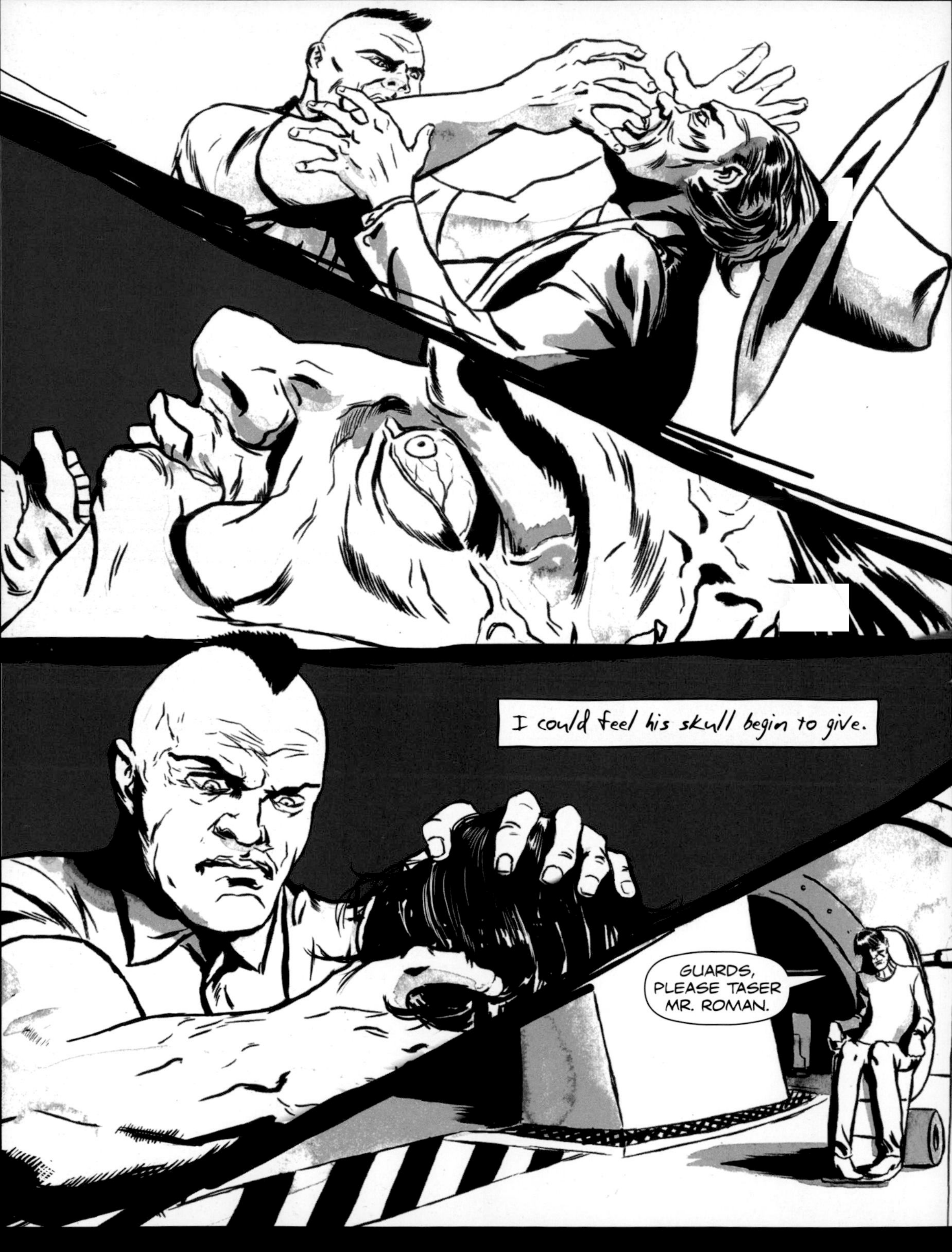
I could feel his skull begin to give.
GUARDS, PLEASE TASER MR. ROMAN.

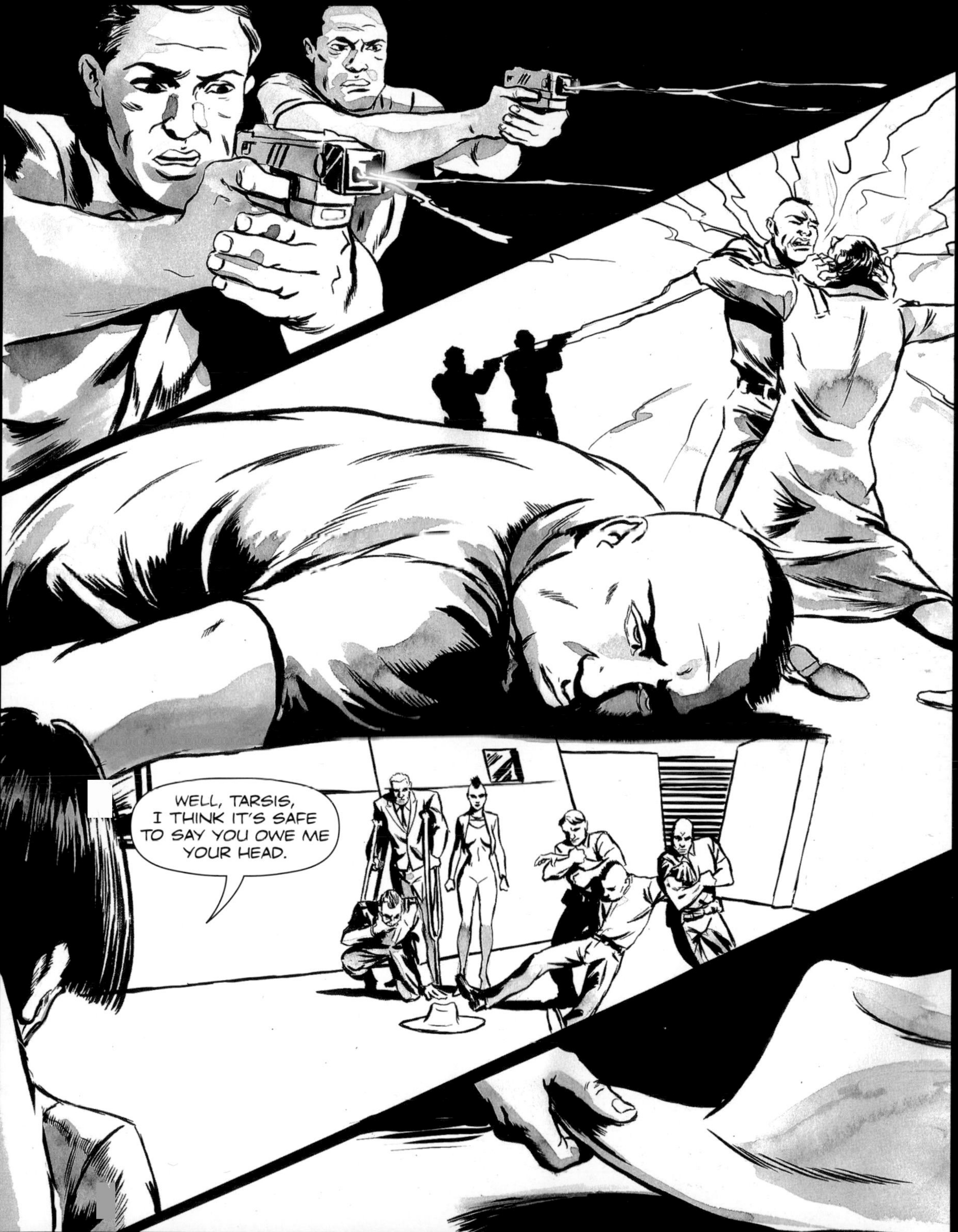
WELL, TARSIS, I THINK IT'S SAFE TO SAY YOU OWE ME YOUR HEAD.

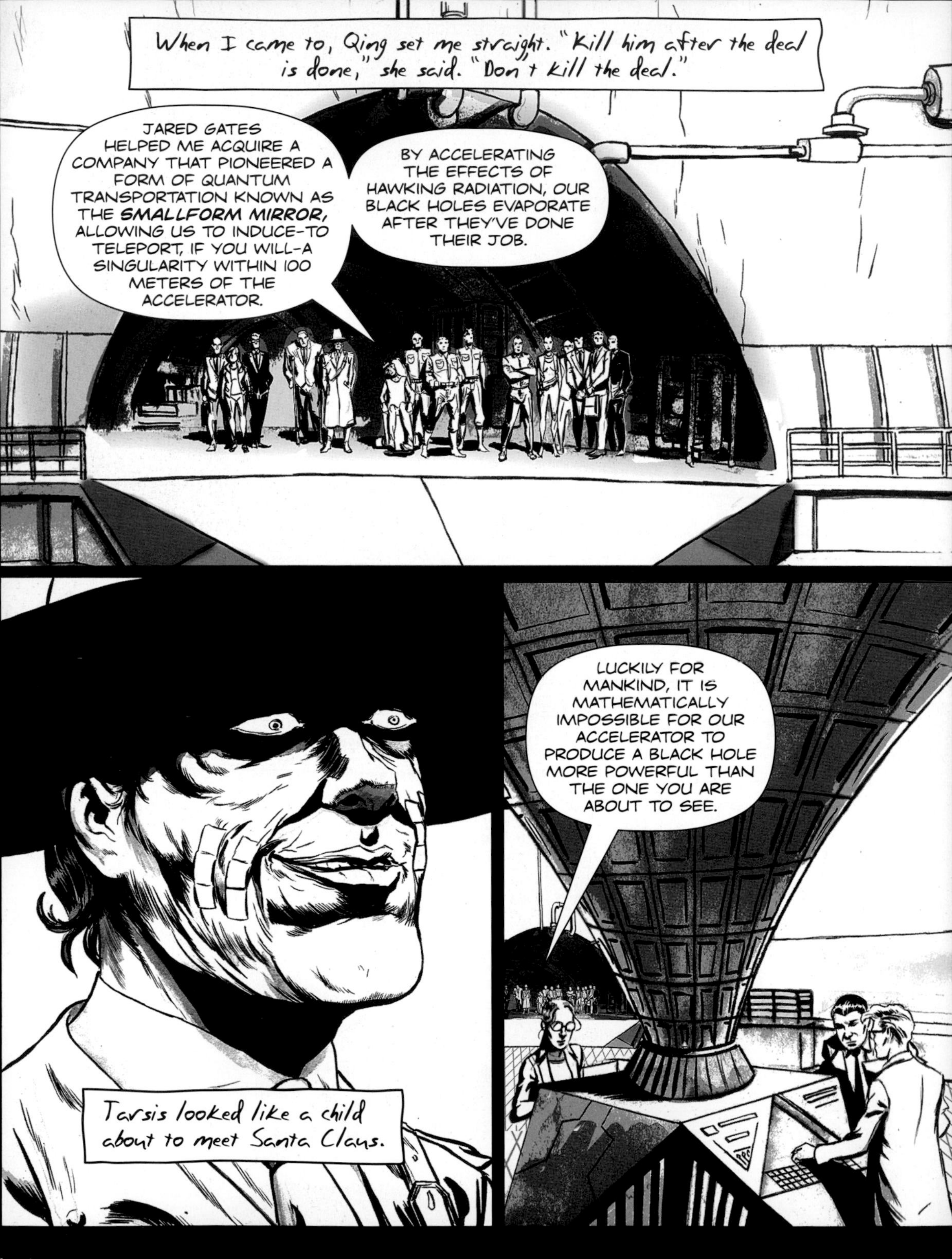
When I came to, Qing set me straight. "Kill him after the deal is done," she said. "Don't kill the deal."
JARED GATES HELPED ME ACQUIRE A COMPANY THAT PIONEERED A FORM OF QUANTUM TRANSPORTATION KNOWN AS THE ***SMALLFORM MIRROR,*** ALLOWING US TO INDUCE—TO TELEPORT, IF YOU WILL—A SINGULARITY WITHIN 100 METERS OF THE ACCELERATOR.
BY ACCELERATING THE EFFECTS OF HAWKING RADIATION, OUR BLACK HOLES EVAPORATE AFTER THEY'VE DONE THEIR JOB.
Tarsis looked like a child about to meet Santa Claus.
LUCKILY FOR MANKIND, IT IS MATHEMATICALLY IMPOSSIBLE FOR OUR ACCELERATOR TO PRODUCE A BLACK HOLE MORE POWERFUL THAN THE ONE YOU ARE ABOUT TO SEE.

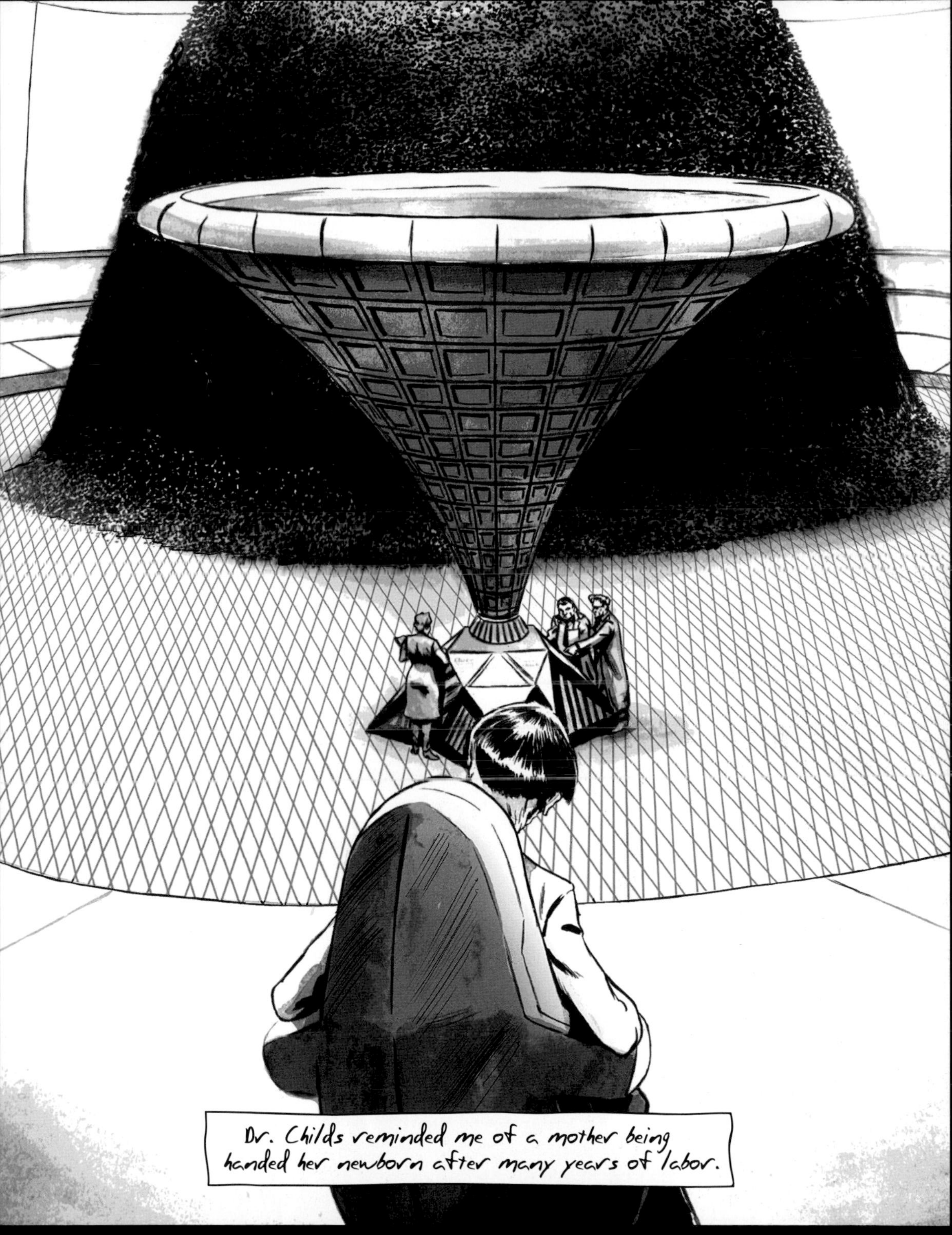
Dr. Childs reminded me of a mother being handed her newborn after many years of labor.

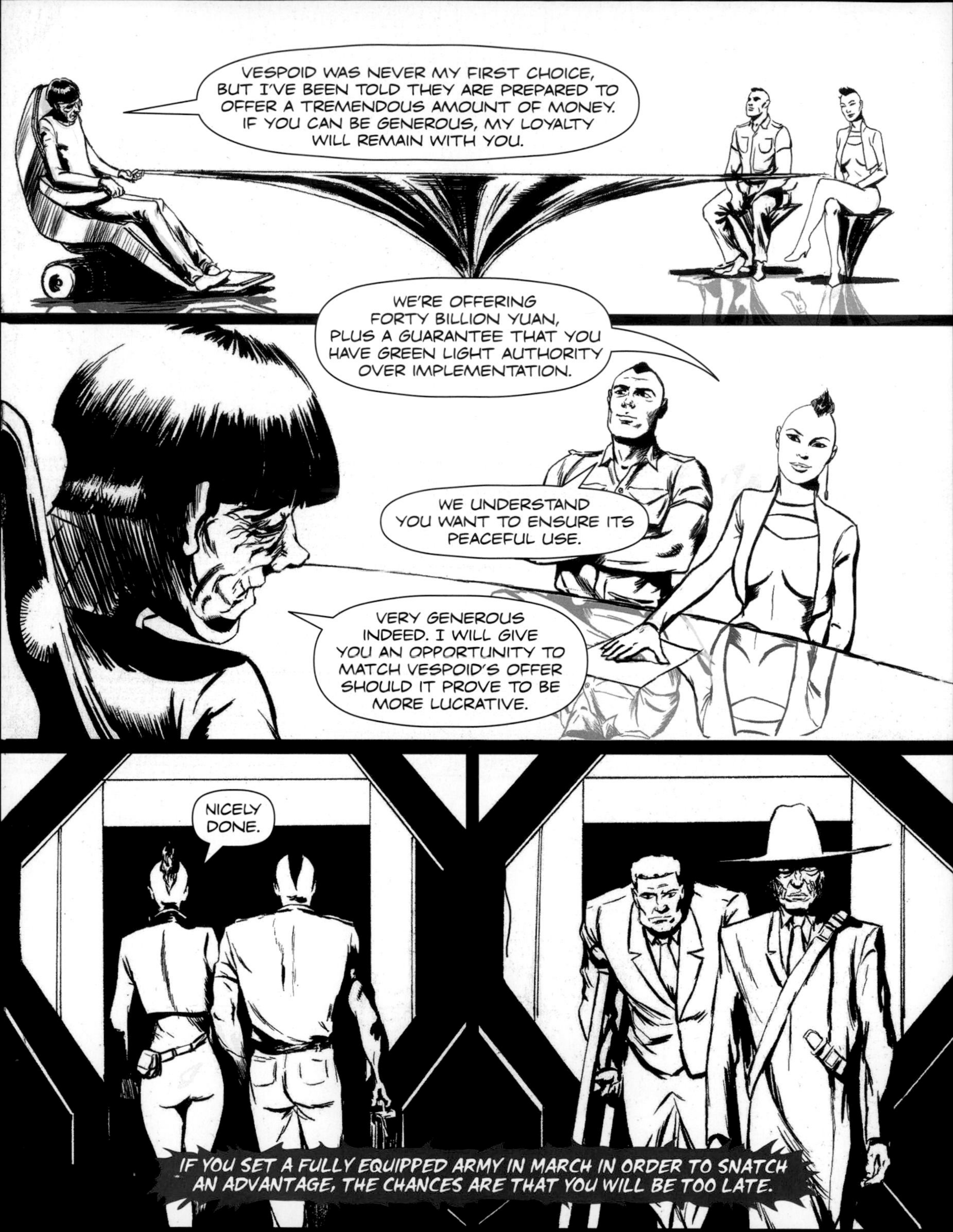
VESPOID WAS NEVER MY FIRST CHOICE, BUT I'VE BEEN TOLD THEY ARE PREPARED TO OFFER A TREMENDOUS AMOUNT OF MONEY. IF YOU CAN BE GENEROUS, MY LOYALTY WILL REMAIN WITH YOU.
WE'RE OFFERING FORTY BILLION YUAN, PLUS A GUARANTEE THAT YOU HAVE GREEN LIGHT AUTHORITY OVER IMPLEMENTATION.
WE UNDERSTAND YOU WANT TO ENSURE ITS PEACEFUL USE.
VERY GENEROUS INDEED. I WILL GIVE YOU AN OPPORTUNITY TO MATCH VESPOID'S OFFER SHOULD IT PROVE TO BE MORE LUCRATIVE.
NICELY DONE.
IF YOU SET A FULLY EQUIPPED ARMY IN MARCH IN ORDER TO SNATCH AN ADVANTAGE, THE CHANCES ARE THAT YOU WILL BE TOO LATE.

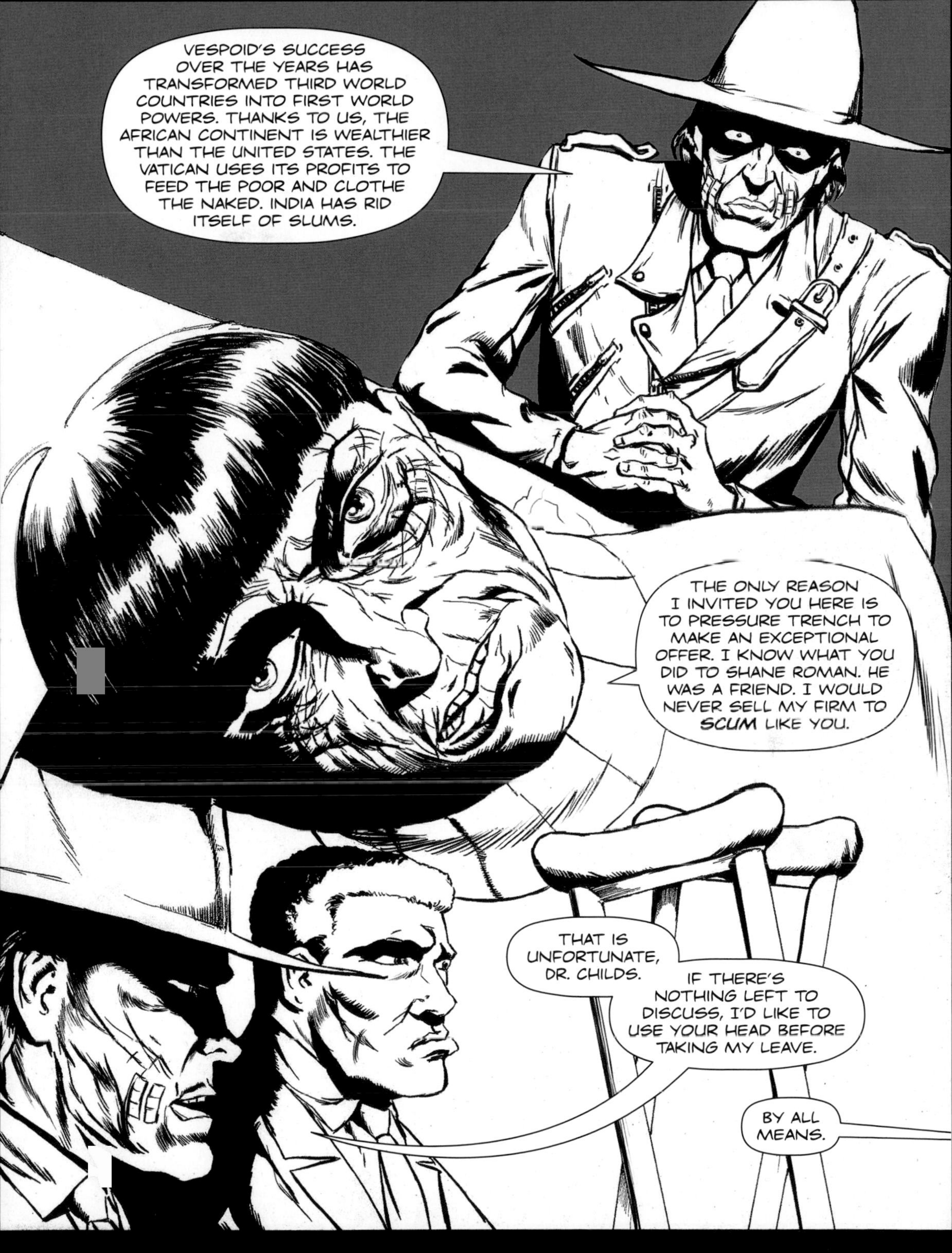
VESPOID'S SUCCESS OVER THE YEARS HAS TRANSFORMED THIRD WORLD COUNTRIES INTO FIRST WORLD POWERS. THANKS TO US, THE AFRICAN CONTINENT IS WEALTHIER THAN THE UNITED STATES. THE VATICAN USES ITS PROFITS TO FEED THE POOR AND CLOTHE THE NAKED. INDIA HAS RID ITSELF OF SLUMS.
THE ONLY REASON I INVITED YOU HERE IS TO PRESSURE TRENCH TO MAKE AN EXCEPTIONAL OFFER. I KNOW WHAT YOU DID TO SHANE ROMAN. HE WAS A FRIEND. I WOULD NEVER SELL MY FIRM TO SCUM LIKE YOU.
THAT IS UNFORTUNATE, DR. CHILDS.
IF THERE'S NOTHING LEFT TO DISCUSS, I'D LIKE TO USE YOUR HEAD BEFORE TAKING MY LEAVE.
BY ALL MEANS.

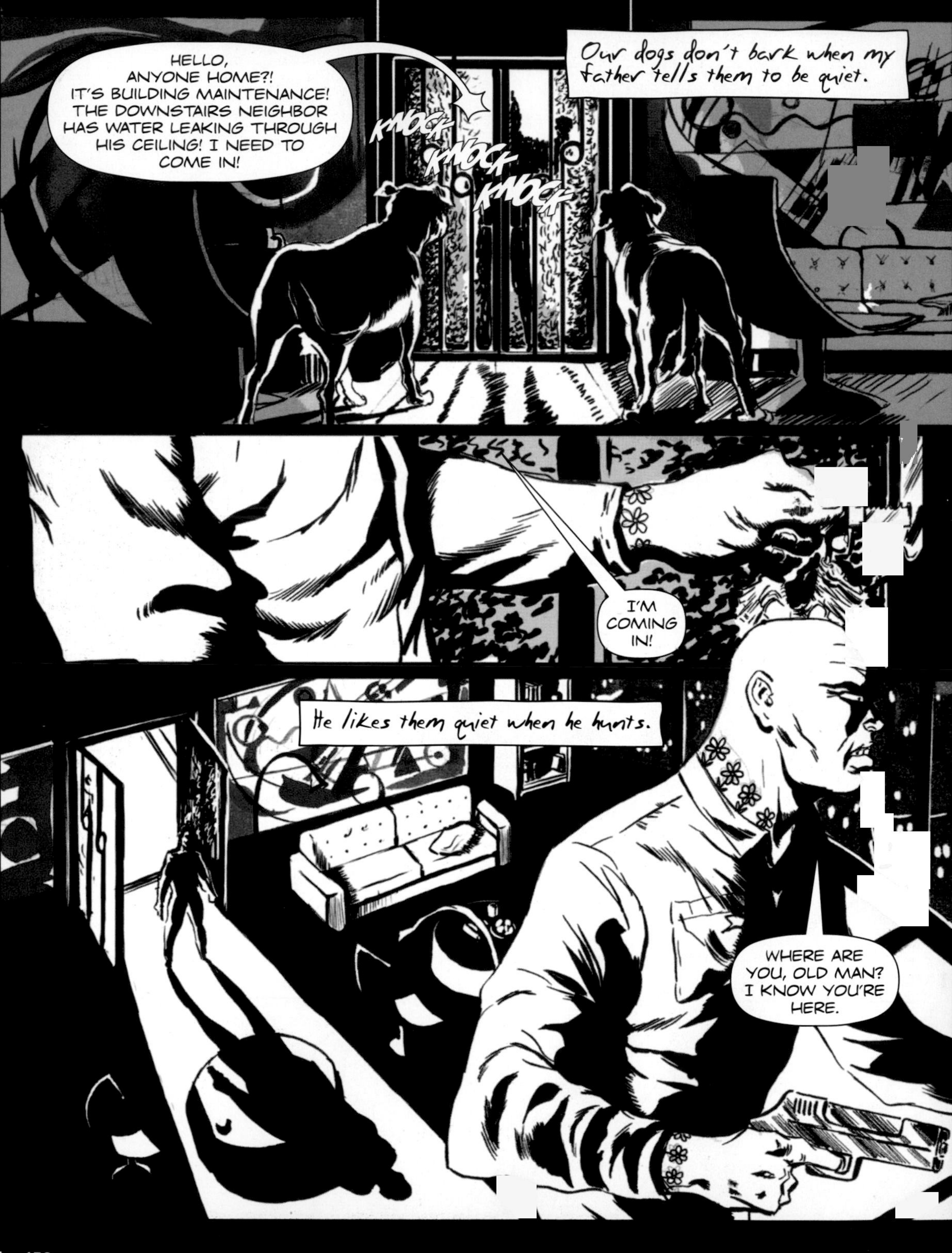
HELLO, ANYONE HOME?! IT'S BUILDING MAINTENANCE! THE DOWNSTAIRS NEIGHBOR HAS WATER LEAKING THROUGH HIS CEILING! I NEED TO COME IN!
Our dogs don't bark when my father tells them to be quiet.
KNOCK KNOCK KNOCK
I'M COMING IN!
He likes them quiet when he hunts.
WHERE ARE YOU, OLD MAN? I KNOW YOU'RE HERE.

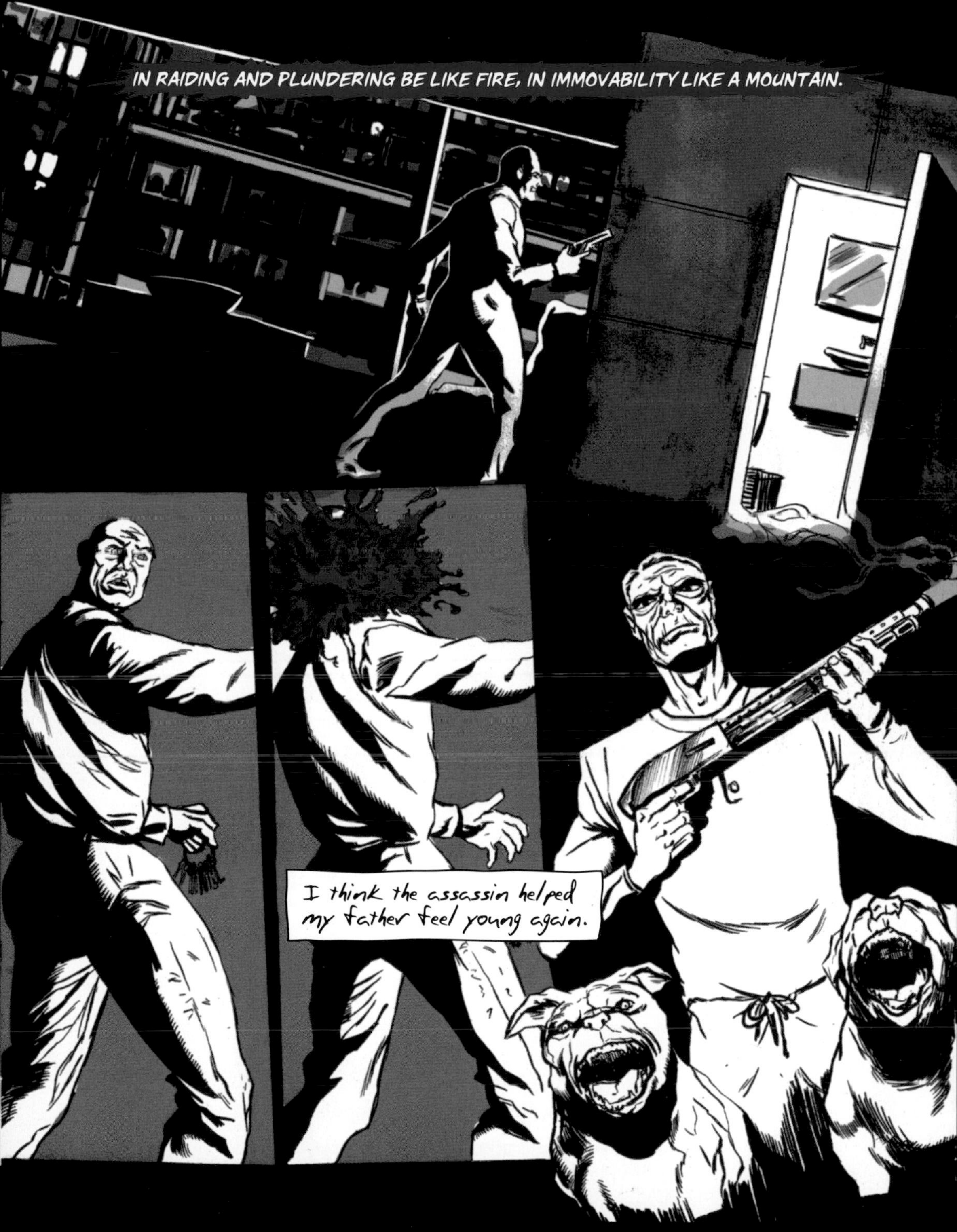
IN RAIDING AND PLUNDERING BE LIKE FIRE, IN IMMOVABILITY LIKE A MOUNTAIN.
I think the assassin helped my father feel young again.

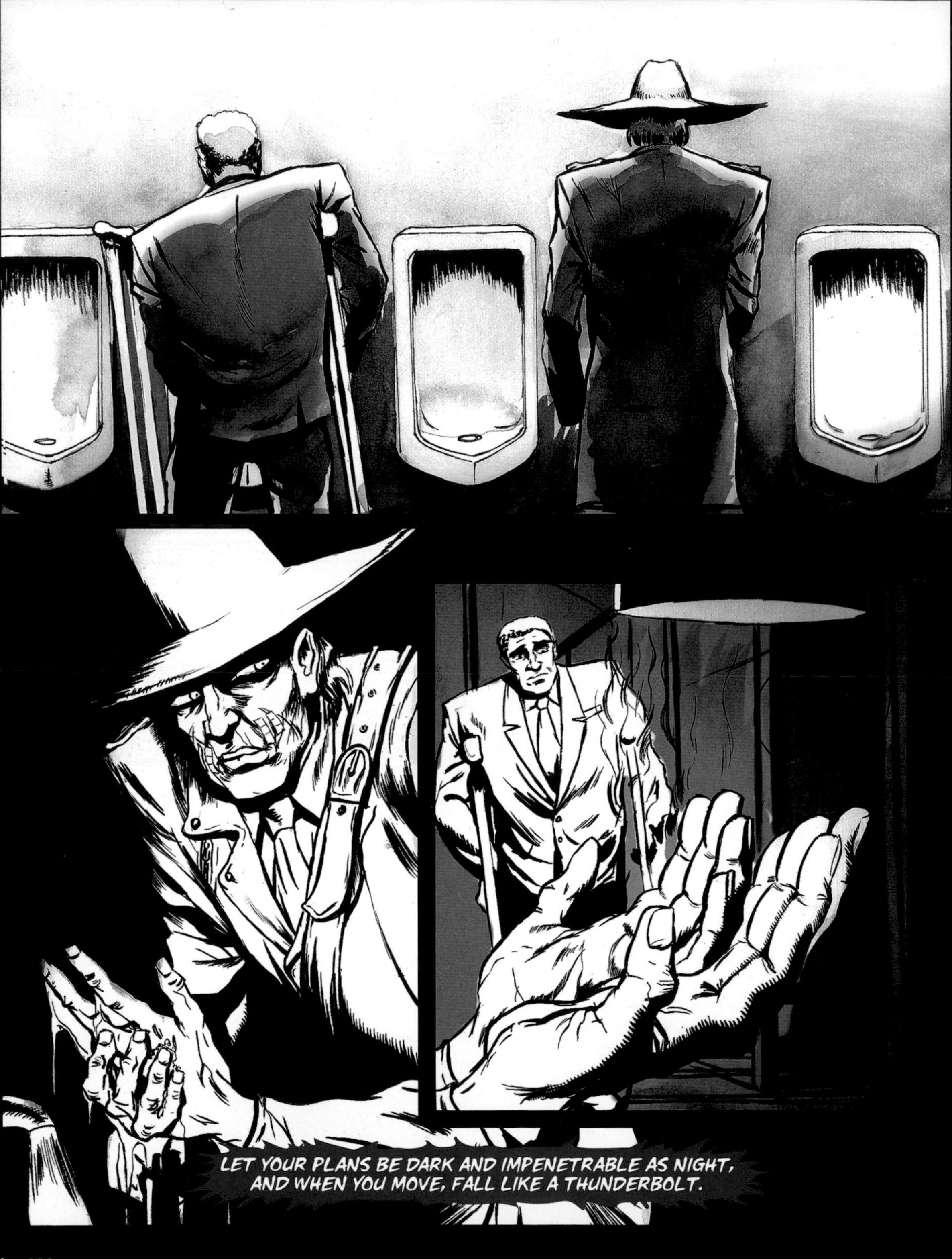
LET YOUR PLANS BE DARK AND IMPENETRABLE AS NIGHT, AND WHEN YOU MOVE, FALL LIKE A THUNDERBOLT.

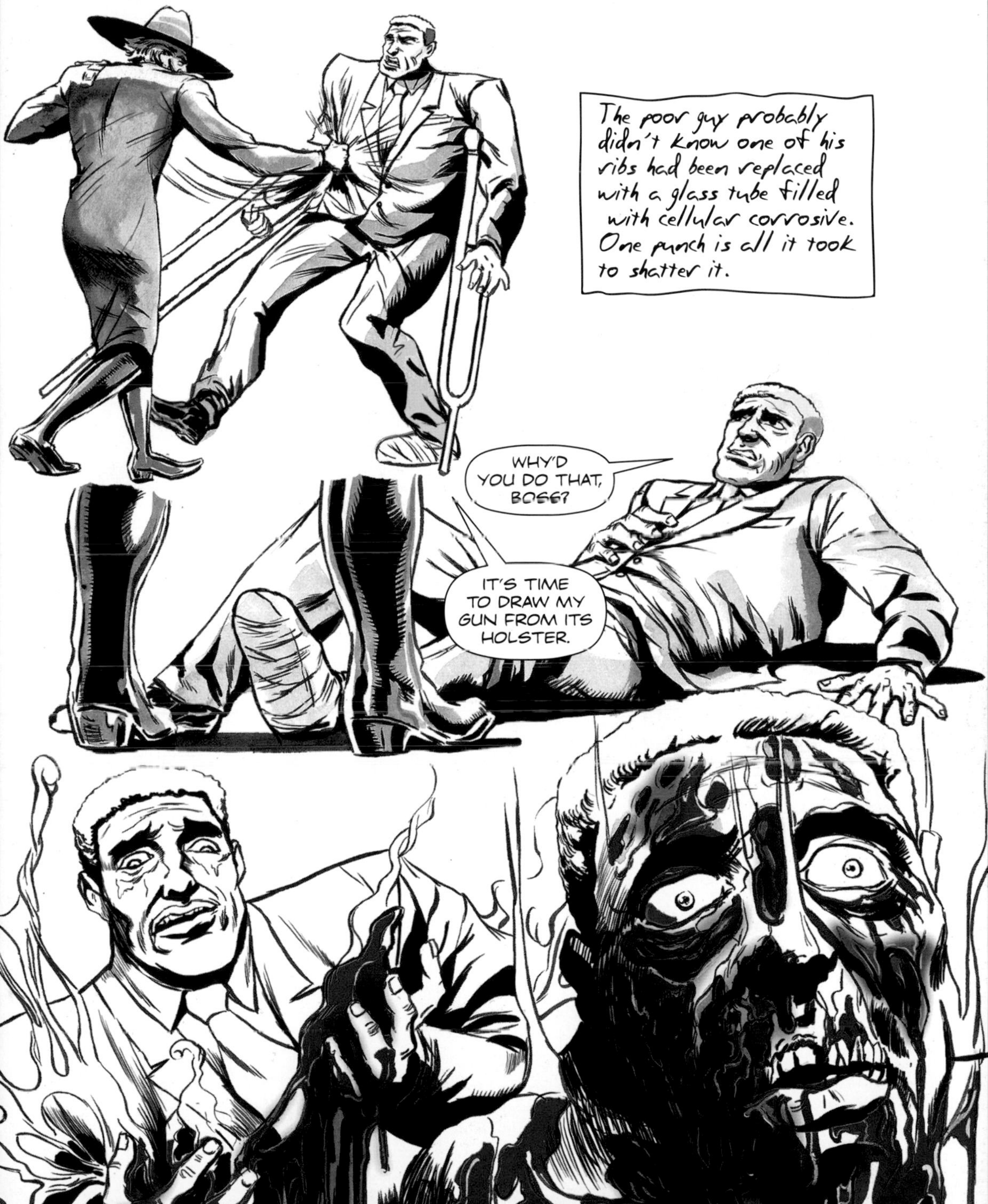
The poor guy probably didn't know one of his ribs had been replaced with a glass tube filled with cellular corrosive. One punch is all it took to shatter it.
WHY'D YOU DO THAT, BOSS?
IT'S TIME TO DRAW MY GUN FROM ITS HOLSTER.

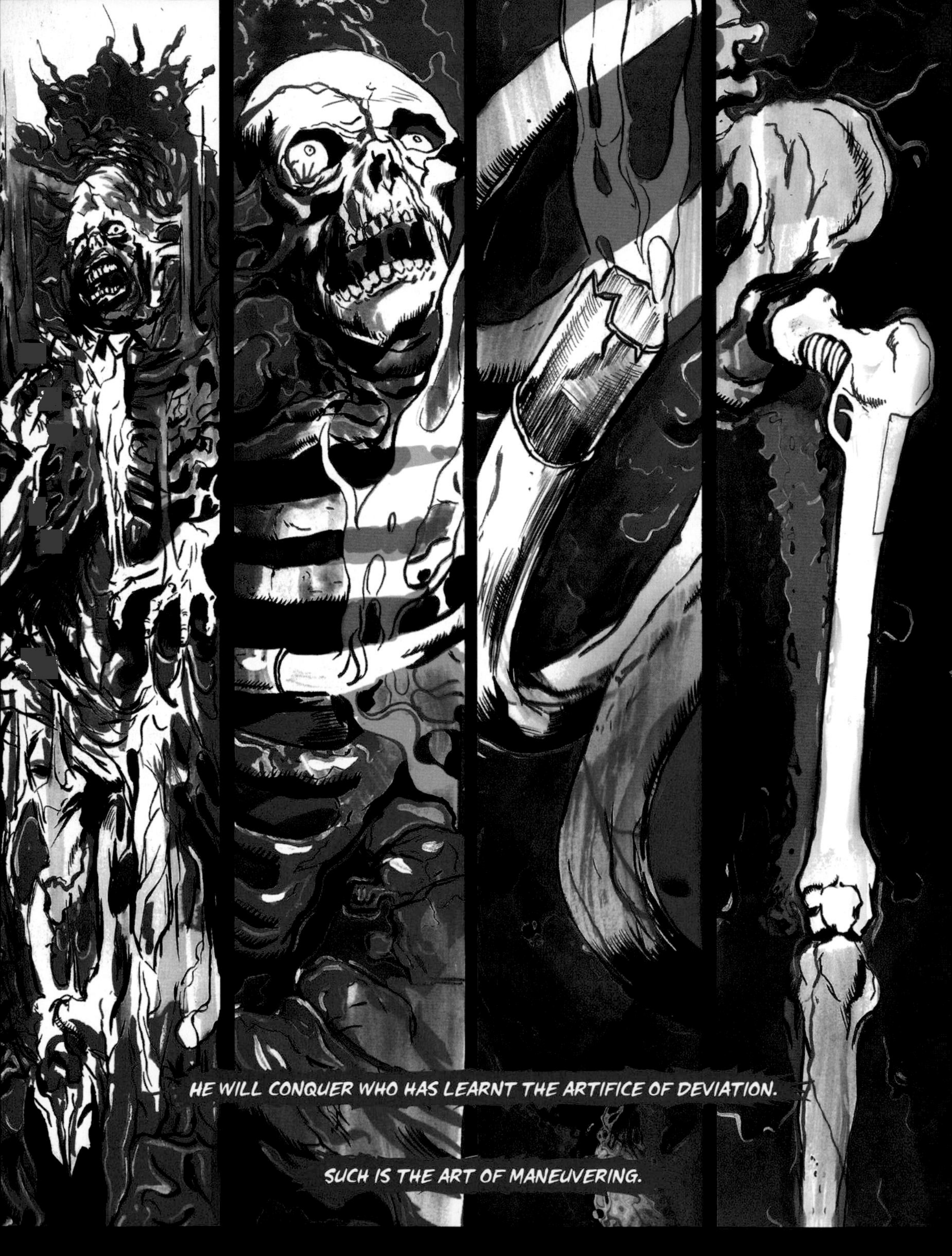
HE WILL CONQUER WHO HAS LEARNT THE ARTIFICE OF DEVIATION.
SUCH IS THE ART OF MANEUVERING.

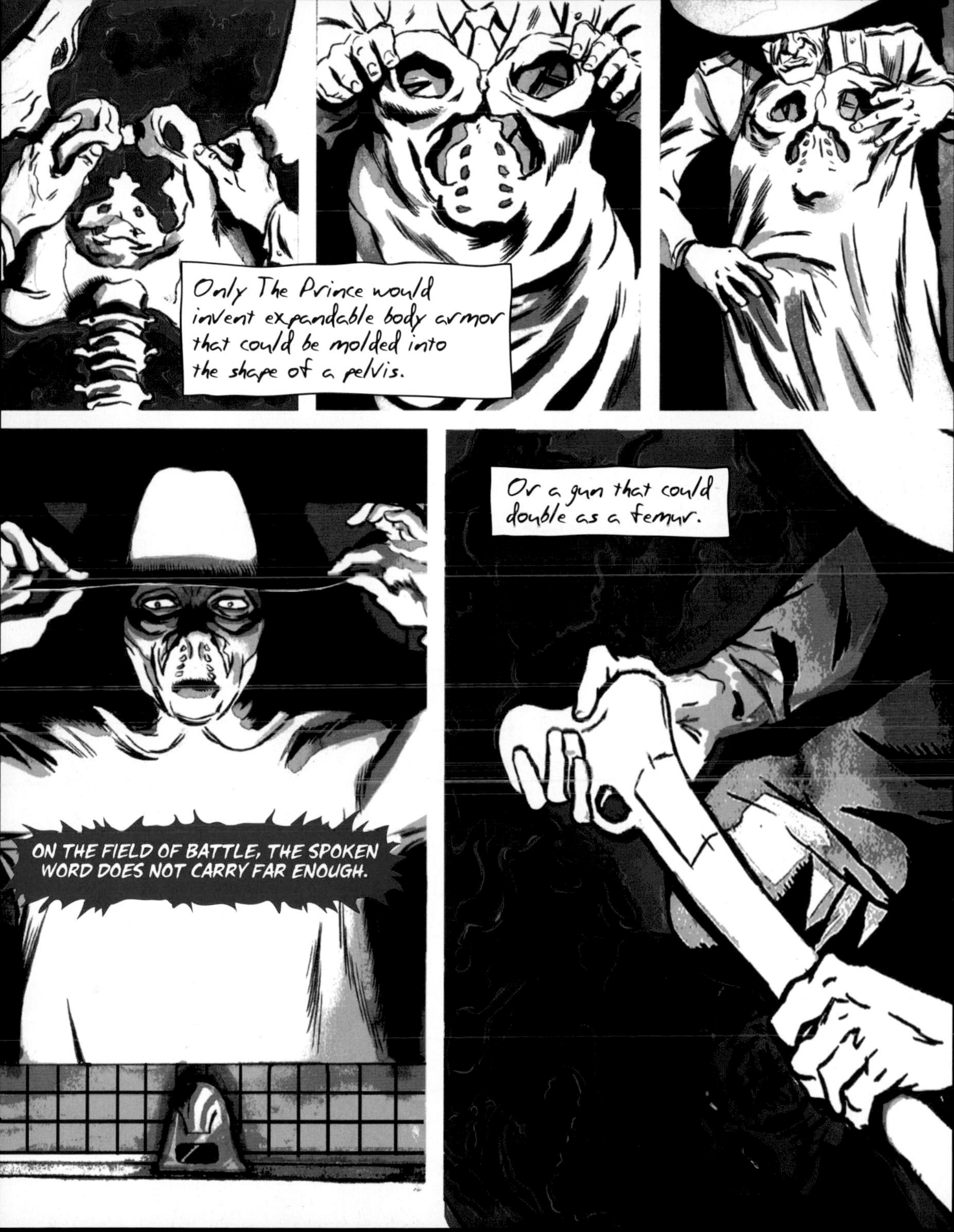
Only The Prince would invent expandable body armor that could be molded into the shape of a pelvis.
Or a gun that could double as a femur.
ON THE FIELD OF BATTLE, THE SPOKEN WORD DOES NOT CARRY FAR ENOUGH.

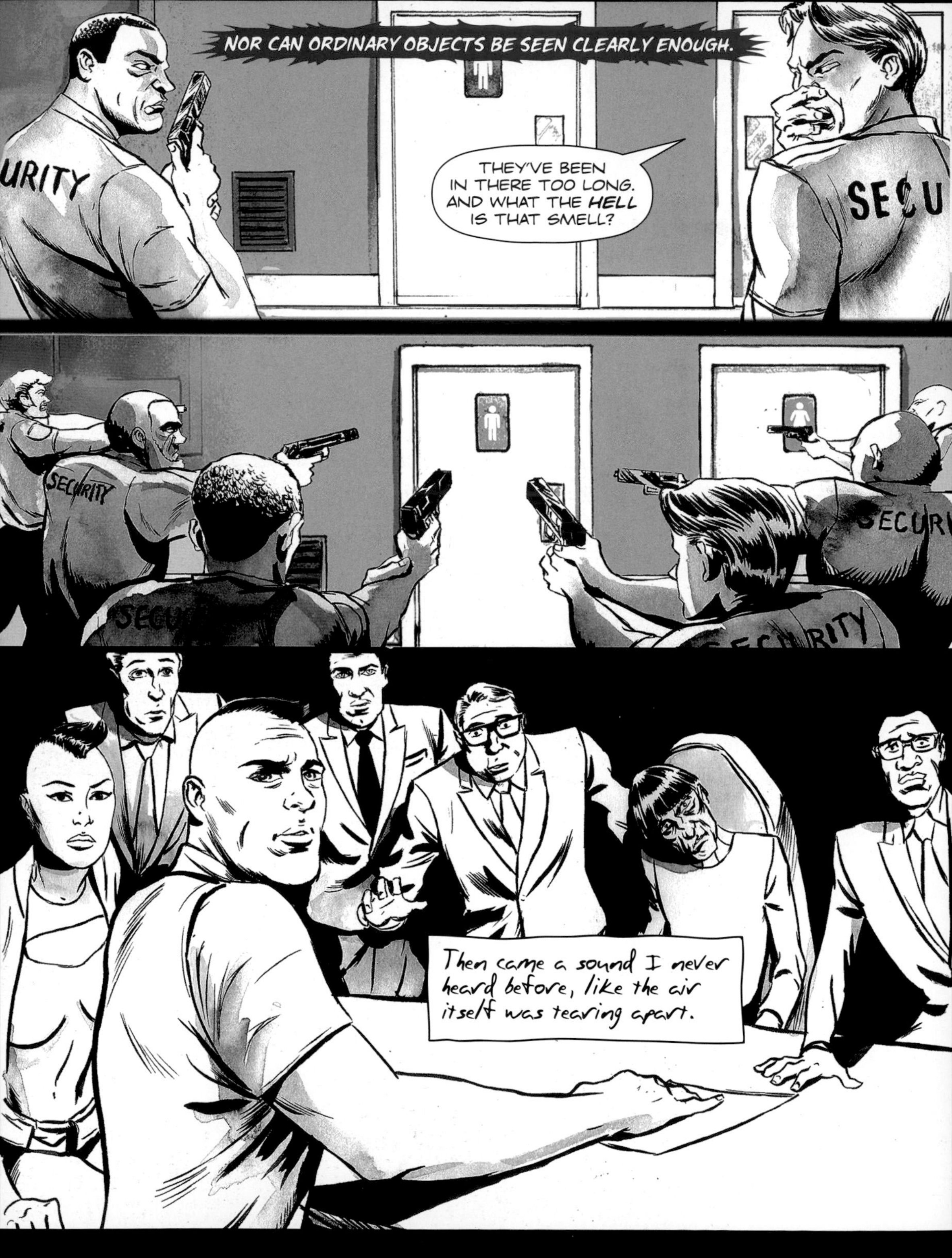
NOR CAN ORDINARY OBJECTS BE SEEN CLEARLY ENOUGH.
THEY'VE BEEN IN THERE TOO LONG. AND WHAT THE HELL IS THAT SMELL?
Then came a sound I never heard before, like the air itself was tearing apart.

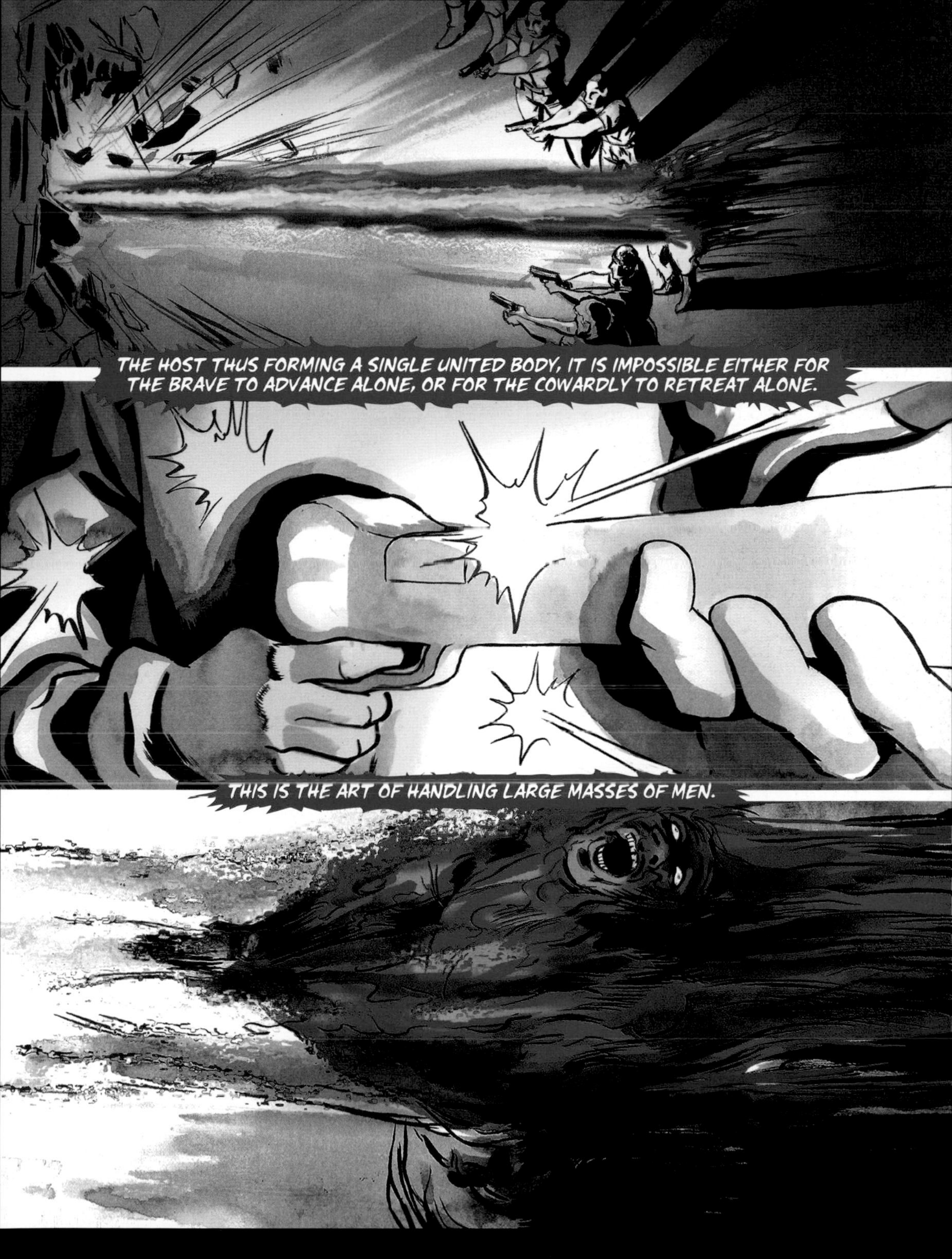
THE HOST THUS FORMING A SINGLE UNITED BODY, IT IS IMPOSSIBLE EITHER FOR THE BRAVE TO ADVANCE ALONE, OR FOR THE COWARDLY TO RETREAT ALONE.
THIS IS THE ART OF HANDLING LARGE MASSES OF MEN.

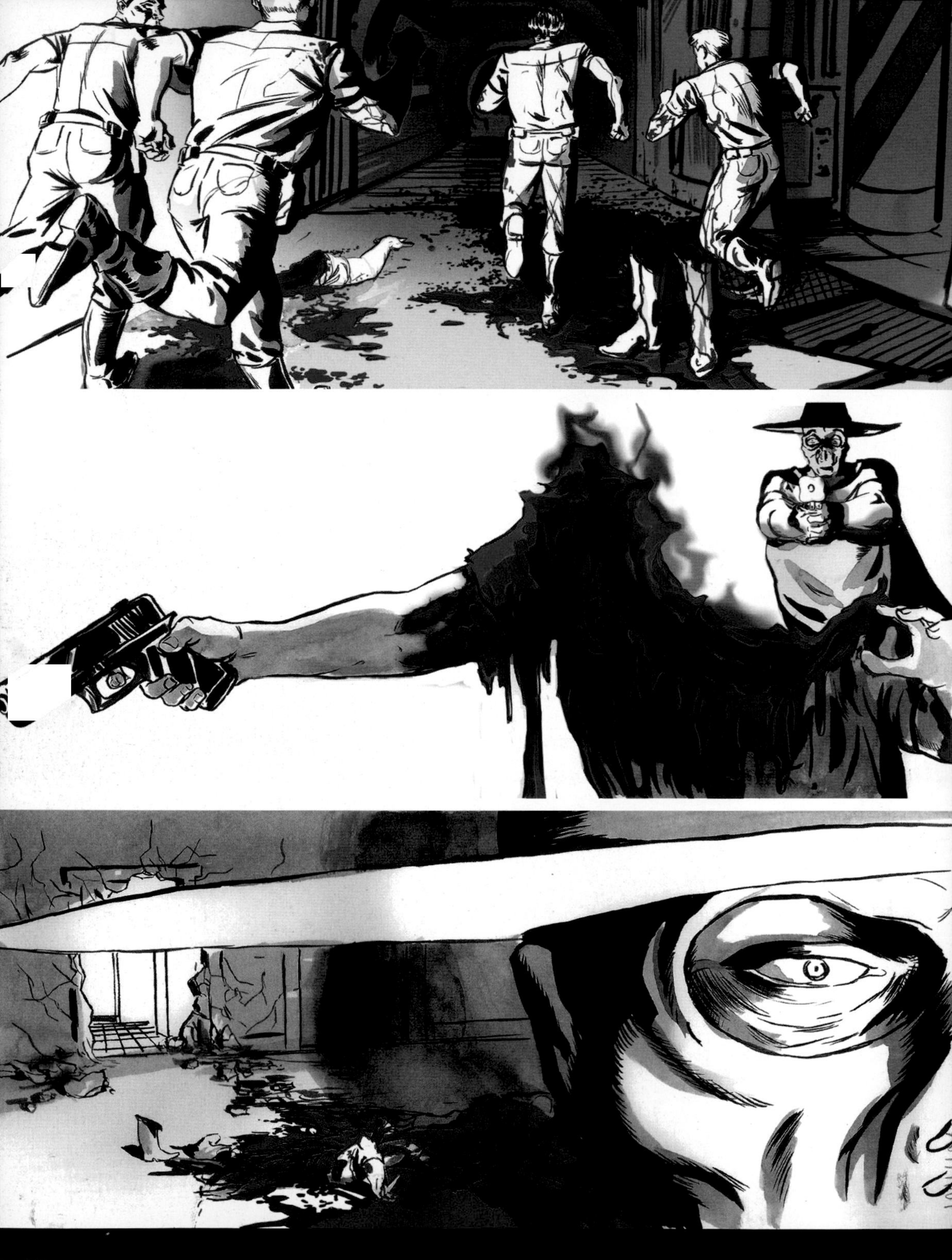

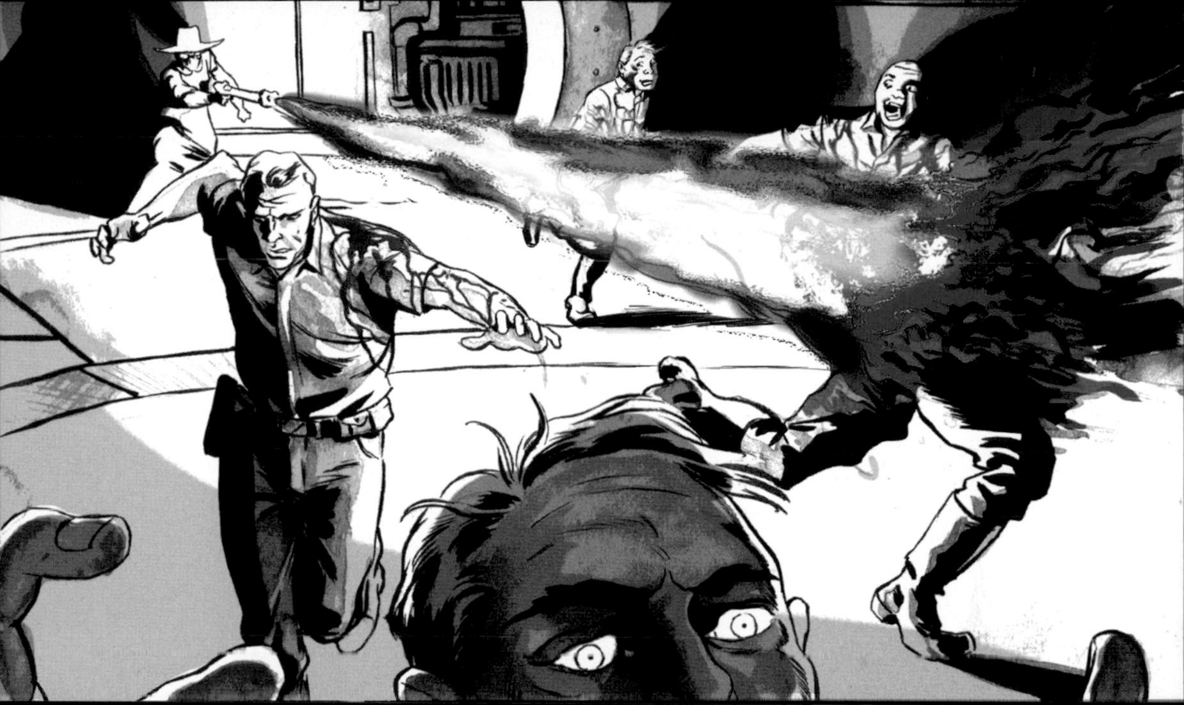

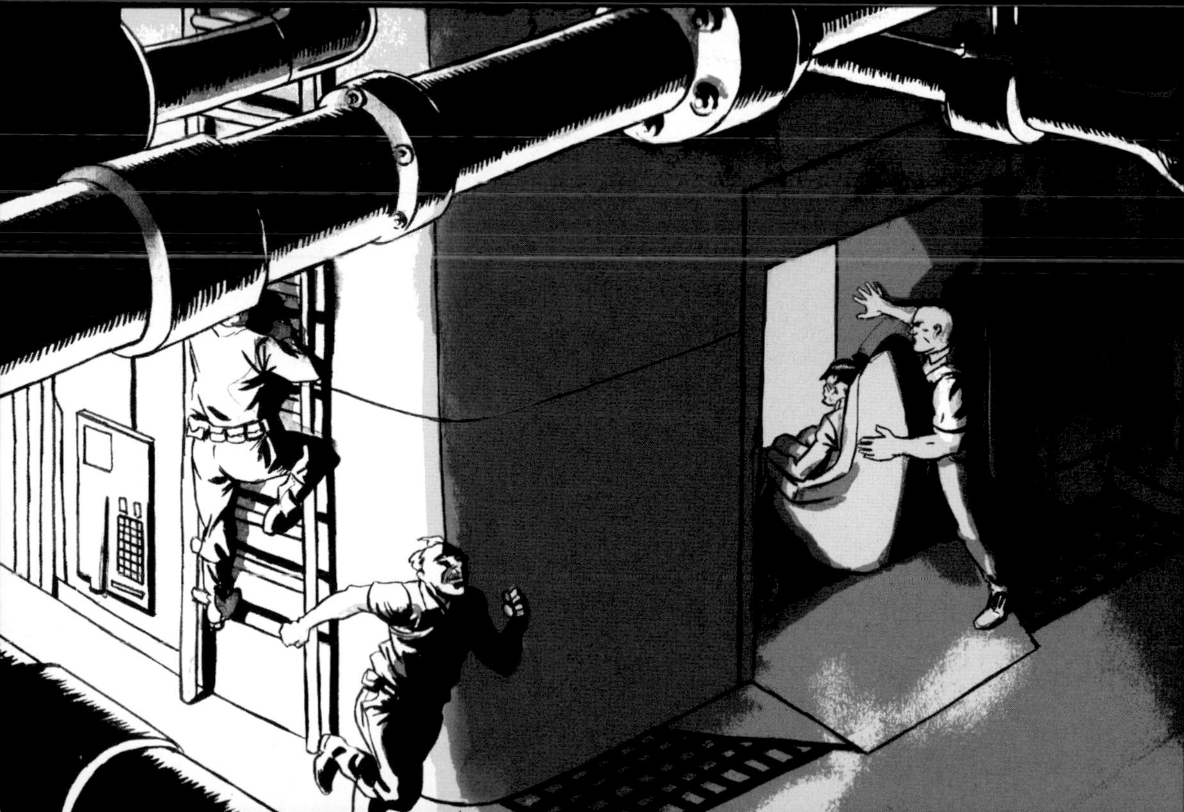

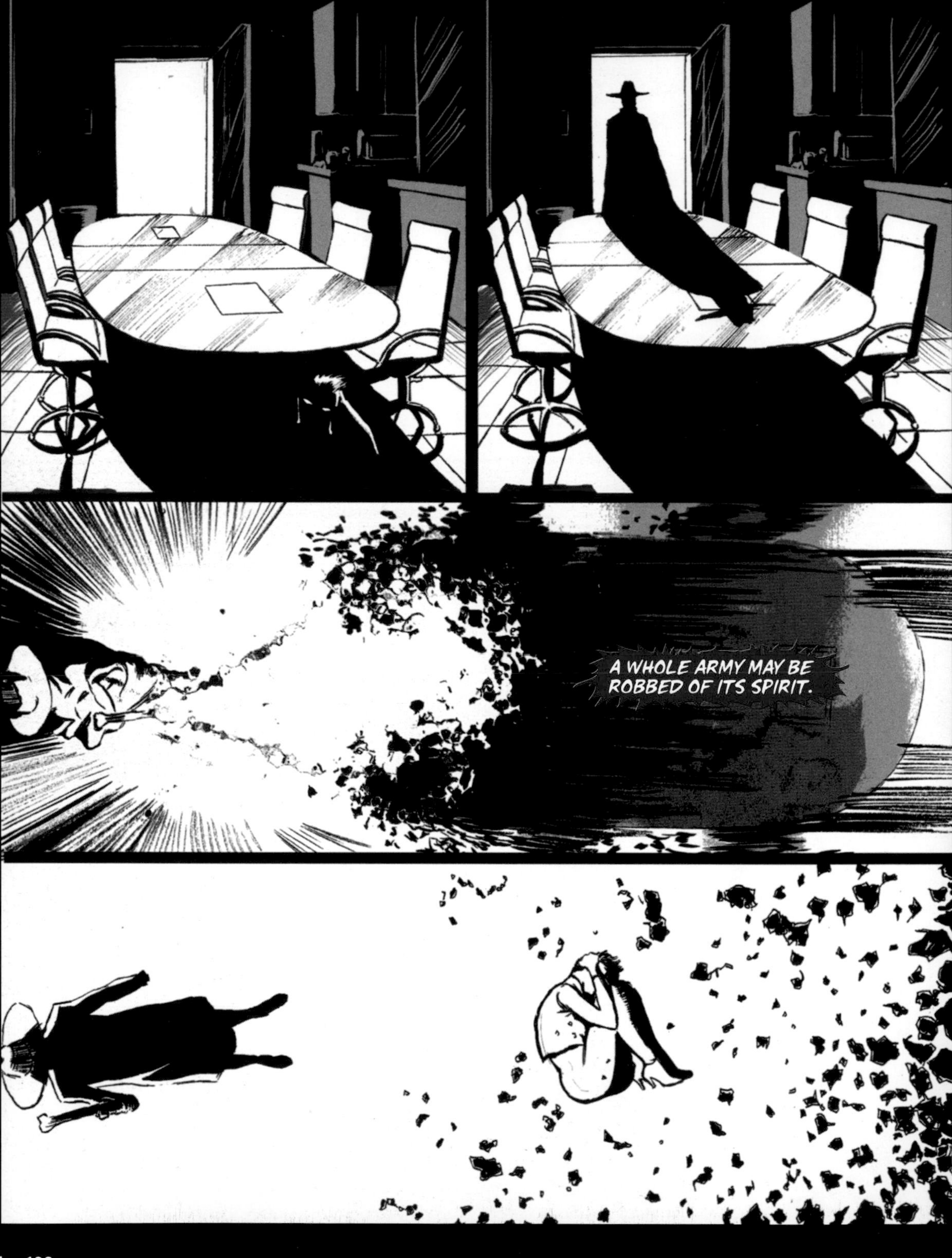
A WHOLE ARMY MAY BE ROBBED OF ITS SPIRIT.

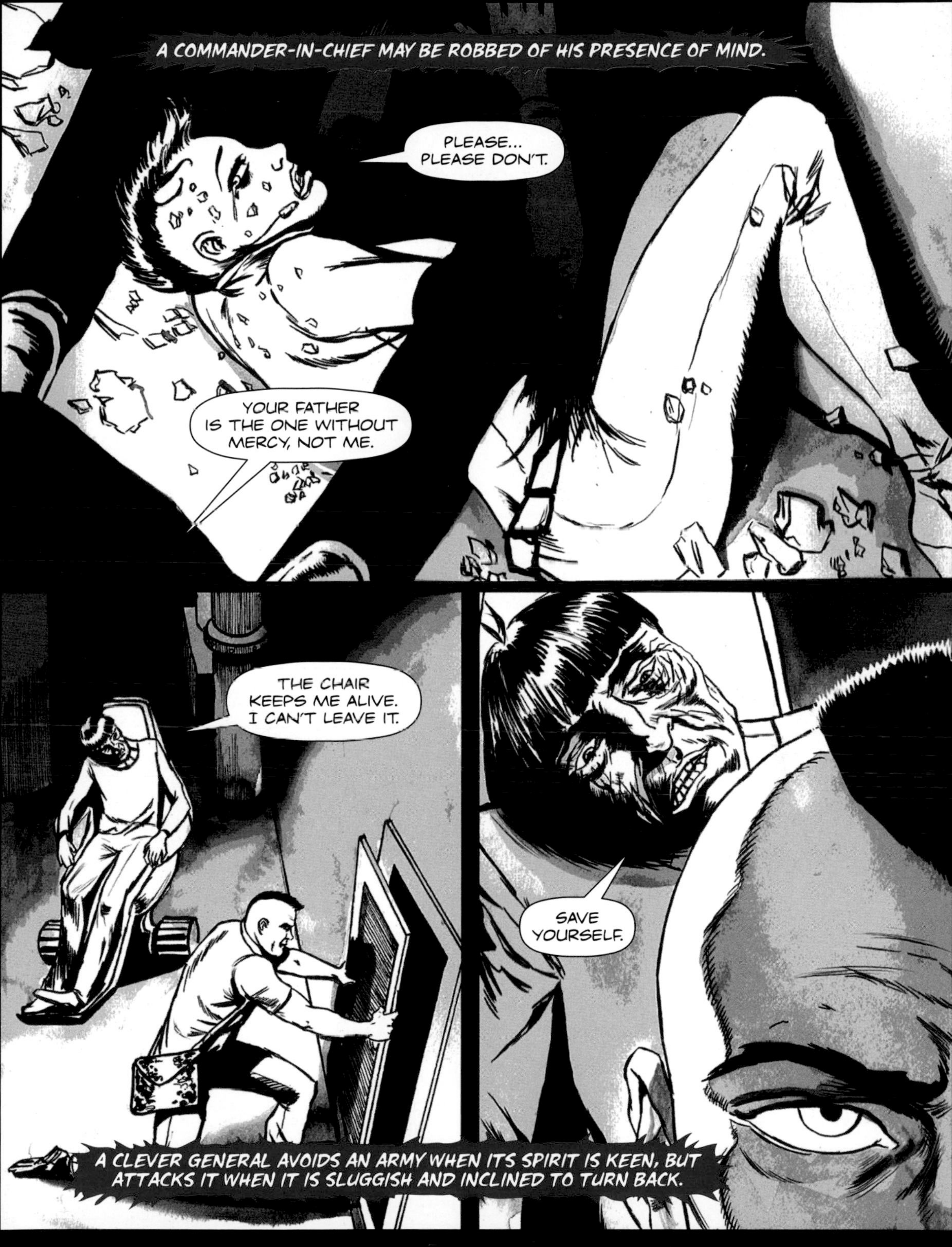
A COMMANDER-IN-CHIEF MAY BE ROBBED OF HIS PRESENCE OF MIND.
PLEASE... PLEASE DON'T.
YOUR FATHER IS THE ONE WITHOUT MERCY, NOT ME.
THE CHAIR KEEPS ME ALIVE. I CAN'T LEAVE IT.
SAVE YOURSELF.
A CLEVER GENERAL AVOIDS AN ARMY WHEN ITS SPIRIT IS KEEN, BUT ATTACKS IT WHEN IT IS SLUGGISH AND INCLINED TO TURN BACK.

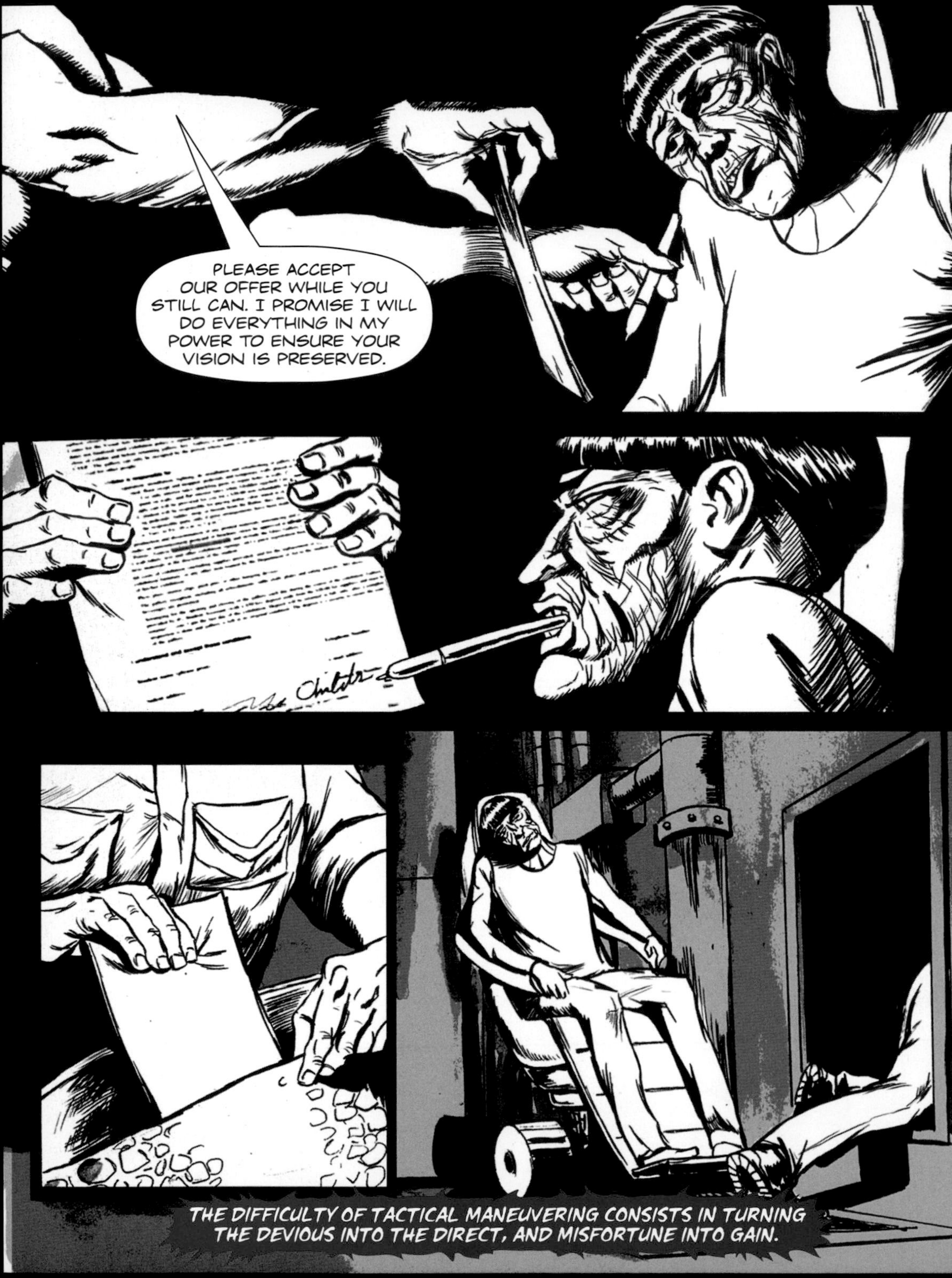
PLEASE ACCEPT OUR OFFER WHILE YOU STILL CAN. I PROMISE I WILL DO EVERYTHING IN MY POWER TO ENSURE YOUR VISION IS PRESERVED.
THE DIFFICULTY OF TACTICAL MANEUVERING CONSISTS IN TURNING THE DEVIOUS INTO THE DIRECT, AND MISFORTUNE INTO GAIN.

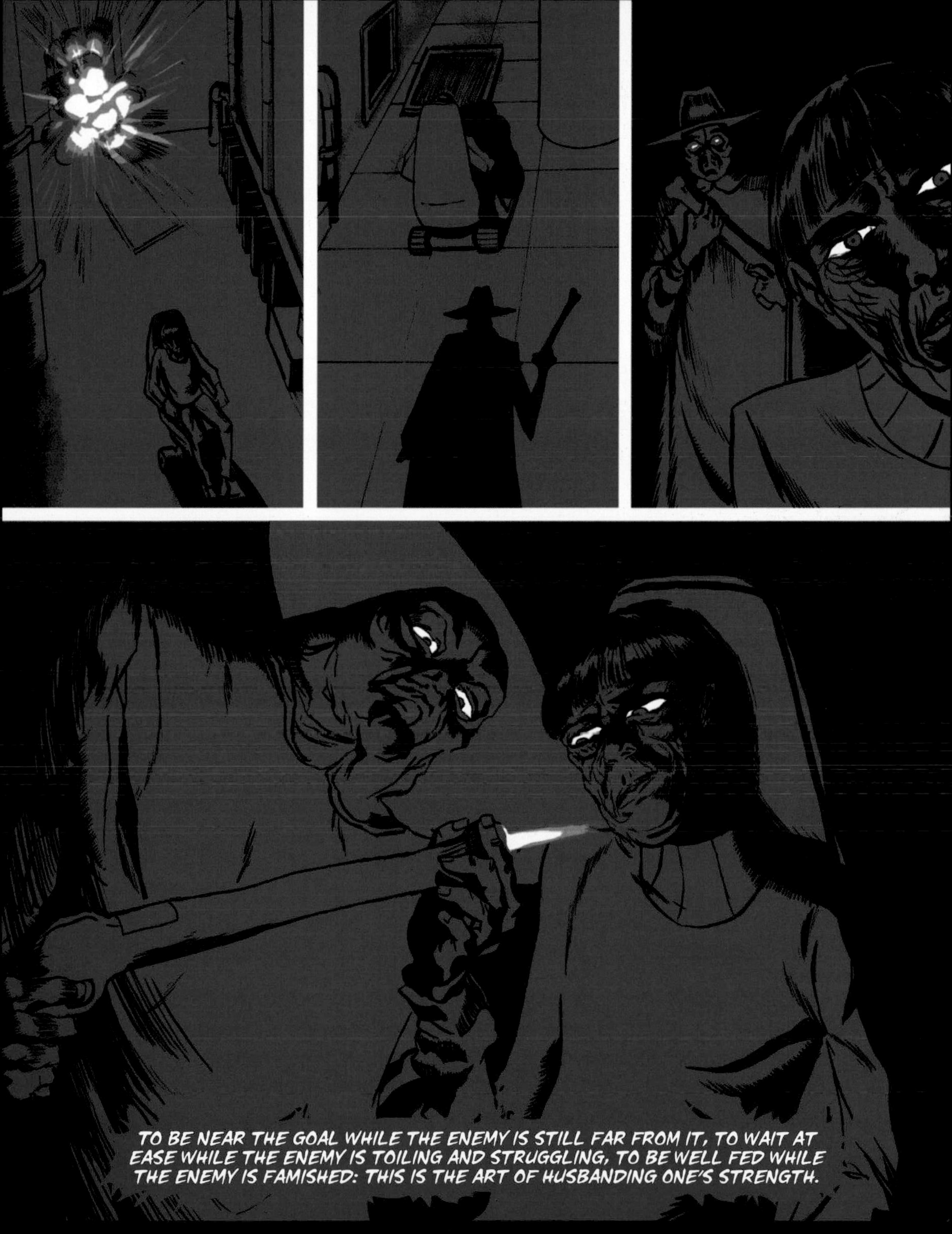
TO BE NEAR THE GOAL WHILE THE ENEMY IS STILL FAR FROM IT, TO WAIT AT EASE WHILE THE ENEMY IS TOILING AND STRUGGLING, TO BE WELL FED WHILE THE ENEMY IS FAMISHED: THIS IS THE ART OF HUSBANDING ONE'S STRENGTH.

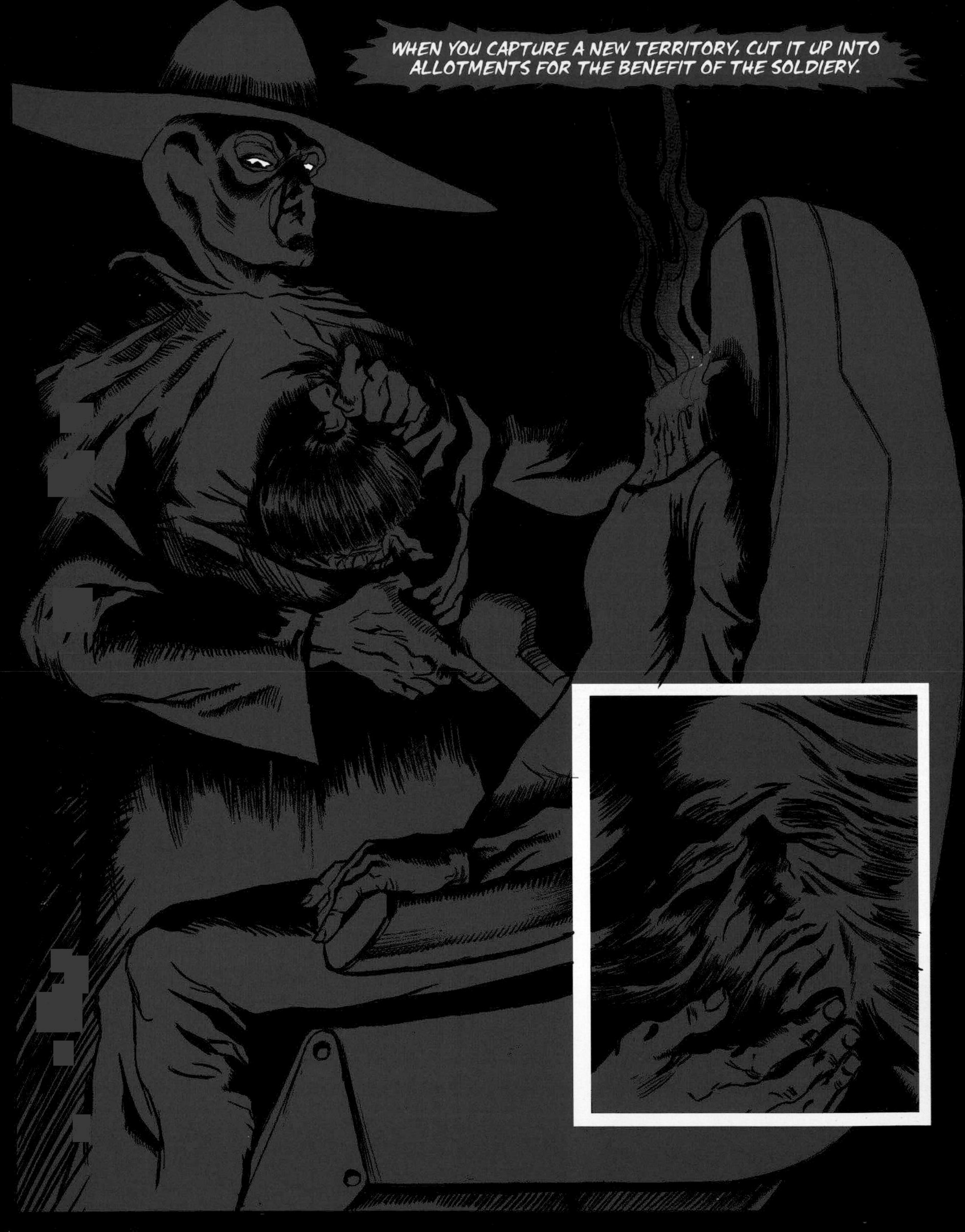
WHEN YOU CAPTURE A NEW TERRITORY, CUT IT UP INTO ALLOTMENTS FOR THE BENEFIT OF THE SOLDIERY.

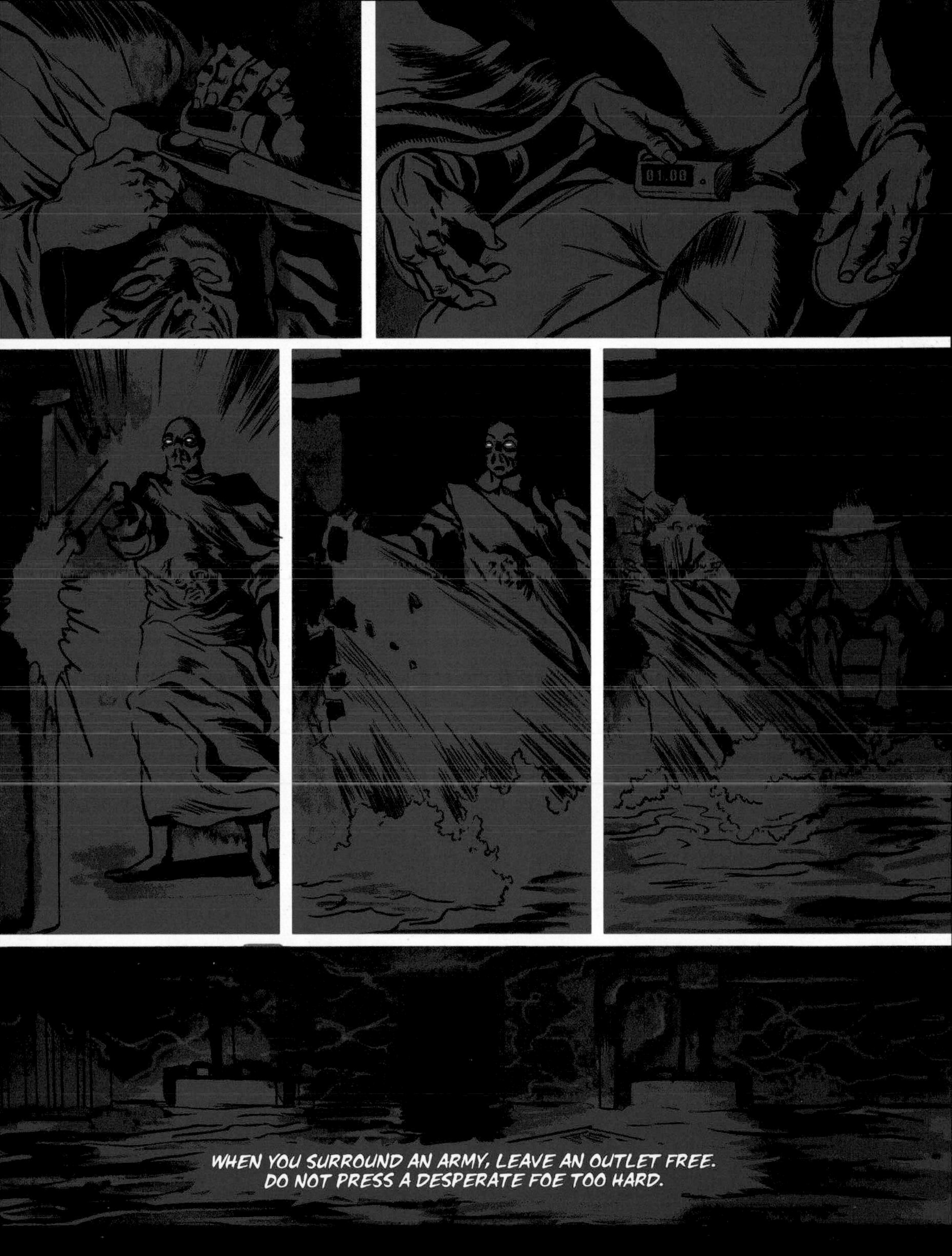
01.00
WHEN YOU SURROUND AN ARMY, LEAVE AN OUTLET FREE.
DO NOT PRESS A DESPERATE FOE TOO HARD.

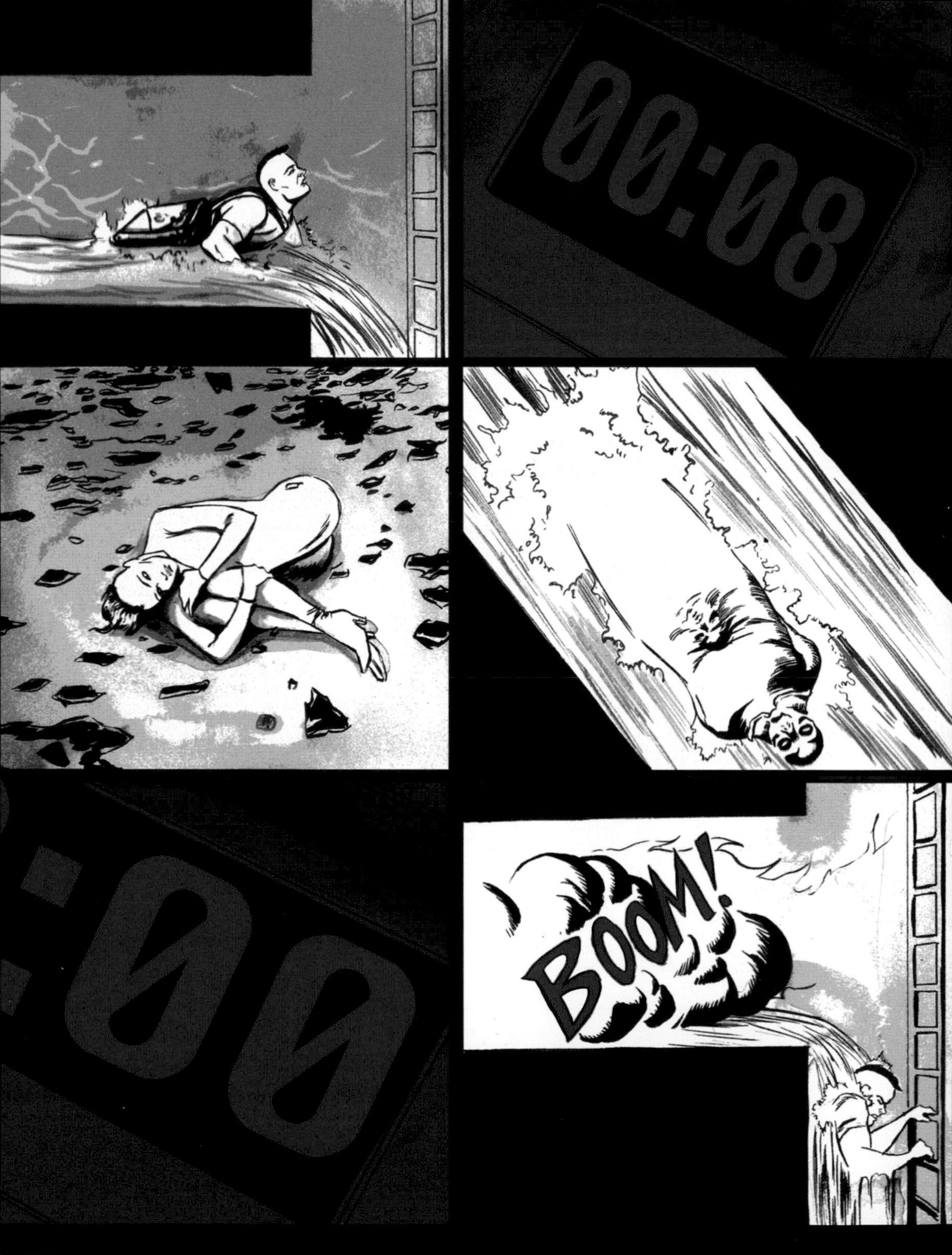
00:08
00
BOOM!

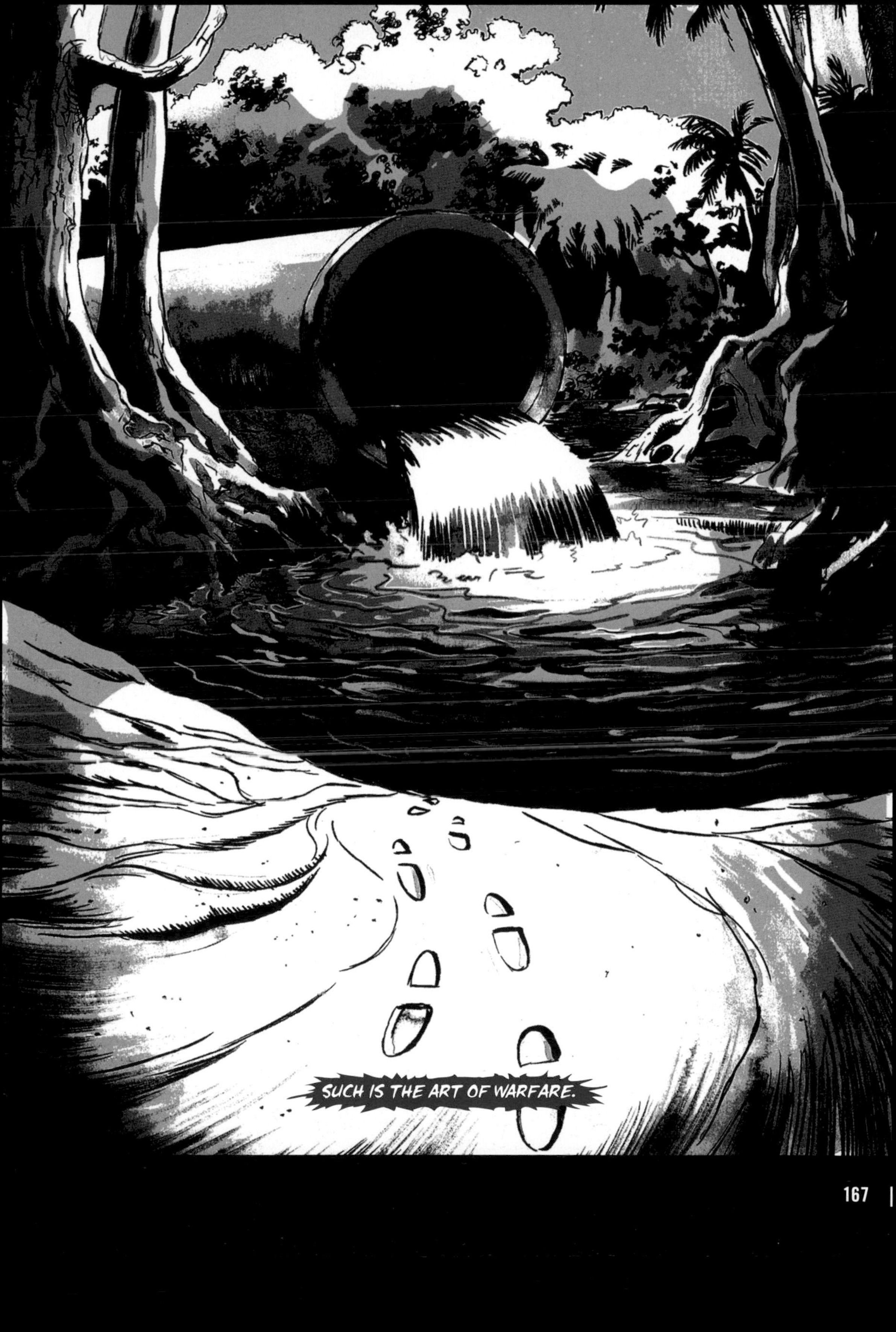
SUCH IS THE ART OF WARFARE.

九變篇

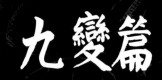

VIII.
VARIATION OF TACTICS

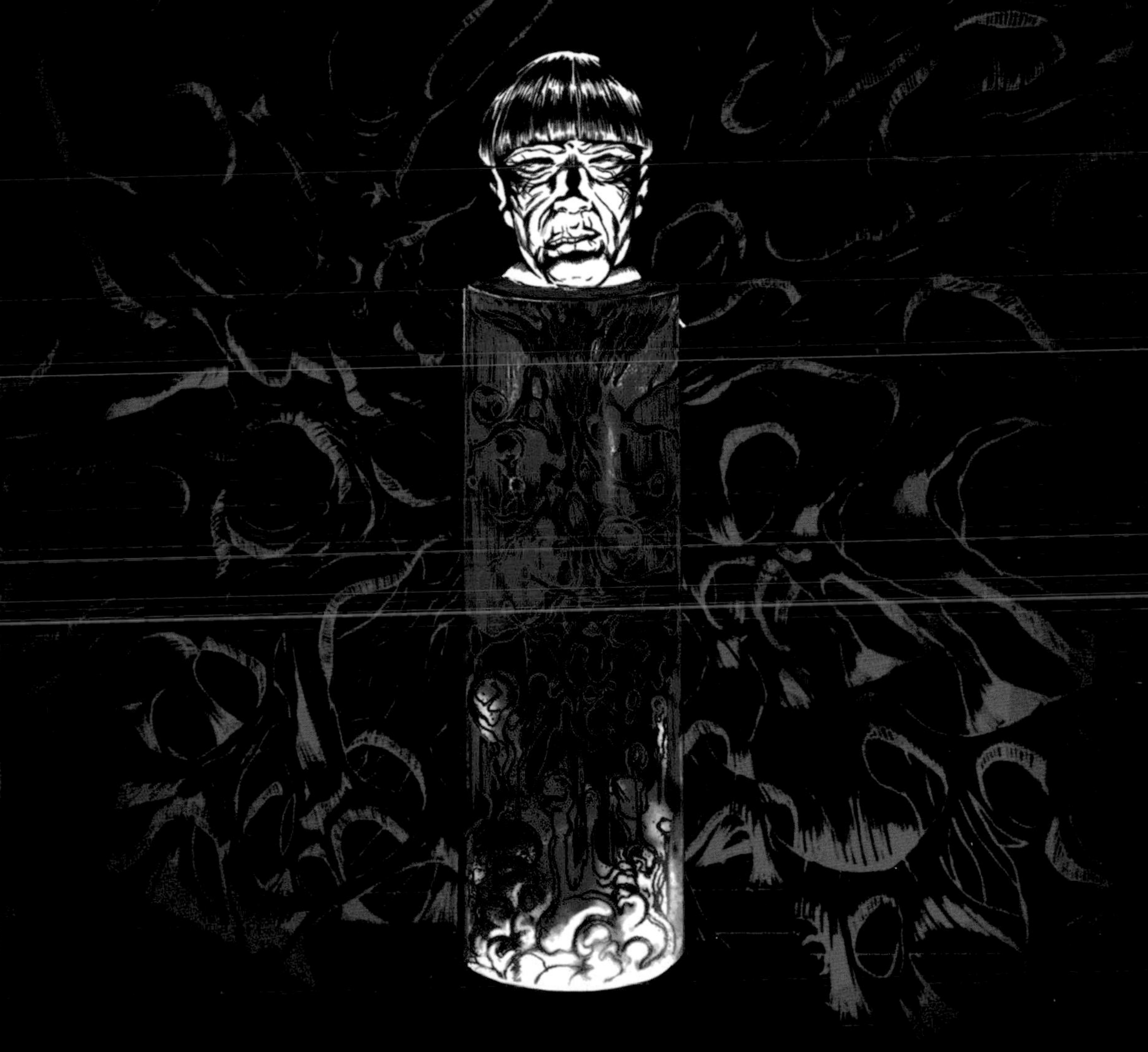

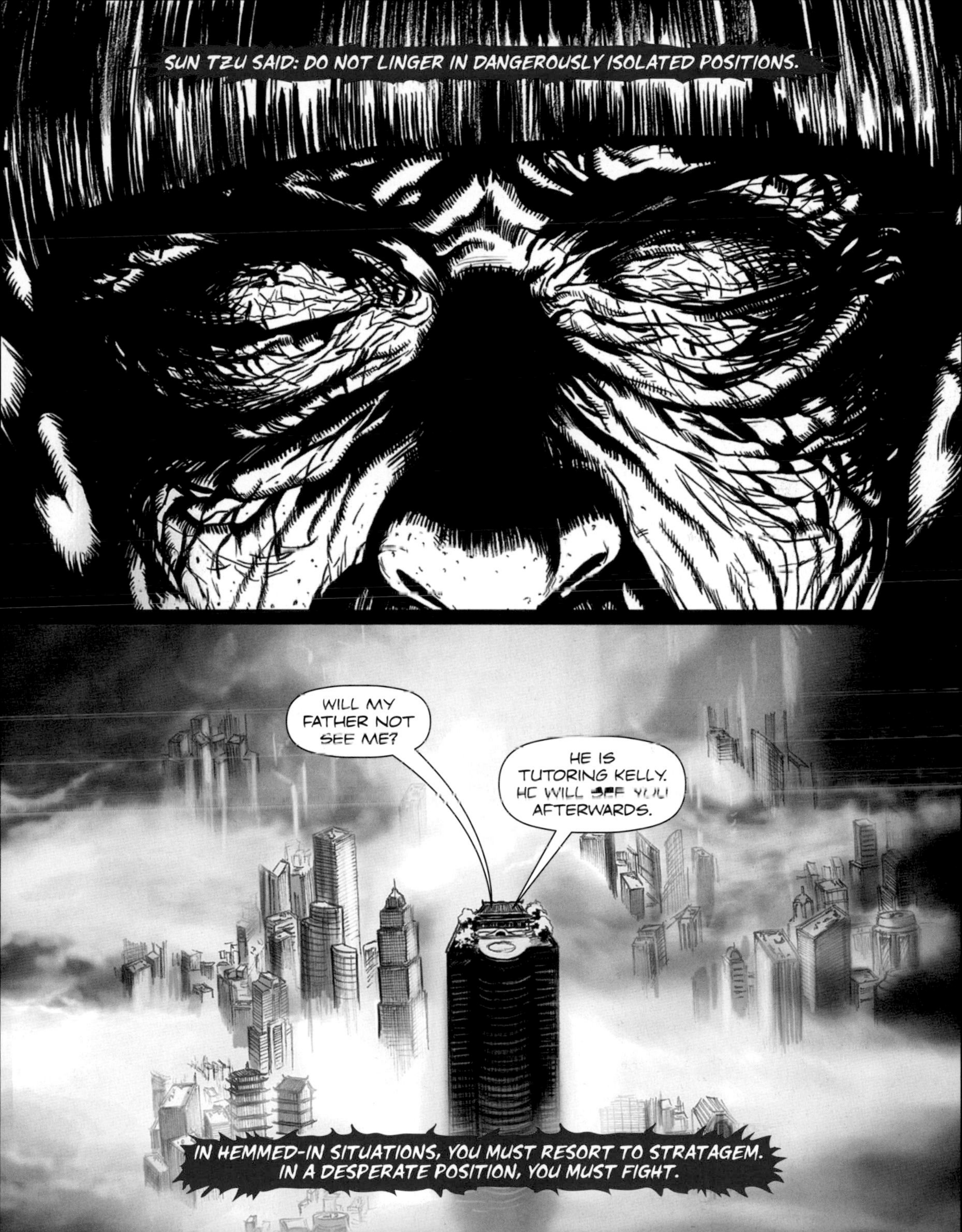
SUN TZU SAID: DO NOT LINGER IN DANGEROUSLY ISOLATED POSITIONS.
WILL MY FATHER NOT SEE ME?
HE IS TUTORING KELLY. HE WILL SEE YOU AFTERWARDS.
IN HEMMED-IN SITUATIONS, YOU MUST RESORT TO STRATAGEM. IN A DESPERATE POSITION, YOU MUST FIGHT.

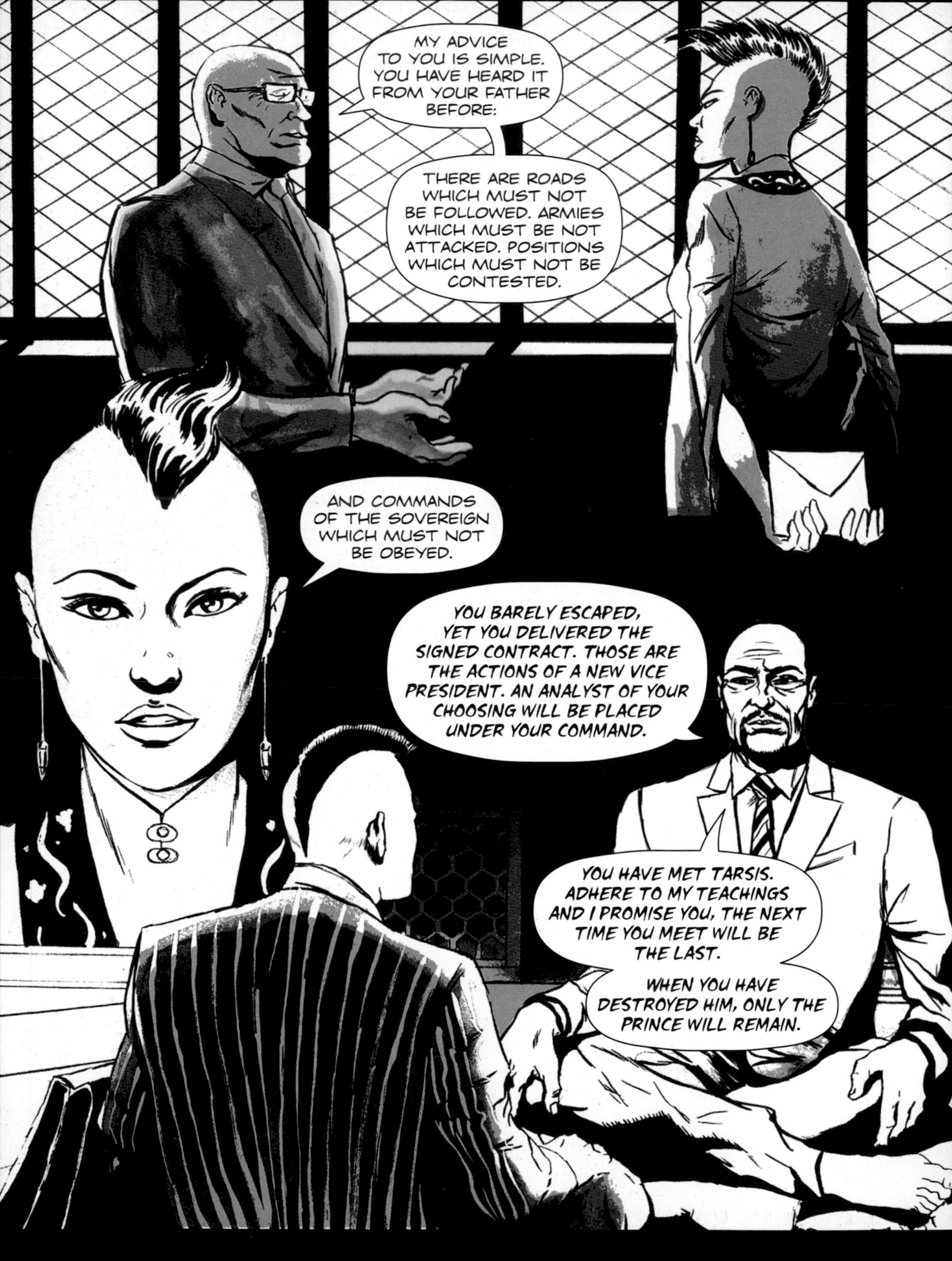
MY ADVICE TO YOU IS SIMPLE. YOU HAVE HEARD IT FROM YOUR FATHER BEFORE:
THERE ARE ROADS WHICH MUST NOT BE FOLLOWED. ARMIES WHICH MUST BE NOT ATTACKED. POSITIONS WHICH MUST NOT BE CONTESTED.
AND COMMANDS OF THE SOVEREIGN WHICH MUST NOT BE OBEYED.
YOU BARELY ESCAPED, YET YOU DELIVERED THE SIGNED CONTRACT. THOSE ARE THE ACTIONS OF A NEW VICE PRESIDENT. AN ANALYST OF YOUR CHOOSING WILL BE PLACED UNDER YOUR COMMAND.
YOU HAVE MET TARSIS. ADHERE TO MY TEACHINGS AND I PROMISE YOU, THE NEXT TIME YOU MEET WILL BE THE LAST.
WHEN YOU HAVE DESTROYED HIM, ONLY THE PRINCE WILL REMAIN.

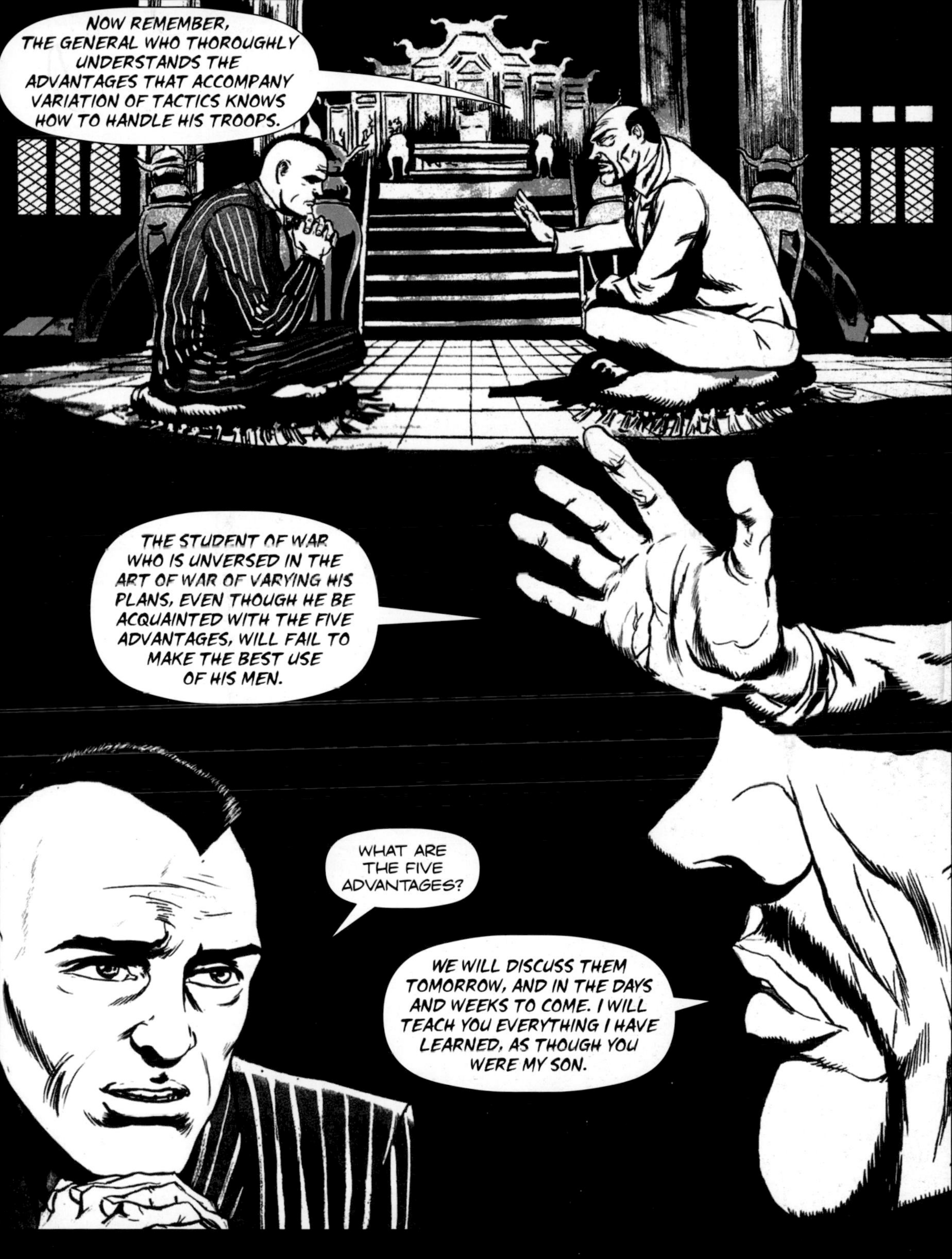
NOW REMEMBER, THE GENERAL WHO THOROUGHLY UNDERSTANDS THE ADVANTAGES THAT ACCOMPANY VARIATION OF TACTICS KNOWS HOW TO HANDLE HIS TROOPS.
THE STUDENT OF WAR WHO IS UNVERSED IN THE ART OF WAR OF VARYING HIS PLANS, EVEN THOUGH HE BE ACQUAINTED WITH THE FIVE ADVANTAGES, WILL FAIL TO MAKE THE BEST USE OF HIS MEN.
WHAT ARE THE FIVE ADVANTAGES?
WE WILL DISCUSS THEM TOMORROW, AND IN THE DAYS AND WEEKS TO COME. I WILL TEACH YOU EVERYTHING I HAVE LEARNED, AS THOUGH YOU WERE MY SON.

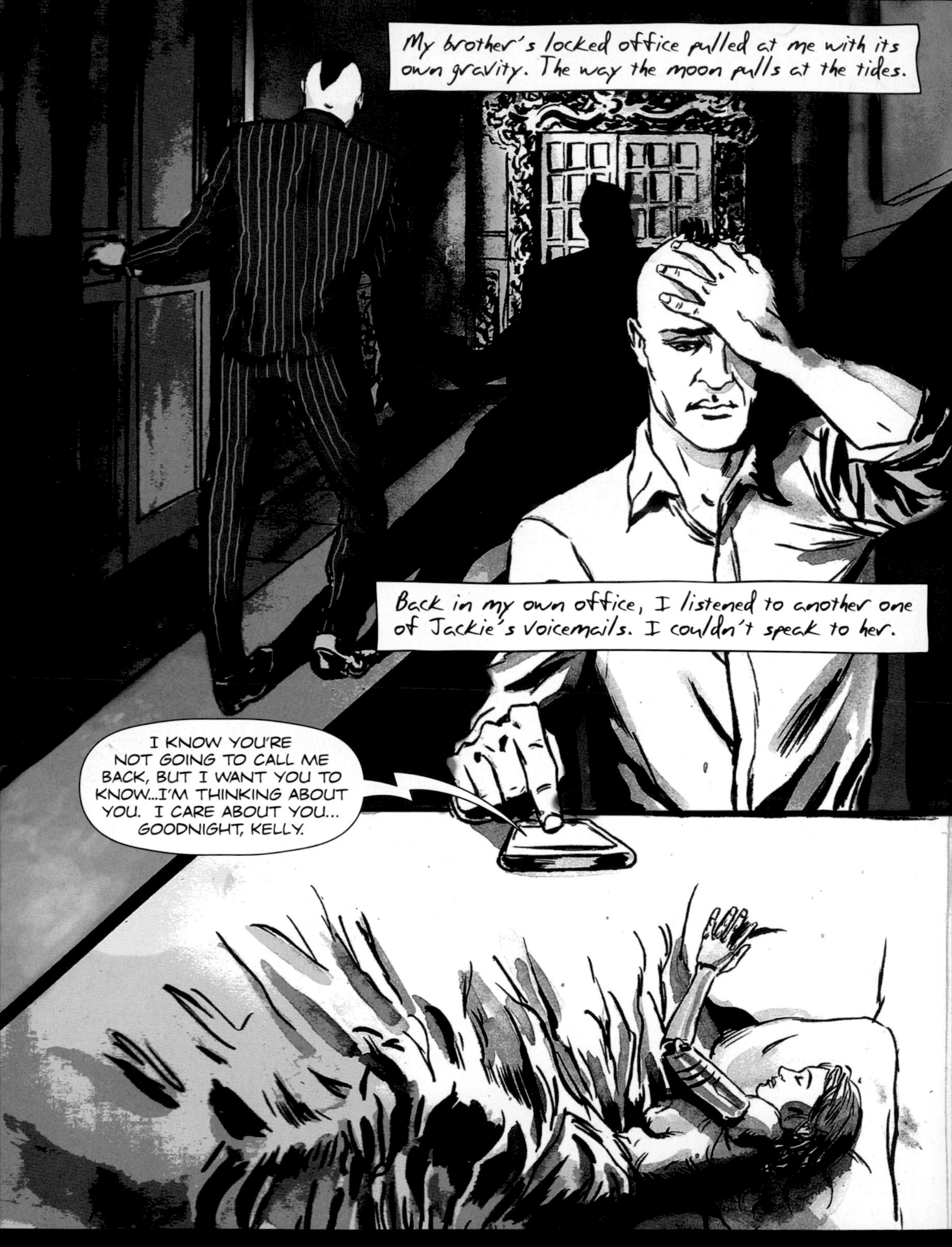
My brother's locked office pulled at me with its own gravity. The way the moon pulls at the tides.
Back in my own office, I listened to another one of Jackie's voicemails. I couldn't speak to her.
I KNOW YOU'RE NOT GOING TO CALL ME BACK, BUT I WANT YOU TO KNOW...I'M THINKING ABOUT YOU. I CARE ABOUT YOU... GOODNIGHT, KELLY.

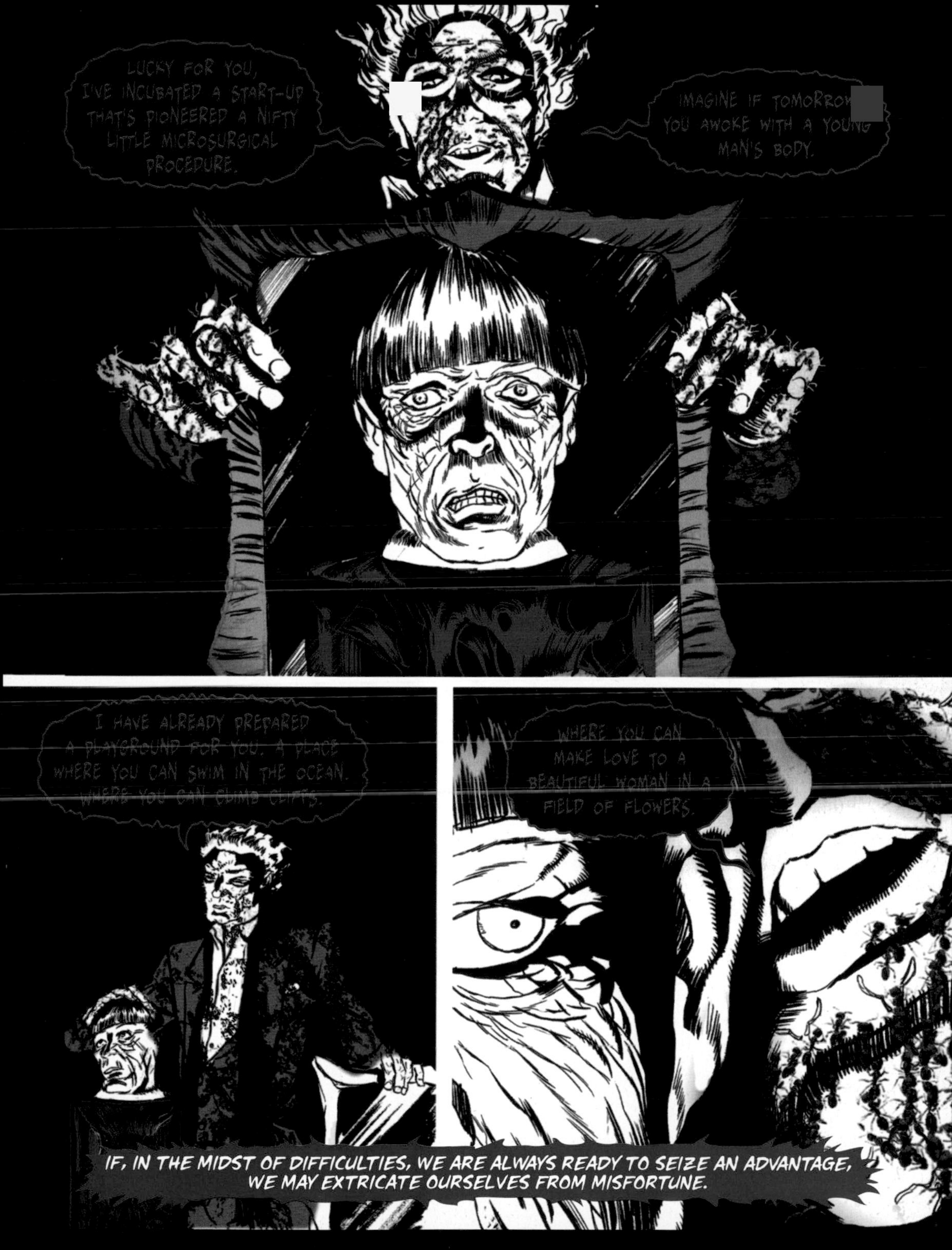
LUCKY FOR YOU, I'VE INCUBATED A START-UP THAT'S PIONEERED A NIFTY LITTLE MICROSURGICAL PROCEDURE.
IMAGINE IF TOMORRO[redacted] YOU AWOKE WITH A YOUNG MAN'S BODY.
I HAVE ALREADY PREPARED A PLAYGROUND FOR YOU. A PLACE WHERE YOU CAN SWIM IN THE OCEAN. WHERE YOU CAN CLIMB CLIFFS.
WHERE YOU CAN MAKE LOVE TO A BEAUTIFUL WOMAN IN A FIELD OF FLOWERS.
IF, IN THE MIDST OF DIFFICULTIES, WE ARE ALWAYS READY TO SEIZE AN ADVANTAGE, WE MAY EXTRICATE OURSELVES FROM MISFORTUNE.

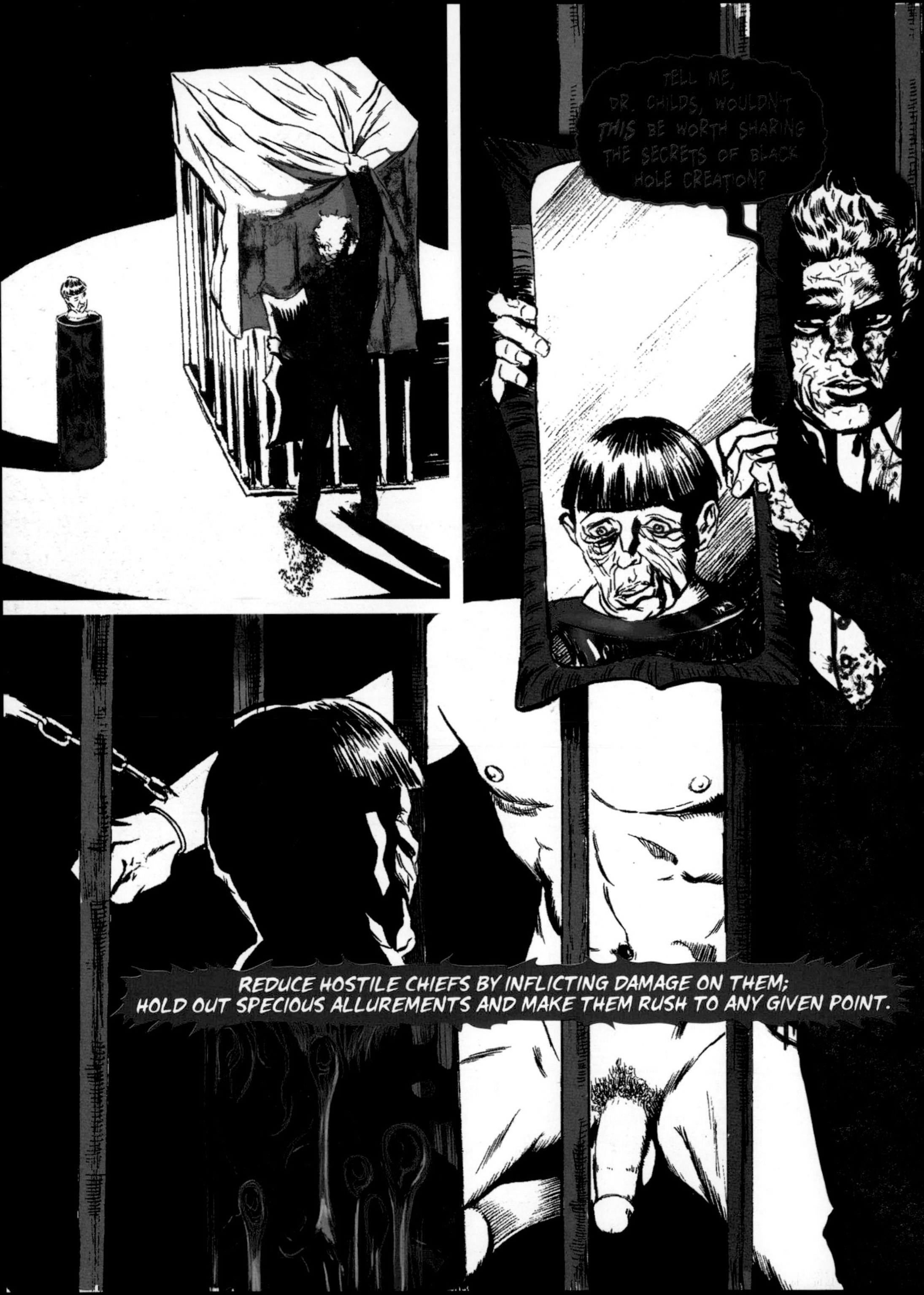
TELL ME, DR. CHILDS, WOULDN'T THIS BE WORTH SHARING THE SECRETS OF BLACK HOLE CREATION?
REDUCE HOSTILE CHIEFS BY INFLICTING DAMAGE ON THEM; HOLD OUT SPECIOUS ALLUREMENTS AND MAKE THEM RUSH TO ANY GIVEN POINT.

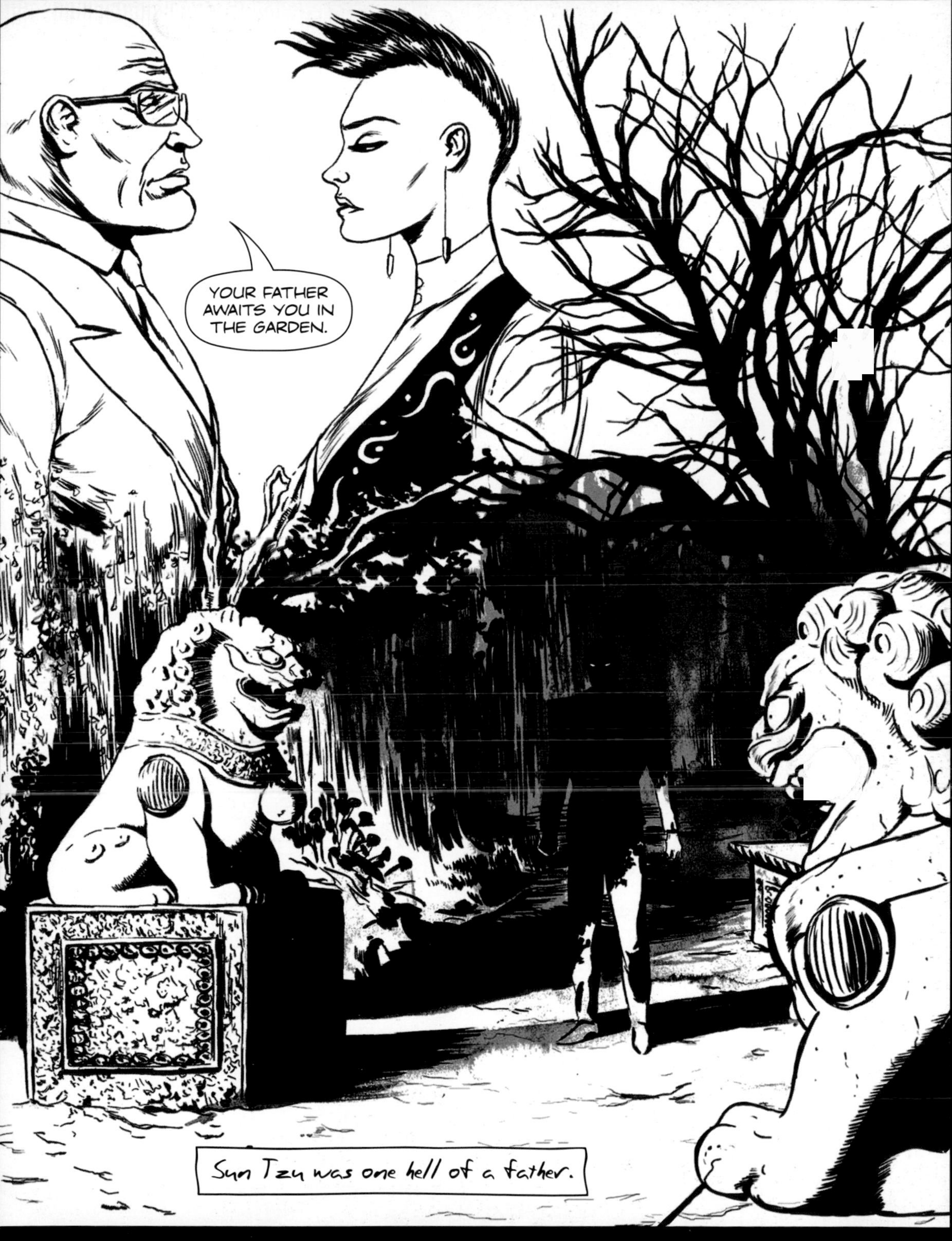
YOUR FATHER AWAITS YOU IN THE GARDEN.
Sun Tzu was one hell of a father.

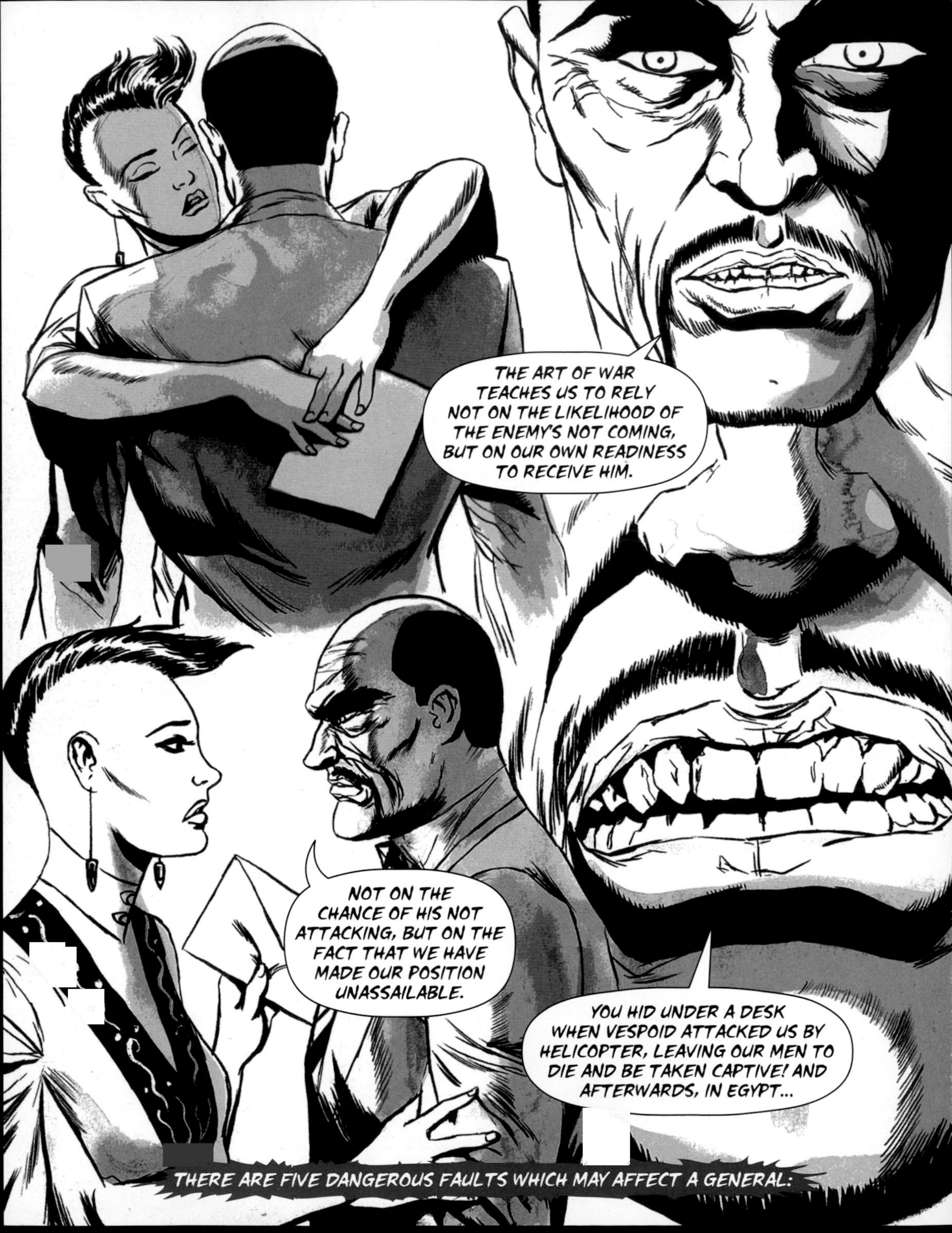
THE ART OF WAR TEACHES US TO RELY NOT ON THE LIKELIHOOD OF THE ENEMY'S NOT COMING, BUT ON OUR OWN READINESS TO RECEIVE HIM.
NOT ON THE CHANCE OF HIS NOT ATTACKING, BUT ON THE FACT THAT WE HAVE MADE OUR POSITION UNASSAILABLE.
YOU HID UNDER A DESK WHEN VESPOID ATTACKED US BY HELICOPTER, LEAVING OUR MEN TO DIE AND BE TAKEN CAPTIVE! AND AFTERWARDS, IN EGYPT...
THERE ARE FIVE DANGEROUS FAULTS WHICH MAY AFFECT A GENERAL:

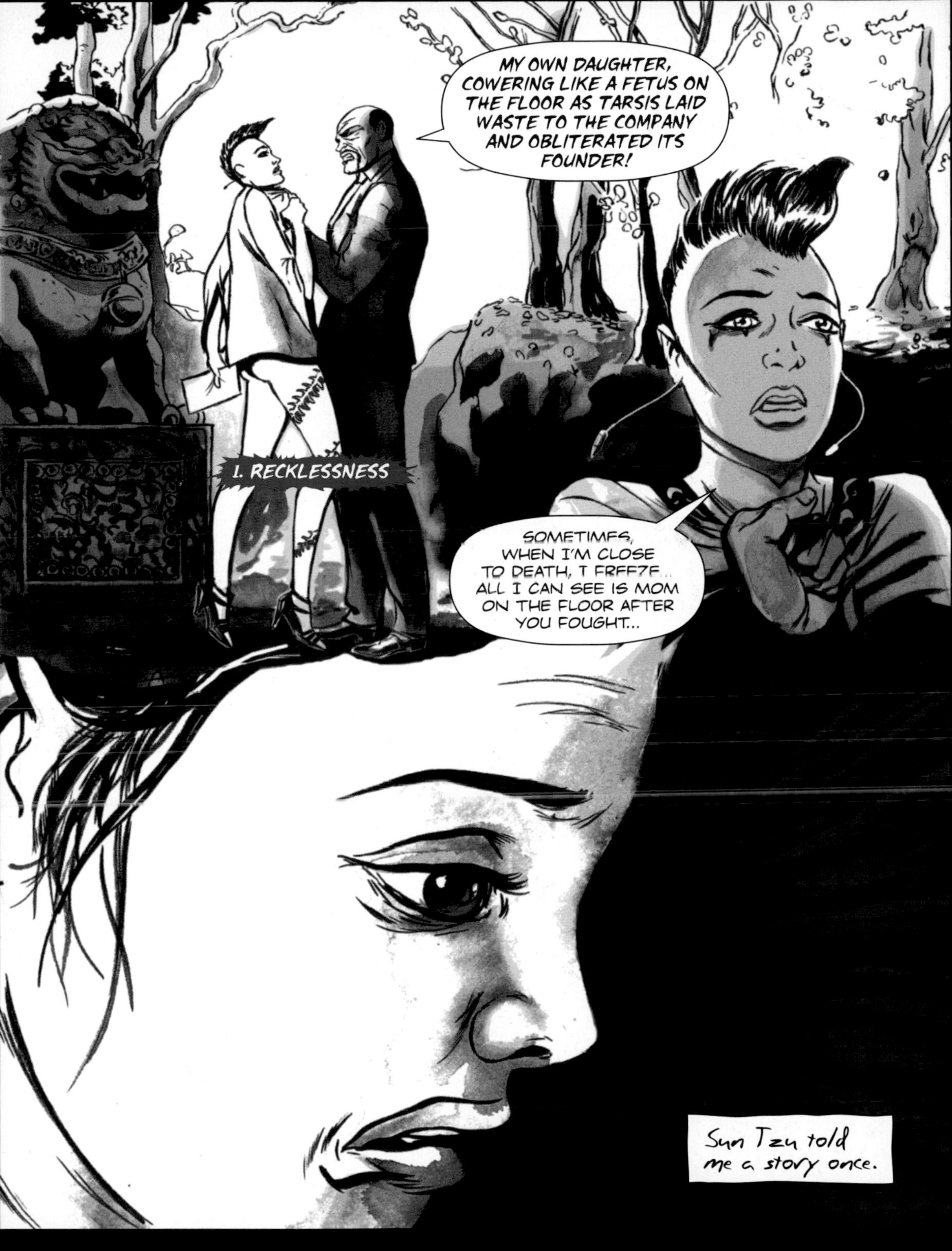
MY OWN DAUGHTER, COWERING LIKE A FETUS ON THE FLOOR AS TARSIS LAID WASTE TO THE COMPANY AND OBLITERATED ITS FOUNDER!
1. RECKLESSNESS
SOMETIMES, WHEN I'M CLOSE TO DEATH, I FREEZE... ALL I CAN SEE IS MOM ON THE FLOOR AFTER YOU FOUGHT...
Sun Tzu told me a story once.

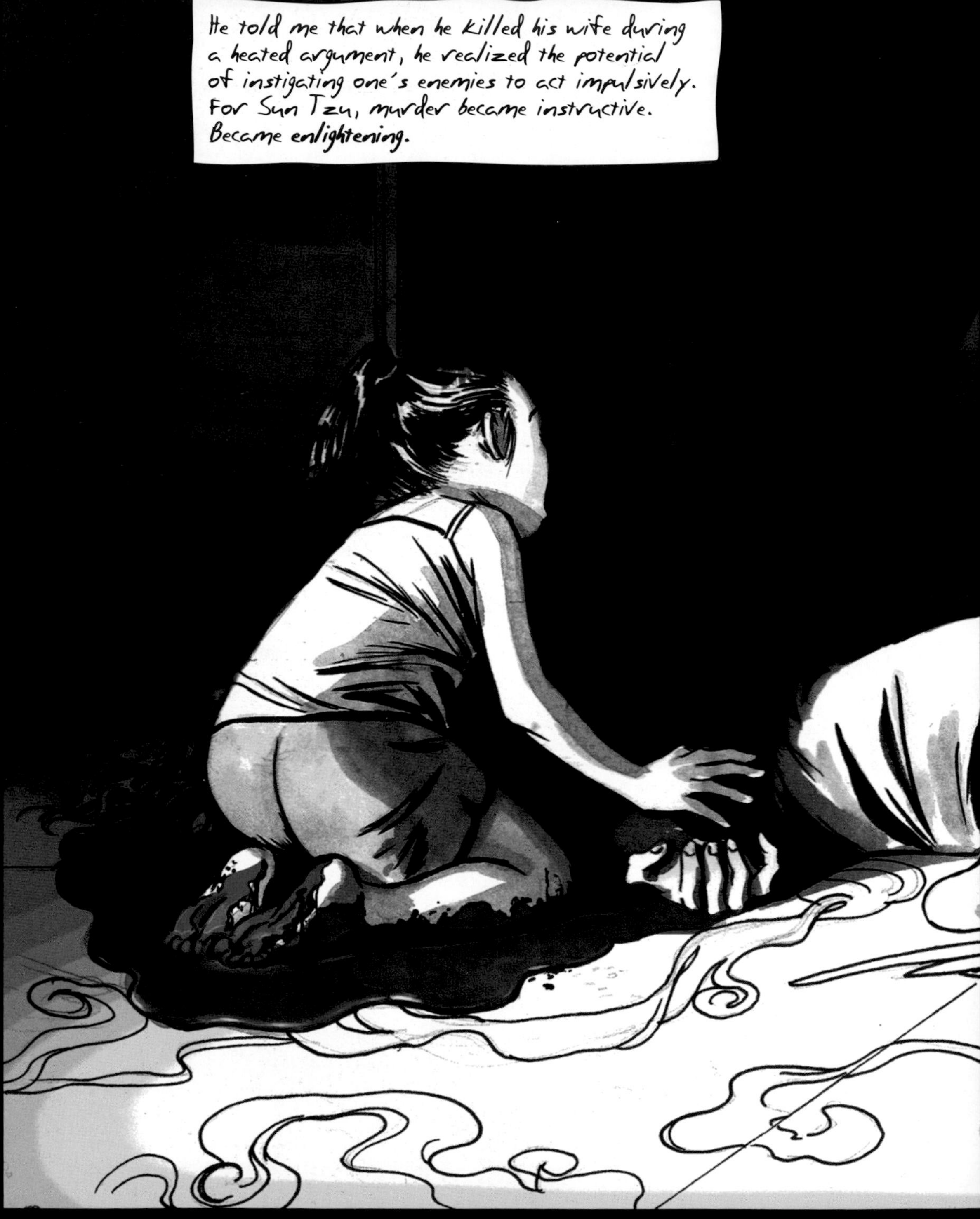
He told me that when he killed his wife during a heated argument, he realized the potential of instigating one's enemies to act impulsively. For Sun Tzu, murder became instructive. Became enlightening.

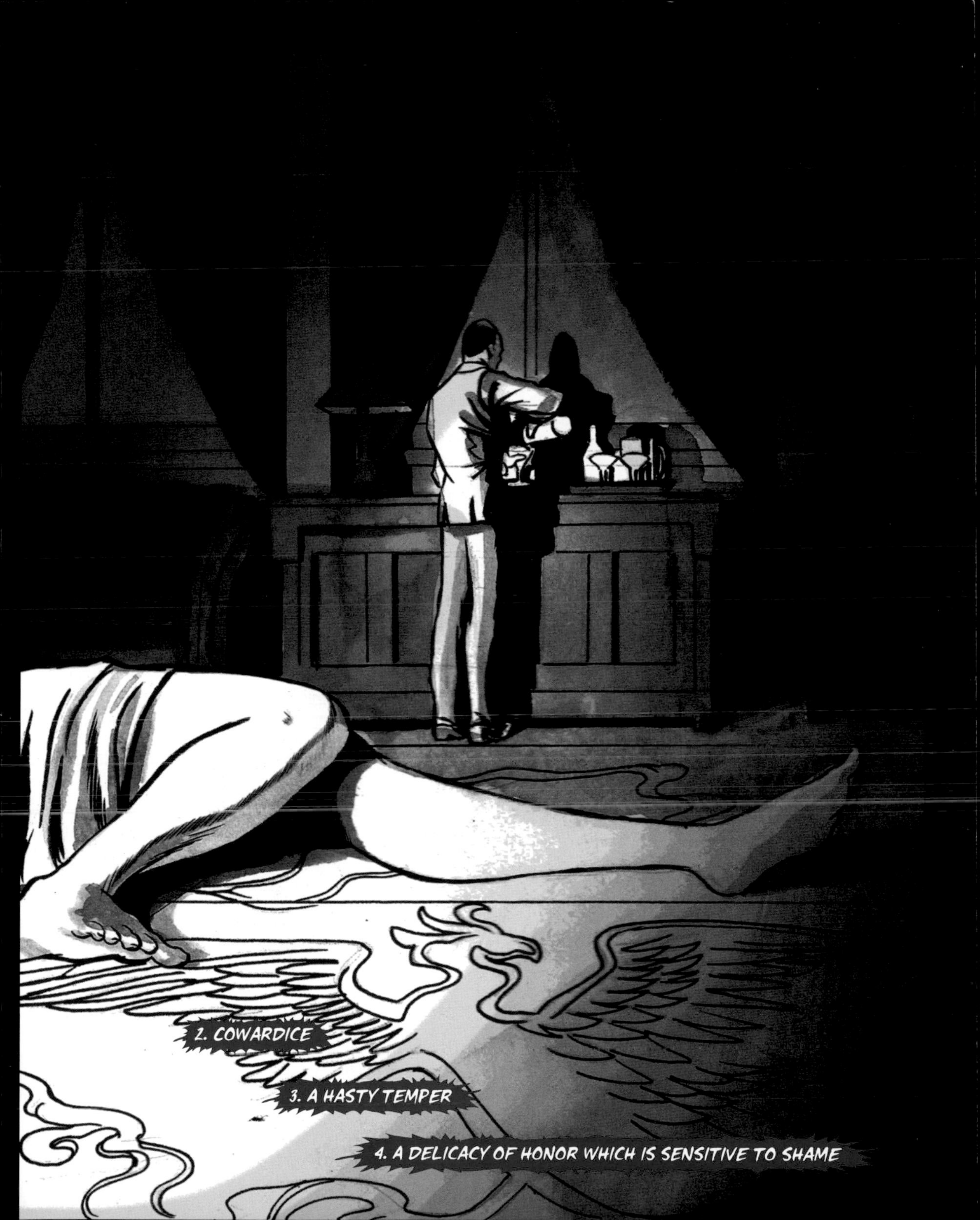
2. COWARDICE
3. A HASTY TEMPER
4. A DELICACY OF HONOR WHICH IS SENSITIVE TO SHAME

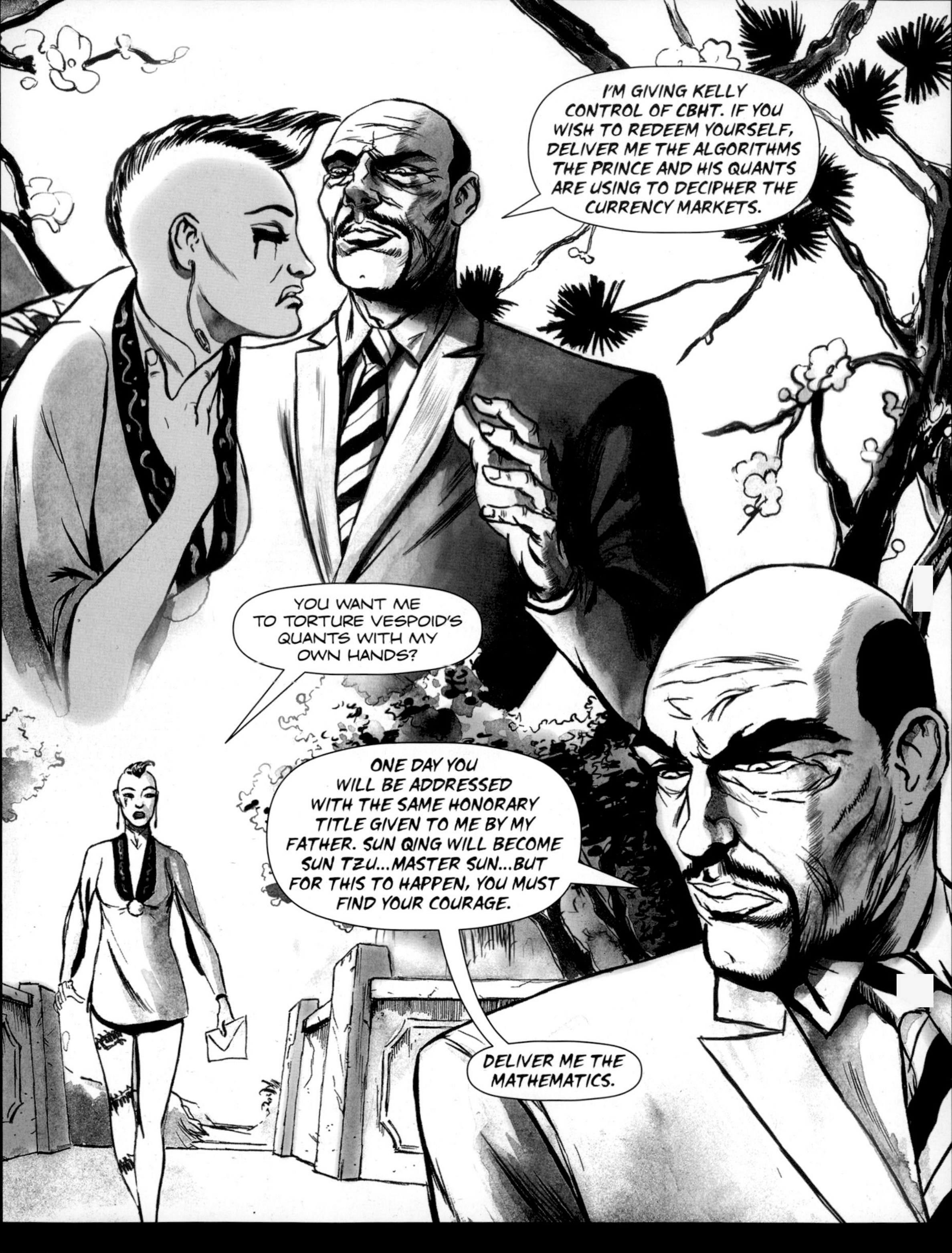
I'M GIVING KELLY CONTROL OF CBHT. IF YOU WISH TO REDEEM YOURSELF, DELIVER ME THE ALGORITHMS THE PRINCE AND HIS QUANTS ARE USING TO DECIPHER THE CURRENCY MARKETS.
YOU WANT ME TO TORTURE VESPOID'S QUANTS WITH MY OWN HANDS?
ONE DAY YOU WILL BE ADDRESSED WITH THE SAME HONORARY TITLE GIVEN TO ME BY MY FATHER. SUN QING WILL BECOME SUN TZU...MASTER SUN...BUT FOR THIS TO HAPPEN, YOU MUST FIND YOUR COURAGE.
DELIVER ME THE MATHEMATICS.

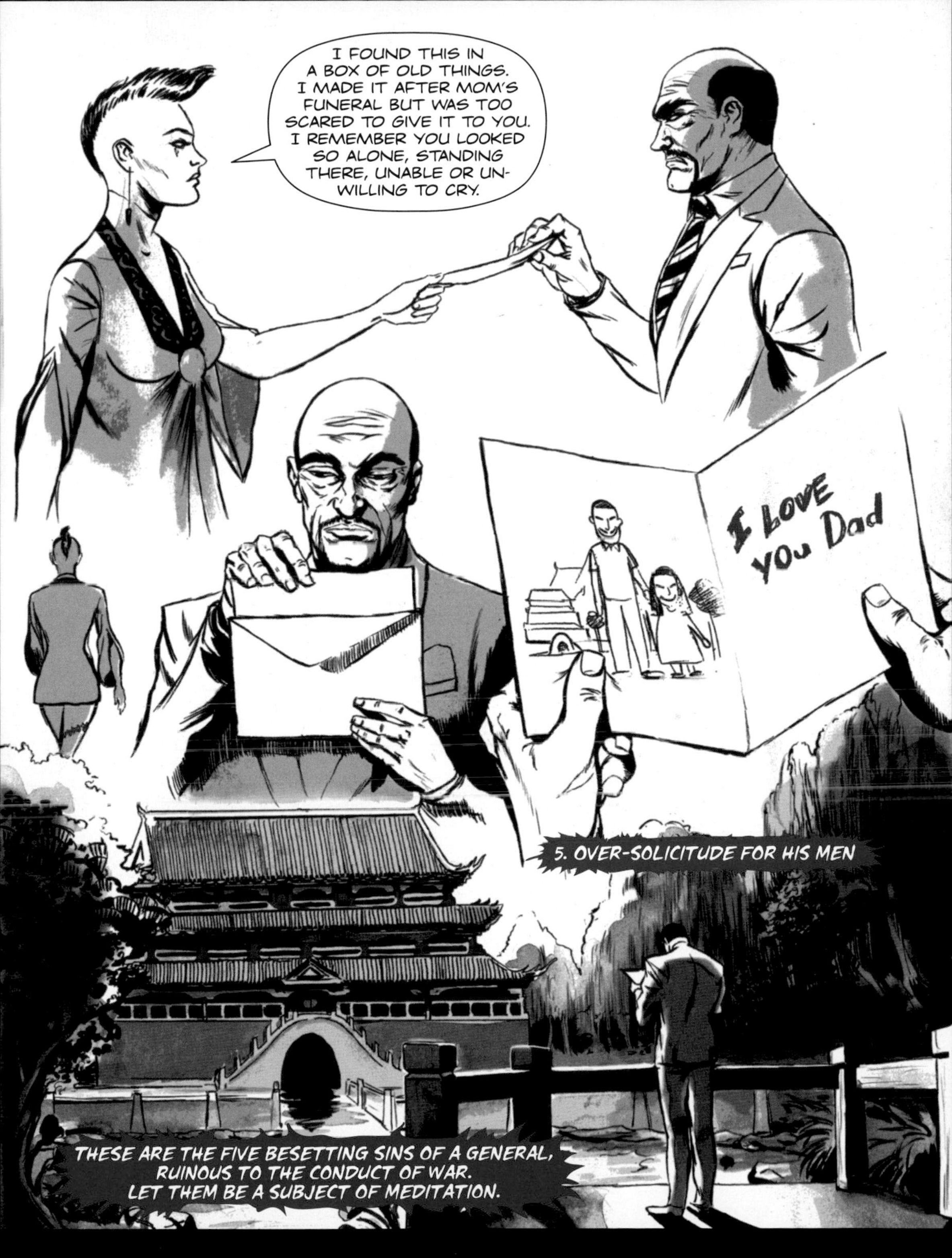
I FOUND THIS IN A BOX OF OLD THINGS. I MADE IT AFTER MOM'S FUNERAL BUT WAS TOO SCARED TO GIVE IT TO YOU. I REMEMBER YOU LOOKED SO ALONE, STANDING THERE, UNABLE OR UNWILLING TO CRY.
I LOVE YOU Dad
5. OVER-SOLICITUDE FOR HIS MEN
THESE ARE THE FIVE BESETTING SINS OF A GENERAL, RUINOUS TO THE CONDUCT OF WAR. LET THEM BE A SUBJECT OF MEDITATION.

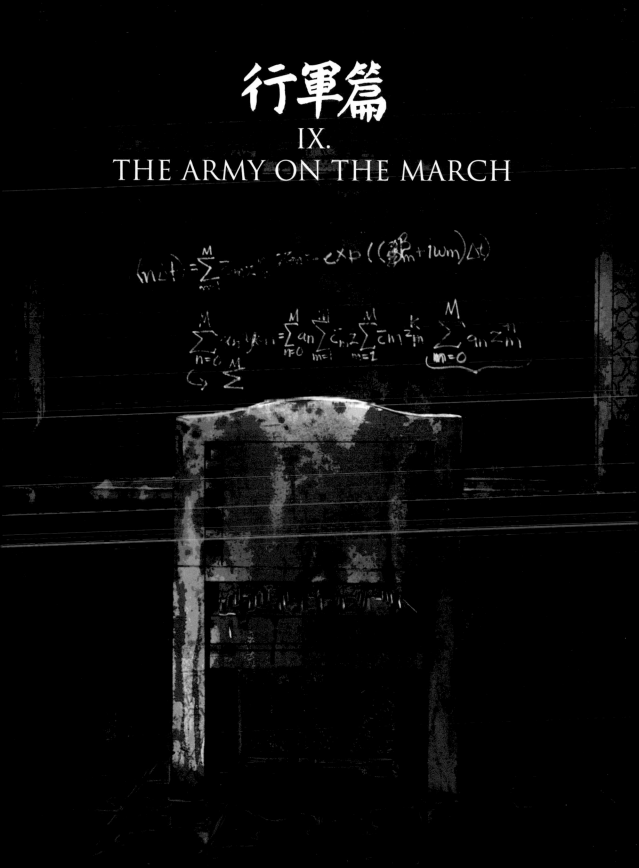

行軍篇

IX.
THE ARMY ON THE MARCH

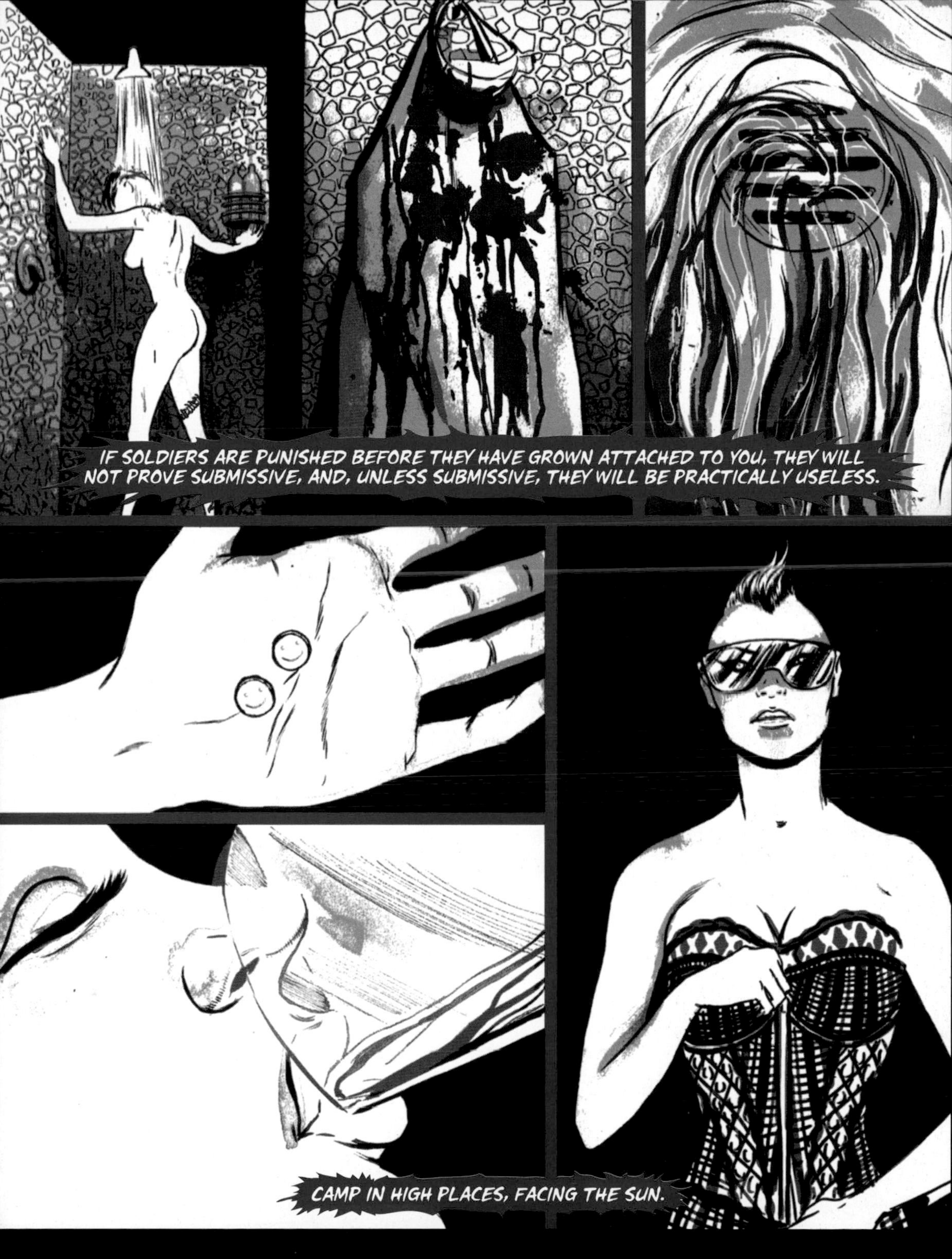
IF SOLDIERS ARE PUNISHED BEFORE THEY HAVE GROWN ATTACHED TO YOU, THEY WILL NOT PROVE SUBMISSIVE, AND, UNLESS SUBMISSIVE, THEY WILL BE PRACTICALLY USELESS.
CAMP IN HIGH PLACES, FACING THE SUN.

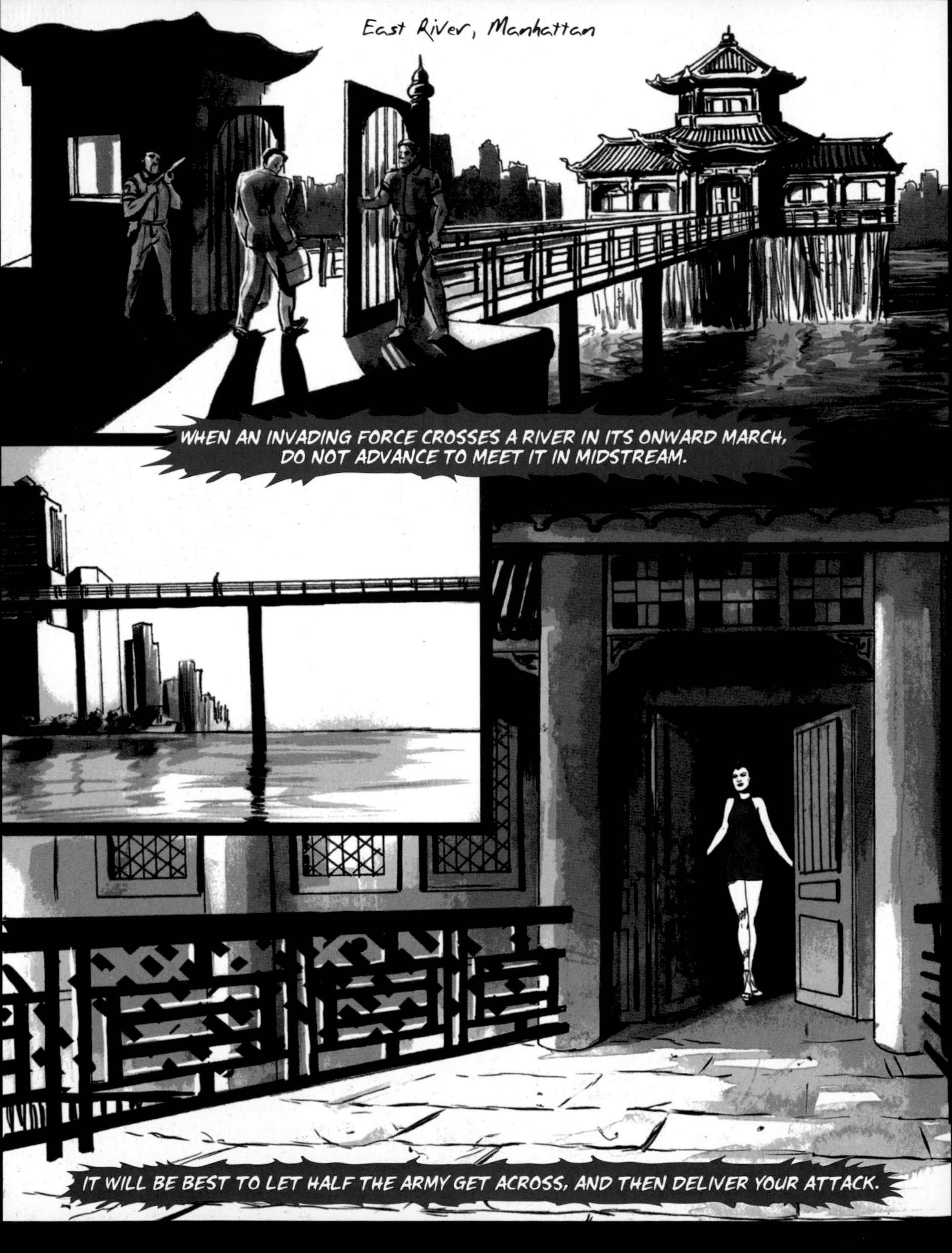
East River, Manhattan
WHEN AN INVADING FORCE CROSSES A RIVER IN ITS ONWARD MARCH, DO NOT ADVANCE TO MEET IT IN MIDSTREAM.
IT WILL BE BEST TO LET HALF THE ARMY GET ACROSS, AND THEN DELIVER YOUR ATTACK.

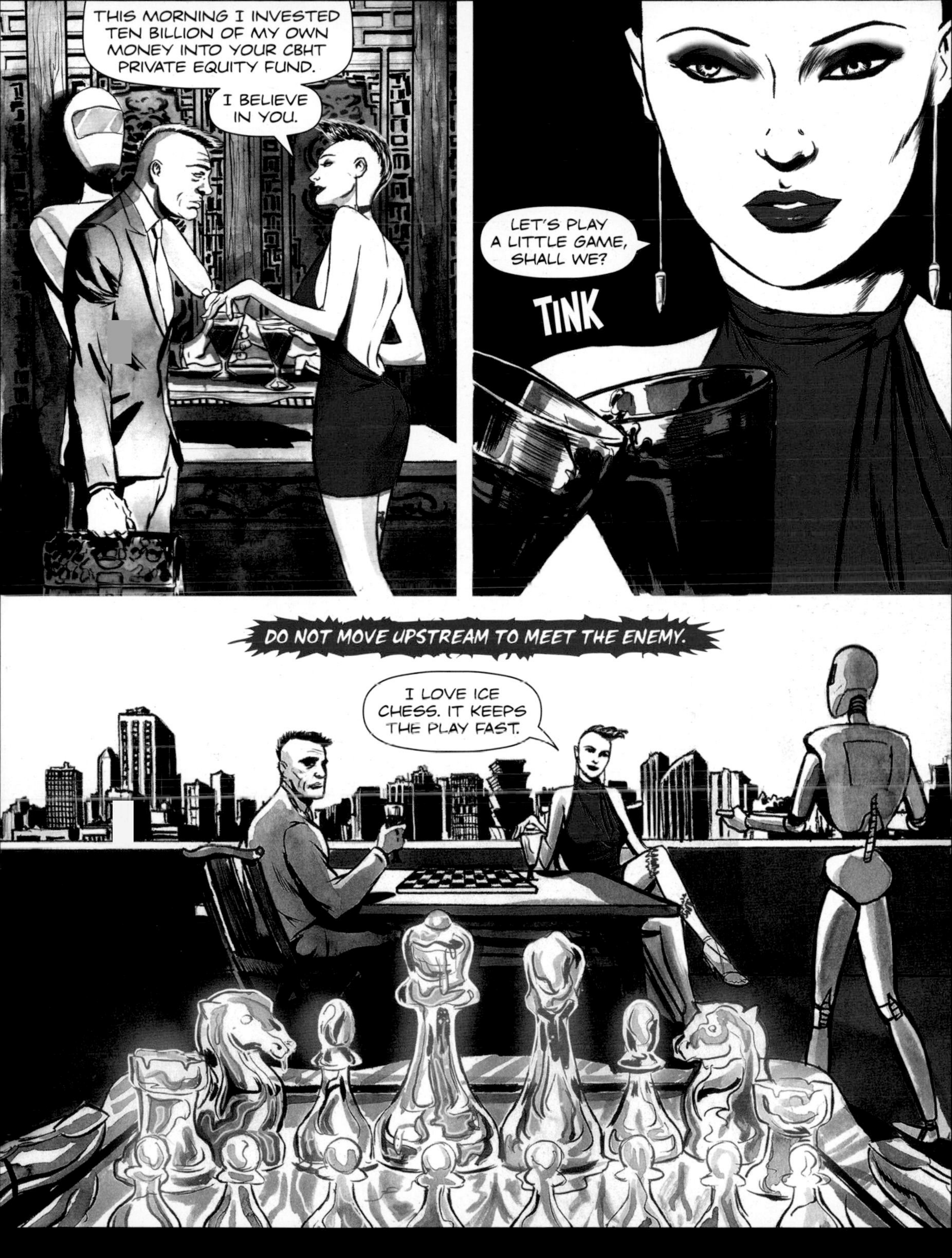
THIS MORNING I INVESTED TEN BILLION OF MY OWN MONEY INTO YOUR CBHT PRIVATE EQUITY FUND.
I BELIEVE IN YOU.
LET'S PLAY A LITTLE GAME, SHALL WE?
TINK
DO NOT MOVE UPSTREAM TO MEET THE ENEMY.
I LOVE ICE CHESS. IT KEEPS THE PLAY FAST.

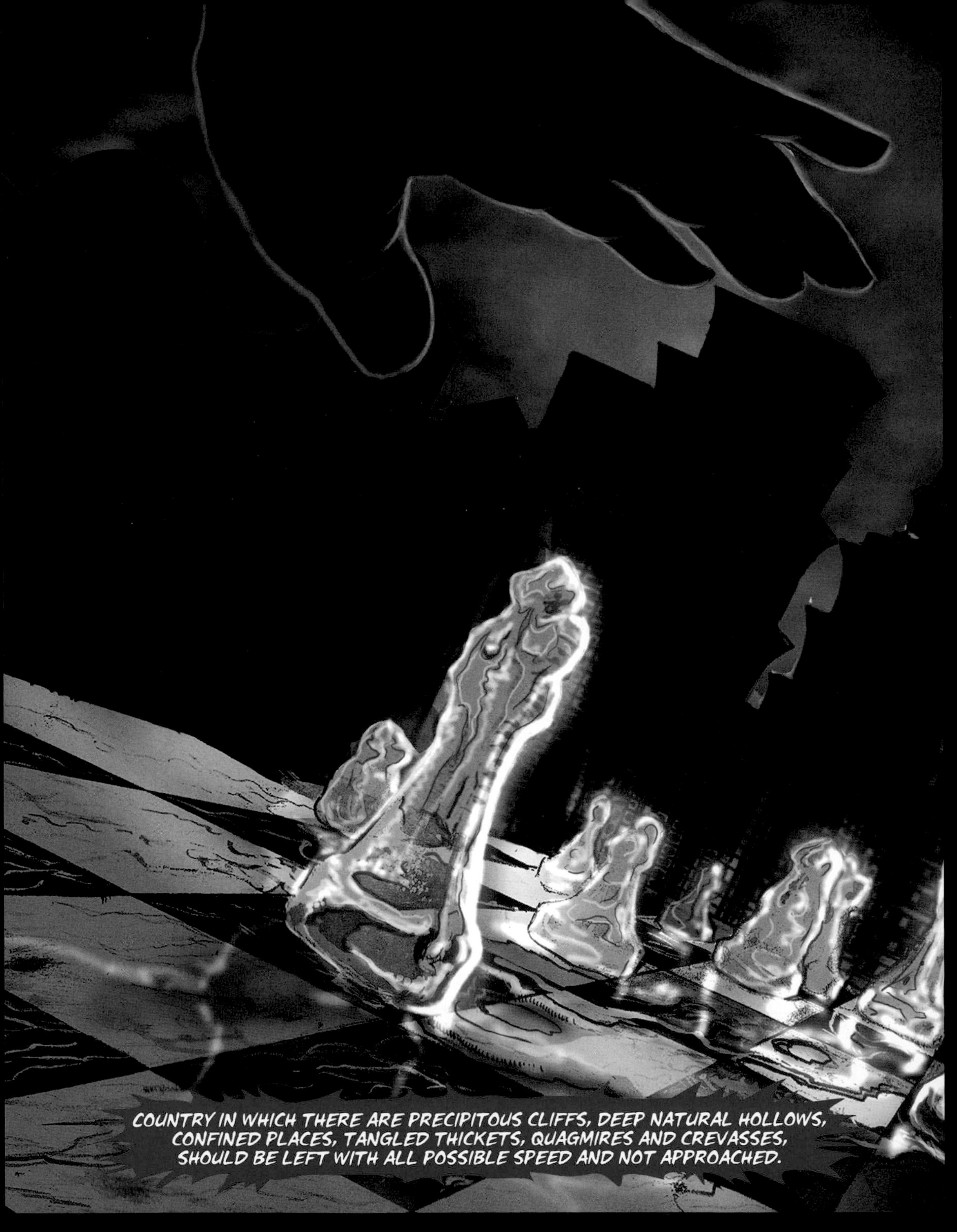
COUNTRY IN WHICH THERE ARE PRECIPITOUS CLIFFS, DEEP NATURAL HOLLOWS, CONFINED PLACES, TANGLED THICKETS, QUAGMIRES AND CREVASSES, SHOULD BE LEFT WITH ALL POSSIBLE SPEED AND NOT APPROACHED.

YOU LOOK EXHAUSTED. WANT SOMETHING THAT REMOVES THE NEED FOR SLEEP?

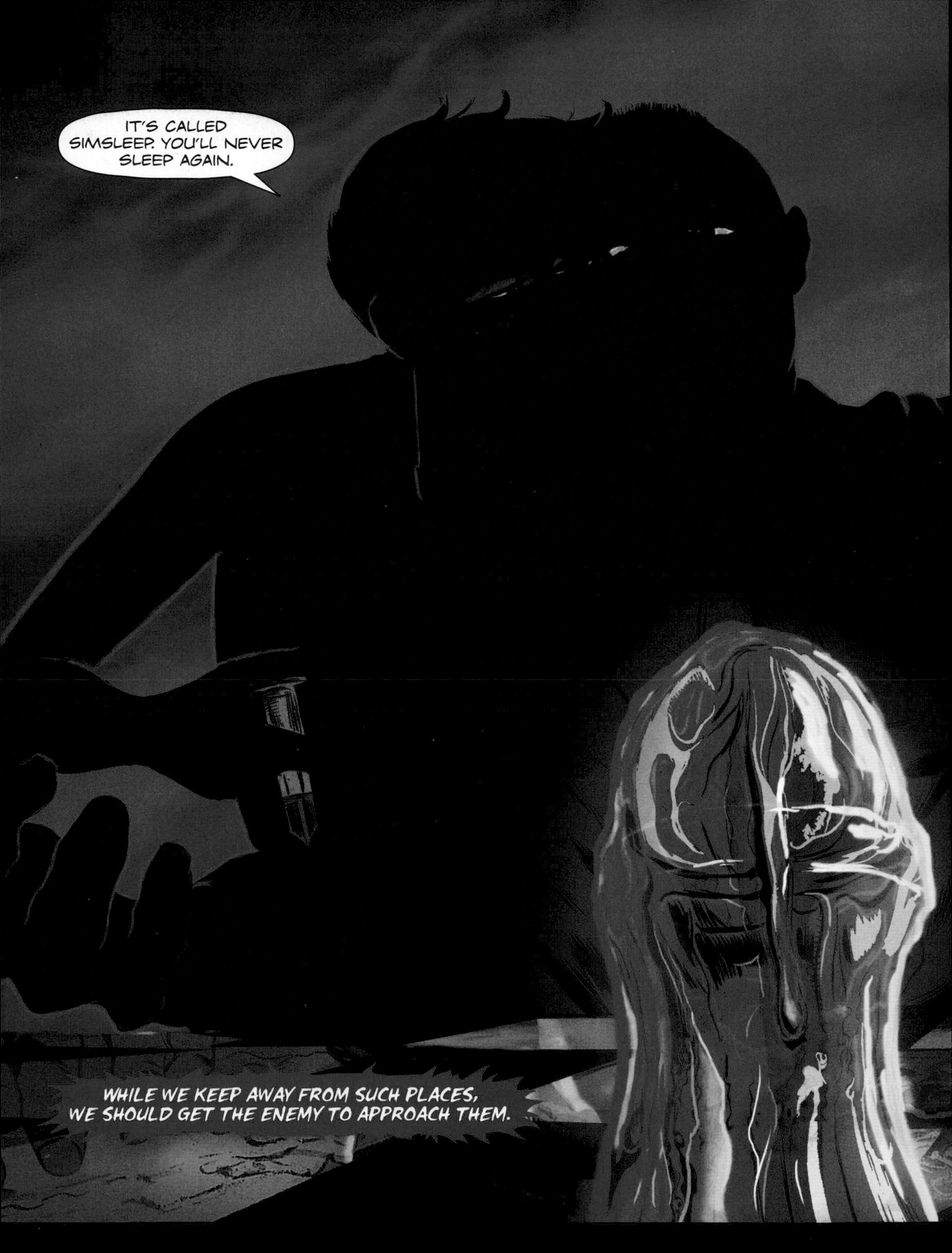
IT'S CALLED SIMSLEEP. YOU'LL NEVER SLEEP AGAIN.
WHILE WE KEEP AWAY FROM SUCH PLACES, WE SHOULD GET THE ENEMY TO APPROACH THEM.

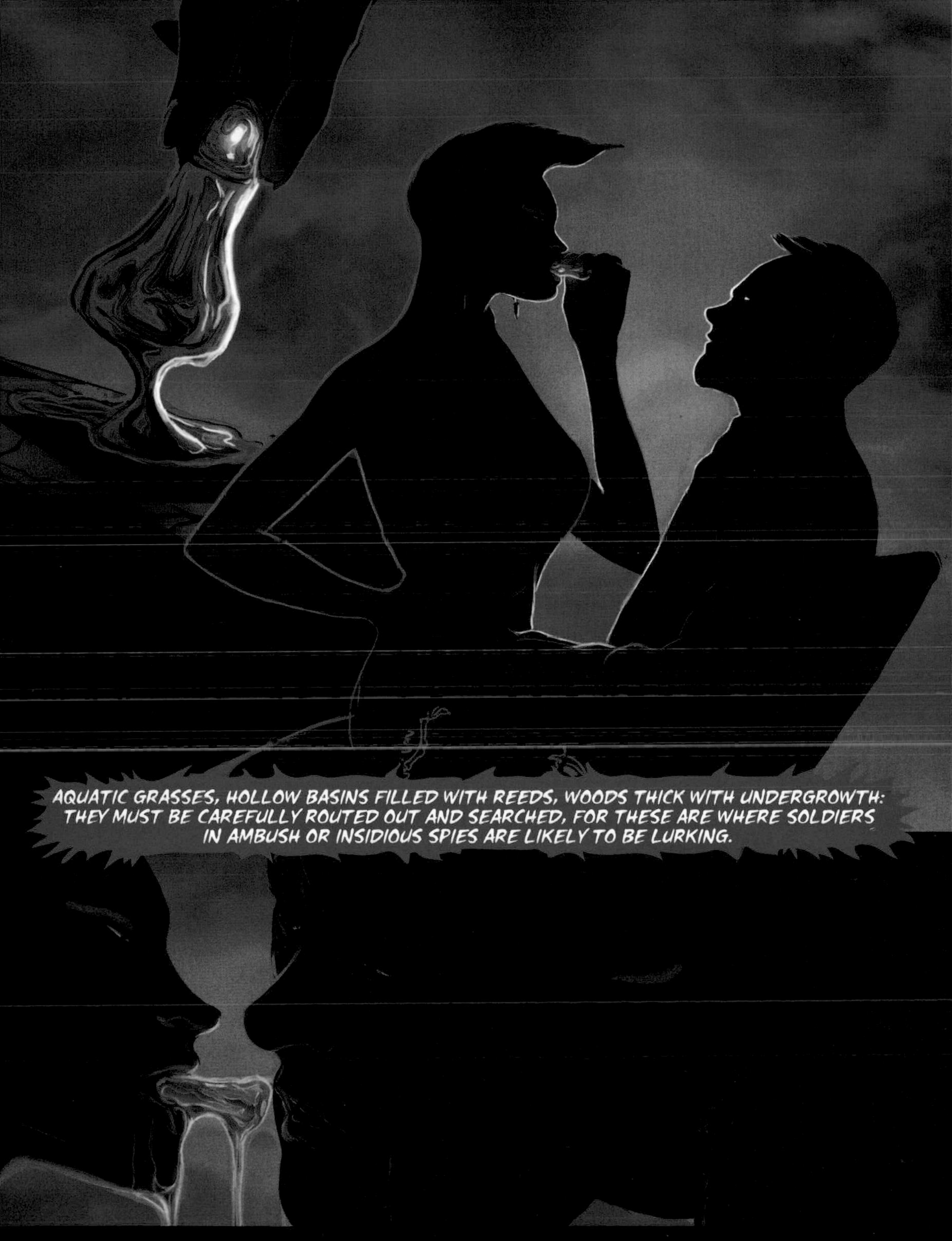
AQUATIC GRASSES, HOLLOW BASINS FILLED WITH REEDS, WOODS THICK WITH UNDERGROWTH: THEY MUST BE CAREFULLY ROUTED OUT AND SEARCHED, FOR THESE ARE WHERE SOLDIERS IN AMBUSH OR INSIDIOUS SPIES ARE LIKELY TO BE LURKING.

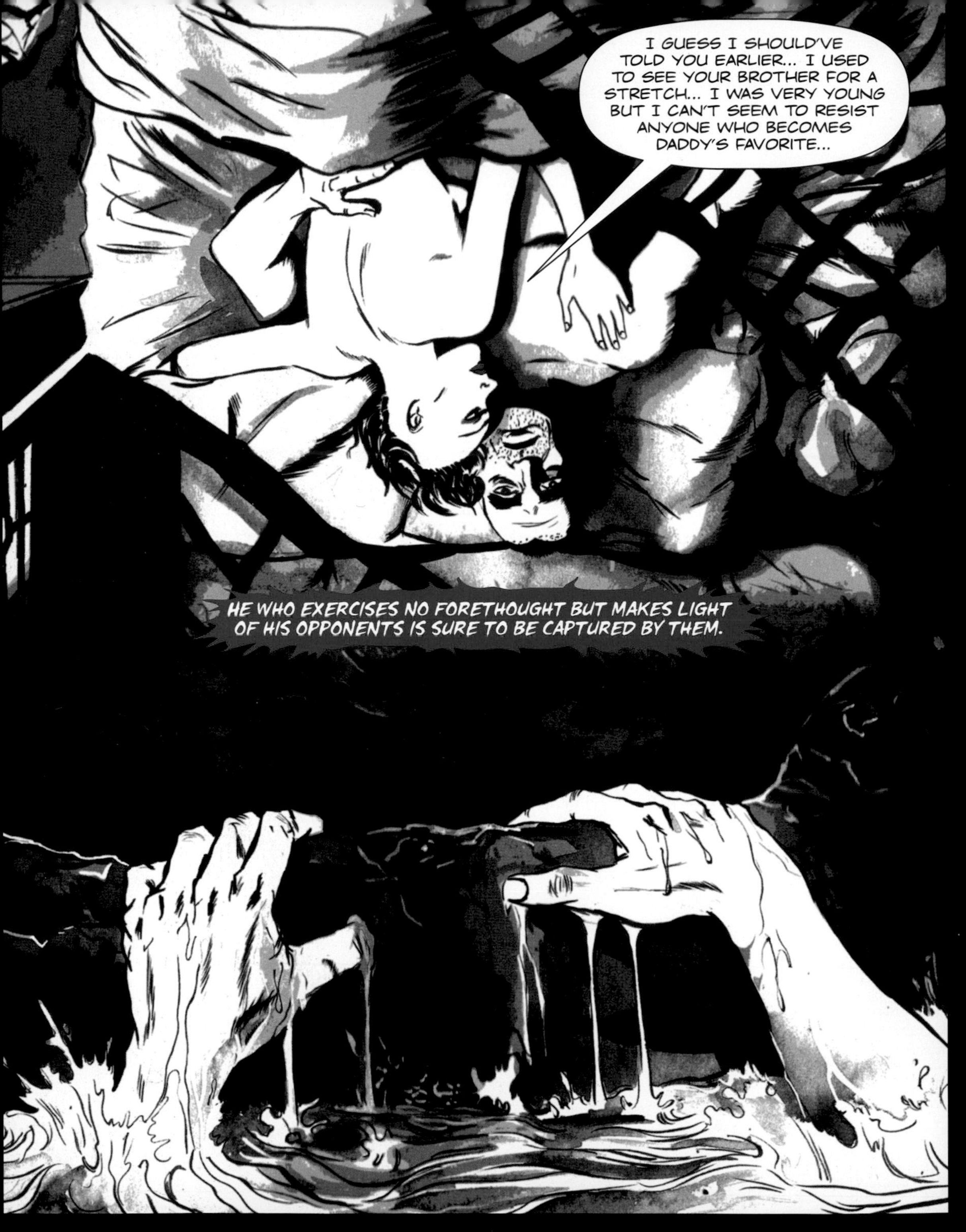
I GUESS I SHOULD'VE TOLD YOU EARLIER... I USED TO SEE YOUR BROTHER FOR A STRETCH... I WAS VERY YOUNG BUT I CAN'T SEEM TO RESIST ANYONE WHO BECOMES DADDY'S FAVORITE...
HE WHO EXERCISES NO FORETHOUGHT BUT MAKES LIGHT OF HIS OPPONENTS IS SURE TO BE CAPTURED BY THEM.

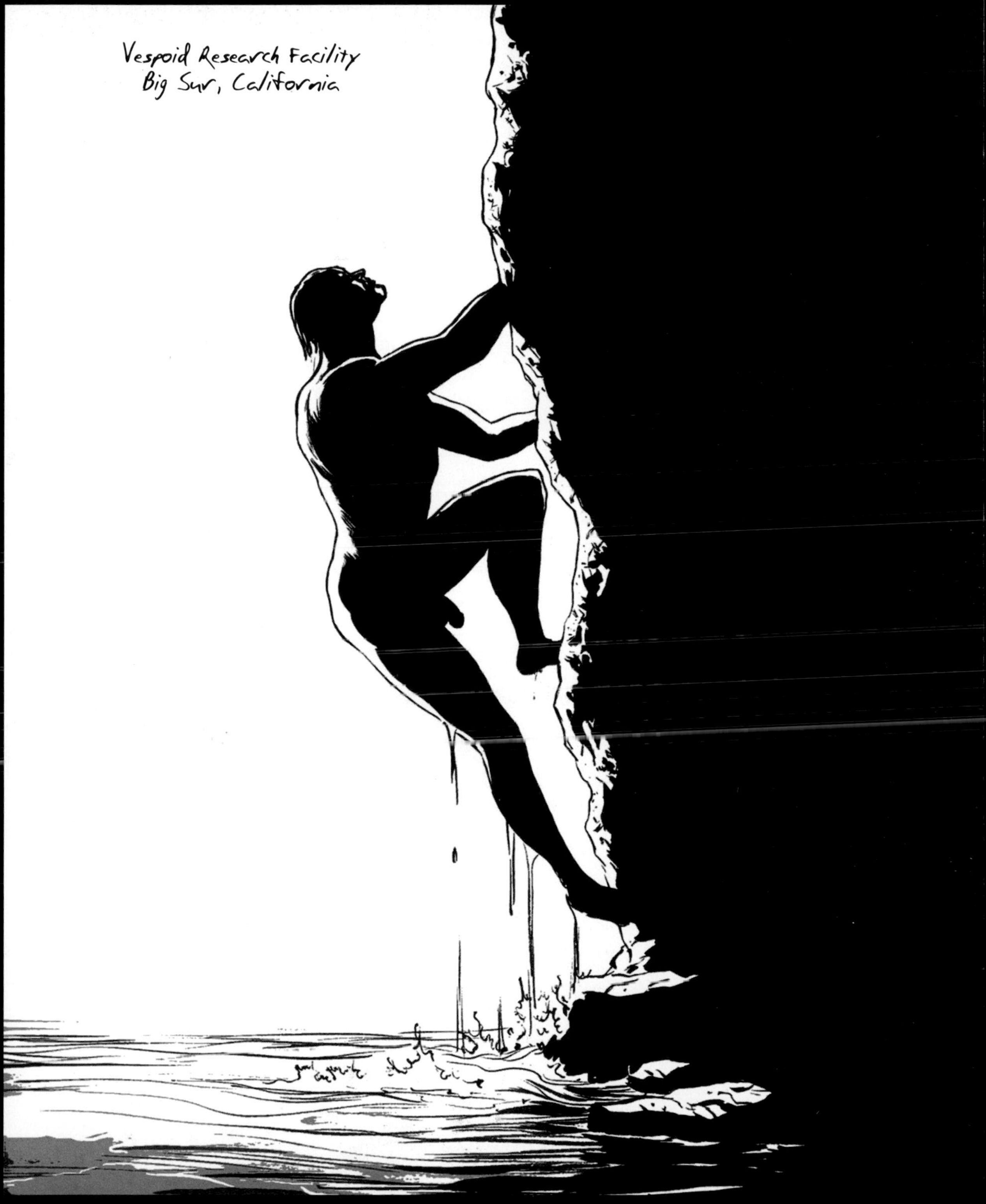
Vespoid Research Facility
Big Sur, California

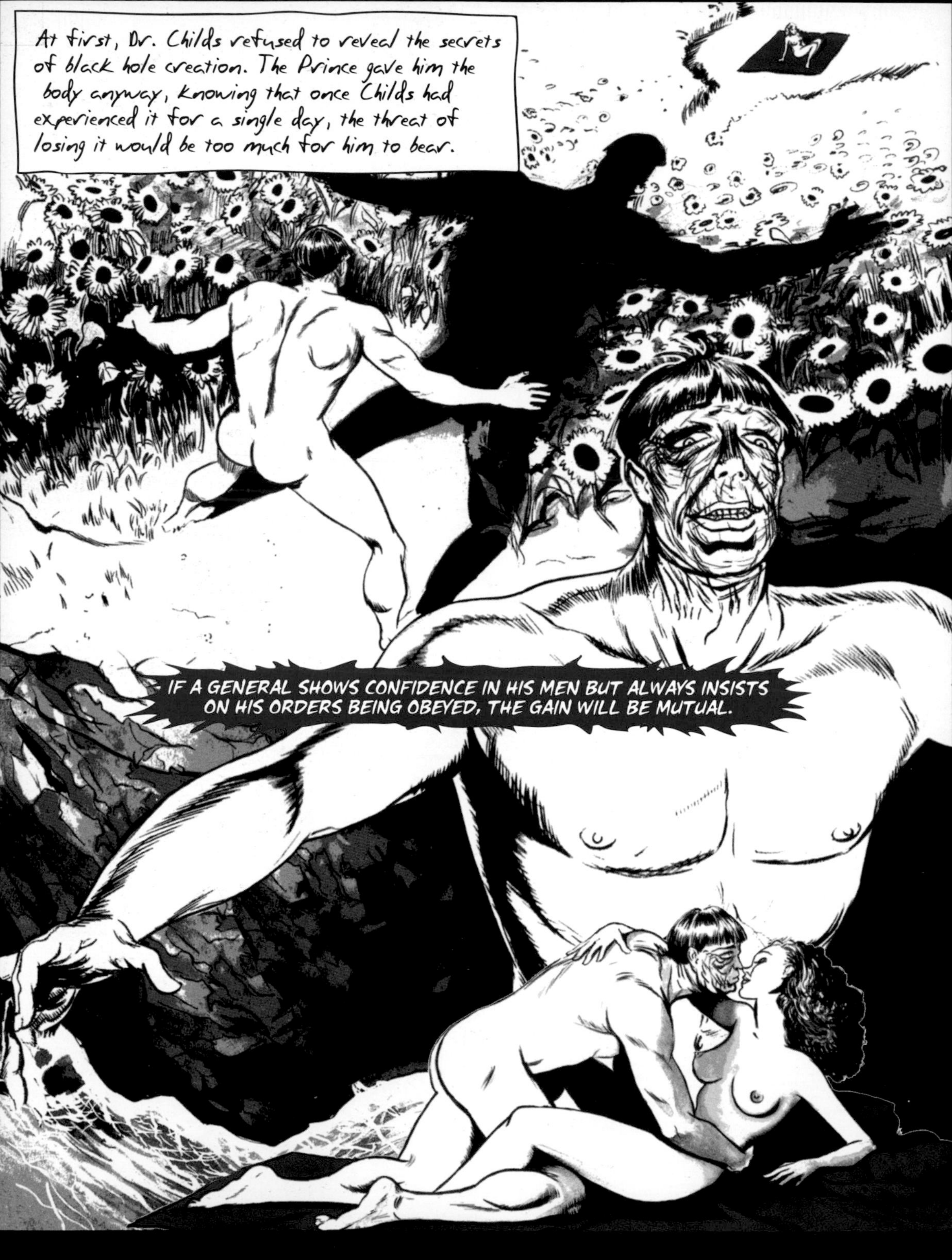
At first, Dr. Childs refused to reveal the secrets of black hole creation. The Prince gave him the body anyway, knowing that once Childs had experienced it for a single day, the threat of losing it would be too much for him to bear.
IF A GENERAL SHOWS CONFIDENCE IN HIS MEN BUT ALWAYS INSISTS ON HIS ORDERS BEING OBEYED, THE GAIN WILL BE MUTUAL.

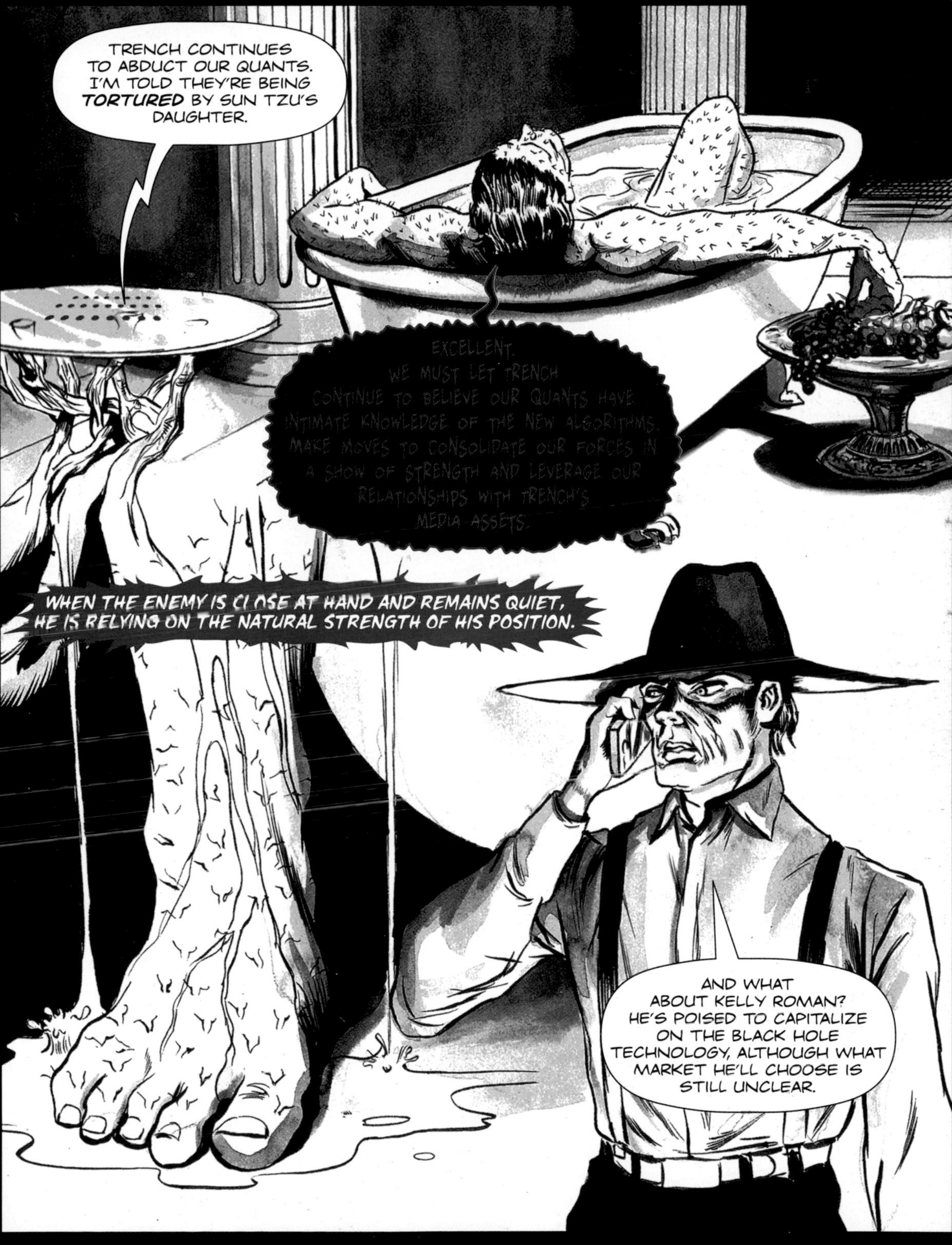
TRENCH CONTINUES TO ABDUCT OUR QUANTS. I'M TOLD THEY'RE BEING **TORTURED** BY SUN TZU'S DAUGHTER.
EXCELLENT. WE MUST LET TRENCH CONTINUE TO BELIEVE OUR QUANTS HAVE INTIMATE KNOWLEDGE OF THE NEW ALGORITHMS. MAKE MOVES TO CONSOLIDATE OUR FORCES IN A SHOW OF STRENGTH AND LEVERAGE OUR RELATIONSHIPS WITH TRENCH'S MEDIA ASSETS.
WHEN THE ENEMY IS CLOSE AT HAND AND REMAINS QUIET, HE IS RELYING ON THE NATURAL STRENGTH OF HIS POSITION.
AND WHAT ABOUT KELLY ROMAN? HE'S POISED TO CAPITALIZE ON THE BLACK HOLE TECHNOLOGY, ALTHOUGH WHAT MARKET HE'LL CHOOSE IS STILL UNCLEAR.

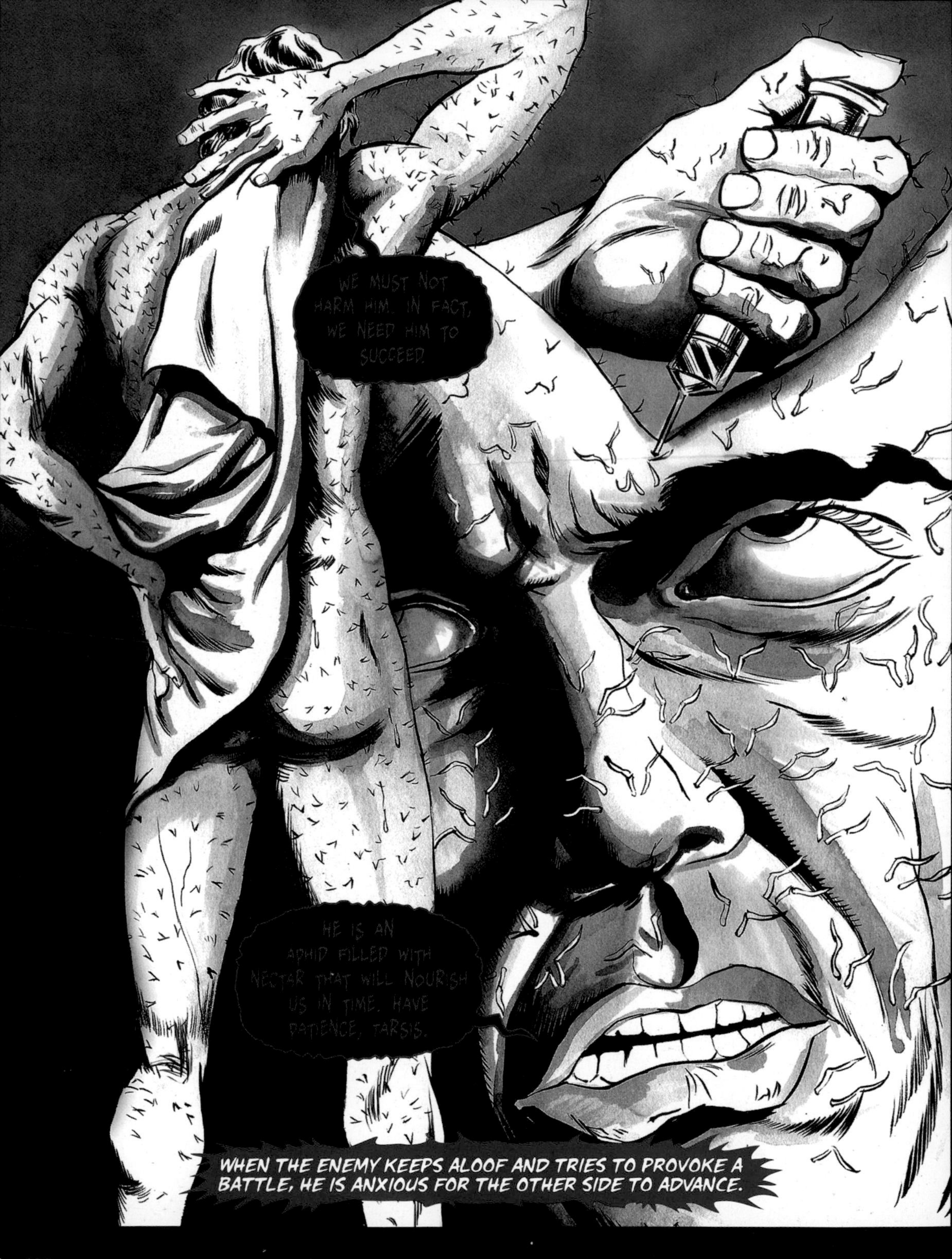
WE MUST NOT HARM HIM. IN FACT, WE NEED HIM TO SUCCEED.
HE IS AN APHID FILLED WITH NECTAR THAT WILL NOURISH US IN TIME. HAVE PATIENCE, TARSIS.
WHEN THE ENEMY KEEPS ALOOF AND TRIES TO PROVOKE A BATTLE, HE IS ANXIOUS FOR THE OTHER SIDE TO ADVANCE.

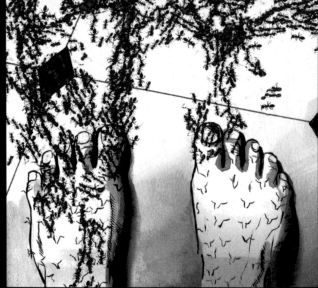

ALTHOUGH SOME OF THEIR INVESTMENTS ARE SUFFERING, VESPOID CONTINUES TO OUTPERFORM ALL OTHERS IN ALGORITHMIC TRADING. AND TODAY WE'VE LEARNED THAT *THE PRINCE* IS TAKING THE DRAMATIC STEP OF RELOCATING HIS QUANTITATIVE ANALYSTS TO INDIA, WHICH HAPPENS TO PROVIDE THE MAJORITY OF VESPOID'S CAPITAL.

Mumbai, India

IF HIS PLACE OF ENCAMPMENT IS EASY OF ACCESS, HE IS TENDERING A BAIT.

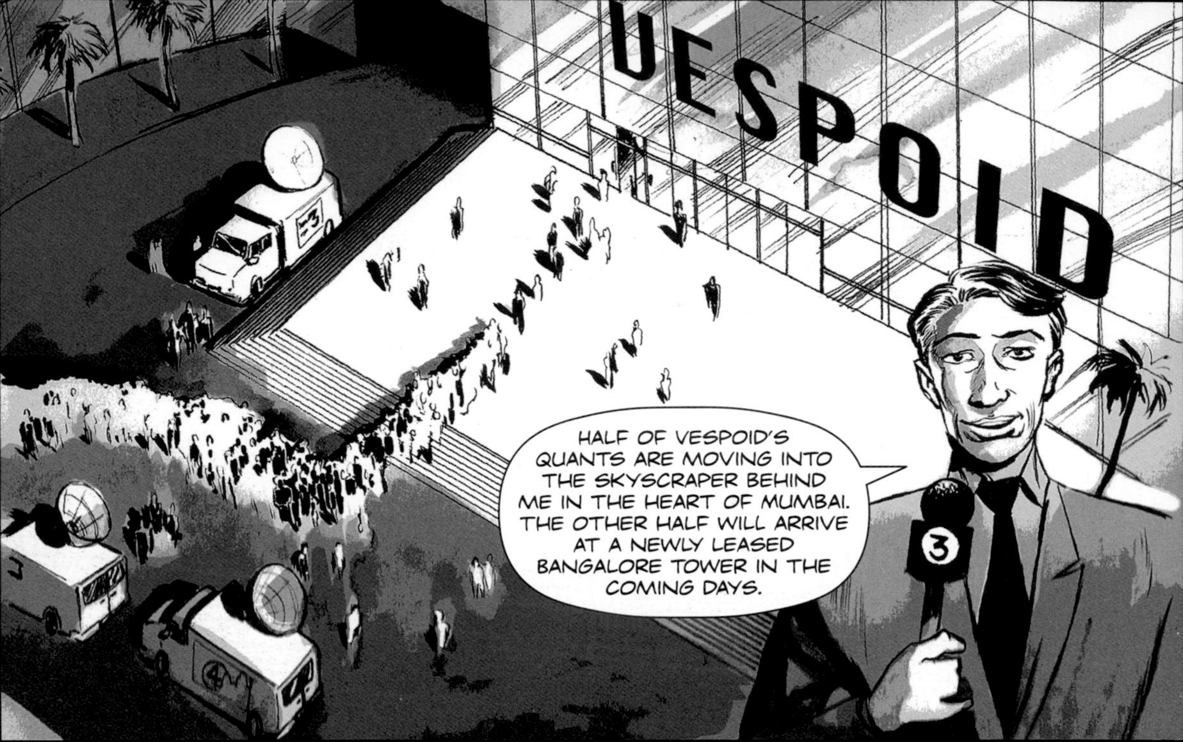
VESPOID
HALF OF VESPOID'S QUANTS ARE MOVING INTO THE SKYSCRAPER BEHIND ME IN THE HEART OF MUMBAI. THE OTHER HALF WILL ARRIVE AT A NEWLY LEASED BANGALORE TOWER IN THE COMING DAYS.

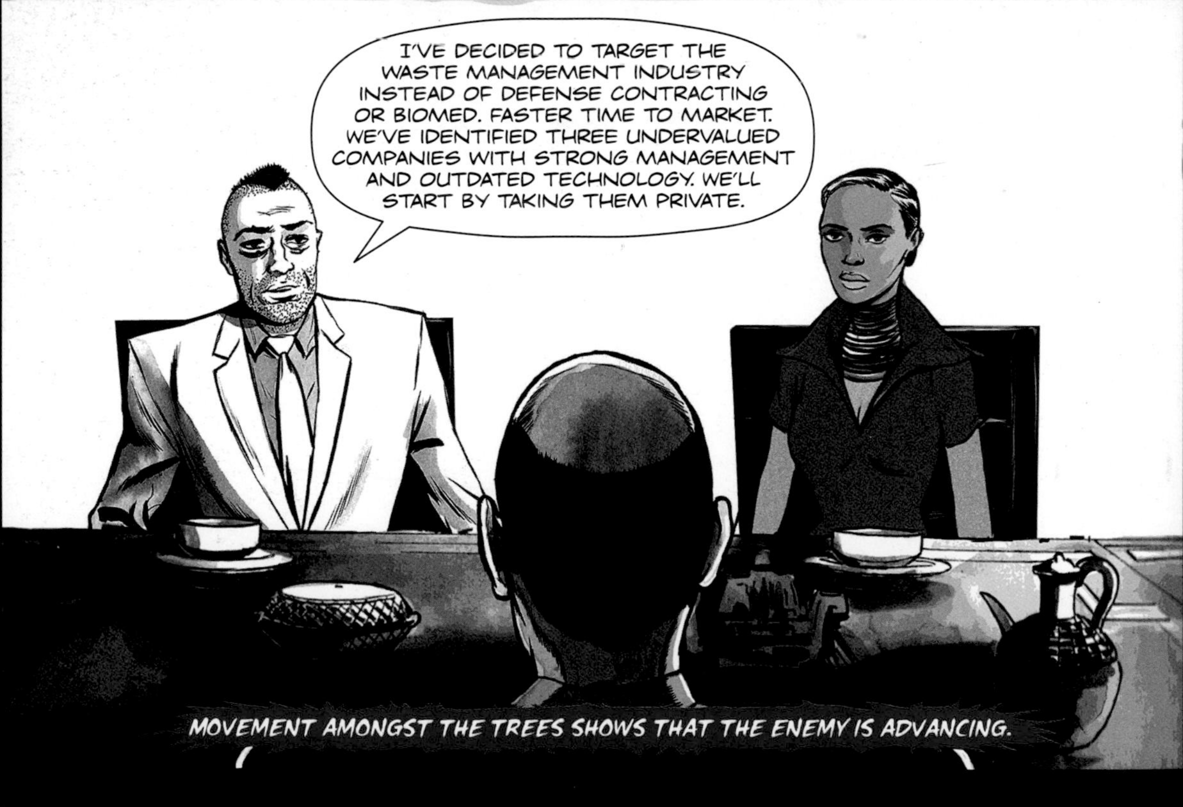
I'VE DECIDED TO TARGET THE WASTE MANAGEMENT INDUSTRY INSTEAD OF DEFENSE CONTRACTING OR BIOMED. FASTER TIME TO MARKET. WE'VE IDENTIFIED THREE UNDERVALUED COMPANIES WITH STRONG MANAGEMENT AND OUTDATED TECHNOLOGY. WE'LL START BY TAKING THEM PRIVATE.
MOVEMENT AMONGST THE TREES SHOWS THAT THE ENEMY IS ADVANCING.

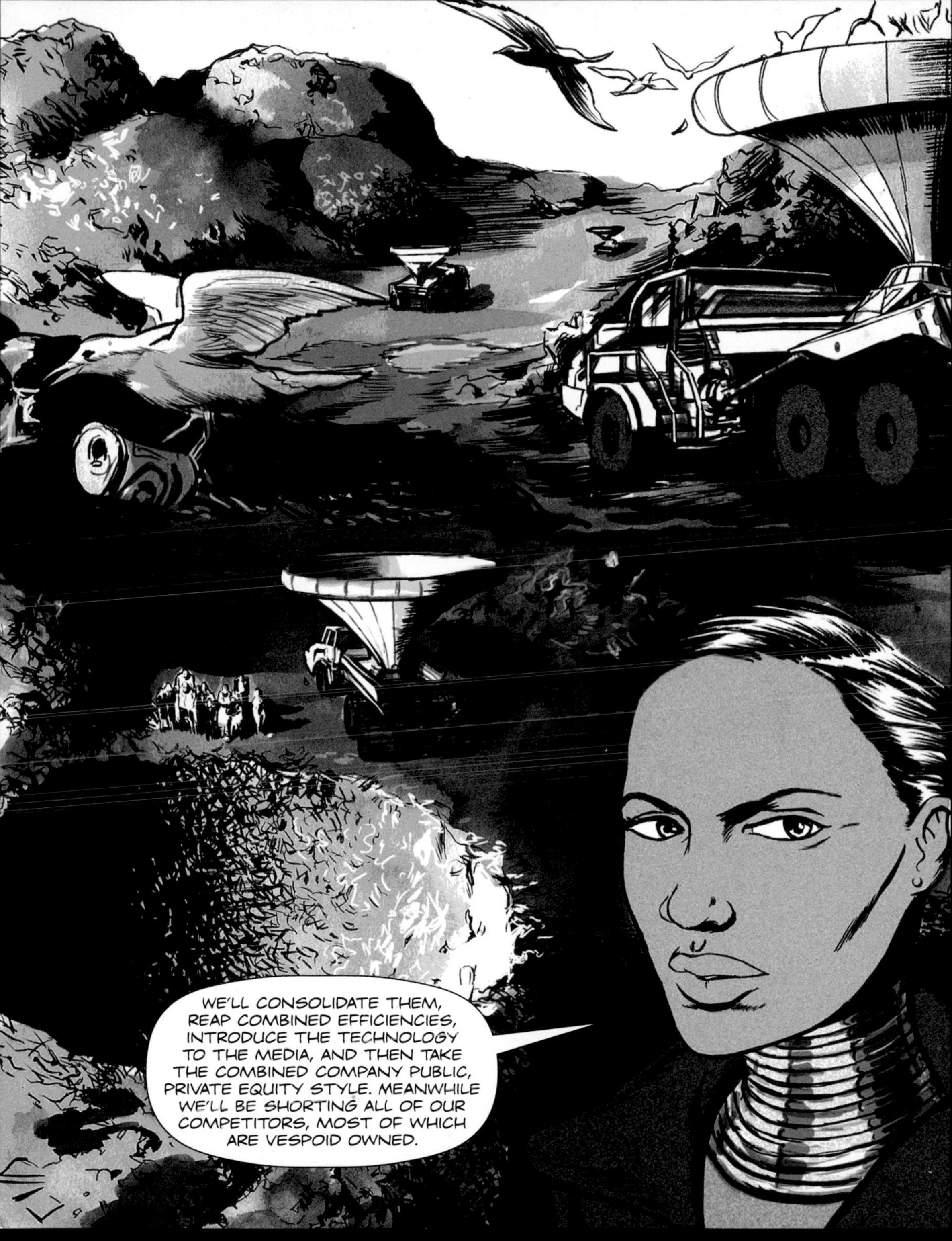
WE'LL CONSOLIDATE THEM, REAP COMBINED EFFICIENCIES, INTRODUCE THE TECHNOLOGY TO THE MEDIA, AND THEN TAKE THE COMBINED COMPANY PUBLIC, PRIVATE EQUITY STYLE. MEANWHILE WE'LL BE SHORTING ALL OF OUR COMPETITORS, MOST OF WHICH ARE VESPOID OWNED.

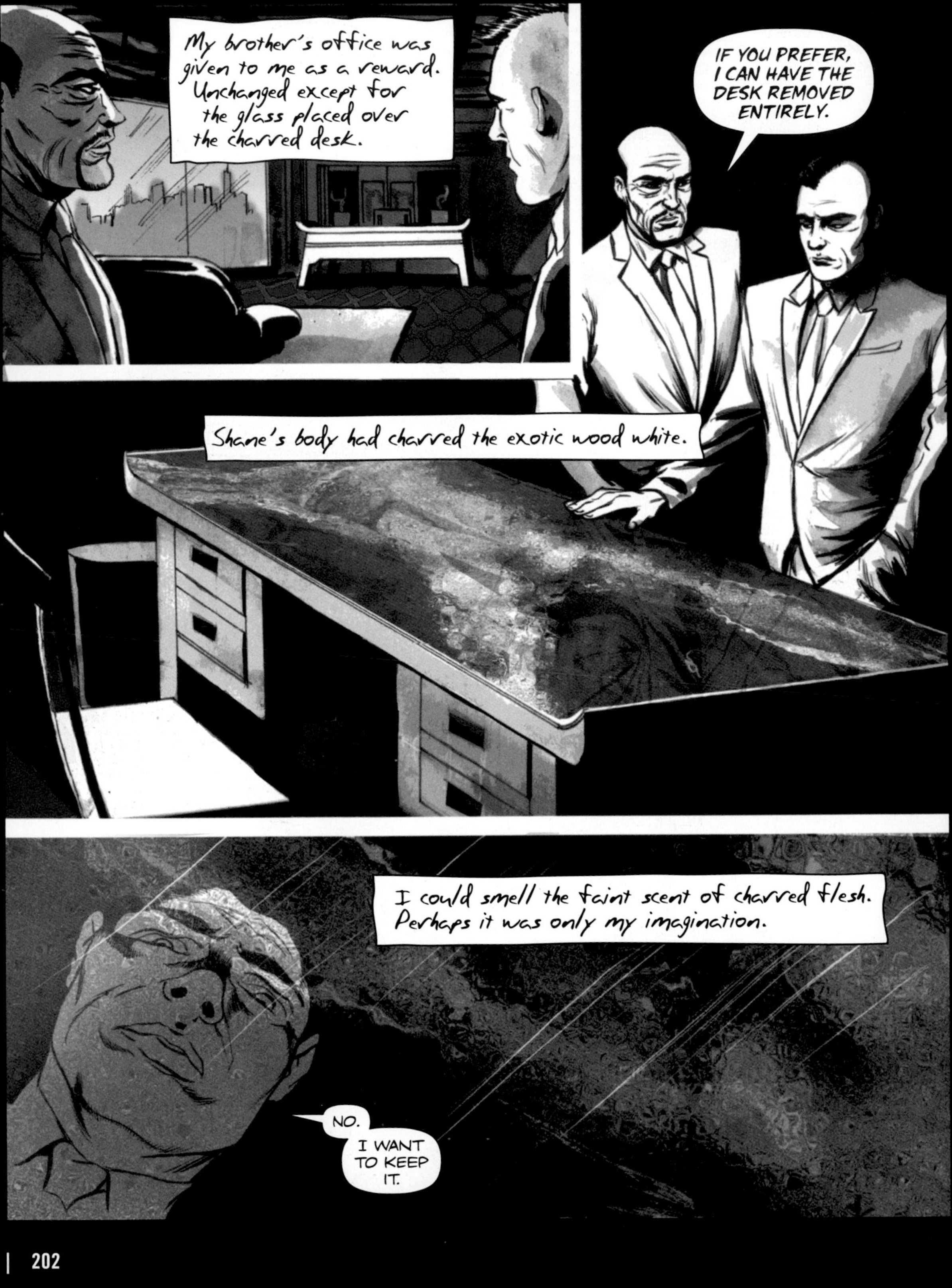
My brother's office was given to me as a reward. Unchanged except for the glass placed over the charred desk.
IF YOU PREFER, I CAN HAVE THE DESK REMOVED ENTIRELY.
Shane's body had charred the exotic wood white.
I could smell the faint scent of charred flesh. Perhaps it was only my imagination.
NO.
I WANT TO KEEP IT.

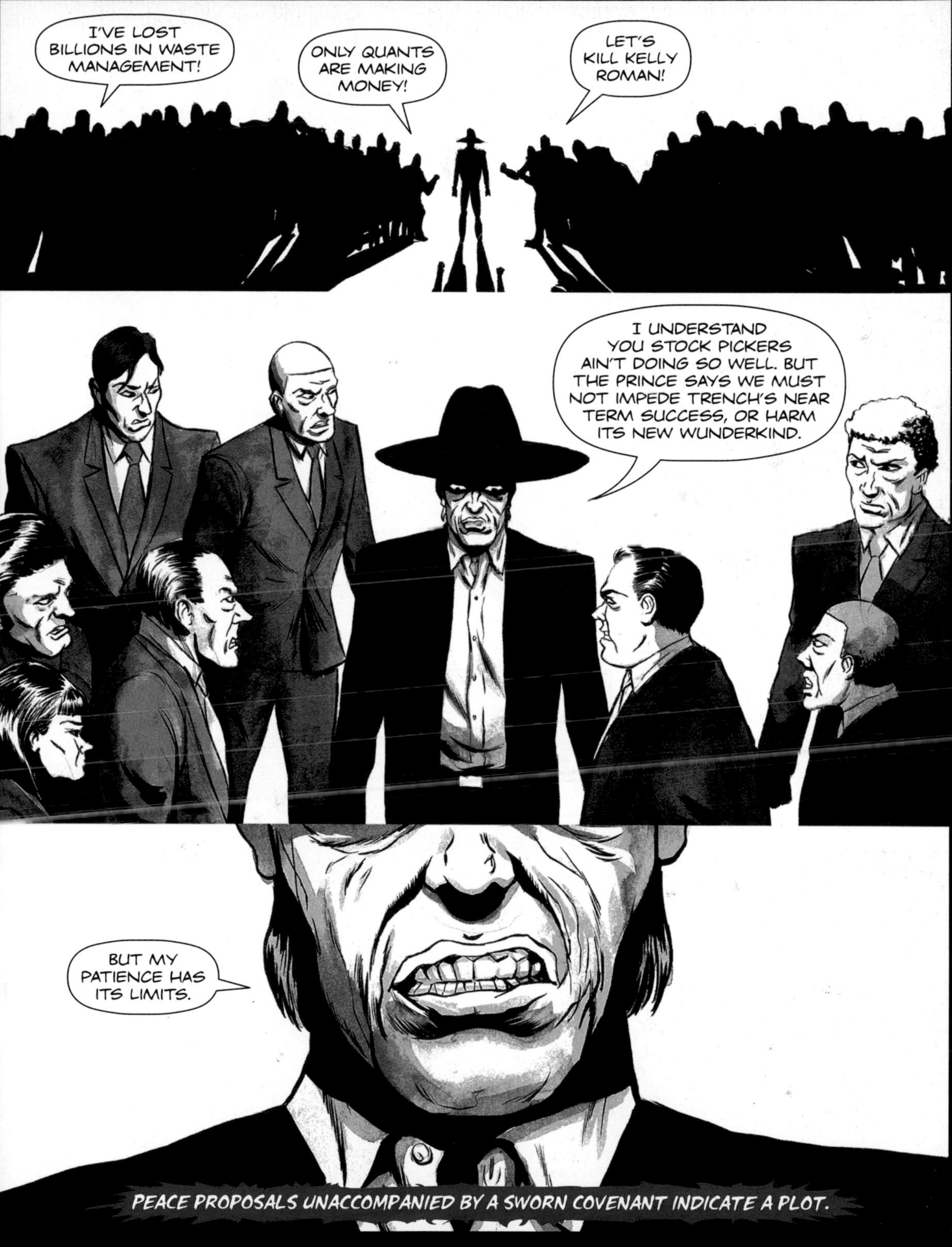
I'VE LOST BILLIONS IN WASTE MANAGEMENT!
ONLY QUANTS ARE MAKING MONEY!
LET'S KILL KELLY ROMAN!
I UNDERSTAND YOU STOCK PICKERS AIN'T DOING SO WELL. BUT THE PRINCE SAYS WE MUST NOT IMPEDE TRENCH'S NEAR TERM SUCCESS, OR HARM ITS NEW WUNDERKIND.
BUT MY PATIENCE HAS ITS LIMITS.
PEACE PROPOSALS UNACCOMPANIED BY A SWORN COVENANT INDICATE A PLOT.

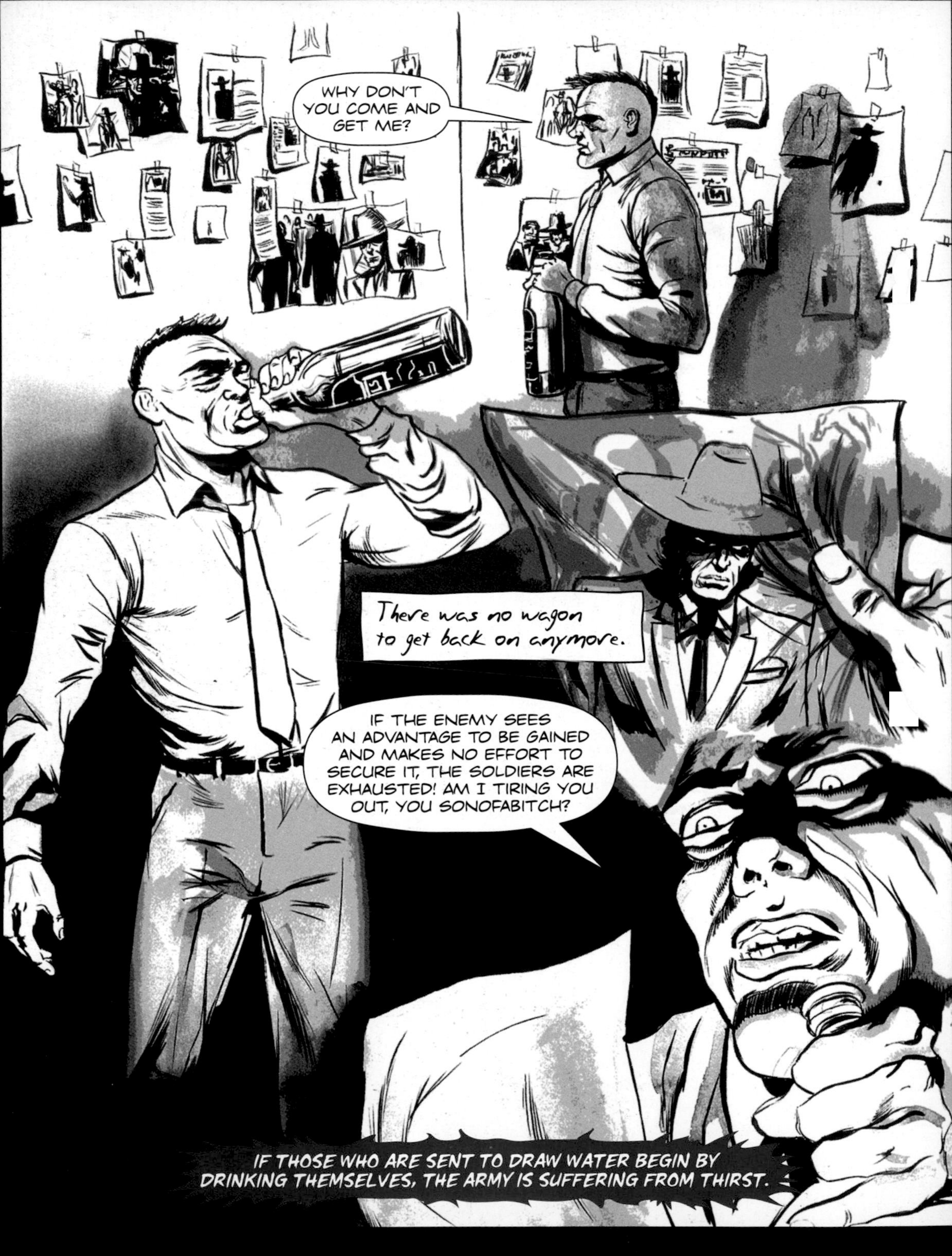
WHY DON'T YOU COME AND GET ME?
There was no wagon to get back on anymore.
IF THE ENEMY SEES AN ADVANTAGE TO BE GAINED AND MAKES NO EFFORT TO SECURE IT, THE SOLDIERS ARE EXHAUSTED! AM I TIRING YOU OUT, YOU SONOFABITCH?
IF THOSE WHO ARE SENT TO DRAW WATER BEGIN BY DRINKING THEMSELVES, THE ARMY IS SUFFERING FROM THIRST.

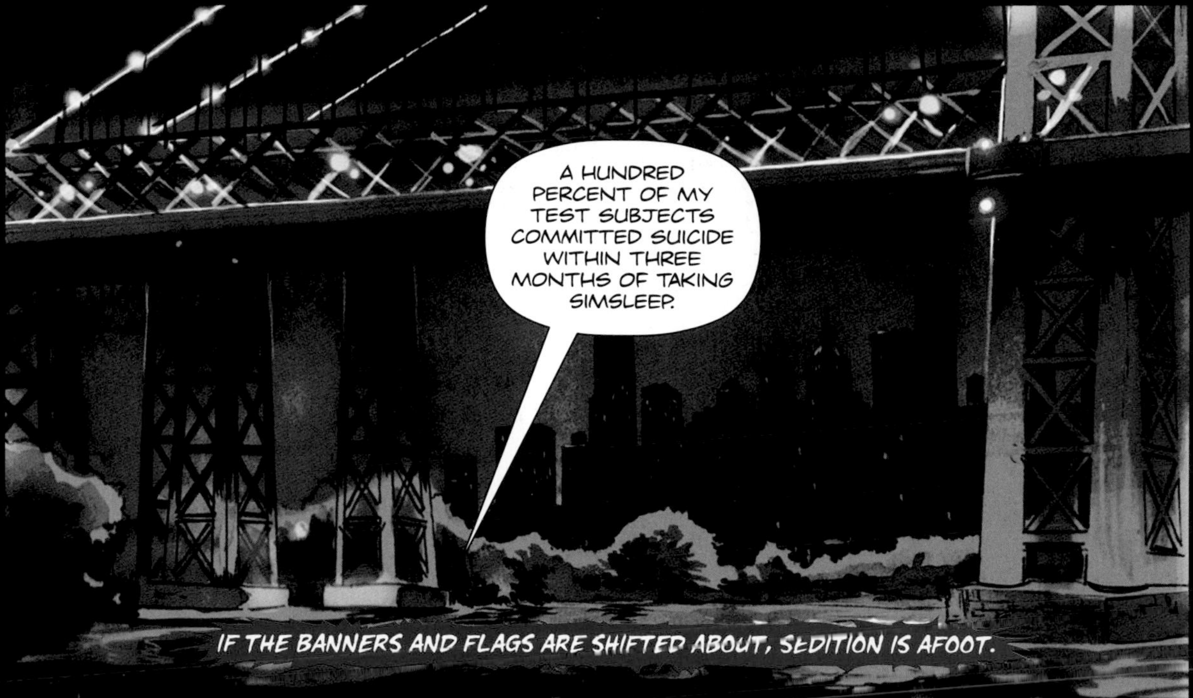
A HUNDRED PERCENT OF MY TEST SUBJECTS COMMITTED SUICIDE WITHIN THREE MONTHS OF TAKING SIMSLEEP.
IF THE BANNERS AND FLAGS ARE SHIFTED ABOUT, SEDITION IS AFOOT.

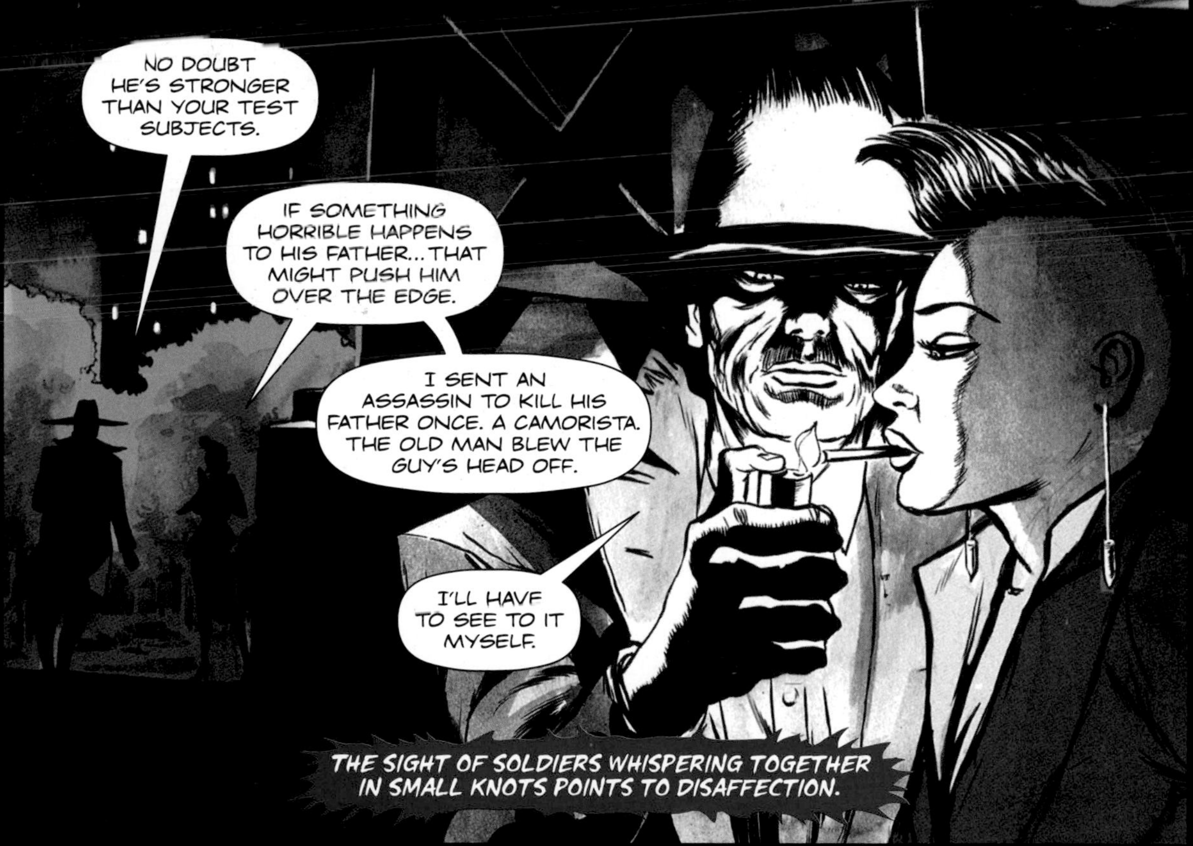
NO DOUBT HE'S STRONGER THAN YOUR TEST SUBJECTS.
IF SOMETHING HORRIBLE HAPPENS TO HIS FATHER... THAT MIGHT PUSH HIM OVER THE EDGE.
I SENT AN ASSASSIN TO KILL HIS FATHER ONCE. A CAMORISTA. THE OLD MAN BLEW THE GUY'S HEAD OFF.
I'LL HAVE TO SEE TO IT MYSELF.
THE SIGHT OF SOLDIERS WHISPERING TOGETHER IN SMALL KNOTS POINTS TO DISAFFECTION.

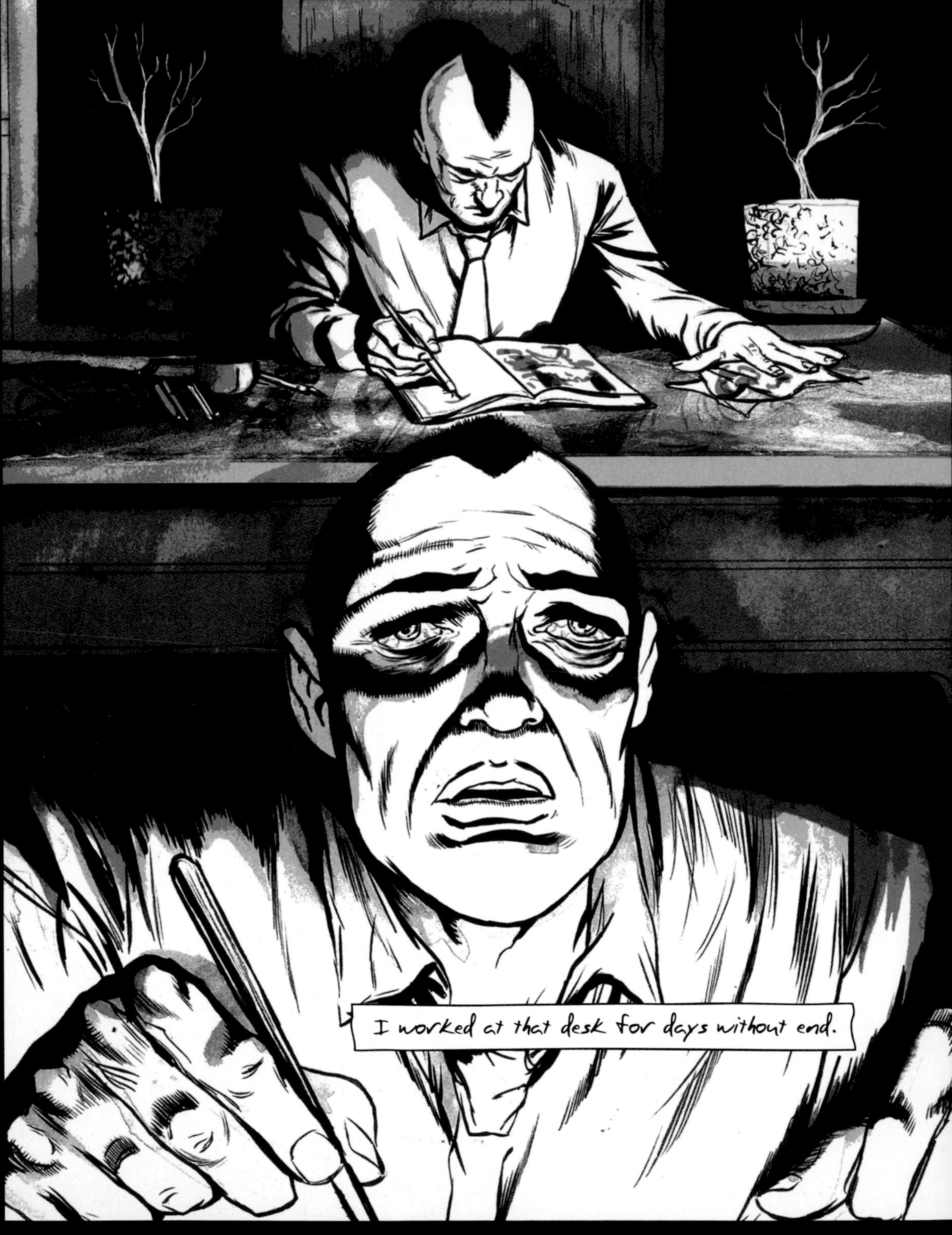
I worked at that desk for days without end.

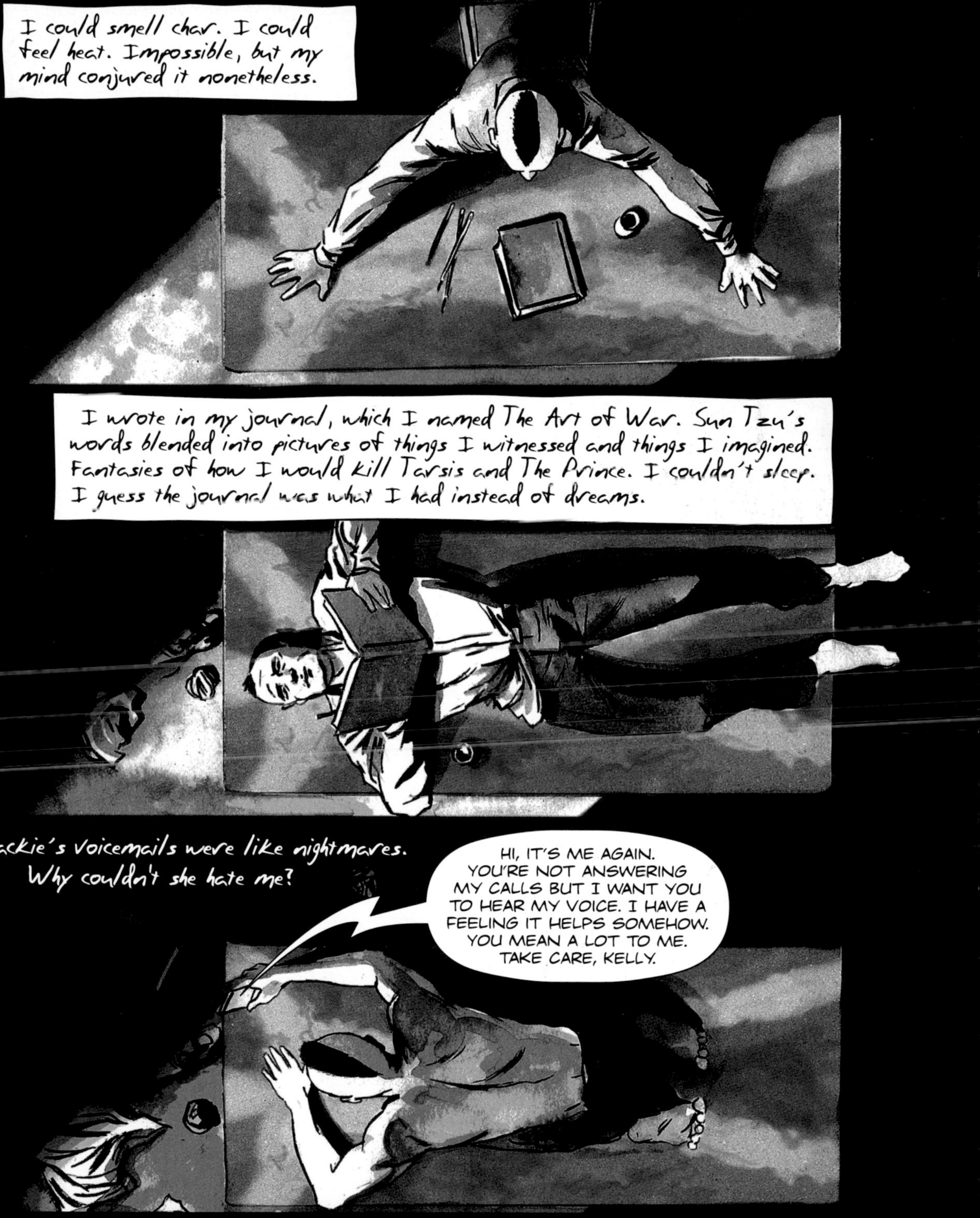
I could smell char. I could feel heat. Impossible, but my mind conjured it nonetheless.
I wrote in my journal, which I named The Art of War. Sun Tzu's words blended into pictures of things I witnessed and things I imagined. Fantasies of how I would kill Tarsis and The Prince. I couldn't sleep. I guess the journal was what I had instead of dreams.
Jackie's voicemails were like nightmares. Why couldn't she hate me?
HI, IT'S ME AGAIN. YOU'RE NOT ANSWERING MY CALLS BUT I WANT YOU TO HEAR MY VOICE. I HAVE A FEELING IT HELPS SOMEHOW. YOU MEAN A LOT TO ME. TAKE CARE, KELLY.

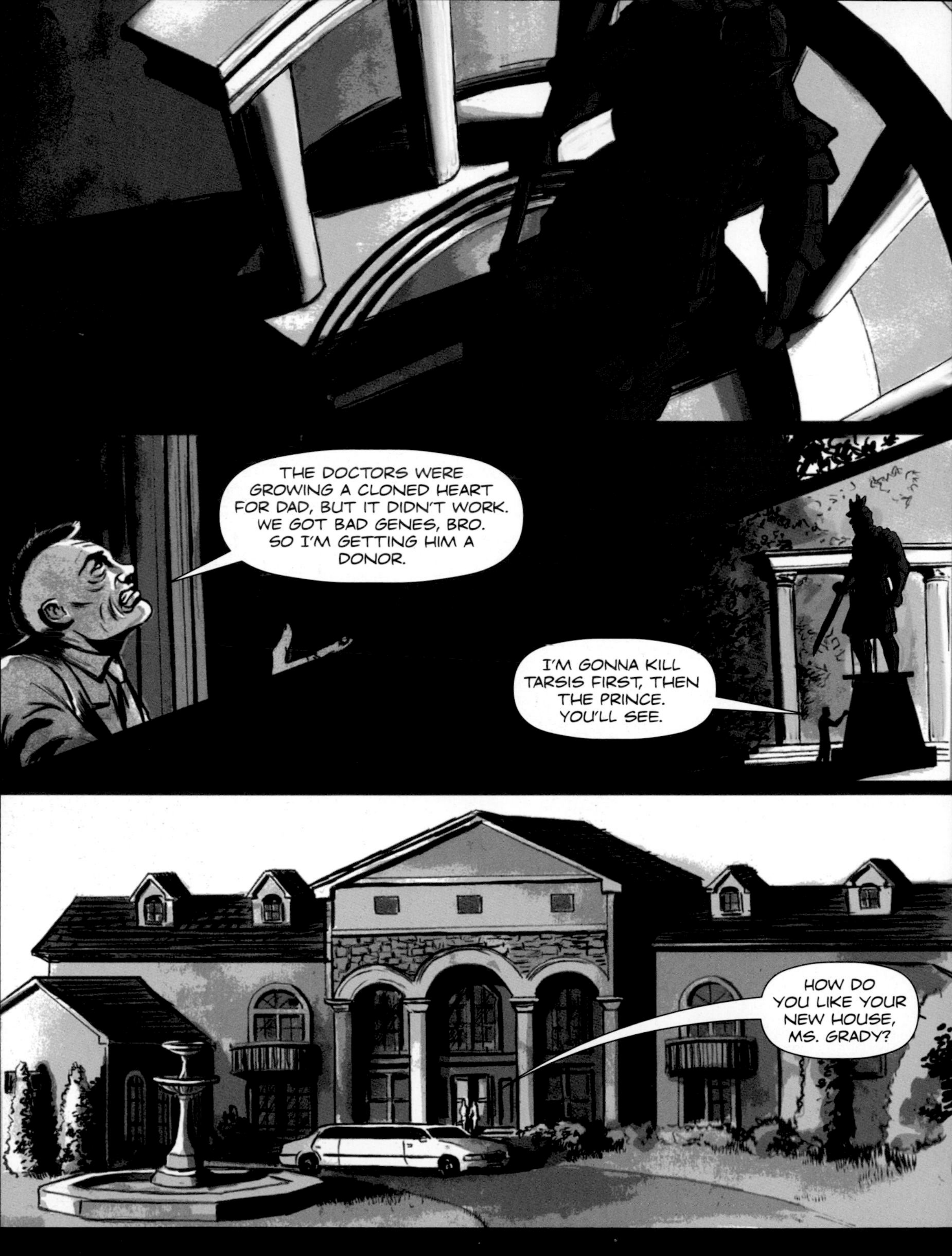
THE DOCTORS WERE GROWING A CLONED HEART FOR DAD, BUT IT DIDN'T WORK. WE GOT BAD GENES, BRO. SO I'M GETTING HIM A DONOR.
I'M GONNA KILL TARSIS FIRST, THEN THE PRINCE. YOU'LL SEE.
HOW DO YOU LIKE YOUR NEW HOUSE, MS. GRADY?

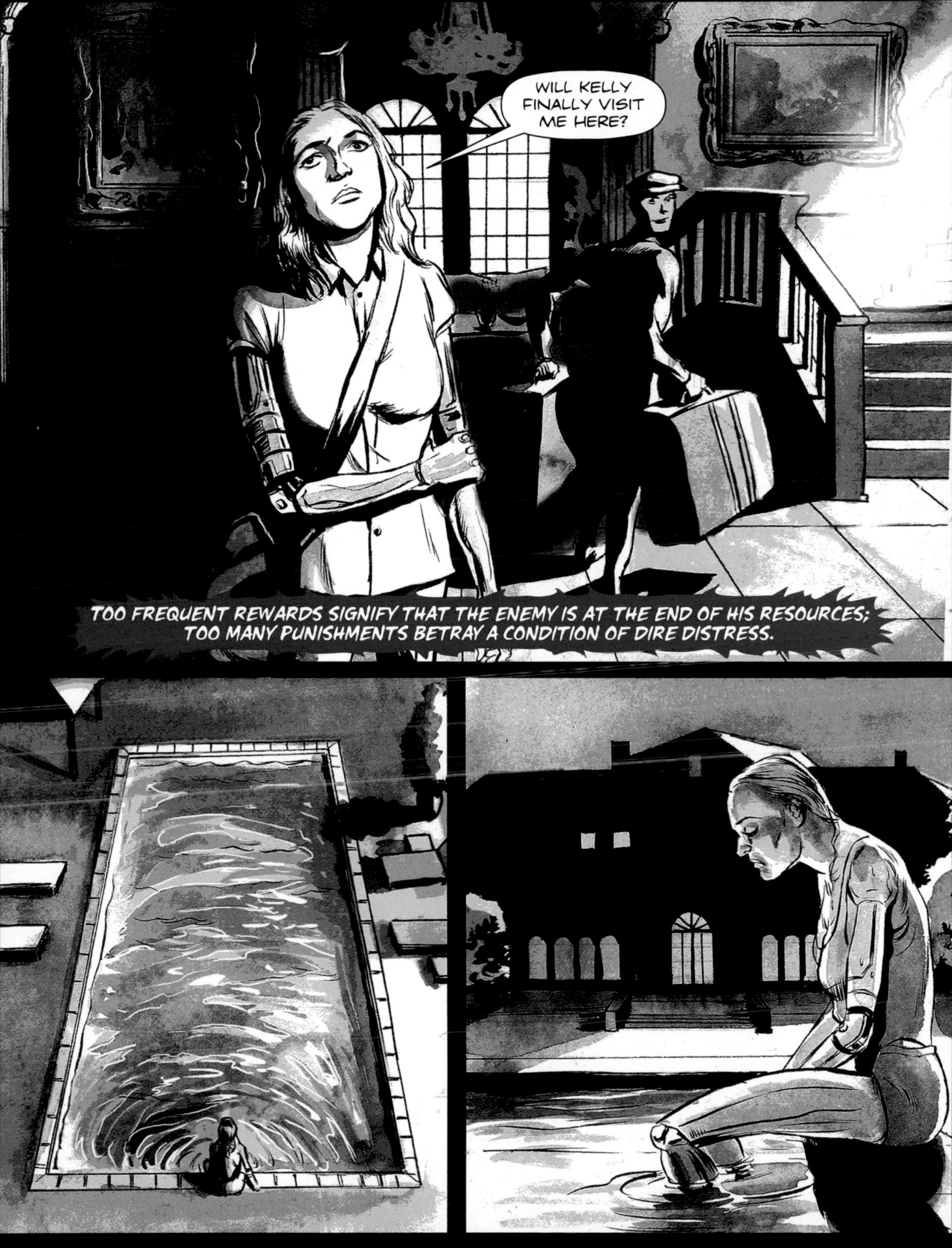
WILL KELLY FINALLY VISIT ME HERE?
TOO FREQUENT REWARDS SIGNIFY THAT THE ENEMY IS AT THE END OF HIS RESOURCES; TOO MANY PUNISHMENTS BETRAY A CONDITION OF DIRE DISTRESS.

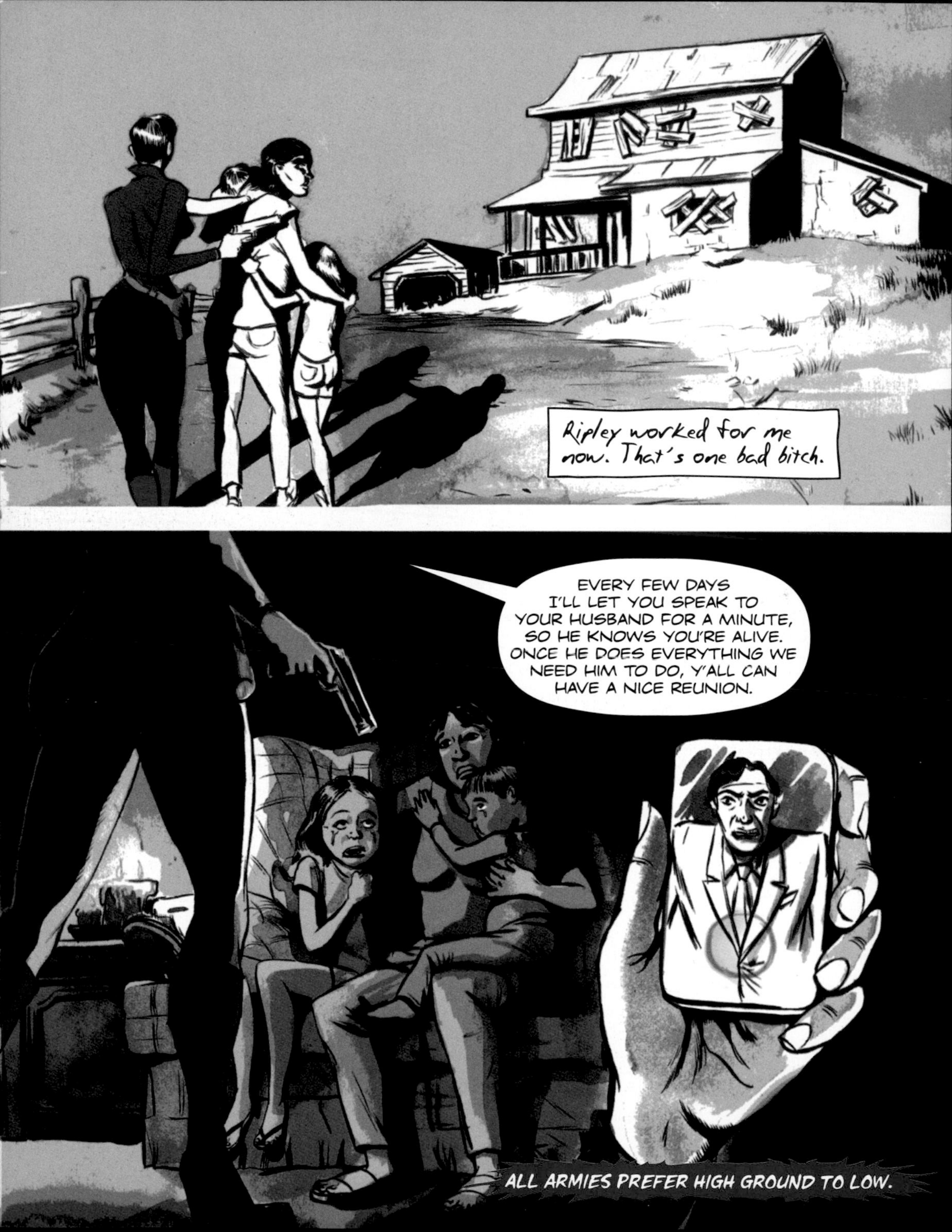
Ripley worked for me now. That's one bad bitch.
EVERY FEW DAYS I'LL LET YOU SPEAK TO YOUR HUSBAND FOR A MINUTE, SO HE KNOWS YOU'RE ALIVE. ONCE HE DOES EVERYTHING WE NEED HIM TO DO, Y'ALL CAN HAVE A NICE REUNION.
ALL ARMIES PREFER HIGH GROUND TO LOW.

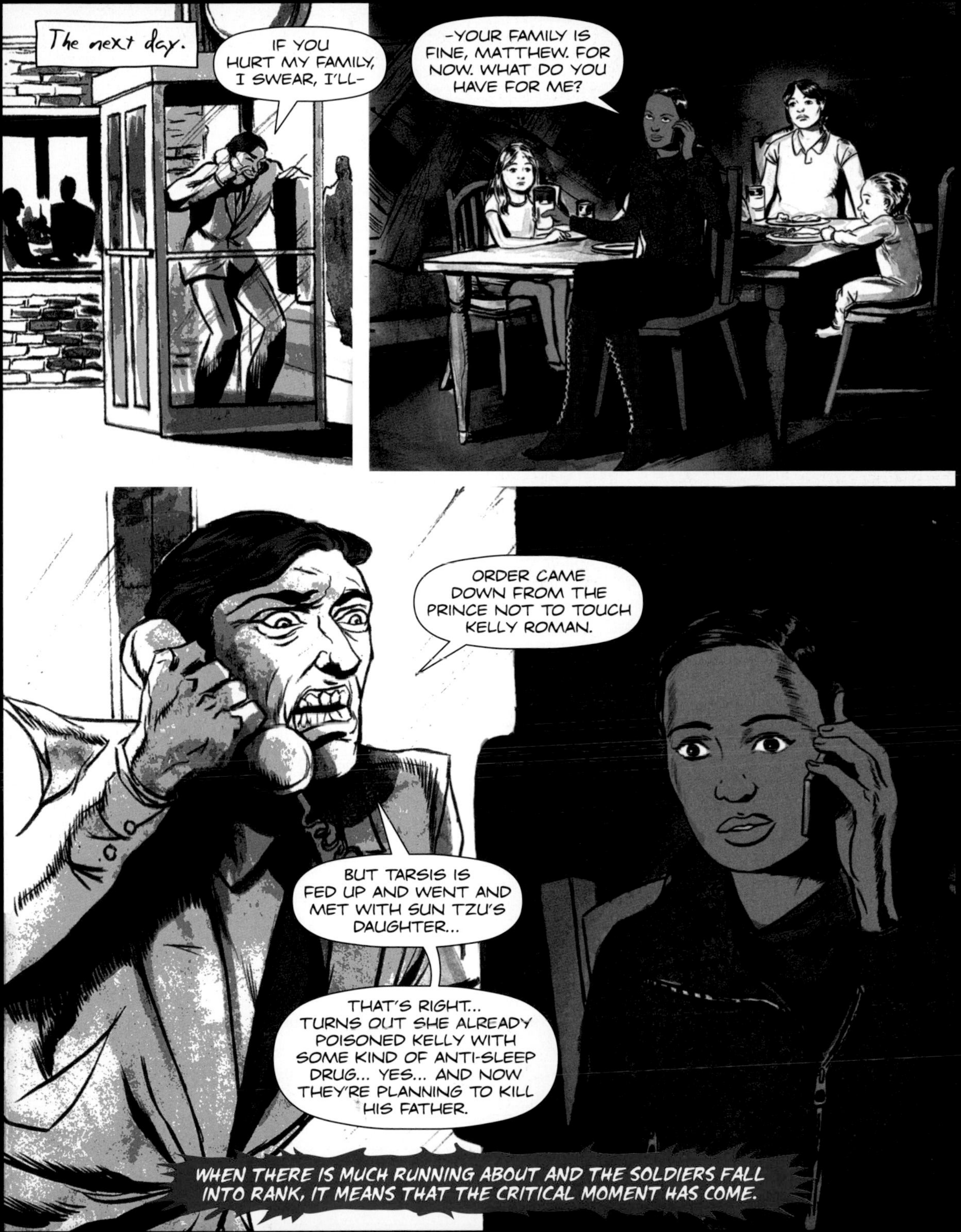
The next day.
IF YOU HURT MY FAMILY, I SWEAR, I'LL-
-YOUR FAMILY IS FINE, MATTHEW. FOR NOW. WHAT DO YOU HAVE FOR ME?
ORDER CAME DOWN FROM THE PRINCE NOT TO TOUCH KELLY ROMAN.
BUT TARSIS IS FED UP AND WENT AND MET WITH SUN TZU'S DAUGHTER...
THAT'S RIGHT... TURNS OUT SHE ALREADY POISONED KELLY WITH SOME KIND OF ANTI-SLEEP DRUG... YES... AND NOW THEY'RE PLANNING TO KILL HIS FATHER.
WHEN THERE IS MUCH RUNNING ABOUT AND THE SOLDIERS FALL INTO RANK, IT MEANS THAT THE CRITICAL MOMENT HAS COME.

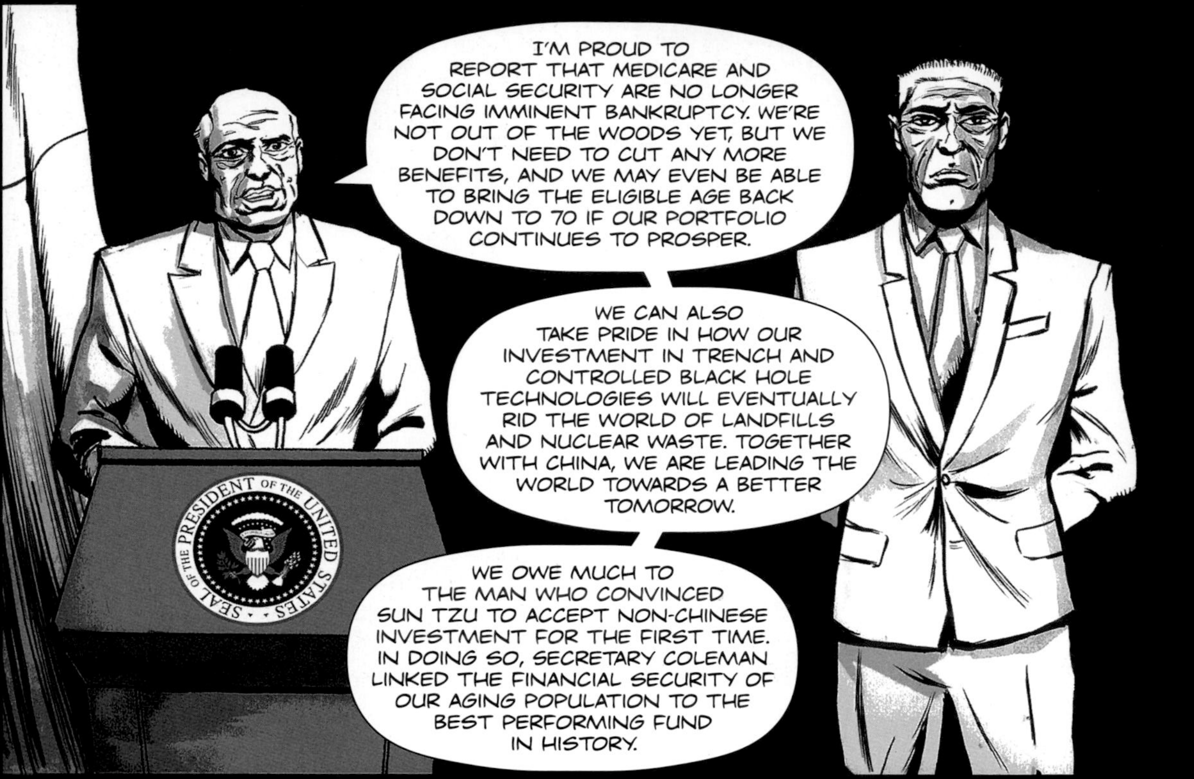
I'M PROUD TO REPORT THAT MEDICARE AND SOCIAL SECURITY ARE NO LONGER FACING IMMINENT BANKRUPTCY. WE'RE NOT OUT OF THE WOODS YET, BUT WE DON'T NEED TO CUT ANY MORE BENEFITS, AND WE MAY EVEN BE ABLE TO BRING THE ELIGIBLE AGE BACK DOWN TO 70 IF OUR PORTFOLIO CONTINUES TO PROSPER.
WE CAN ALSO TAKE PRIDE IN HOW OUR INVESTMENT IN TRENCH AND CONTROLLED BLACK HOLE TECHNOLOGIES WILL EVENTUALLY RID THE WORLD OF LANDFILLS AND NUCLEAR WASTE. TOGETHER WITH CHINA, WE ARE LEADING THE WORLD TOWARDS A BETTER TOMORROW.
WE OWE MUCH TO THE MAN WHO CONVINCED SUN TZU TO ACCEPT NON-CHINESE INVESTMENT FOR THE FIRST TIME. IN DOING SO, SECRETARY COLEMAN LINKED THE FINANCIAL SECURITY OF OUR AGING POPULATION TO THE BEST PERFORMING FUND IN HISTORY.
SEAL OF THE PRESIDENT OF THE UNITED STATES
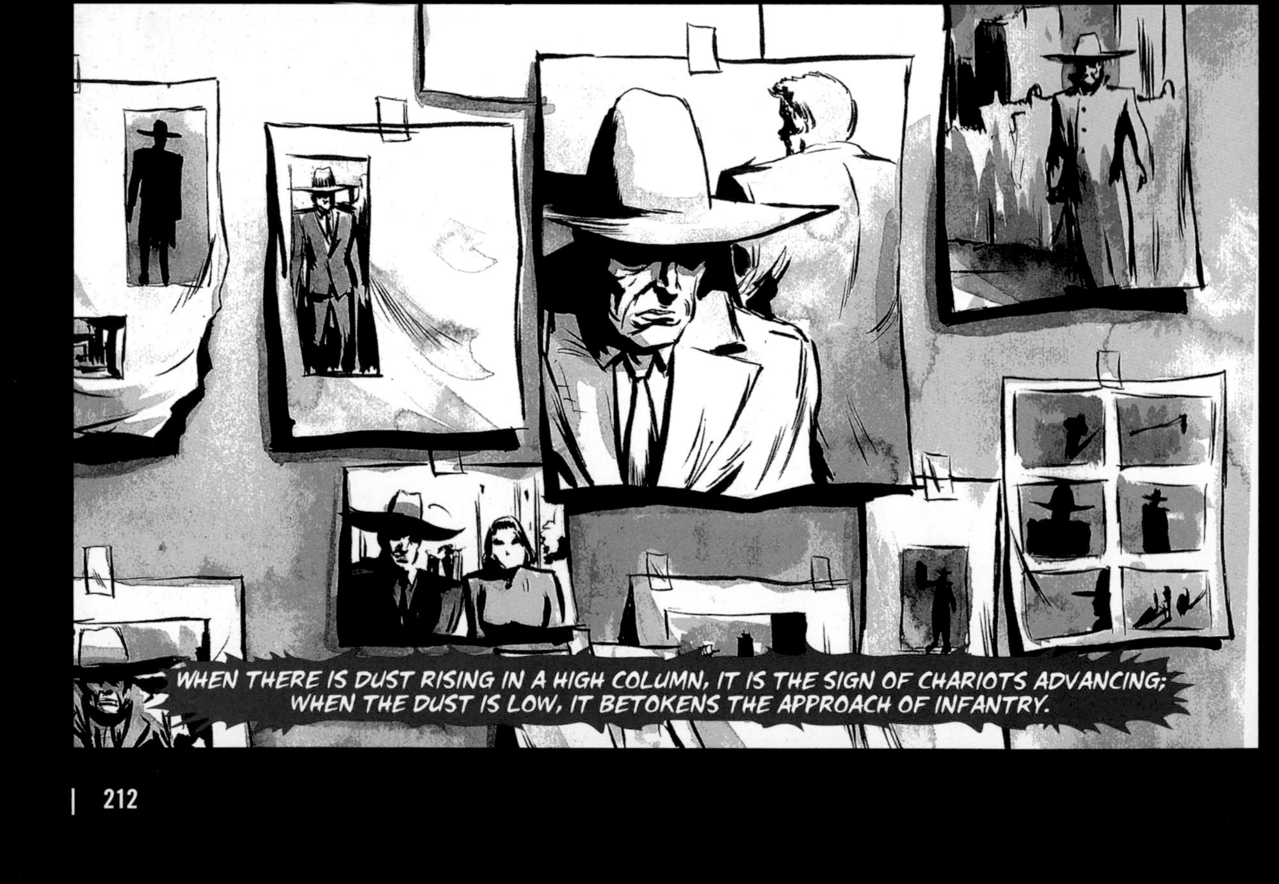
WHEN THERE IS DUST RISING IN A HIGH COLUMN, IT IS THE SIGN OF CHARIOTS ADVANCING; WHEN THE DUST IS LOW, IT BETOKENS THE APPROACH OF INFANTRY.

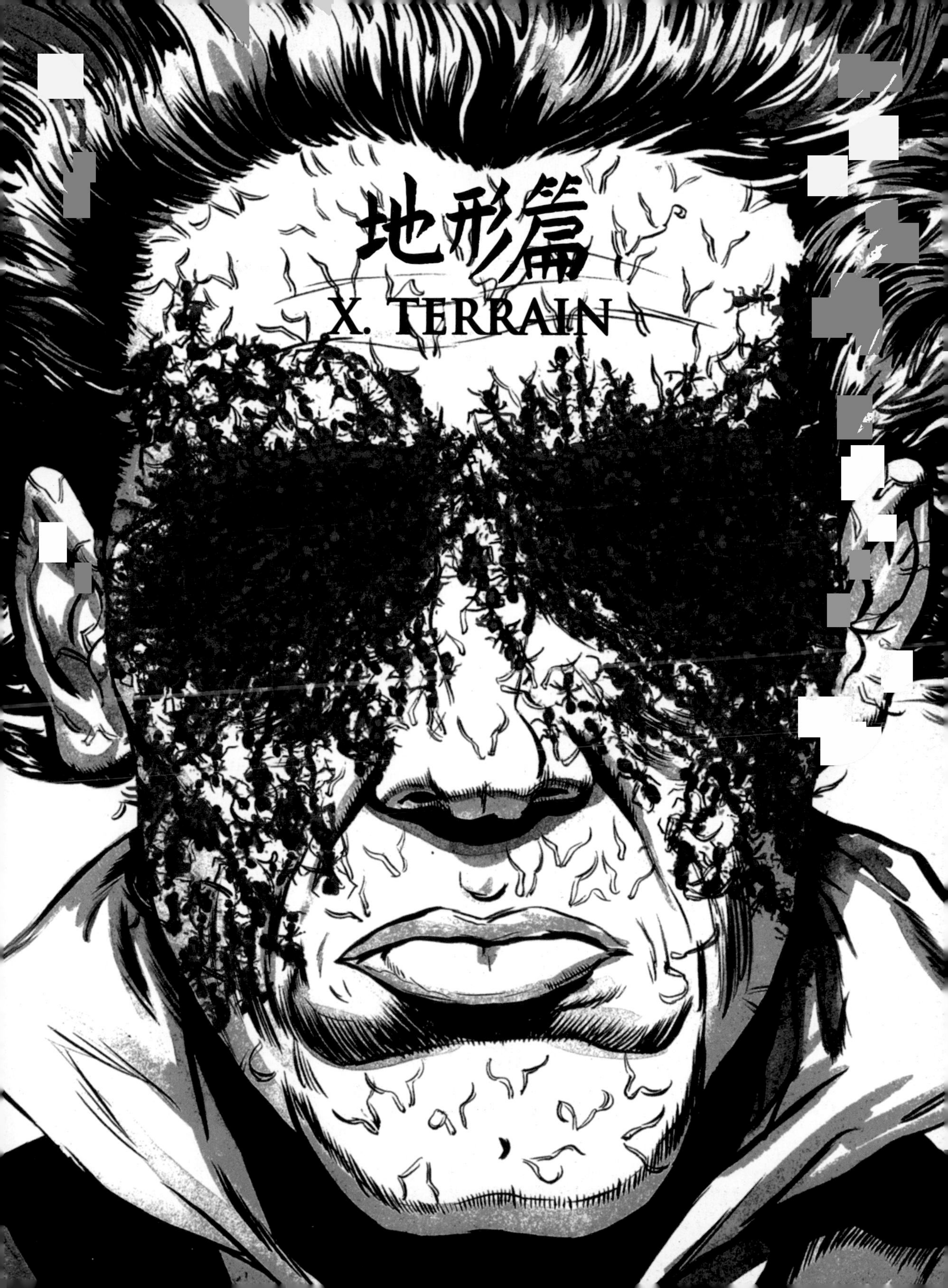
地形篇
X. TERRAIN

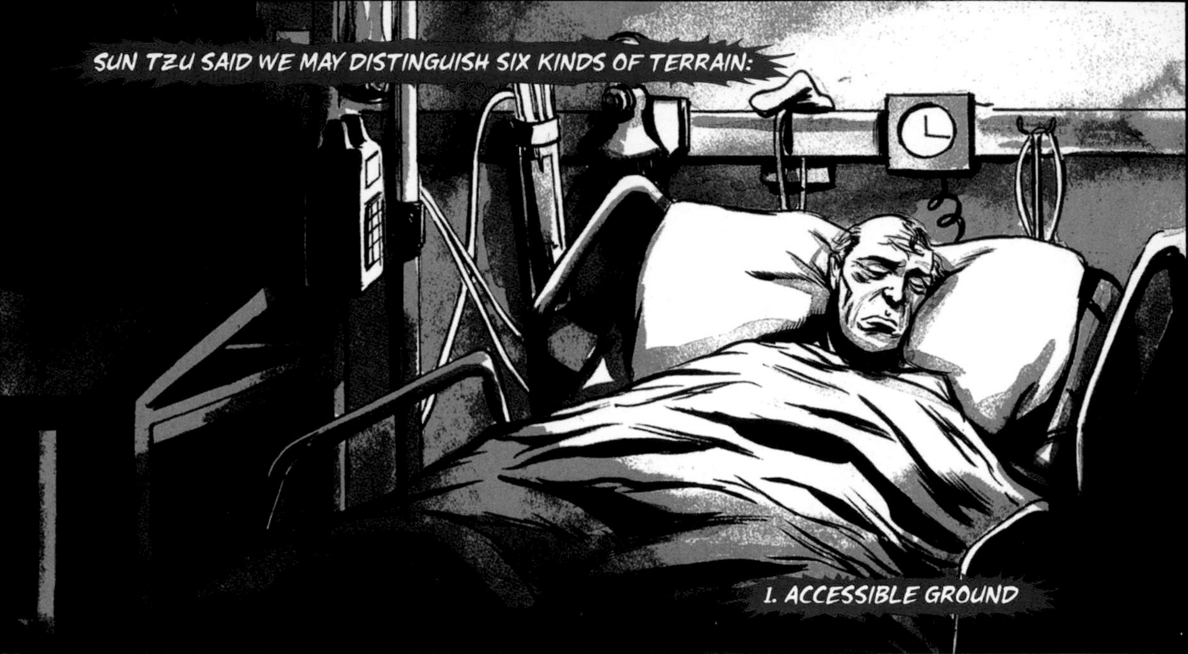
SUN TZU SAID WE MAY DISTINGUISH SIX KINDS OF TERRAIN:
1. ACCESSIBLE GROUND

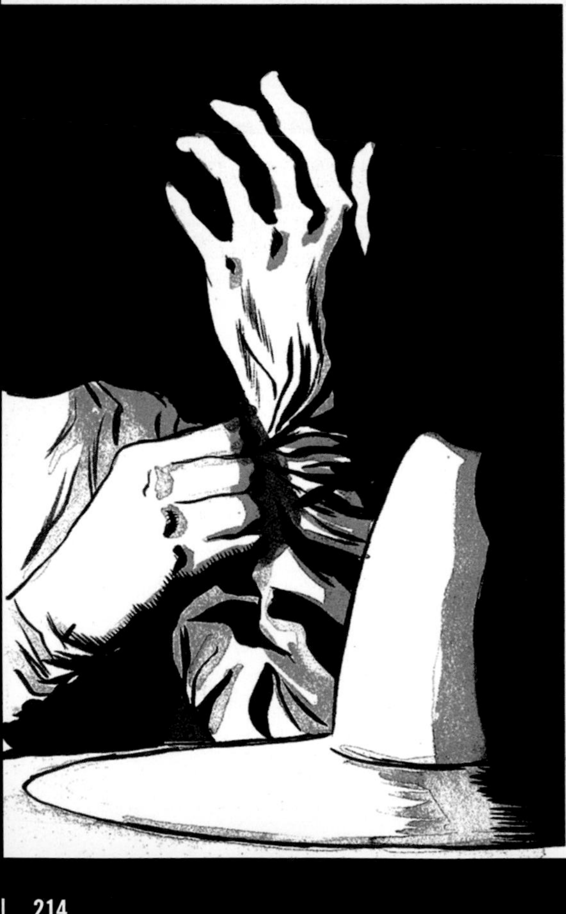

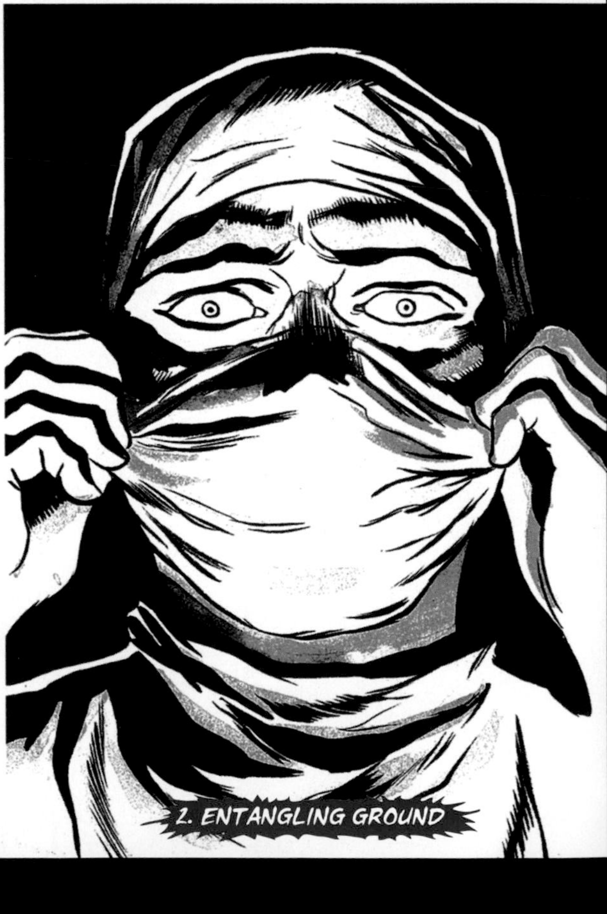
2. ENTANGLING GROUND

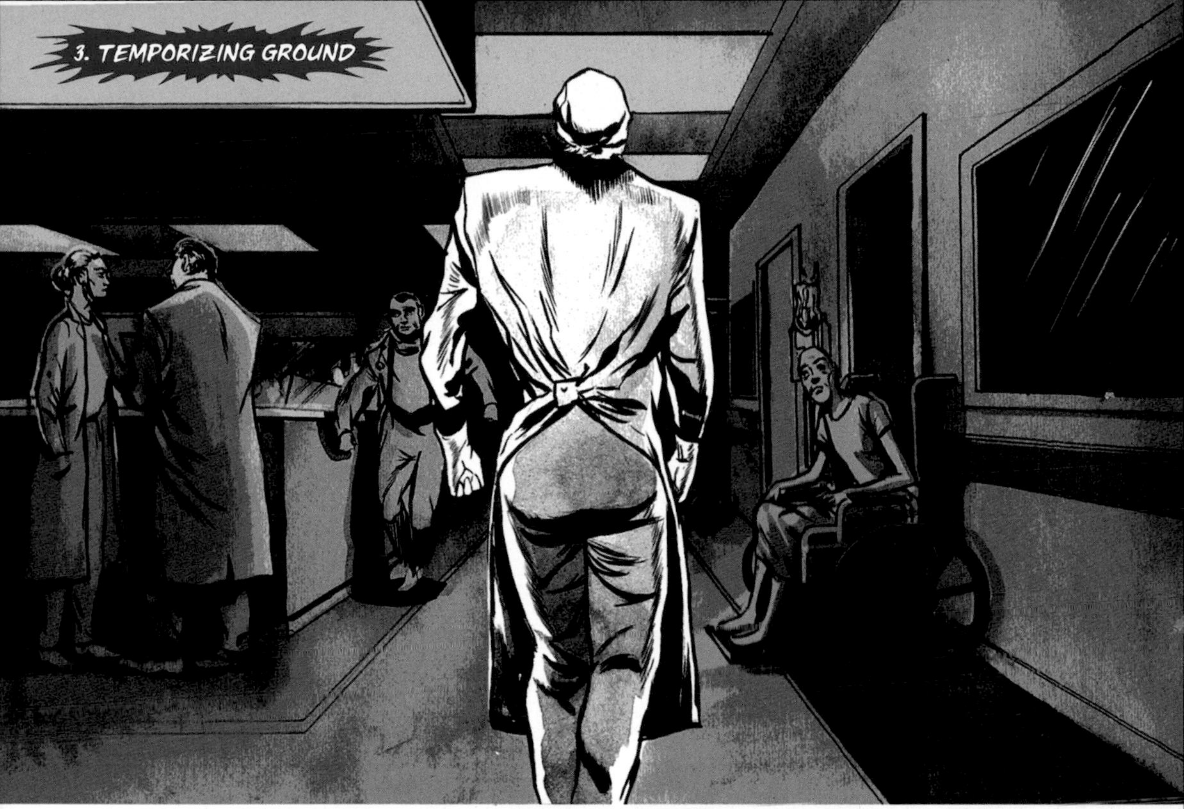
3. TEMPORIZING GROUND

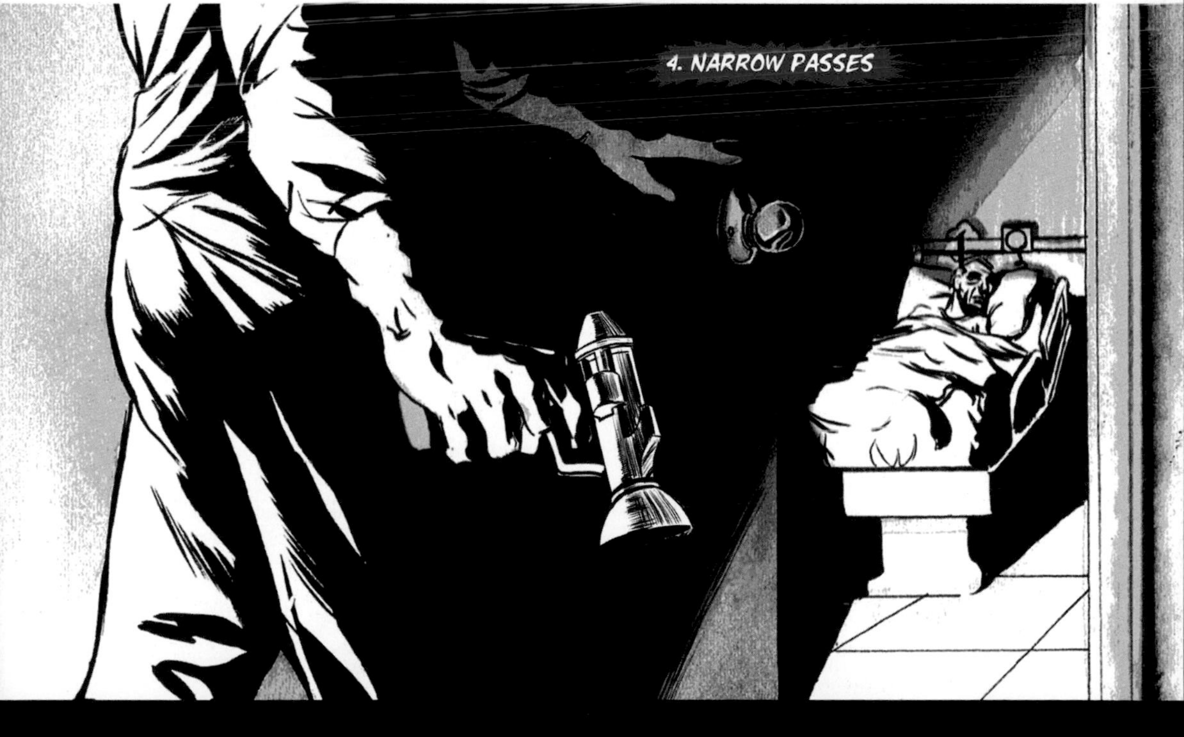
4. NARROW PASSES

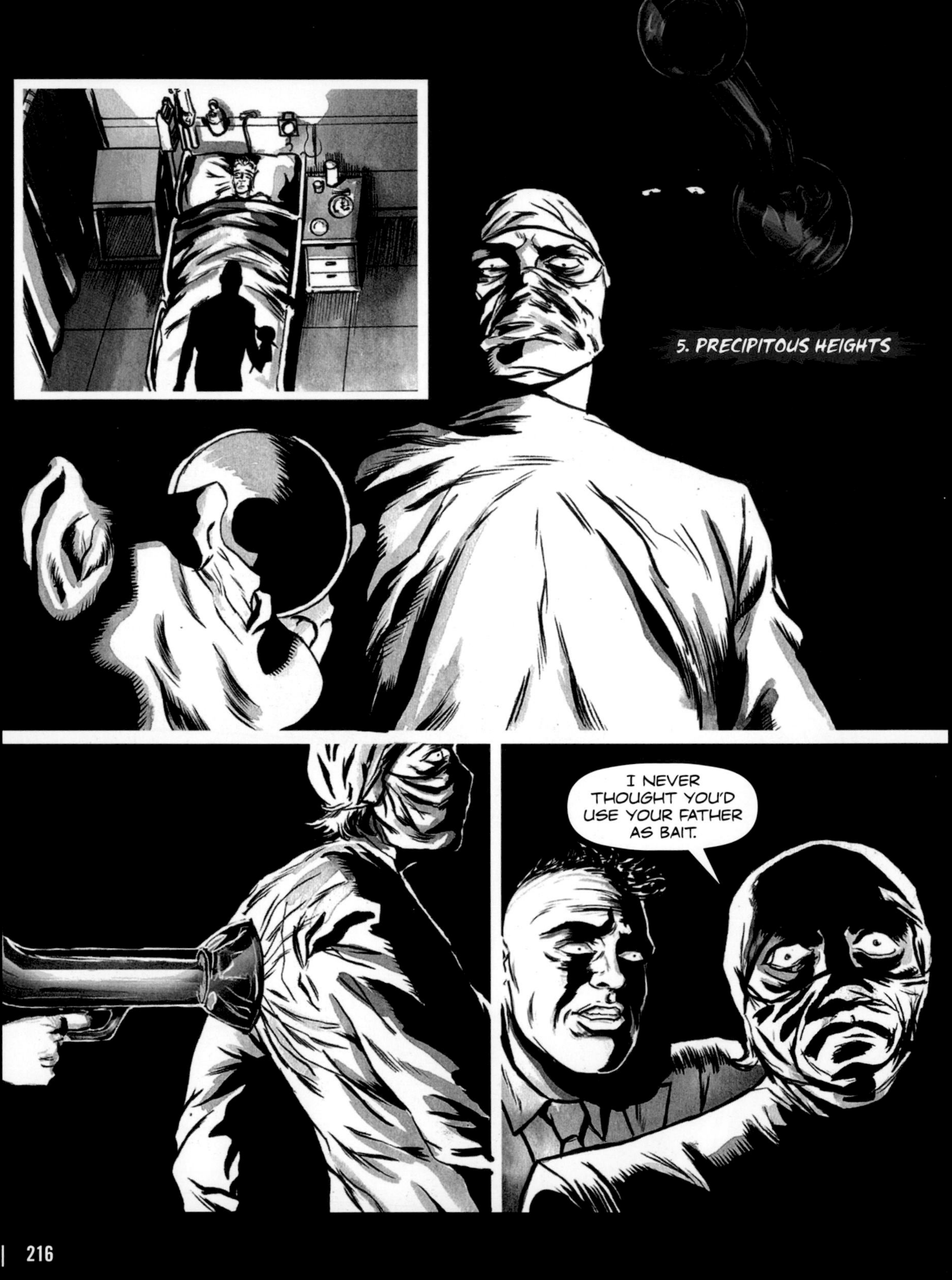
5. PRECIPITOUS HEIGHTS
I NEVER THOUGHT YOU'D USE YOUR FATHER AS BAIT.

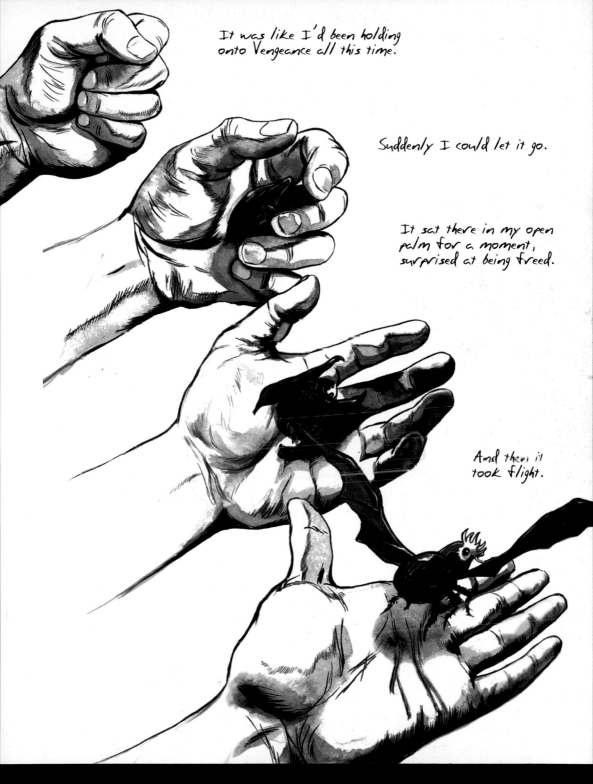

It was like I'd been holding onto Vengeance all this time.

Suddenly I could let it go.

It sat there in my open palm for a moment, surprised at being freed.

And then it took flight.

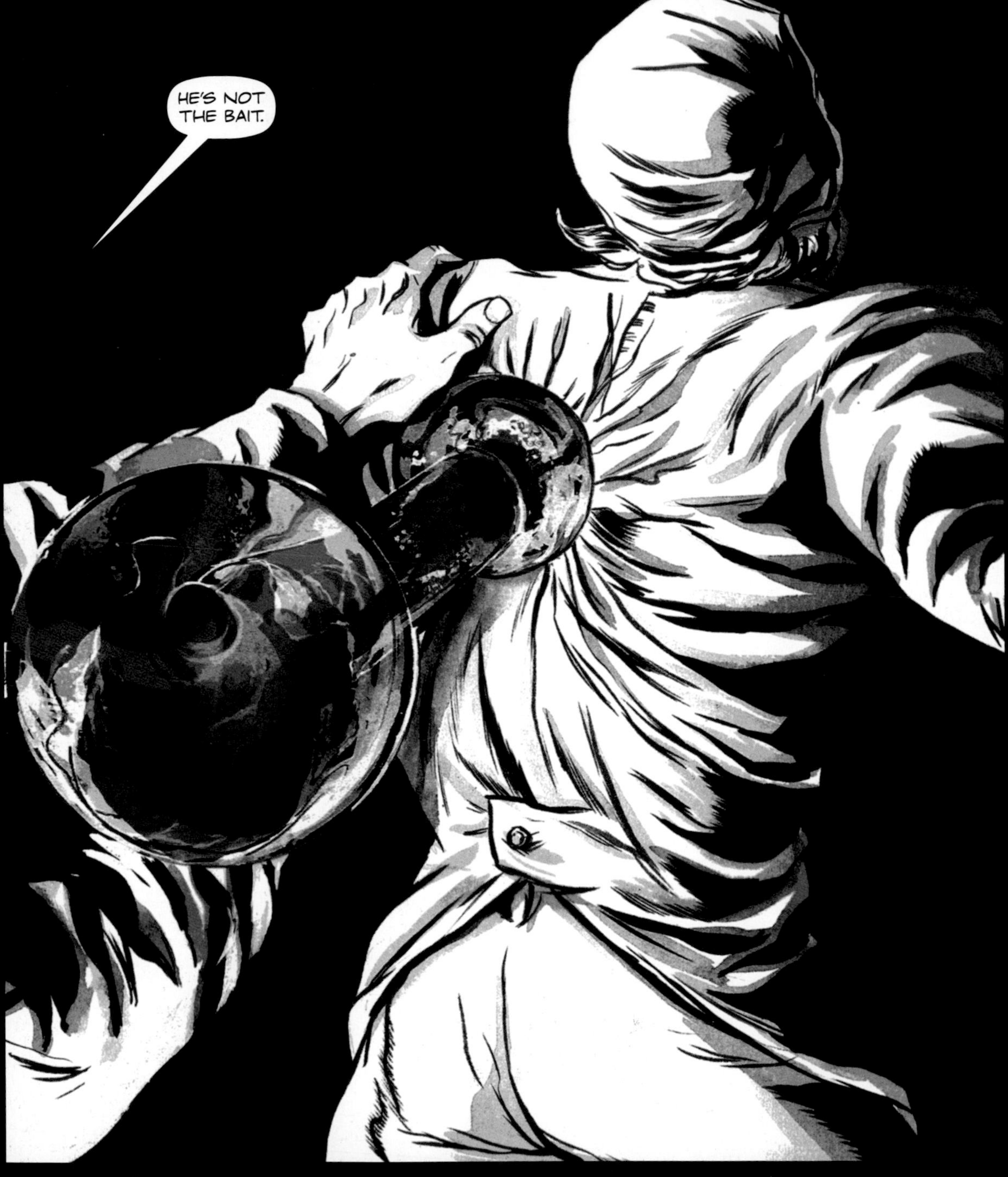
HE'S NOT THE BAIT.

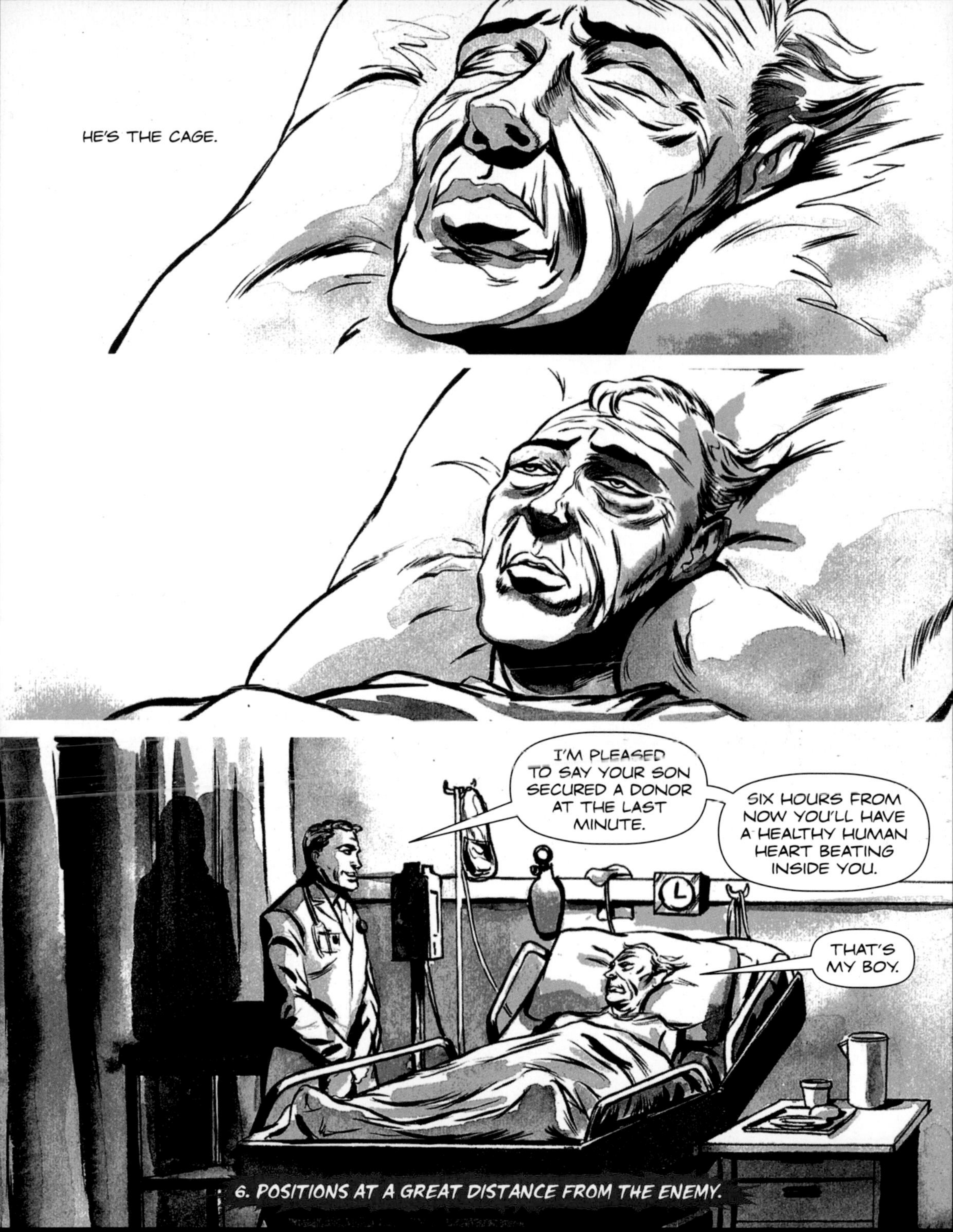
HE'S THE CAGE.
I'M PLEASED TO SAY YOUR SON SECURED A DONOR AT THE LAST MINUTE.
SIX HOURS FROM NOW YOU'LL HAVE A HEALTHY HUMAN HEART BEATING INSIDE YOU.
THAT'S MY BOY.
6. POSITIONS AT A GREAT DISTANCE FROM THE ENEMY.

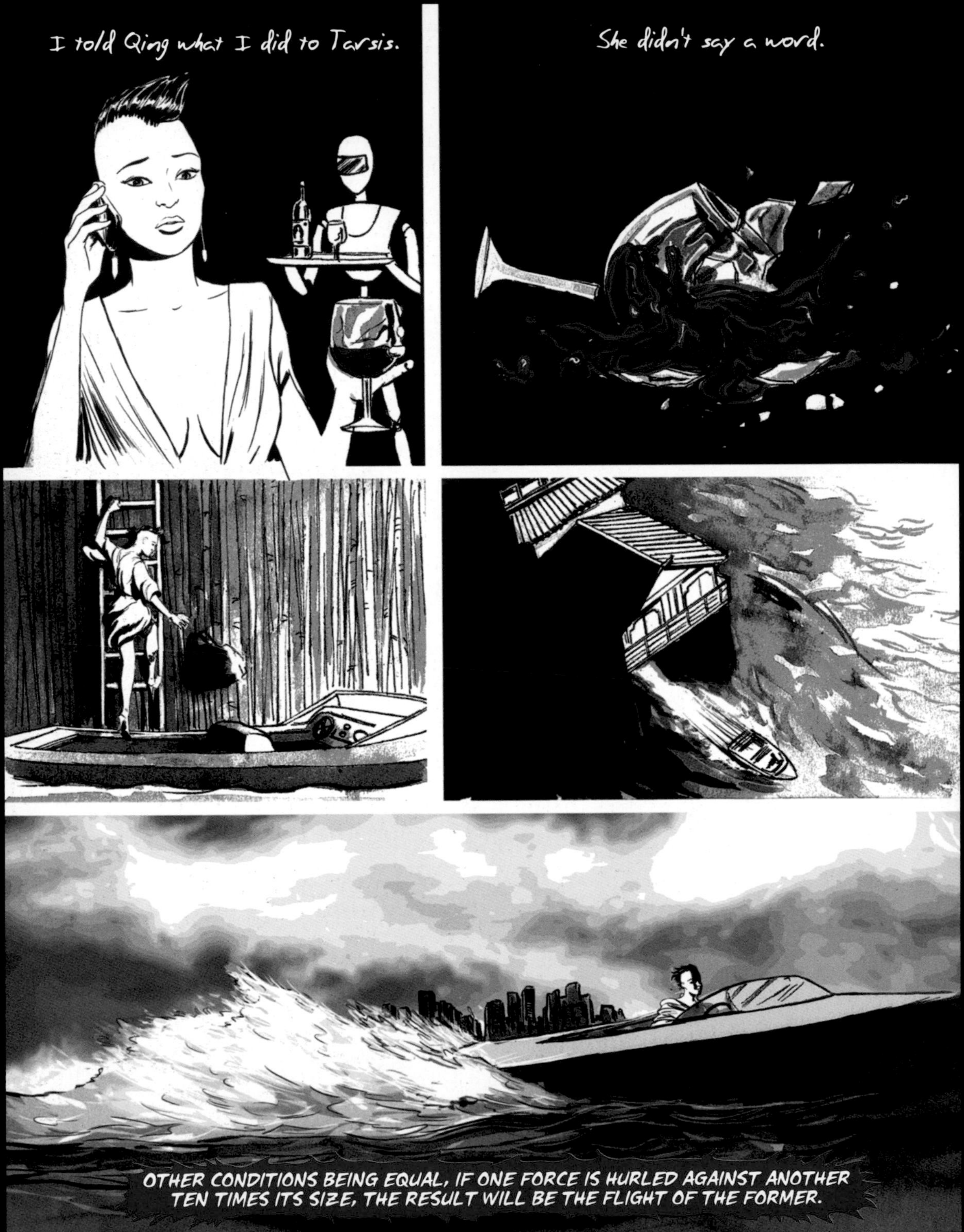
I told Qing what I did to Tarsis.
She didn't say a word.
OTHER CONDITIONS BEING EQUAL, IF ONE FORCE IS HURLED AGAINST ANOTHER TEN TIMES ITS SIZE, THE RESULT WILL BE THE FLIGHT OF THE FORMER.

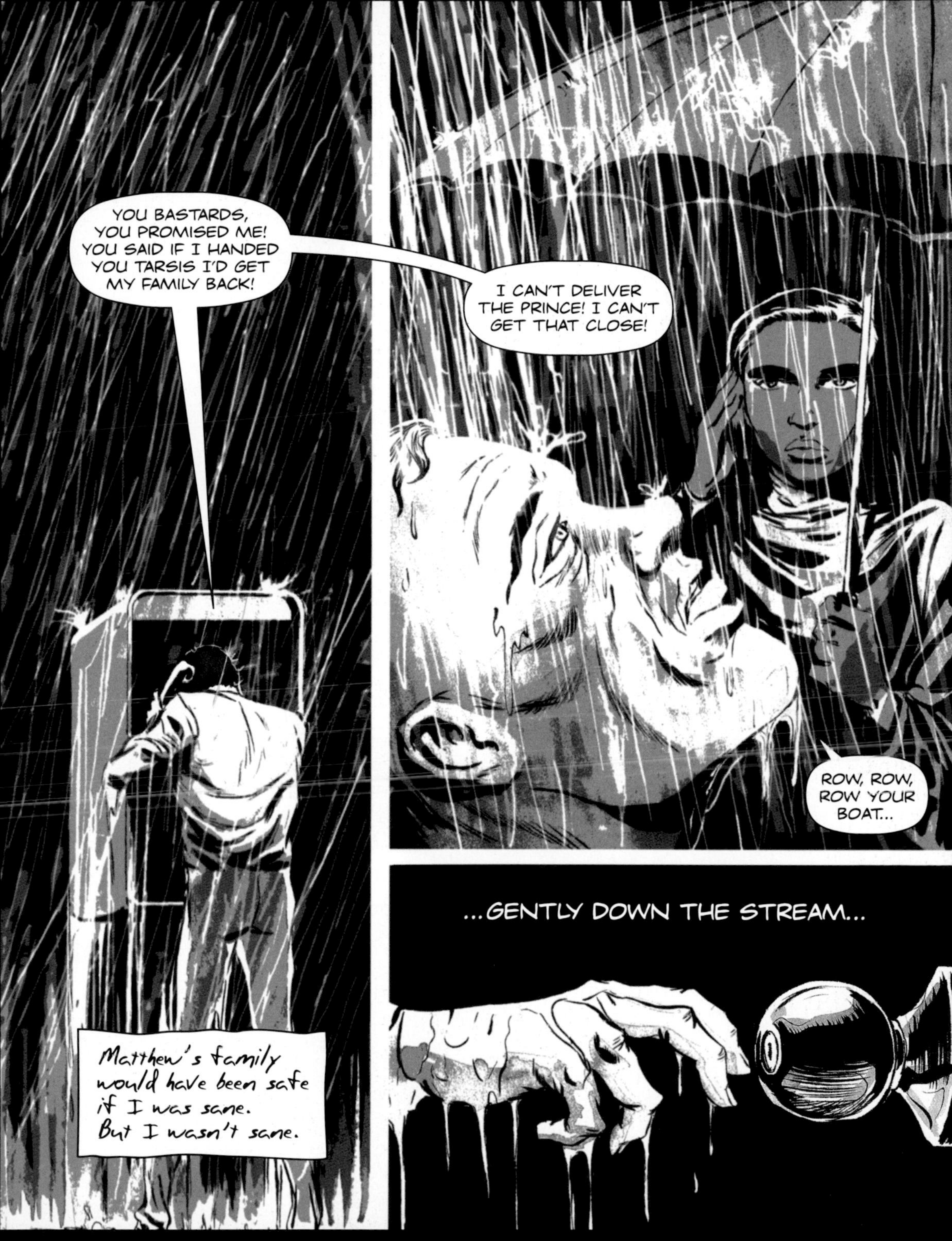
YOU BASTARDS, YOU PROMISED ME! YOU SAID IF I HANDED YOU TARSIS I'D GET MY FAMILY BACK!
I CAN'T DELIVER THE PRINCE! I CAN'T GET THAT CLOSE!
ROW, ROW, ROW YOUR BOAT...
Matthew's family would have been safe if I was sane. But I wasn't sane.
...GENTLY DOWN THE STREAM...

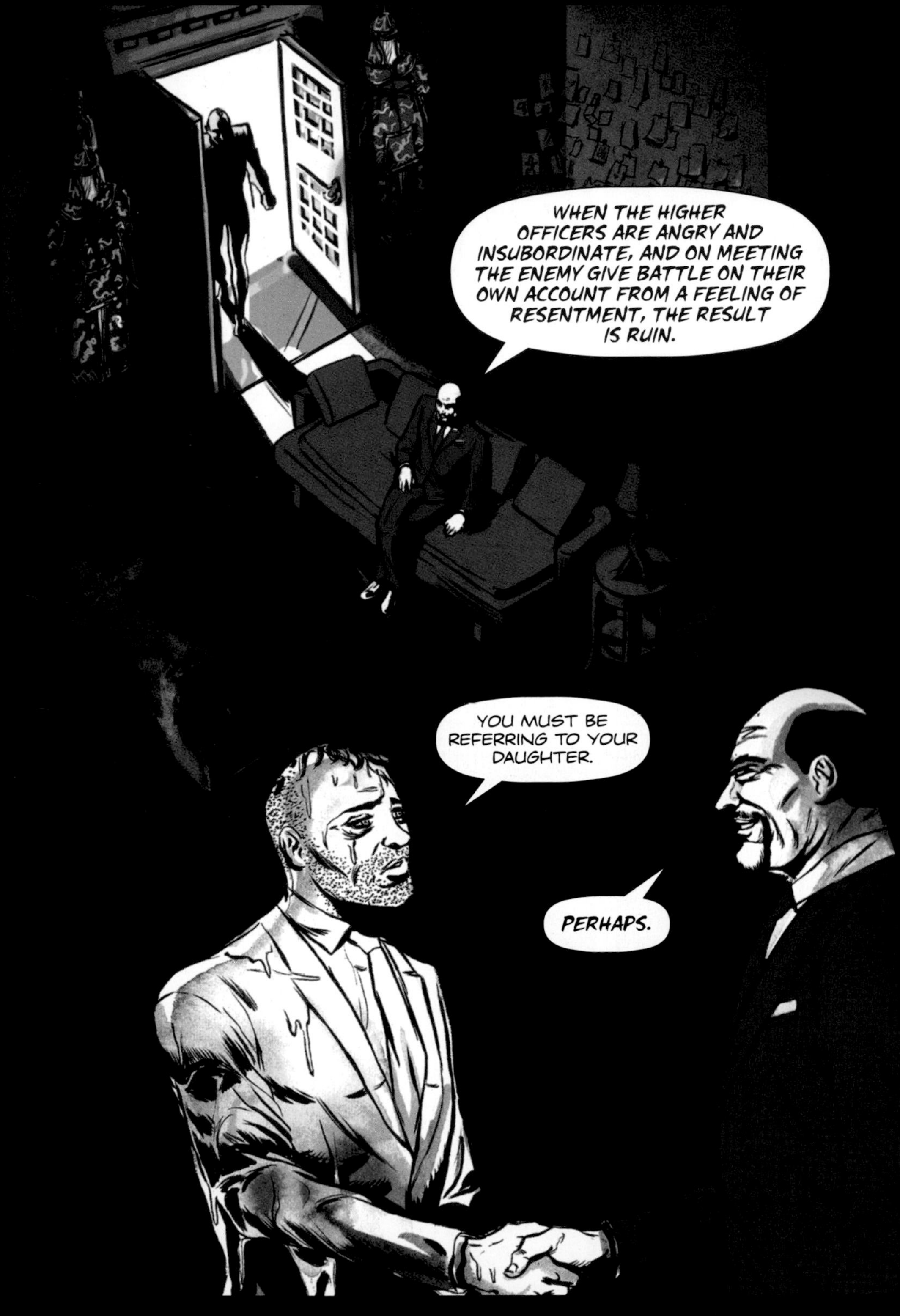
WHEN THE HIGHER OFFICERS ARE ANGRY AND INSUBORDINATE, AND ON MEETING THE ENEMY GIVE BATTLE ON THEIR OWN ACCOUNT FROM A FEELING OF RESENTMENT, THE RESULT IS RUIN.
YOU MUST BE REFERRING TO YOUR DAUGHTER.
PERHAPS.

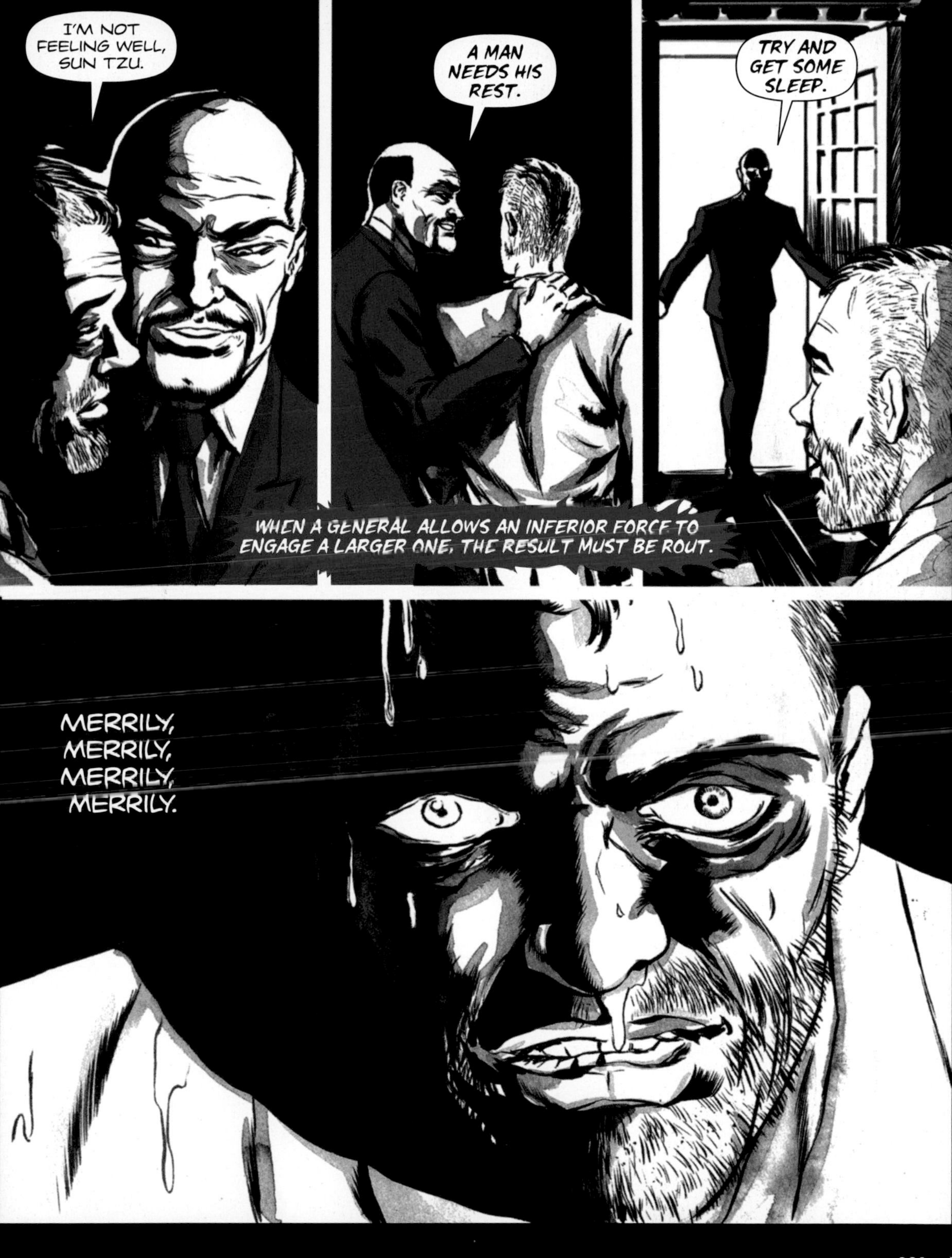
I'M NOT FEELING WELL, SUN TZU.
A MAN NEEDS HIS REST.
TRY AND GET SOME SLEEP.
WHEN A GENERAL ALLOWS AN INFERIOR FORCE TO ENGAGE A LARGER ONE, THE RESULT MUST BE ROUT.
MERRILY, MERRILY, MERRILY, MERRILY.

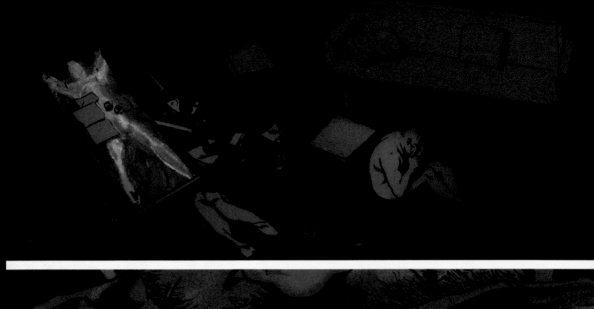

Life is but
a dream.

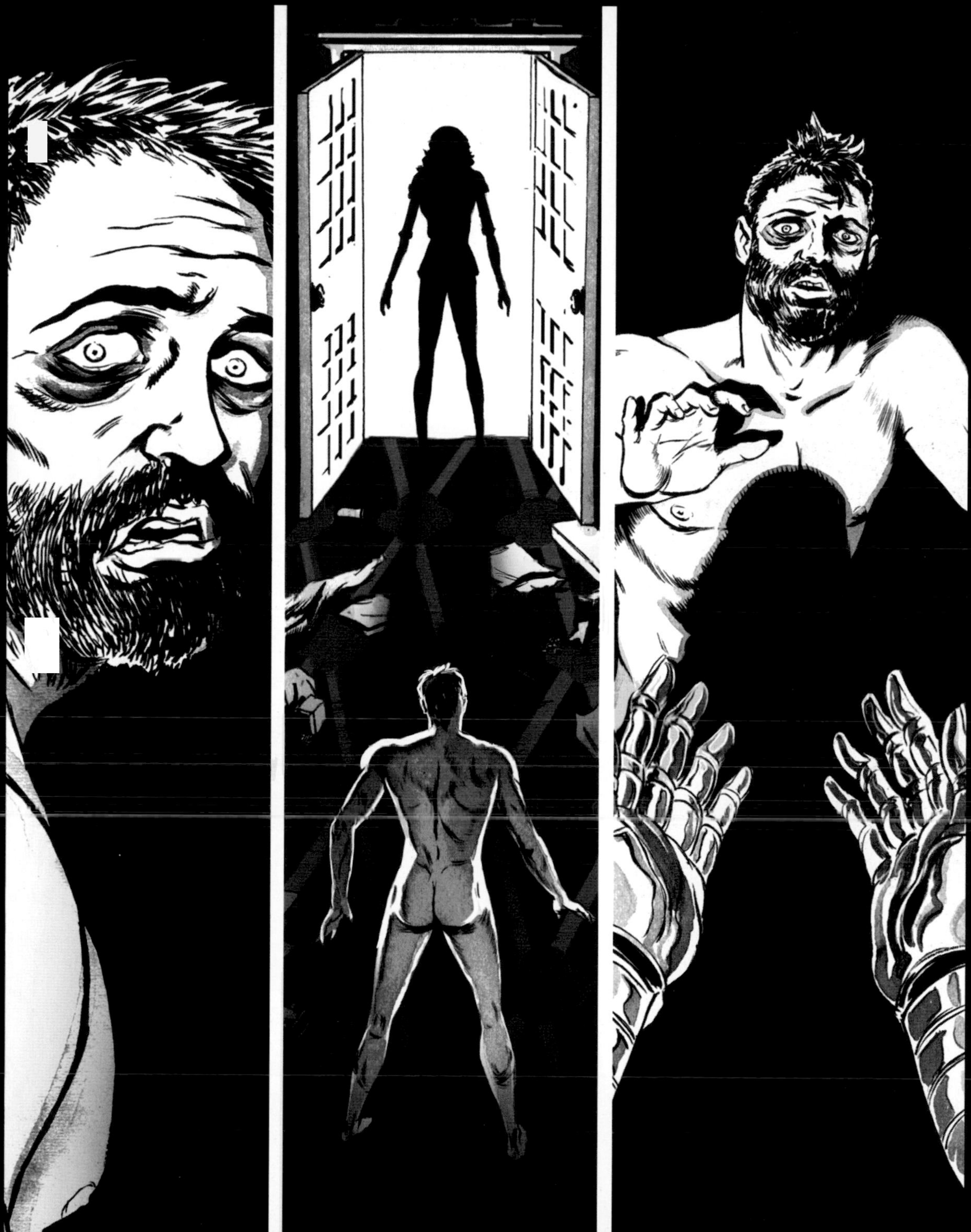

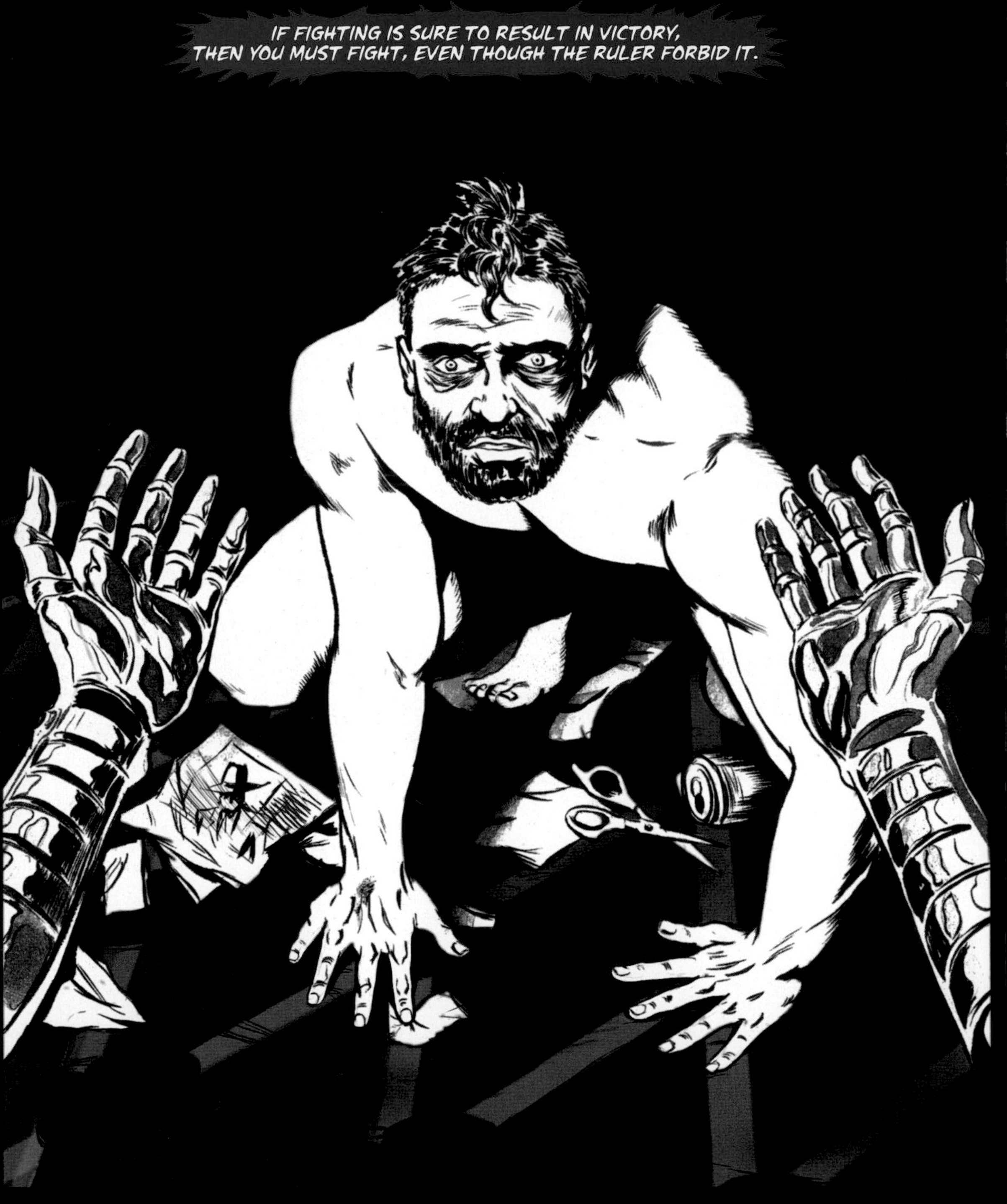
IF FIGHTING IS SURE TO RESULT IN VICTORY, THEN YOU MUST FIGHT, EVEN THOUGH THE RULER FORBID IT.

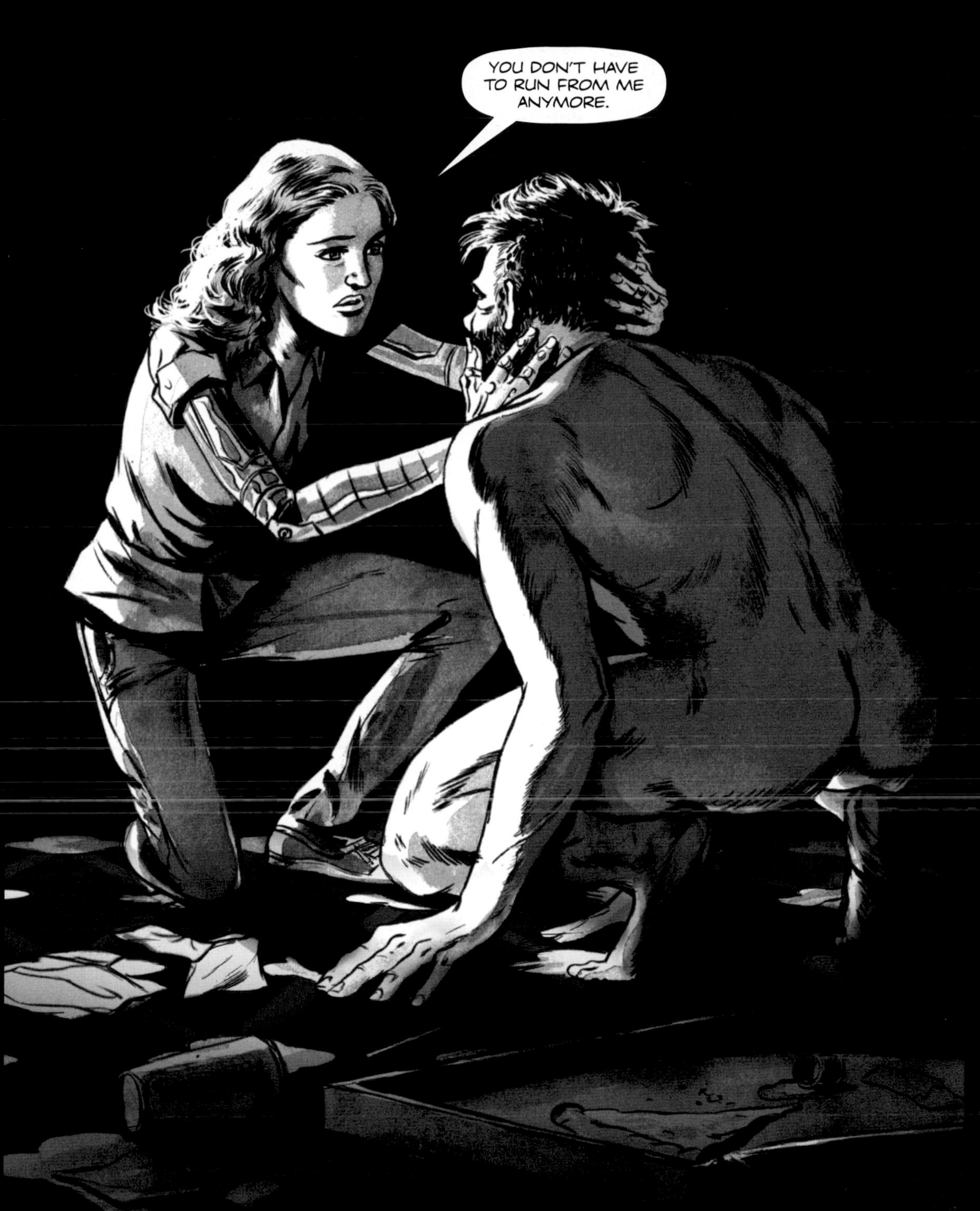
YOU DON'T HAVE TO RUN FROM ME ANYMORE.

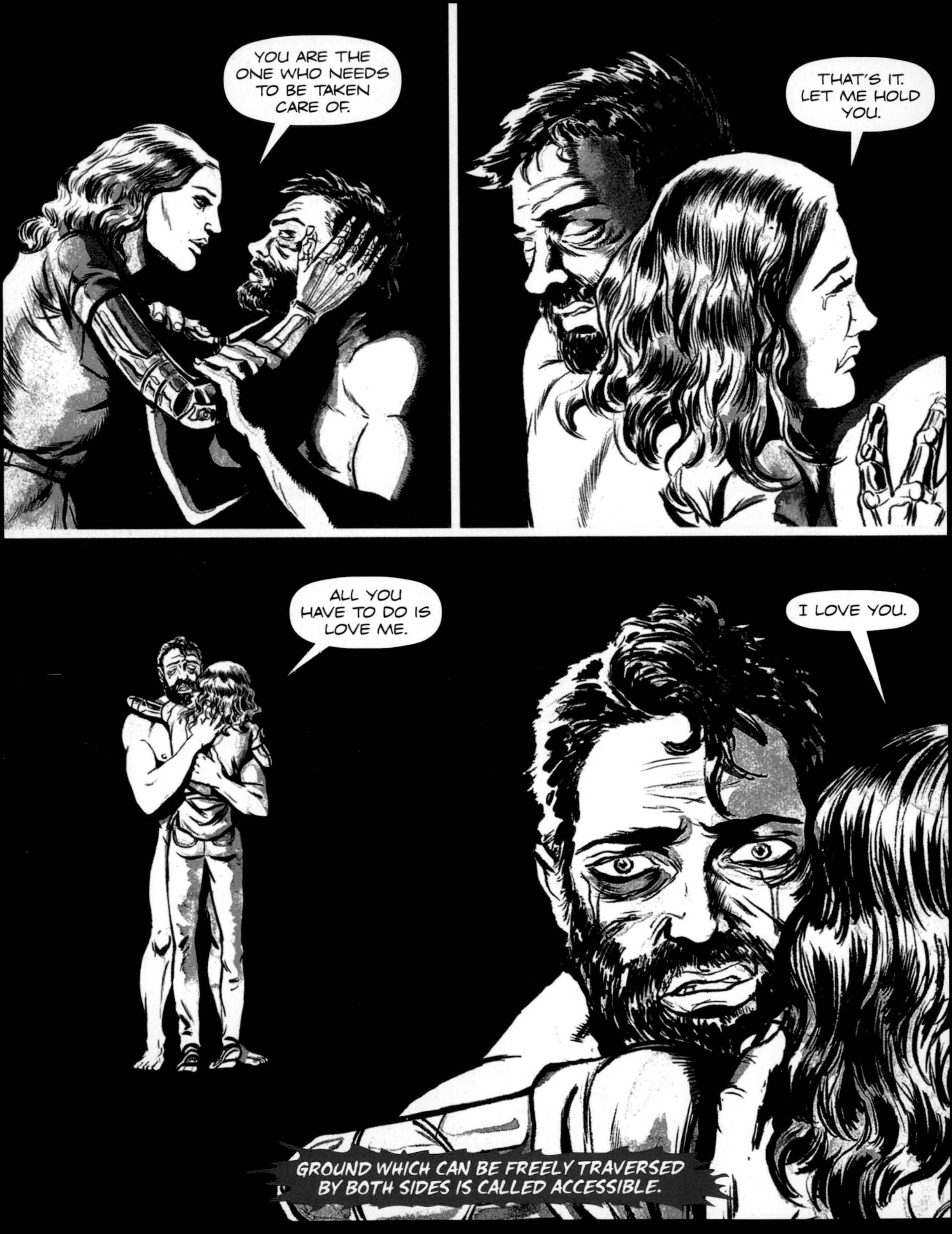
YOU ARE THE ONE WHO NEEDS TO BE TAKEN CARE OF.
THAT'S IT. LET ME HOLD YOU.
ALL YOU HAVE TO DO IS LOVE ME.
I LOVE YOU.
GROUND WHICH CAN BE FREELY TRAVERSED BY BOTH SIDES IS CALLED ACCESSIBLE.

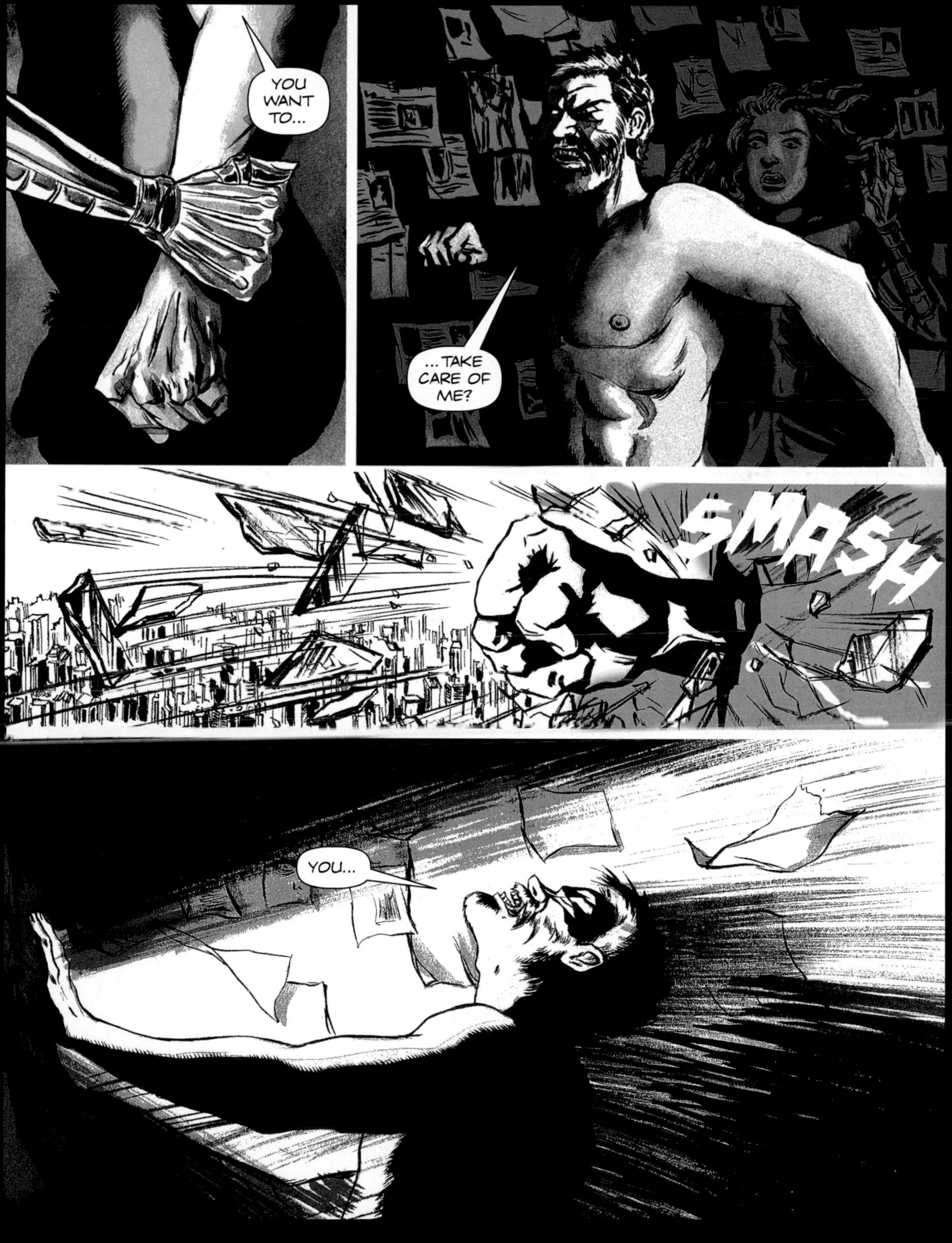
YOU WANT TO...
...TAKE CARE OF ME?
SMASH
YOU...

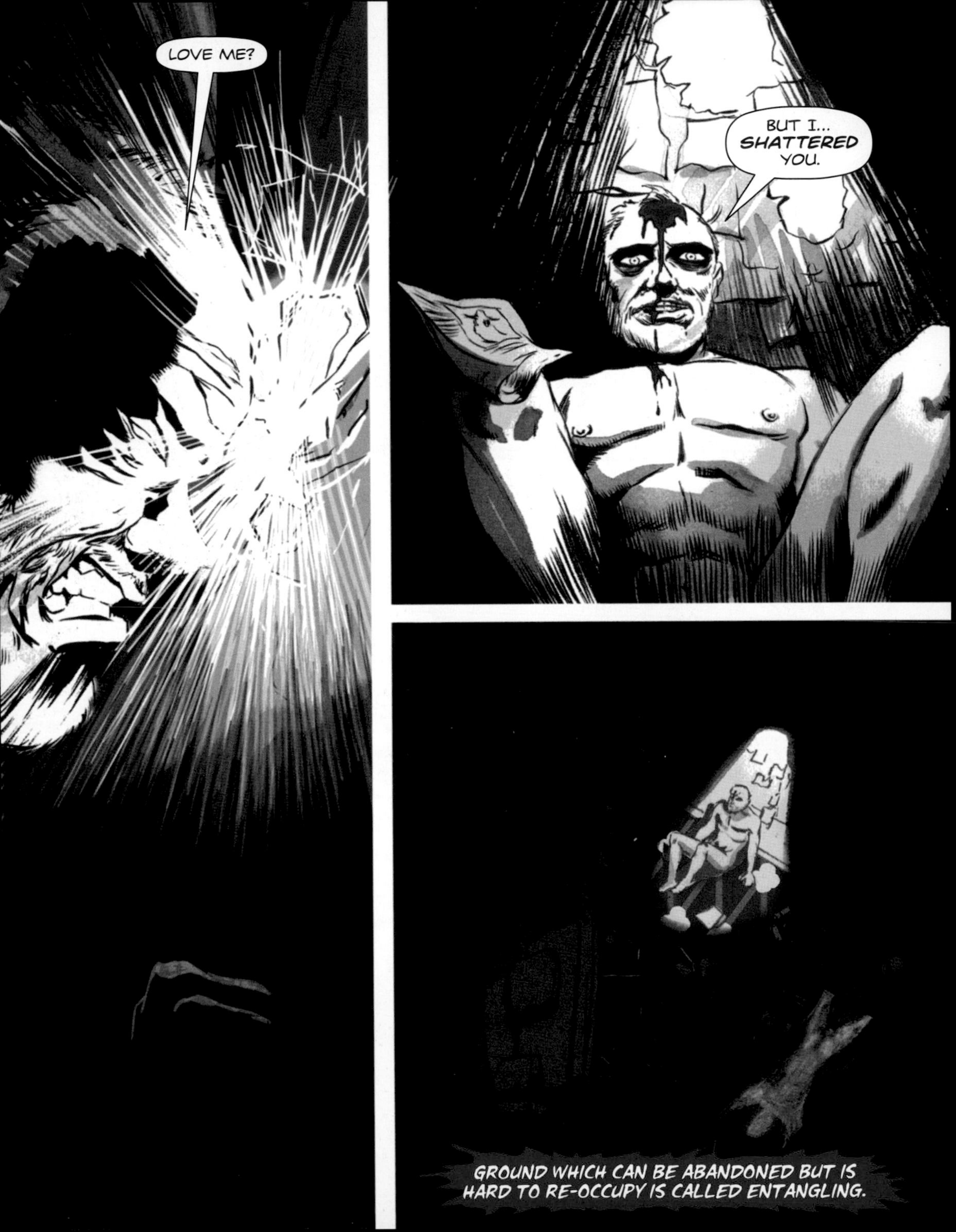
LOVE ME?
BUT I... SHATTERED YOU.
GROUND WHICH CAN BE ABANDONED BUT IS HARD TO RE-OCCUPY IS CALLED ENTANGLING.

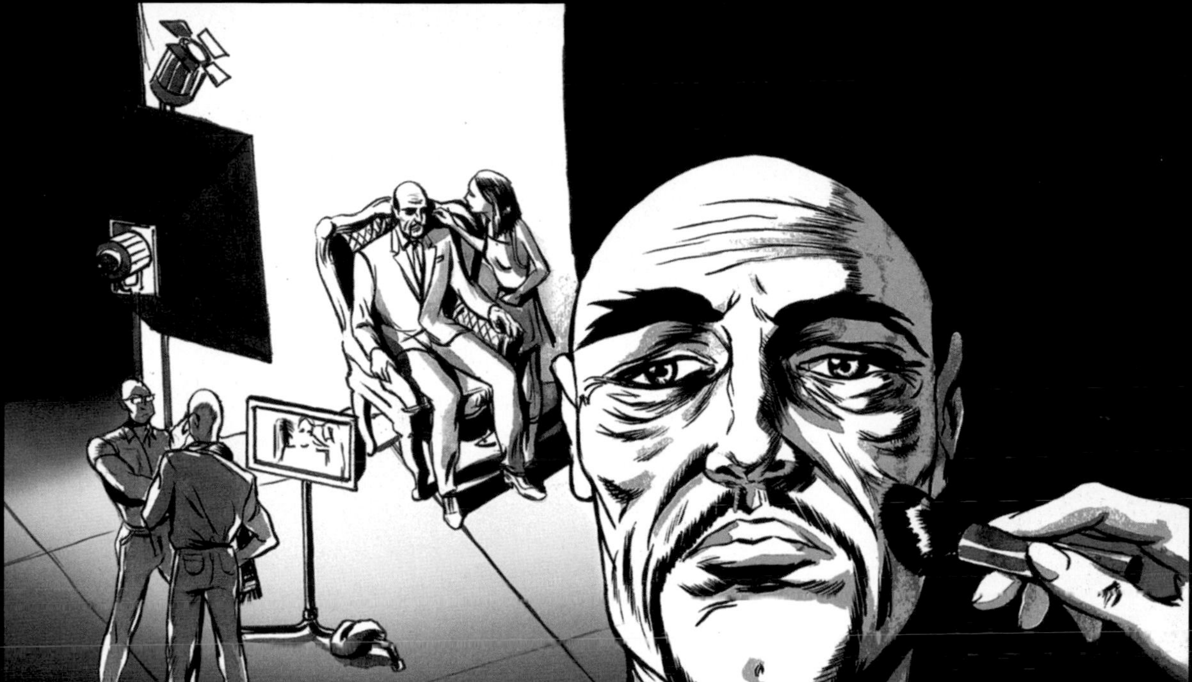
THE GENERAL WHO ADVANCES WITHOUT COVETING FAME AND RETREATS WITHOUT FEARING DISGRACE, WHOSE ONLY THOUGHT IS TO PROTECT HIS COUNTRY, IS THE JEWEL OF THE KINGDOM.

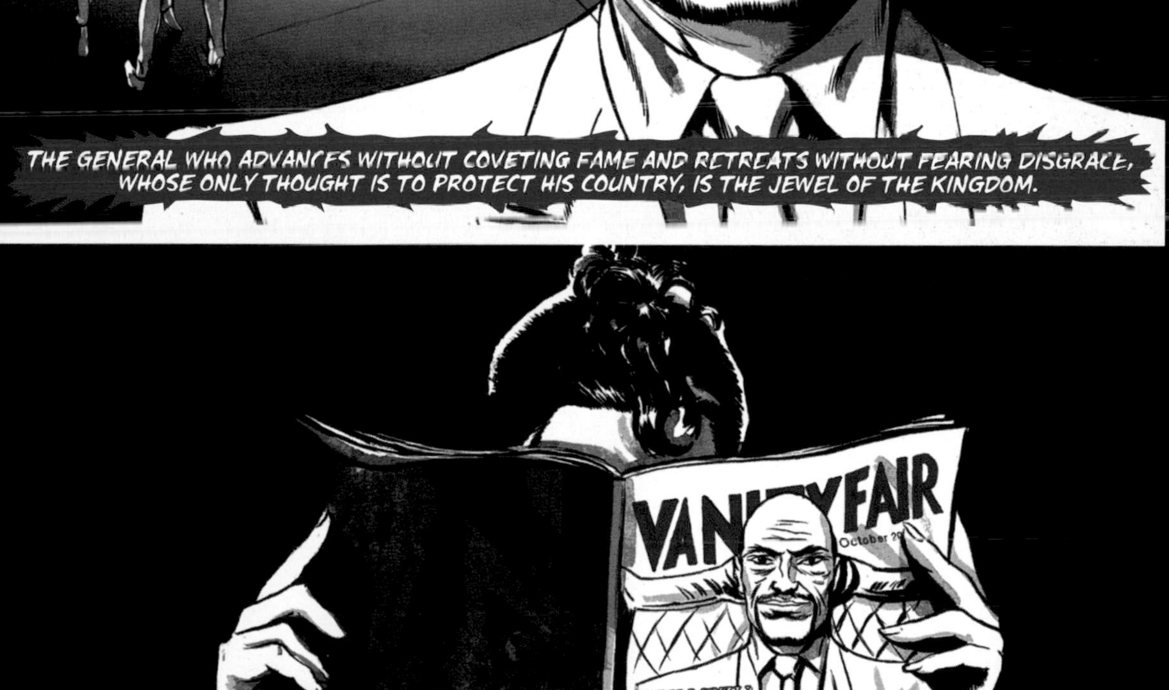
SUN TZU
"AMERICA'S WHITE KNIGHT"
REGARD YOUR SOLDIERS AS YOUR CHILDREN, AND THEY WILL FOLLOW YOU INTO THE DEEPEST VALLEYS; LOOK UPON THEM AS YOUR OWN BELOVED SONS, AND THEY WILL STAND BY YOU EVEN UNTO DEATH.

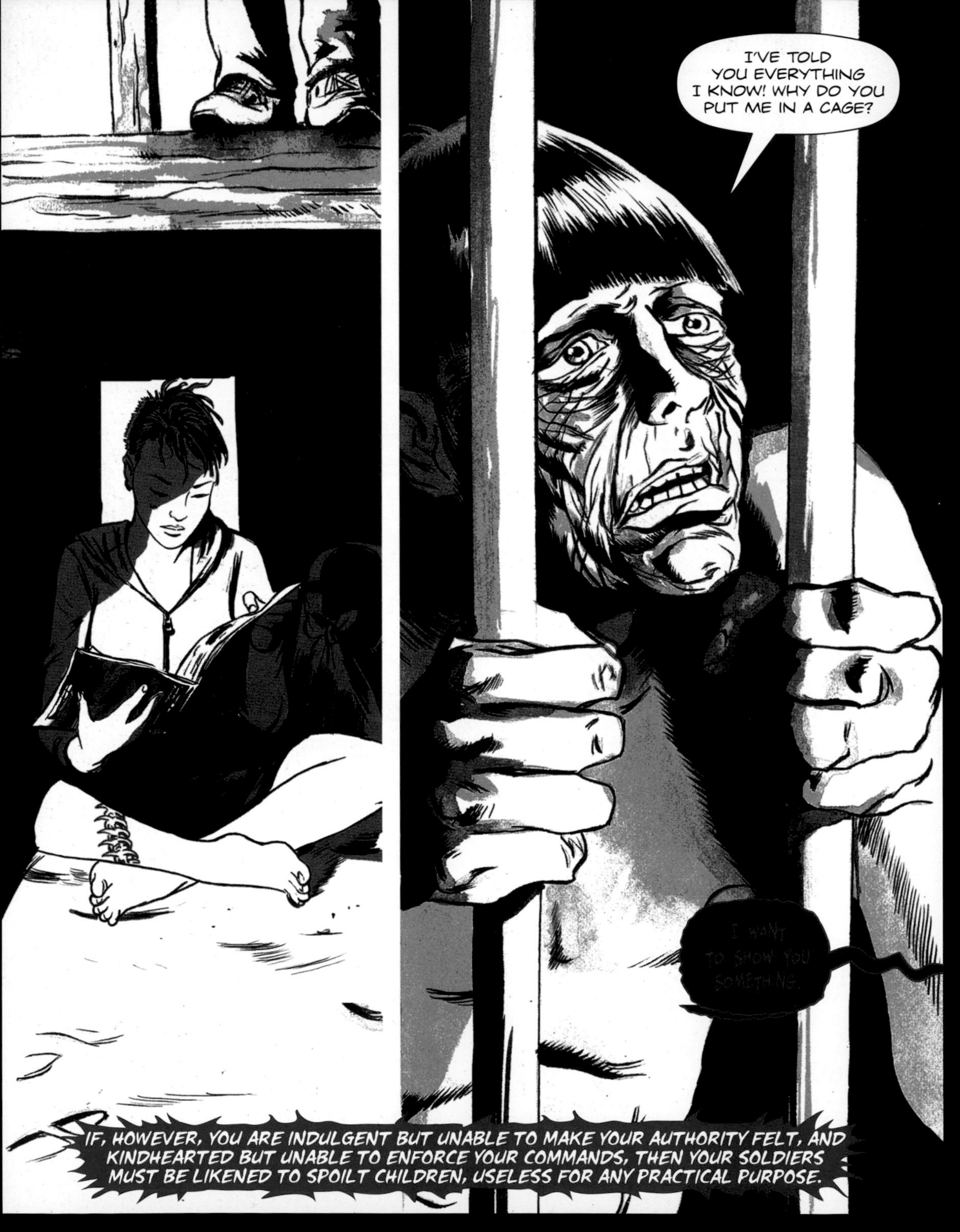
I'VE TOLD YOU EVERYTHING I KNOW! WHY DO YOU PUT ME IN A CAGE?
I WANT TO SHOW YOU SOMETHING.
IF, HOWEVER, YOU ARE INDULGENT BUT UNABLE TO MAKE YOUR AUTHORITY FELT, AND KINDHEARTED BUT UNABLE TO ENFORCE YOUR COMMANDS, THEN YOUR SOLDIERS MUST BE LIKENED TO SPOILT CHILDREN, USELESS FOR ANY PRACTICAL PURPOSE.

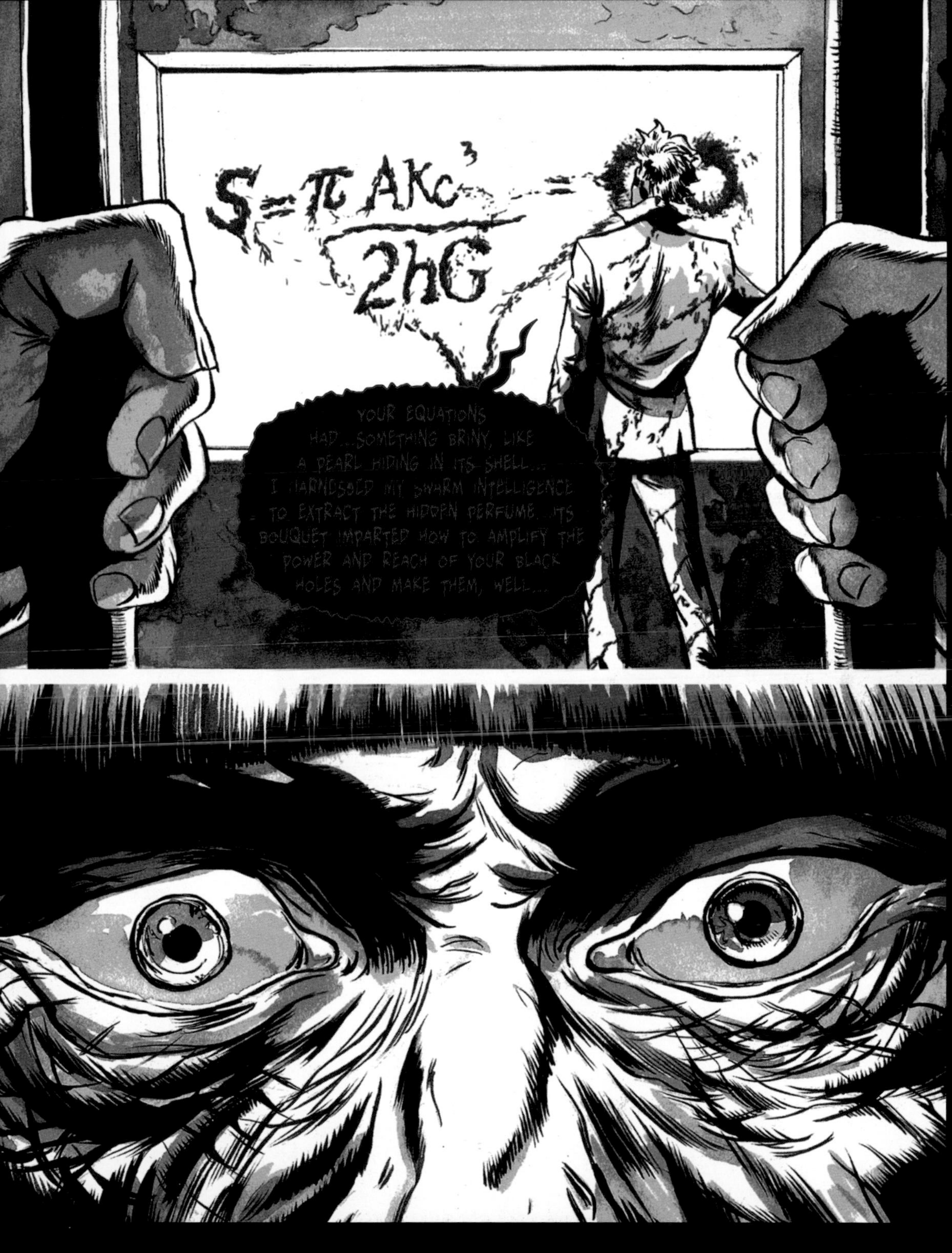

$S = \frac{\pi A K c^3}{2hG}$
YOUR EQUATIONS HAD...SOMETHING BRINY, LIKE A PEARL HIDING IN ITS SHELL... I HARNESSED MY SWARM INTELLIGENCE TO EXTRACT THE HIDDEN PERFUME...ITS BOUQUET IMPARTED HOW TO AMPLIFY THE POWER AND REACH OF YOUR BLACK HOLES AND MAKE THEM, WELL...

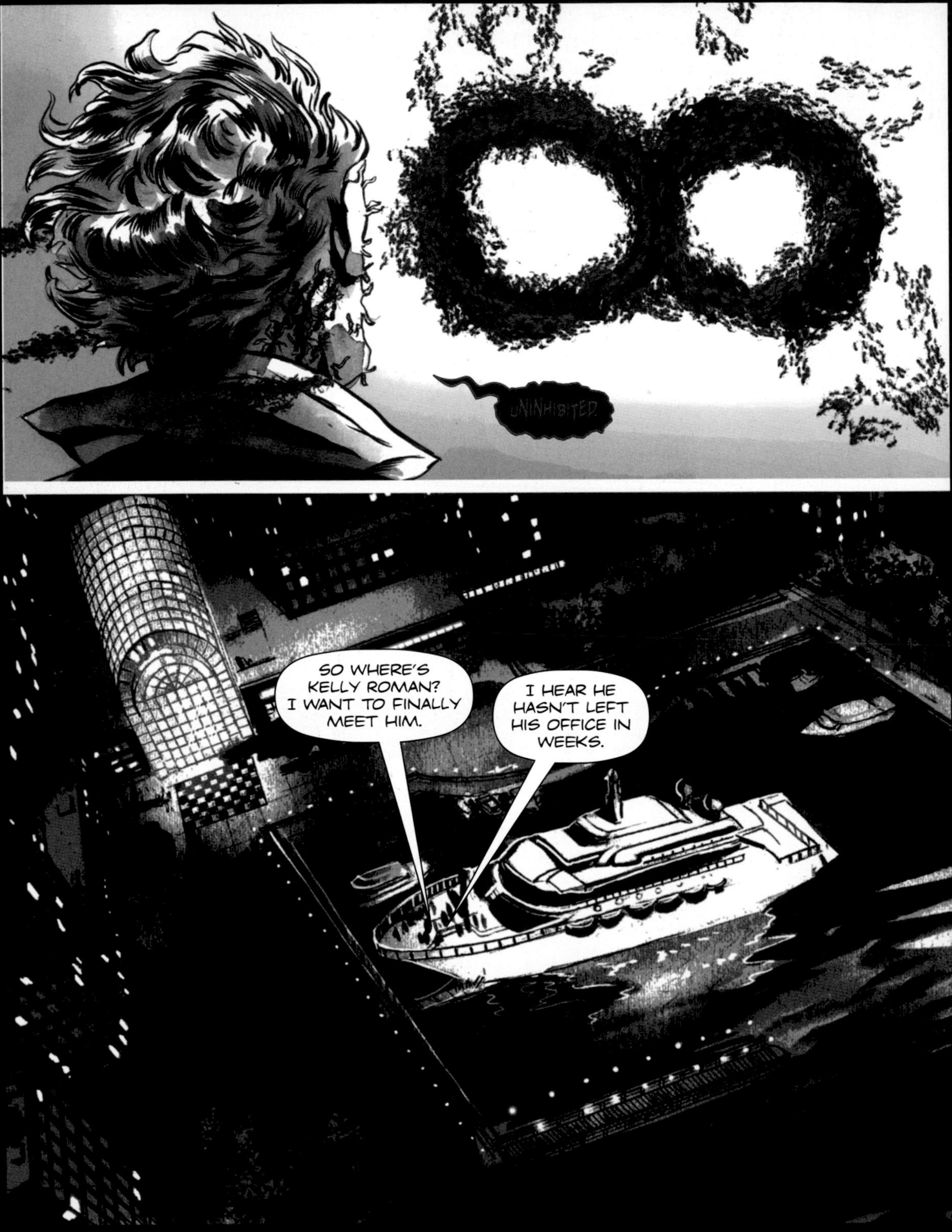
UNINHIBITED.
SO WHERE'S KELLY ROMAN? I WANT TO FINALLY MEET HIM.
I HEAR HE HASN'T LEFT HIS OFFICE IN WEEKS.

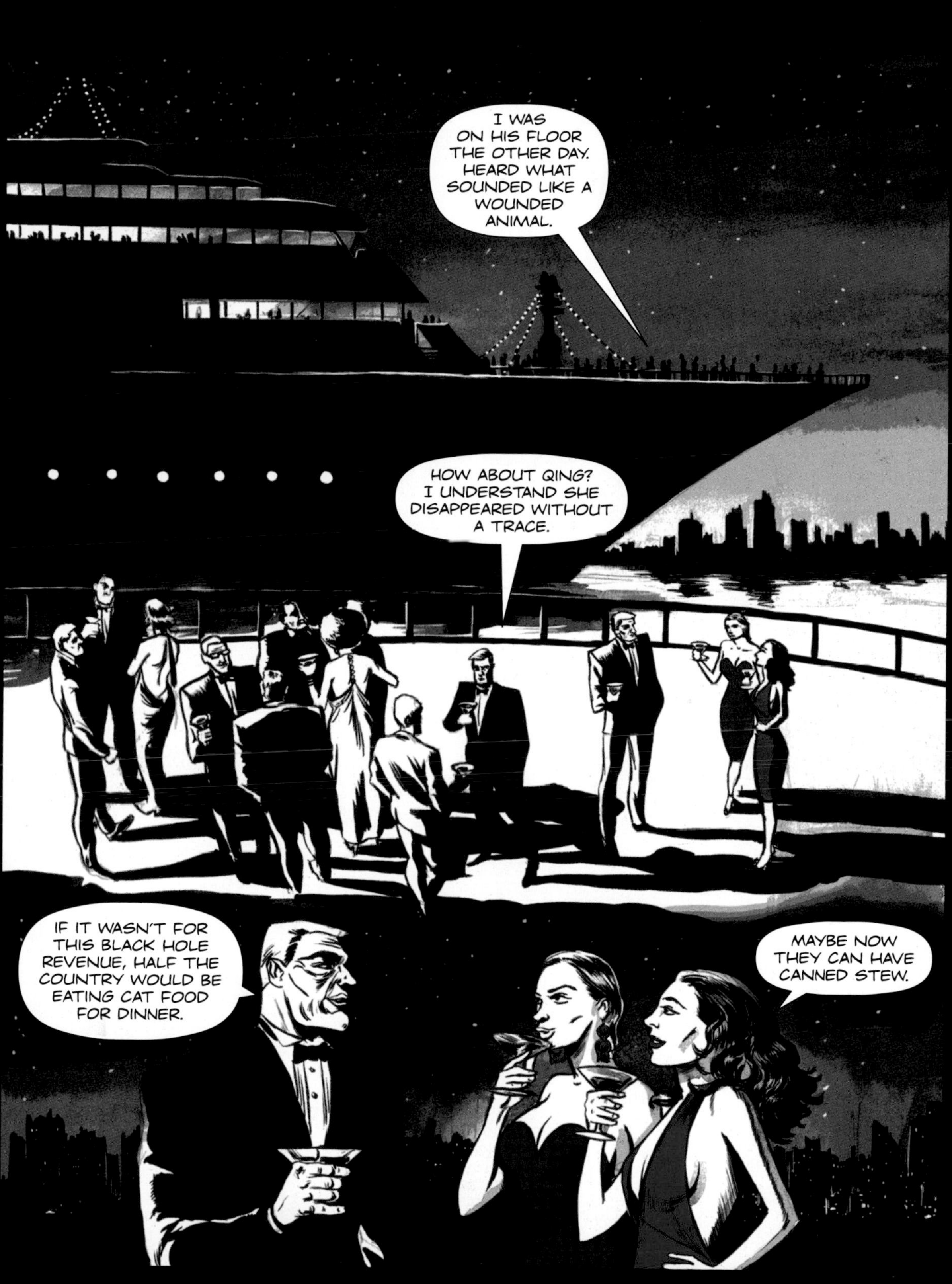
I WAS ON HIS FLOOR THE OTHER DAY. HEARD WHAT SOUNDED LIKE A WOUNDED ANIMAL.
HOW ABOUT QING? I UNDERSTAND SHE DISAPPEARED WITHOUT A TRACE.
IF IT WASN'T FOR THIS BLACK HOLE REVENUE, HALF THE COUNTRY WOULD BE EATING CAT FOOD FOR DINNER.
MAYBE NOW THEY CAN HAVE CANNED STEW.

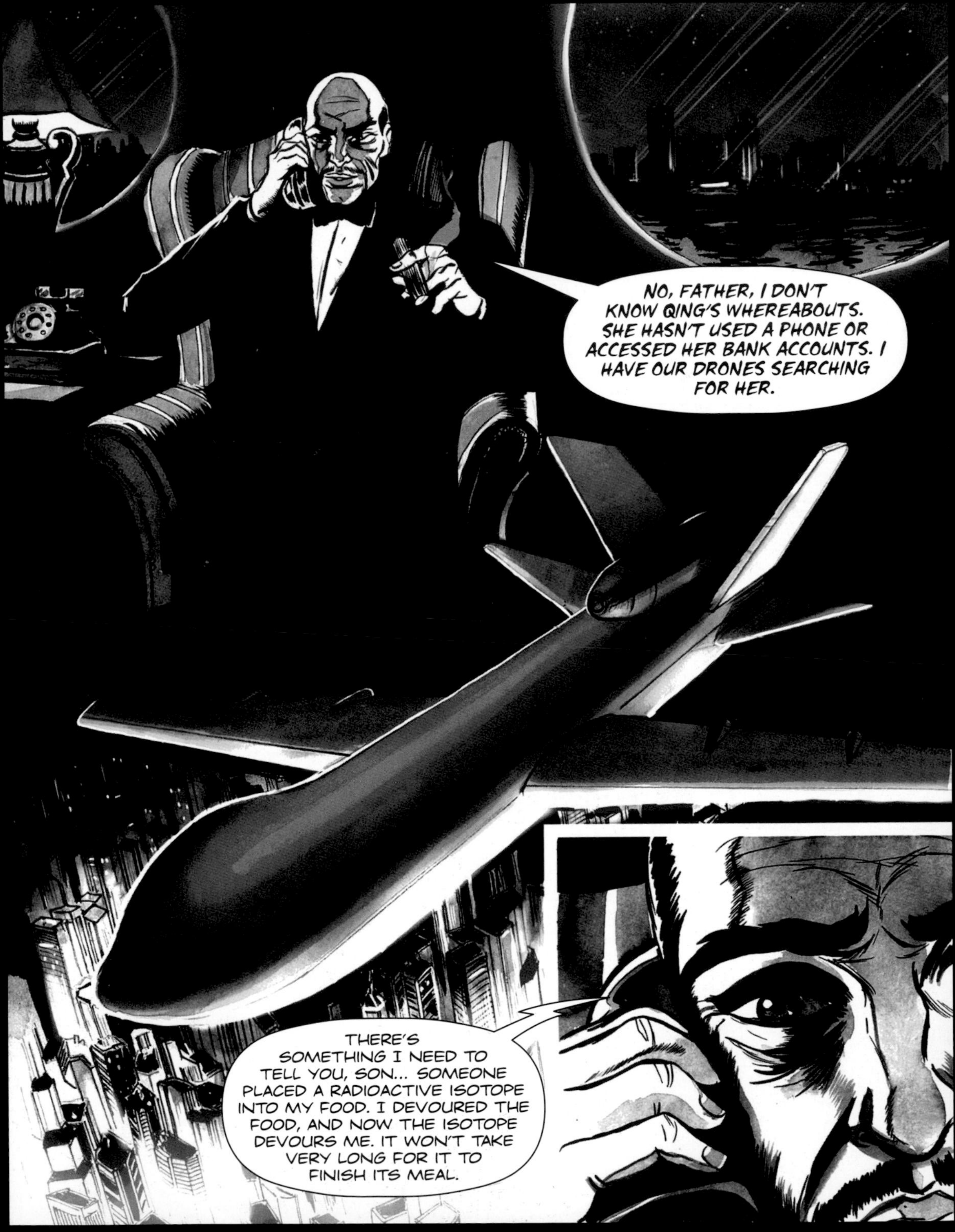
NO, FATHER, I DON'T KNOW QING'S WHEREABOUTS. SHE HASN'T USED A PHONE OR ACCESSED HER BANK ACCOUNTS. I HAVE OUR DRONES SEARCHING FOR HER.
THERE'S SOMETHING I NEED TO TELL YOU, SON... SOMEONE PLACED A RADIOACTIVE ISOTOPE INTO MY FOOD. I DEVOURED THE FOOD, AND NOW THE ISOTOPE DEVOURS ME. IT WON'T TAKE VERY LONG FOR IT TO FINISH ITS MEAL.

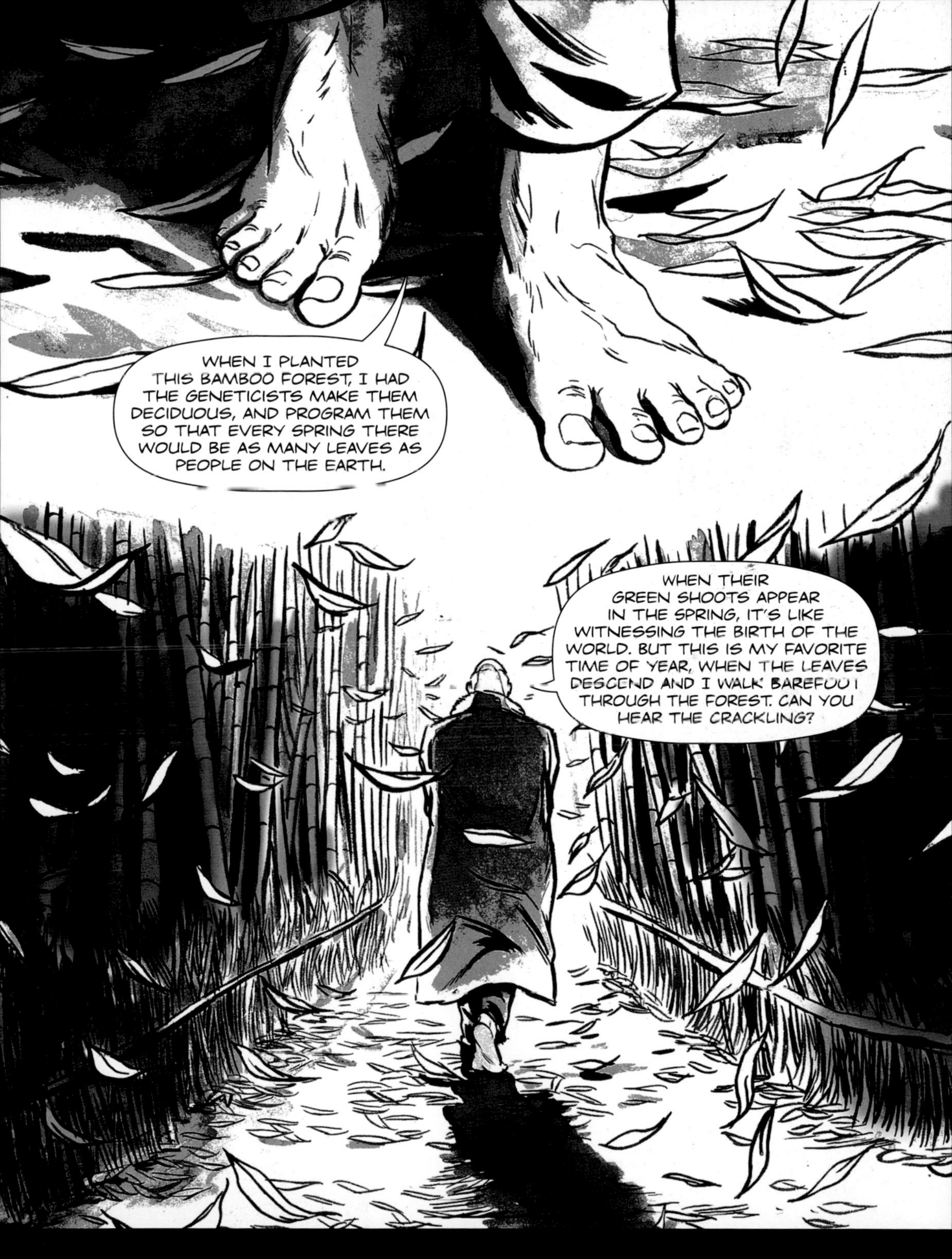
WHEN I PLANTED THIS BAMBOO FOREST, I HAD THE GENETICISTS MAKE THEM DECIDUOUS, AND PROGRAM THEM SO THAT EVERY SPRING THERE WOULD BE AS MANY LEAVES AS PEOPLE ON THE EARTH.
WHEN THEIR GREEN SHOOTS APPEAR IN THE SPRING, IT'S LIKE WITNESSING THE BIRTH OF THE WORLD. BUT THIS IS MY FAVORITE TIME OF YEAR, WHEN THE LEAVES DESCEND AND I WALK BAREFOOT THROUGH THE FOREST. CAN YOU HEAR THE CRACKLING?

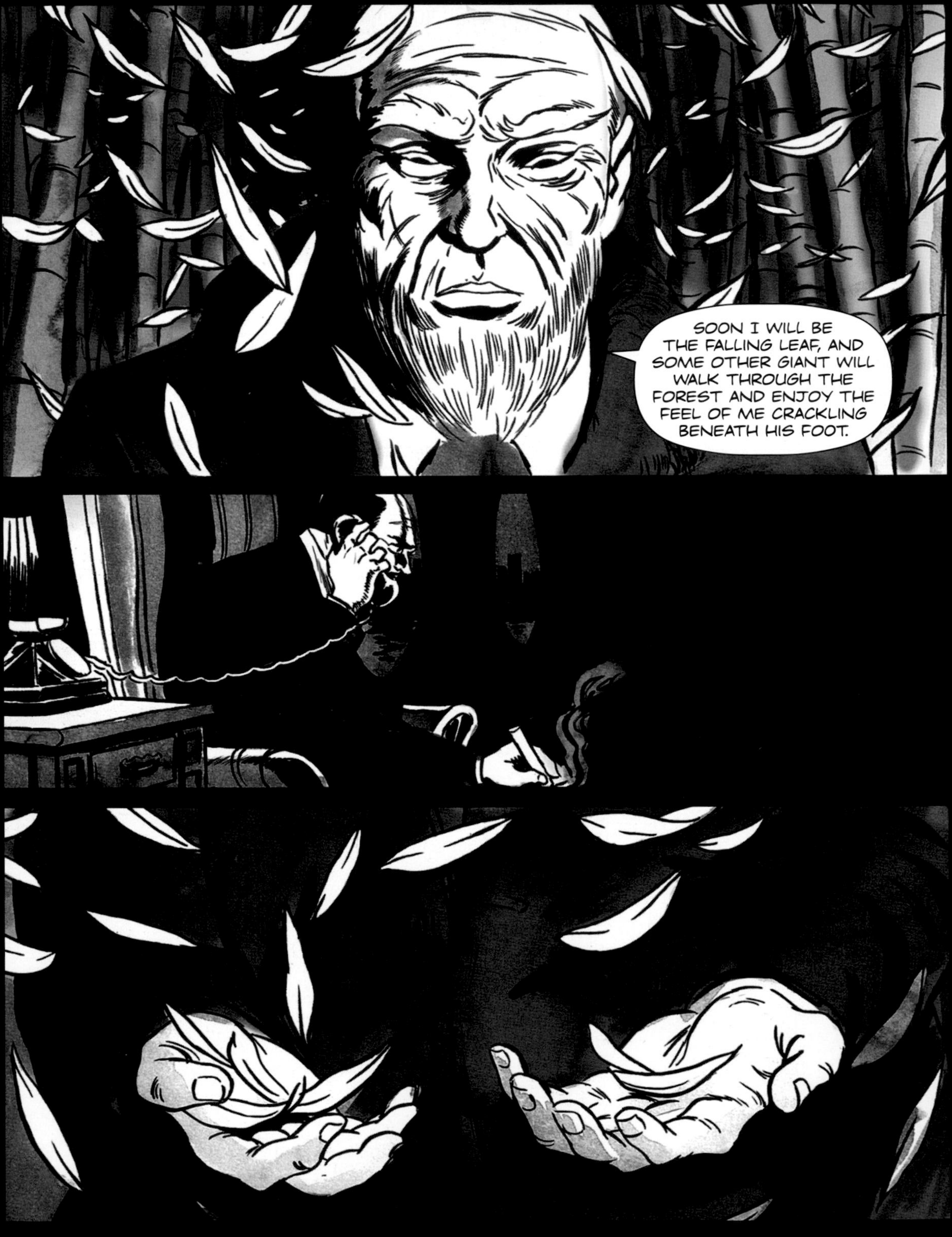
SOON I WILL BE THE FALLING LEAF, AND SOME OTHER GIANT WILL WALK THROUGH THE FOREST AND ENJOY THE FEEL OF ME CRACKLING BENEATH HIS FOOT.

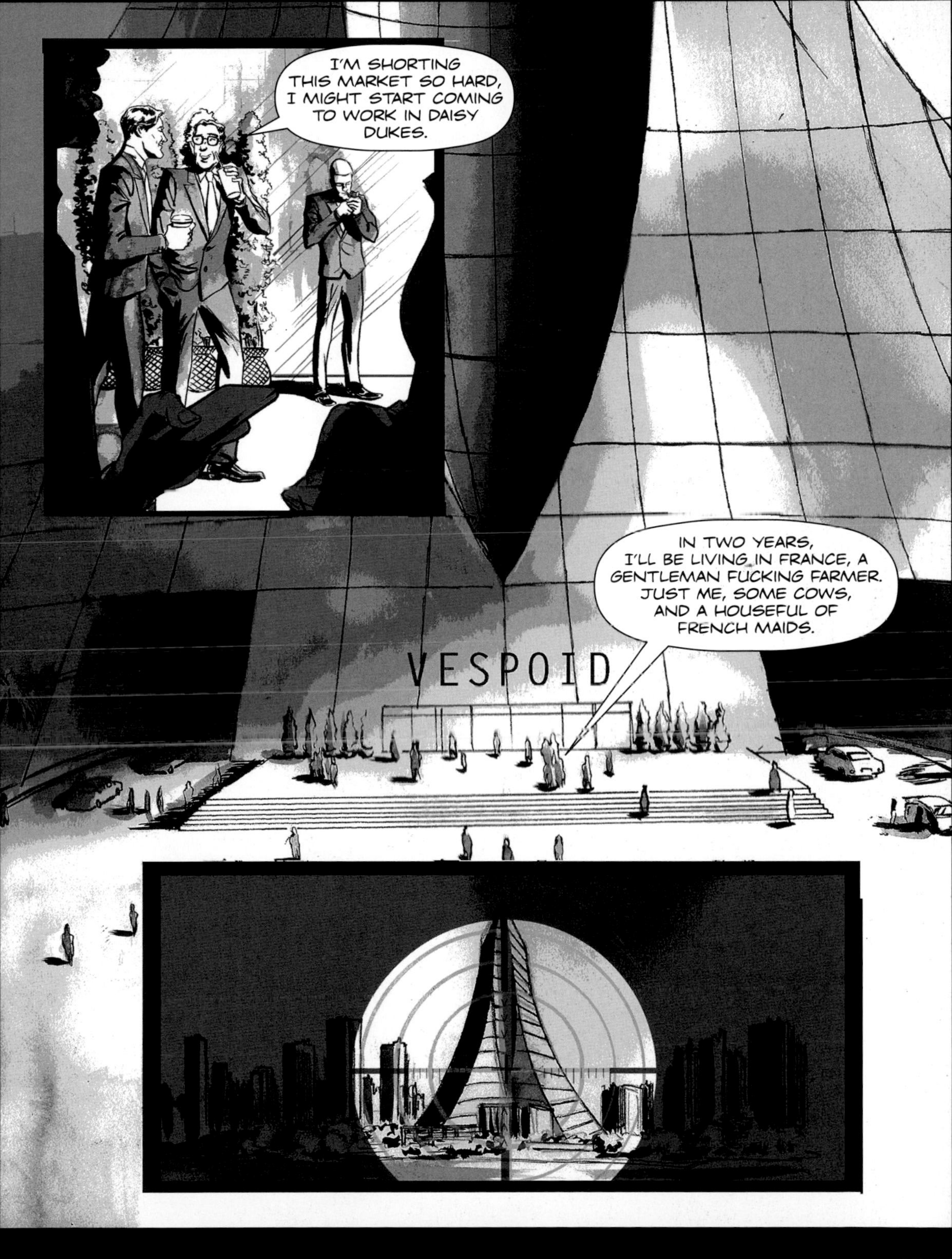
I'M SHORTING THIS MARKET SO HARD, I MIGHT START COMING TO WORK IN DAISY DUKES.
IN TWO YEARS, I'LL BE LIVING IN FRANCE, A GENTLEMAN FUCKING FARMER. JUST ME, SOME COWS, AND A HOUSEFUL OF FRENCH MAIDS.
VESPOID

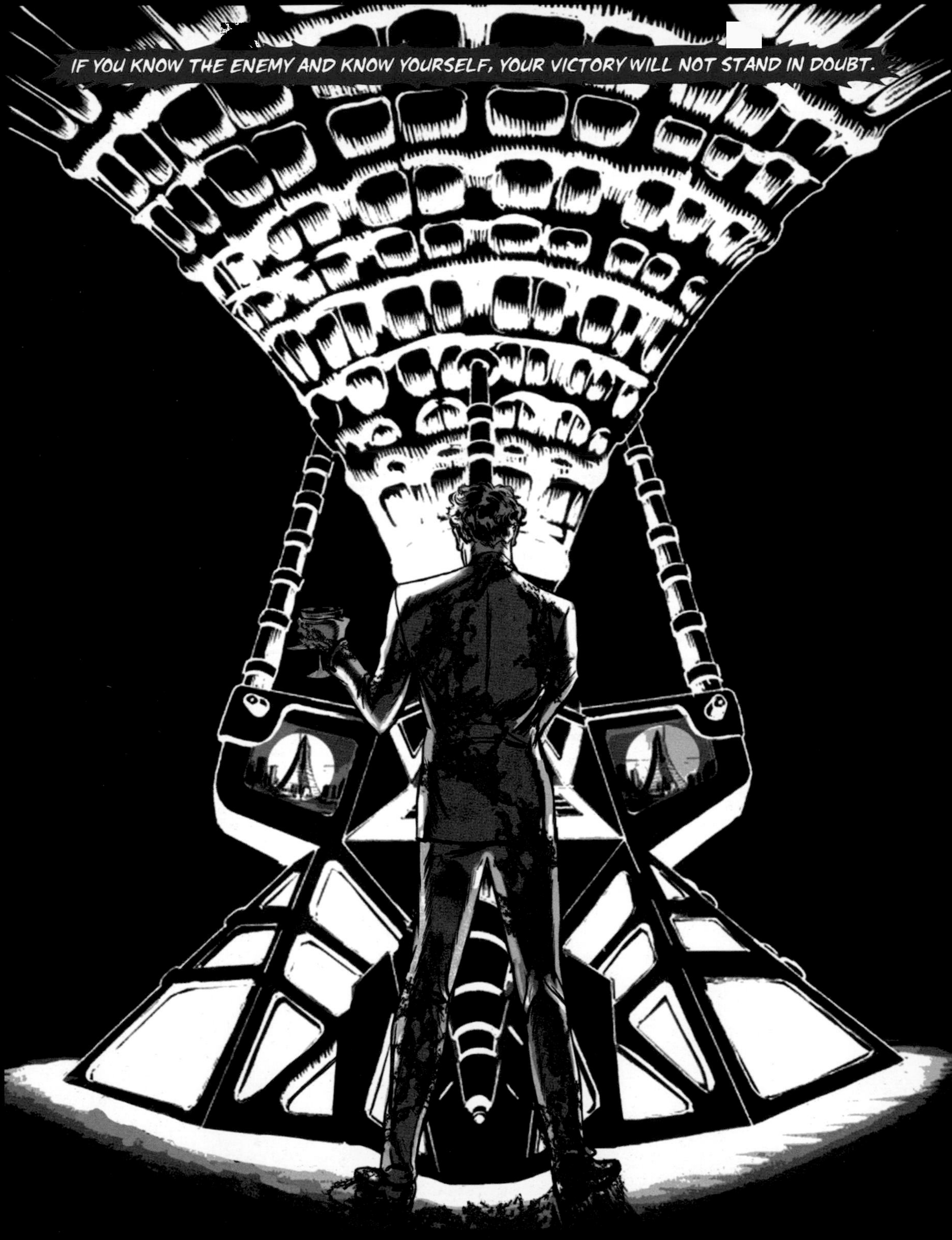
IF YOU KNOW THE ENEMY AND KNOW YOURSELF, YOUR VICTORY WILL NOT STAND IN DOUBT.

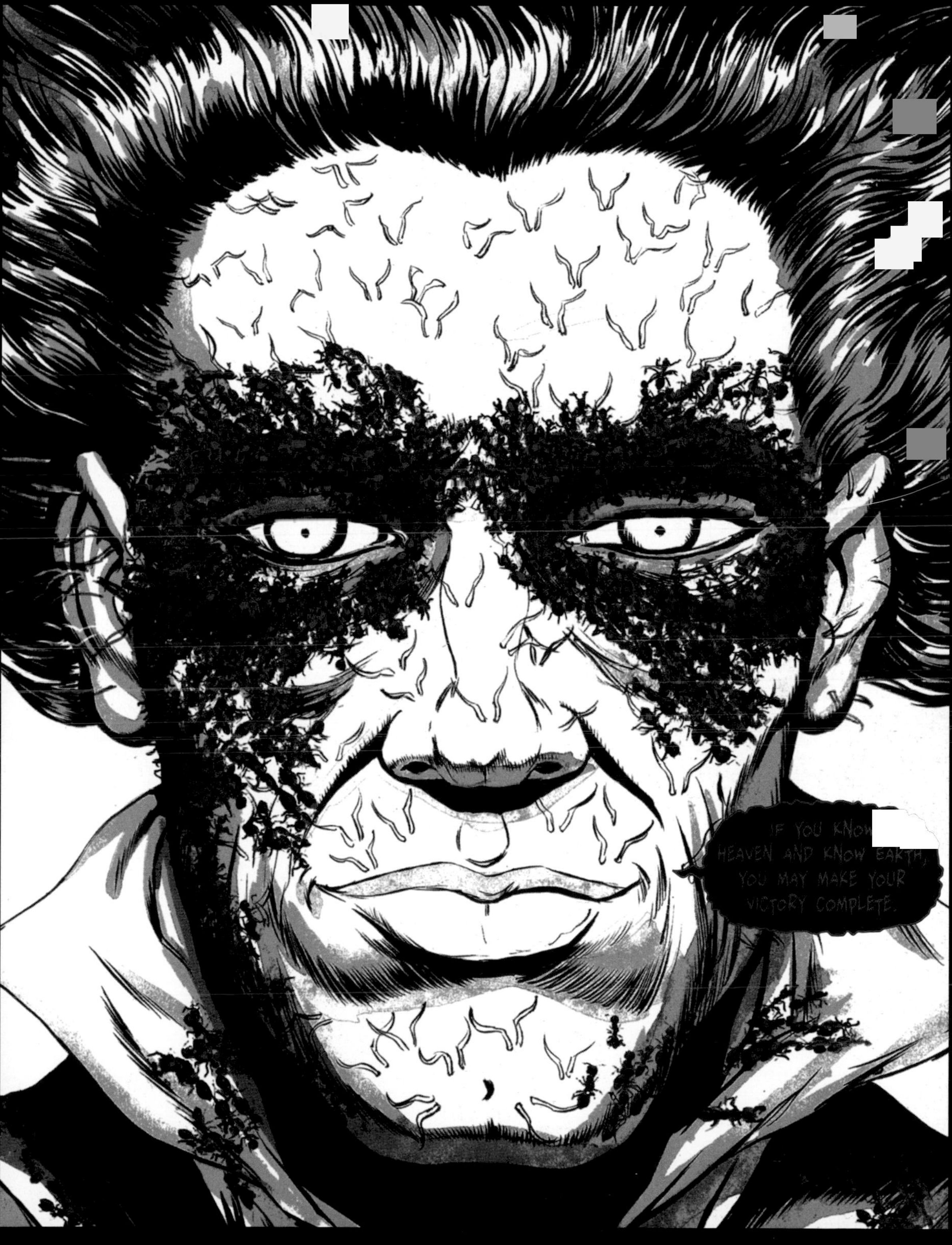
IF YOU KNOW HEAVEN AND KNOW EARTH, YOU MAY MAKE YOUR VICTORY COMPLETE.

九地篇

XI. THE NINE SITUATIONS

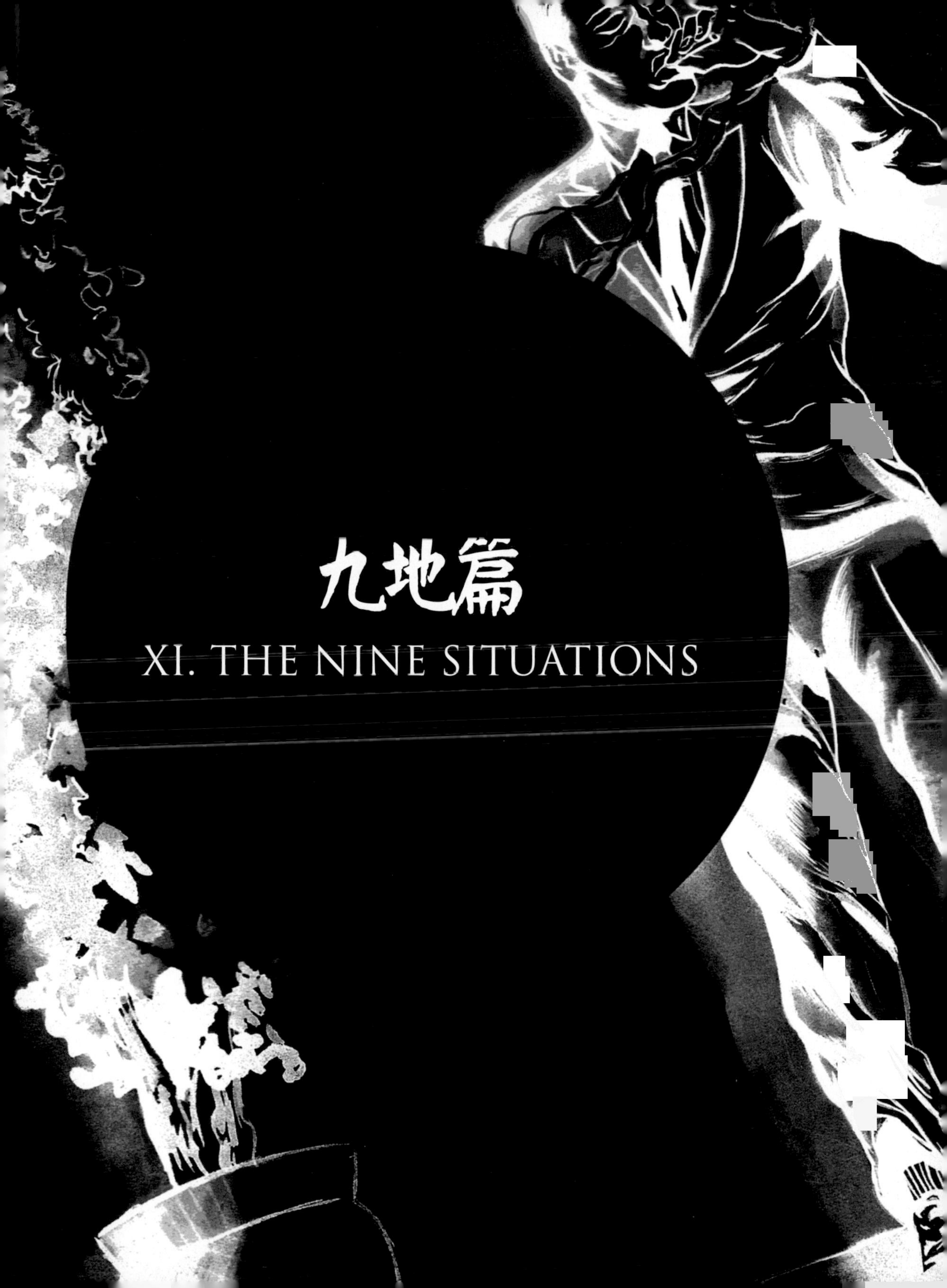

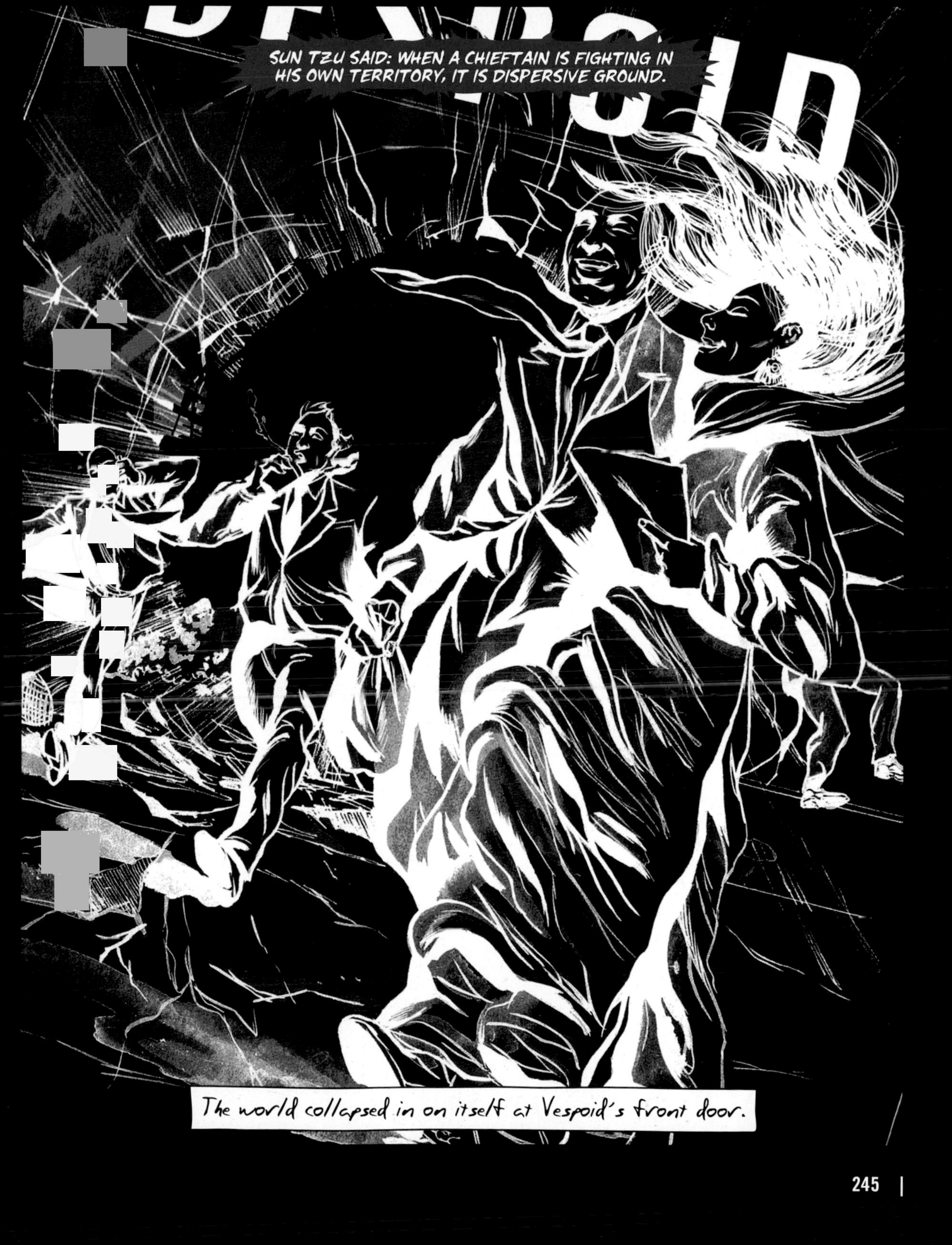
SUN TZU SAID: WHEN A CHIEFTAIN IS FIGHTING IN HIS OWN TERRITORY, IT IS DISPERSIVE GROUND.
The world collapsed in on itself at Vespoid's front door.

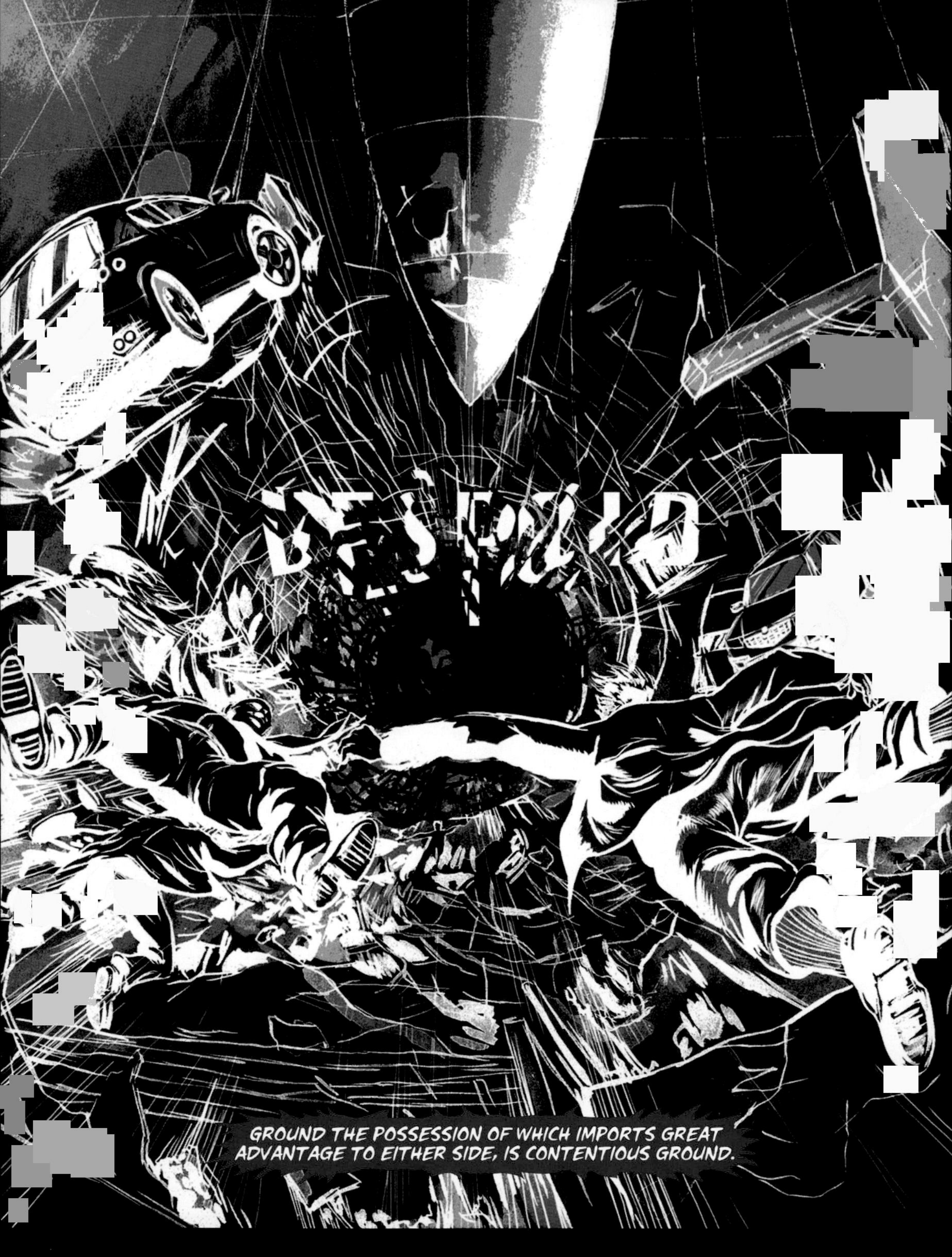
GROUND THE POSSESSION OF WHICH IMPORTS GREAT ADVANTAGE TO EITHER SIDE, IS CONTENTIOUS GROUND.

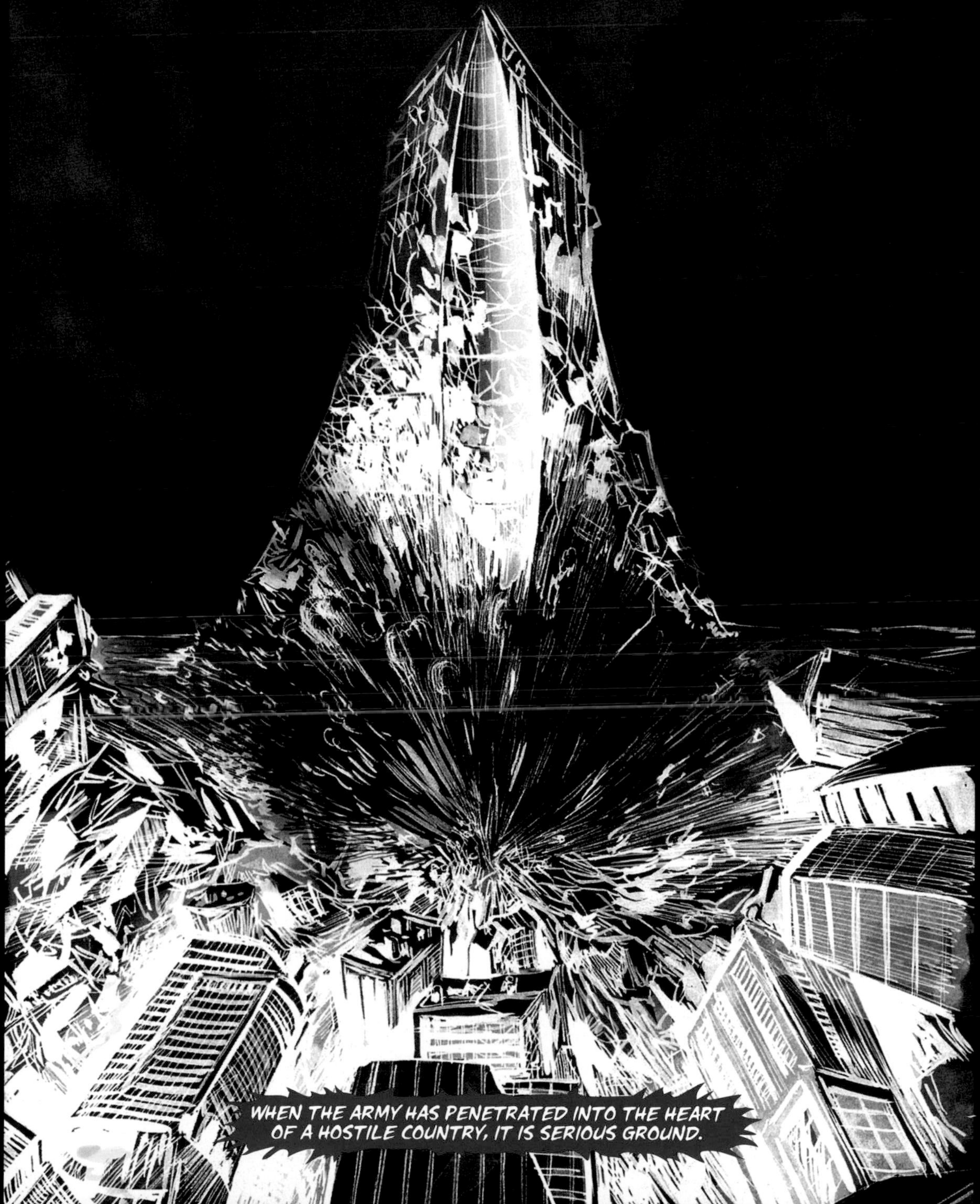
WHEN THE ARMY HAS PENETRATED INTO THE HEART OF A HOSTILE COUNTRY, IT IS SERIOUS GROUND.

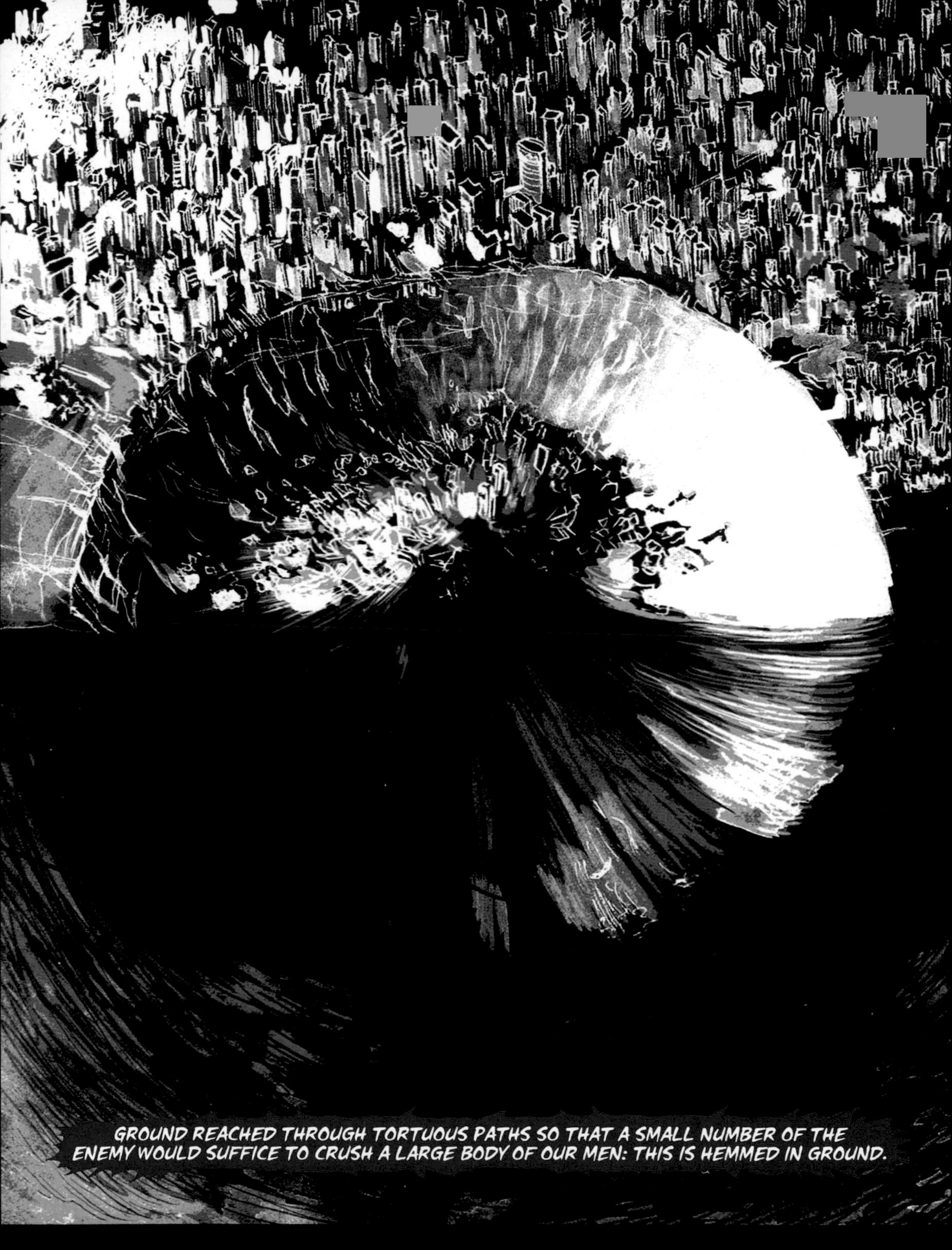
GROUND REACHED THROUGH TORTUOUS PATHS SO THAT A SMALL NUMBER OF THE ENEMY WOULD SUFFICE TO CRUSH A LARGE BODY OF OUR MEN: THIS IS HEMMED IN GROUND.

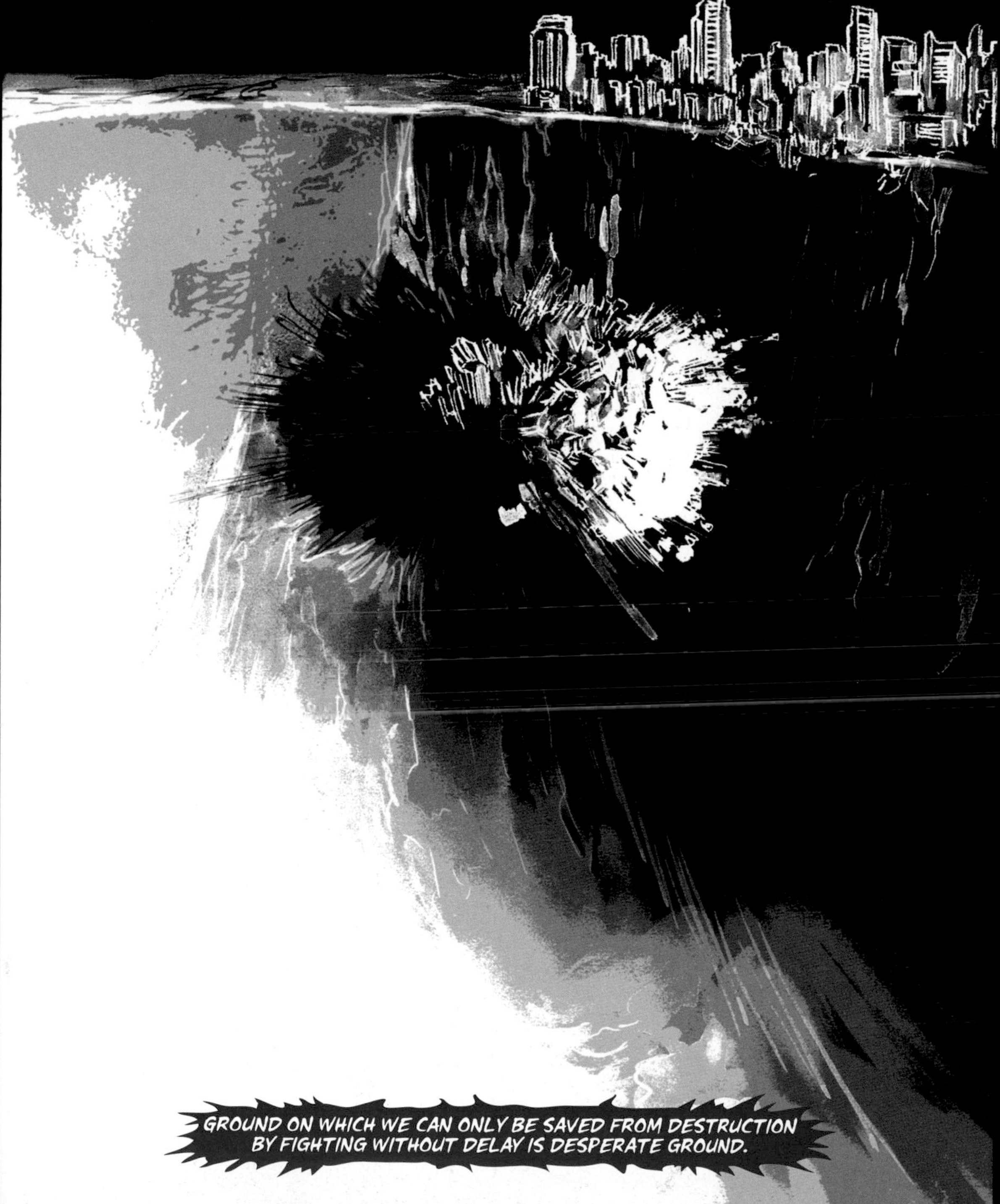
GROUND ON WHICH WE CAN ONLY BE SAVED FROM DESTRUCTION BY FIGHTING WITHOUT DELAY IS DESPERATE GROUND.

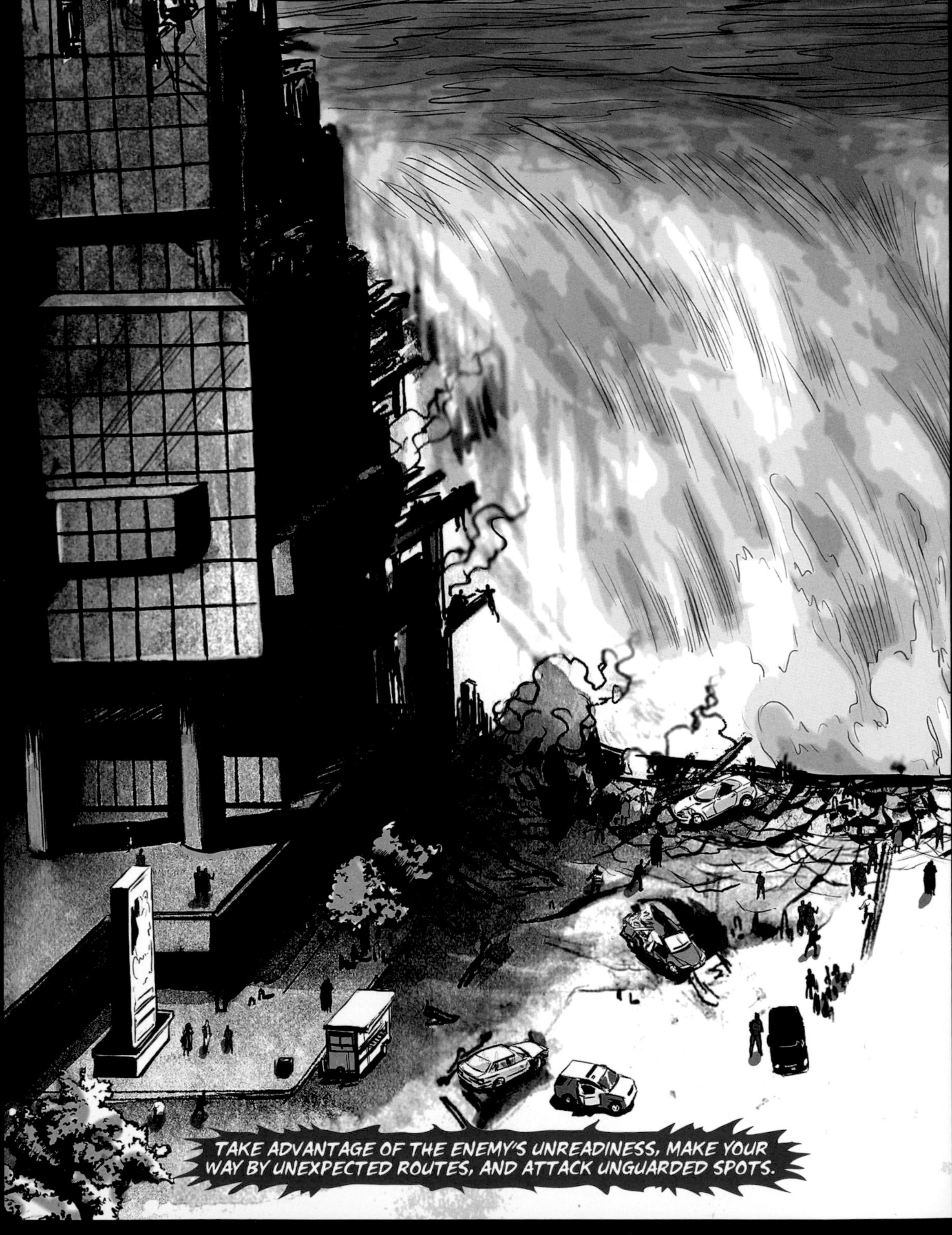
TAKE ADVANTAGE OF THE ENEMY'S UNREADINESS, MAKE YOUR WAY BY UNEXPECTED ROUTES, AND ATTACK UNGUARDED SPOTS.

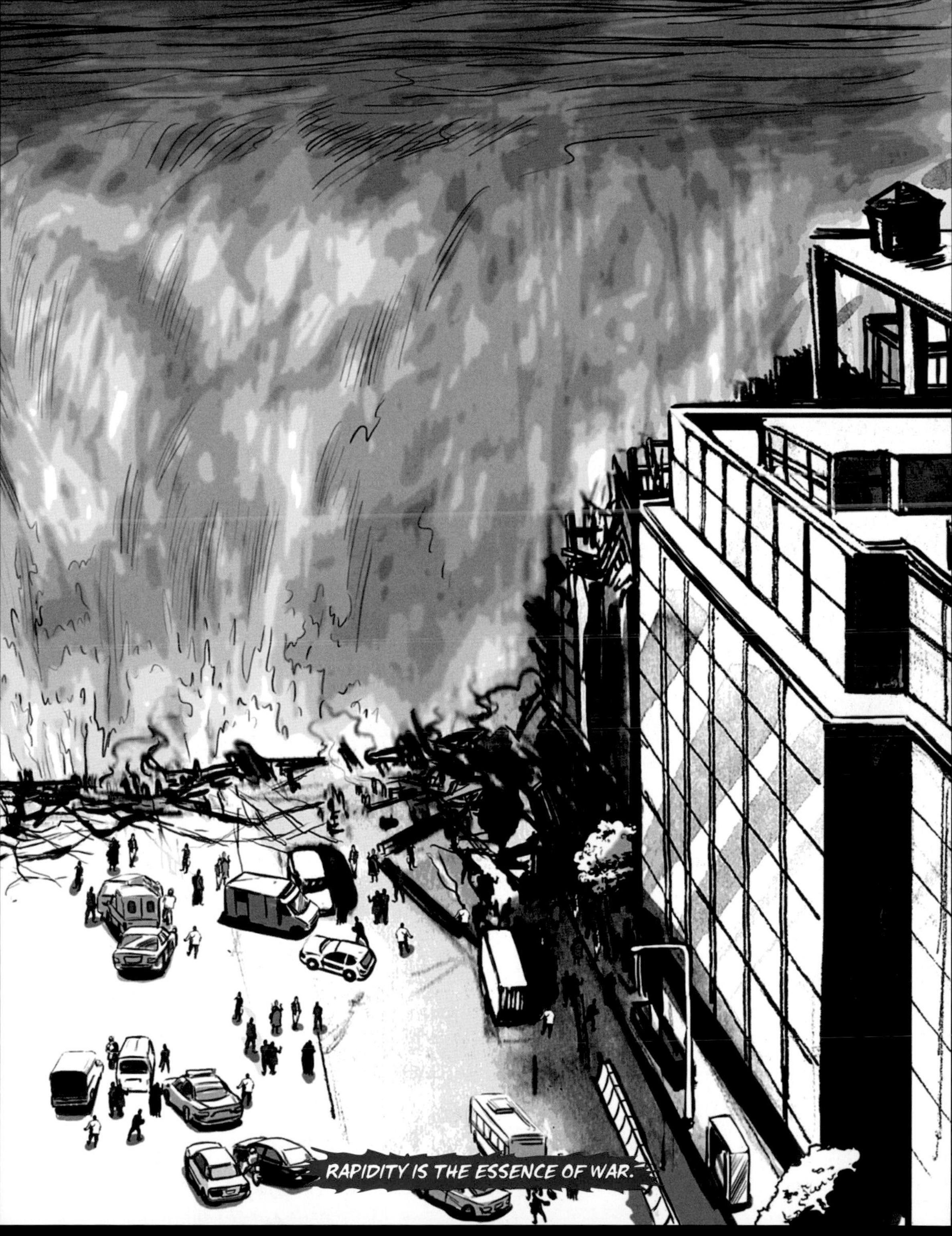
RAPIDITY IS THE ESSENCE OF WAR.

Ministry of Finance, Beijing
A BLACK HOLE JUST IMPLODED MUMBAI'S FINANCIAL DISTRICT. VESPOID'S OFFICES WERE AT THE EPICENTER. THE INDIAN GOVERNMENT HAS BEGUN EVACUATING BANGALORE, THE OTHER CITY HOME TO VESPOID.
TRENCH IS THE ONLY FUND KNOWN TO POSSESS BLACK HOLE TECHNOLOGY. THE INDIANS ARE INTERPRETING THIS AS AN ATTACK BY CHINA AND THE UNITED STATES. THEY HAVE ARMED THEIR NUCLEAR WEAPONS.
EVEN IF MY SON IS INNOCENT, HIS DENIAL WILL NOT MEAN MUCH. NOT WITH VESPOID'S DEVASTATION.
LEAVE ME FOR A MOMENT.

THE EARTH HAS BECOME TOO SMALL A BATTLEFIELD FOR YOU, MY SON.
ON THE GROUND OF INTERSECTING HIGHWAYS, JOIN HANDS WITH YOUR ALLIES.

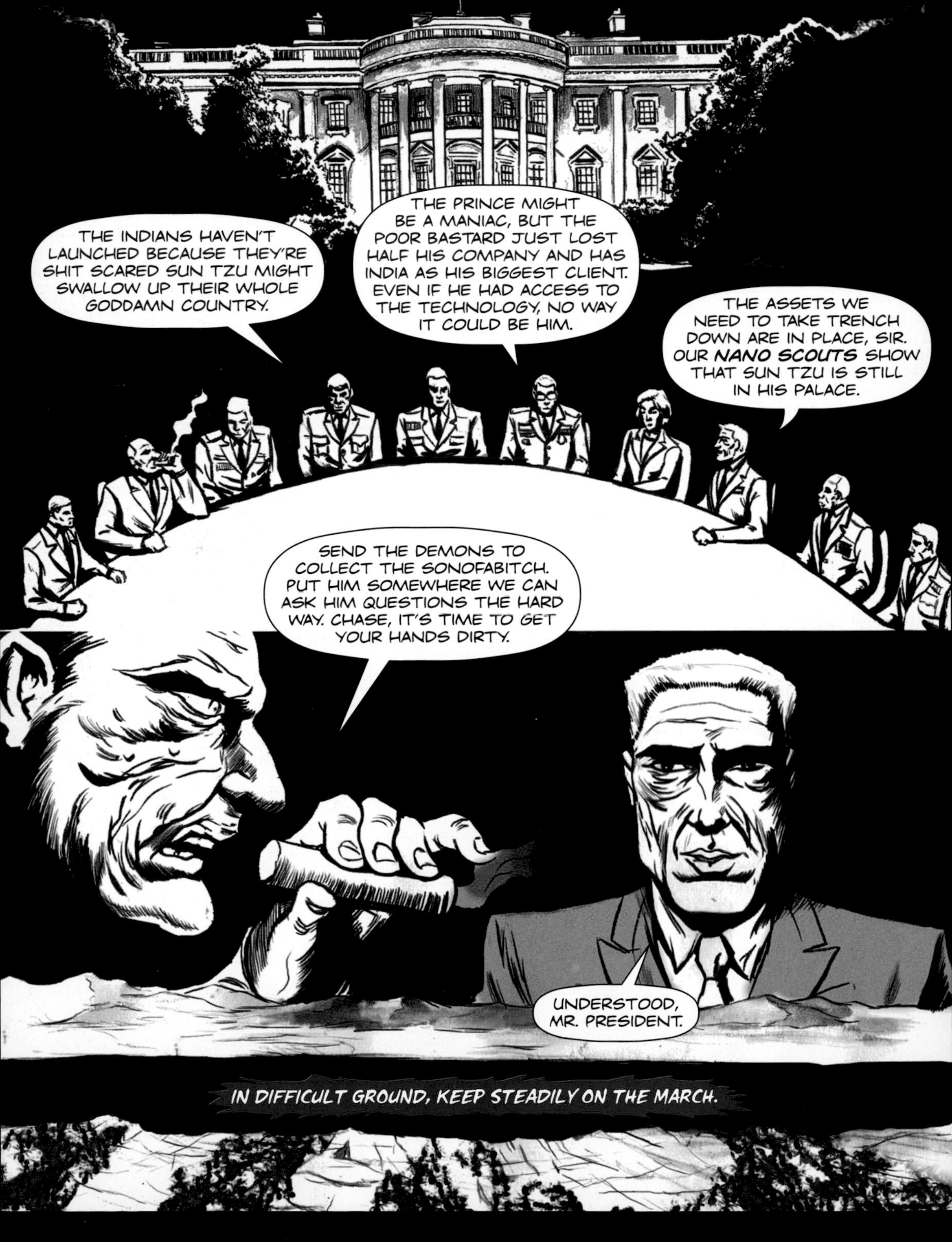
THE INDIANS HAVEN'T LAUNCHED BECAUSE THEY'RE SHIT SCARED SUN TZU MIGHT SWALLOW UP THEIR WHOLE GODDAMN COUNTRY.
THE PRINCE MIGHT BE A MANIAC, BUT THE POOR BASTARD JUST LOST HALF HIS COMPANY AND HAS INDIA AS HIS BIGGEST CLIENT. EVEN IF HE HAD ACCESS TO THE TECHNOLOGY, NO WAY IT COULD BE HIM.
THE ASSETS WE NEED TO TAKE TRENCH DOWN ARE IN PLACE, SIR. OUR **NANO SCOUTS** SHOW THAT SUN TZU IS STILL IN HIS PALACE.
SEND THE DEMONS TO COLLECT THE SONOFABITCH. PUT HIM SOMEWHERE WE CAN ASK HIM QUESTIONS THE HARD WAY. CHASE, IT'S TIME TO GET YOUR HANDS DIRTY.
UNDERSTOOD, MR. PRESIDENT.
IN DIFFICULT GROUND, KEEP STEADILY ON THE MARCH.

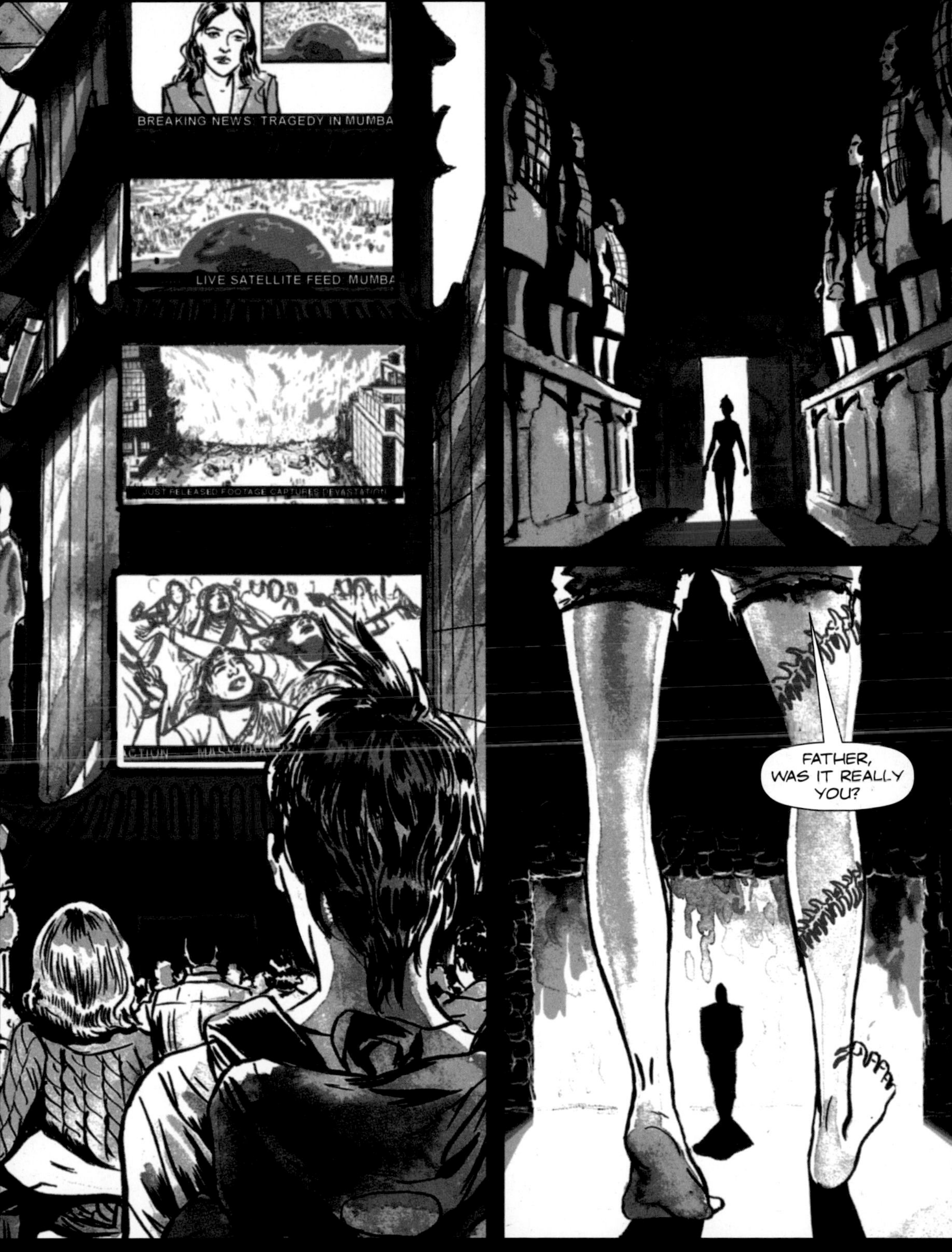
BREAKING NEWS: TRAGEDY IN MUMBA
LIVE SATELLITE FEED: MUMBA
JUST RELEASED FOOTAGE CAPTURES DEVASTATION
FATHER, WAS IT REALLY YOU?

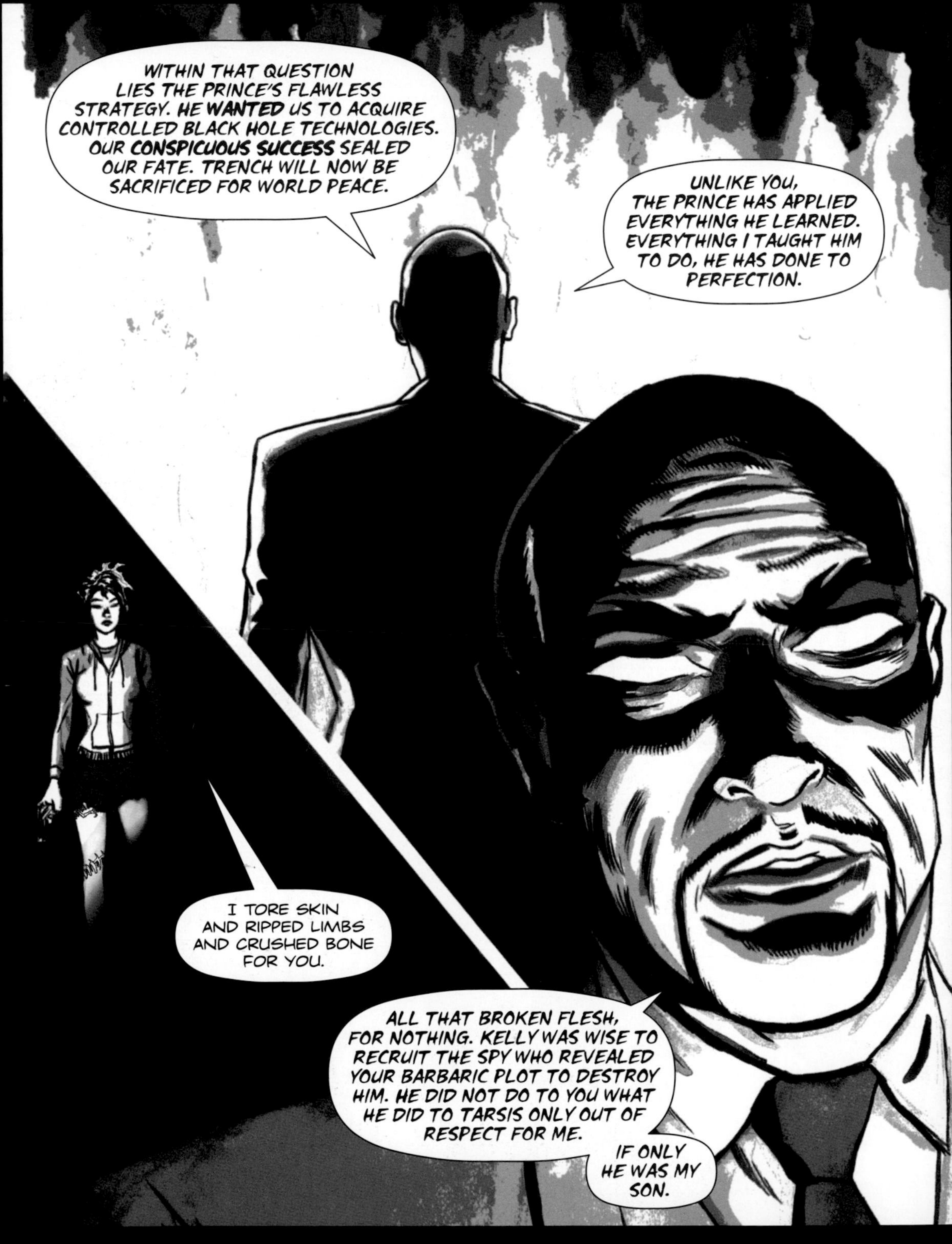
WITHIN THAT QUESTION LIES THE PRINCE'S FLAWLESS STRATEGY. HE WANTED US TO ACQUIRE CONTROLLED BLACK HOLE TECHNOLOGIES. OUR CONSPICUOUS SUCCESS SEALED OUR FATE. TRENCH WILL NOW BE SACRIFICED FOR WORLD PEACE.
UNLIKE YOU, THE PRINCE HAS APPLIED EVERYTHING HE LEARNED. EVERYTHING I TAUGHT HIM TO DO, HE HAS DONE TO PERFECTION.
I TORE SKIN AND RIPPED LIMBS AND CRUSHED BONE FOR YOU.
ALL THAT BROKEN FLESH, FOR NOTHING. KELLY WAS WISE TO RECRUIT THE SPY WHO REVEALED YOUR BARBARIC PLOT TO DESTROY HIM. HE DID NOT DO TO YOU WHAT HE DID TO TARSIS ONLY OUT OF RESPECT FOR ME.
IF ONLY HE WAS MY SON.

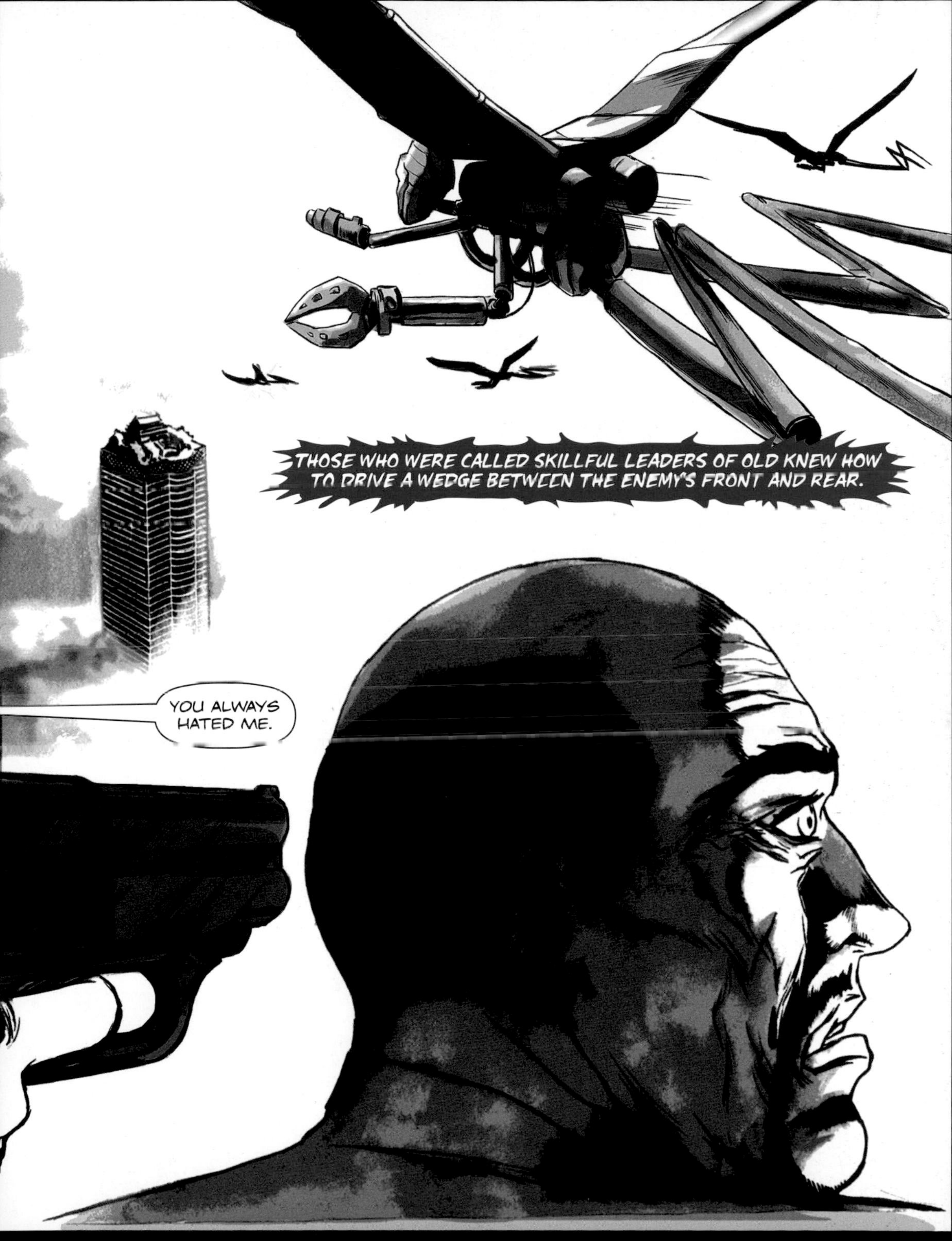
THOSE WHO WERE CALLED SKILLFUL LEADERS OF OLD KNEW HOW TO DRIVE A WEDGE BETWEEN THE ENEMY'S FRONT AND REAR.
YOU ALWAYS HATED ME.

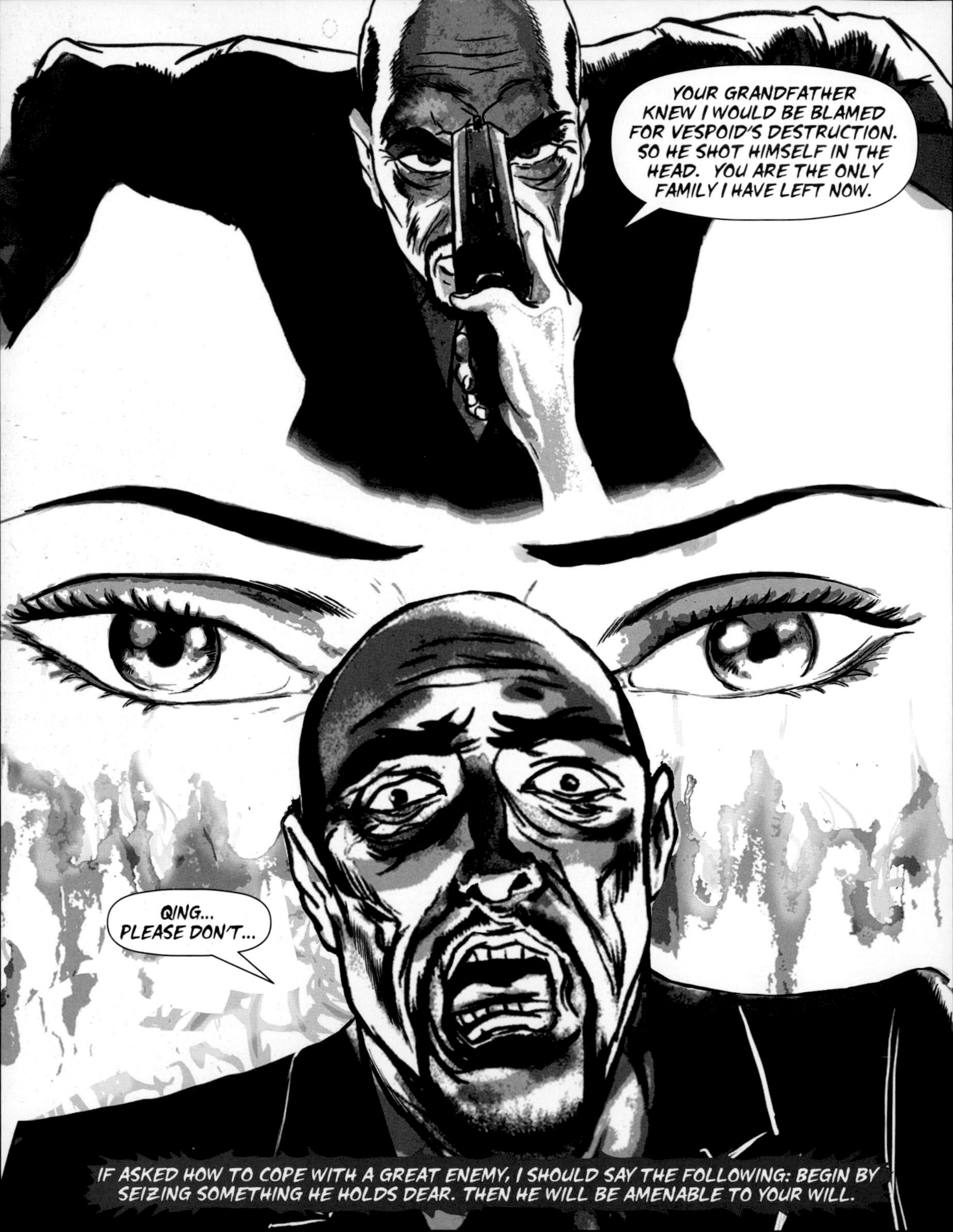
YOUR GRANDFATHER KNEW I WOULD BE BLAMED FOR VESPOID'S DESTRUCTION. SO HE SHOT HIMSELF IN THE HEAD. YOU ARE THE ONLY FAMILY I HAVE LEFT NOW.
QING... PLEASE DON'T...
IF ASKED HOW TO COPE WITH A GREAT ENEMY, I SHOULD SAY THE FOLLOWING: BEGIN BY SEIZING SOMETHING HE HOLDS DEAR. THEN HE WILL BE AMENABLE TO YOUR WILL.

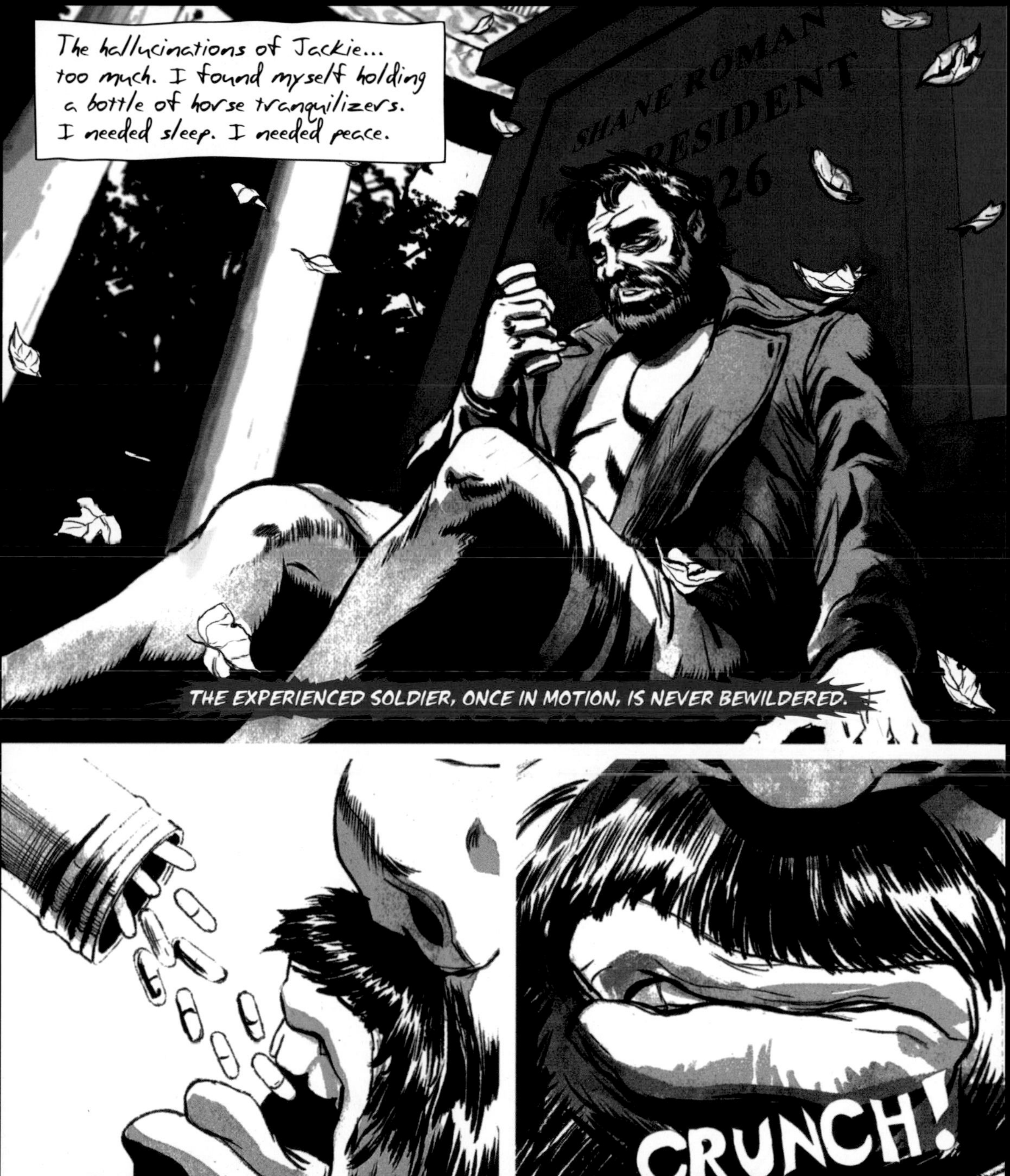
The hallucinations of Jackie... too much. I found myself holding a bottle of horse tranquilizers. I needed sleep. I needed peace.
THE EXPERIENCED SOLDIER, ONCE IN MOTION, IS NEVER BEWILDERED.
CRUNCH!

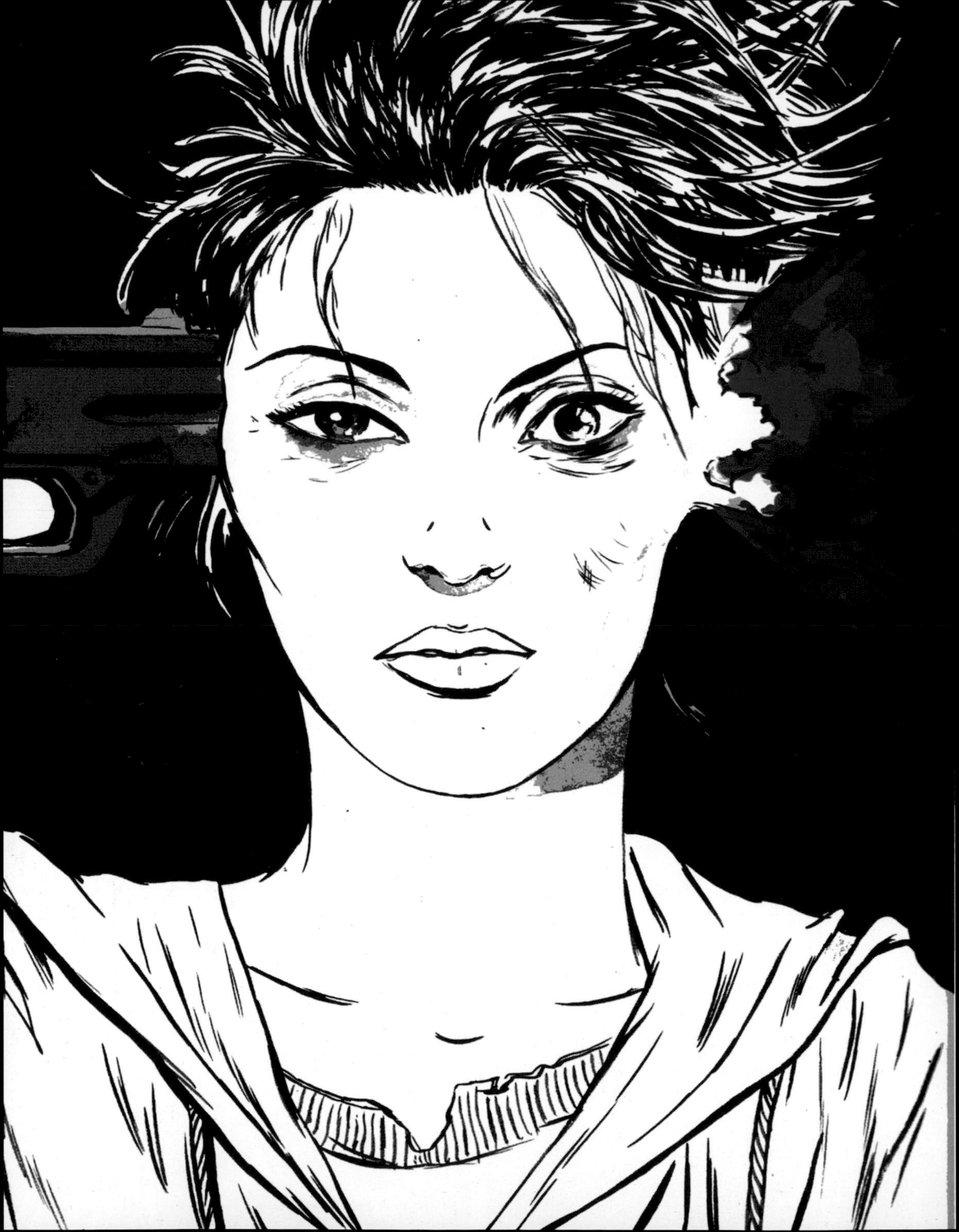

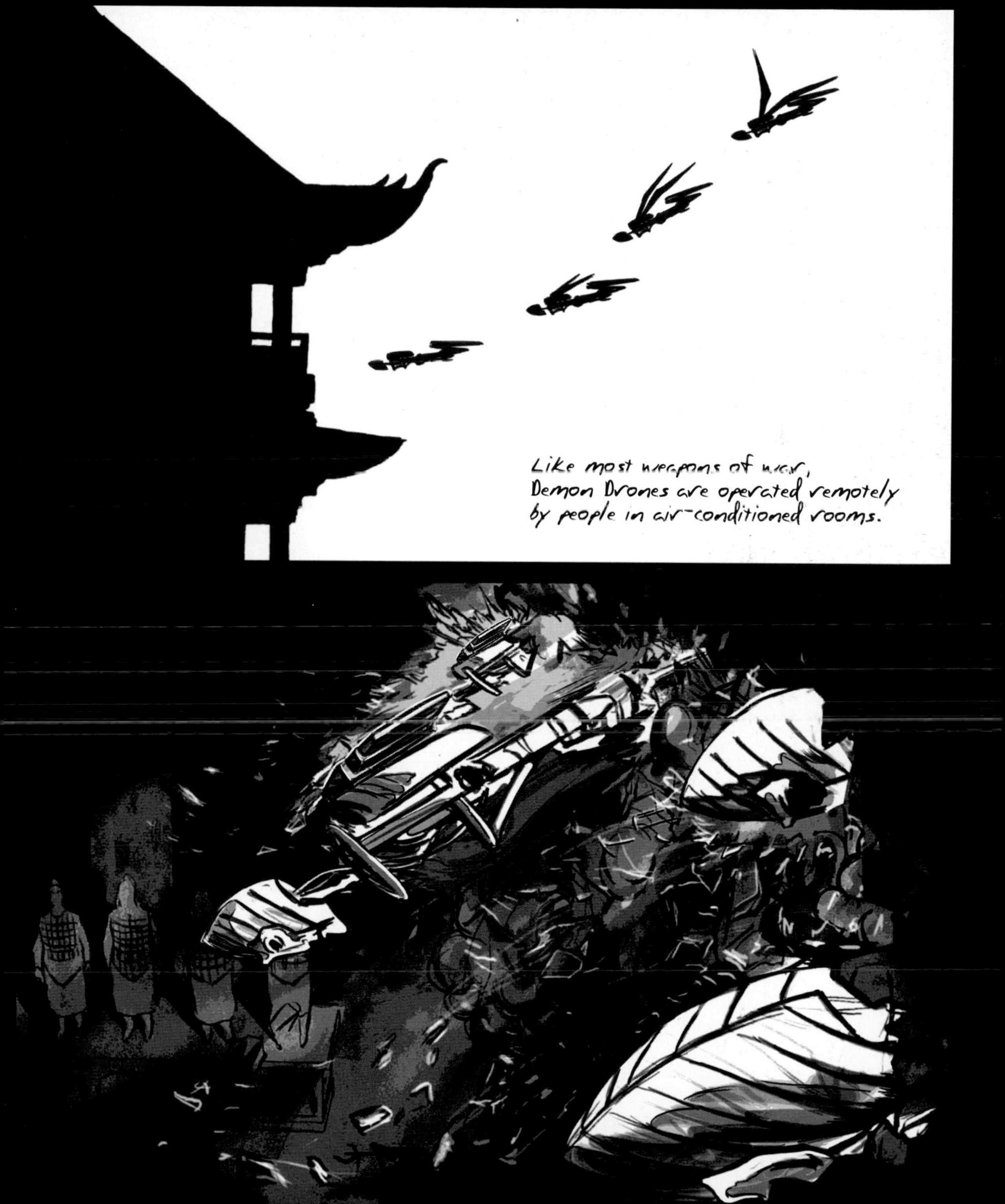
Like most weapons of war, Demon Drones are operated remotely by people in air-conditioned rooms.

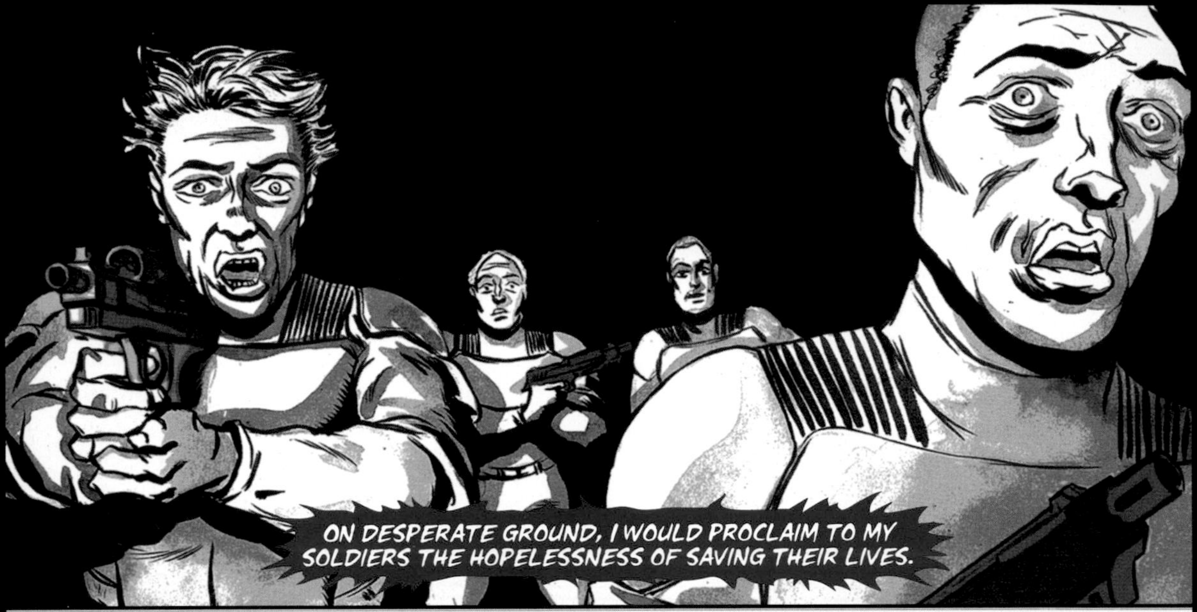
ON DESPERATE GROUND, I WOULD PROCLAIM TO MY SOLDIERS THE HOPELESSNESS OF SAVING THEIR LIVES.

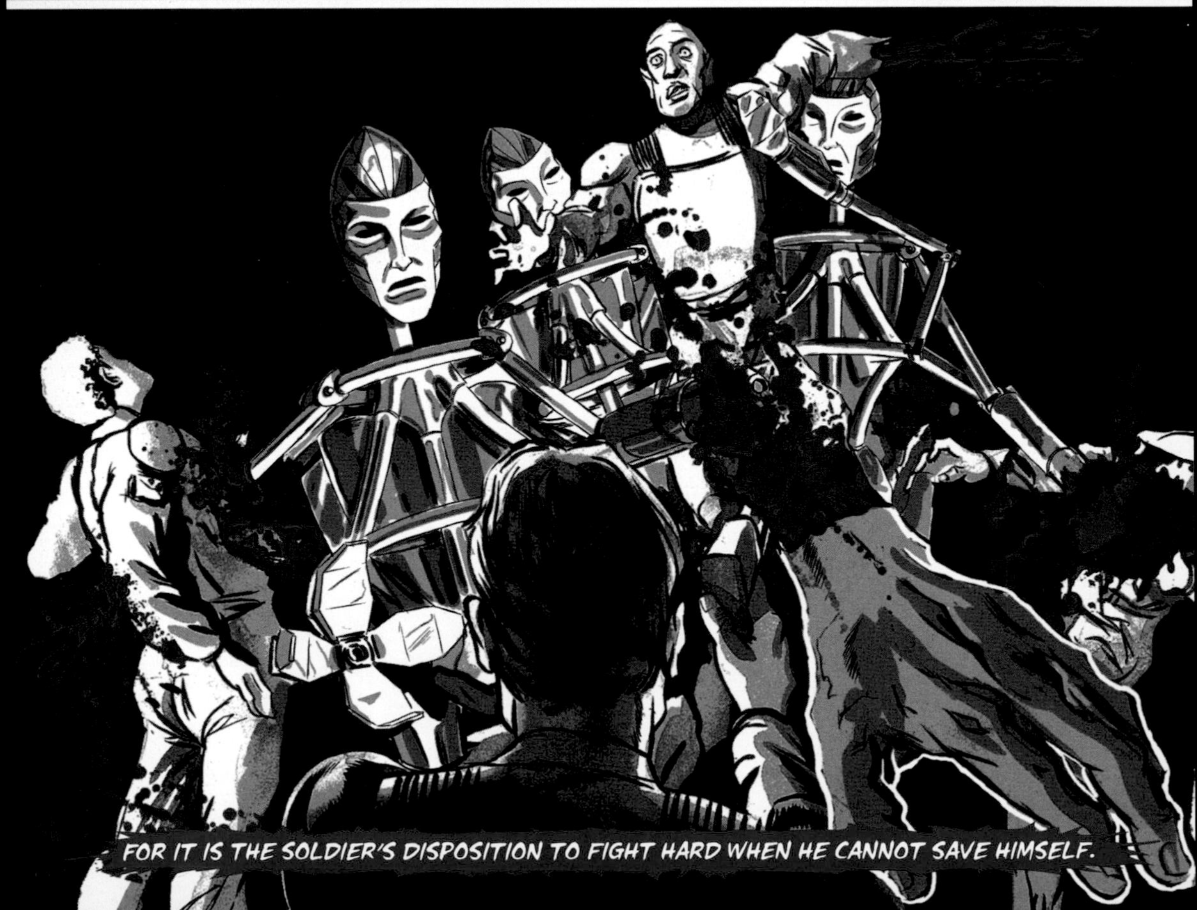
FOR IT IS THE SOLDIER'S DISPOSITION TO FIGHT HARD WHEN HE CANNOT SAVE HIMSELF.

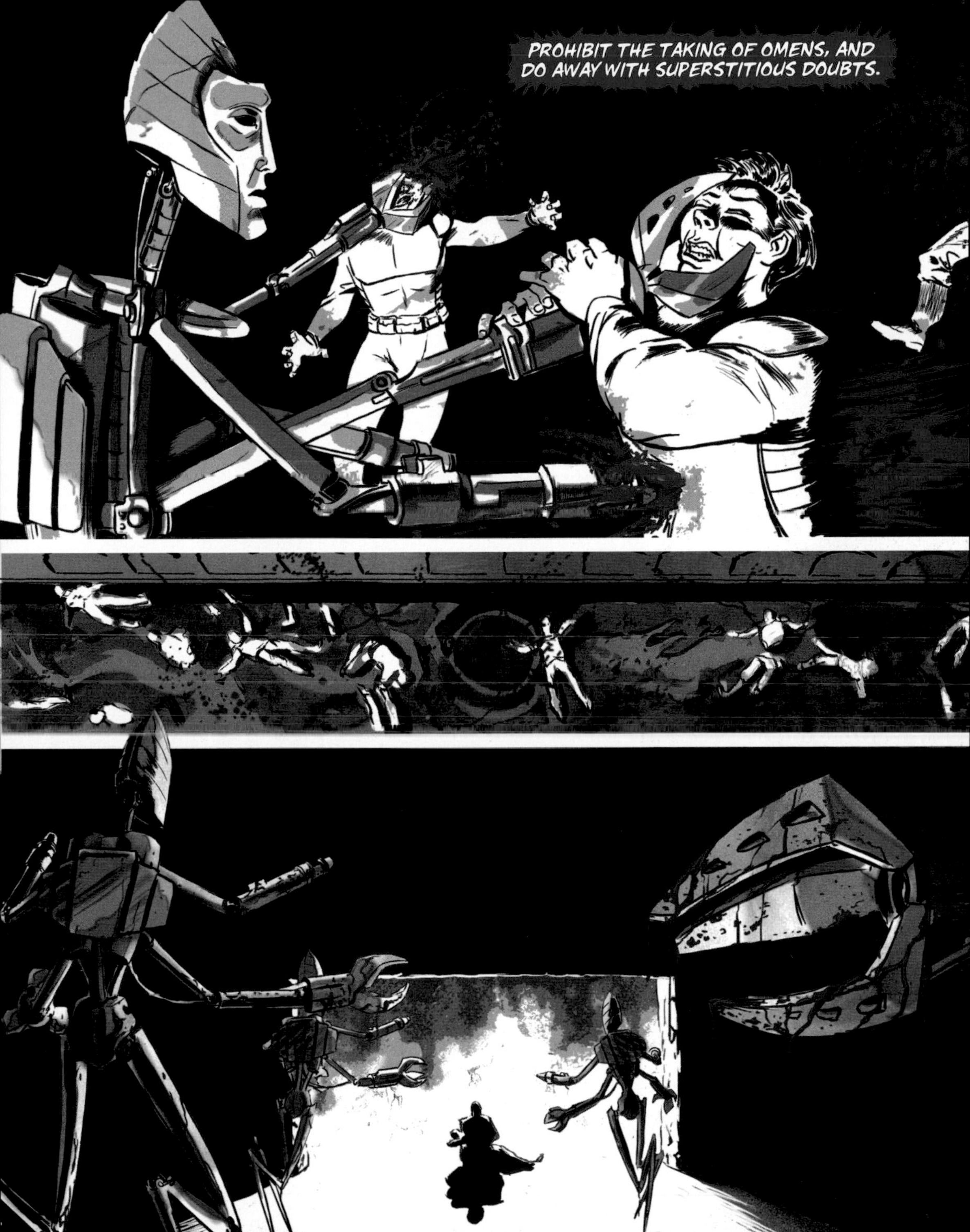
PROHIBIT THE TAKING OF OMENS, AND DO AWAY WITH SUPERSTITIOUS DOUBTS.

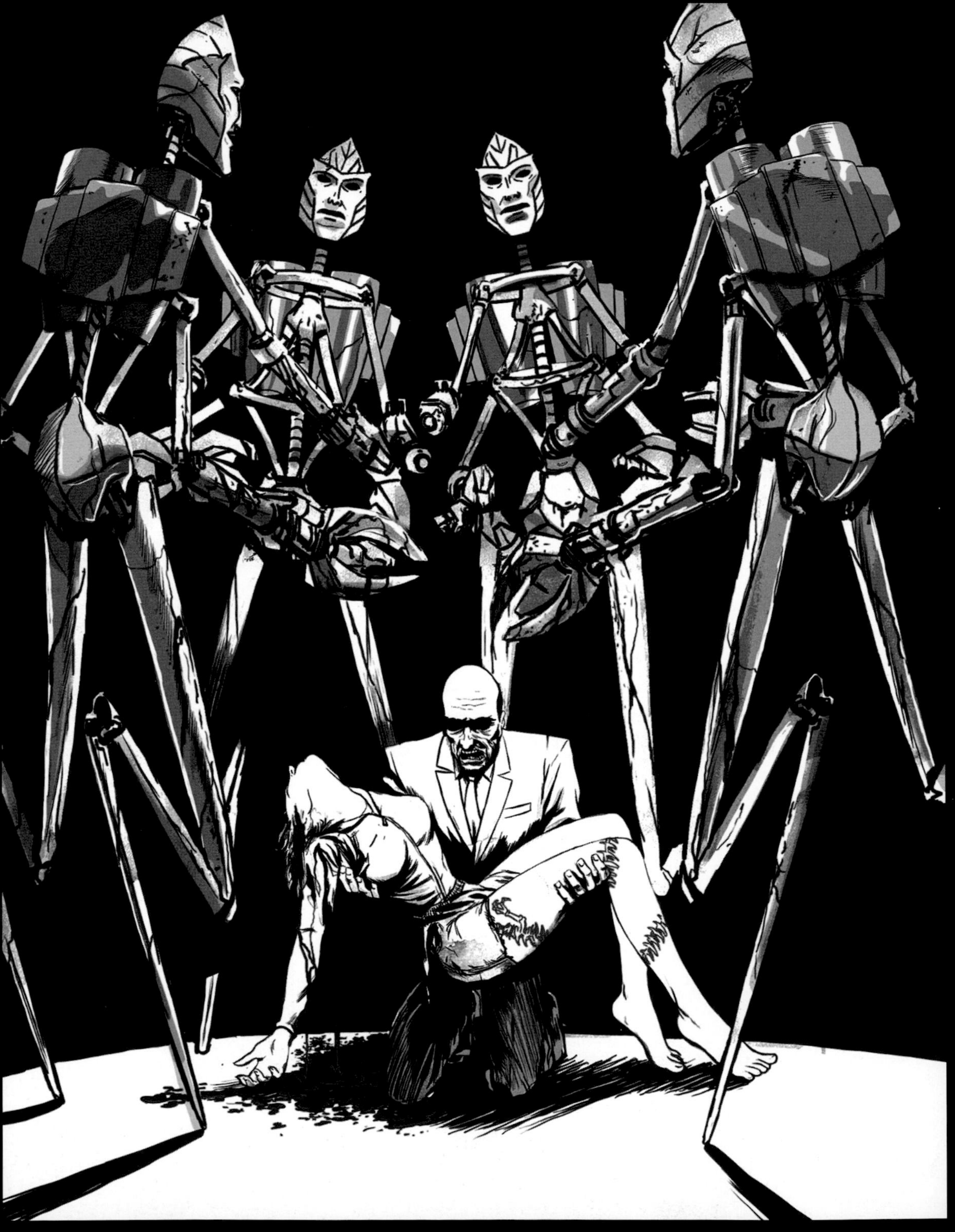

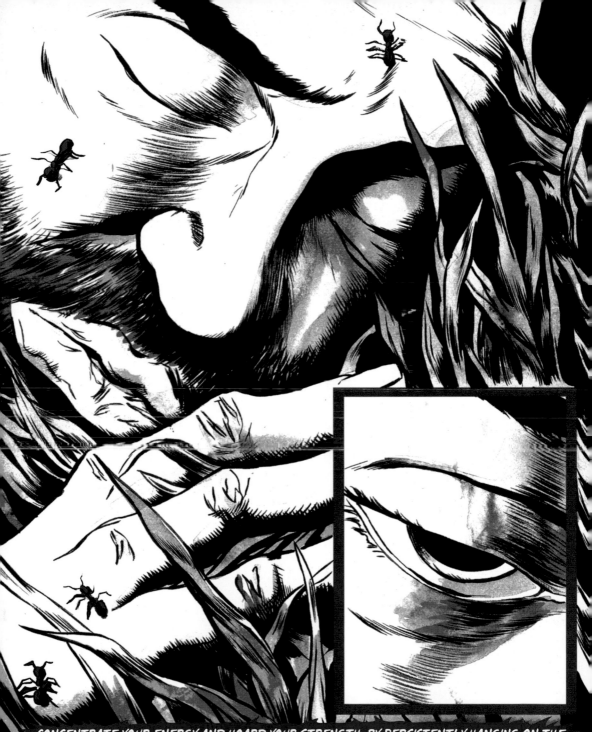

CONCENTRATE YOUR ENERGY AND HOARD YOUR STRENGTH. BY PERSISTENTLY HANGING ON THE ENEMY'S FLANK, WE SHALL SUCCEED IN THE LONG RUN IN KILLING THE COMMANDER-IN-CHIEF.

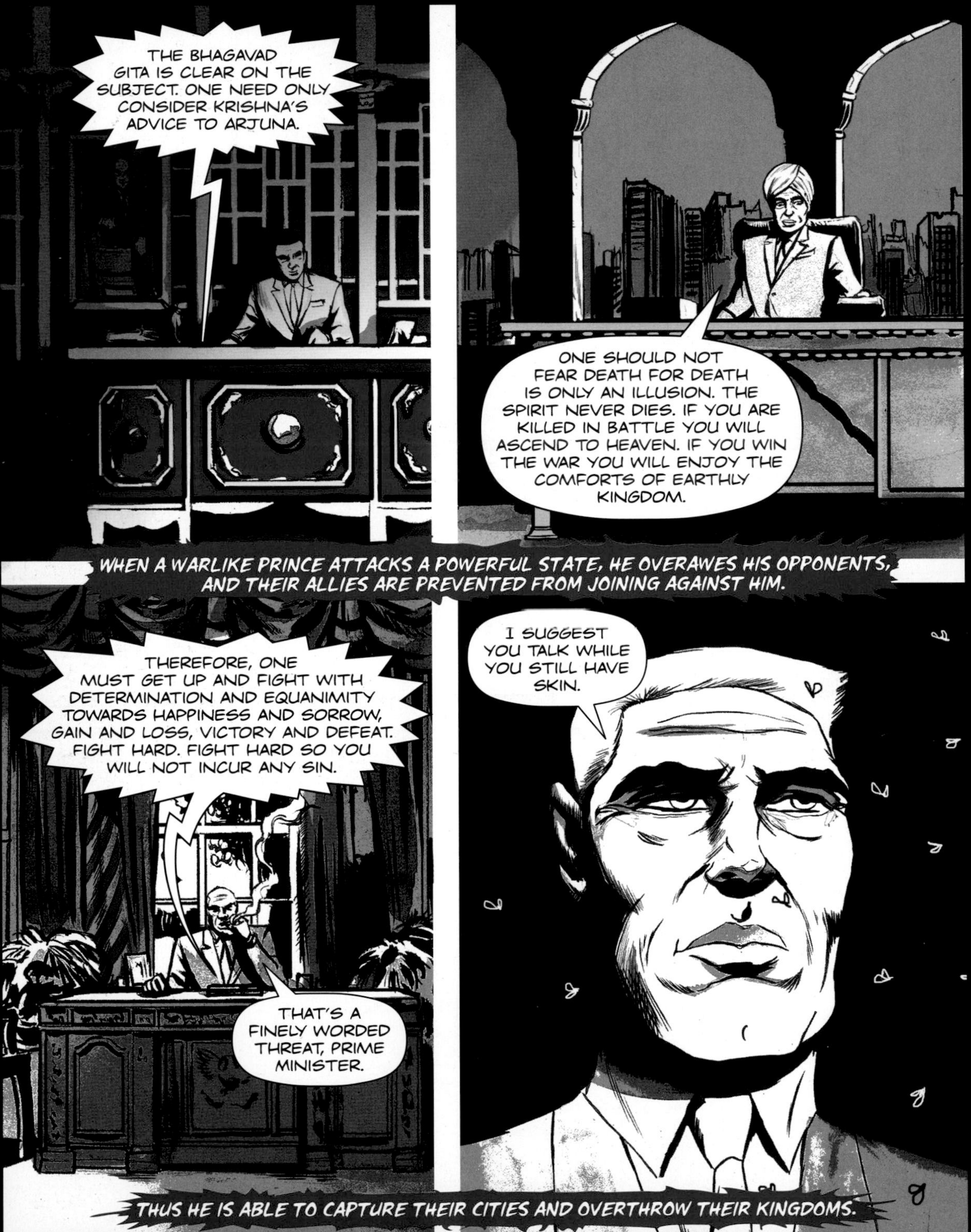
THE BHAGAVAD GITA IS CLEAR ON THE SUBJECT. ONE NEED ONLY CONSIDER KRISHNA'S ADVICE TO ARJUNA.
ONE SHOULD NOT FEAR DEATH FOR DEATH IS ONLY AN ILLUSION. THE SPIRIT NEVER DIES. IF YOU ARE KILLED IN BATTLE YOU WILL ASCEND TO HEAVEN. IF YOU WIN THE WAR YOU WILL ENJOY THE COMFORTS OF EARTHLY KINGDOM.
WHEN A WARLIKE PRINCE ATTACKS A POWERFUL STATE, HE OVERAWES HIS OPPONENTS, AND THEIR ALLIES ARE PREVENTED FROM JOINING AGAINST HIM.
THEREFORE, ONE MUST GET UP AND FIGHT WITH DETERMINATION AND EQUANIMITY TOWARDS HAPPINESS AND SORROW, GAIN AND LOSS, VICTORY AND DEFEAT. FIGHT HARD. FIGHT HARD SO YOU WILL NOT INCUR ANY SIN.
THAT'S A FINELY WORDED THREAT, PRIME MINISTER.
I SUGGEST YOU TALK WHILE YOU STILL HAVE SKIN.
THUS HE IS ABLE TO CAPTURE THEIR CITIES AND OVERTHROW THEIR KINGDOMS.

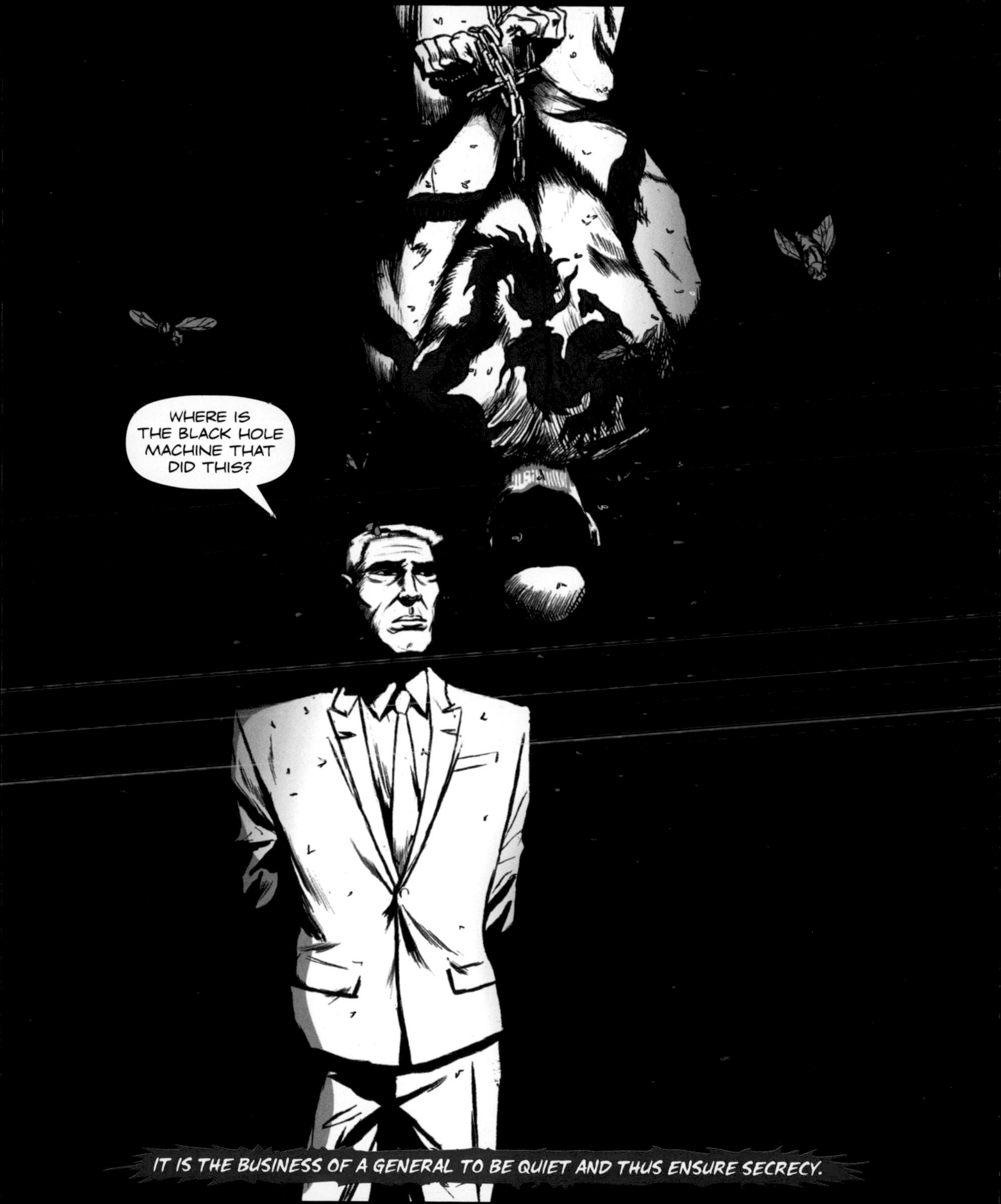
WHERE IS THE BLACK HOLE MACHINE THAT DID THIS?
IT IS THE BUSINESS OF A GENERAL TO BE QUIET AND THUS ENSURE SECRECY.

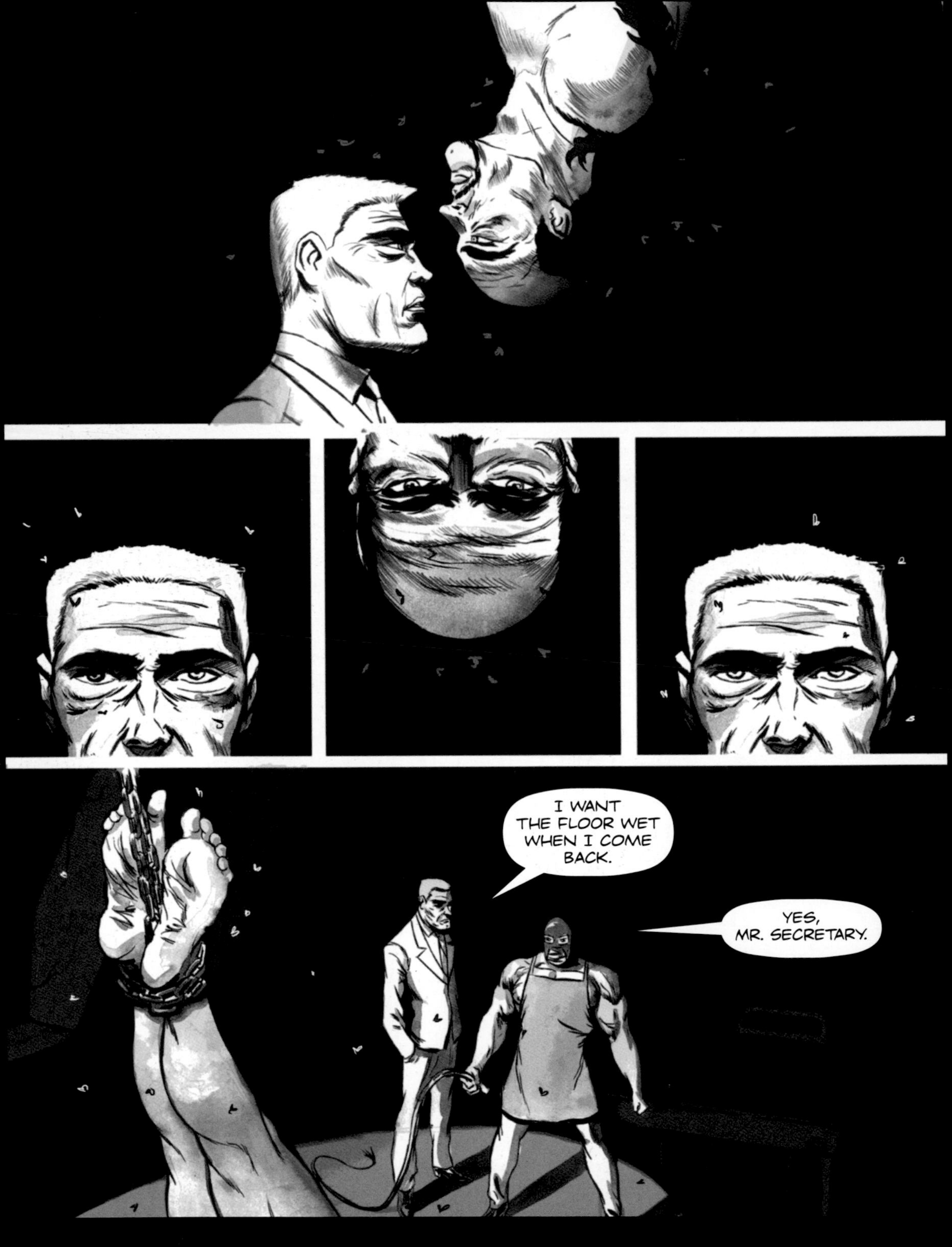
I WANT THE FLOOR WET WHEN I COME BACK.
YES, MR. SECRETARY.

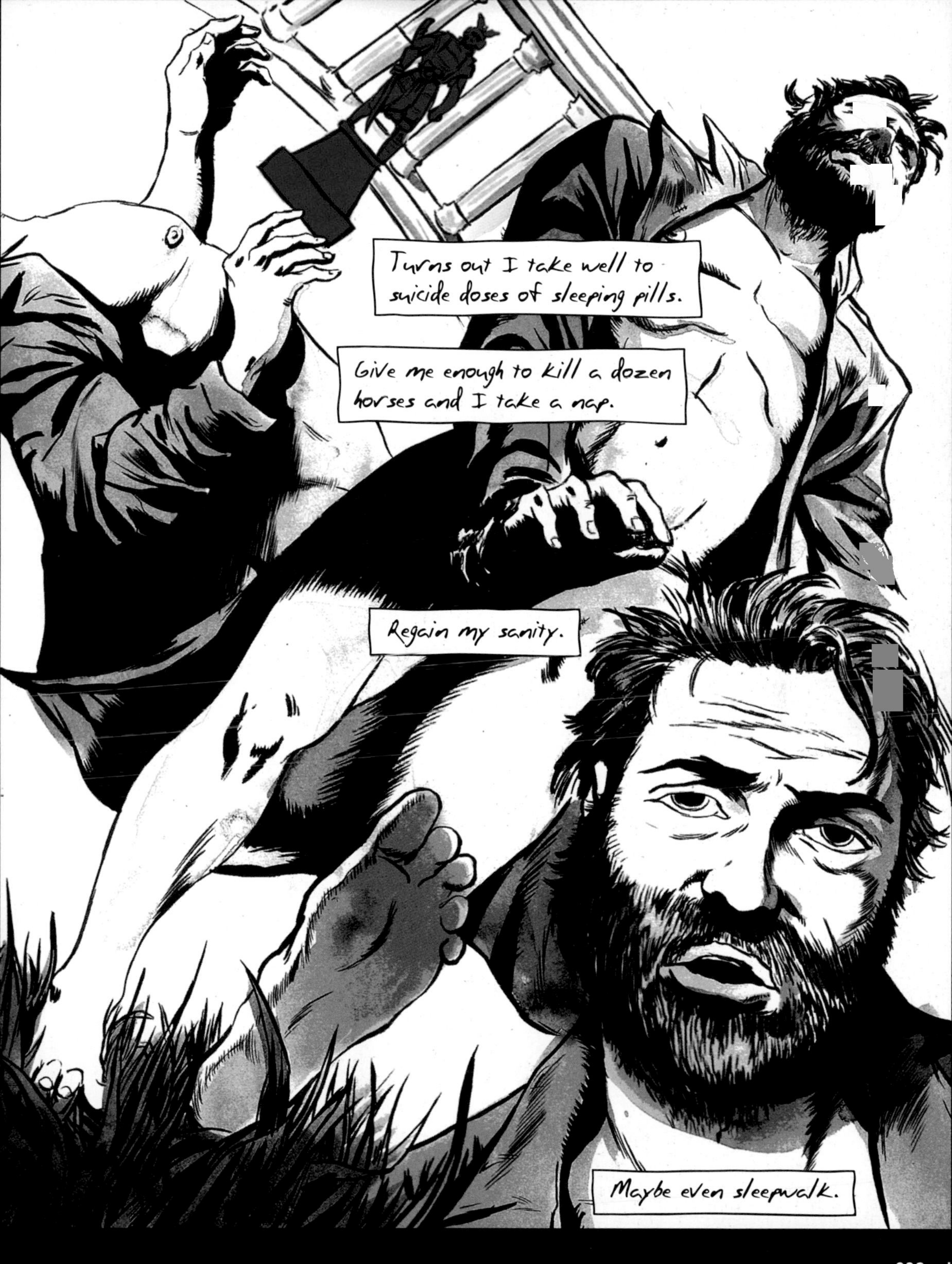
Turns out I take well to suicide doses of sleeping pills.
Give me enough to kill a dozen horses and I take a nap.
Regain my sanity.
Maybe even sleepwalk.

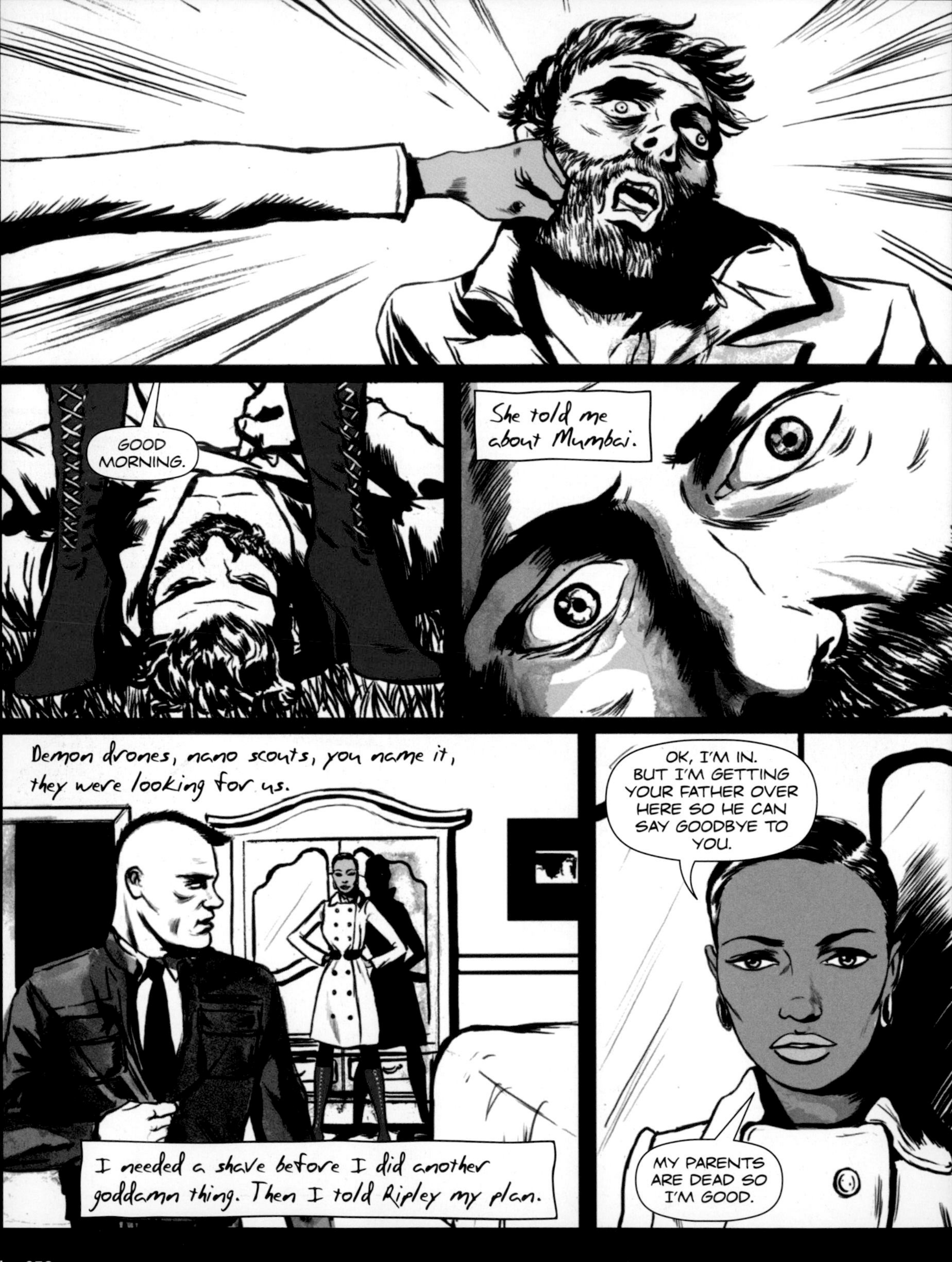
GOOD MORNING.
She told me about Mumbai.
Demon drones, nano scouts, you name it, they were looking for us.
I needed a shave before I did another goddamn thing. Then I told Ripley my plan.
OK, I'M IN. BUT I'M GETTING YOUR FATHER OVER HERE SO HE CAN SAY GOODBYE TO YOU.
MY PARENTS ARE DEAD SO I'M GOOD.

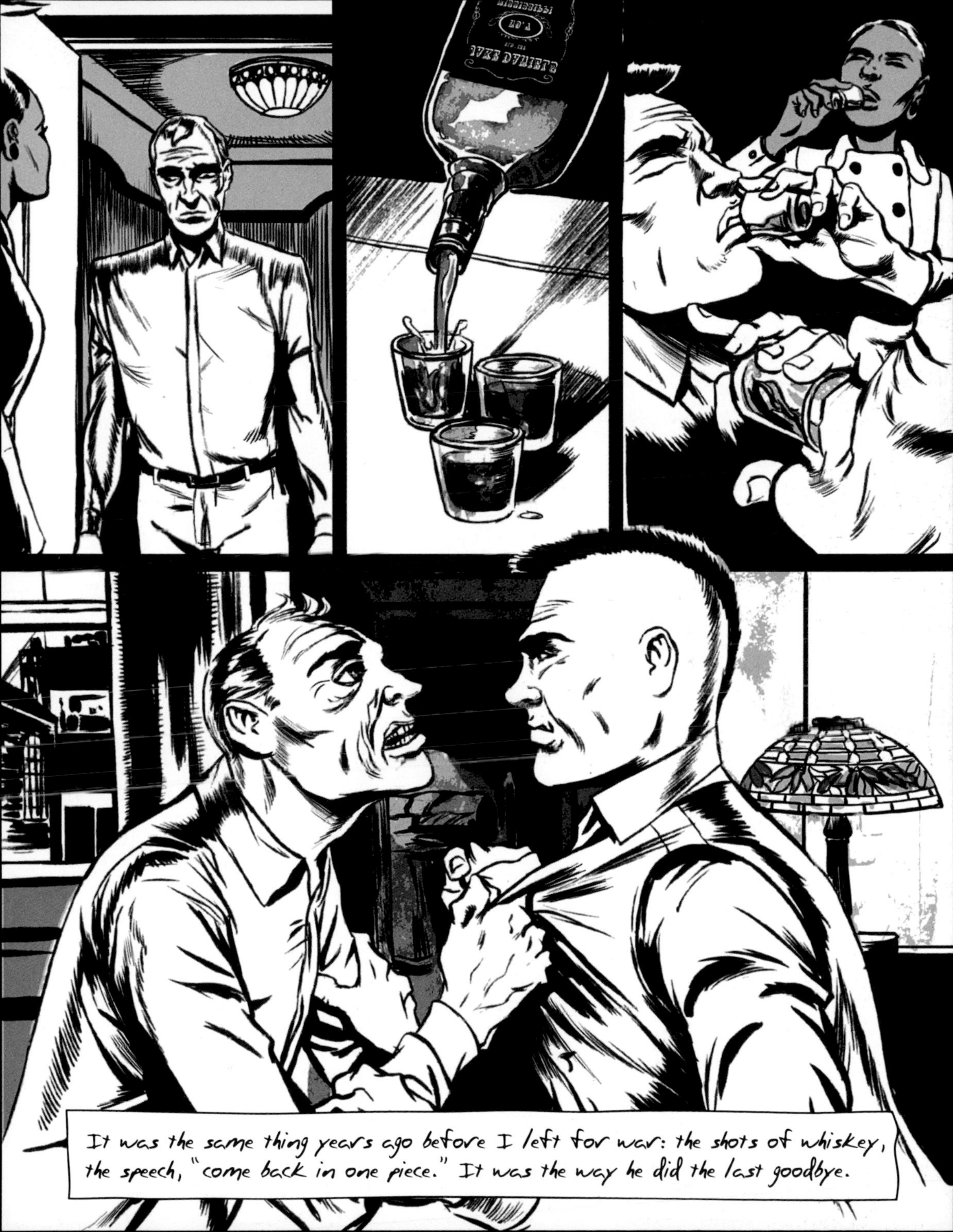
It was the same thing years ago before I left for war: the shots of whiskey, the speech, "come back in one piece." It was the way he did the last goodbye.

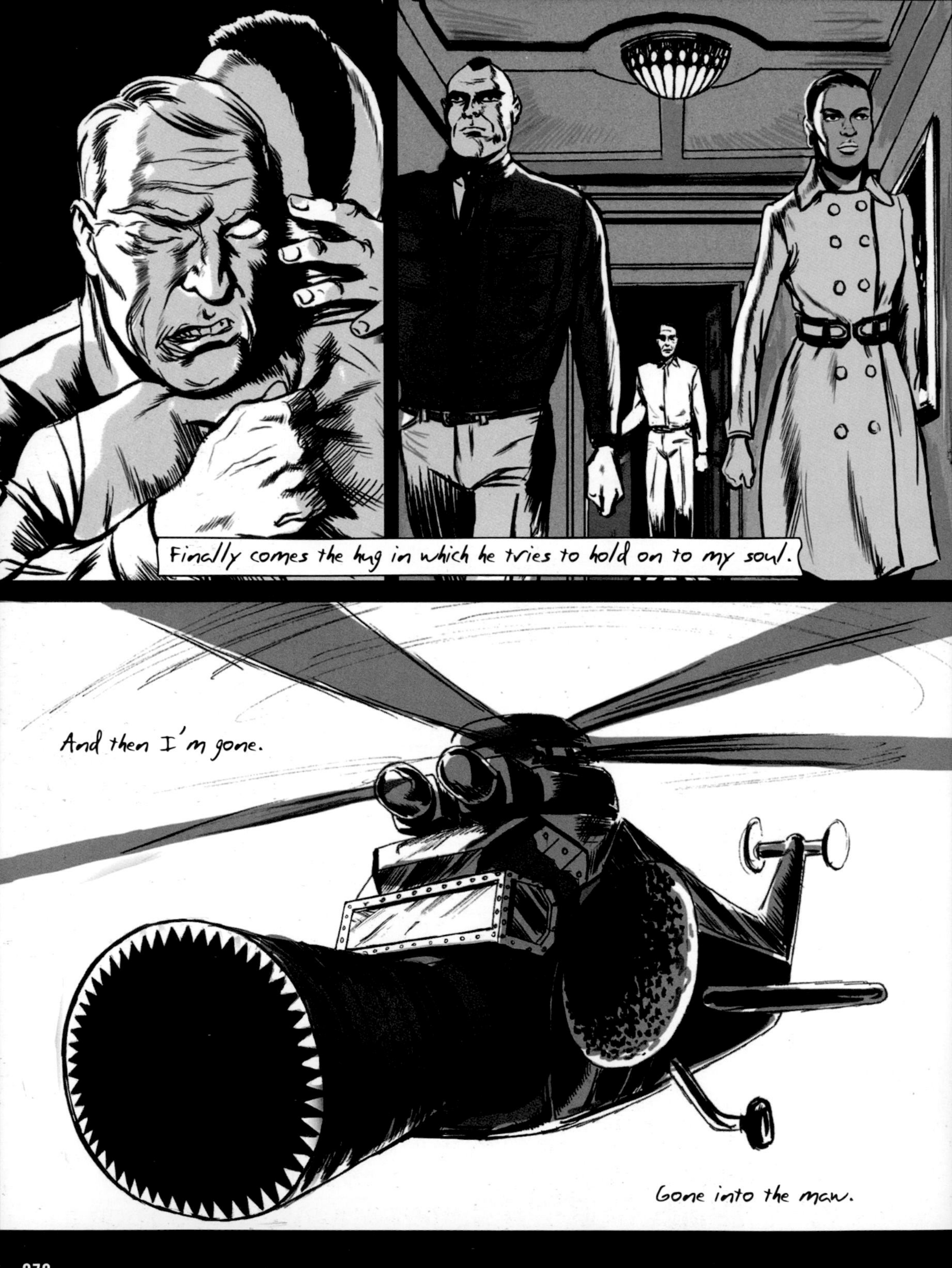
Finally comes the hug in which he tries to hold on to my soul.
And then I'm gone.
Gone into the maw.

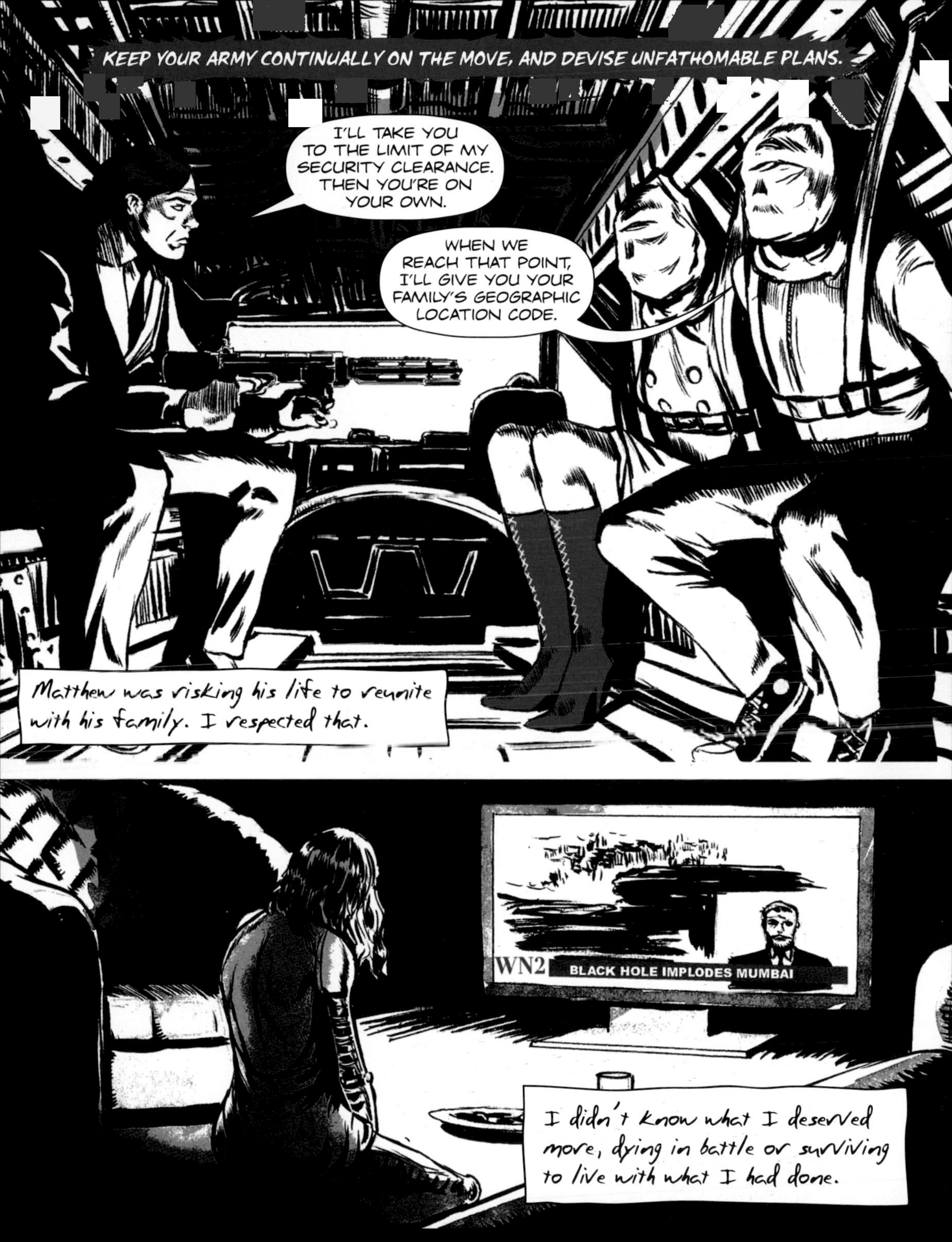
KEEP YOUR ARMY CONTINUALLY ON THE MOVE, AND DEVISE UNFATHOMABLE PLANS.
I'LL TAKE YOU TO THE LIMIT OF MY SECURITY CLEARANCE. THEN YOU'RE ON YOUR OWN.
WHEN WE REACH THAT POINT, I'LL GIVE YOU YOUR FAMILY'S GEOGRAPHIC LOCATION CODE.
Matthew was risking his life to reunite with his family. I respected that.
WN2
BLACK HOLE IMPLODES MUMBAI
I didn't know what I deserved more, dying in battle or surviving to live with what I had done.

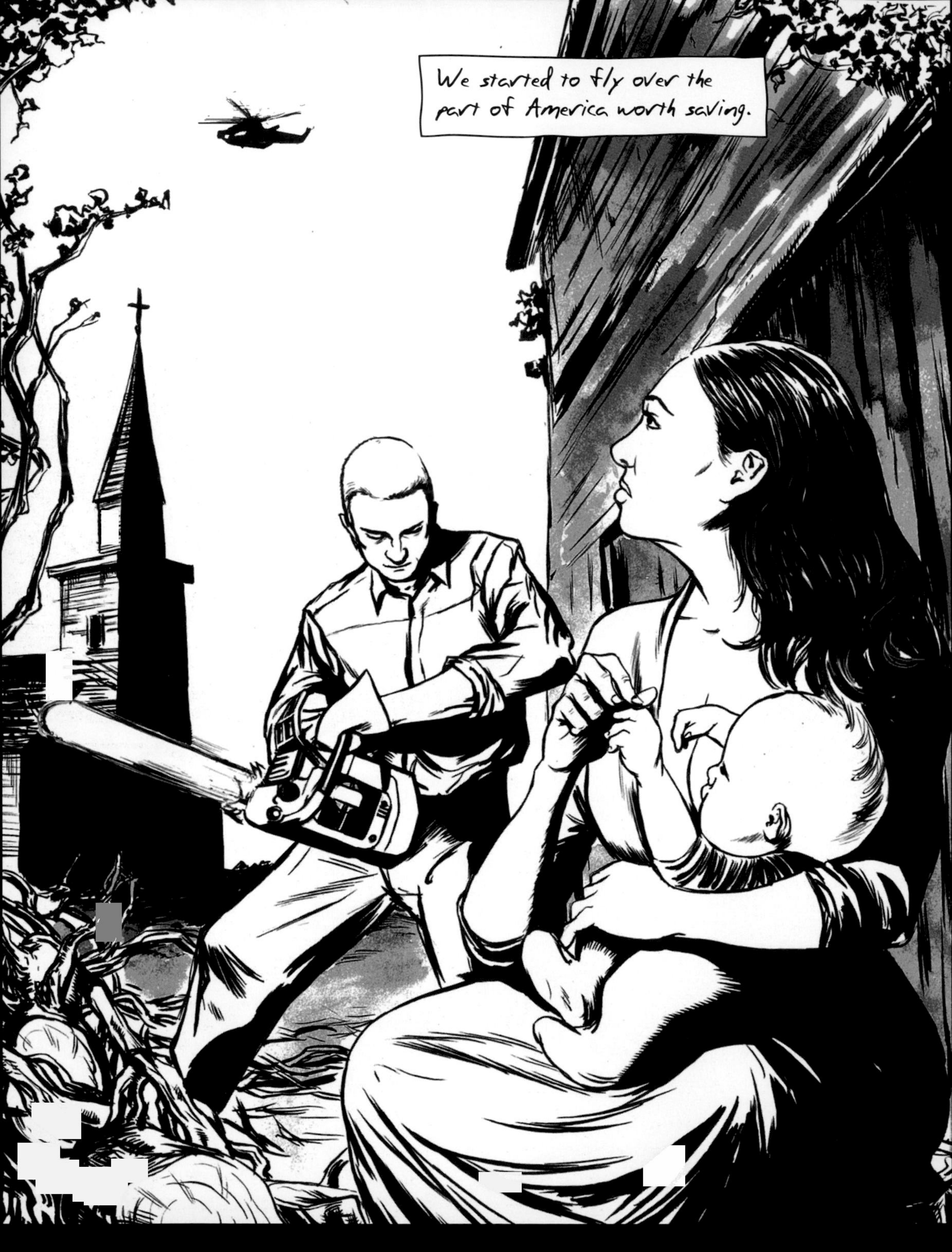
We started to fly over the part of America worth saving.

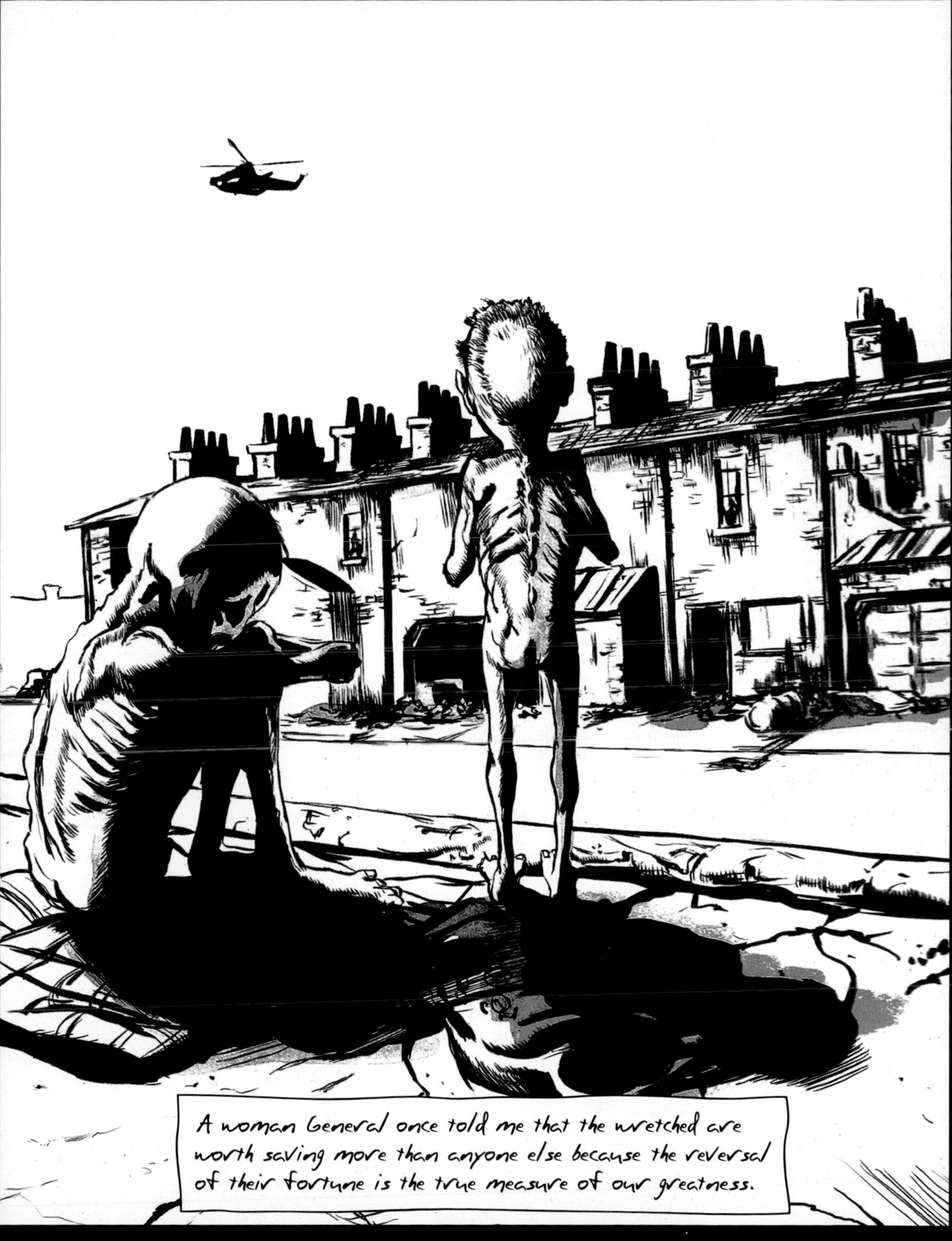
A woman General once told me that the wretched are worth saving more than anyone else because the reversal of their fortune is the true measure of our greatness.

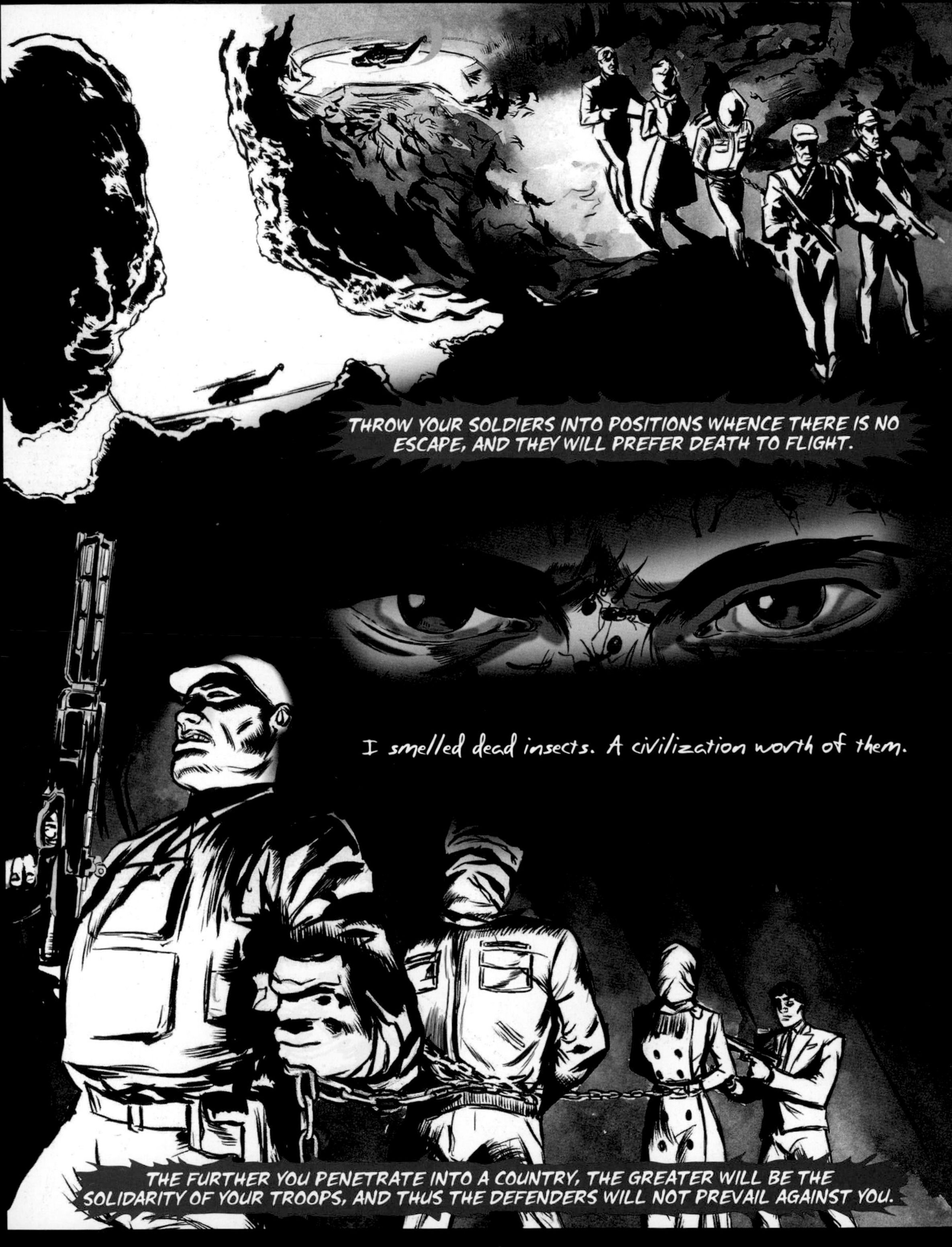
THROW YOUR SOLDIERS INTO POSITIONS WHENCE THERE IS NO ESCAPE, AND THEY WILL PREFER DEATH TO FLIGHT.
I smelled dead insects. A civilization worth of them.
THE FURTHER YOU PENETRATE INTO A COUNTRY, THE GREATER WILL BE THE SOLIDARITY OF YOUR TROOPS, AND THUS THE DEFENDERS WILL NOT PREVAIL AGAINST YOU.

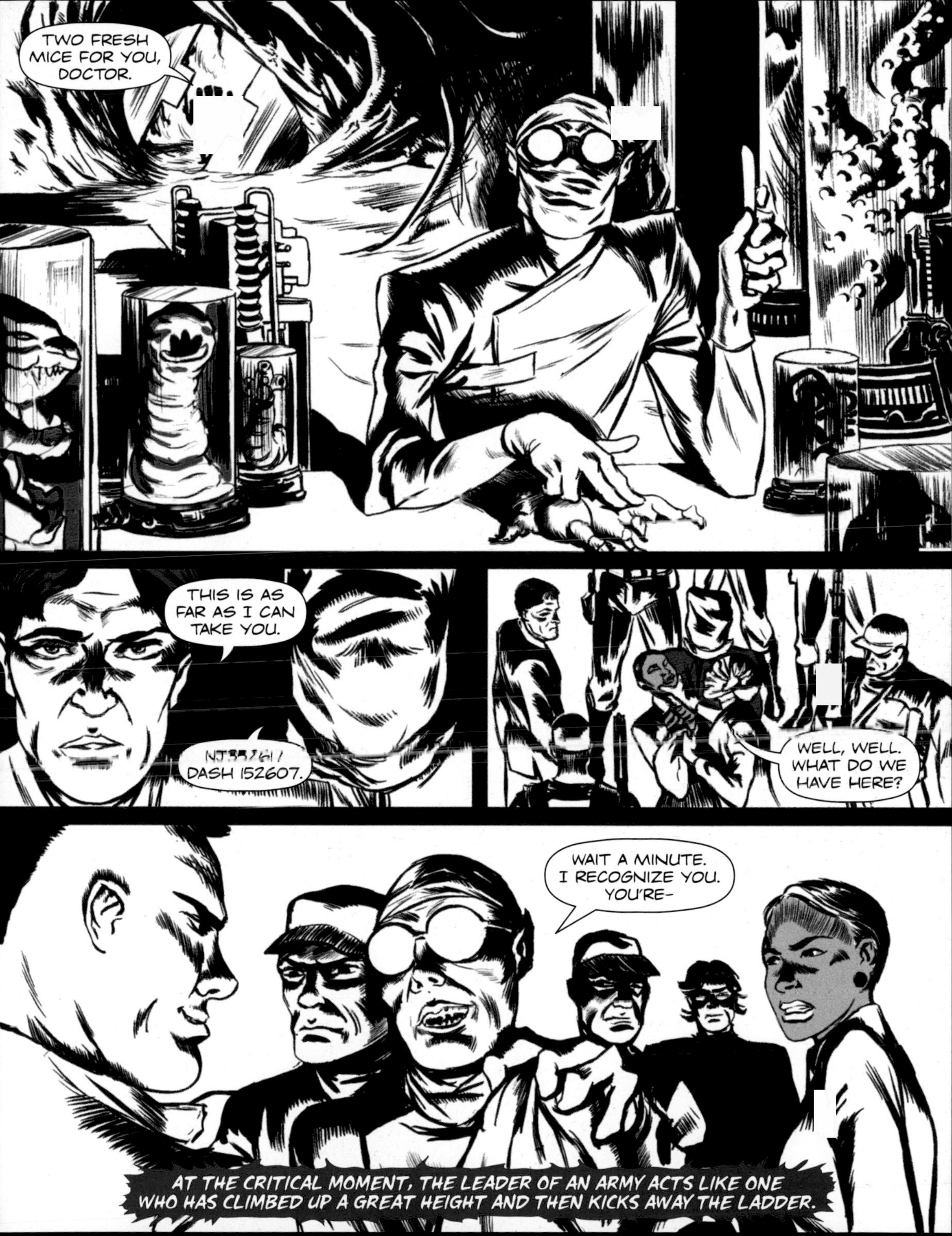
TWO FRESH MICE FOR YOU, DOCTOR.
THIS IS AS FAR AS I CAN TAKE YOU.
DASH 152607.
WELL, WELL. WHAT DO WE HAVE HERE?
WAIT A MINUTE. I RECOGNIZE YOU. YOU'RE-
AT THE CRITICAL MOMENT, THE LEADER OF AN ARMY ACTS LIKE ONE WHO HAS CLIMBED UP A GREAT HEIGHT AND THEN KICKS AWAY THE LADDER.

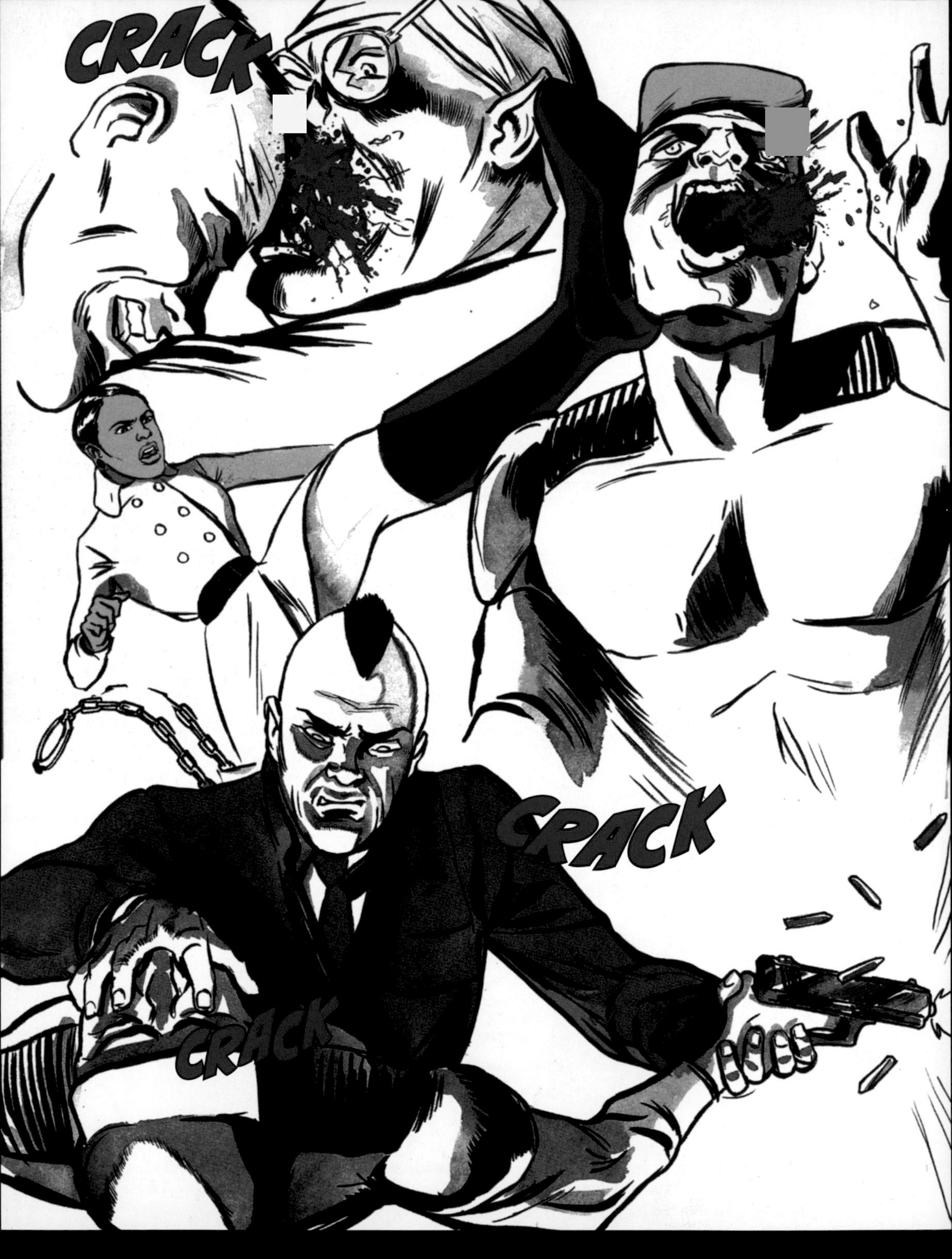
CRACK
CRACK
CRACK

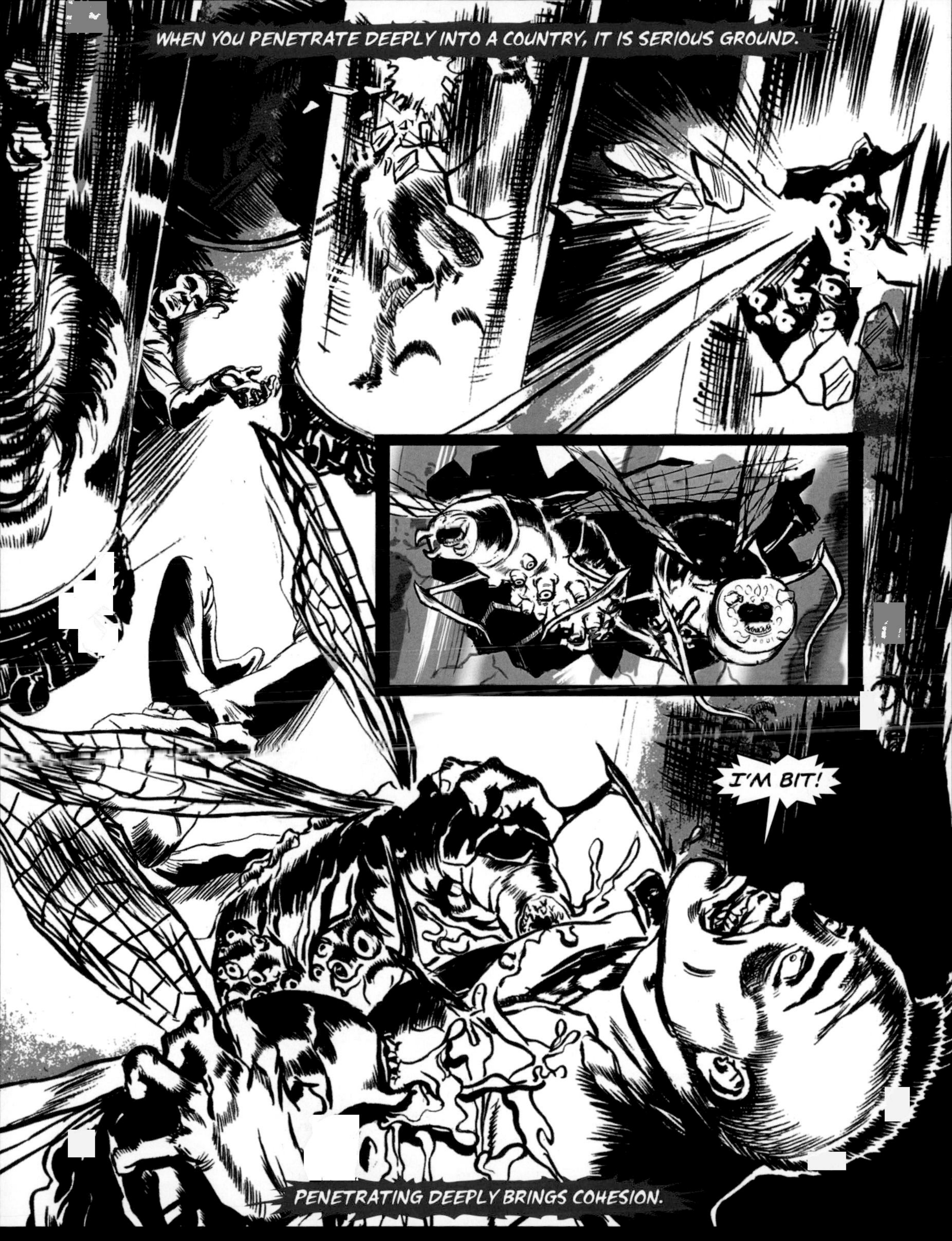

WHEN YOU PENETRATE DEEPLY INTO A COUNTRY, IT IS SERIOUS GROUND.
I'M BIT!
PENETRATING DEEPLY BRINGS COHESION.

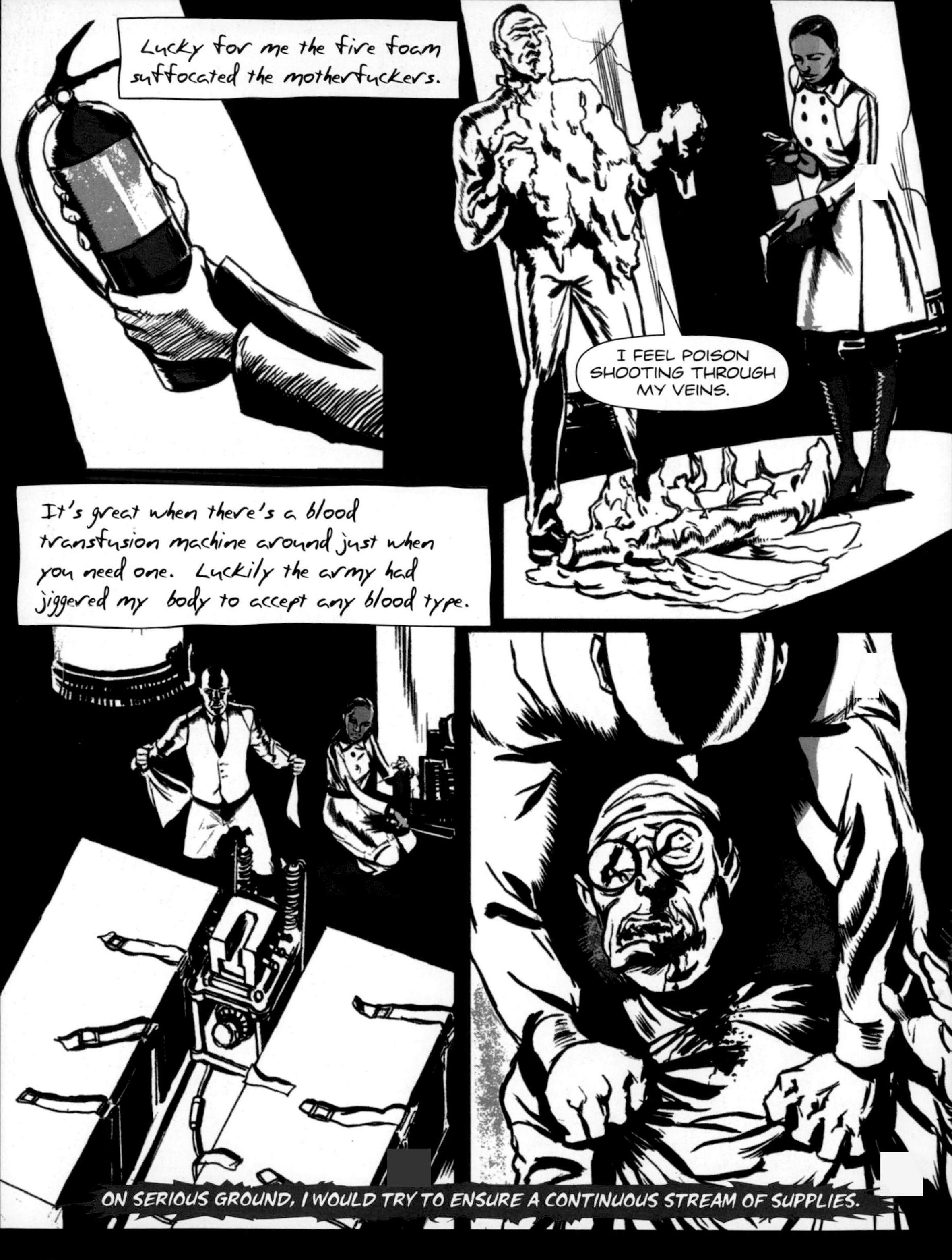
Lucky for me the fire foam suffocated the motherfuckers.
I FEEL POISON SHOOTING THROUGH MY VEINS.
It's great when there's a blood transfusion machine around just when you need one. Luckily the army had jiggered my body to accept any blood type.
ON SERIOUS GROUND, I WOULD TRY TO ENSURE A CONTINUOUS STREAM OF SUPPLIES.

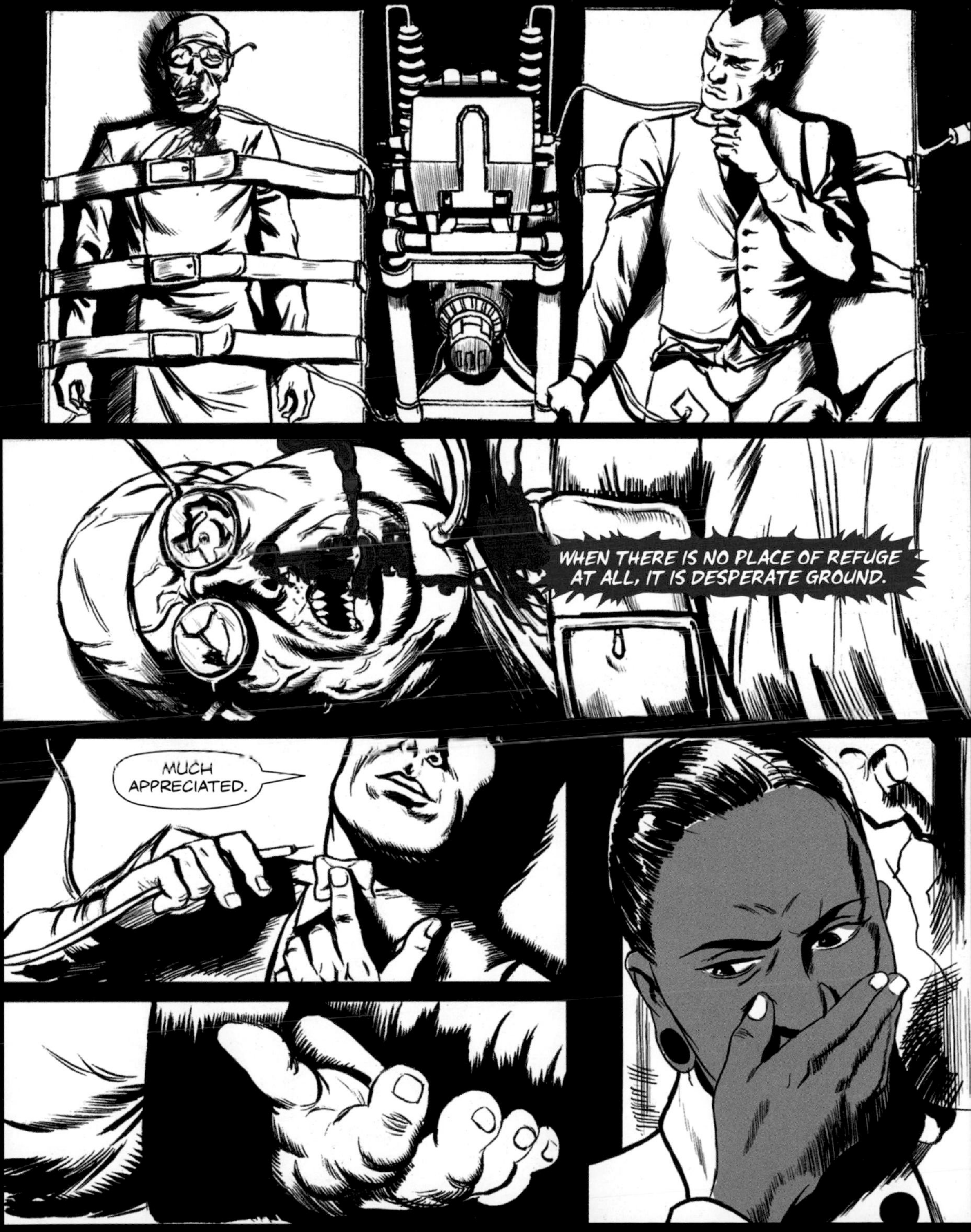
WHEN THERE IS NO PLACE OF REFUGE AT ALL, IT IS DESPERATE GROUND.
MUCH APPRECIATED.

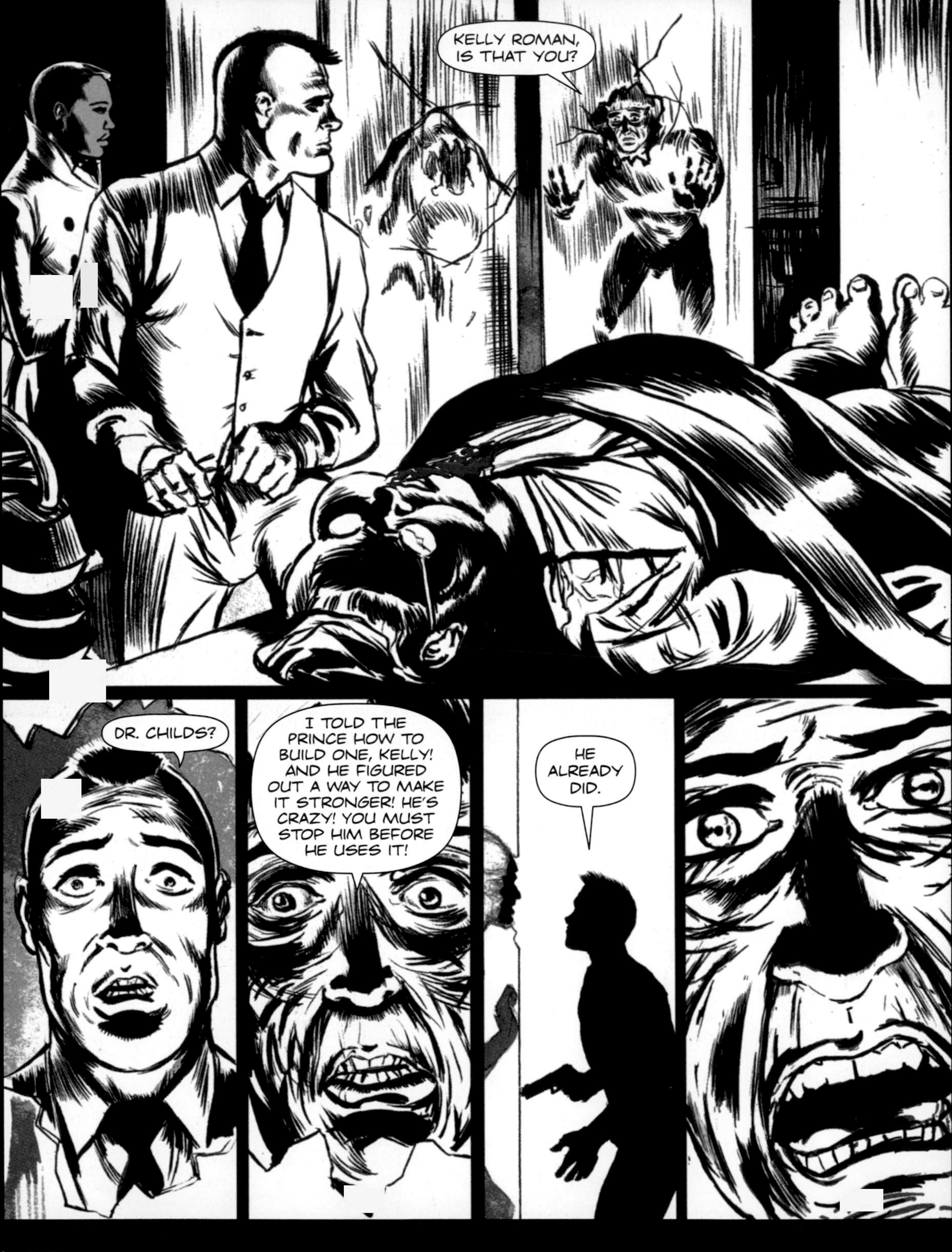
KELLY ROMAN, IS THAT YOU?
DR. CHILDS?
I TOLD THE PRINCE HOW TO BUILD ONE, KELLY! AND HE FIGURED OUT A WAY TO MAKE IT STRONGER! HE'S CRAZY! YOU MUST STOP HIM BEFORE HE USES IT!
HE ALREADY DID.

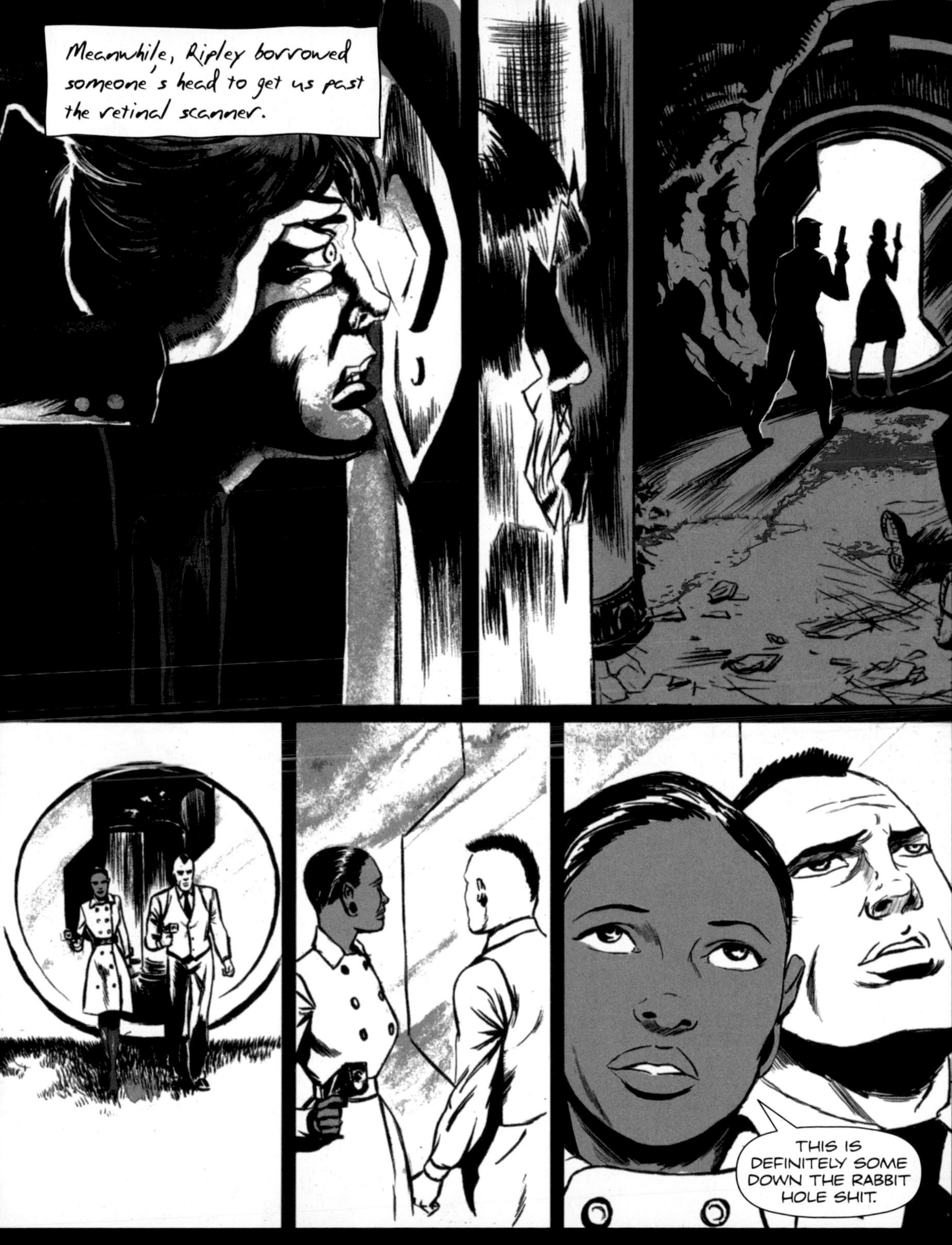
Meanwhile, Ripley borrowed someone's head to get us past the retinal scanner.
THIS IS DEFINITELY SOME DOWN THE RABBIT HOLE SHIT.

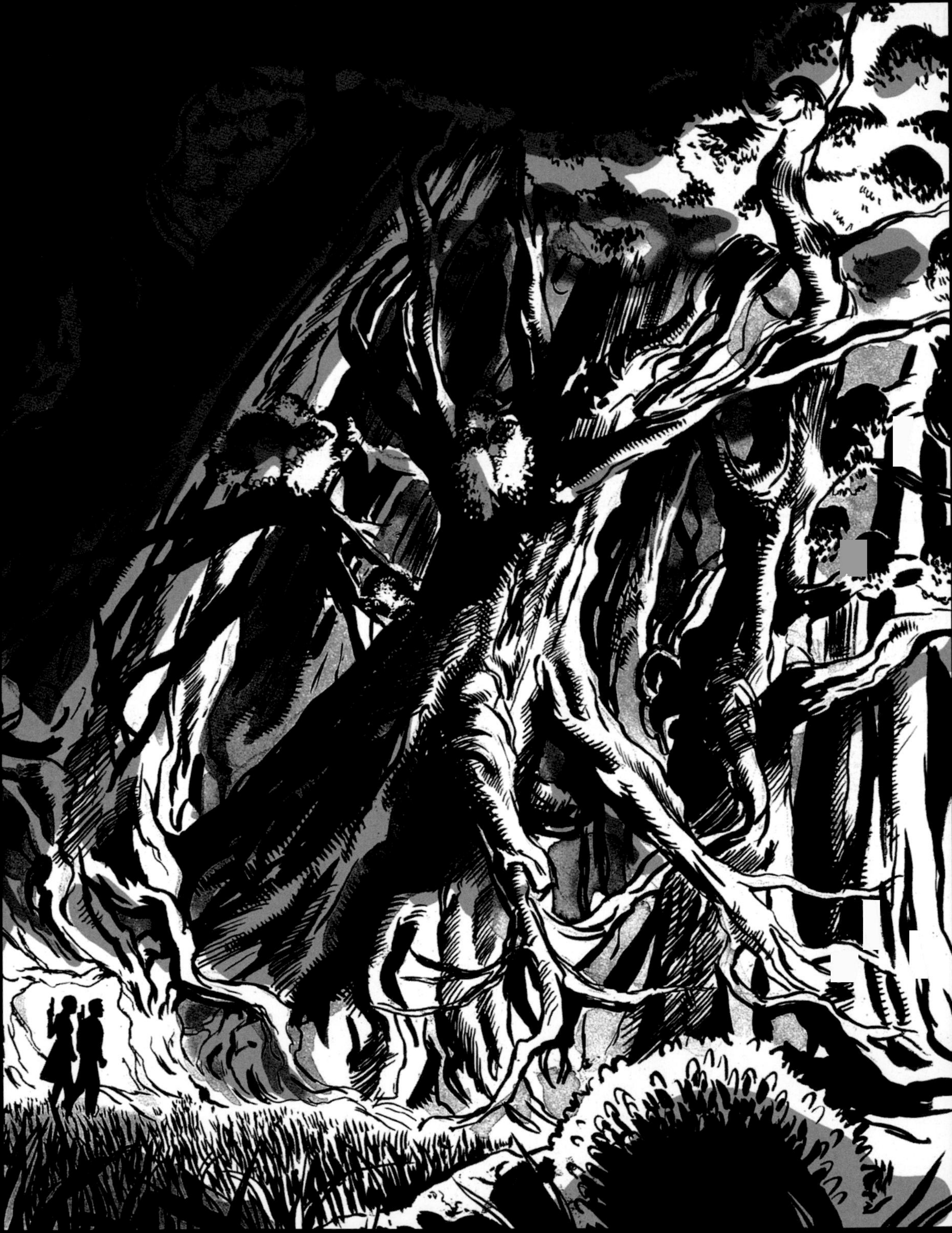

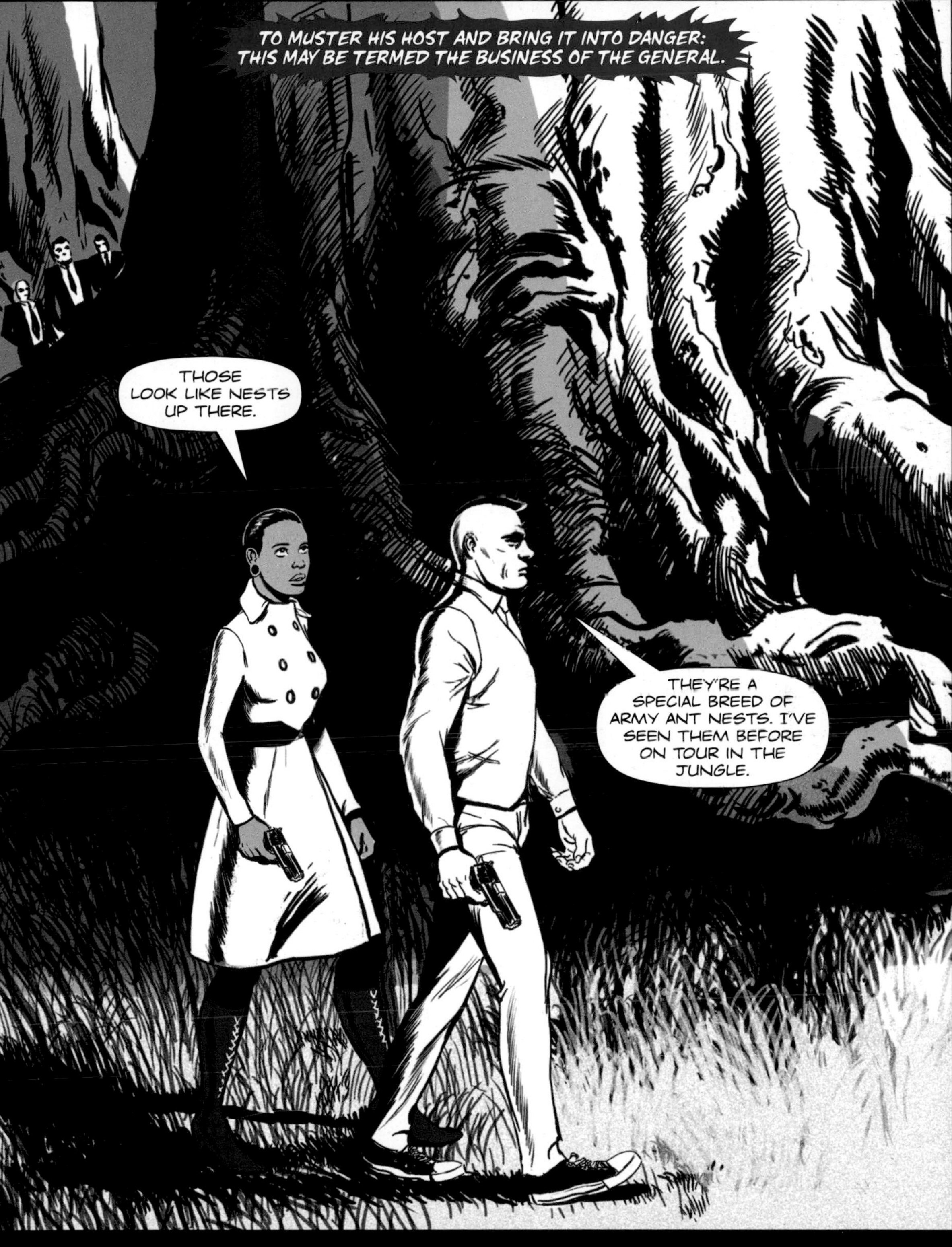
TO MUSTER HIS HOST AND BRING IT INTO DANGER: THIS MAY BE TERMED THE BUSINESS OF THE GENERAL.
THOSE LOOK LIKE NESTS UP THERE.
THEY'RE A SPECIAL BREED OF ARMY ANT NESTS. I'VE SEEN THEM BEFORE ON TOUR IN THE JUNGLE.

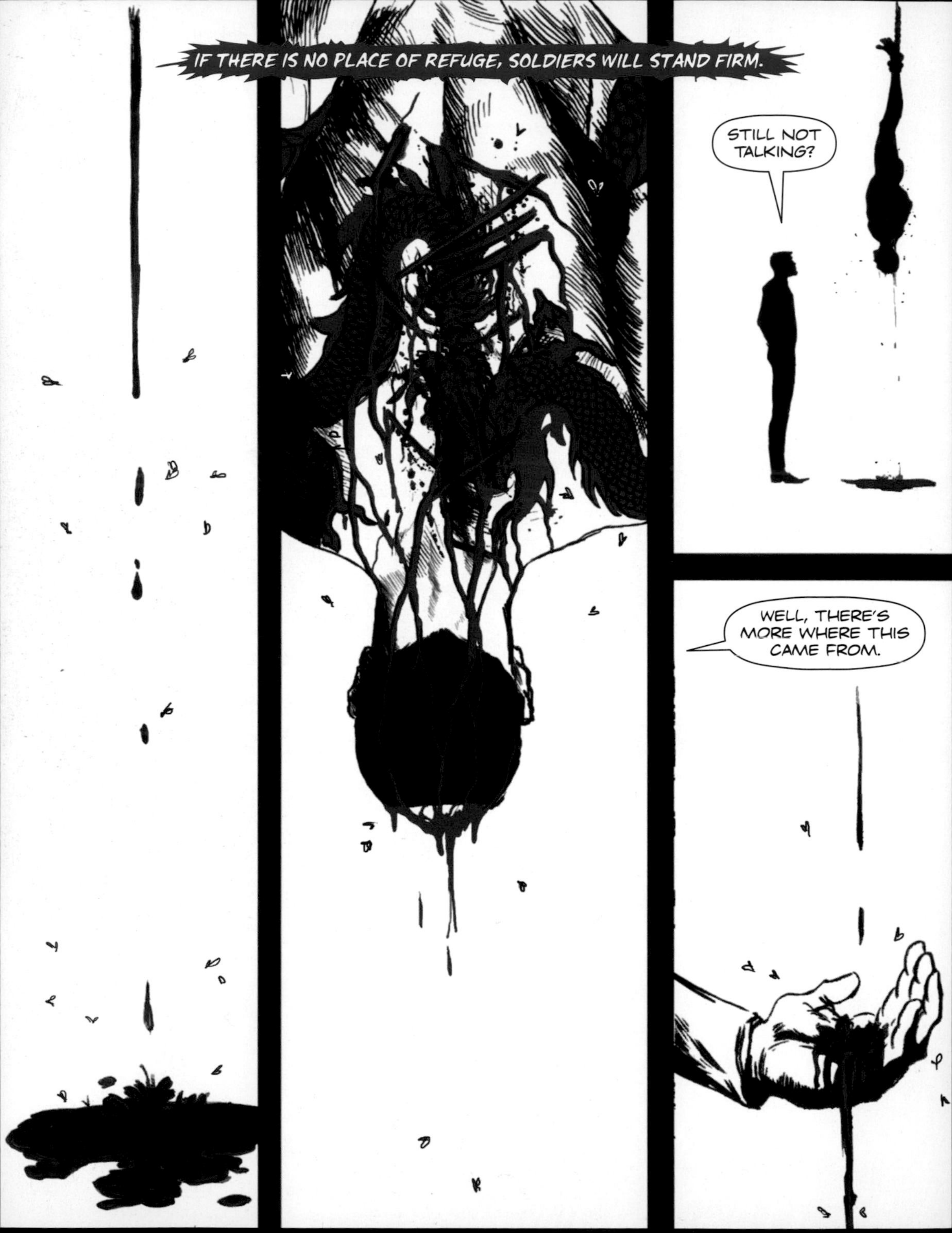
IF THERE IS NO PLACE OF REFUGE, SOLDIERS WILL STAND FIRM.
STILL NOT TALKING?
WELL, THERE'S MORE WHERE THIS CAME FROM.

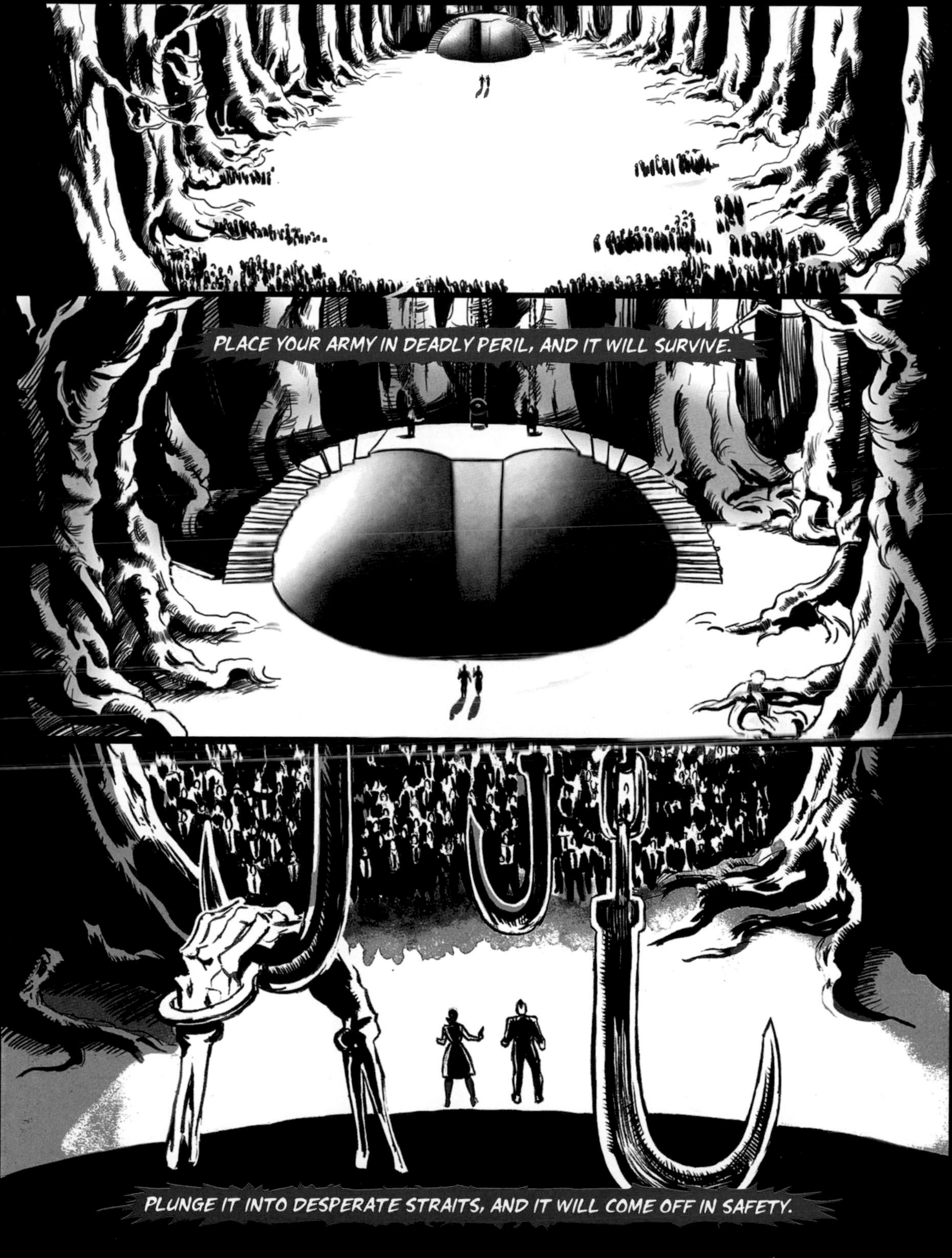
PLACE YOUR ARMY IN DEADLY PERIL, AND IT WILL SURVIVE.
PLUNGE IT INTO DESPERATE STRAITS, AND IT WILL COME OFF IN SAFETY.

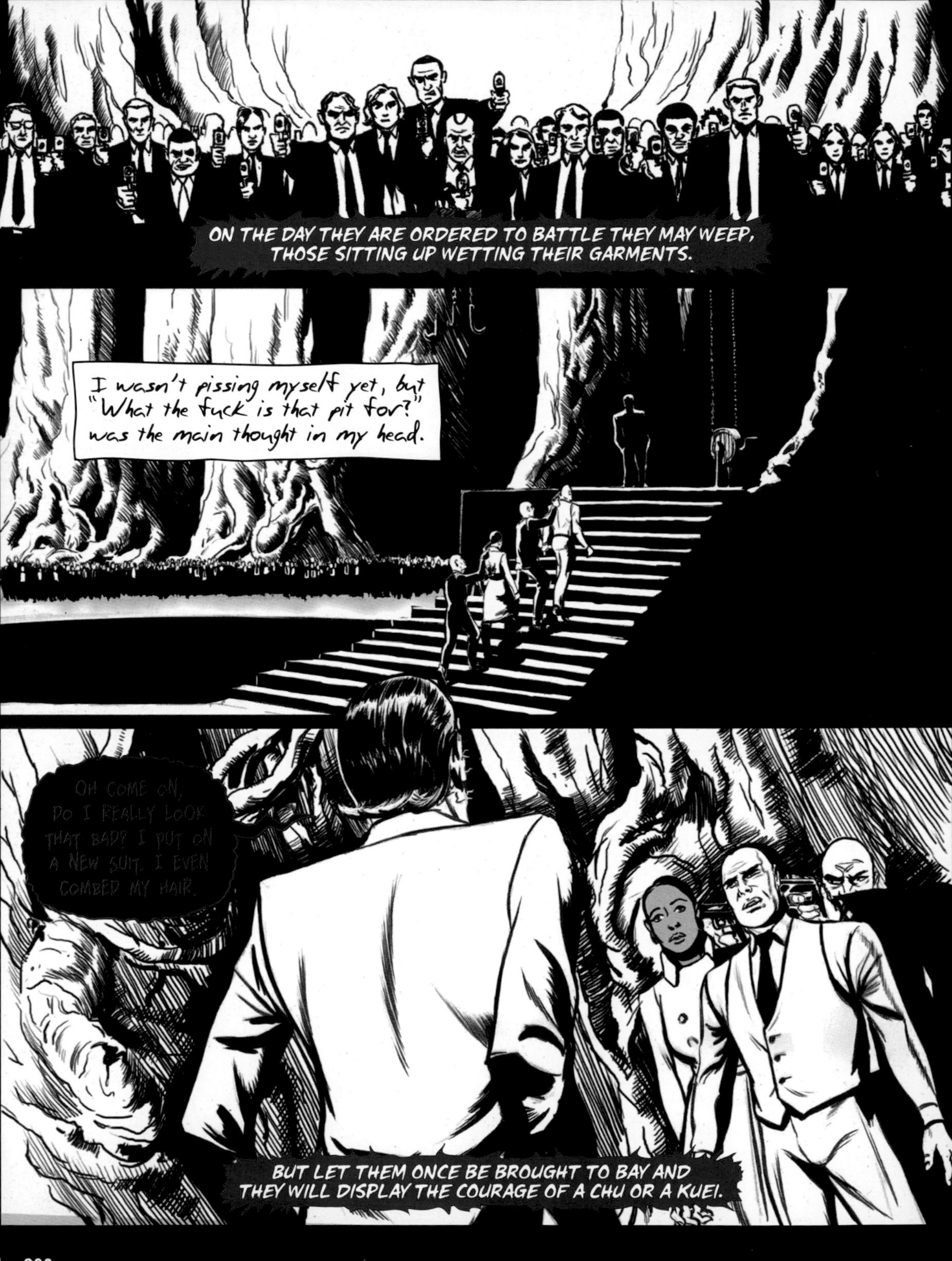
ON THE DAY THEY ARE ORDERED TO BATTLE THEY MAY WEEP, THOSE SITTING UP WETTING THEIR GARMENTS.
I wasn't pissing myself yet, but "What the fuck is that pit for?" was the main thought in my head.
OH COME ON, DO I REALLY LOOK THAT BAD? I PUT ON A NEW SUIT. I EVEN COMBED MY HAIR.
BUT LET THEM ONCE BE BROUGHT TO BAY AND THEY WILL DISPLAY THE COURAGE OF A CHU OR A KUEI.

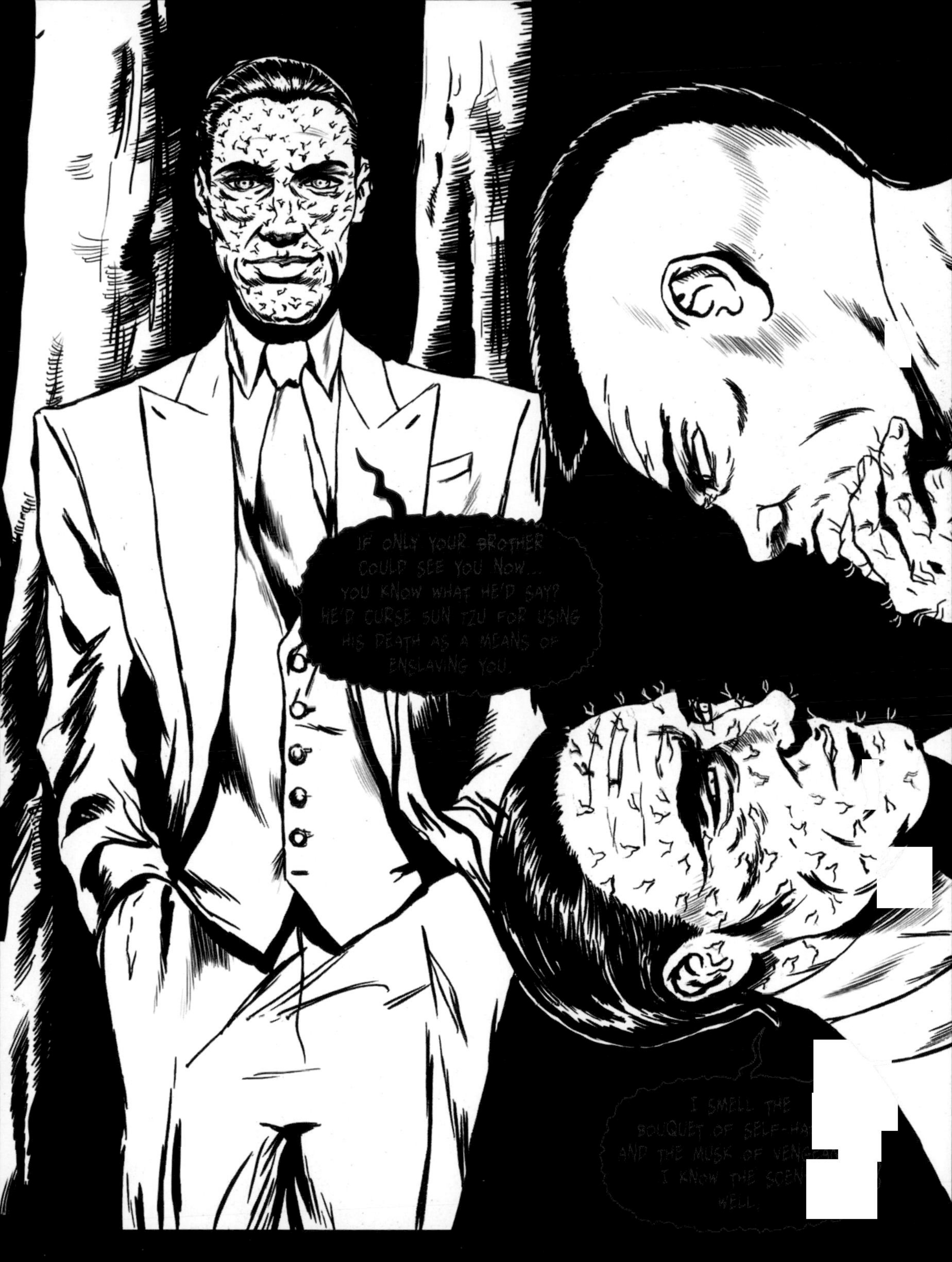
IF ONLY YOUR BROTHER COULD SEE YOU NOW... YOU KNOW WHAT HE'D SAY? HE'D CURSE SUN TZU FOR USING HIS DEATH AS A MEANS OF ENSLAVING YOU.
I SMELL THE BOUQUET OF SELF-HA AND THE MUSK OF VENG I KNOW THE SCEN WELL.

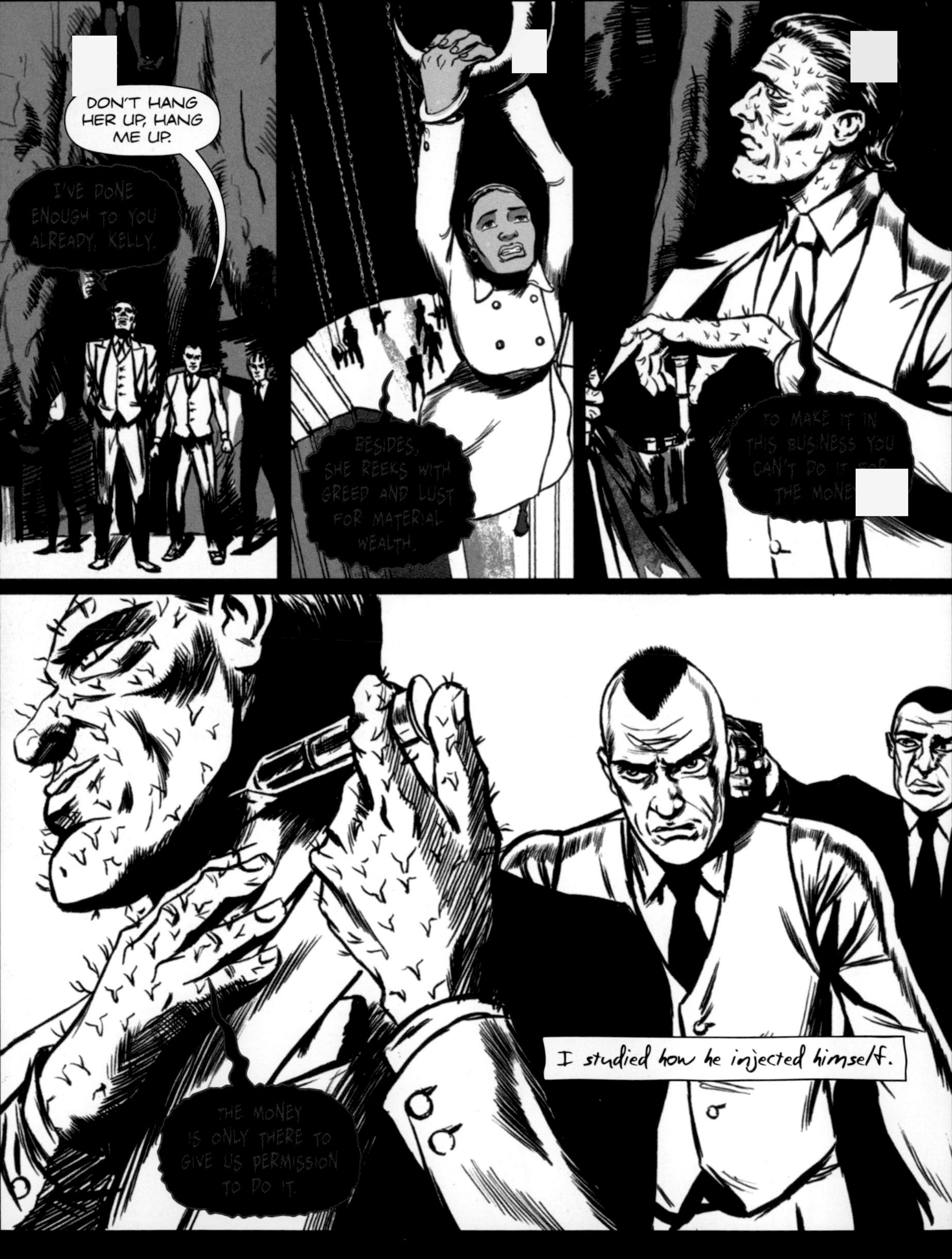
DON'T HANG HER UP, HANG ME UP.
I'VE DONE ENOUGH TO YOU ALREADY, KELLY.
BESIDES, SHE REEKS WITH GREED AND LUST FOR MATERIAL WEALTH.
TO MAKE IT IN THIS BUSINESS YOU CAN'T DO IT
I studied how he injected himself.
THE MONEY IS ONLY THERE TO GIVE US PERMISSION TO DO IT.

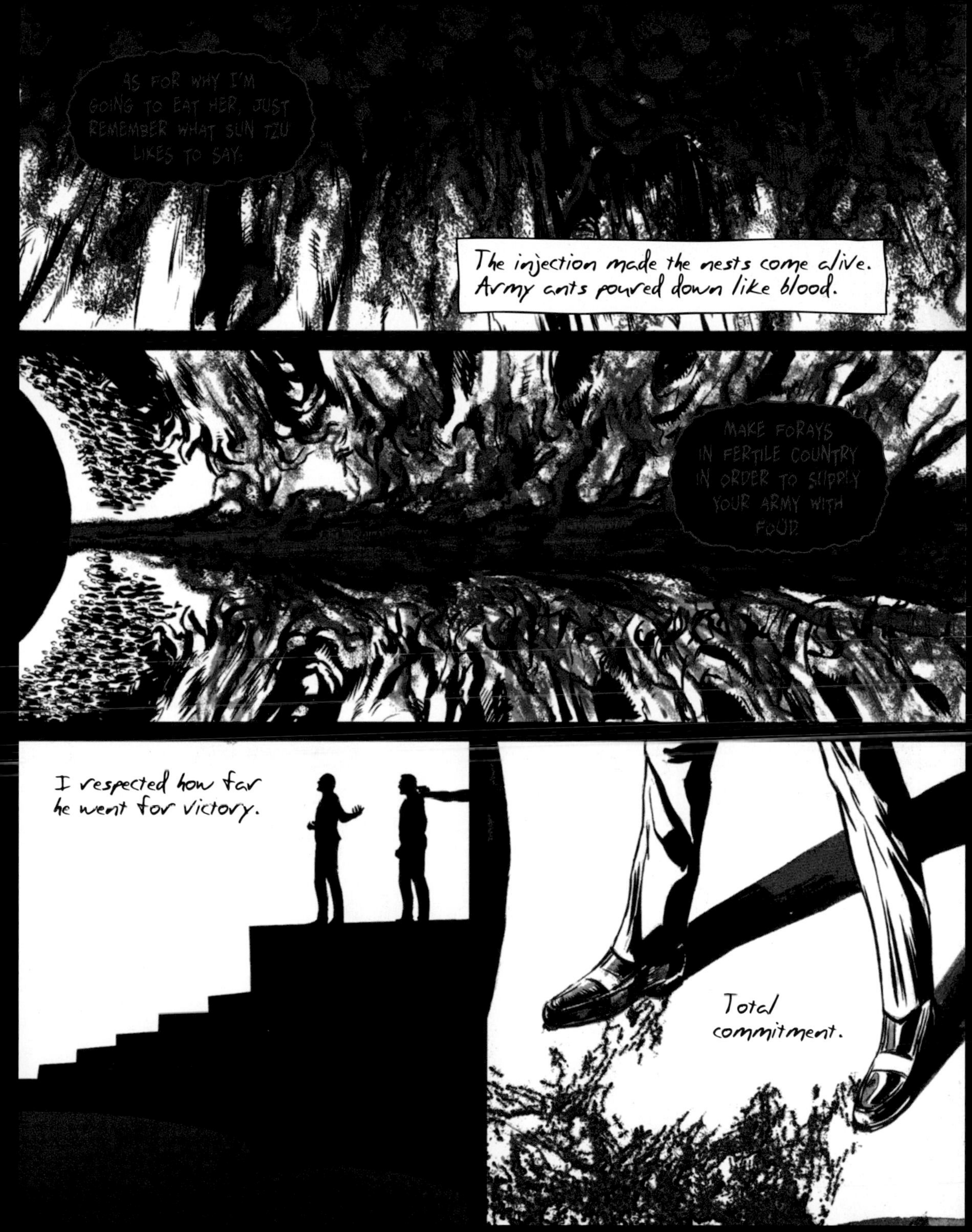
AS FOR WHY I'M GOING TO EAT HER, JUST REMEMBER WHAT SUN TZU LIKES TO SAY:
The injection made the nests come alive. Army ants poured down like blood.
MAKE FORAYS IN FERTILE COUNTRY IN ORDER TO SUPPLY YOUR ARMY WITH FOOD.
I respected how far he went for victory.
Total commitment.

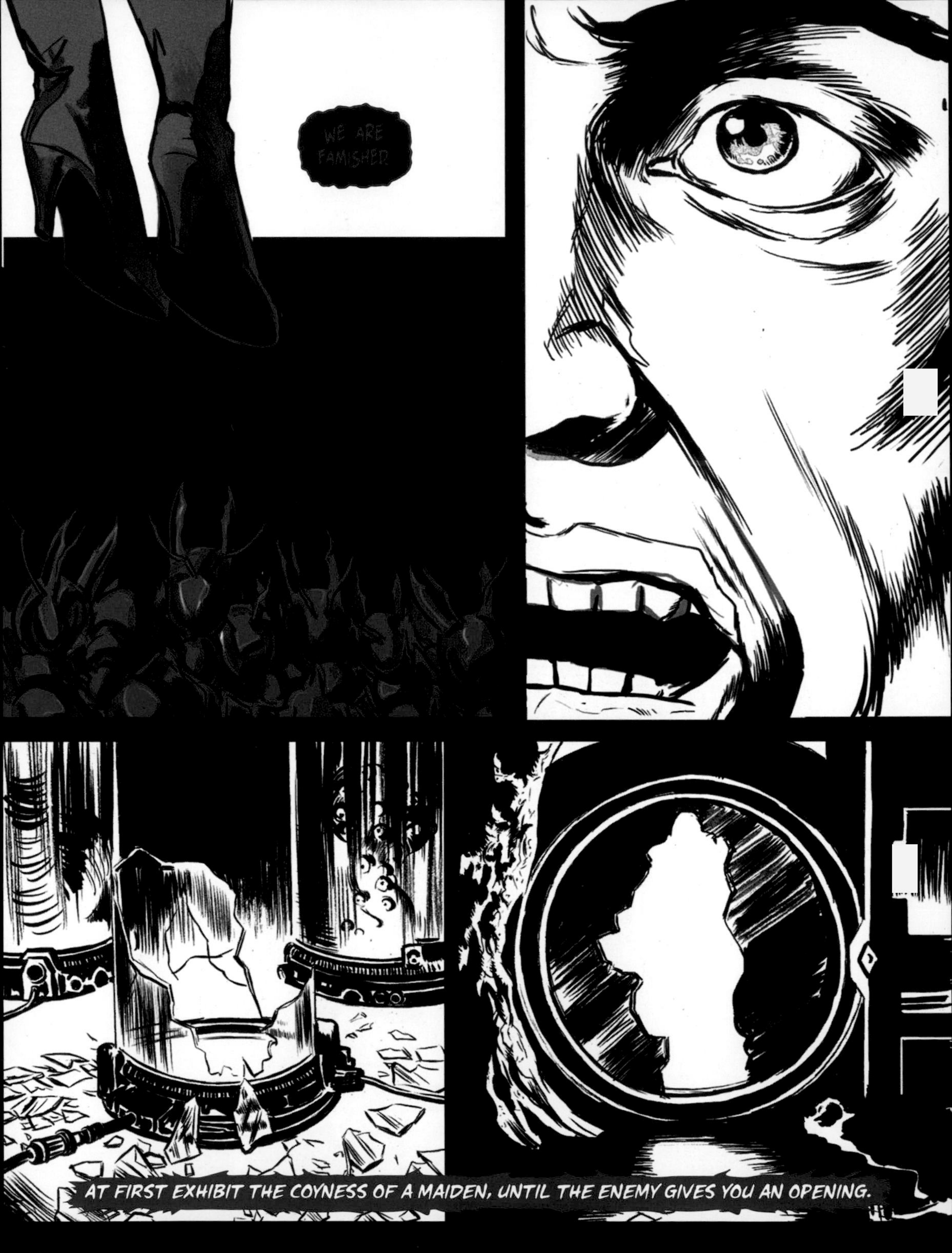
WE ARE FAMISHED
AT FIRST EXHIBIT THE COYNESS OF A MAIDEN, UNTIL THE ENEMY GIVES YOU AN OPENING.

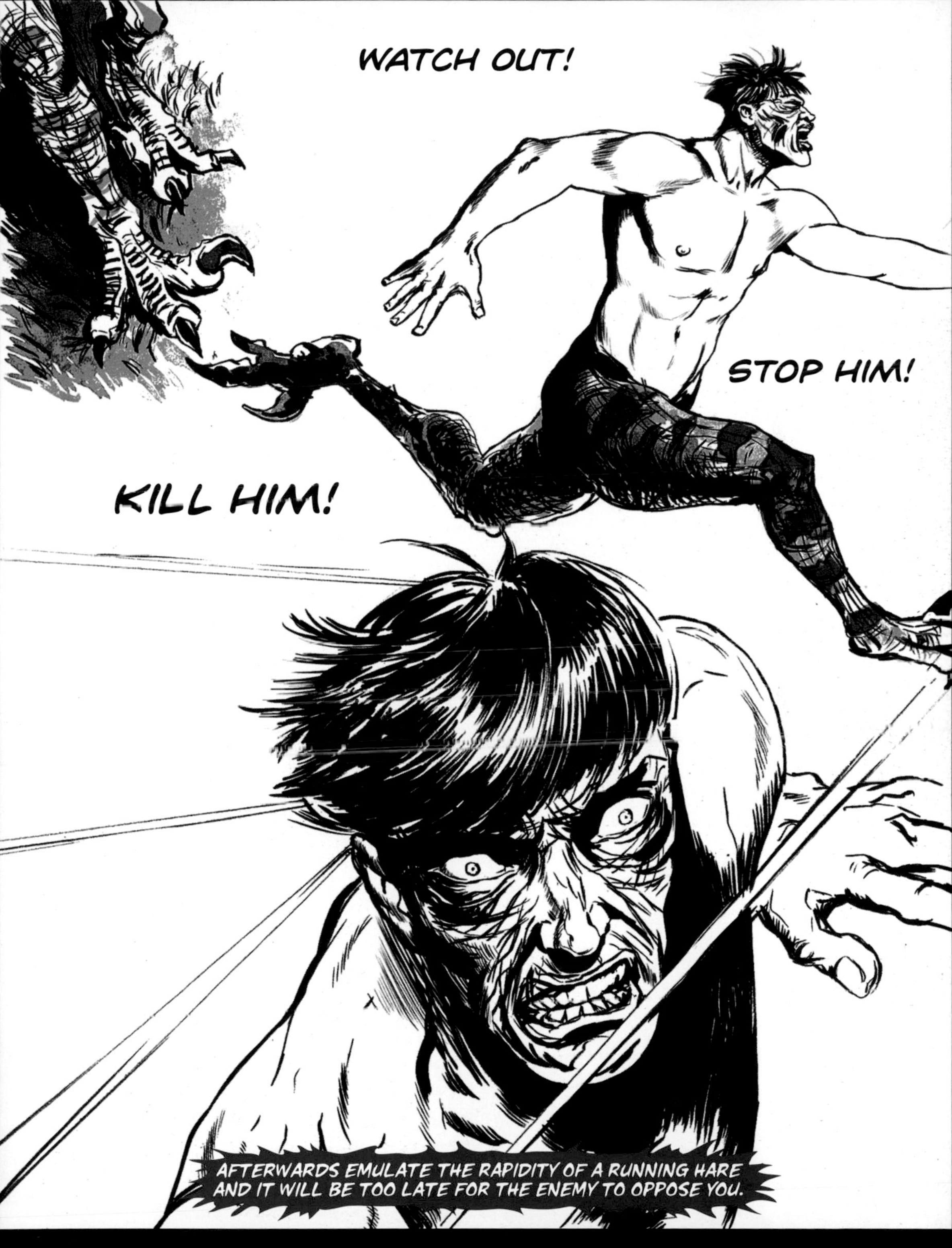
WATCH OUT!
STOP HIM!
KILL HIM!
AFTERWARDS EMULATE THE RAPIDITY OF A RUNNING HARE AND IT WILL BE TOO LATE FOR THE ENEMY TO OPPOSE YOU.

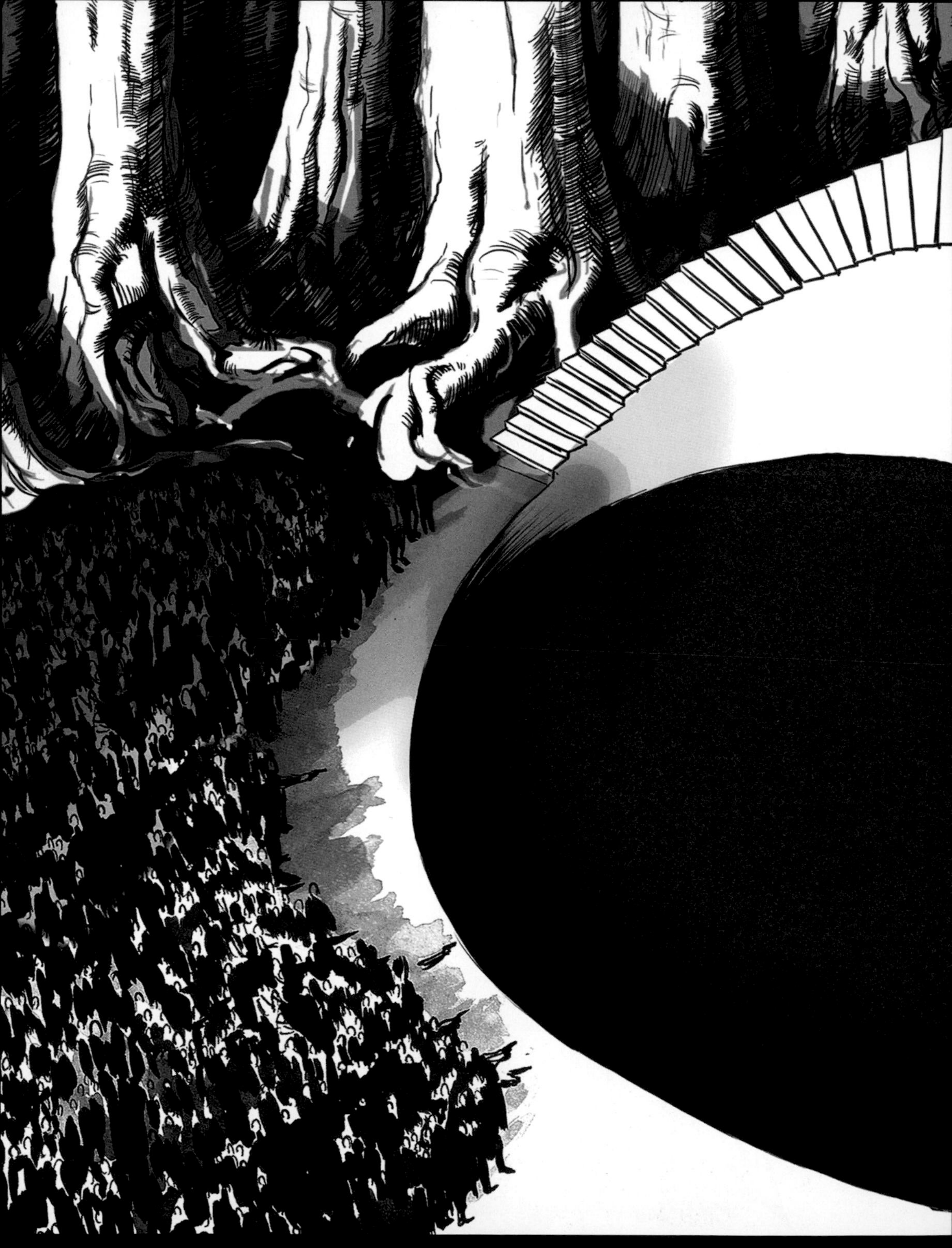

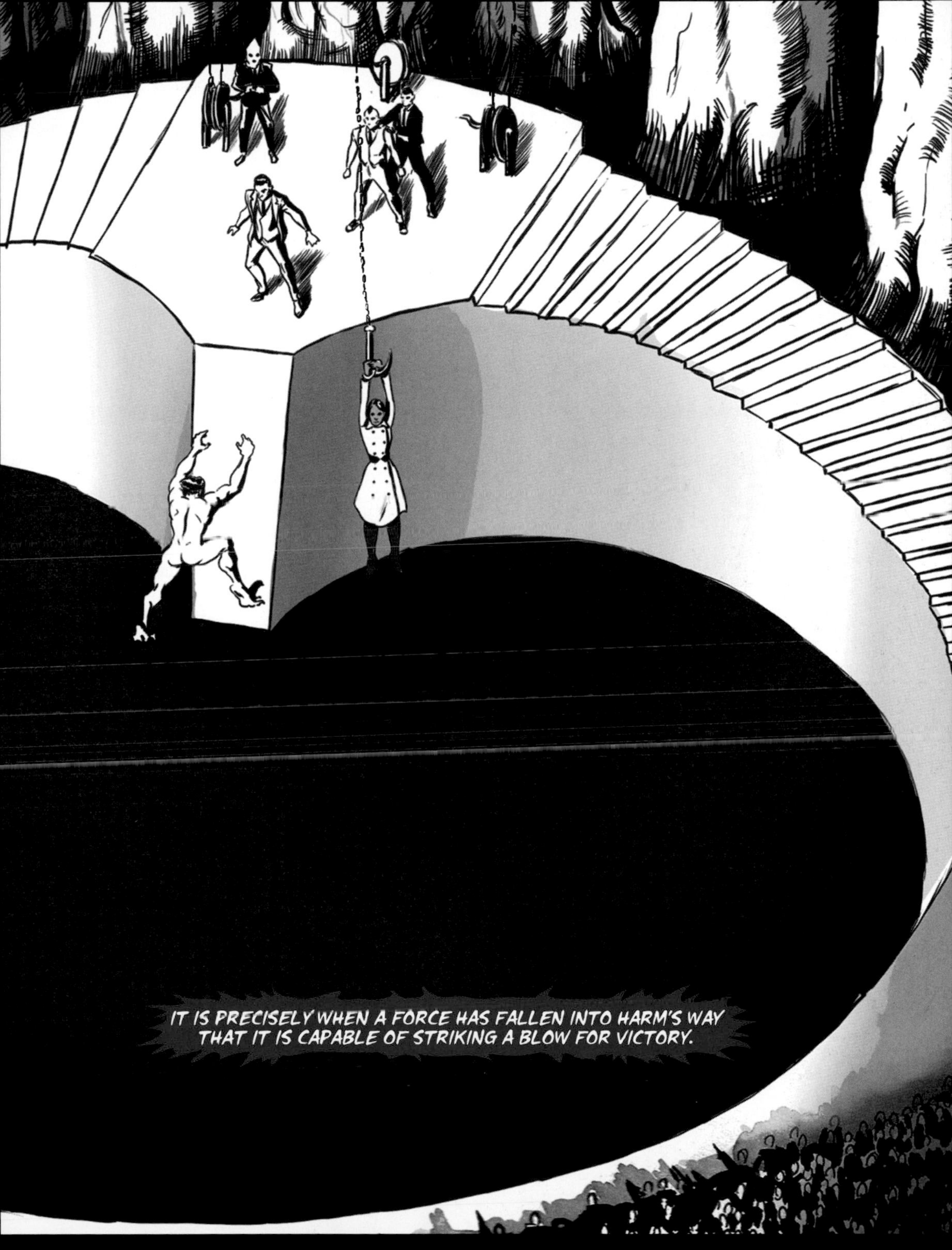
IT IS PRECISELY WHEN A FORCE HAS FALLEN INTO HARM'S WAY
THAT IT IS CAPABLE OF STRIKING A BLOW FOR VICTORY.

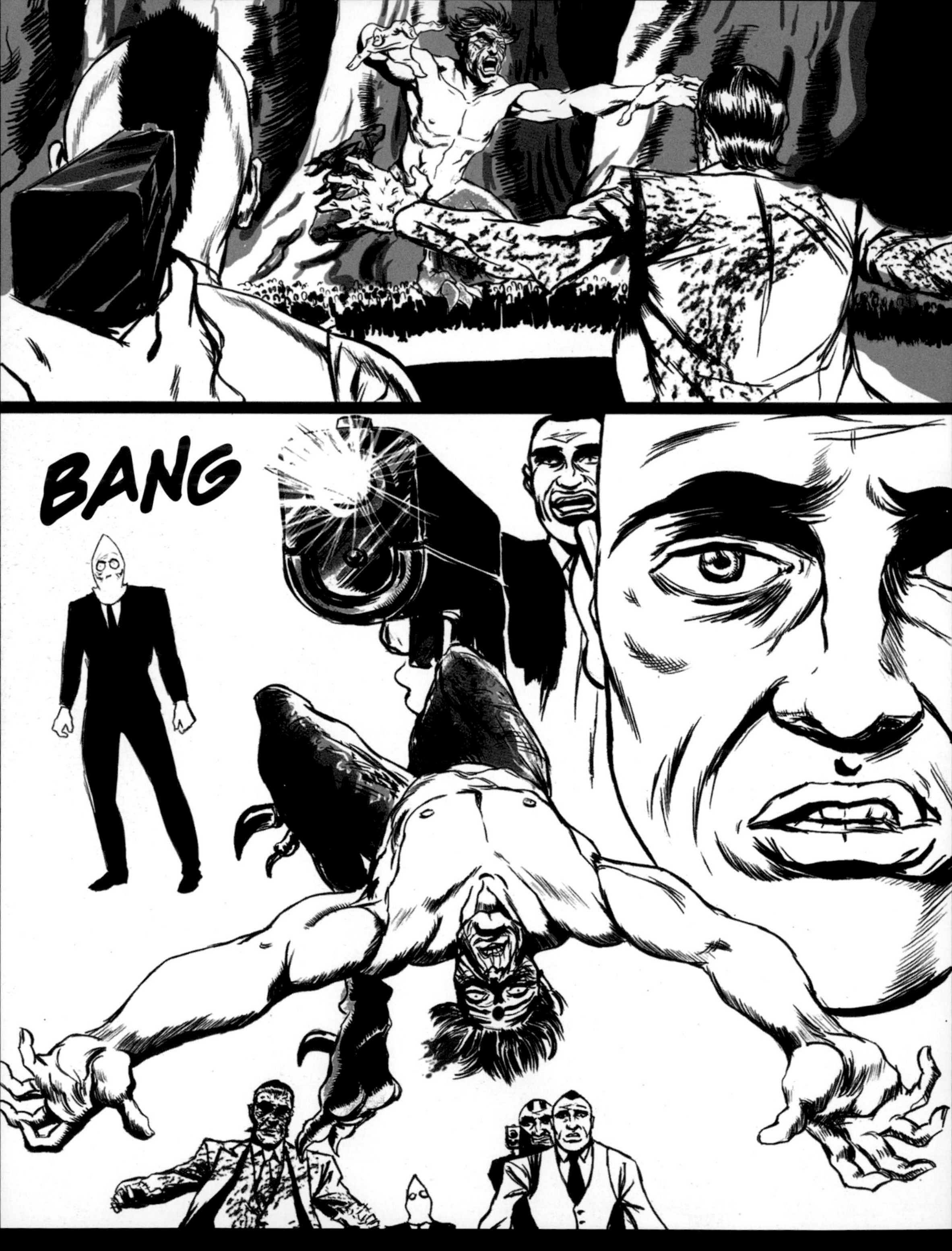
BANG

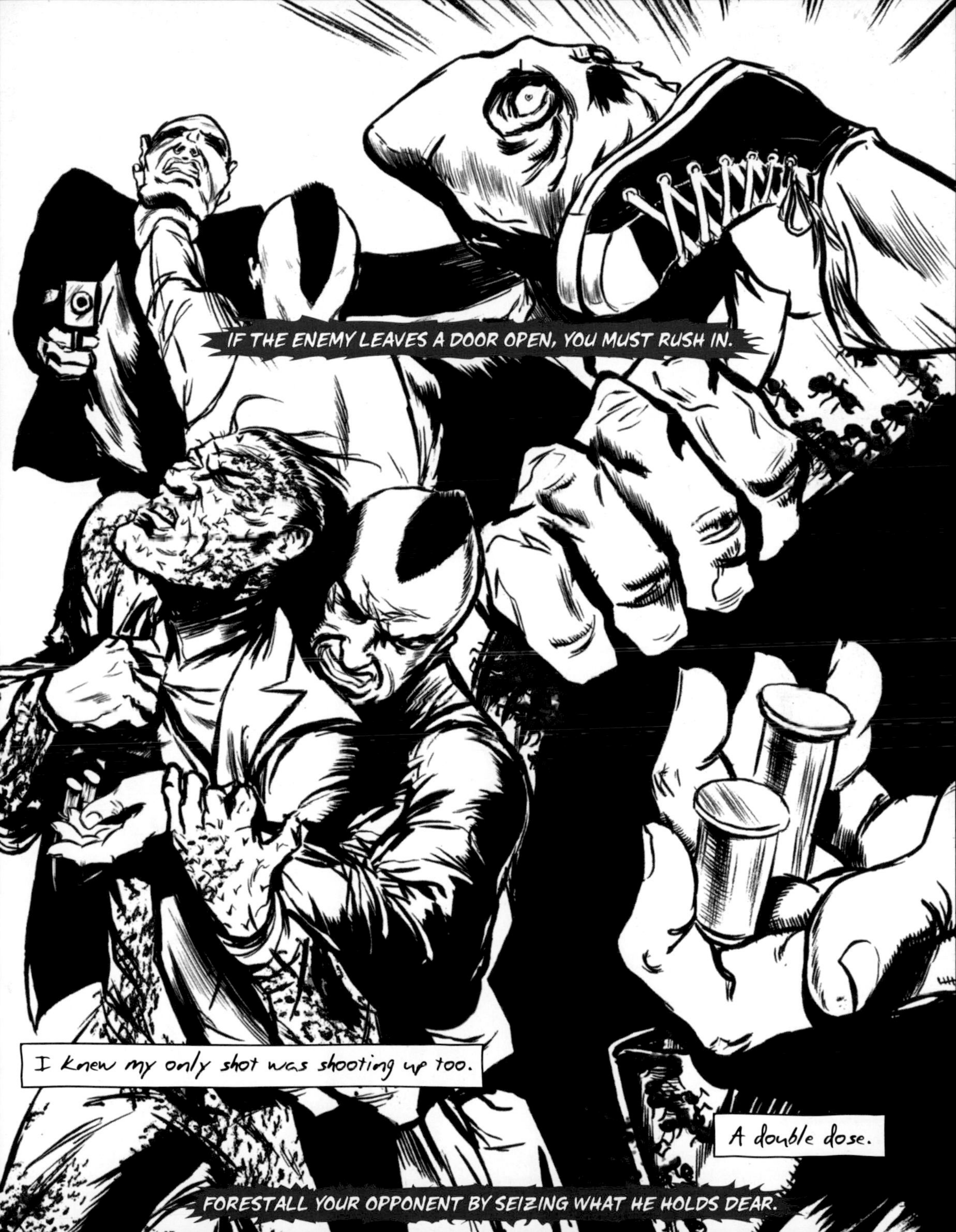
IF THE ENEMY LEAVES A DOOR OPEN, YOU MUST RUSH IN.
I knew my only shot was shooting up too.
A double dose.
FORESTALL YOUR OPPONENT BY SEIZING WHAT HE HOLDS DEAR.

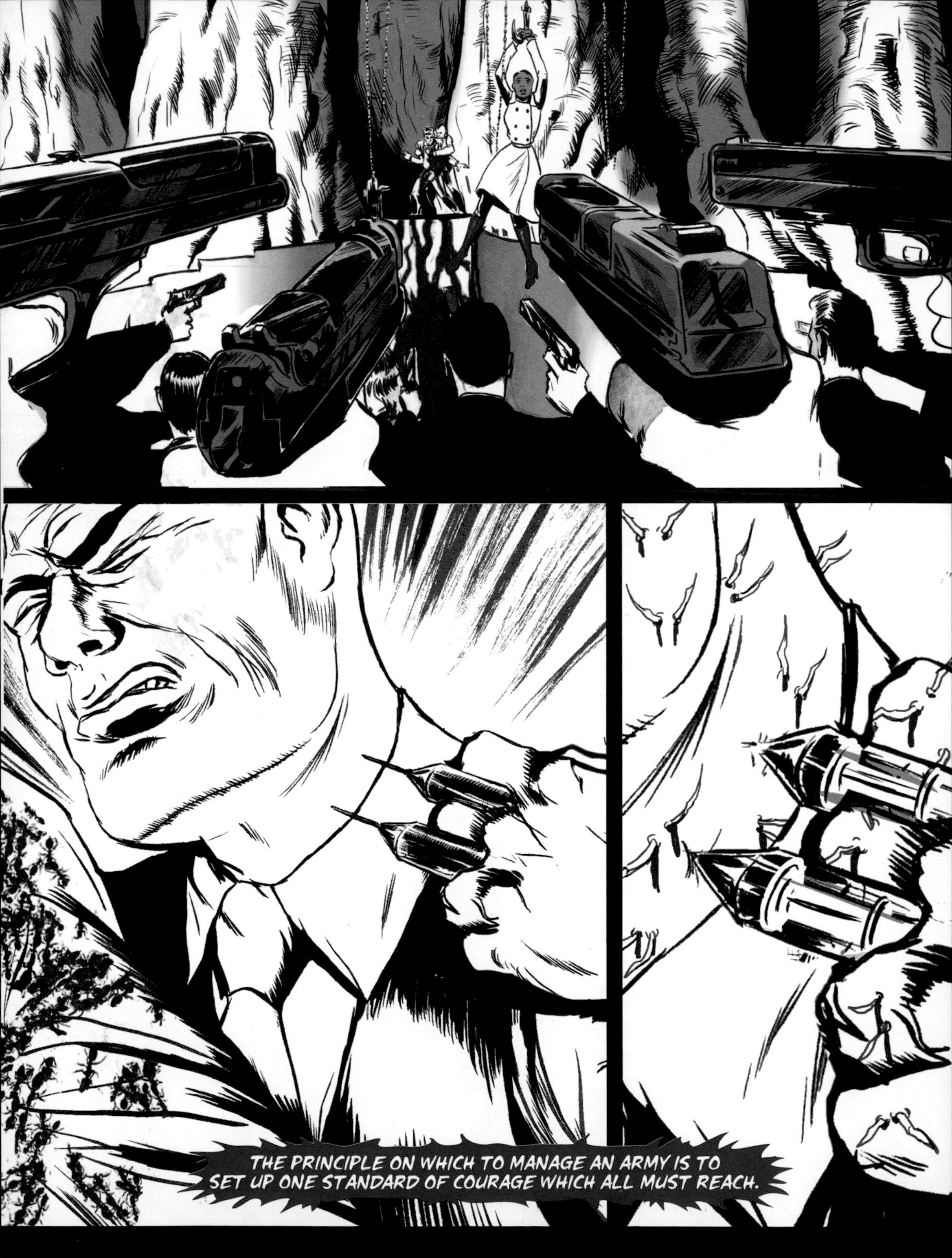
THE PRINCIPLE ON WHICH TO MANAGE AN ARMY IS TO SET UP ONE STANDARD OF COURAGE WHICH ALL MUST REACH.

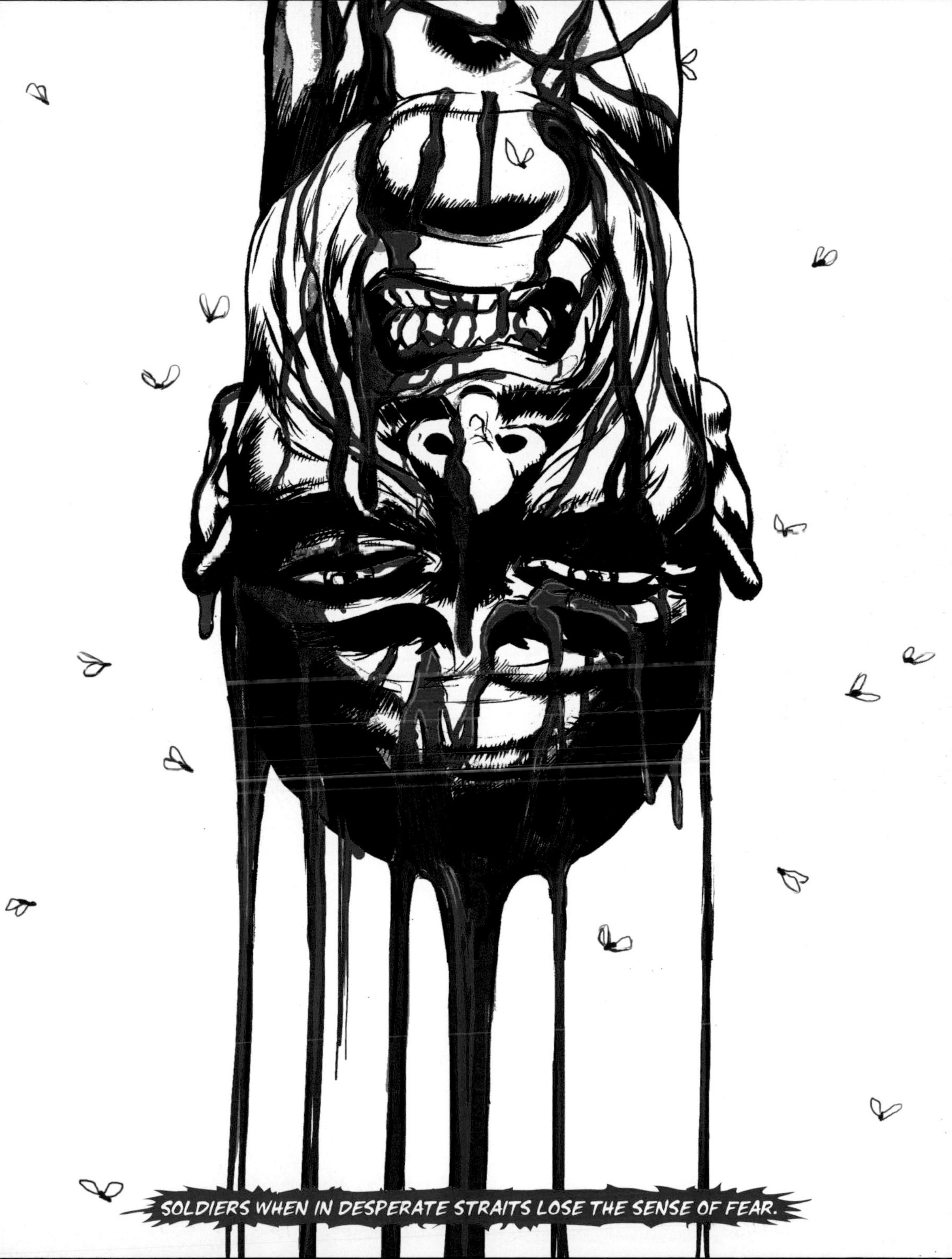
SOLDIERS WHEN IN DESPERATE STRAITS LOSE THE SENSE OF FEAR.

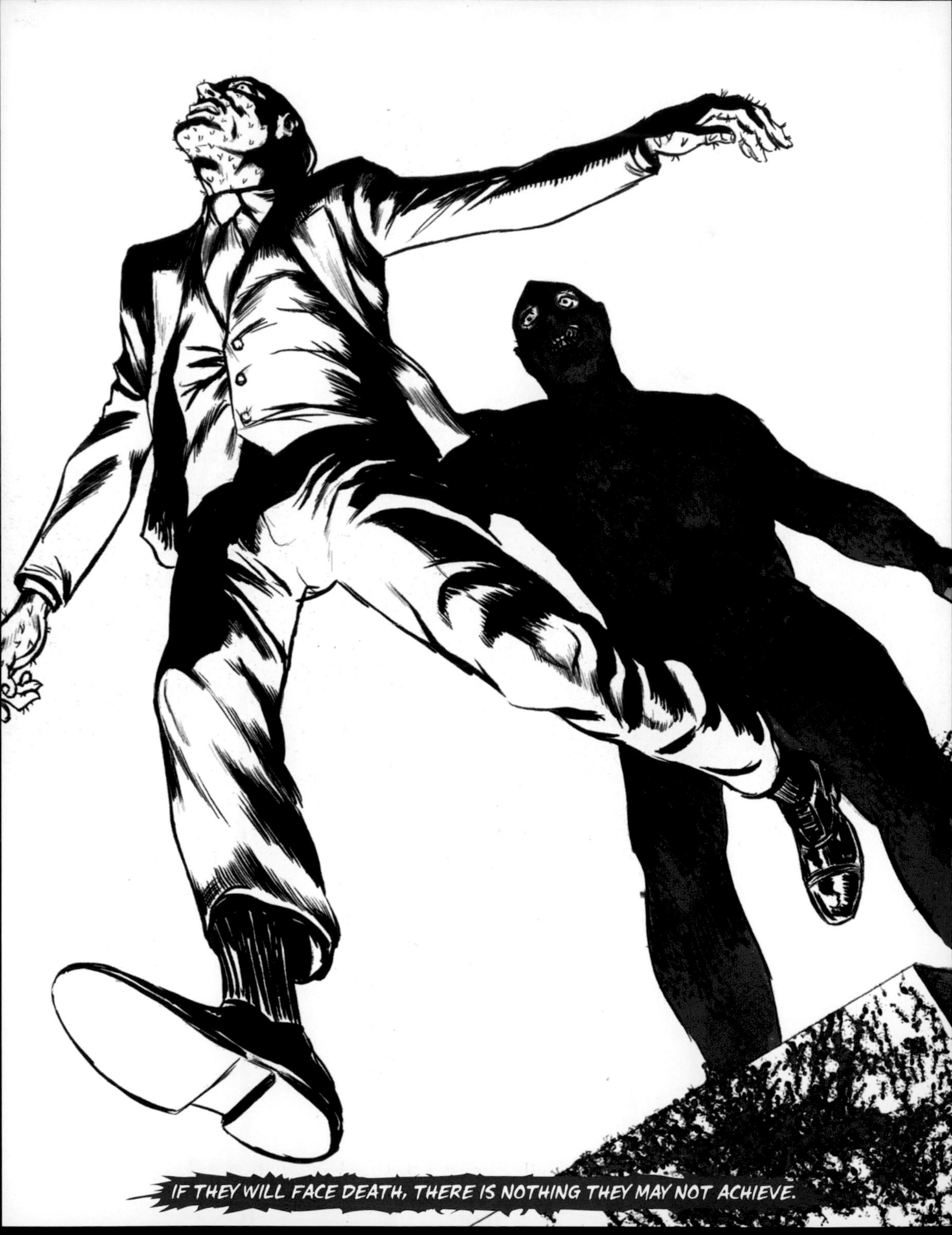
IF THEY WILL FACE DEATH, THERE IS NOTHING THEY MAY NOT ACHIEVE.

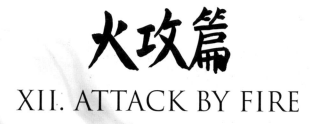

火攻篇

XII. ATTACK BY FIRE

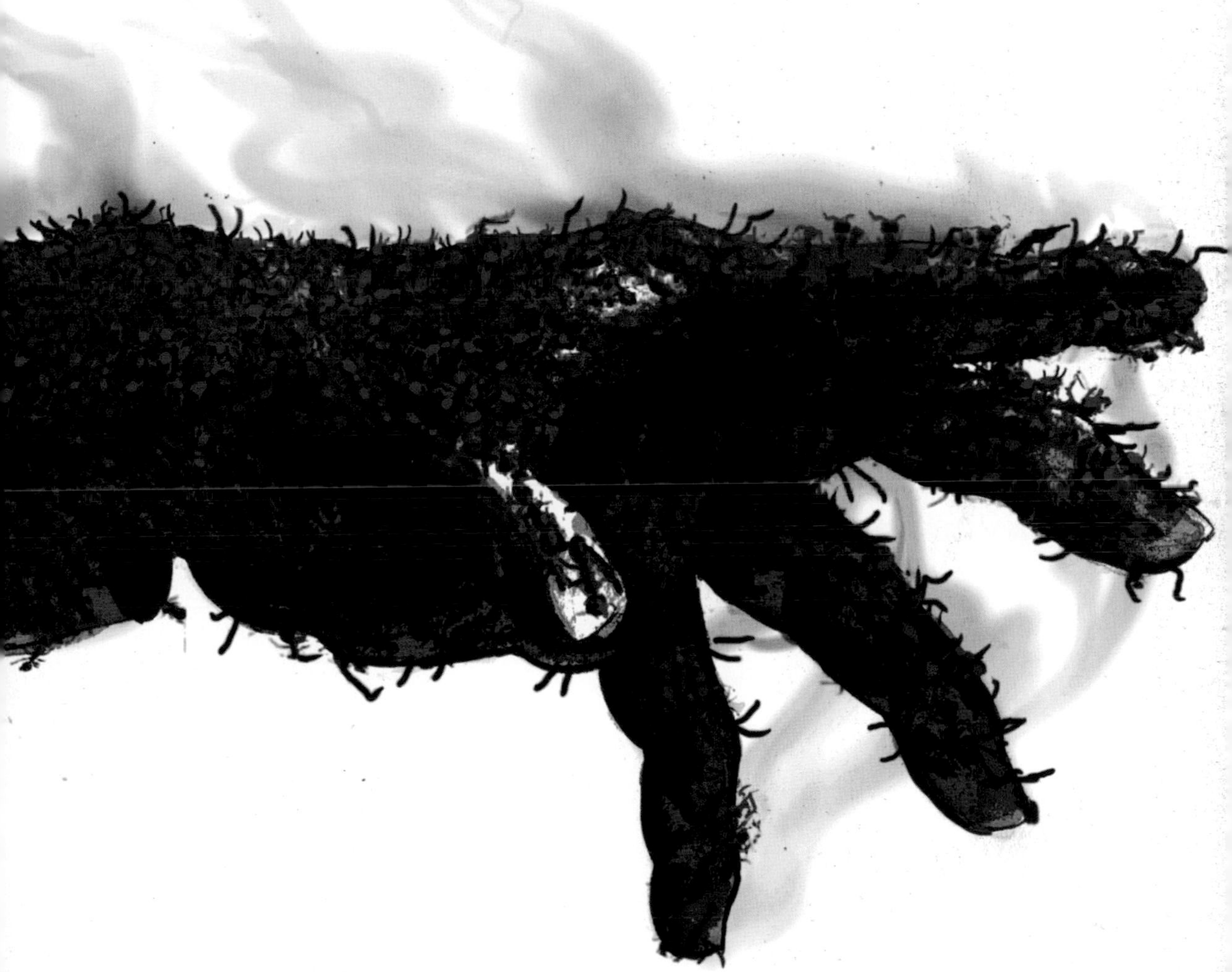

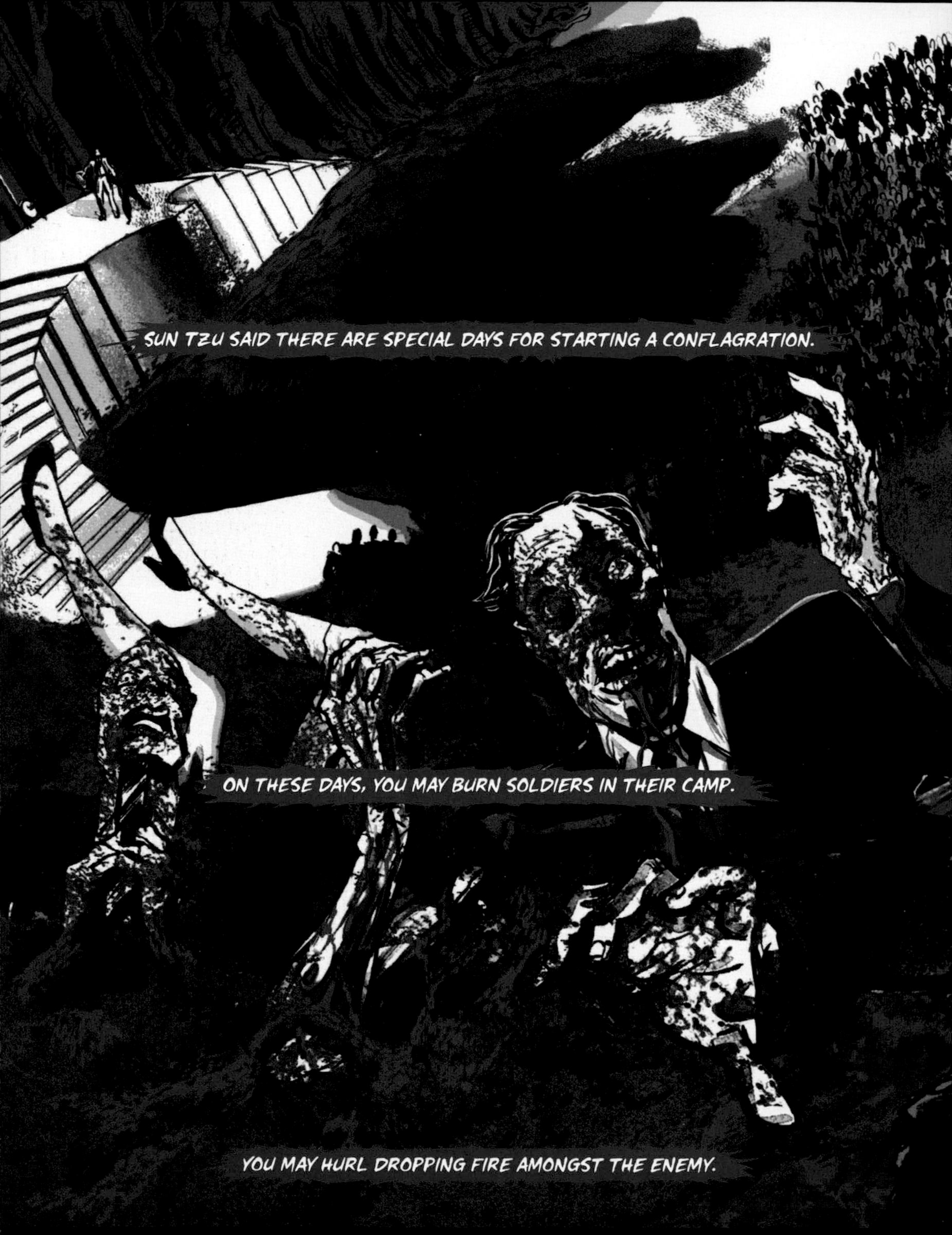
SUN TZU SAID THERE ARE SPECIAL DAYS FOR STARTING A CONFLAGRATION.
ON THESE DAYS, YOU MAY BURN SOLDIERS IN THEIR CAMP.
YOU MAY HURL DROPPING FIRE AMONGST THE ENEMY.

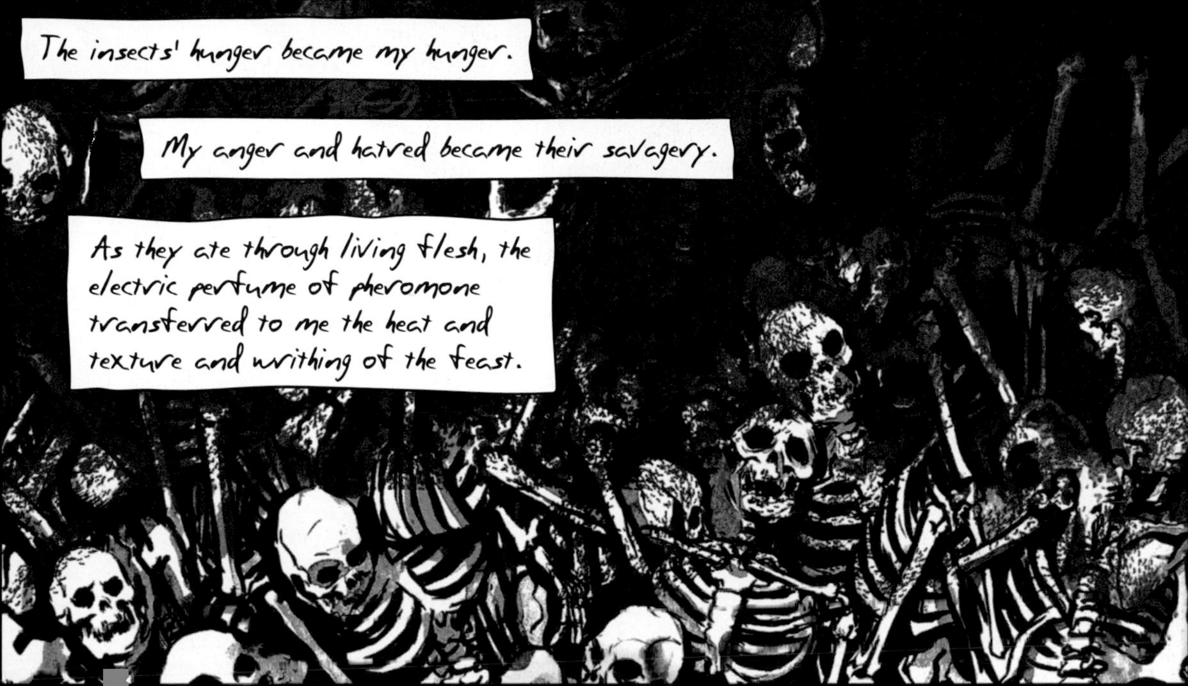
The insects' hunger became my hunger.
My anger and hatred became their savagery.
As they ate through living flesh, the electric perfume of pheromone transferred to me the heat and texture and writhing of the feast.

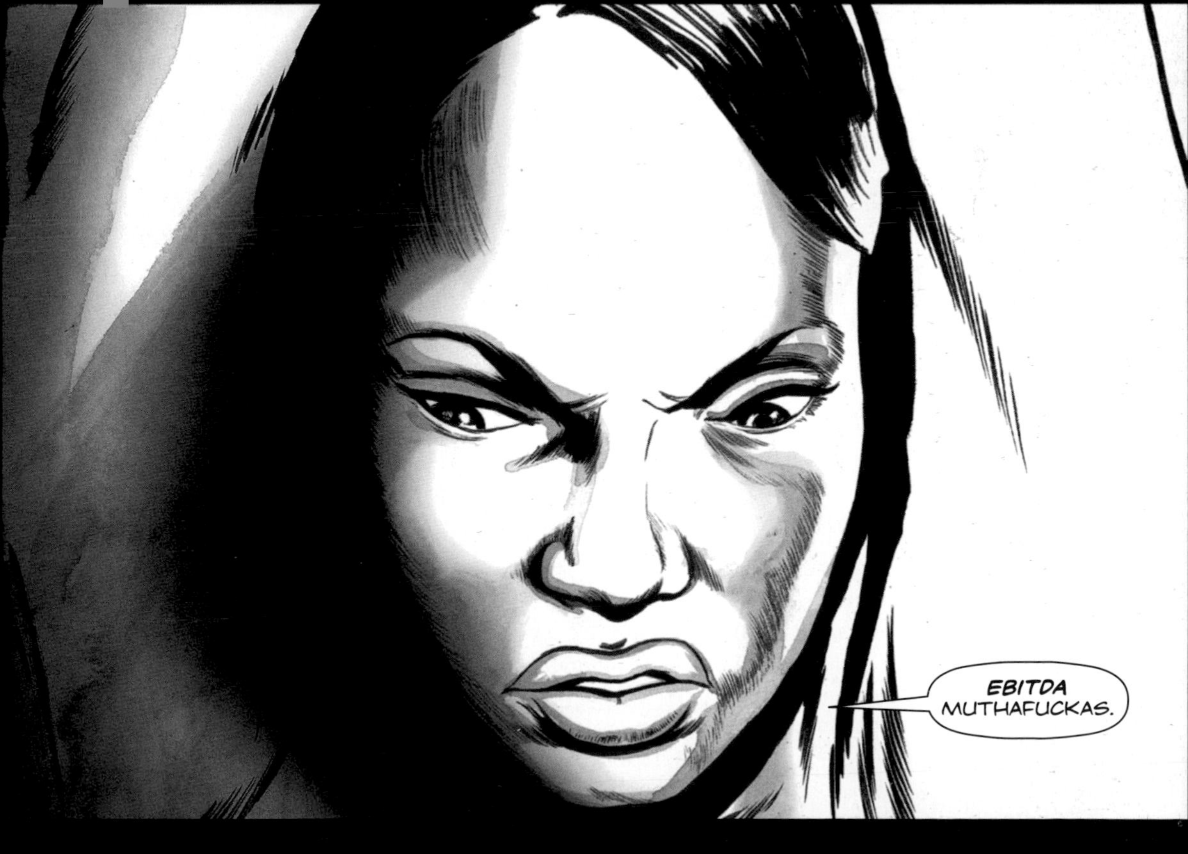
EBITDA MUTHAFUCKAS.

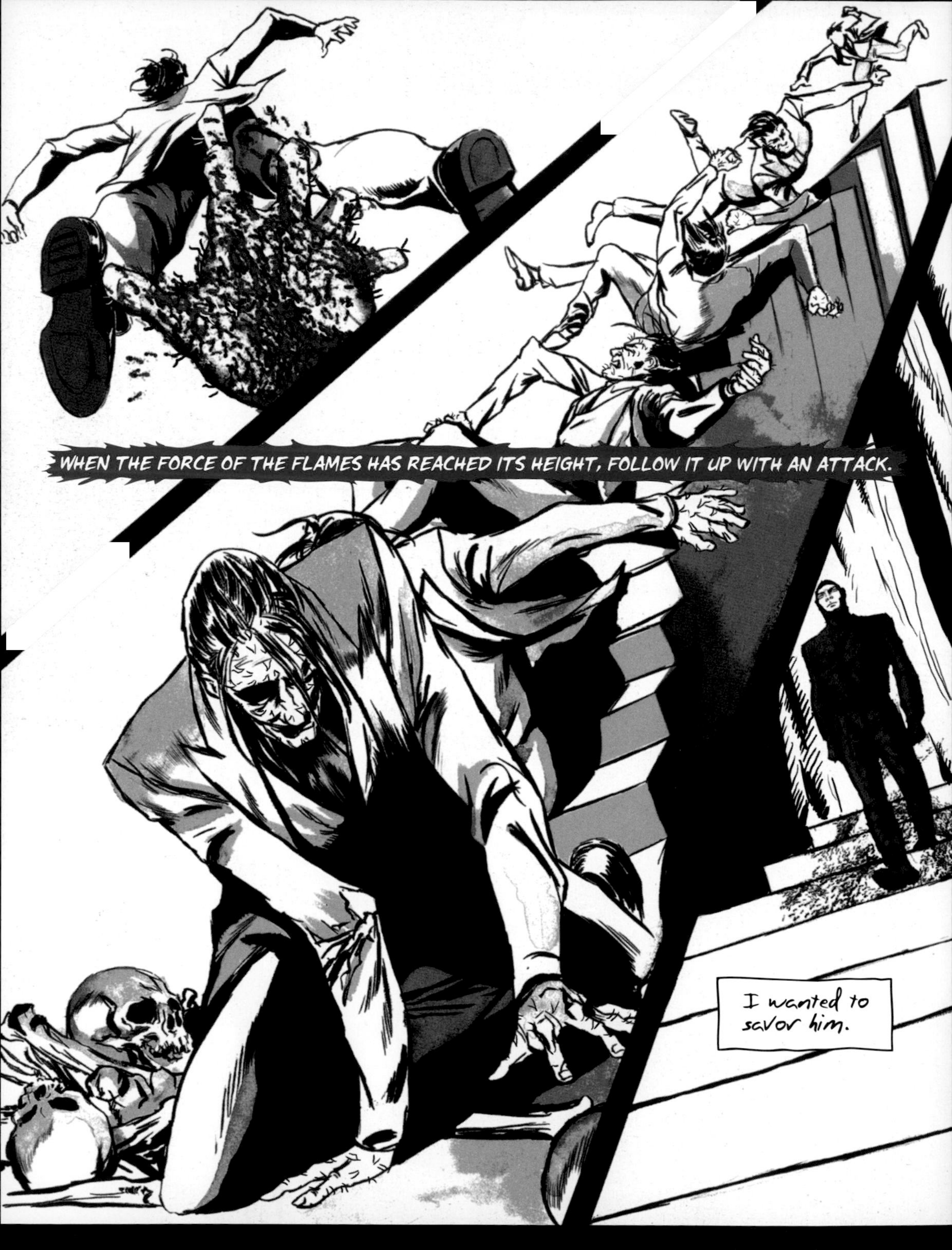
WHEN THE FORCE OF THE FLAMES HAS REACHED ITS HEIGHT, FOLLOW IT UP WITH AN ATTACK.
I wanted to savor him.

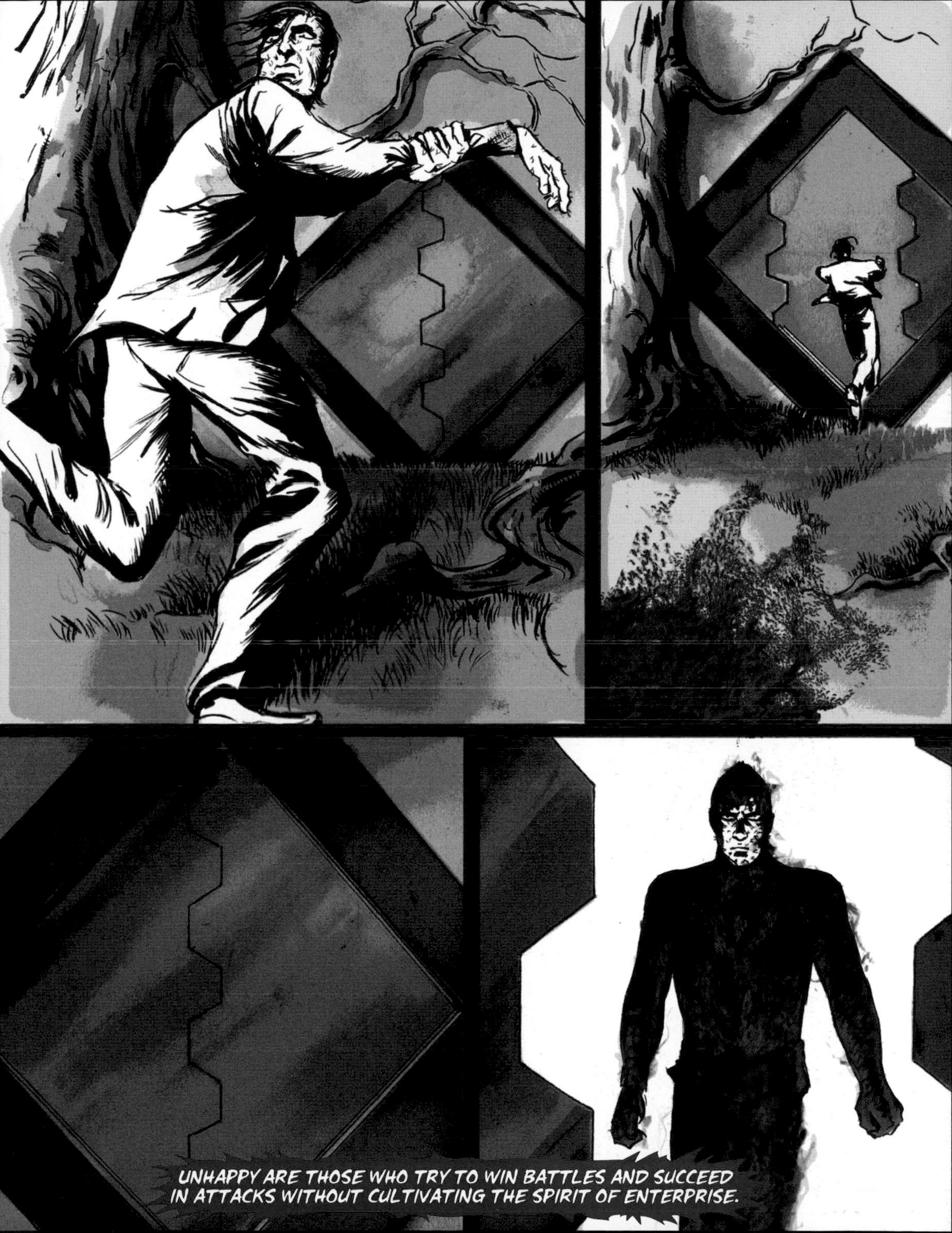
UNHAPPY ARE THOSE WHO TRY TO WIN BATTLES AND SUCCEED IN ATTACKS WITHOUT CULTIVATING THE SPIRIT OF ENTERPRISE.

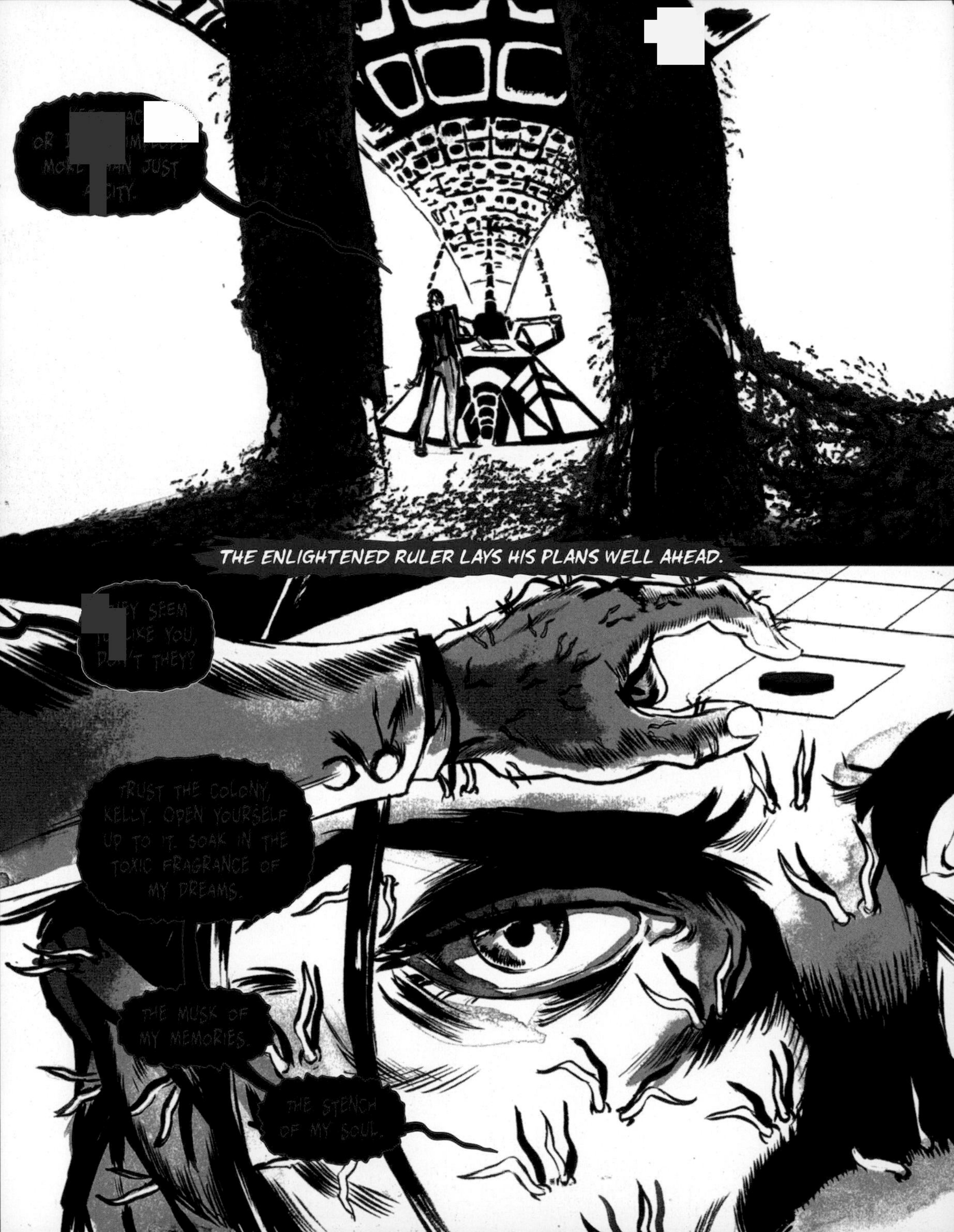
[redacted] OR [redacted] MORE [redacted]AN JUST [redacted] CITY.
THE ENLIGHTENED RULER LAYS HIS PLANS WELL AHEAD.
[redacted]EY SEEM [redacted]LIKE YOU, [redacted]'T THEY?
TRUST THE COLONY, KELLY. OPEN YOURSELF UP TO IT. SOAK IN THE TOXIC FRAGRANCE OF MY DREAMS.
THE MUSK OF MY MEMORIES.
THE STENCH OF MY SOUL.

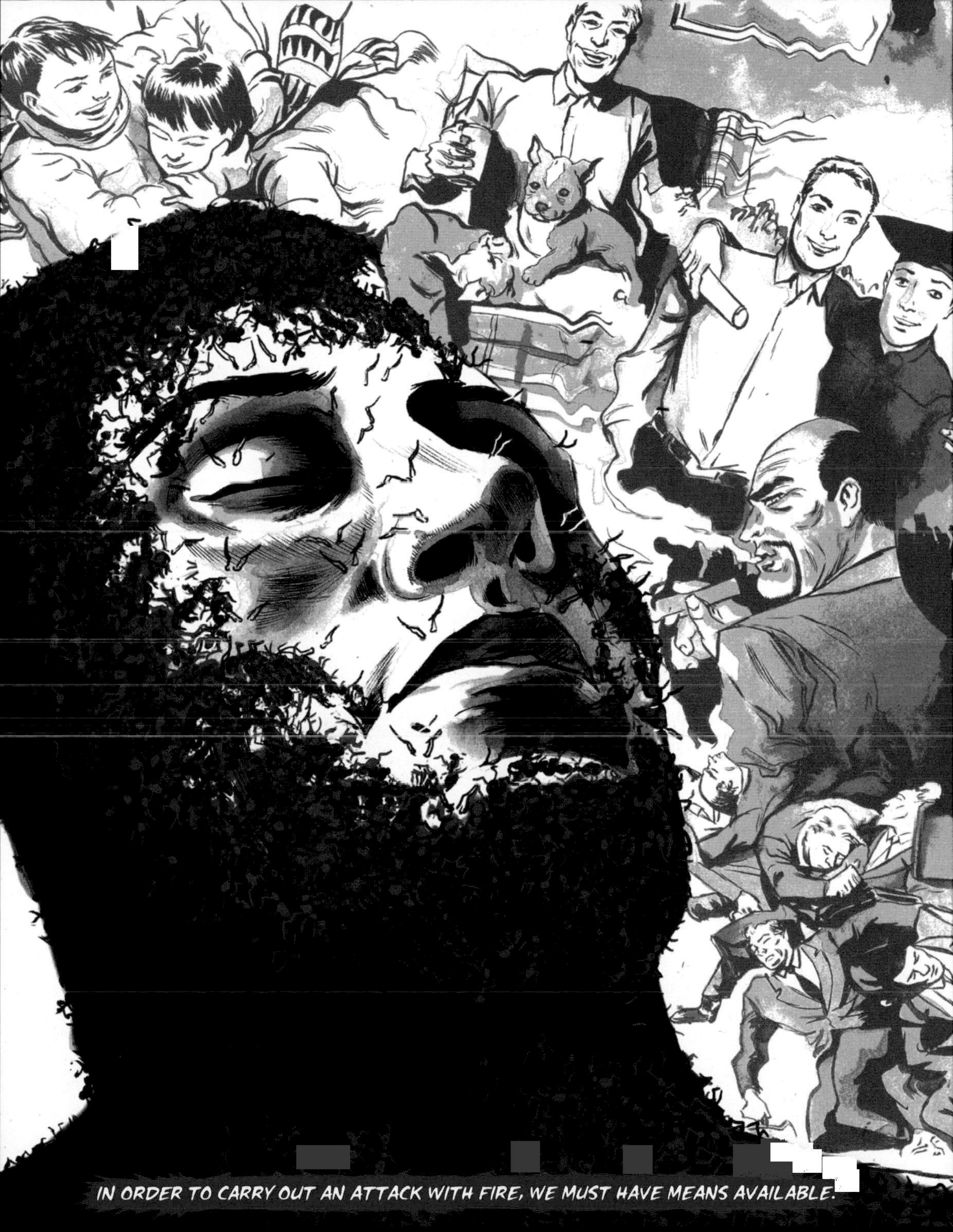
IN ORDER TO CARRY OUT AN ATTACK WITH FIRE, WE MUST HAVE MEANS AVAILABLE.

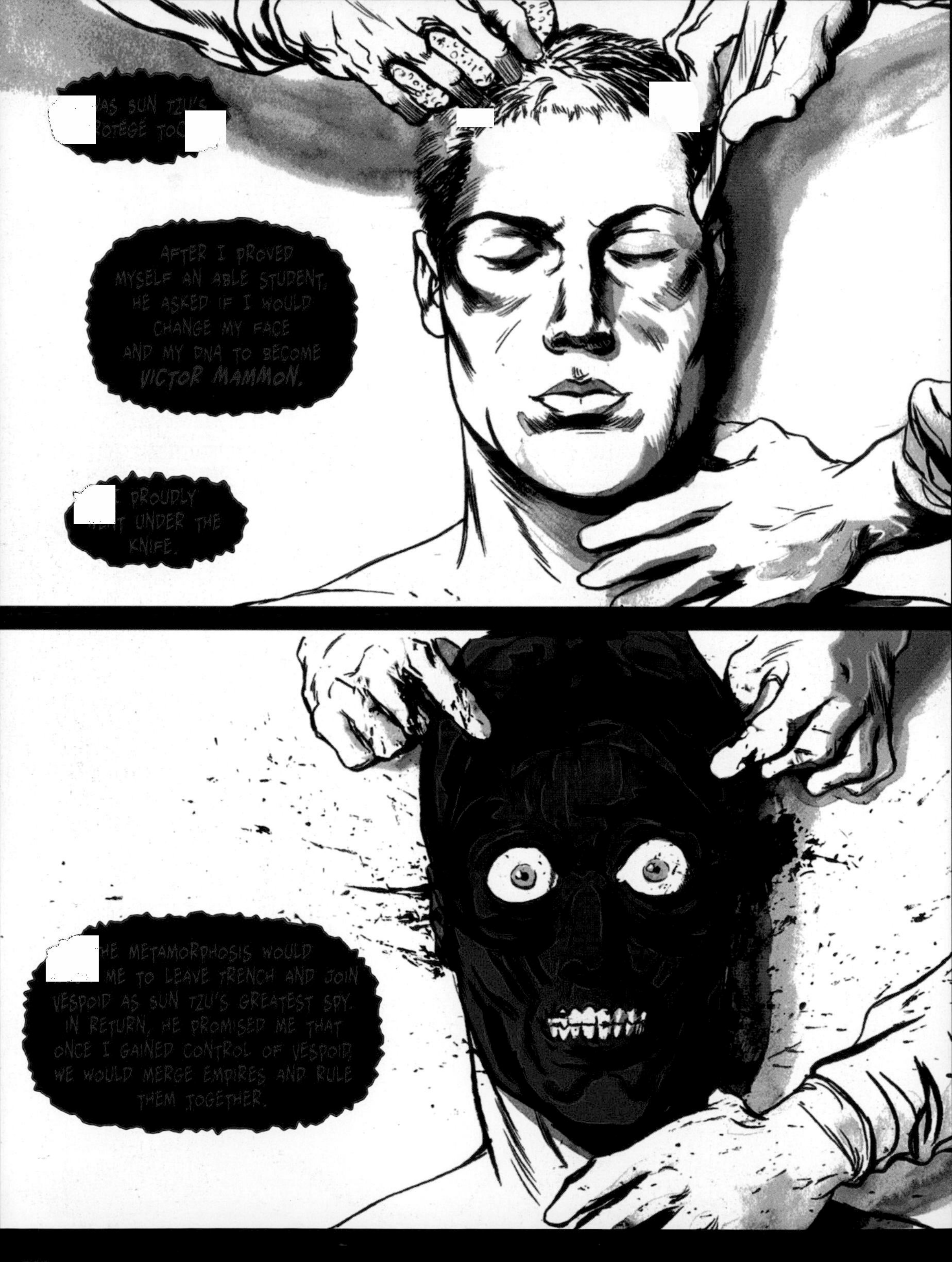
[redacted]AS SUN TZU'S [redacted]ROTÉGÉ TO[redacted]
AFTER I PROVED MYSELF AN ABLE STUDENT, HE ASKED IF I WOULD CHANGE MY FACE AND MY DNA TO BECOME VICTOR MAMMON.
[redacted] PROUDLY [redacted] UNDER THE KNIFE.
[redacted]HE METAMORPHOSIS WOULD [redacted] ME TO LEAVE TRENCH AND JOIN VESPOID AS SUN TZU'S GREATEST SPY. IN RETURN, HE PROMISED ME THAT ONCE I GAINED CONTROL OF VESPOID, WE WOULD MERGE EMPIRES AND RULE THEM TOGETHER.

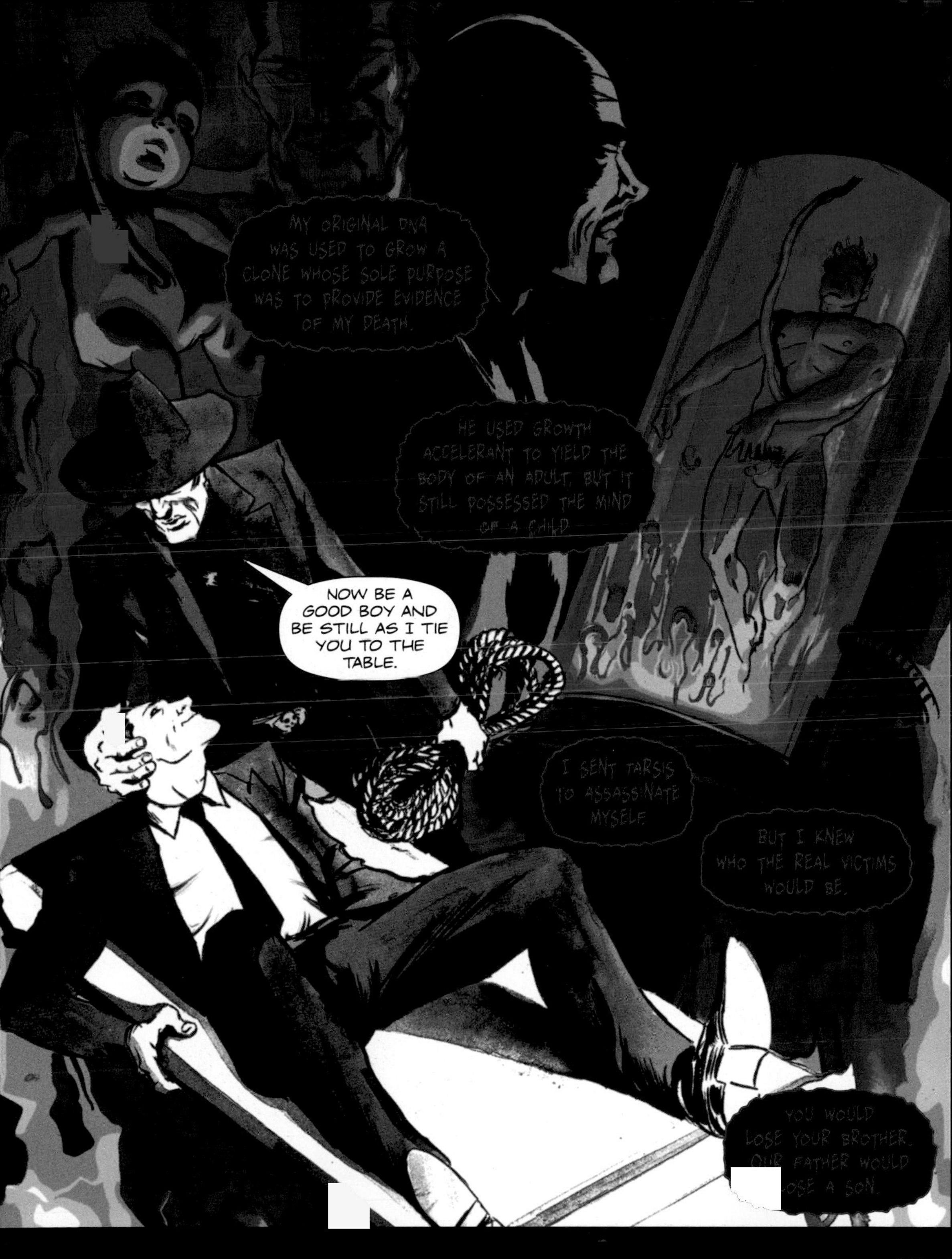
MY ORIGINAL DNA WAS USED TO GROW A CLONE WHOSE SOLE PURPOSE WAS TO PROVIDE EVIDENCE OF MY DEATH.
HE USED GROWTH ACCELERANT TO YIELD THE BODY OF AN ADULT, BUT IT STILL POSSESSED THE MIND OF A CHILD.
NOW BE A GOOD BOY AND BE STILL AS I TIE YOU TO THE TABLE.
I SENT TARSIS TO ASSASSINATE MYSELF.
BUT I KNEW WHO THE REAL VICTIMS WOULD BE.
YOU WOULD LOSE YOUR BROTHER. OUR FATHER WOULD
OSE A SON.

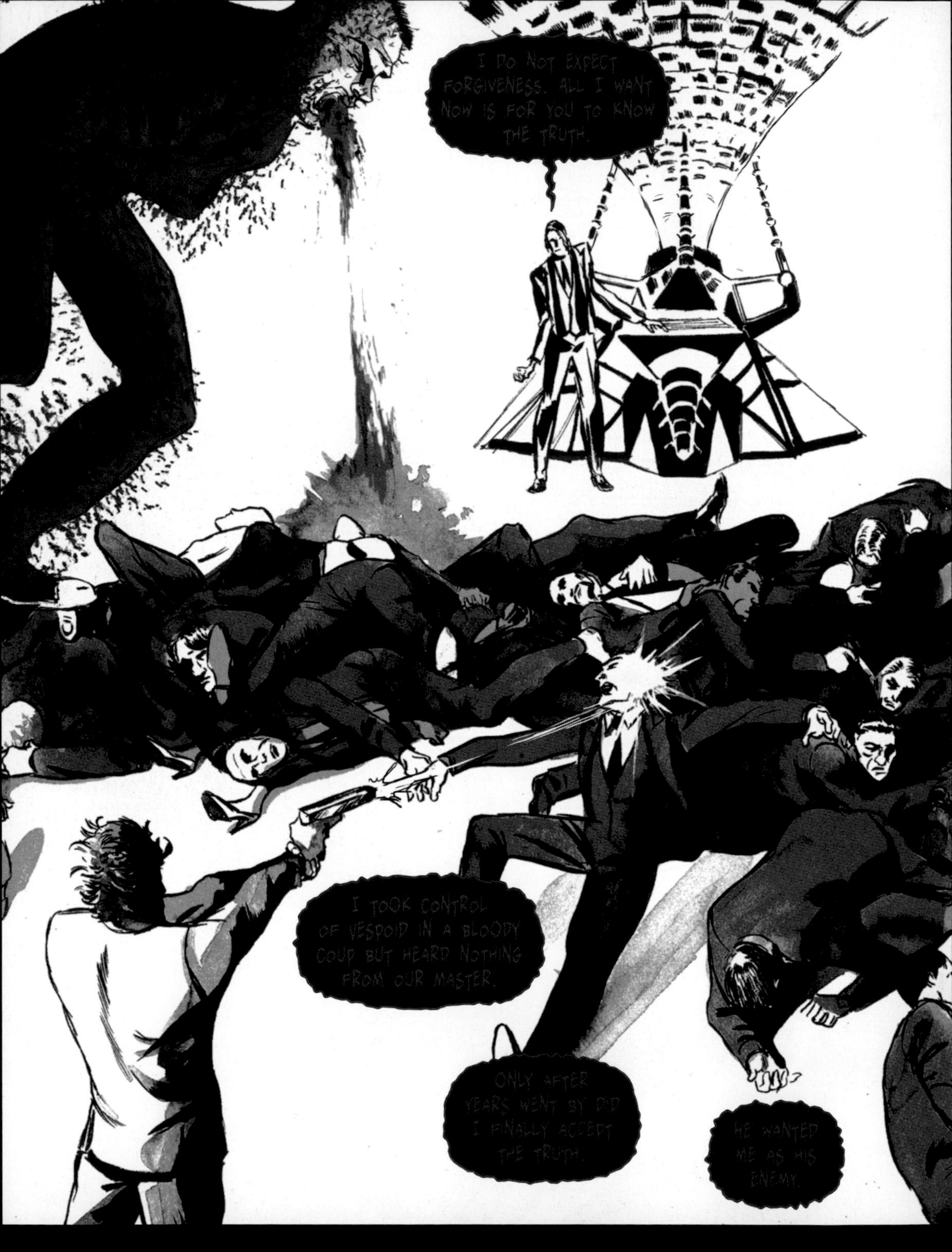
I DO NOT EXPECT FORGIVENESS. ALL I WANT NOW IS FOR YOU TO KNOW THE TRUTH.
I TOOK CONTROL OF VESPOID IN A BLOODY COUP BUT HEARD NOTHING FROM OUR MASTER.
ONLY AFTER YEARS WENT BY DID I FINALLY ACCEPT THE TRUTH.
HE WANTED ME AS HIS ENEMY.

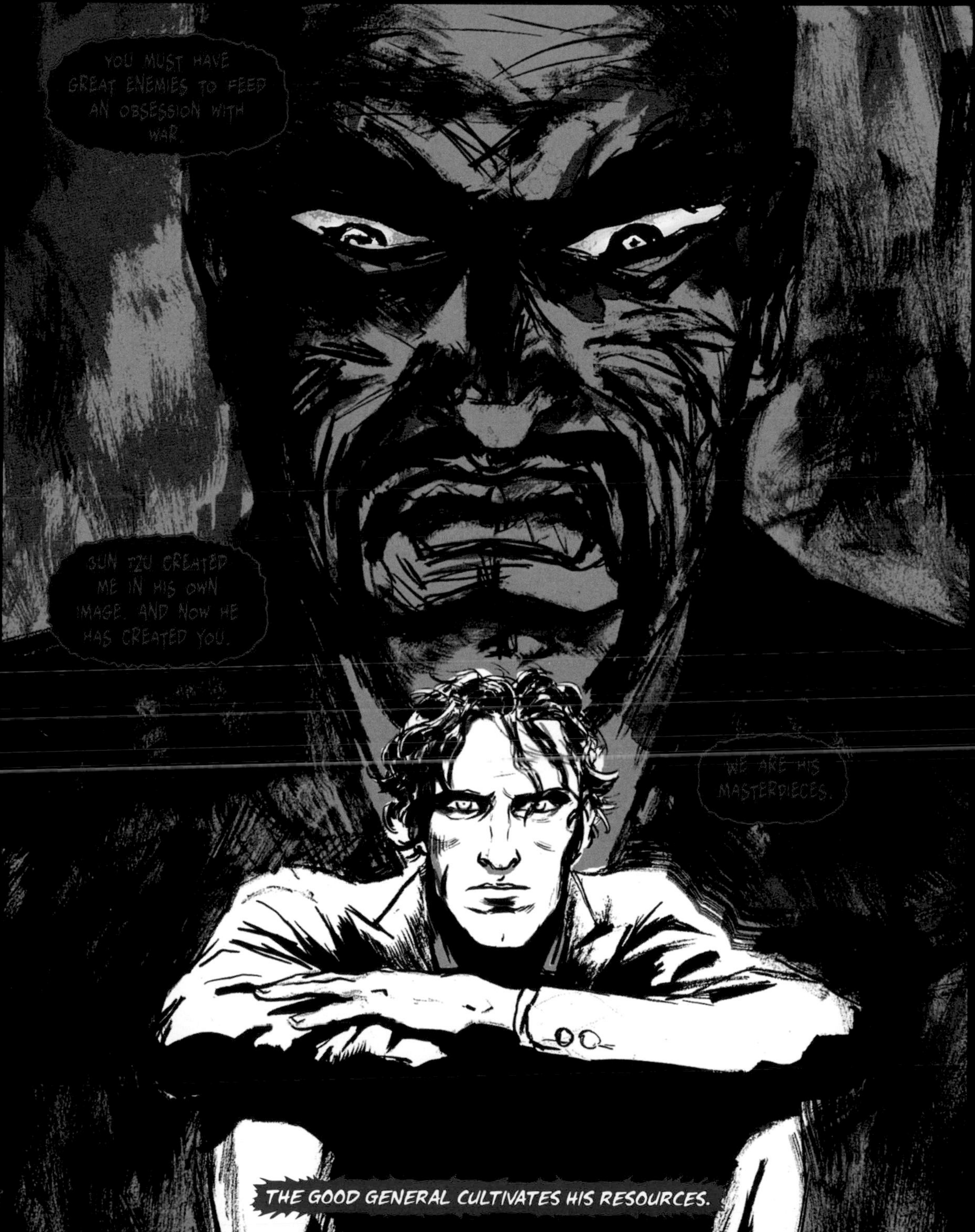
YOU MUST HAVE GREAT ENEMIES TO FEED AN OBSESSION WITH WAR.
SUN TZU CREATED ME IN HIS OWN IMAGE. AND NOW HE HAS CREATED YOU.
WE ARE HIS MASTERPIECES.
THE GOOD GENERAL CULTIVATES HIS RESOURCES.

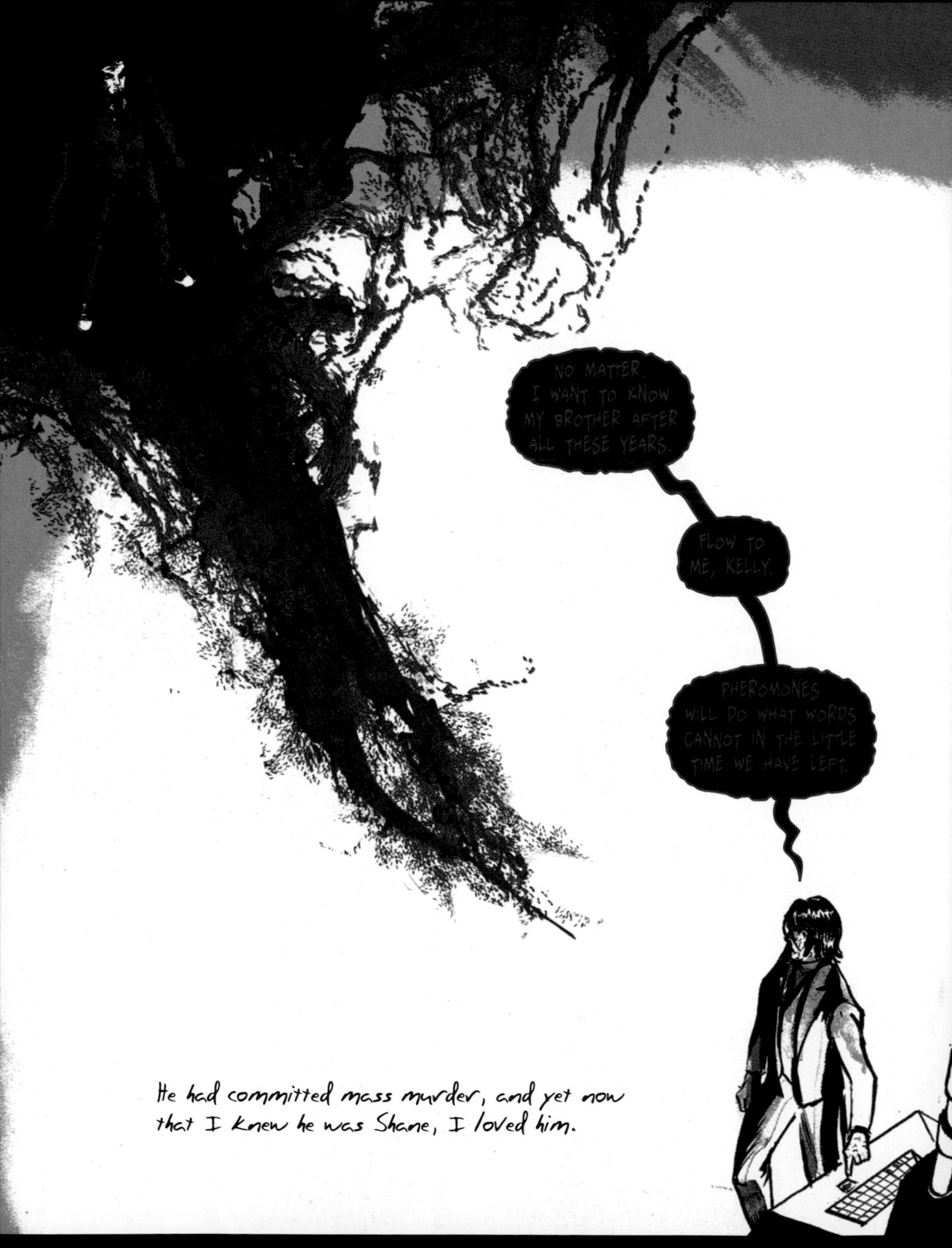
NO MATTER. I WANT TO KNOW MY BROTHER AFTER ALL THESE YEARS.
FLOW TO ME, KELLY.
PHEROMONES WILL DO WHAT WORDS CANNOT IN THE LITTLE TIME WE HAVE LEFT.
He had committed mass murder, and yet now that I knew he was Shane, I loved him.

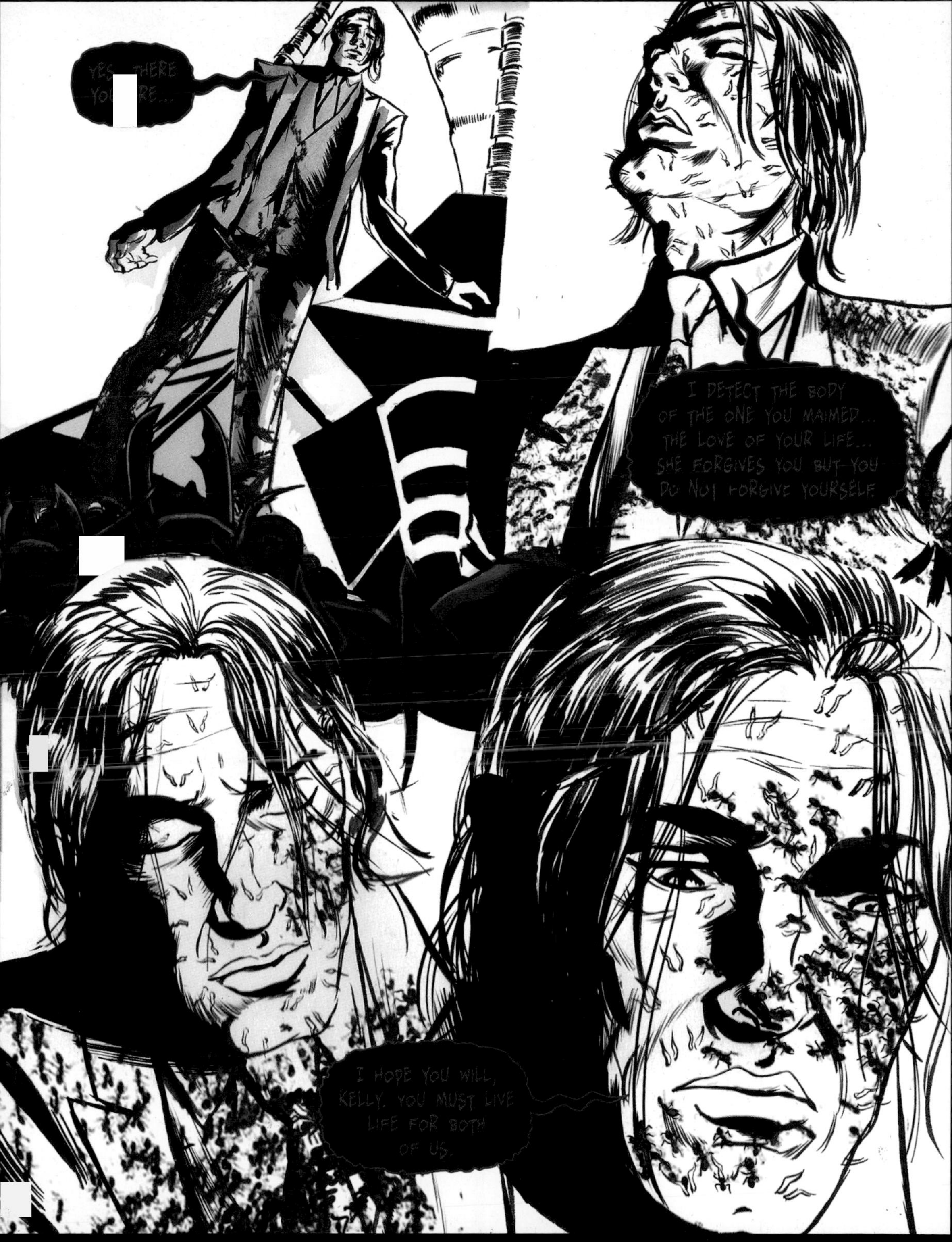
YES, THERE YOU RE...
I DETECT THE BODY OF THE ONE YOU MAIMED... THE LOVE OF YOUR LIFE... SHE FORGIVES YOU BUT YOU DO NOT FORGIVE YOURSELF.
I HOPE YOU WILL, KELLY. YOU MUST LIVE LIFE FOR BOTH OF US.

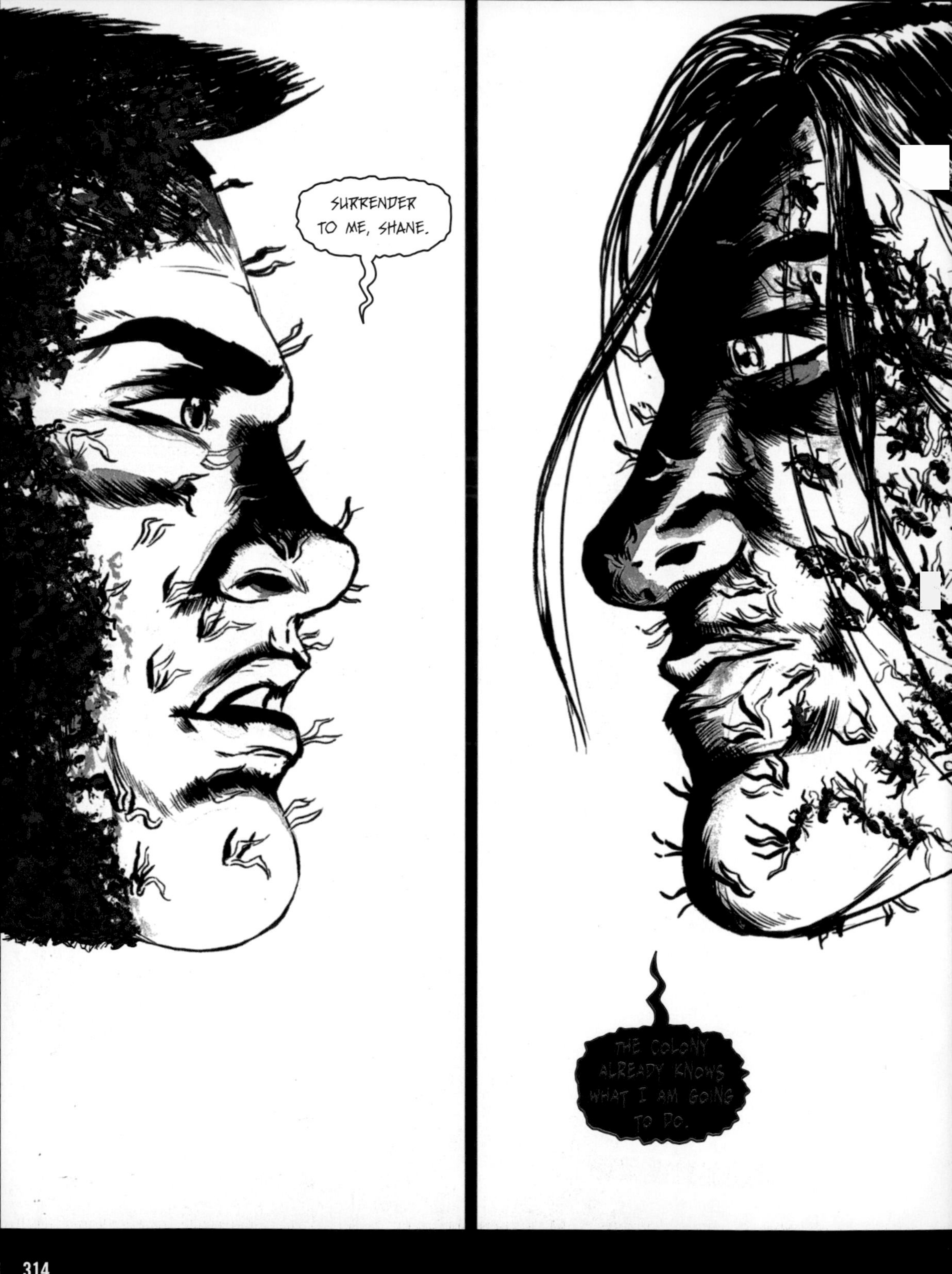
SURRENDER TO ME, SHANE.
THE COLONY ALREADY KNOWS WHAT I AM GOING TO DO.

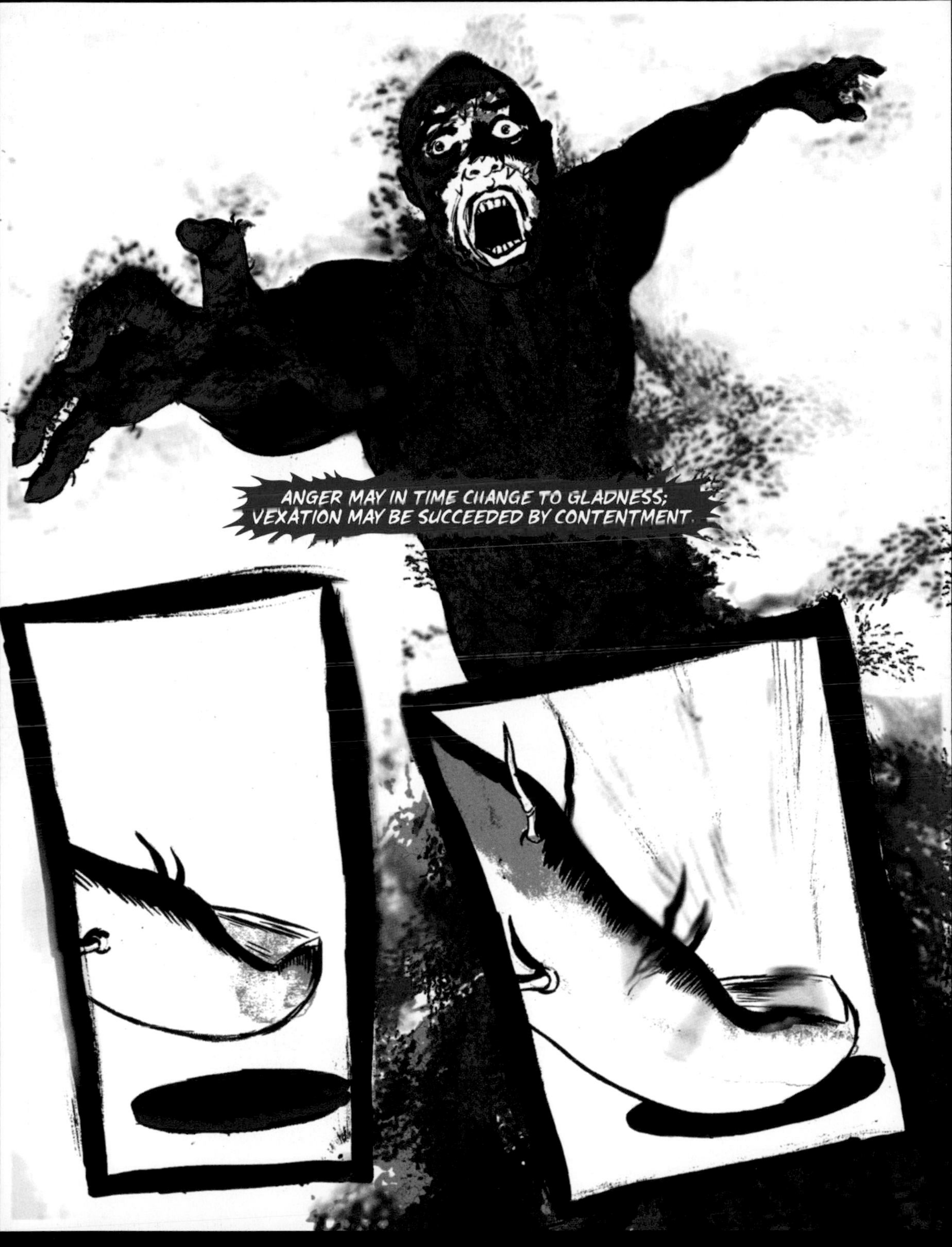
ANGER MAY IN TIME CHANGE TO GLADNESS; VEXATION MAY BE SUCCEEDED BY CONTENTMENT.

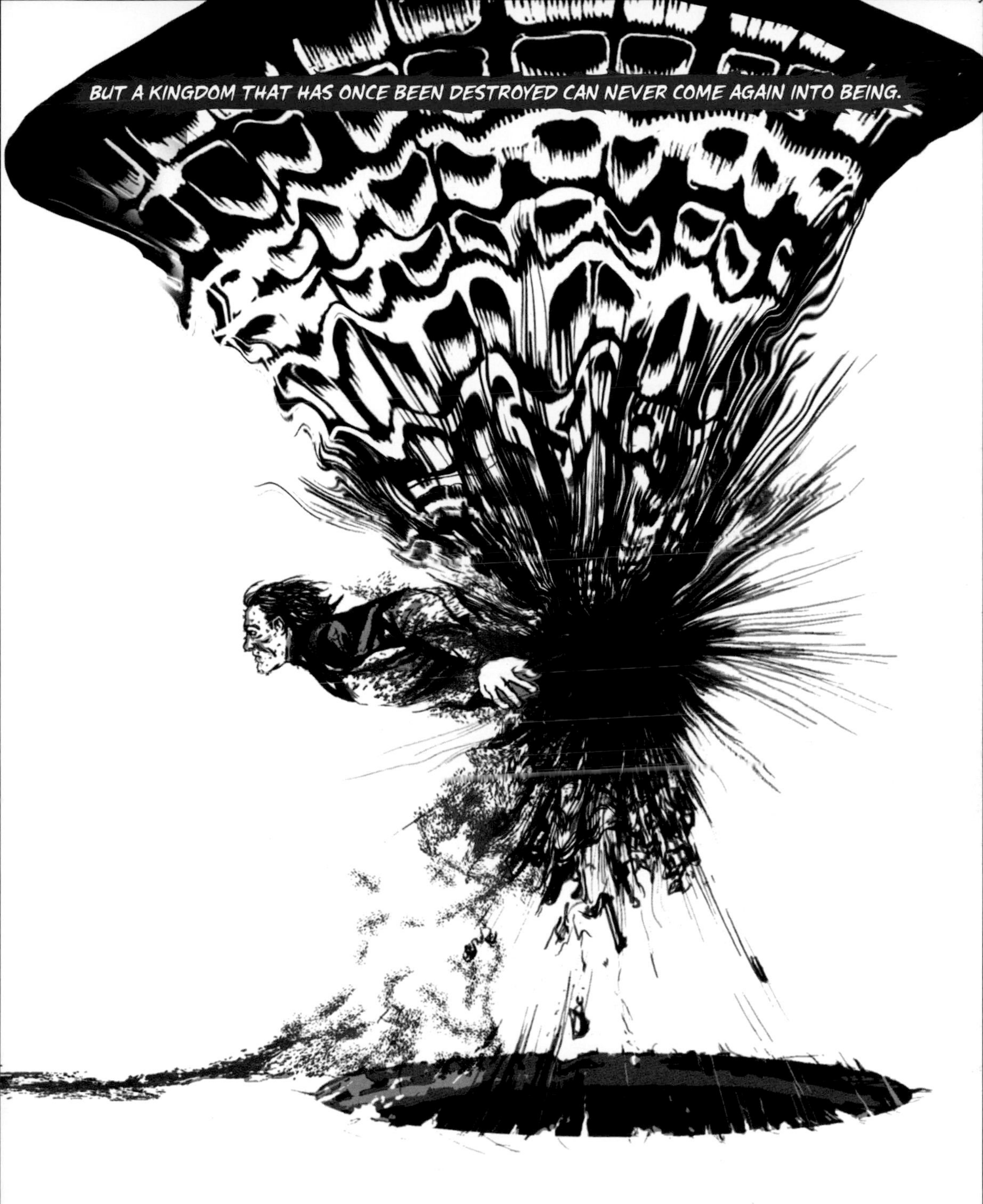
BUT A KINGDOM THAT HAS ONCE BEEN DESTROYED CAN NEVER COME AGAIN INTO BEING.

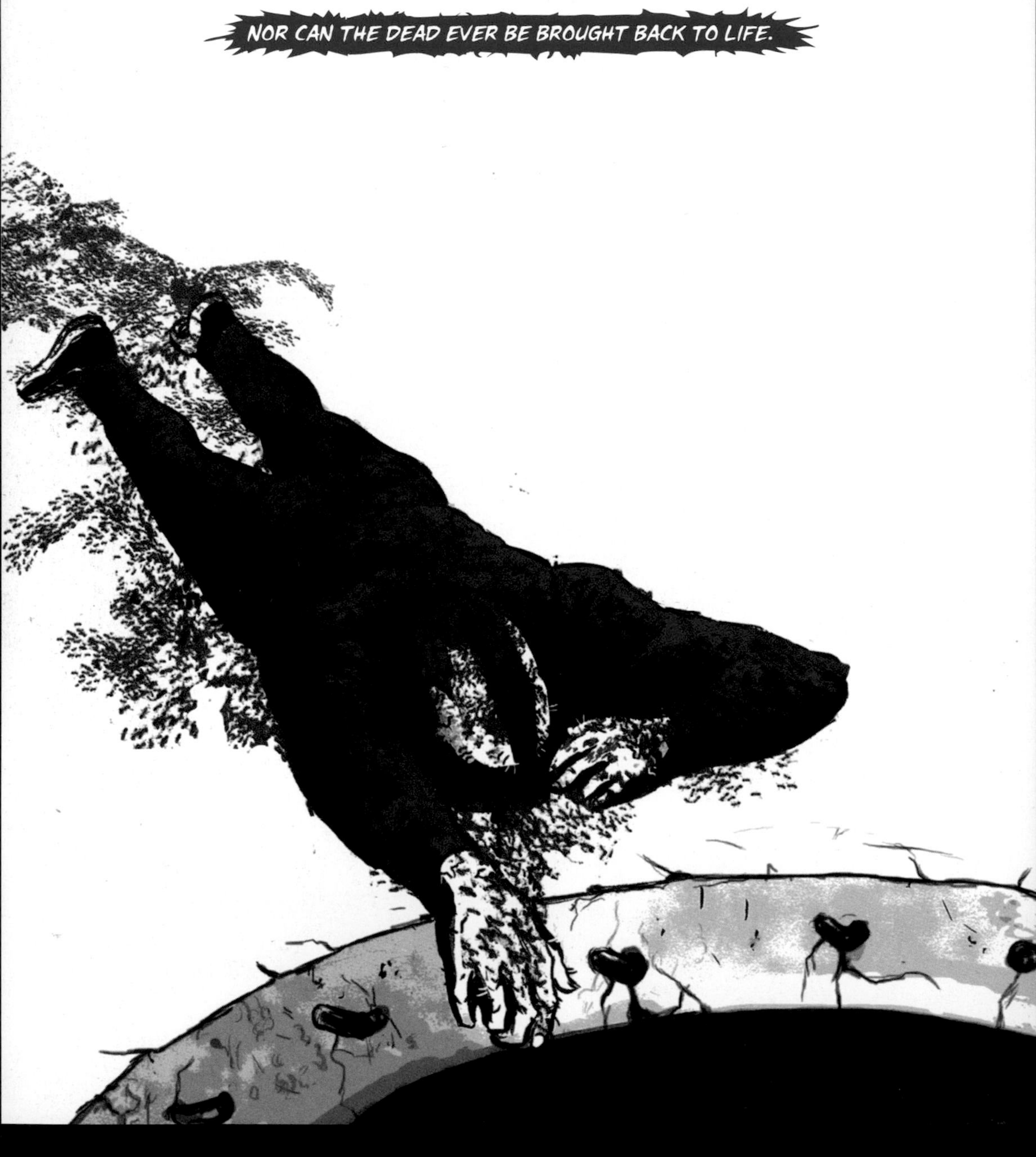
NOR CAN THE DEAD EVER BE BROUGHT BACK TO LIFE.

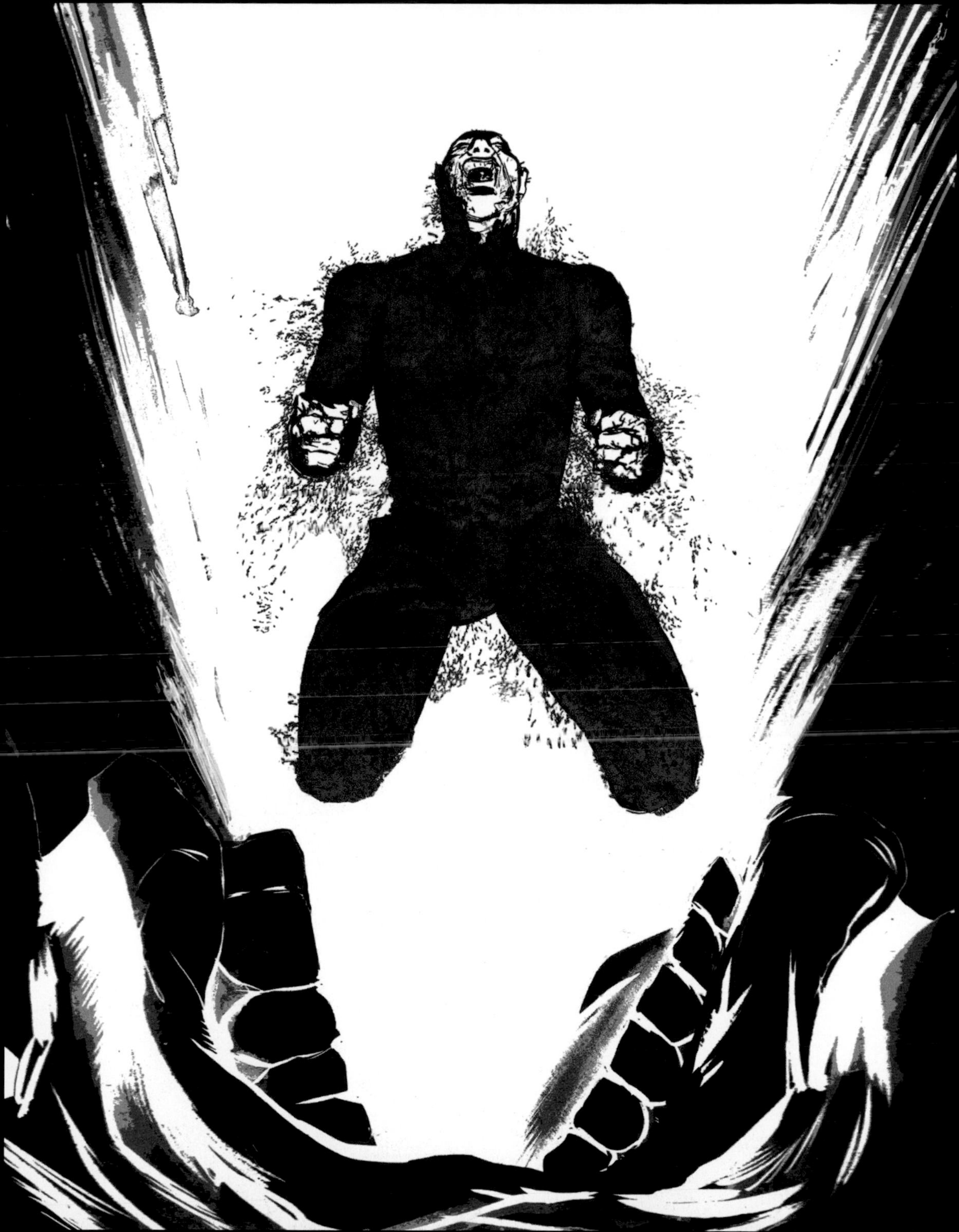

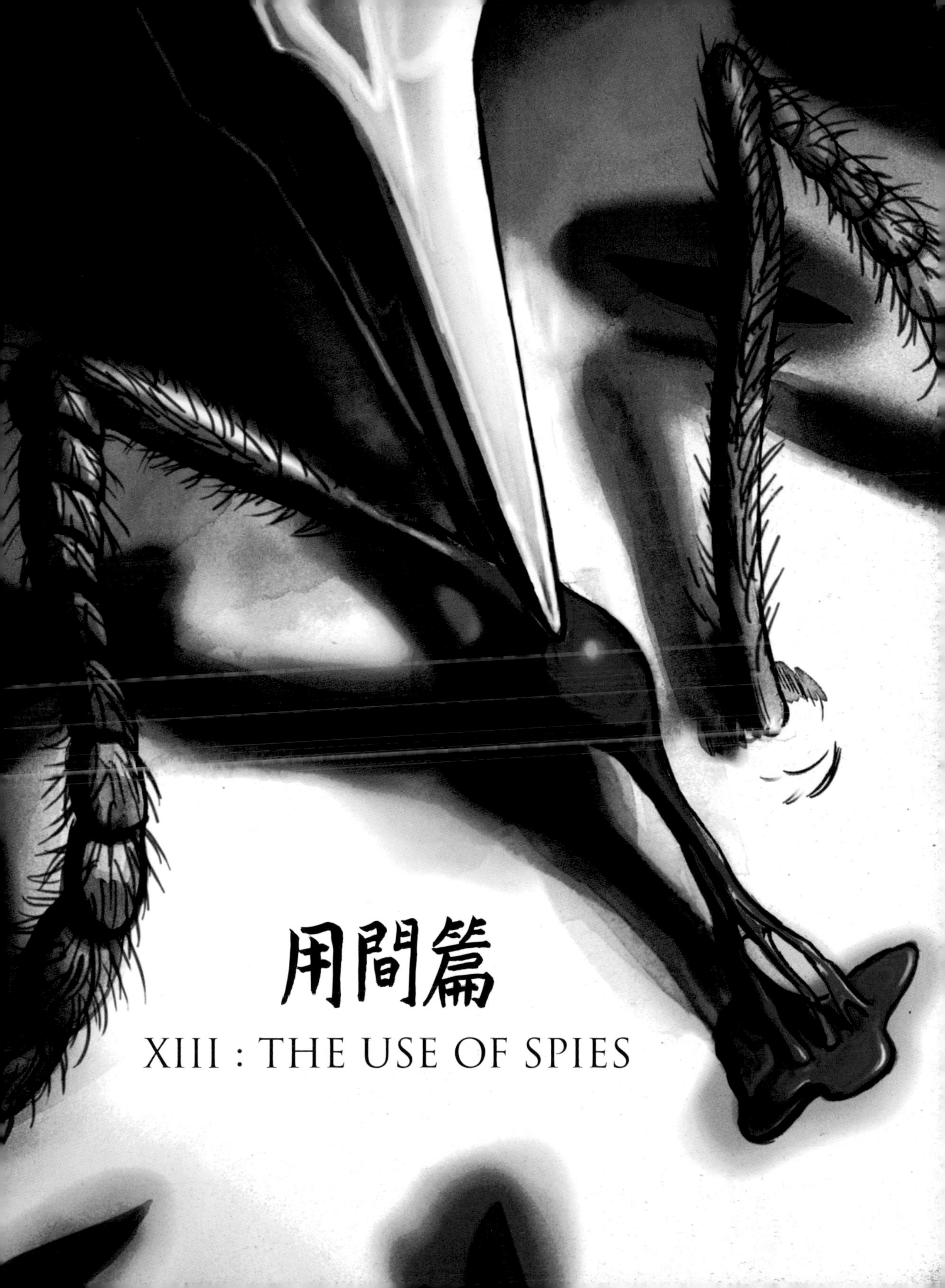

用間篇

XIII : THE USE OF SPIES

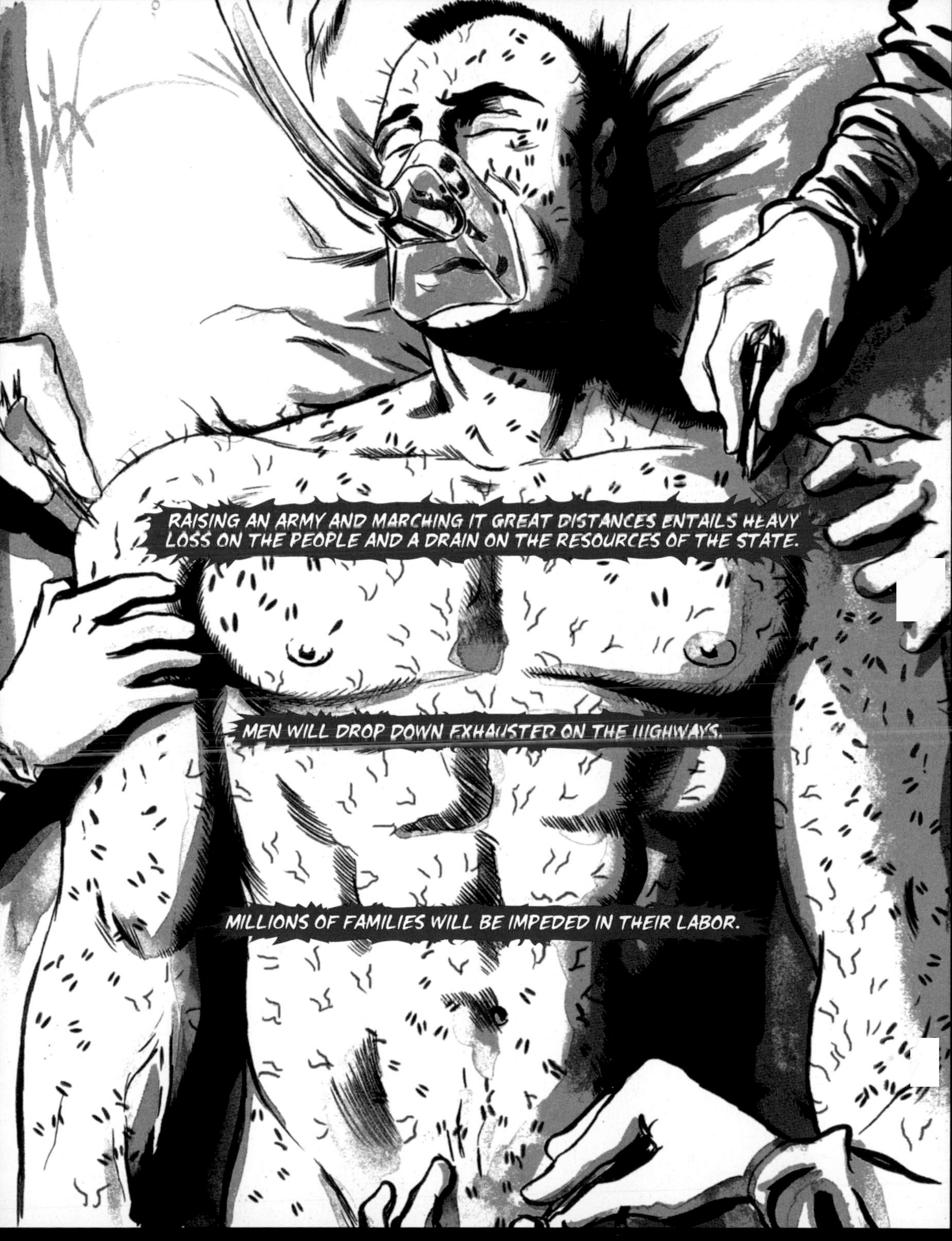
RAISING AN ARMY AND MARCHING IT GREAT DISTANCES ENTAILS HEAVY LOSS ON THE PEOPLE AND A DRAIN ON THE RESOURCES OF THE STATE.
MEN WILL DROP DOWN EXHAUSTED ON THE HIGHWAYS.
MILLIONS OF FAMILIES WILL BE IMPEDED IN THEIR LABOR.

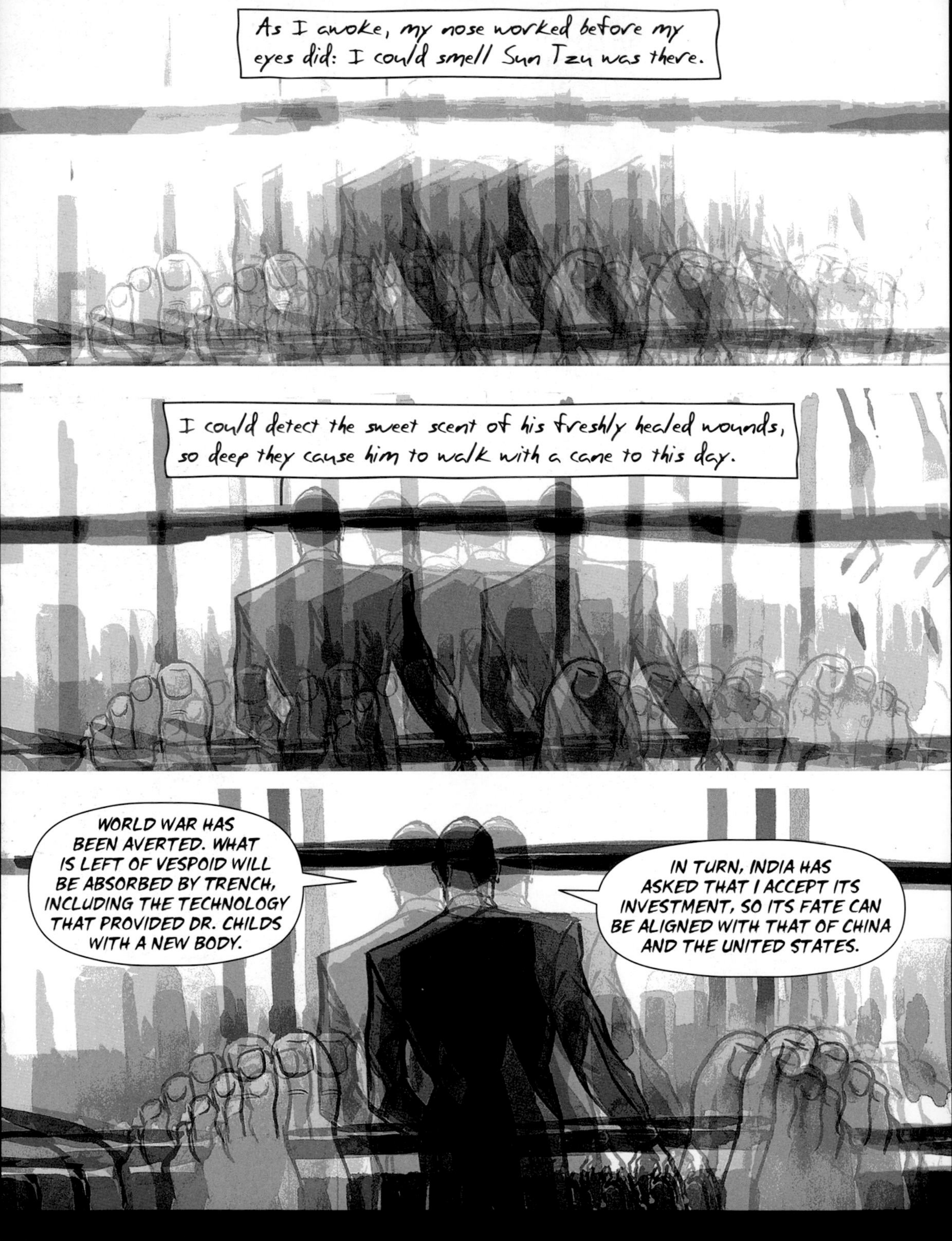
As I awoke, my nose worked before my eyes did: I could smell Sun Tzu was there.
I could detect the sweet scent of his freshly healed wounds, so deep they cause him to walk with a cane to this day.
WORLD WAR HAS BEEN AVERTED. WHAT IS LEFT OF VESPOID WILL BE ABSORBED BY TRENCH, INCLUDING THE TECHNOLOGY THAT PROVIDED DR. CHILDS WITH A NEW BODY.
IN TURN, INDIA HAS ASKED THAT I ACCEPT ITS INVESTMENT, SO ITS FATE CAN BE ALIGNED WITH THAT OF CHINA AND THE UNITED STATES.

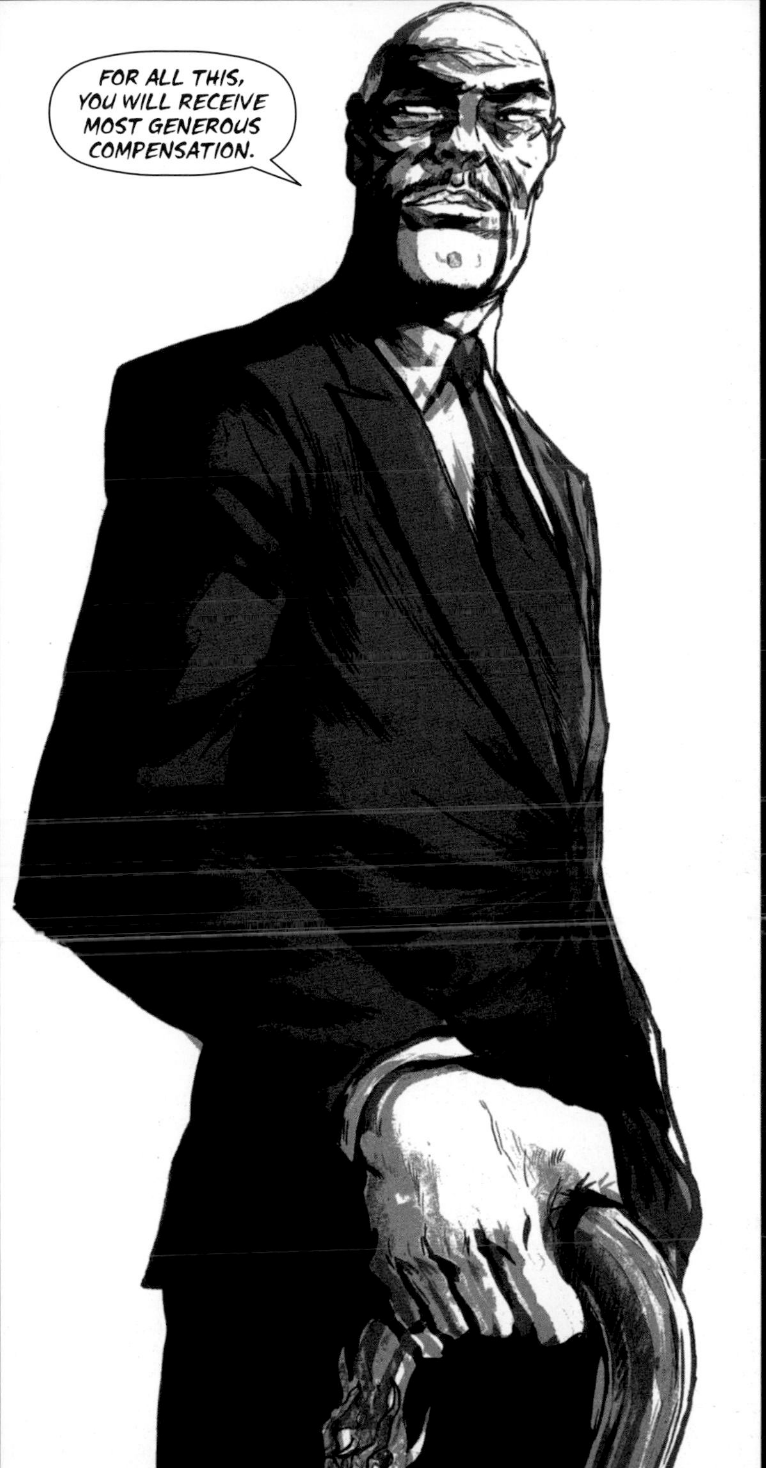
FOR ALL THIS, YOU WILL RECEIVE MOST GENEROUS COMPENSATION.
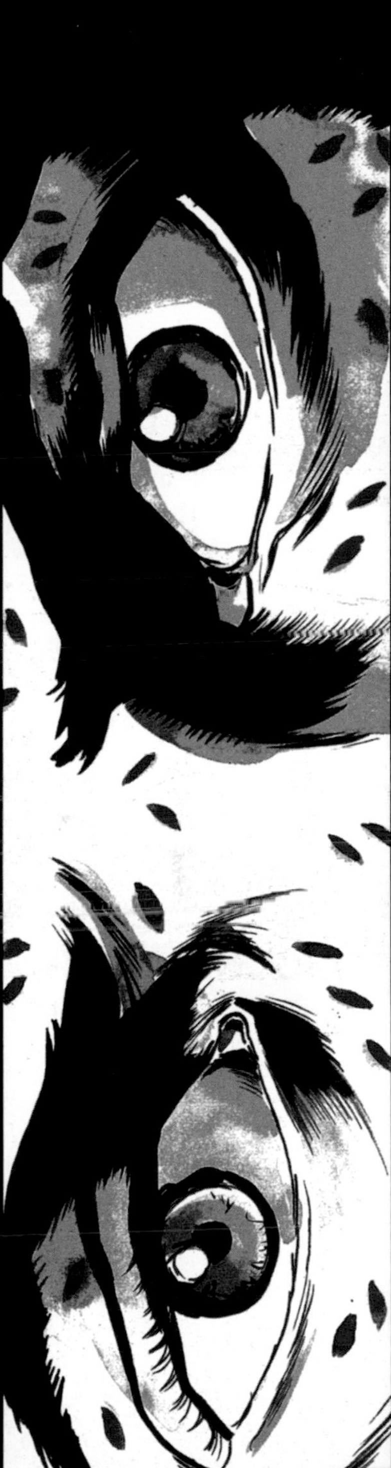

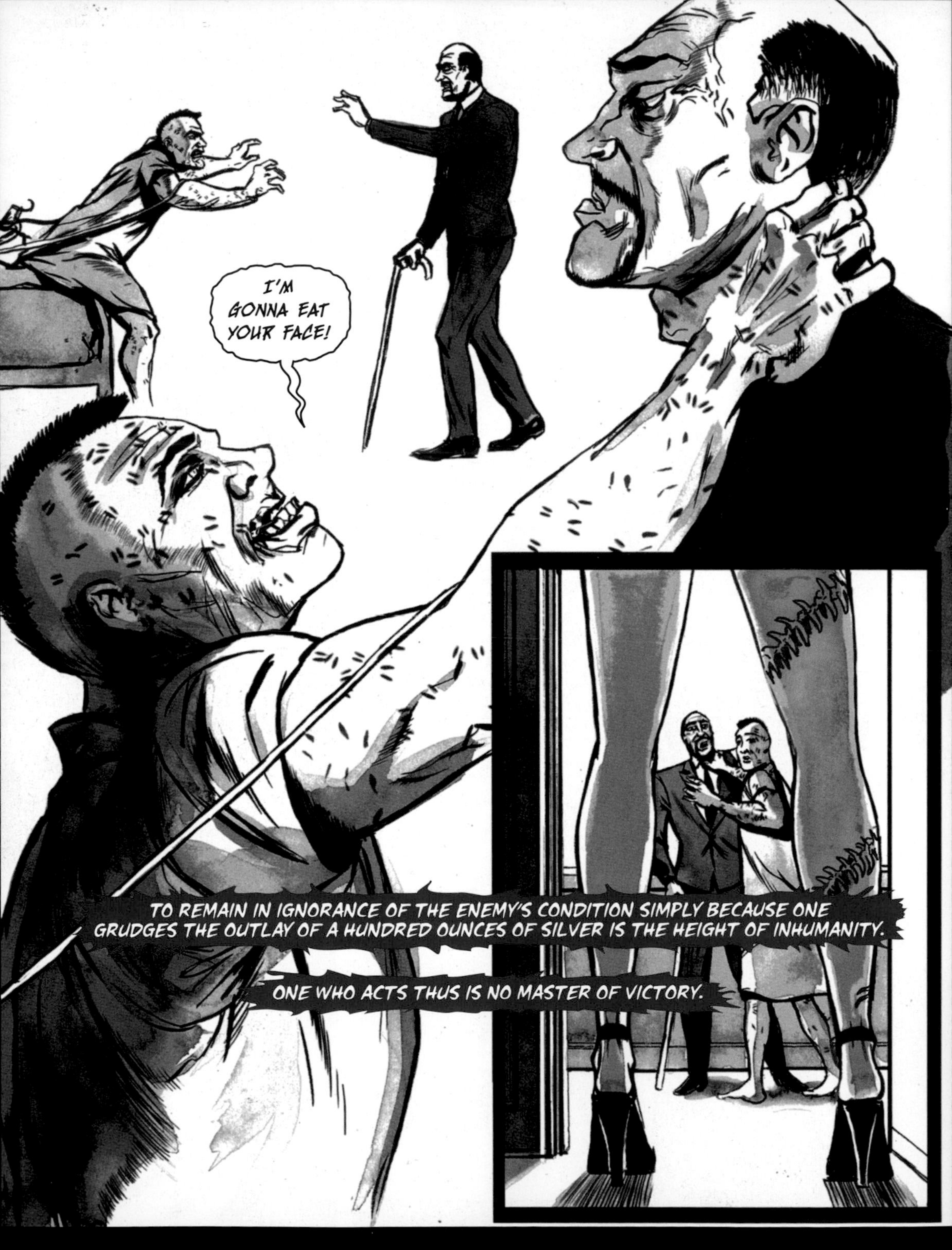
I'M GONNA EAT YOUR FACE!
TO REMAIN IN IGNORANCE OF THE ENEMY'S CONDITION SIMPLY BECAUSE ONE GRUDGES THE OUTLAY OF A HUNDRED OUNCES OF SILVER IS THE HEIGHT OF INHUMANITY.
ONE WHO ACTS THUS IS NO MASTER OF VICTORY.

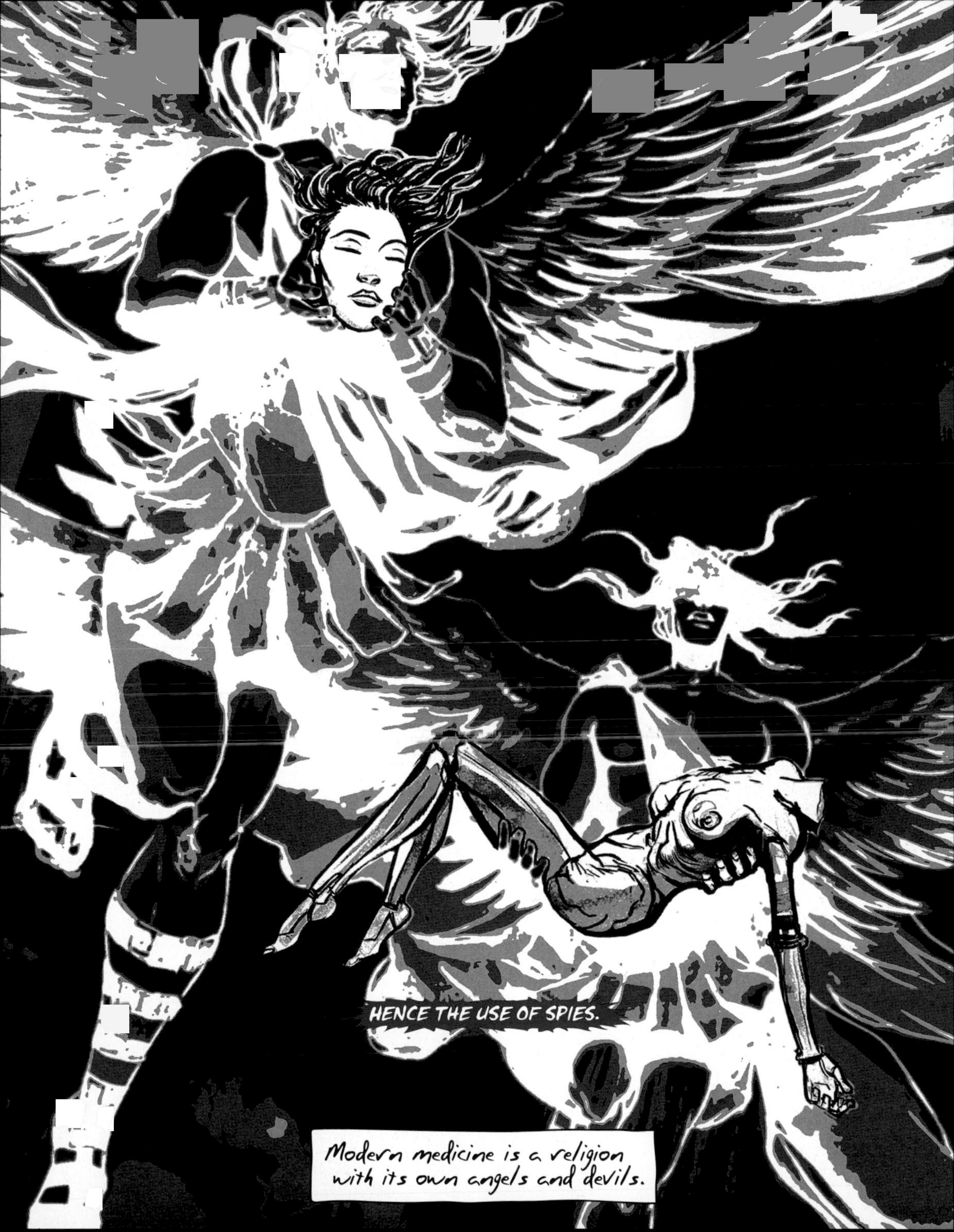
HENCE THE USE OF SPIES.
Modern medicine is a religion with its own angels and devils.

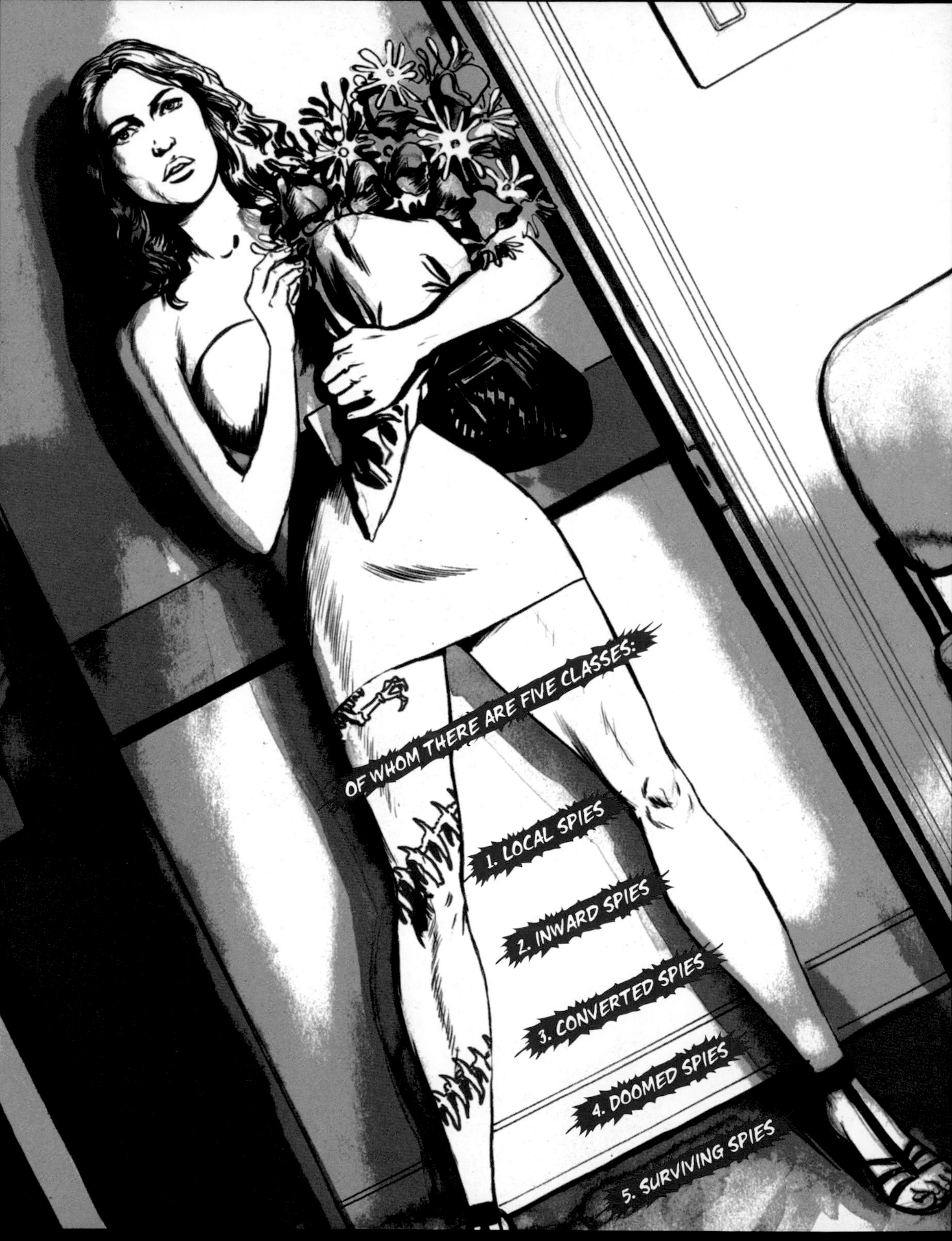
OF WHOM THERE ARE FIVE CLASSES:
1. LOCAL SPIES
2. INWARD SPIES
3. CONVERTED SPIES
4. DOOMED SPIES
5. SURVIVING SPIES

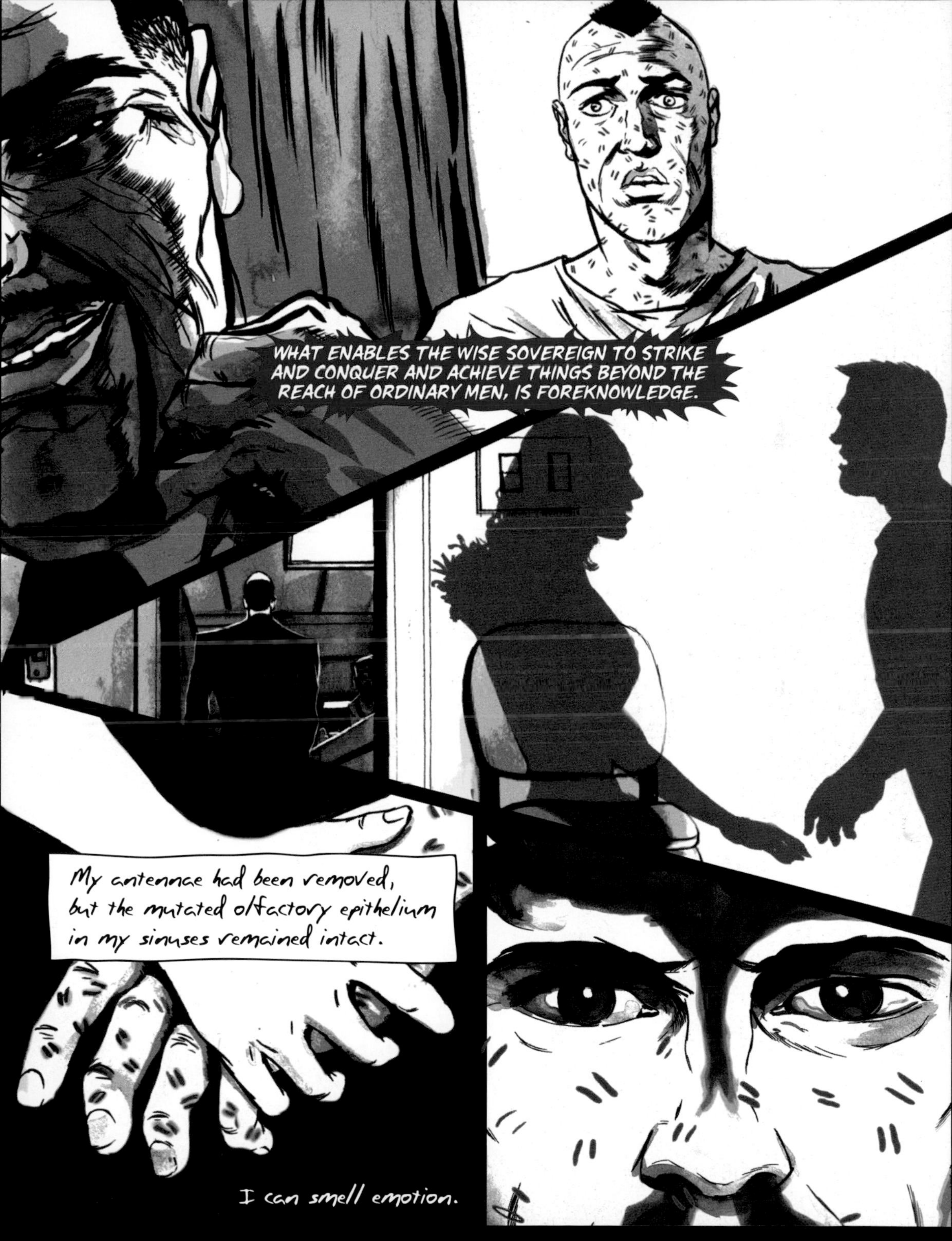
WHAT ENABLES THE WISE SOVEREIGN TO STRIKE AND CONQUER AND ACHIEVE THINGS BEYOND THE REACH OF ORDINARY MEN, IS FOREKNOWLEDGE.
My antennae had been removed, but the mutated olfactory epithelium in my sinuses remained intact.
I can smell emotion.

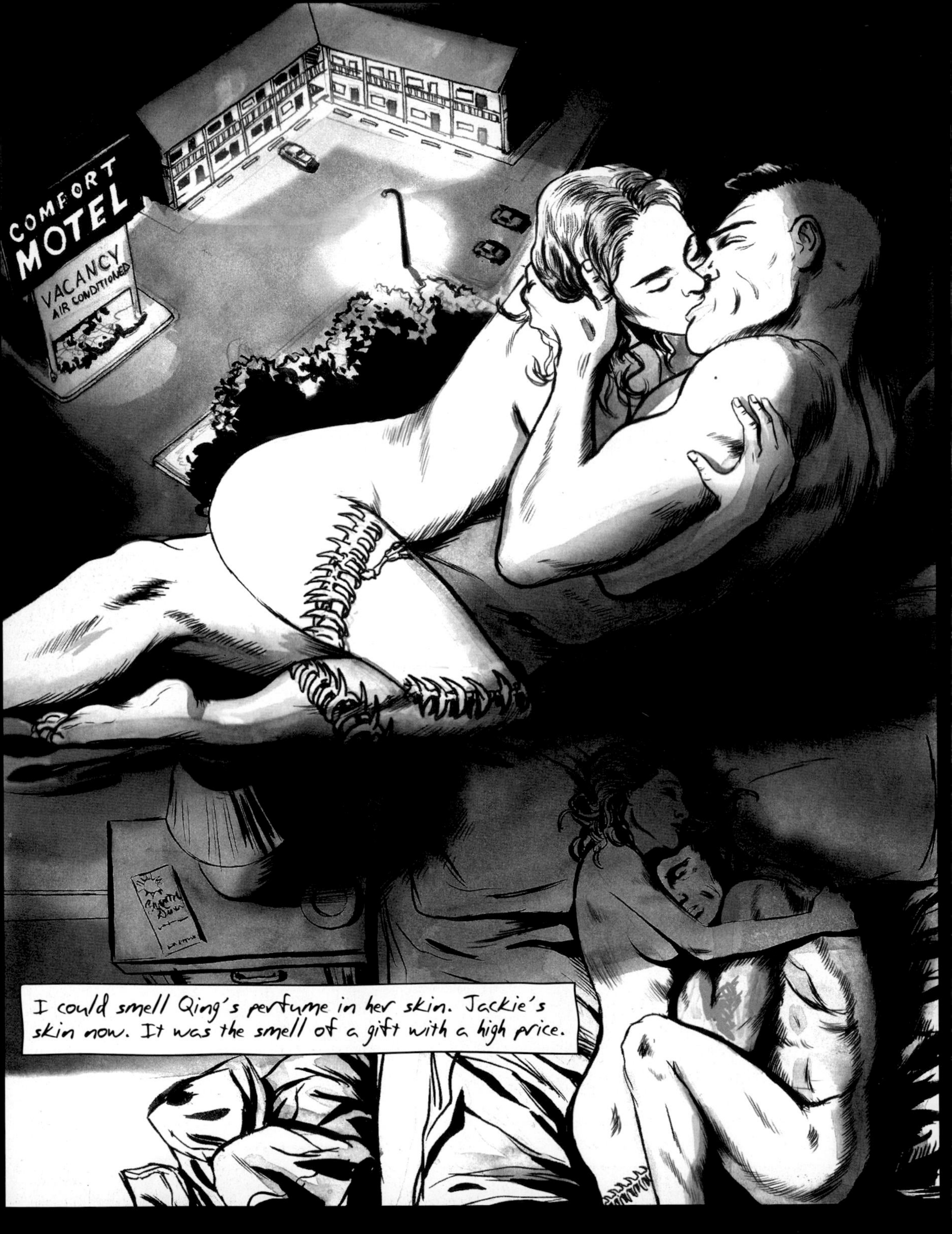
COMFORT
MOTEL
VACANCY
AIR CONDITIONED
I could smell Qing's perfume in her skin. Jackie's skin now. It was the smell of a gift with a high price.

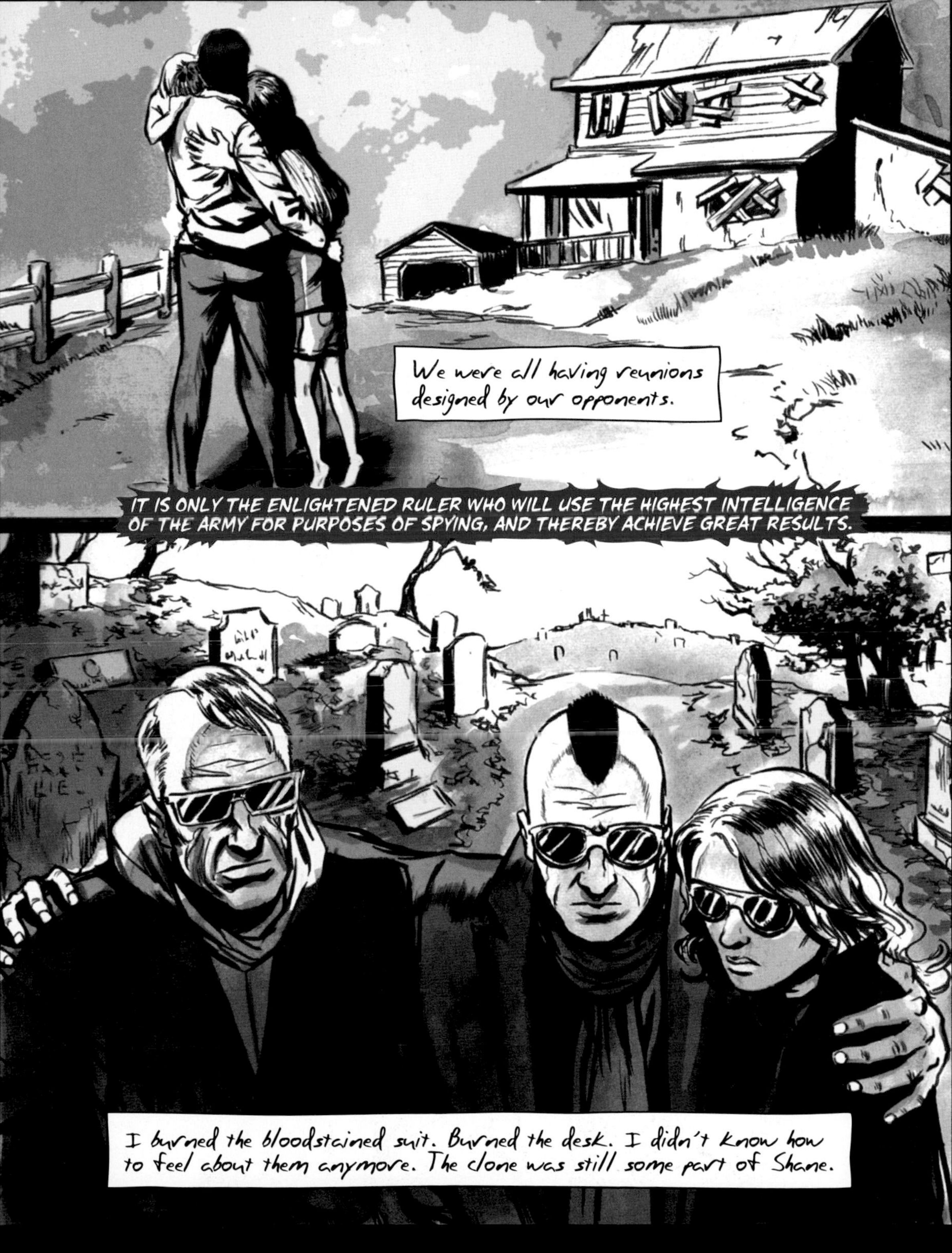
We were all having reunions designed by our opponents.
IT IS ONLY THE ENLIGHTENED RULER WHO WILL USE THE HIGHEST INTELLIGENCE OF THE ARMY FOR PURPOSES OF SPYING, AND THEREBY ACHIEVE GREAT RESULTS.
I burned the bloodstained suit. Burned the desk. I didn't know how to feel about them anymore. The clone was still some part of Shane.

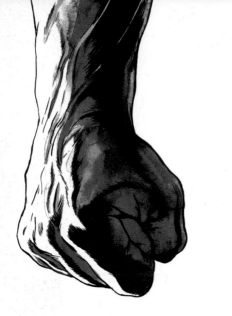

Sun Tzu's betrayal caused me to grip vengeance too tightly.

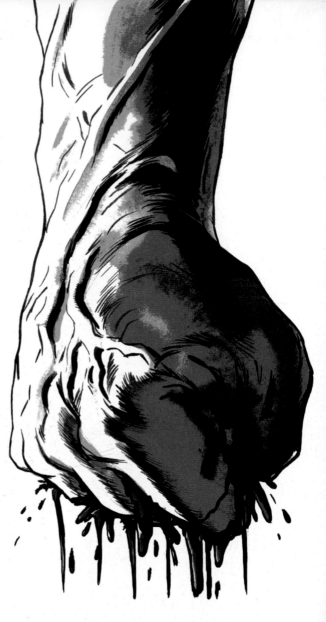

Now it is impossible to set free.

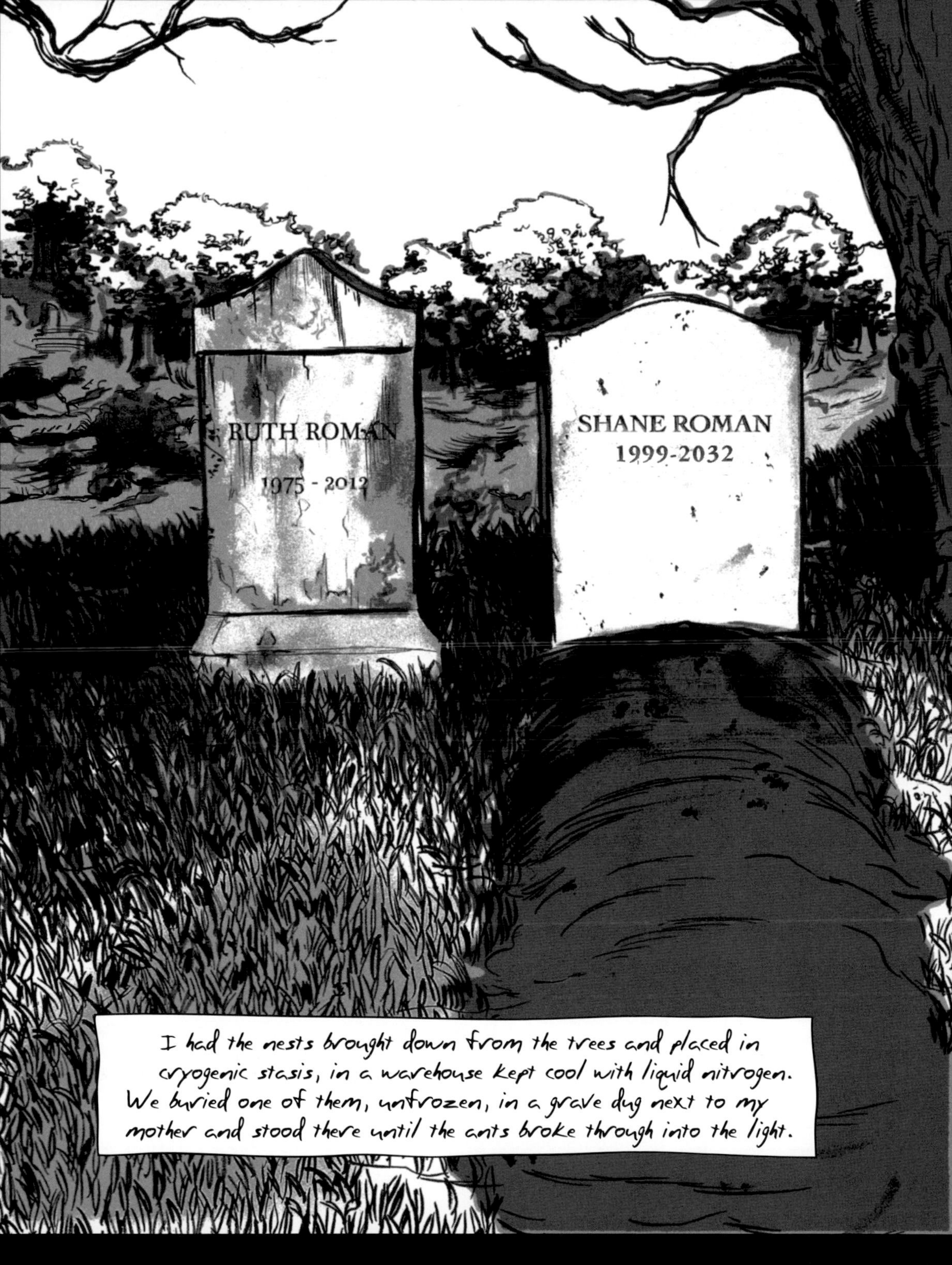
RUTH ROMAN
1975 - 2012
SHANE ROMAN
1999-2032
I had the nests brought down from the trees and placed in cryogenic stasis, in a warehouse kept cool with liquid nitrogen. We buried one of them, unfrozen, in a grave dug next to my mother and stood there until the ants broke through into the light.

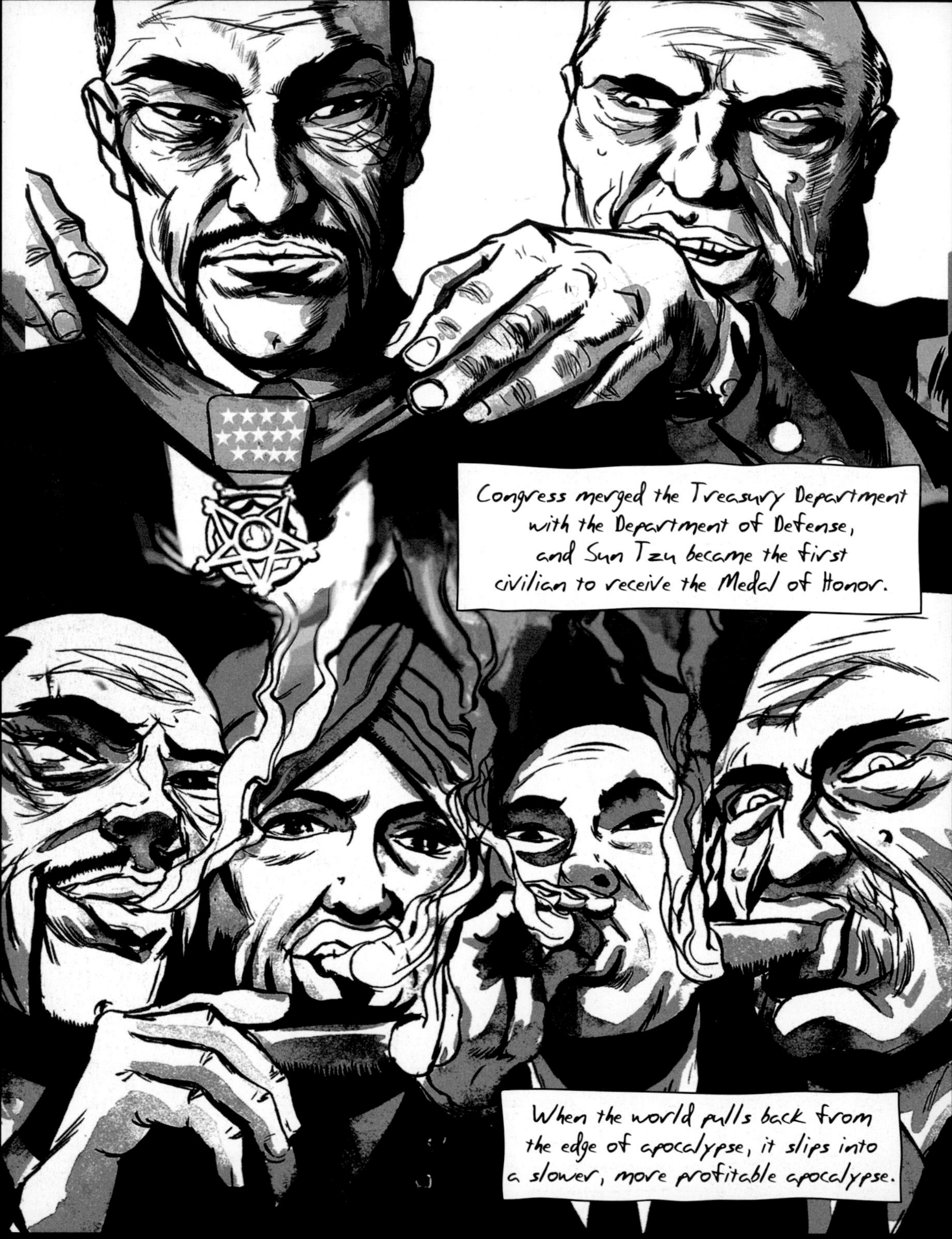
Congress merged the Treasury Department with the Department of Defense, and Sun Tzu became the first civilian to receive the Medal of Honor.
When the world pulls back from the edge of apocalypse, it slips into a slower, more profitable apocalypse.

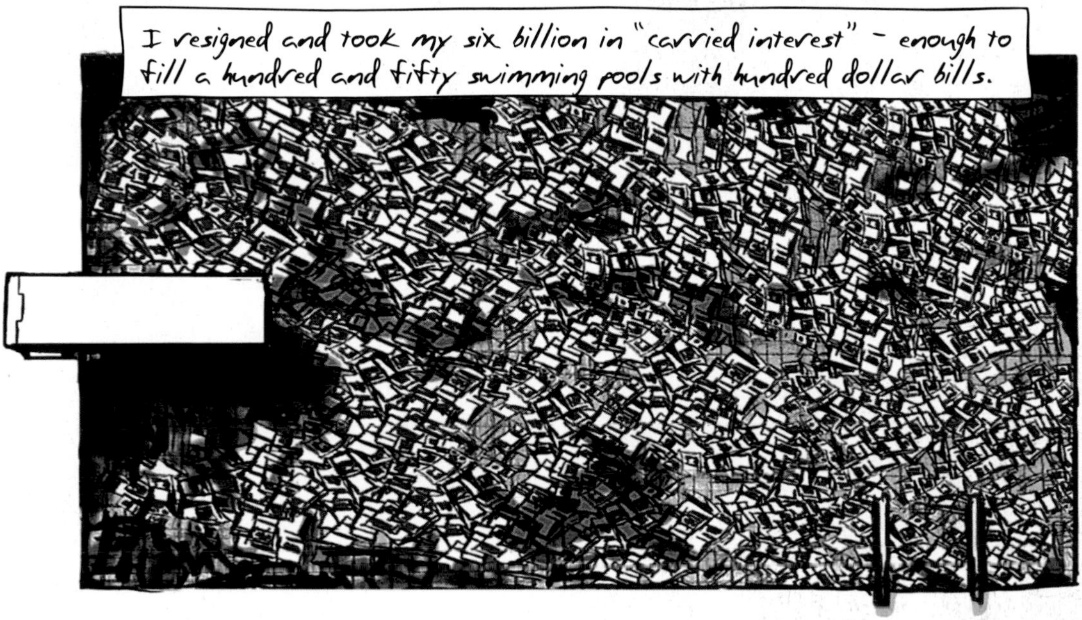
I resigned and took my six billion in "carried interest" - enough to fill a hundred and fifty swimming pools with hundred dollar bills.

Sun Tzu mailed me the journal I left on my desk - the one you are holding.

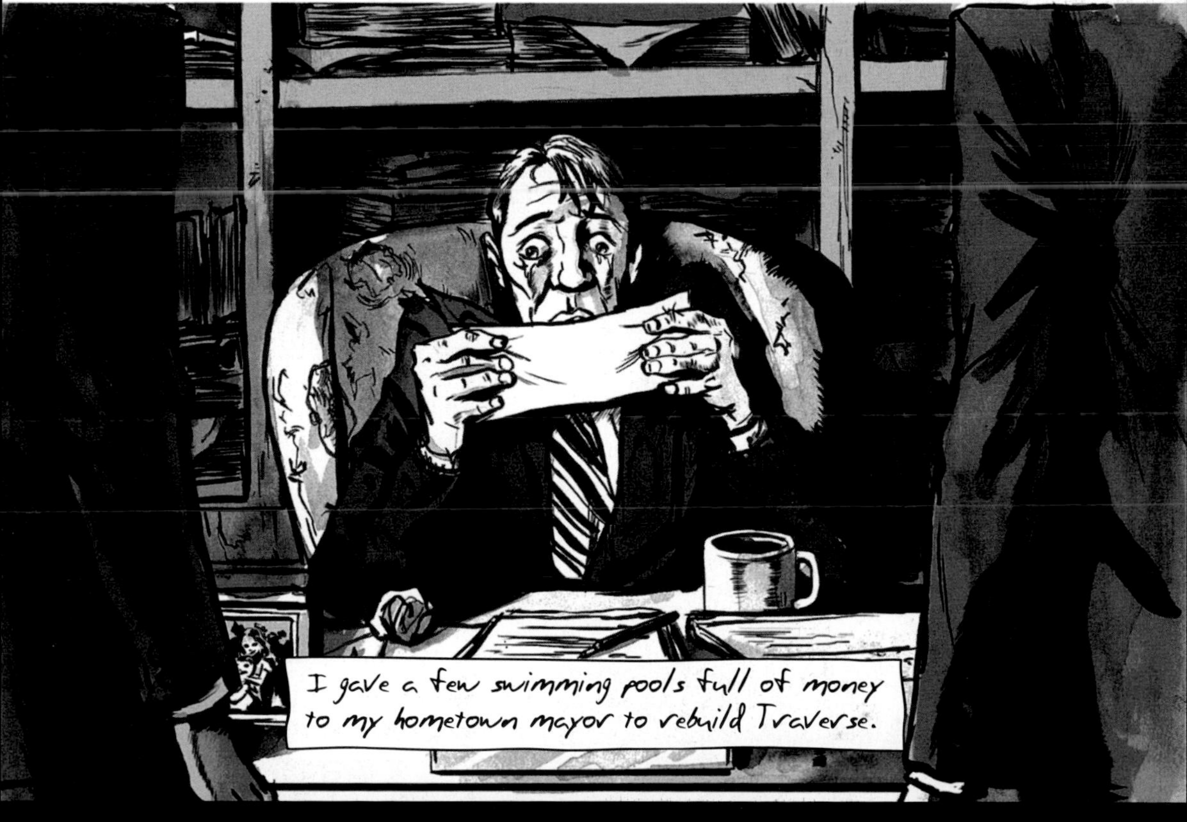
I gave a few swimming pools full of money to my hometown mayor to rebuild Traverse.

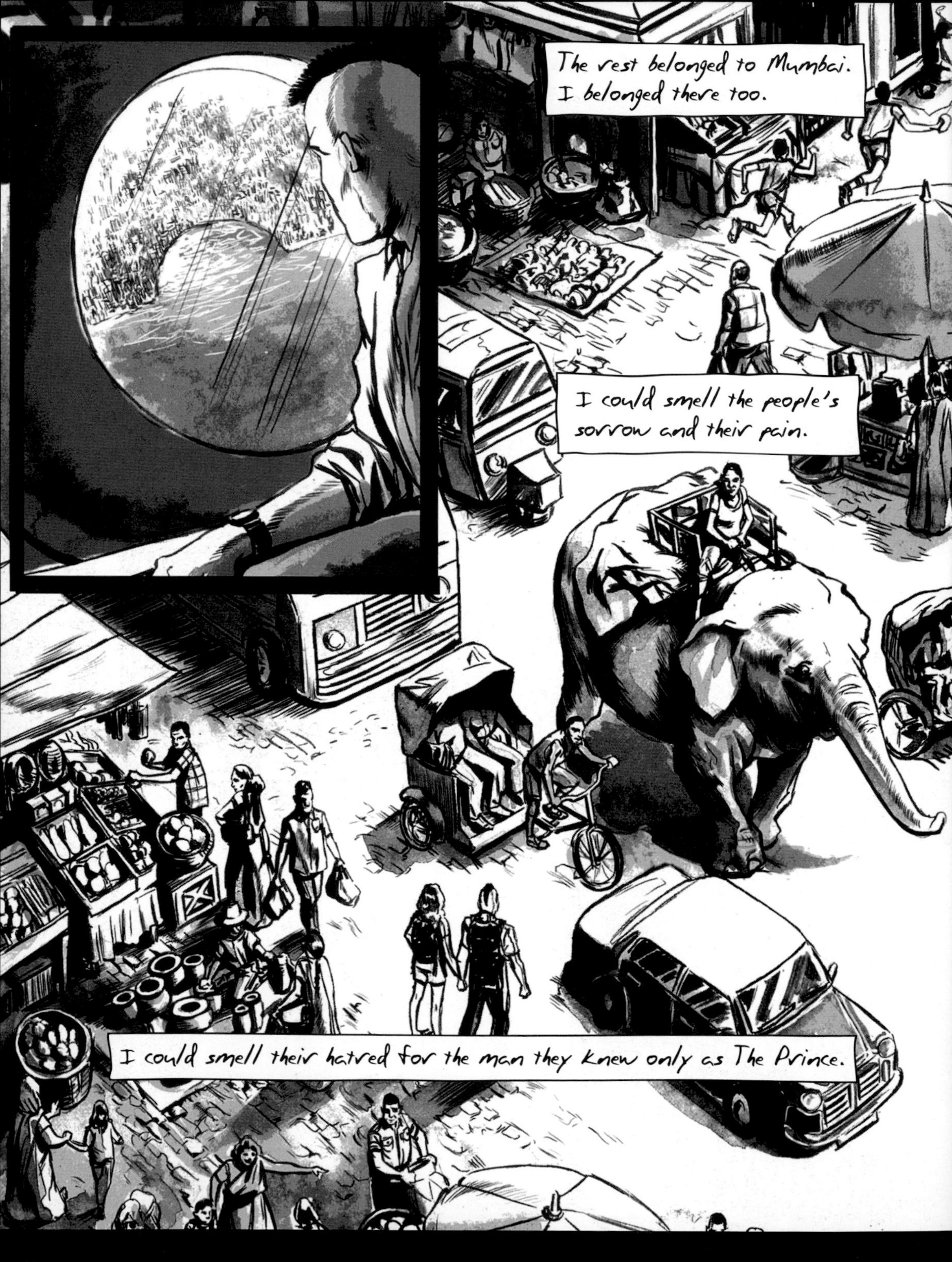
The rest belonged to Mumbai.
I belonged there too.
I could smell the people's sorrow and their pain.
I could smell their hatred for the man they knew only as The Prince.

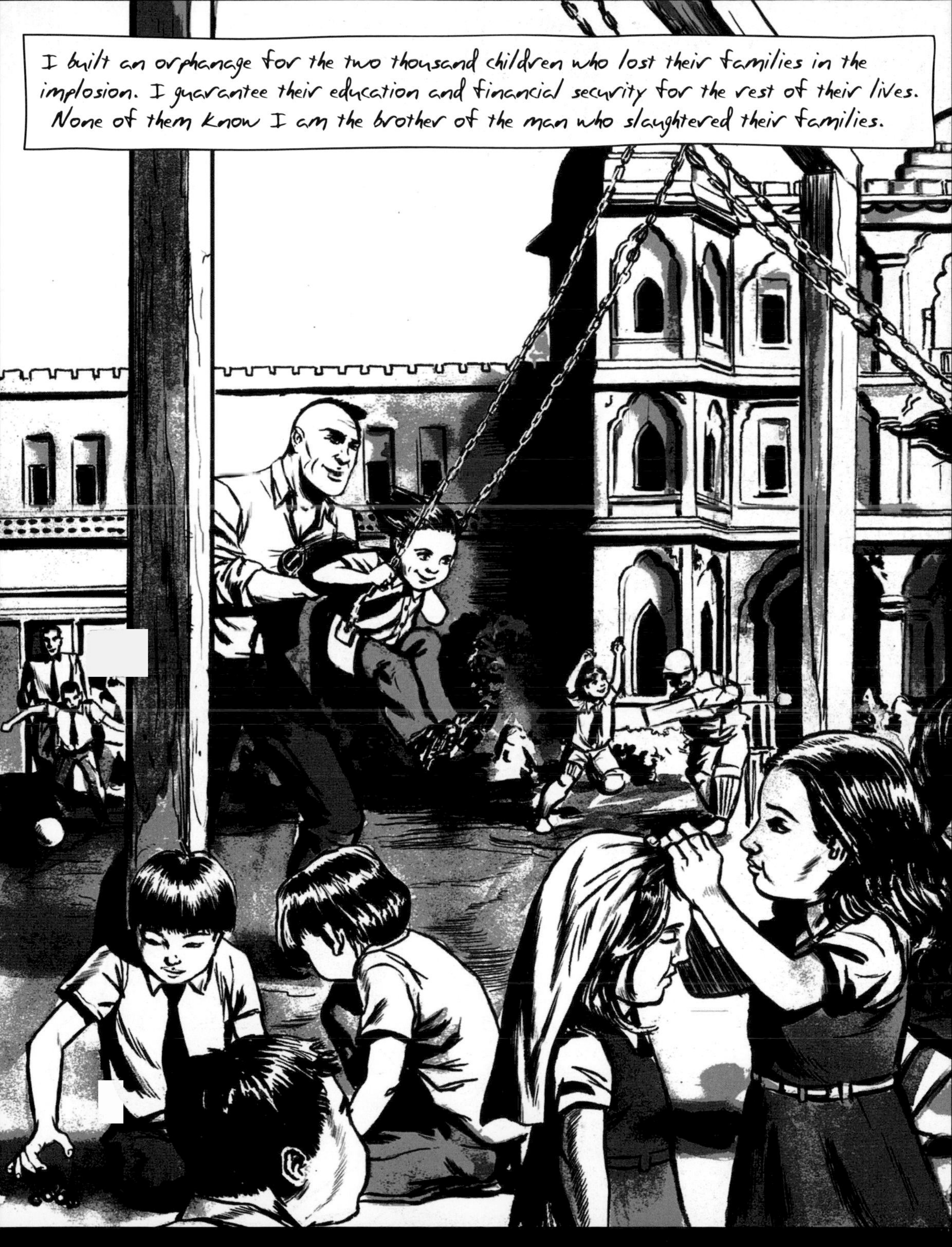
I built an orphanage for the two thousand children who lost their families in the implosion. I guarantee their education and financial security for the rest of their lives. None of them know I am the brother of the man who slaughtered their families.

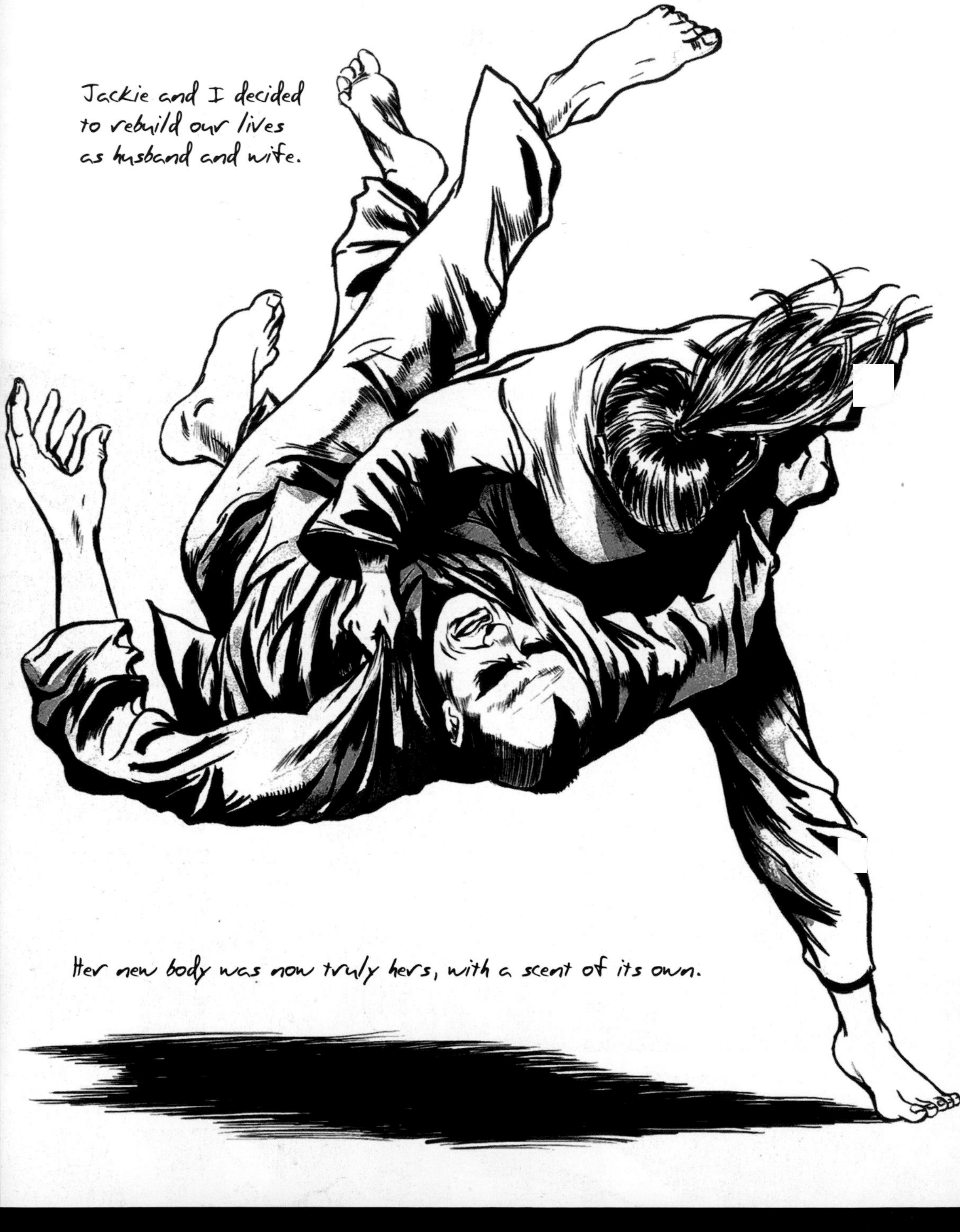
Jackie and I decided to rebuild our lives as husband and wife.
Her new body was now truly hers, with a scent of its own.

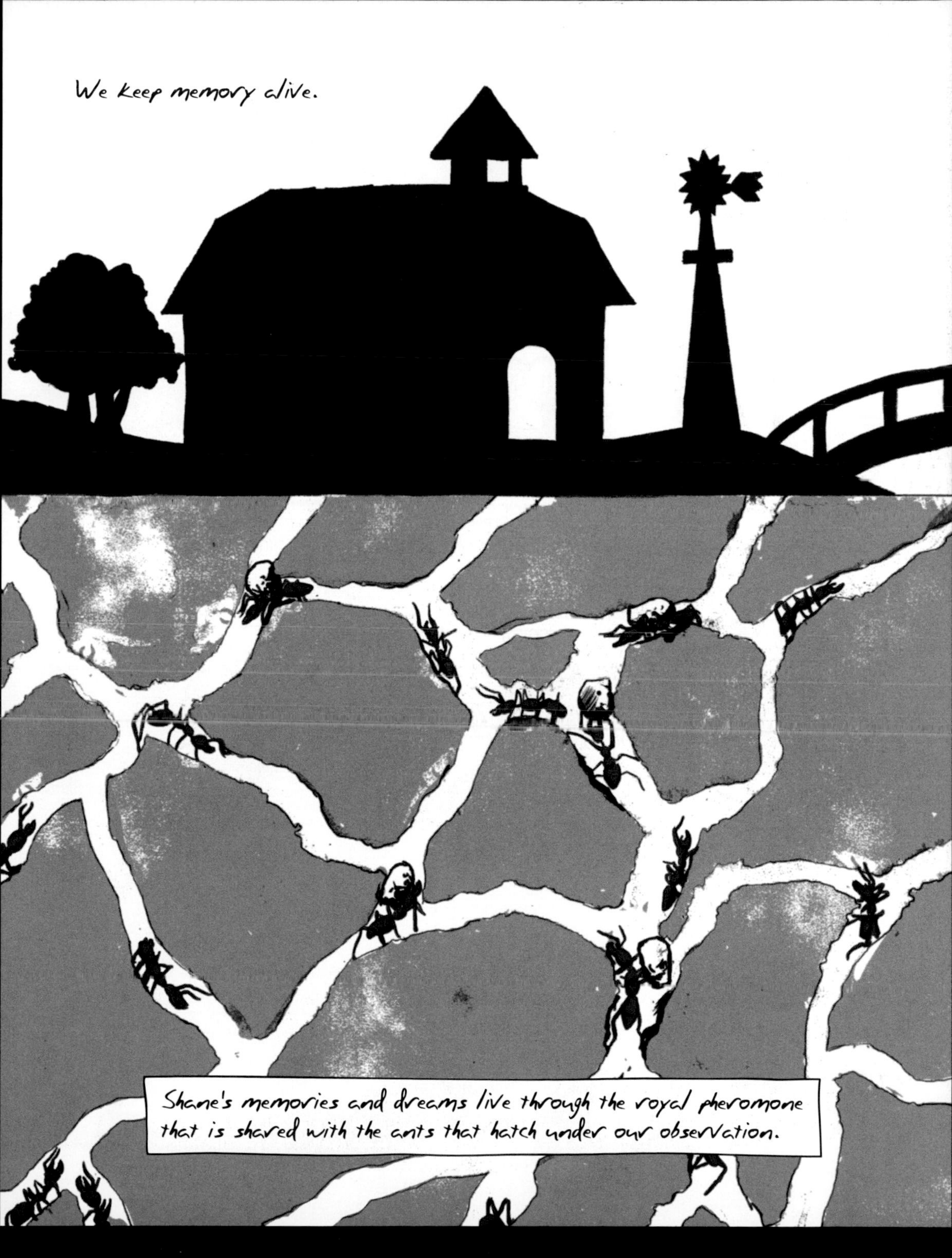
We keep memory alive.
Shane's memories and dreams live through the royal pheromone that is shared with the ants that hatch under our observation.

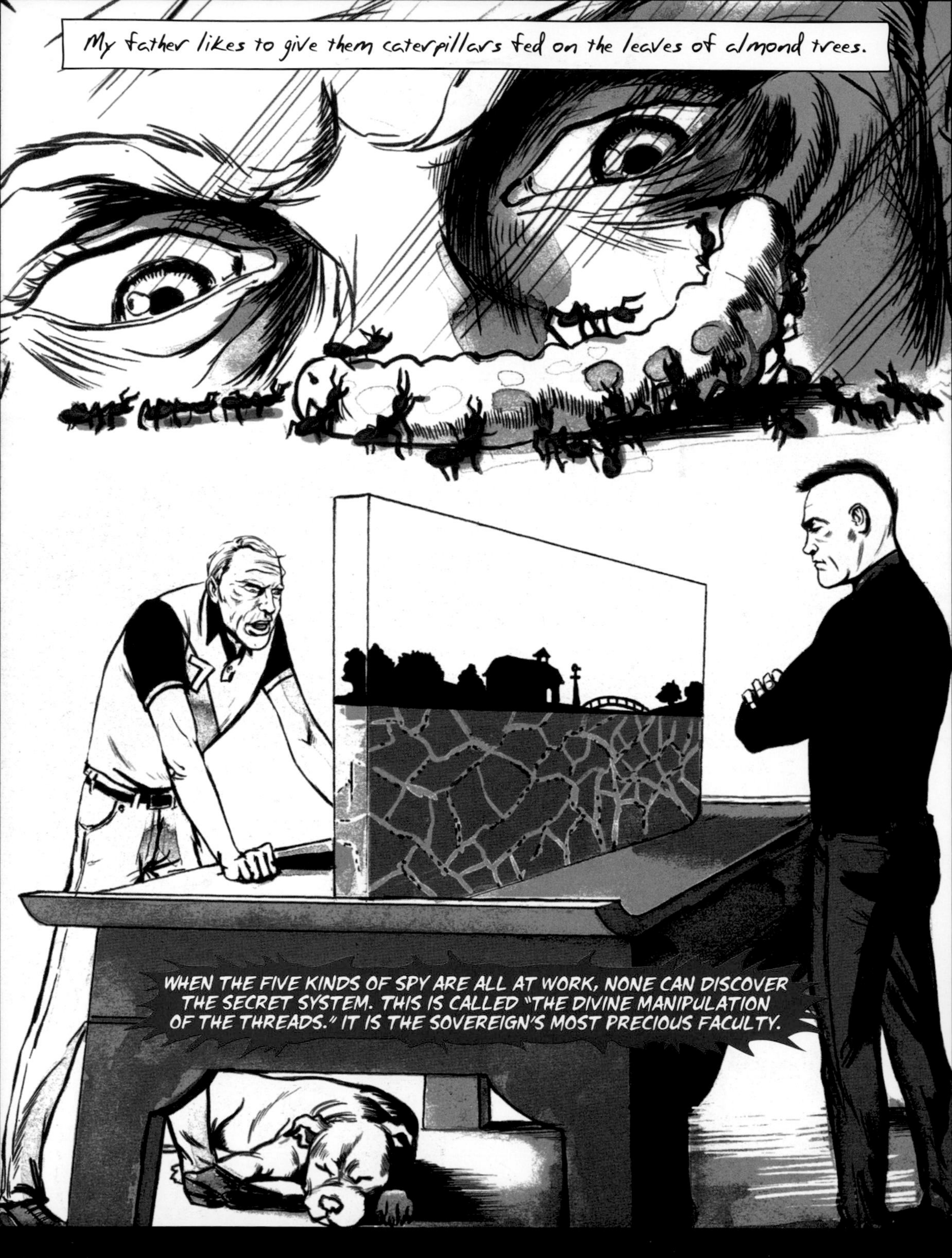
My father likes to give them caterpillars fed on the leaves of almond trees.
WHEN THE FIVE KINDS OF SPY ARE ALL AT WORK, NONE CAN DISCOVER THE SECRET SYSTEM. THIS IS CALLED "THE DIVINE MANIPULATION OF THE THREADS." IT IS THE SOVEREIGN'S MOST PRECIOUS FACULTY.

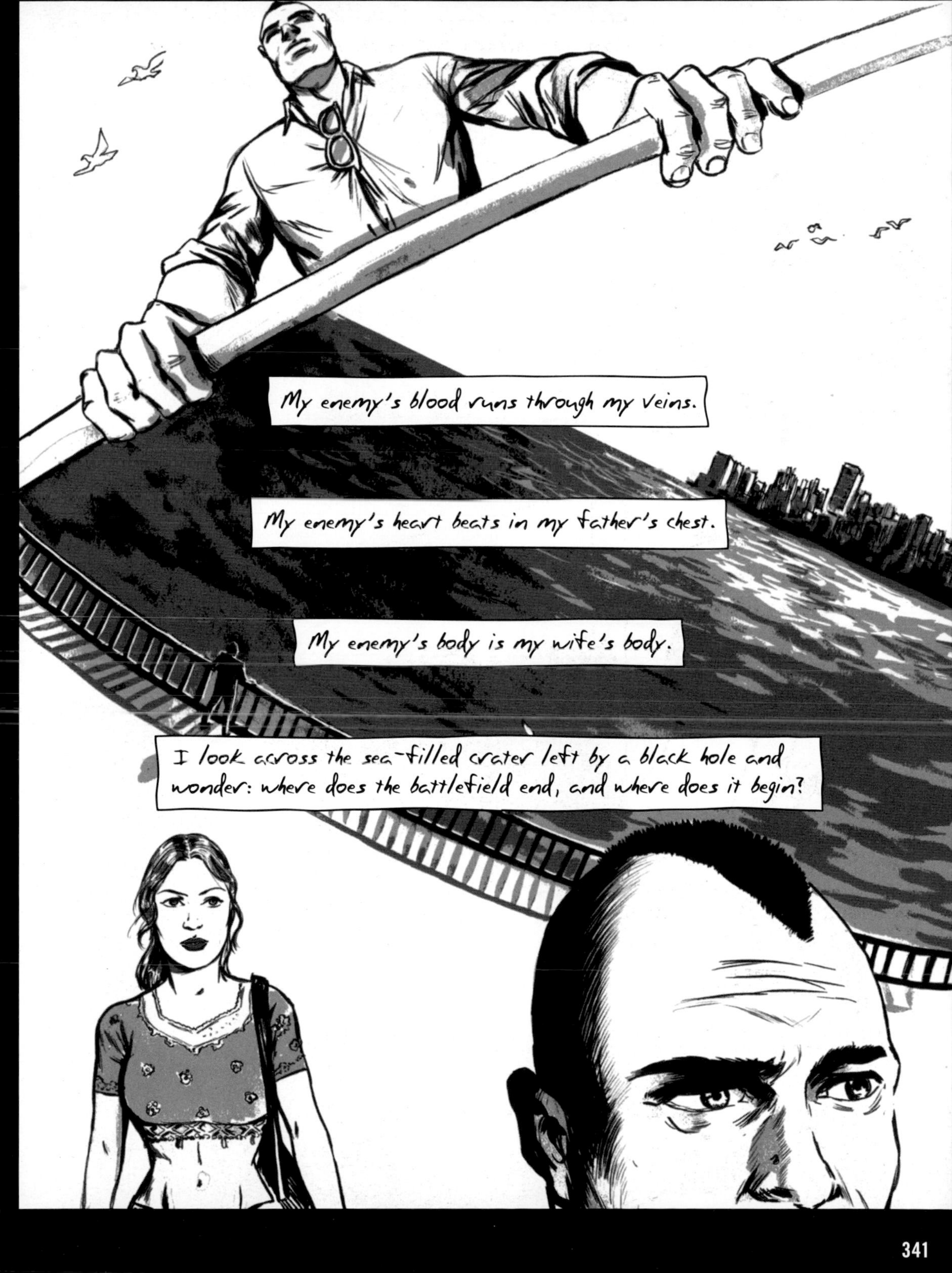
My enemy's blood runs through my veins.
My enemy's heart beats in my father's chest.
My enemy's body is my wife's body.
I look across the sea-filled crater left by a black hole and wonder: where does the battlefield end, and where does it begin?

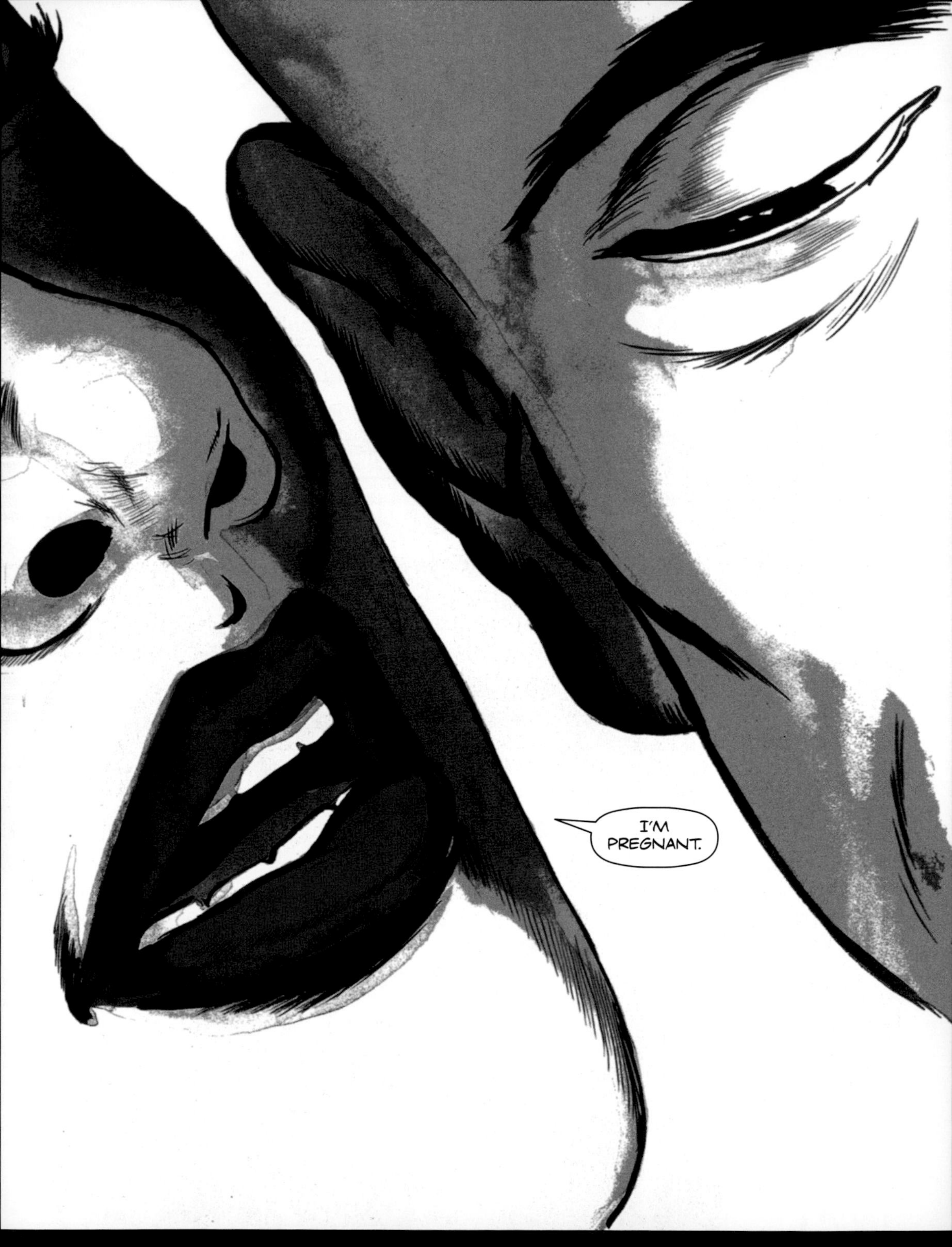
I'M PREGNANT.

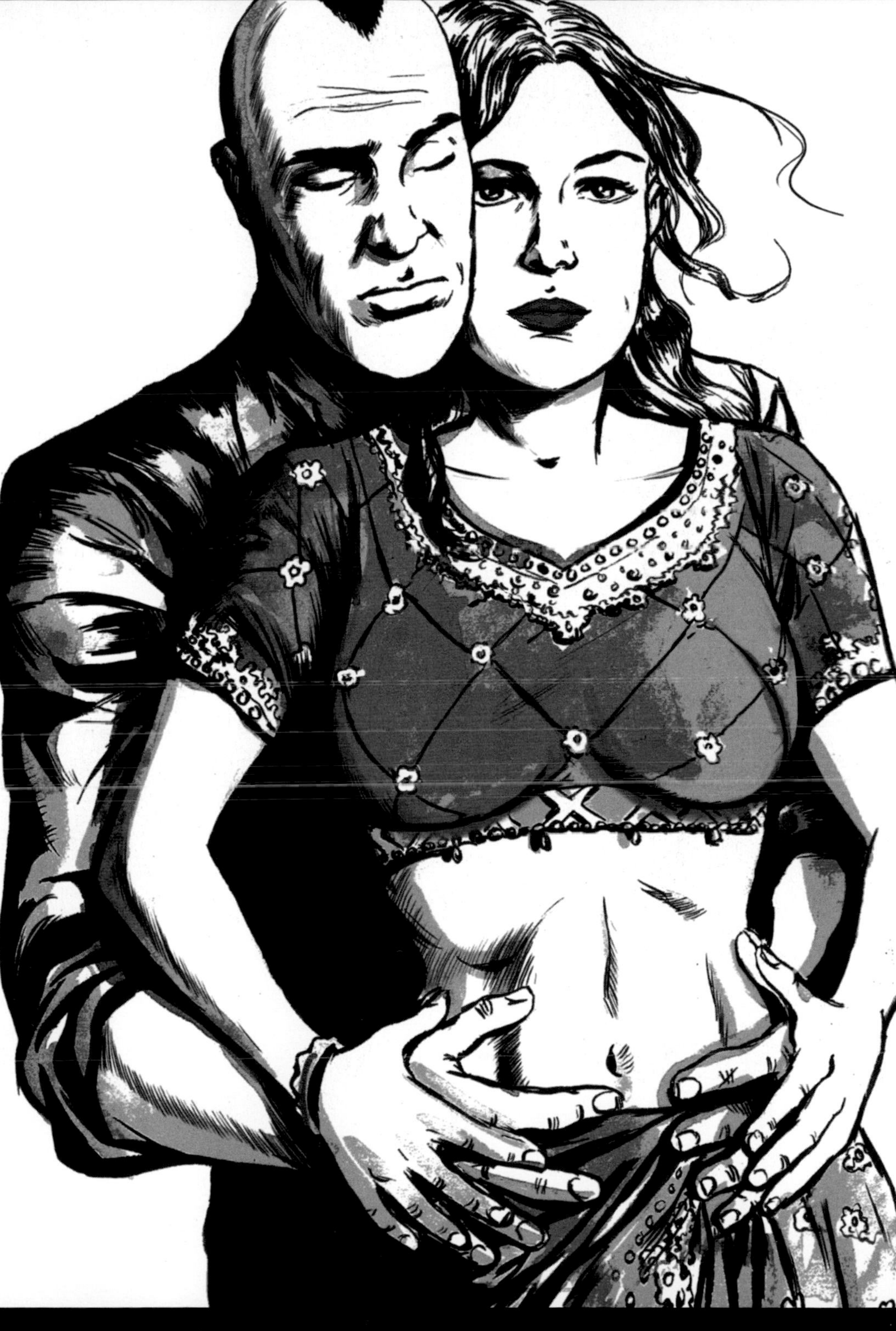

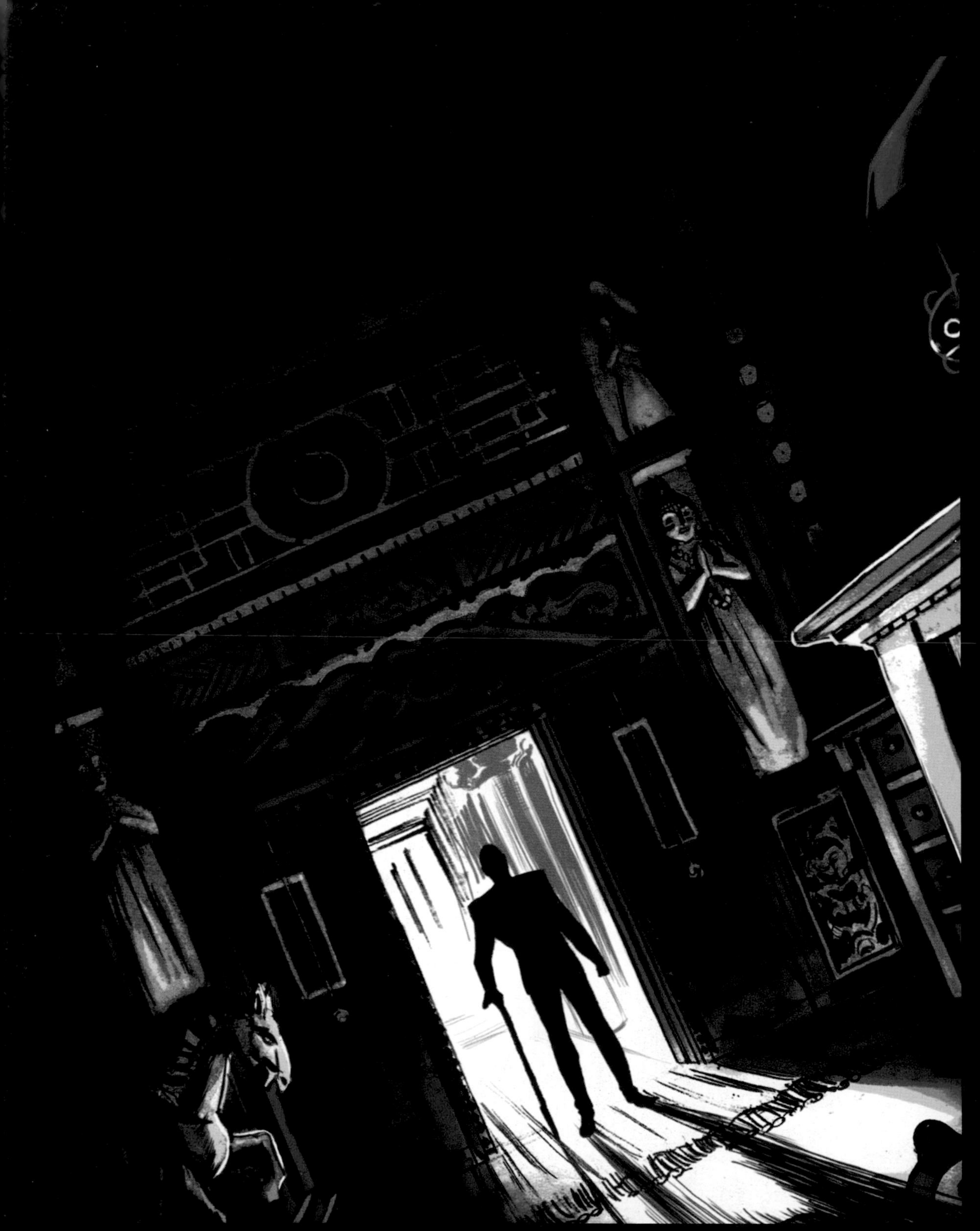

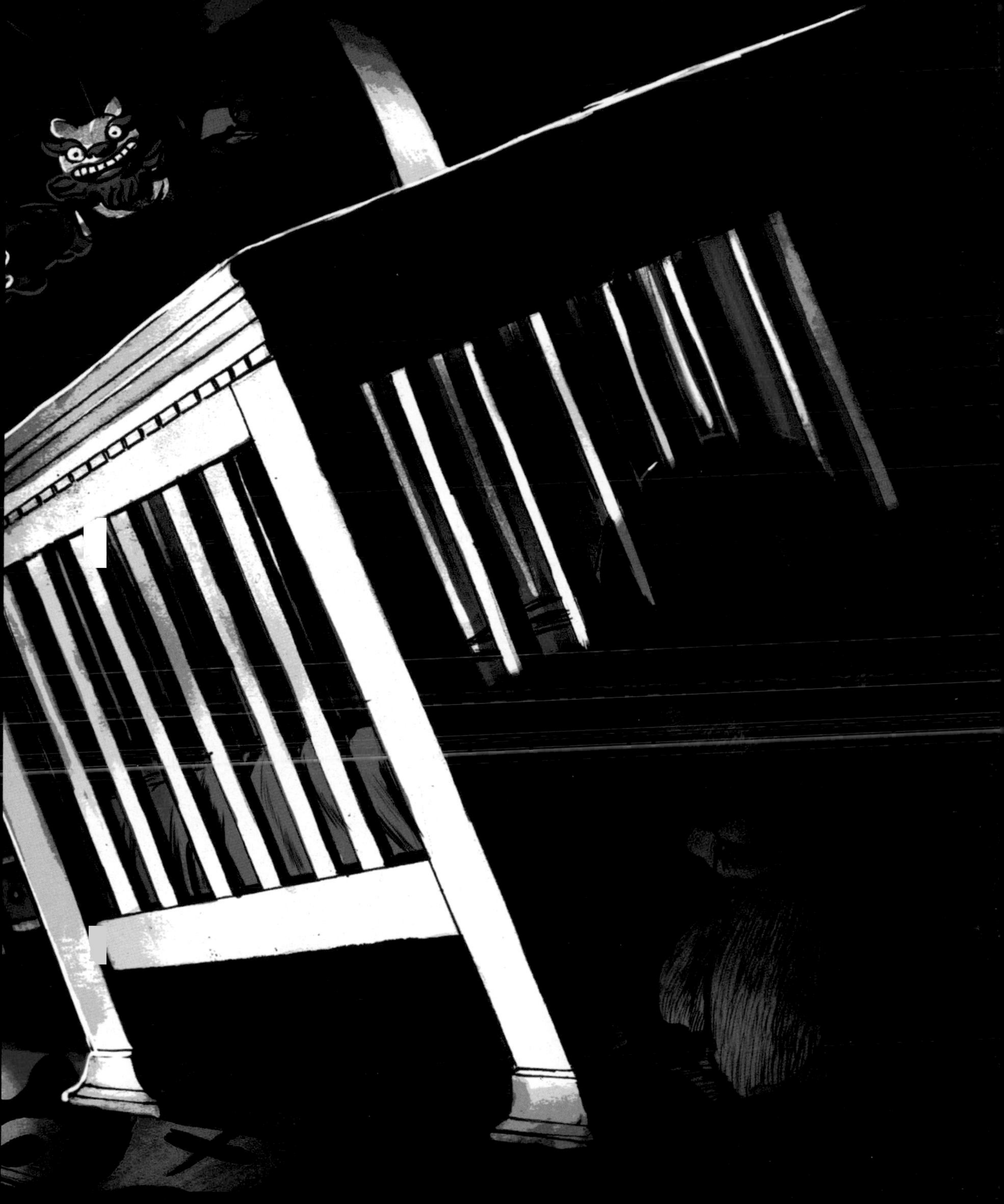

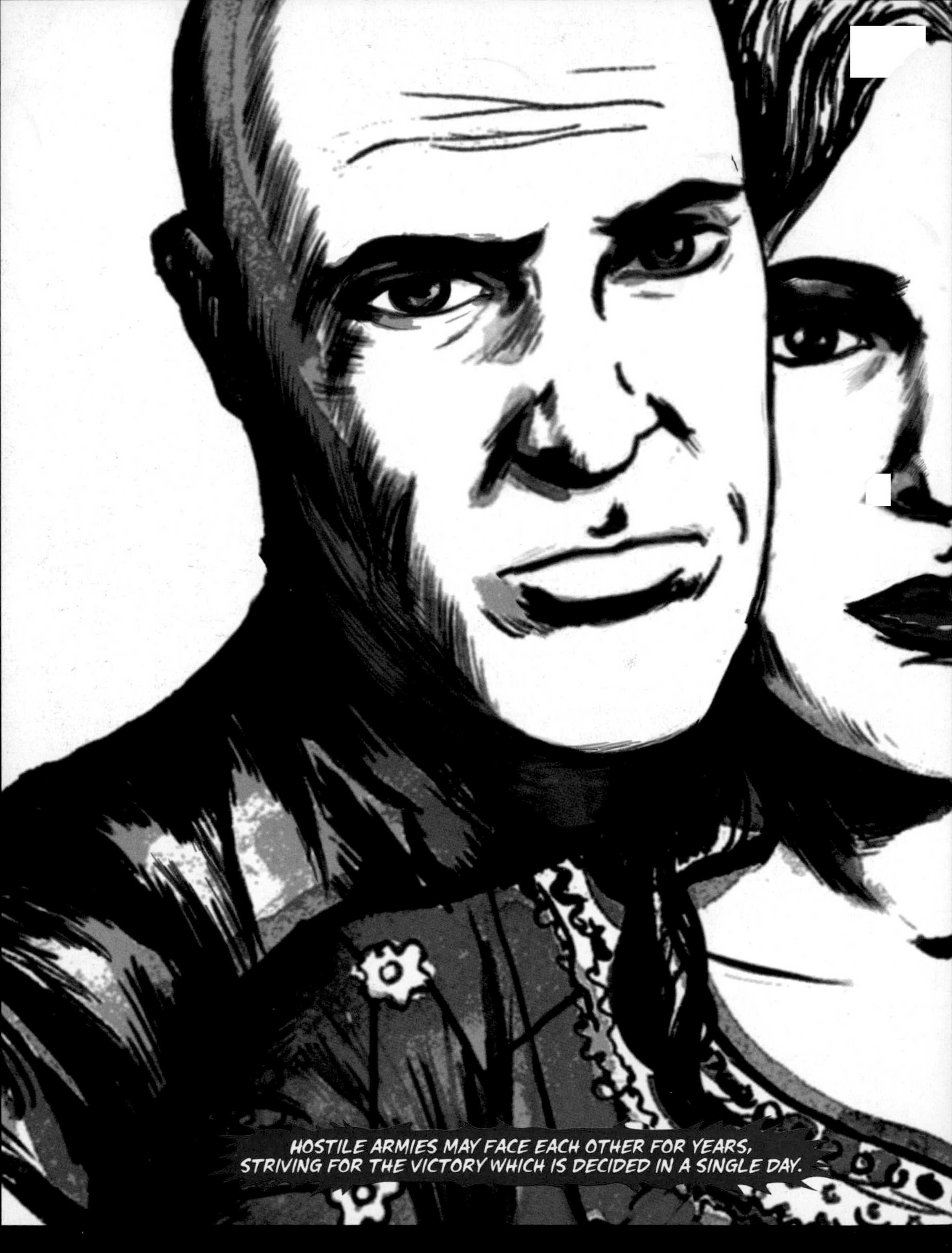
HOSTILE ARMIES MAY FACE EACH OTHER FOR YEARS, STRIVING FOR THE VICTORY WHICH IS DECIDED IN A SINGLE DAY.

Edited by Will Hinton and Mauro DiPreta

Lettered by Jason Arthur

Calligraphy by Ming Sheng Wang

Color conversion by Crawford Hart

Original text by Sun Tzu, translated by Lionel Giles

Special thanks to Robyn Rubenstein for early draft editing and support.

Thanks to Ryan FitzSimons, Julian Hill-Wood, Lorraine Roman, Joseph Roman, Timothy Engelland, Richard Ford, Jim Hart, Randy Becker, Mollie Glick, Josie Freedman, Lisa Lu Britton, Jay Rohrs, and Ben Chabala.

Michael DeWeese would also like to thank John, Nancy, and Nikita Susens, Mary Colston, Casey Aksoy, Adam Wilson, Katherine Murray Satchell, Emily Kwong, Melvin and Dolores DeWeese, Justine Ericksen, Donna and Derek Nance, and Leonida DeWeese.